KU-689-849

A Collection distributed by Heron Books

CHARLES DICKENS

COMPLETE
WORKS

CENTENNIAL EDITION

Charles Dickens

CHARLES DICKENS

LITTLE DORRIT

I

Introduction by
Lionel Trilling

Illustrations by
Phiz

Distributed by
HERON BOOKS

*The introduction to this book
was originally published for the
Oxford Illustrated Dickens,
published by
the Oxford University Press.*

Edito-Service S.A., Geneva, Publishers

INTRODUCTION

Little Dorrit *is one of the three great novels of Dickens's great last period, but of the three it is perhaps the least established with modern readers. When it first appeared—in monthly parts from December 1855 to June 1857—its success was even more decisive than that of* Bleak House, *but the suffrage of later audiences has gone the other way, and of all Dickens's later works it is* Bleak House *that has come to be the best known. As for* Our Mutual Friend, *after having for some time met with adverse critical opinion among the enlightened—one recalls that the youthful Henry James attacked it for standing in the way of art and truth—it has of recent years been regarded with evergrowing admiration. But* Little Dorrit *seems to have retired to the background and shadow of our consciousness of Dickens.*

This does not make an occasion for concern or indignation. With a body of work as large and as enduring as that of Dickens, taste and opinion will never be done. They will shift and veer as they have shifted and veered with the canon of Shakespeare, and each generation will have its special favourites and make its surprised discoveries. Little Dorrit, *one of the most profound of*

LITTLE DORRIT

Dickens's novels and one of the most significant works of the nineteenth century, will not fail to be thought of as speaking with a peculiar and passionate intimacy to our own time.

Little Dorrit *is about society, which certainly does not distinguish it from the rest of Dickens's novels unless we go on to say, as we must, that it is* more *about society than any other of the novels, that it is about society in its very essence. This essential quality of the book has become apparent as many of the particular social conditions to which it refers have passed into history. Some of these conditions were already of the past when Dickens wrote, for although imprisonment for debt was indeed not wholly given up until 1869, yet imprisonment for small debts was done away with in 1844, the prison of the Marshalsea was abolished in 1842 and the Court of the Marshalsea in 1849. Bernard Shaw said of* Little Dorrit *that it converted him to socialism; it is not likely that any contemporary English reader would feel it appropriate to respond to its social message in the same way. The dead hand of outworn tradition no longer supports special privilege in England; for good or bad, in scarcely any country in the world can the whole art of government be said to be How Not To Do It. Mrs. General cannot impose the genteel discipline of Prunes and Prisms, and no prestige whatever attaches to 'the truly refined mind' of her definition—'one that will seem to be ignorant of the existence of anything that is not perfectly proper, placid, and pleasant'. At no point, perhaps, do the particular abuses and absurdities upon which Dickens directed his terrible cold anger represent the problems of social life as we must now conceive them.*

Yet this makes Little Dorrit *not less but more relevant to our sense of things. As the particulars seem less immediate to our case, the general force of the novel becomes greater, and* Little Dorrit *is seen to be about a problem which does not yield easily to time. It is about society in relation to the individual human will. This is certainly a matter general enough—general to the point of tautology, were it not for the bitterness with which the tautology is articulated, were it not for the specificity, and the subtlety, and the boldness with which the human will is anatomized.*

INTRODUCTION

The subject of Little Dorrit *is borne in upon us by the inform-
ing symbol, or emblem, of the book, which is the prison. The
story opens in a prison in Marseilles. It goes on to the Marshalsea, which in effect it never leaves. The second of the two parts
of the novel begins in what we are urged to think of as a sort of
prison, the monastery of the Great St. Bernard. The Circumlocution Office is the prison of the creative mind of England. Mr.
Merdle is shown habitually holding himself by the wrist, taking
himself into custody, and in a score of ways the theme of incarceration is carried out, persons and classes being imprisoned by
their notions of predestined fate or of religious duty, or by their
occupations, their life-schemes, their ideas of themselves, their
very habits of language.*

*Symbolic or emblematic devices are used by Dickens to one
degree or another in several of the novels of his late period, but
nowhere to such good effect as in* Little Dorrit. *The fog of* Bleak
House, *the dust-heap and the river of* Our Mutual Friend *are
very striking, but they scarcely equal in force the prison image
which dominates* Little Dorrit. *This is because the prison is an
actuality before it is ever a symbol; its connexion with the will
is real, it is the practical instrument for the negation of man's
will which the will of society has contrived. As such, the prison
haunted the mind of the nineteenth century, which may be
said to have had its birth at the fall of the Bastille. The genius
of the age, conceiving itself as creative will, naturally thought of
the prisons from which it must be freed, and the trumpet call
of the* Lenore *overture sounds through the century, the signal
for the opening of the gates, for a general deliverance, although
it grows fainter as men come to think of the prison not as a
political instrument merely, but as the ineluctable condition of
life in society. 'Most men in a brazen prison live'—the line in
which Matthew Arnold echoes Wordsworth's 'shades of the
prison-house begin to close Upon the growing boy', might have
served as the epigraph of* Little Dorrit. *In the mind of Dickens
himself the idea of the prison was obsessive, not merely because
of his own boyhood experience of prison life through his father's
three months in the Marshalsea (although this must be given
great weight in our understanding of his intense preoccupation*

with the theme), but because of his own consciousness of the force and scope of his will.

If we speak of the place which the image of the prison occupied in the mind of the nineteenth century, we ought to recollect a certain German picture of the time, inconsiderable in itself but made significant by its use in a famous work of the early twentieth century. It represents a man lying in a medieval dungeon; he is asleep, his head pillowed on straw, and we know that he dreams of freedom because the bars of his window are shown being sawed by gnomes. This picture serves as the frontispiece to Freud's Introductory Lectures on Psychoanalysis—Freud uses it to make plain one of the more elementary ideas of his psychology, the idea of the fulfilment in dream or fantasy of impulses of the will that cannot be fulfilled in actuality. His choice of this particular picture is not fortuitous; other graphic representations of wish-fulfilment exist which might have served equally well his immediate didactic purpose, but Freud's general conception of the mind does indeed make the prison-image peculiarly appropriate. And Freud is in point here because in a passage of Little Dorrit Dickens anticipates one of Freud's ideas, and not one of the simplest but nothing less bold and inclusive than the essential theory of the neurosis; and the quality of mind that makes this striking anticipation is at work everywhere in Little Dorrit.

The brief passage to which I make reference occurs in the course of Arthur Clennam's pursuit of the obsessive notion that his family is in some way guilty, that its fortune, although now greatly diminished, has been built on injury done to someone. And he conjectures that the injured person is William Dorrit, who has been confined for debt in the Marshalsea for twenty years. Clennam is not wholly wrong in his supposition—there is indeed guilt in the family, incurred by Arthur's mother, and it consists in part of an injury done to a member of the Dorrit family. But he is not wholly right, for Mr. Dorrit has not been imprisoned through the wish or agency of Mrs. Clennam. The reasoning by which Arthur reaches his partly mistaken conclusion is of the greatest interest. It is based upon the fact that his mother, although mentally very vigorous, has lived as an invalid

. *for many years. She has been imprisoned in a single room of her house, confined to her chair, which she leaves only for her bed. And her son conjectures that her imprisoning illness is the price she pays for the guilty gratification of keeping William Dorrit in his prison. In order to have the right to injure another, she must injure herself in an equivalent way. 'A swift thought shot into [Arthur Clennam's] mind. In that long imprisonment here [i.e. Mr. Dorrit's] and in her long confinement to her room, did his mother find a balance to be struck? I admit that I was accessory to that man's captivity. I have suffered it in kind. He has decayed in his prison; I in mine. I have paid the penalty.'*

I have dwelt on this detail because it suggests, even more than the naked fact of the prison itself, the nature of the vision of society of Little Dorrit. *One way of describing Freud's conception of the mind is to say that it is based upon the primacy of the will, and that the organization of the internal life is in the form, often fantastically parodic, of a criminal process in which the mind is at once the criminal, the victim, the police, the judge, and the executioner. And this is a fair description of Dickens's own view of the mind, as, having received the social impress, it becomes in turn the matrix of society.*

In emphasizing the psychological aspects of the representation of society of Little Dorrit *I do not wish to slight those more immediate institutional aspects of which earlier readers of the novel were chiefly aware. These are of as great importance now as they ever were in Dickens's career. Dickens is far from having lost his sense of the cruelty and stupidity of institutions and functionaries, his sense of the general rightness of the people as a whole and of the general wrongness of those who are put in authority over then. He certainly has not moved to that specious position in which all injustice is laid at the door of the original old Adam in each of us, not to be done away with until we shall all, at the same movement, become the new Adam. The Circumlocution Office is a constraint upon the life of England which nothing can justify. Mr. Dorrit's suffering and the injustice done to him are not denied or mitigated by his passionate commitment to some of the worst aspects of the society which deals with him so badly.*

Yet the emphasis on the internal life and on personal respon-
sibility is very strong in Little Dorrit. *Thus, to take but one*
example, in the matter of the Circumlocution Office Dickens is
at pains to remind us that the responsibility for its existence lies
even with so good a man as Mr. Meagles. In his alliance with
Daniel Doyce against the torpor of the Office, Mr. Meagles has
been undeviatingly faithful. Yet Clennam finds occasion to
wonder whether there might not be 'in the breast of this honest,
affectionate, and cordial Mr. Meagles, any microscopic portion
of the mustard-seed that had sprung up into the great tree of
the Circumlocution Office'. He is led to this speculation by his
awareness that Mr. Meagles feels 'a general superiority to Daniel
Doyce, which seemed to be founded, not so much on anything
in Doyce's personal character, as on the mere fact of [Doyce's]
being an originator and a man out of the beaten track of other
men'.

Perhaps the single best index of the degree of complexity with
which Dickens views society in Little Dorrit *is afforded by the*
character of Blandois and his place in the novel. Blandois is
wholly wicked, the embodiment of evil; he is, indeed, a devil.
One of the effects of his presence in Little Dorrit *is to complicate*
our response to the theme of the prison, to deprive us of the
comfortable, philanthropic thought that prisons are nothing but
instruments of injustice. Because Blandois exists, prisons are
necessary. The generation of readers that preceded our own was
inclined, I think, to withhold credence from Blandois—they did
not believe in his aesthetic actuality because they did not believe
in his moral actuality, the less so because they coud not account
for his existence in specific terms of social causation. But we
have been forced to believe that there really are people who
seem entirely wicked, and almost unaccountably so; the social
causes of their badness lie so far back that they can scarcely be
reached, and causation pales into irrelevance before the effects
of their action; our 'understanding' becomes a mere form of
thought.

In this novel about the will and society, the devilish nature of
Blandois is confirmed by his maniac insistence upon his gen-
tility, his mad reiteration that it is the right and necessity of his

INTRODUCTION

*existence to be served by others. He is the exemplification of
the line in* Lear: *'The prince of darkness is a gentleman.' The
influence of Dickens upon Dostoievski is perhaps nowhere
exhibited in a more detailed way than in the similarities between
Blandois and the shabby-genteel devil of* The Brothers Kara-
mazov *and also Smerdyakov of the same novel. It is of consequence to Dickens as to Dostoievski that the evil of the unmiti-
gated social will should own no country, yet that the flavour of
its cosmopolitanism should be 'French'—that is, rationalistic
and subversive of the very assumption of society. Blandois
enfolds himself in the soiled tatters of the revolutionary pathos.
So long as he can play the game in his chosen style, he is nature's
gentleman dispossessed of his rightful place, he is the natural
genius against whom the philistine world closes its dull ranks.
And when the disguise, which deceives no one, is off, he makes
use of the classic social rationalization: Society has made him
what he is; he does in his own person only what society does
in its corporate form and with its corporate self-justification.
'Society sells itself and sells me: and I sell society.'*

*Around Blandois are grouped certain characters of the novel
of whose manner of life he is the pure principle. In these people
the social will, the will to status, is the ruling faculty. To be
recognized, deferred to, and served—this is their master passion.
Money is of course of great consequence in the exercise of this
passion, yet in* Little Dorrit *the desire for money is subordinated
to the desire for deference. The Midas figure of Mr. Merdle
must not mislead us on this point—should, indeed, guide us
aright, for Mr. Merdle, despite his destructive power, is an
innocent and passive man among those who live by the social
will. It is to be noted of all these people that they justify their
insensate demand for status by some version of Blandois's
pathos; they are confirmed in their lives by self-pity, they rely
on the great modern strategy of being the insulted and injured.
Mr. Dorrit is too soft a man for his gentility-mania ever to be
quite diabolical, but his younger daughter Fanny sells herself
to the devil, damns herself entirely in order to torture the woman
who once questioned her social position. Henry Gowan, the
cynical, incompetent gentleman-artist who associates himself*

with Blandois in order to épater society, is very nearly as diabolical as his companion. From his mother—who must dismiss once for all any lingering doubt of Dickens's ability to portray what Chesterton calls the delicate or deadly in human character—he has learned to base his attack on society upon the unquestionable rightness of wronged gentility. Miss Wade lives a life of tortured self-commiseration which gives her licence to turn her hatred and her hand against everyone, and she imposes her principle of judgement and conduct upon Tattycoram.

In short, it is part of the complexity of this novel which deals so bitterly with society that those of its characters who share its social bitterness are by that very fact condemned. And yet— so much further does the complexity extend—the subversive pathos of self-pity is by no means wholly dismissed, the devil has not wholly lied. No reader of Little Dorrit can possibly conclude that the rage of envy which Tattycoram feels is not justified in some degree, or that Miss Wade is wholly wrong in pointing out to her the insupportable ambiguity of her position as the daughter-servant of Mr. and Mrs. Meagles and the sister-servant of Pet Meagles. Nor is it possible to read Miss Wade's account of her life, 'The History of a Self Tormentor', without an understanding that amounts to sympathy. We feel this the more—Dickens meant us to feel it the more—because the two young women have been orphaned from infancy, and illegitimate. Their bitterness is seen to be the perversion of the desire for love. The self-torture of Miss Wade—who becomes the more interesting if we think of her as the exact inversion of Esther Summerson of Bleak House—is the classic manœuvre of the child who is unloved, or believes herself to be unloved—she refuses to be lovable, she elects to be hateful. The sense of injustice precedes the sense of justice by many years. It haunts the infancy of all of us, and even the most dearly loved of children may conceive themselves to be oppressed. Such is the nature of the human will, so perplexed is it by the disparity between what it desires and what it is allowed to have. With Dickens as with Blake, the perfect image of injustice is the unhappy child, and, like the historian Burckhardt, he connects the fate of nations with the treatment of children. It is a common-

INTRODUCTION

place of the biography and criticism of Dickens that this reflects his own sense of having been unjustly treated by his parents, specifically in ways which injured his own sense of social status, his own gentility; the general force of Dickens's social feelings derives from their being rooted in childhood experience, and something of the special force of Little Dorrit *derives from Dickens having discovered its matter in the depths of his own social will.*

At this point we become aware of the remarkable number of false and inadequate parents in Little Dorrit. *To what pains Dickens goes to represent delinquent parenthood, with what an elaboration of irony he sets it forth! The Father of the Marshalsea—this is the style borne by Mr. Dorrit, who, preoccupied by the gratification of being the First Gentleman of a prison, is unable to exercise the simplest paternal function; who corrupts two of his children by his dream of gentility; who will accept any sacrifice from his saintly daughter Amy, Little Dorrit, to whom he is the beloved child to be cherished and forgiven. The Patriarch—this is the title bestowed upon Mr. Casby, who stands as a parody of all Dickens's benevolent old gentlemen from Mr. Pickwick through the Cherrybles to John Jarndyce, an astounding unreality of a man who, living only to grip and grind, has convinced the world by the iconography of his dress and mien that he is the repository of all benevolence. The primitive appropriateness of the strange, the unEnglish, punishment which Mr. Pancks metes out to this hollow paternity, the cutting off of his long hair and the broad brim of his hat, will be understood by any reader with the least tincture of psychoanalytical knowledge. Then the Meagles, however solicitous of their own daughter, are, as we have seen, but indifferent parents to Tattycoram. Mrs. Gowan's rearing of her son is the root of his corruption. It is Fanny Dorrit's complaint of her enemy, Mrs. Merdle, that she refuses to surrender the appearance of youth, as a mother should. And at the very centre of the novel is Mrs. Clennam, a false mother in more ways than one; she does not deny love but she perverts and prevents it by denying all that love feeds on— liberty, demonstrative tenderness, joy, and, what for Dickens is the guardian of love in society, art. It is her harsh rearing of her* son that has given him cause to say in his fortieth year, 'I have no will.'

Some grace—it is, of course, the secret of his birth, of his being really a child of love and art—has kept Arthur Clennam from responding to the will of his mother with a bitter, clenched will of his own. The alternative he has chosen has not, contrary to his declaration, left him no will at all. He has by no means been robbed of his ethical will, he can exert energy to help others, and for the sake of Mr. Dorrit or Daniel Doyce's invention he can haunt the Circumlocution Office with his mild, stubborn 'I want to know—.' But the very accent of that phrase seems to forecast the terrible 'I prefer not to' of Bartleby the Scrivener in Melville's great story of the will in its ultimate fatigue.

It is impossible, I think, not to find in Arthur Clennam the evidence of Dickens's deep personal involvement in Little Dorrit. If we ask what Charles Dickens has to do with poor Clennam, what The Inimitable has to do with this sad depleted failure, the answer must be—Nothing, save what is implied by Clennam's consciousness that he has passed the summit of life and that the path henceforward leads down, by his belief that the pleasures of love are not for him, by his 'I want to know—', by his wish to negate the will in death. Arthur Clennam is that mode of Dickens's existence at the time of Little Dorrit which makes it possible for him to write to his friend Macready, 'However strange it is never to be at rest, and never satisfied, and ever trying after something that is never reached, and to be always laden with plot and plan and care and worry, how clear it is that it must be, and that one is driven by an irresistible might until the journey is worked out.' And somewhat earlier and with a yet more poignant relevance : 'Why is it, that as with poor David, a sense always comes crushing upon me now, when I fall into low spirits, as of one happiness I have missed in life, and one friend and companion I have never made?'

If we become aware of an autobiographical element in Little Dorrit, we must of course take notice of the fact that the novel was conceived after the famous incident of Maria Beadnell, who, poor woman, was the original of Arthur Clennam's Flora Finching. She was the first love of Dicken's proud, unfledged *youth; she had married what Dickens has taught us to call Another, and now, after twenty years, she had chosen to come back into his life. Familiarity with the story cannot diminish our amazement at it—Dickens was a subtle and worldly man, but his sophistication was not proof against his passionate senti- mentality, and he fully expected the past to come back to him, borne in the little hands of the adorable Maria. The actuality had a quite extreme effect upon him, and Flora, fat and foolish, is his monument to the discovered discontinuity between youth and middle age, she is the nonsensical spirit of the anti-climax of the years. And if she is in some degree forgiven, being repre- sented as the kindest of foolish women, yet it is not without meaning that she is everywhere attended by Mr. F's Aunt, one of Dicken's most astonishing ideas, the embodiment of senile rage and spite, flinging to the world the crusts of her buttered toast. 'He has proud stomach, this chap', she cries when poor Arthur hesitates over her dreadful gift. 'Give him a meal of chaff!' It is the voice of one of the Parcae.*

It did not, of course, need the sad comedy of Maria Beadnell for Dickens to conceive that something in his life had come to an end. It did not even need his growing certainty that, after so many years and so many children, his relations with his wife were insupportable—this realization was as much a consequence as it was a cause of the sense of termination. He was forty-three years old and at the pinnacle of a success unique in the history of letters. The wildest ambitions of his youth could not have comprehended the actuality of his fame. But the last infirmity of noble mind may lead to the first infirmity of noble will. Dickens, to be sure, never lost his love of fame, or of whatever of life's goods his miraculous powers might bring him, but there came a moment when the old primitive motive could no longer serve, when the joy of impressing his powers on the world no longer seemed delightful in itself, and when the first, simple, honest, vulgar energy of desire no longer seemed appropriate to his idea of himself.

We may say of Dickens that at the time of Little Dorrit *he was at a crisis of the will which is expressed in the characters and forces of the novel, in the extremity of its bitterness against* the social will, in its vision of peace and selflessness. This moral crisis is most immediately represented by the condition of Arthur Clennam's will, by his sense of guilt, by his belief that he is unloved and unlovable, by his retirement to the Marshalsea as by an act of choice, by his sickness unto death. We have here the analogy to the familiar elements of a religious crisis. This is not the place to raise the question of Dickens's relation to the Christian religion, which was a complicated one. But we cannot speak of Little Dorrit without taking notice of its reference to Christian feeling, if only because this is of considerable importance in its effect upon the aesthetic of the novel.

It has been observed of Little Dorrit that certain of Dickens's characteristic delights are not present in their usual force. Something of his gusto is diminished in at least one of its aspects. We do not have the amazing thickness of fact and incident that marks, say, Bleak House or Our Mutual Friend—not that we do not have sufficient thickness, but we do not have what Dickens usually gives us. We do not have the great population of characters from whom shines the freshness of their autonomous life. Mr. Pancks and Mrs. Plornish and Flora Finching and Flintwinch are interesting and amusing, but they seem to be the fruit of conscious intention rather than of free creation. This is sometimes explained by saying that Dickens was fatigued. Perhaps so, but if we are aware that Dickens is here expending less of one kind of creative energy, we must at the same time be aware that he is expending more than ever before of another kind. The imagination of Little Dorrit is marked not so much by its powers of particularization as by its powers of generalization and abstraction. It is an imagination under the dominion of a great articulated idea, a moral idea which tends to find its full development in a religious experience. It is an imagination akin to that which created Piers Plowman and The Pilgrim's Progress. And, indeed, it is akin to the imagination of The Divine Comedy. Never before has Dickens made so full, so Dantean, a claim for the virtue of the artist, and there is a Dantean pride and a Dantean reason in what he says of Daniel Doyce, who, although an engineer, stands for the creative mind in general and for its appropriate virtue: 'His dismissal of *himself [was] remarkable. He never said, I discovered this adaptation or invented that combination; but showed the whole thing as if the Divine artificer had made it, and he had happened to find it. So modest was he about it, such a pleasant touch of respect was mingled with his quiet admiration of it, and so calmly convinced was he that it was established on irrefragable laws.' Like much else that might be pointed to, this confirms us in the sense that the whole energy of the imagination of* Little Dorrit *is directed to finding the non-personal will in which shall be our peace.*

We must accept—and we easily do accept, if we do not permit critical cliché to interfere—the aesthetic of such an imagination, which will inevitably tend to a certain formality of pattern and to the generalization and the abstraction we have remarked. In a novel in which a house falls physically to ruins from the moral collapse of its inhabitants, in which the heavens open over London to show a crown of thorns, in which there are characters named nothing else than Bar, Bishop, Physician, we are quite content to accept the existence of a devil. And we do not reject, for all our inevitable first impulse to do so, the character of Little Dorrit herself. Her untinctured goodness does not appal us or make us misdoubt her, as we expect it to do. This novel at its best is only incidentally realistic, its finest power of imagination appears in the great general images whose abstractness is their actuality, like Mr. Merdle's dinner parties, or the Circumlocution Office itself, and in such a context we understand Little Dorrit to be the Beatrice of the Comedy, the Paraclete in female form. Even the physical littleness of this grown woman, an attribute which is insisted on and which seems so likely to repel us, does not do so, for we perceive it to be the sign that she not only is the Child of the Marshalsea, as she is called, but also the Child of the Parable, the negation of the social will.

Lionel Trilling

1952

PREFACE

I was occupied with this story, during many working hours of two years. I must have been very ill employed, if I could not leave its merits and demerits as a whole, to express themselves on its being read as a whole.

If I might offer any apology for so exaggerated a fiction as the Barnacles and the Circumlocution Office, I would seek it in the common experience of an Englishman, without presuming to mention the unimportant fact of my having done that violence to good manners, in the days of a Russian war, and of a Court of Enquiry at Chelsea. If I might make so bold as to defend that extravagant conception, Mr. Merdle, I would hint that it originated after the Railroad-share epoch, in the times of a certain Irish bank, and of one or two other equally laudable enterprises. If I were to plead anything in mitigation of the preposterous fancy that a bad design will sometimes claim to be a good and an expressly religious design, it would be the curious coincidence that such fancy was brought to its climax in these pages, in the days of the public examination of late Directors of a Royal British Bank. But, I submit myself to suffer judgment to go by default on all these counts, if need be, and to accept the assurance (on good authority) that nothing like them was ever known in this land.

Some of my readers may have an interest in being informed

whether or no any portions of the Marshalsea Prison are yet standing. I myself did not know, until I was approaching the end of this story, when I went to look. I found the outer front court-yard, often mentioned here, metamorphosed into a butter shop; and I then almost gave up every brick of the jail for lost. Wandering, however, down a certain adjacent " Angel Court, leading to Bermondsey," I came to " Marshalsea Place : " the houses in which I recognised, not only as the great block of the former prison, but as preserving the rooms that arose in my mind's-eye when I became Little Dorrit's Biographer. The smallest boy I ever conversed with, carrying the largest baby I ever saw, offered a supernaturally intelligent explanation of the locality in its old uses, and was very nearly correct. How this young Newton (for such I judge him to be) came by his information, I don't know; he was a quarter of a century too young to know anything about it of himself. I pointed to the window of the room where Little Dorrit was born, and where her father lived so long, and asked him what was the name of the lodger who tenanted that apartment at present? He said, " Tom Pythick." I asked him who was Tom Pythick? and he said, " Joe Pythick's uncle."

A little further on, I found the older and smaller wall, which used to enclose the pent-up inner prison where nobody was put, except for ceremony. Whosoever goes into Marshalsea Place, turning out of Angel Court, leading to Bermondsey, will find his feet on the very paving-stones of the extinct Marshalsea jail; will see its narrow yard to the right and to the left, very little altered if at all, except that the walls were lowered when the place got free ; will look upon the rooms in which the debtors lived ; will stand among the crowding ghosts of many miserable years.

CONTENTS

BOOK THE FIRST: POVERTY

CHAPTER I
Sun and Shadow 1

CHAPTER II
Fellow-travellers 18

CHAPTER III
Home 34

CHAPTER IV
Mrs. Flintwinch has a Dream 50

CHAPTER V
Family Affairs 54

CHAPTER VI
The Father of the Marshalsea 68

CONTENTS

CHAPTER VII

PAGE

The Child of the Marshalsea 81

CHAPTER VIII

The Lock 95

CHAPTER IX

Little Mother 109

CHAPTER X

Containing the whole Science of Government 126

CHAPTER XI

Let Loose 151

CHAPTER XII

Bleeding Heart Yard 164

CHAPTER XIII

Patriarchal 175

CHAPTER XIV

Little Dorrit's Party 203

CHAPTER XV

Mrs. Flintwinch has another Dream 218

CHAPTER XVI

Nobody's Weakness 230

CONTENTS

CHAPTER XVII.

PAGE

Nobody's Rival 247

CHAPTER XVIII

Little Dorrit's Lover 259

CHAPTER XIX

The Father of the Marshalsea in two or three Relations . . 271

CHAPTER XX

Moving in Society 285

CHAPTER XXI

Mr. Merdle's Complaint 302

CHAPTER XXII

A Puzzle 313

CHAPTER XXIII

Machinery in Motion 325

CHAPTER XXIV

Fortune-telling 345

CHAPTER XXV

Conspirators and Others 365

CHAPTER XXVI

Nobody's State of Mind 378

CONTENTS

CHAPTER XXVII

PAGE

Five-and-twenty 395

CHAPTER XXVIII

Nobody's Disappearance 411

CHAPTER XXIX

Mrs. Flintwinch goes on Dreaming 421

CHAPTER XXX

The Word of a Gentleman 431

CHAPTER XXXI

Spirit 451

CHAPTER XXXII

More Fortune-telling 470

CHAPTER XXXIII

Mrs. Merdle's Complaint 482

CHAPTER XXXIV

A Shoal of Barnacles 495

CHAPTER XXXV

What was behind Mr. Pancks on Little Dorrit's Hand . . . 507

CHAPTER XXXVI

The Marshalsea becomes an Orphan 524

LIST OF ILLUSTRATIONS

	PAGE
THE BIRDS IN THE CAGE	6
UNDER THE MICROSCOPE	32
MR. FLINTWINCH MEDIATES AS A FRIEND OF THE FAMILY	62
LITTLE MOTHER	122
MAKING OFF	162
MR. F'S AUNT IS CONDUCTED INTO RETIREMENT	194
LITTLE DORRIT'S PARTY	216
THE FERRY	248
THE BROTHERS	272
MISS DORRIT AND LITTLE DORRIT	288
VISITORS AT THE WORKS	330
THE STORY OF THE PRINCESS	362
FIVE-AND-TWENTY	408
MR. FLINTWINCH HAS A MILD ATTACK OF IRRITABILITY	432
THE PENSIONER ENTERTAINMENT	464
SOCIETY EXPRESSES ITS VIEWS ON A QUESTION OF MARRIAGE	484

BOOK THE FIRST
POVERTY

CHAPTER I

SUN AND SHADOW

THIRTY years ago, Marseilles lay burning in the sun, one day.

A blazing sun upon a fierce August day was no greater rarity in southern France then, than at any other time, before or since. Everything in Marseilles, and about Marseilles, had stared at the fervid sky, and been stared at in return, until a staring habit had become universal there. Strangers were stared out of countenance by staring white houses, staring white walls, staring white streets, staring tracts of arid road, staring hills from which verdure was burnt away. The only things to be seen not fixedly staring and glaring were the vines drooping under their load of grapes. These did occasionally wink a little, as the hot air barely moved their faint leaves.

There was no wind to make a ripple on the foul water within the harbour, or on the beautiful sea without. The line of demarcation between the two colours, black and blue, showed the point which the pure sea would not pass; but

1

it lay as quiet as the abominable pool, with which it never
mixed. Boats without awnings were too hot to touch; ships
blistered at their moorings; the stones of the quays had not
cooled, night or day, for months. Hindoos, Russians, Chinese,
Spaniards, Portuguese, Englishmen, Frenchmen, Genoese,
Neapolitans, Venetians, Greeks, Turks, descendants from all
the builders of Babel, come to trade at Marseilles, sought the
shade alike—taking refuge in any hiding-place from a sea too
intensely blue to be looked at, and a sky of purple, set with
one great flaming jewel of fire.

The universal stare made the eyes ache. Towards the
distant line of Italian coast, indeed, it was a little relieved
by light clouds of mist, slowly rising from the evaporation
of the sea, but it softened nowhere else. Far away the
staring roads, deep in dust, stared from the hill-side, stared
from the hollow, stared from the interminable plain. Far
away the dusty vines overhanging wayside cottages, and the
monotonous wayside avenues of parched trees without shade,
drooped beneath the stare of earth and sky. So did the
horses with drowsy bells, in long files of carts, creeping
slowly towards the interior; so did their recumbent drivers,
when they were awake, which rarely happened; so did the
exhausted labourers in the fields. Everything that lived or
grew, was oppressed by the glare; except the lizard, passing
swiftly over rough stone walls, and the cicala, chirping his
dry hot chirp, like a rattle. The very dust was scorched
brown, and something quivered in the atmosphere as if the
air itself were panting.

Blinds, shutters, curtains, awnings, were all closed and
drawn to keep out the stare. Grant it but a chink or keyhole, and it shot in like a white-hot arrow. The churches
were the freest from it. To come out of the twilight of
pillars and arches—dreamily dotted with winking lamps,
dreamily peopled with ugly old shadows piously dozing,
spitting, and begging—was to plunge into a fiery river, and
swim for life to the nearest strip of shade. So, with people

2

lounging and lying wherever shade was, with but little hum of tongues or barking of dogs, with occasional jangling of discordant church bells, and rattling of vicious drums, Marseilles, a fact to be strongly smelt and tasted, lay broiling in the sun one day.

In Marseilles that day there was a villainous prison. In one of its chambers, so repulsive a place that even the obtrusive stare blinked at it, and left it to such refuse of reflected light as it could find for itself, were two men. Besides the two men, a notched and disfigured bench, im-movable from the wall, with a draught-board rudely hacked upon it with a knife, a set of draughts, made of old buttons and soup bones, a set of dominoes, two mats, and two or three wine bottles. That was all the chamber held, exclusive of rats and other unseen vermin, in addition to the seen vermin, the two men.

It received such light as it got, through a grating of iron bars, fashioned like a pretty large window, by means of which it could be always inspected from the gloomy staircase on which the grating gave. There was a broad strong ledge of stone to this grating, where the bottom of it was let into the masonry, three or four feet above the ground. Upon it, one of the two men lolled, half sitting and half lying, with his knees drawn up, and his feet and shoulders planted against the opposite sides of the aperture. The bars were wide enough apart to admit of his thrusting his arm through to the elbow; and so he held on negligently, for his greater ease.

A prison taint was on everything there. The imprisoned air, the imprisoned light, the imprisoned damps, the im-prisoned men, were all deteriorated by confinement. As the captive men were faded and haggard, so the iron was rusty, the stone was slimy, the wood was rotten, the air was faint, the light was dim. Like a well, like a vault, like a tomb, the prison had no knowledge of the brightness outside; and would have kept its polluted atmosphere intact, in one of the spice islands of the Indian ocean.

The man who lay on the ledge of the grating was even chilled. He jerked his great cloak more heavily upon him by an impatient movement of one shoulder, and growled, "To the devil with this Brigand of a Sun that never shines in here!"

He was waiting to be fed; looking sideways through the bars, that he might see the further down the stairs, with much of the expression of a wild beast in similar expectation. But his eyes, too close together, were not so nobly set in his head as those of the king of beasts are in his, and they were sharp rather than bright—pointed weapons with little surface to betray them. They had no depth or change; they glittered, and they opened and shut. So far, and waiving their use to himself, a clockmaker could have made a better pair. He had a hook nose, handsome after its kind, but too high between the eyes, by probably just as much as his eyes were too near to one another. For the rest, he was large and tall in frame, had thin lips, where his thick moustache showed them at all, and a quantity of dry hair, of no definable colour, in its shaggy state, but shot with red. The hand with which he held the grating (seamed all over the back with ugly scratches newly healed), was unusually small and plump; would have been unusually white, but for the prison grime.

The other man was lying on the stone floor, covered with a coarse brown coat.

"Get up, pig!" growled the first. "Don't sleep when I am hungry."

"It's all one, master," said the pig, in a submissive manner, and not without cheerfulness; "I can wake when I will, I can sleep when I will. It's all the same."

As he said it, he rose, shook himself, scratched himself, tied his brown coat loosely round his neck by the sleeves (he had previously used it as a coverlet), and sat down upon the pavement yawning, with his back against the wall opposite to the grating.

THE BIRDS

"Say what the hour is," grumbled the first man.

"The mid-day bells will ring——in forty minutes." When he made the little pause, he had looked round the prison-room, as if for certain information.

"You are a clock. How is it that you always know?"

"How can I say? I always know what the hour is, and where I am. I was brought in here at night, and out of a boat, but I know where I am. See here! Marseilles harbour;" on his knees on the pavement, mapping it all out with a swarthy forefinger; "Toulon (where the galleys are), Spain over there, Algiers over *there*. Creeping away to the left here, Nice. Round by the Cornice to Genoa. Genoa Mole and Harbour. Quarantine Ground. City there; terrace gardens blushing with the bella donna. Here, Porto Fino. Stand out for Leghorn. Out again for Civita Vecchia. So away to——hey! there's no room for Naples;" he had got to the wall by this time; "but it's all one; it's in there!"

He remained on his knees, looking up at his fellow-prisoner with a lively look for a prison. A sunburnt, quick, lithe, little man, though rather thick-set. Earrings in his brown ears, white teeth lighting up his grotesque brown face, intensely black hair clustering about his brown throat, a ragged red shirt open at his brown breast. Loose, seaman-like trousers, decent shoes, a long red cap, a red sash round his waist, and a knife in it.

"Judge if I come back from Naples as I went! See here, my master! Civita Vecchia, Leghorn, Porto Fino, Genoa, Cornice, Off Nice (which is in there), Marseilles, you and me. The apartment of the jailer and his keys is where I put this thumb; and here at my wrist they keep the national razor in its case—the guillotine locked up."

The other man spat suddenly on the pavement, and gurgled in his throat.

Some lock below gurgled in *its* throat immediately after-wards, and then a door clashed. Slow steps began ascending the stairs; the prattle of a sweet little voice mingled with the noise they made; and the prison-keeper appeared carrying his daughter, three or four years old, and a basket.

"How goes the world this forenoon, gentlemen? My little one, you see, going round with me to have a peep at her father's birds. Fie, then! Look at the birds, my pretty, look at the birds."

He looked sharply at the birds himself, as he held the child up at the grate, especially at the little bird, whose activity he seemed to mistrust. "I have brought your bread, Signor John Baptist," said he (they all spoke in French, but the little man was an Italian); "and if I might recommend you not to game——"

"You don't recommend the master!" said John Baptist, showing his teeth as he smiled.

"Oh! but the master wins," returned the jailer, with a passing look of no particular liking at the other man, "and you lose. It's quite another thing. You get husky bread and sour drink by it; and he gets sausage of Lyons, veal in savoury jelly, white bread, strachino cheese, and good wine by it. Look at the birds, my pretty!"

"Poor birds!" said the child.

The fair little face, touched with divine compassion, as it peeped shrinkingly through the grate, was like an angel's in the prison. John Baptist rose and moved towards it, as if it had a good attraction for him. The other bird remained as before, except for an impatient glance at the basket.

"Stay!" said the jailer, putting his little daughter on the outer ledge of the grate, "she shall feed the birds. This big loaf is for Signor John Baptist. We must break it to get it through into the cage. So, there's a tame bird to kiss the little hand! This sausage in a vine-leaf is for Monsieur Rigaud. Again—this veal in savoury jelly is for Monsieur Rigaud. Again—these three white little loaves are for Monsieur Rigaud. Again, this cheese—again, this wine— again, this tobacco—all for Monsieur Rigaud. Lucky bird!"

The Birds in the Cage

MONSIEUR RIGAUD AND JOHN BAPTIST

The child put all these things between the bars into the soft, smooth, well-shaped hand, with evident dread—more than once drawing back her own and looking at the man with her fair brow roughened into an expression half of fright and half of anger. Whereas she had put the lump of coarse bread into the swart, scaled, knotted hands of John Baptist (who had scarcely as much nail on his eight fingers and two thumbs as would have made out one for Monsieur Rigaud), with ready confidence; and, when he kissed her hand, had herself passed it caressingly over his face. Monsieur Rigaud, indifferent to this distinction, propitiated the father by laughing and nodding at the daughter as often as she gave him anything; and, so soon as he had all his viands about him in convenient nooks of the ledge on which he rested, began to eat with an appetite.

When Monsieur Rigaud laughed, a change took place in his face, that was more remarkable than prepossessing. His moustache went up under his nose, and his nose came down over his moustache, in a very sinister and cruel manner.

"There!" said the jailer, turning his basket upside down to beat the crumbs out, "I have expended all the money I received; here is the note of it, and *that's* a thing accomplished. Monsieur Rigaud, as I expected yesterday, the President will look for the pleasure of your society at an hour after mid-day, to-day."

"To try me, eh?" said Rigaud, pausing, knife in hand and morsel in mouth.

"You have said it. To try you."

"There is no news for me?" asked John Baptist, who had begun, contentedly, to munch his bread.

The jailer shrugged his shoulders.

"Lady of mine! Am I to lie here all my life, my father?"

"What do I know!" cried the jailer, turning upon him with southern quickness, and gesticulating with both his hands and all his fingers, as if he were threatening to tear him to pieces. "My friend, how is it possible for me to tell

7

how long you are to lie here? What do I know, John Baptist Cavalletto? Death of my life! There are prisoners here sometimes, who are not in such a devil of a hurry to be tried."

He seemed to glance obliquely at Monsieur Rigaud in this remark; but Monsieur Rigaud had already resumed his meal, though not with quite so quick an appetite as before.

"Adieu, my birds!" said the keeper of the prison, taking his pretty child in his arms, and dictating the words with a kiss.

"Adieu, my birds!" the pretty child repeated.

Her innocent face looked back so brightly over his shoulder, as he walked away with her, singing her the song of the child's game:

> "Who passes by this road so late?
> Compagnon de la Majolaine!
> Who passes by this road so late?
> Always gay!"

that John Baptist felt it a point of honour to reply at the grate, and in good time and tune, though a little hoarsely:

> "Of all the king's knights 'tis the flower,
> Compagnon de la Majolaine!
> Of all the king's knights 'tis the flower,
> Always gay!"

Which accompanied them so far down the few steep stairs, that the prison-keeper had to stop at last for his little daughter to hear the song out, and repeat the Refrain while they were yet in sight. Then the child's head disappeared, and the prison-keeper's head disappeared, but the little voice prolonged the strain until the door clashed.

Monsieur Rigaud, finding the listening John Baptist in his way before the echoes had ceased (even the echoes were the weaker for imprisonment, and seemed to lag), reminded him with a push of his foot that he had better resume his own darker place. The little man sat down again upon the pavement, with the negligent ease of one who was thoroughly accustomed to pavements; and placing three hunks of coarse

8

bread before himself, and falling to upon a fourth, began contentedly to work his way through them, as if to clear them off were a sort of game.

Perhaps he glanced at the Lyons sausage, and perhaps he glanced at the veal in savoury jelly, but they were not there long, to make his mouth water; Monsieur Rigaud soon dispatched them, in spite of the president and tribunal, and proceeded to suck his fingers as clean as he could, and to wipe them on his vine-leaves. Then, as he paused in his drink to contemplate his fellow-prisoner, his moustache went up, and his nose came down.

" How do you find the bread ? "

" A little dry, but I have my old sauce here," returned John Baptist, holding up his knife.

" How sauce ? "

" I can cut my bread so—like a melon. Or so—like an omelette. Or so—like a fried fish. Or so—like Lyons sausage," said John Baptist, demonstrating the various cuts on the bread he held, and soberly chewing what he had in his mouth.

" Here ! " cried Monsieur Rigaud. " You may drink. You may finish this."

It was no great gift, for there was mighty little wine left; but Signor Cavalletto, jumping to his feet, received the bottle gratefully, turned it upside down at his mouth, and smacked his lips.

" Put the bottle by with the rest," said Rigaud.

The little man obeyed his orders, and stood ready to give him a lighted match; for he was now rolling his tobacco into cigarettes, by the aid of little squares of paper which had been brought in with it.

" Here ! You may have one."

" A thousand thanks, my master ! " John Baptist said it in his own language, and with the quick conciliatory manner of his own countrymen.

Monsieur Rigaud arose, lighted a cigarette, put the rest

of his stock into a breast-pocket, and stretched himself out at full length upon the bench. Cavalletto sat down on the pavement, holding one of his ankles in each hand, and smoking peacefully. There seemed to be some uncomfortable attraction of Monsieur Rigaud's eyes to the immediate neighbourhood of that part of the pavement where the thumb had been in the plan. They were so drawn in that direction, that the Italian more than once followed them to and back from the pavement in some surprise.

"What an infernal hole this is!" said Monsieur Rigaud, breaking a long pause. "Look at the light of day. Day? the light of yesterday week, the light of six months ago, the light of six years ago. So slack and dead!"

It came languishing down a square funnel that blinded a window in the staircase wall, through which the sky was never seen—nor anything else.

"Cavalletto," said Monsieur Rigaud, suddenly withdrawing his gaze from this funnel to which they had both involuntarily turned their eyes, "you know me for a gentleman?"

"Surely, surely!"

"How long have we been here?"

"I, eleven weeks, to-morrow night at midnight. You, nine weeks and three days, at five this afternoon."

"Have I ever done anything here? Ever touched the broom, or spread the mats, or rolled them up, or found the draughts, or collected the dominoes, or put my hand to any kind of work?"

"Never!"

"Have you ever thought of looking to me to do any kind of work?"

John Baptist answered with that peculiar back-handed shake of the right forefinger which is the most expressive negative in the Italian language.

"No! You knew from the first moment when you saw me here, that I was a gentleman?"

"ALTRO!" returned John Baptist, closing his eyes and

10

giving his head a most vehement toss. The word being, according to its Genoese emphasis, a confirmation, a contradiction, an assertion, a denial, a taunt, a compliment, a joke, and fifty other things, became in the present instance, with a significance beyond all power of written expression, our familiar English " I believe you !"

" Haha ! You are right ! A gentleman I am, a gentleman I'll live, and a gentleman I'll die ! It's my intent to be a gentleman. It's my game. Death of my soul, I play it out wherever I go ! "

He changed his posture to a sitting one, crying with a triumphant air :

" Here I am ! See me ! Shaken out of destiny's dice-box into the company of a mere smuggler ;—shut up with a poor little contraband trader, whose papers are wrong, and whom the police lay hold of besides, for placing his boat (as a means of getting beyond the frontier) at the disposition of other little people whose papers are wrong ; and he instinctively recognises my position, even by this light and in this place. It's well done ! By Heaven ! I win, however the game goes."

Again his moustache went up, and his nose came down.

" What's the hour now ? " he asked, with a dry hot pallor upon him, rather difficult of association with merriment.

" A little half-hour after mid-day."

" Good ! The President will have a gentleman before him soon. Come ! Shall I tell you on what accusation ? It must be now, or never, for I shall not return here. Either I shall go free, or I shall go to be made ready for shaving. You know where they keep the razor."

Signor Cavalletto took his cigarette from between his parted lips, and showed more momentary discomfiture than might have been expected.

" I am a "—Monsieur Rigaud stood up to say it—" I am a cosmopolitan gentleman. I own no particular country. My father was Swiss—Canton de Vaud. My mother was

French by blood, English by birth. I myself was born in Belgium. I am a citizen of the world."

His theatrical air, as he stood with one arm on his hip, within the folds of his cloak, together with his manner of disregarding his companion and addressing the opposite wall instead, seemed to intimate that he was rehearsing for the President, whose examination he was shortly to undergo, rather than troubling himself merely to enlighten so small a person as John Baptist Cavalletto.

"Call me five-and-thirty years of age. I have seen the world. I have lived here, and lived there, and lived like a gentleman everywhere. I have been treated and respected as a gentleman universally. If you try to prejudice me, by making out that I have lived by my wits—how do your lawyers live—your politicians—your intriguers—your men of the Exchange?"

He kept his small smooth hand in constant requisition, as if it were a witness to his gentility that had often done him good service before.

"Two years ago I came to Marseilles. I admit that I was poor; I had been ill. When your lawyers, your politicians, your intriguers, your men of the Exchange fall ill, and have not scraped money together, *they* become poor. I put up at the Cross of Gold,—kept then by Monsieur Henri Barronneau—sixty-five at least, and in a failing state of health. I had lived in the house some four months, when Monsieur Henri Barronneau had the misfortune to die;—at any rate, not a rare misfortune, that. It happens without any aid of mine, pretty often."

John Baptist having smoked his cigarette down to his fingers' ends, Monsieur Rigaud had the magnanimity to throw him another. He lighted the second at the ashes of the first, and smoked on, looking sideways at his companion, who, pre-occupied with his own case, hardly looked at him.

"Monsieur Barronneau left a widow. She was two-and-twenty. She had gained a reputation for beauty, and (which

12

is often another thing) was beautiful. I continued to live at the Cross of Gold. I married Madame Barronneau. It is not for me to say whether there was any great disparity in such a match. Here I stand, with the contamination of a jail upon me; but it is possible that you may think me better suited to her than her former husband was."

He had a certain air of being a handsome man—which he was not; and a certain air of being a well-bred man—which he was not. It was mere swagger and challenge; but in this particular, as in many others, blustering assertion goes for proof, half over the world.

"Be it as it may, Madame Barronneau approved of me. *That* is not to prejudice me, I hope?"

His eye happening to light upon John Baptist with this inquiry, that little man briskly shook his head in the negative, and repeated in an argumentative tone under his breath, altro, altro, altro, altro—an infinite number of times.

"Now came the difficulties of our position. I am proud. I say nothing in defence of pride, but I am proud. It is also my character to govern. I can't submit; I must govern. Unfortunately, the property of Madame Rigaud was settled upon herself. Such was the insane act of her late husband. More unfortunately still, she had relations. When a wife's relations interpose against a husband who is a gentleman, who is proud, and who must govern, the consequences are inimical to peace. There was yet another source of difference between us. Madame Rigaud was unfortunately a little vulgar. I sought to improve her manners and ameliorate her general tone; she (supported in this likewise by her relations) resented my endeavours. Quarrels began to arise between us; and, propagated and exaggerated by the slanders of the relations of Madame Rigaud, to become notorious to the neighbours. It has been said that I treated Madame Rigaud with cruelty. I may have been seen to slap her face —nothing more. I have a light hand; and if I have been seen apparently to correct Madame Rigaud in that manner, I have done it almost playfully."

If the playfulness of Monsieur Rigaud were at all expressed by his smile at this point, the relations of Madame Rigaud might have said that they would have much preferred his correcting that unfortunate woman seriously.

"I am sensitive and brave. I do not advance it as a merit to be sensitive and brave, but it is my character. If the male relations of Madame Rigaud had put themselves forward openly, I should have known how to deal with them. They knew that, and their machinations were conducted in secret; consequently, Madame Rigaud and I were brought into frequent and unfortunate collision. Even when I wanted any little sum of money for my personal expenses, I could not obtain it without collision—and I, too, a man whose character it is to govern! One night, Madame Rigaud and myself were walking amicably—I may say like lovers—on a height overhanging the sea. An evil star occasioned Madame Rigaud to advert to her relations; I reasoned with her on that subject, and remonstrated on the want of duty and devotion manifested in her allowing herself to be influenced by their jealous animosity towards her husband. Madame Rigaud retorted; I retorted; Madame Rigaud grew warm; I grew warm, and provoked her. I admit it. Frankness is a part of my character. At length, Madame Rigaud, in an access of fury that I must ever deplore, threw herself upon me with screams of passion (no doubt those that were overheard at some distance), tore my clothes, tore my hair, lacerated my hands, trampled and trod the dust, and finally leaped over, dashing herself to death upon the rocks below. Such is the train of incidents which malice has perverted into my endeavouring to force from Madame Rigaud a relinquishment of her rights; and, on her persistence in a refusal to make the concession I required, struggling with her—assassinating her!"

He stepped aside to the ledge where the vine-leaves yet

lay strewn about, collected two or three, and stood wiping his hands upon them, with his back to the light.

"Well," he demanded after a silence, "have you nothing to say to all that?"

"It's ugly," returned the little man, who had risen, and was brightening his knife upon his shoe, as he leaned an arm against the wall.

"What do you mean?"

John Baptist polished his knife in silence.

"Do you mean that I have not represented the case correctly?"

"Al-tro!" returned John Baptist. The word was an apology now, and stood for "Oh, by no means?"

"What then?"

"Presidents and tribunals are so prejudiced."

"Well," cried the other, uneasily flinging the end of his cloak over his shoulder with an oath, "let them do their worst!"

"Truly I think they will," murmured John Baptist to himself, as he bent his head to put his knife in his sash.

Nothing more was said on either side, though they both began walking to and fro, and necessarily crossed at every turn. Monsieur Rigaud sometimes half stopped, as if he were going to put his case in a new light, or make some irate remonstrance; but Signor Cavalletto continuing to go slowly to and fro at a grotesque kind of jog-trot pace, with his eyes turned downward, nothing came of these inclinings.

By-and-by the noise of the key in the lock arrested them both. The sound of voices succeeded, and the tread of feet. The door clashed, the voices and the feet came on, and the prison-keeper slowly ascended the stairs, followed by a guard of soldiers.

"Now, Monsieur Rigaud," said he, pausing for a moment at the grate, with his keys in his hands, "have the goodness to come out."

"I am to depart in state, I see?"

"Why, unless you did," returned the jailer, "you might

depart in so many pieces that it would be difficult to get you together again. There's a crowd, Monsieur Rigaud, and it doesn't love you."

He passed on out of sight, and unlocked and unbarred a low door in the corner of the chamber. "Now," said he, as he opened it and appeared within, "come out."

There is no sort of whiteness in all the hues under the sun at all like the whiteness of Monsieur Rigaud's face as it was then. Neither is there any expression of the human countenance at all like that expression, in every little line of which the frightened heart is seen to beat. Both are conventionally compared with death; but the difference is the whole deep gulf between the struggle done, and the fight at its most desperate extremity.

He lighted another of his paper cigars at his companion's; put it tightly between his teeth; covered his head with a soft slouched hat; threw the end of his cloak over his shoulder again; and walked out into the side gallery on which the door opened, without taking any further notice of Signor Cavalletto. As to that little man himself, his whole attention had become absorbed in getting near the door, and looking out at it. Precisely as a beast might approach the opened gate of his den and eye the freedom beyond, he passed those few moments in watching and peering, until the door was closed upon him.

There was an officer in command of the soldiers; a stout, serviceable, profoundly calm man, with his drawn sword in his hand, smoking a cigar. He very briefly directed the placing of Monsieur Rigaud in the midst of the party, put himself with consummate indifference at their head, gave the word "march!" and so they all went jingling down the staircase. The door clashed—the key turned—and a ray of unusual light, and a breath of unusual air, seemed to have passed through the jail, vanishing in a tiny wreath of smoke from the cigar.

Still, in his captivity, like a lower animal—like some

16

impatient ape, or roused bear of the smaller species—the prisoner, now left solitary, had jumped upon the ledge, to lose no glimpse of this departure. As he yet stood clasping the grate with both hands, an uproar broke upon his hearing; yells, shrieks, oaths, threats, execrations, all comprehended in it, though (as in a storm) nothing but a raging swell of sound distinctly heard.

Excited into a still greater resemblance to a caged wild animal by his anxiety to know more, the prisoner leaped nimbly down, ran round the chamber, leaped nimbly up again, clasped the grate and tried to shake it, leaped down and ran, leaped up and listened, and never rested until the noise, becoming more and more distant, had died away. How many better prisoners have worn their noble hearts out so ; no man thinking of it ; not even the beloved of their souls realising it ; great kings and governors, who had made them captive, careering in the sunlight jauntily, and men cheering them on. Even the said great personages dying in bed, making exemplary ends and sounding speeches ; and polite history, more servile than their instruments, embalming them !

At last, John Baptist, now able to choose his own spot within the compass of those walls, for the exercise of his faculty of going to sleep when he would, lay down upon the bench, with his face turned over on his crossed arms, and slumbered. In his submission, in his lightness, in his good humour, in his short-lived passion, in his easy content-ment with hard bread and hard stones, in his ready sleep, in his fits and starts altogether, a true son of the land that gave him birth.

The wide stare stared itself out for one while ; the sun went down in a red, green, golden glory ; the stars came out in the heavens, and the fire-flies mimicked them in the lower air, as men may feebly imitate the goodness of a better order of beings ; the long dusty roads and the interminable plains were in repose—and so deep a hush was on the sea, that it scarcely whispered of the time when it shall give up its dead.

17

CHAPTER II

"No more of yesterday's howling, over yonder, to-day, sir; is there?"

"I have heard none."

"Then you may be sure there *is* none. When these people howl, they howl to be heard."

"Most people do, I suppose."

"Ah! but these people are always howling. Never happy otherwise."

"Do you mean the Marseilles people?"

"I mean the French people. They're always at it. As to Marseilles, we know what Marseilles is. It sent the most insurrectionary tune into the world that was ever composed. It couldn't exist without allonging and marshonging to something or other—victory or death, or blazes, or something."

The speaker, with a whimsical good humour on him all the time, looked over the parapet-wall with the greatest disparagement of Marseilles; and taking up a determined position by putting his hands in his pockets, and rattling his money at it, apostrophised it with a short laugh.

"Allong and marshong, indeed. It would be more creditable to you, I think, to let other people allong and marshong about their lawful business, instead of shutting 'em up in quarantine!"

"Tiresome enough," said the other. "But we shall be out to-day."

18

"Out to-day!" repeated the first. "It's almost an aggravation of the enormity, that we shall be out to-day. Out? What have we ever been in for?"

"For no very strong reason, I must say. But as we come from the East, and as the East is the country of the plague—"

"The plague!" repeated the other. "That's my grievance. I have had the plague continually, ever since I have been here. I am like a sane man shut up in a madhouse; I can't stand the suspicion of the thing. I came here as well as ever I was in my life; but to suspect me of the plague is to give me the plague. And I have had it—and I have got it."

"You bear it very well, Mr. Meagles," said the second speaker, smiling.

"No. If you knew the real state of the case, that's the last observation you would think of making. I have been waking up, night after night, and saying, *now* I have got it, *now* it has developed itself, *now* I am in for it, *now* these fellows are making out their case for their precautions. Why, I'd as soon have a spit put through me, and be stuck upon a card in a collection of beetles, as lead the life I have been leading here."

"Well, Mr. Meagles, say no more about it, now it's over," urged a cheerful feminine voice.

"Over!" repeated Mr. Meagles, who appeared (though without any ill-nature) to be in that peculiar state of mind in which the last word spoken by anybody else is a new injury. "Over! and why should I say no more about it because it's over?"

It was Mrs. Meagles who had spoken to Mr. Meagles; and Mrs. Meagles was, like Mr. Meagles, comely and healthy, with a pleasant English face which had been looking at homely things for five-and-fifty years or more, and shone with a bright reflection of them.

"There! Never mind, Father, never mind!" said Mrs. Meagles. "For goodness sake content yourself with Pet."

" With Pet?" repeated Mr. Meagles in his injured vein. Pet, however, being close behind him, touched him on the shoulder, and Mr. Meagles immediately forgave Marseilles from the bottom of his heart.

Pet was about twenty. A fair girl with rich brown hair hanging free in natural ringlets. A lovely girl, with a frank face, and wonderful eyes ; so large, so soft, so bright, set to such perfection in her kind good head. She was round and fresh and dimpled and spoilt, and there was in Pet an air of timidity and dependence which was the best weakness in the world, and gave her the only crowning charm a girl so pretty and pleasant could have been without.

" Now, I ask you," said Mr. Meagles in the blandest confidence, falling back a step himself, and handing his daughter a step forward to illustrate his question : " I ask you simply, as between man and man, you know, DID you ever hear of such damned nonsense as putting Pet in quarantine?"

" It has had the result of making even quarantine enjoyable."

" Come!" said Mr. Meagles, " that's something to be sure. I am obliged to you for that remark. Now, Pet, my darling, you had better go along with Mother and get ready for the boat. The officer of health and a variety of humbugs, in cocked hats, are coming off to let us out of this at last : and all we jail-birds are to breakfast together in something approaching to a Christian style again, before we take wing for our different destinations. Tattycoram, stick you close to your young mistress."

He spoke to a handsome girl with lustrous dark hair and eyes, and very neatly dressed, who replied with a half curtsey as she passed off in the train of Mrs. Meagles and Pet. They crossed the bare scorched terrace all three together, and disappeared through a staring white archway. Mr. Meagles's companion, a grave dark man of forty, still stood looking towards this archway after they were gone ; until Mr. Meagles tapped him on the arm.

" I beg your pardon," said he, starting.

" Not at all," said Mr. Meagles.

They took one silent turn backward and forward in the shade of the wall, getting, at the height on which the quarantine barracks are placed, what cool refreshment of sea breeze there was, at seven in the morning. Mr. Meagles's companion resumed the conversation.

" May I ask you," he said, " what is the name of— "

" Tattycoram ? " Mr. Meagles struck in. " I have not the least idea."

" I thought," said the other, " that— "

" Tattycoram ? " suggested Mr. Meagles again.

" Thank you—that Tattycoram was a name ; and I have several times wondered at the oddity of it."

" Why, the fact is," said Mr. Meagles, " Mrs. Meagles and myself are, you see, practical people."

" That, you have frequently mentioned in the course of the agreeable and interesting conversations we have had together, walking up and down on these stones," said the other, with a half smile breaking through the gravity of his dark face.

" Practical people. So one day, five or six years ago now, when we took Pet to church at the Foundling—you have heard of the Foundling Hospital in London ? Similar to the Institution for the Found Children in Paris ? "

" I have seen it."

" Well ! One day when we took Pet to church there to hear the music—because, as practical people, it is the business of our lives to show her everything that we think can please her—Mother (my usual name for Mrs. Meagles) began to cry so, that it was necessary to take her out. ' What's the matter, Mother ? ' said I, when we had brought her a little round ; ' you are frightening Pet, my dear.' ' Yes, I know that, Father,' says Mother, ' but I think it's through my loving her so much, that it ever came into my head.' ' That ever what came into your head, Mother ? ' ' O dear, dear ! ' cried Mother, breaking out again, ' when I saw all those children

21

ranged tier above tier, and appealing from the father none of them has ever known on earth, to the great Father of us all in Heaven, I thought, does any wretched mother ever come here, and look among those young faces, wondering which is the poor child she brought into this forlorn world, never through all its life to know her love, her kiss, her face, her voice, even her name!' Now that was practical in Mother, and I told her so. I said, 'Mother, that's what I call practical in you, my dear.'"

The other, not unmoved, assented.

"So I said next day: Now, Mother, I have a proposition to make that I think you'll approve of. Let us take one of those same children to be a little maid to Pet. We are practical people. So if we should find her temper a little defective, or any of her ways a little wide of ours, we shall know what we have to take into account. We shall know what an immense deduction must be made from all the influences and experiences that have formed us—no parents, no child-brother or sister, no individuality of home, no Glass Slipper, or Fairy Godmother. And that's the way we came by Tattycoram."

"And the name itself—"

"By George!" said Mr. Meagles, "I was forgetting the name itself. Why, she was called in the Institution, Harriet Beadle—an arbitrary name, of course. Now, Harriet we changed into Hattey, and then into Tatty, because, as practical people, we thought even a playful name might be a new thing to her, and might have a softening and affectionate kind of effect, don't you see? As to Beadle, that I needn't say was wholly out of the question. If there is anything that is not to be tolerated on any terms, anything that is a type of Jack-in-office insolence and absurdity, anything that represents in coats, waistcoats, and big sticks, our English holding-on by nonsense, after every one has found it out, it is a beadle. You haven't seen a beadle lately?"

22

"As an Englishman, who has been more than twenty years in China, no."

"Then," said Mr. Meagles, laying his forefinger on his companion's breast with great animation, "don't you see a beadle, now, if you can help it. Whenever I see a beadle in full fig, coming down a street on a Sunday at the head of a charity school, I am obliged to turn and run away, or I should hit him. The name of Beadle being out of the question, and the originator of the Institution for these poor foundlings having been a blessed creature of the name of Coram, we gave that name to Pet's little maid. At one time she was Tatty, and at one time she was Coram, until we got into a way of mixing the two names together, and now she is always Tattycoram."

"Your daughter," said the other, when they had taken another silent turn to and fro, and after standing for a moment at the wall glancing down at the sea, had resumed their walk, "is your only child, I know, Mr. Meagles. May I ask you—in no impertinent curiosity, but because I have had so much pleasure in your society, may never in this labyrinth of a world exchange a quiet word with you again, and wish to preserve an accurate remembrance of you and yours—may I ask you, if I have not gathered from your good wife that you have had other children?"

"No. No," said Mr. Meagles. "Not exactly other children. One other child."

"I am afraid I have inadvertently touched upon a tender theme."

"Never mind," said Mr. Meagles. "If I am grave about it, I am not at all sorrowful. It quiets me for a moment, but does not make me unhappy. Pet had a twin sister who died when we could just see her eyes—exactly like Pet's—above the table, as she stood on tiptoe holding by it."

"Ah! indeed, indeed!"

"Yes, and being practical people, a result has gradually sprung up in the minds of Mrs. Meagles and myself which perhaps you may—or perhaps you may not—understand. Pet and her baby sister were so exactly alike, and so completely one, that in our thoughts we have never been able to separate them since. It would be of no use to tell us that our dead child was a mere infant. We have changed that child according to the changes in the child spared to us, and always with us. As Pet has grown, that child has grown; as Pet has become more sensible and womanly, her sister has become more sensible and womanly, by just the same degrees. It would be as hard to convince me that if I was to pass into the other world to-morrow, I should not, through the mercy of God, be received there by a daughter, just like Pet, as to persuade me that Pet herself is not a reality at my side."

"I understand you," said the other, gently.

"As to her," pursued her father, "the sudden loss of her little picture and playfellow, and her early association with that mystery in which we all have our equal share, but which is not often so forcibly presented to a child, has necessarily had some influence on her character. Then, her mother and I were not young when we married, and Pet has always had a sort of grown-up life with us, though we have tried to adapt ourselves to her. We have been advised more than once when she has been a little ailing, to change climate and air for her as often as we could—especially at about this time of her life—and to keep her amused. So, as I have no need to stick at a bank-desk now (though I have been poor enough in my time I assure you, or I should have married Mrs. Meagles long before), we go trotting about the world. This is how you found us staring at the Nile, and the Pyramids, and the Sphinxes, and the Desert, and all the rest of it; and this is how Tattycoram will be a greater traveller in course of time than Captain Cook."

"I thank you," said the other, "very heartily for your confidence."

"Don't mention it," returned Mr. Meagles, "I am sure

you are quite welcome. And now, Mr. Clennam, perhaps I may ask you, whether you have yet come to a decision where to go next ? "

" Indeed, no. I am such a waif and stray everywhere, that I am liable to be drifted where any current may set."

" It's extraordinary to me—if you'll excuse my freedom in saying so—that you don't go straight to London," said Mr. Meagles, in the tone of a confidential adviser.

" Perhaps I shall."

" Ay! But I mean with a will."

" I have no will. That is to say," he coloured a little, " next to none that I can put in action now. Trained by main force; broken, not bent; heavily ironed with an object on which I was never consulted and which was never mine; shipped away to the other end of the world before I was of age, and exiled there until my father's death there, a year ago; always grinding in a mill I always hated; what is to be expected from *me* in middle life? Will, purpose, hope? All those lights were extinguished before I could sound the words."

" Light 'em up again!" said Mr. Meagles.

" Ah! Easily said. I am the son, Mr. Meagles, of a hard father and mother. I am the only child of parents who weighed, measured, and priced everything; for whom what could not be weighed, measured, and priced, had no existence. Strict people as the phrase is, professors of a stern religion, their very religion was a gloomy sacrifice of tastes and sympathies that were never their own, offered up as a part of a bargain for the security of their possessions. Austere faces, inexorable discipline, penance in this world and terror in the next—nothing graceful or gentle anywhere, and the void in my cowed heart everywhere—this was my childhood, if I may so misuse the word as to apply it to such a beginning of life."

" Really though ? " said Mr. Meagles, made very uncomfortable by the picture offered to his imagination. " That was a tough commencement. But come! You must now study, and profit by all that lies beyond it, like a practical man."

"If the people who are usually called practical, were practical in your direction—"

"Why, so they are!" said Mr. Meagles.

"Are they indeed?"

"Well, I suppose so," returned Mr. Meagles, thinking about it. "Eh? One can but *be* practical, and Mrs. Meagles and myself are nothing else."

"My unknown course is easier and more hopeful than I had expected to find it then," said Clennam, shaking his head with his grave smile. "Enough of me. Here is the boat."

The boat was filled with the cocked hats to which Mr. Meagles entertained a national objection; and the wearers of those cocked hats landed and came up the steps, and all the impounded travellers congregated together. There was then a mighty production of papers on the part of the cocked hats, and a calling over of names, and great work of signing, sealing, stamping, inking, and sanding, with exceedingly blurred, gritty, and undecipherable results. Finally, everything was done according to rule, and the travellers were at liberty to depart whithersoever they would.

They made little account of stare and glare, in the new pleasure of recovering their freedom, but flitted across the harbour in gay boats, and re-assembled at a great hotel, whence the sun was excluded by closed lattices, and where bare paved floors, lofty ceilings, and resounding corridors, tempered the intense heat. There, a great table in a great room was soon profusely covered with a superb repast; and the quarantine quarters became bare indeed, remembered among dainty dishes, southern fruits, cooled wines, flowers from Genoa, snow from the mountain tops, and all the colours of the rainbow flashing in the mirrors.

"But I bear those monotonous walls no ill-will now," said Mr. Meagles. "One always begins to forgive a place as soon as it's left behind; I dare say a prisoner begins to relent towards his prison, after he is let out."

They were about thirty in company, and all talking; but necessarily in groups. Father and Mother Meagles sat with their daughter between them, the last three on one side of the table: on the opposite side sat Mr. Clennam; a tall French gentleman with raven hair and beard, of a swart and terrible, not to say genteely diabolical aspect, but who had shown himself the mildest of men; and a handsome young Englishwoman, travelling quite alone, who had a proud observant face, and had either withdrawn herself from the rest or been avoided by the rest—nobody, herself excepted perhaps, could have quite decided which. The rest of the party were of the usual materials. Travellers on business, and travellers for pleasure; officers from India on leave; merchants in the Greek and Turkey trades; a clerical English husband in a meek strait-waistcoat, on a wedding trip with his young wife; a majestic English mama and papa, of the patrician order, with a family of three growing-up daughters, who were keeping a journal for the confusion of their fellow-creatures; and a deaf old English mother tough in travel, with a very decidedly grown-up daughter indeed, which daughter went sketching about the universe in the expectation of ultimately toning herself off into the married state.

The reserved Englishwoman took up Mr. Meagles in his last remark.

"Do you mean that a prisoner forgives his prison?" said she, slowly and with emphasis.

"That was my speculation, Miss Wade. I don't pretend to know positively how a prisoner might feel. I never *was* one before."

"Mademoiselle doubts," said the French gentleman in his own language, "its being so easy to forgive?"

"I do."

Pet had to translate this passage to Mr. Meagles, who

never by any accident acquired any knowledge whatever of the language of any country into which he travelled. "Oh!" said he. "Dear me! But that's a pity, isn't it?"

"That I am not credulous?" said Miss Wade.

"Not exactly that. Put it another way. That you can't believe it easy to forgive."

"My experience," she quietly returned, "has been correcting my belief in many respects, for some years. It is our natural progress, I have heard."

"Well, well! But it's not natural to bear malice, I hope?" said Mr. Meagles, cheerily.

"If I had been shut up in any place to pine and suffer, I should always hate that place and wish to burn it down, or raze it to the ground. I know no more."

"Strong, sir?" said Mr. Meagles to the Frenchman; it being another of his habits to address individuals of all nations in idiomatic English, with a perfect conviction that they were bound to understand it somehow. "Rather forcible in our fair friend, you'll agree with me, I think?"

The French gentleman courteously replied, "Plait-il?" To which Mr. Meagles returned with much satisfaction, "You are right. My opinion."

The breakfast beginning by-and-by to languish, Mr. Meagles made the company a speech. It was short enough and sensible enough, considering that it was a speech at all, and hearty. It merely went to the effect that as they had all been thrown together by chance, and had all preserved a good understanding together, and were now about to disperse, and were not likely ever to find themselves all together again, what could they do better than bid farewell to one another, and give one another good-speed, in a simultaneous glass of cool champagne all round the table? It was done, and with a general shaking of hands the assembly broke up for ever.

The solitary young lady all this time had said no more. She rose with the rest, and silently withdrew to a remote corner of the great room, where she sat herself on a couch in a window, seeming to watch the reflection of the water, as it made a silver quivering on the bars of the lattice. She sat, turned away from the whole length of the apartment, as if she were lonely of her own haughty choice. And yet it would have been as difficult as ever to say, positively, whether she avoided the rest, or was avoided.

The shadow in which she sat, falling like a gloomy veil across her forehead, accorded very well with the character of her beauty. One could hardly see the face, so still and scornful, set off by the arched dark eyebrows, and the folds of dark hair, without wondering what its expression would be if a change came over it. That it could soften or relent, appeared next to impossible. That it could deepen into anger or any extreme of defiance, and that it must change in that direction when it changed at all, would have been its peculiar impression upon most observers. It was dressed and trimmed into no ceremony of expression. Although not an open face, there was no pretence in it. I am self-contained and self-reliant; your opinion is nothing to me; I have no interest in you, care nothing for you, and see and hear you with indifference—this it said plainly. It said so in the proud eyes, in the lifted nostril, in the handsome, but compressed and even cruel mouth. Cover either two of those channels of expression, and the third would have said so still. Mask them all, and the mere turn of the head would have shown an unsubduable nature.

Pet had moved up to her (she had been the subject of remark among her family and Mr. Clennam, who were now the only other occupants of the room), and was standing at her side.

"Are you"—she turned her eyes, and Pet faltered— "expecting any one to meet you here, Miss Wade?"

"I? No."

"Father is sending to the Poste Restante. Shall he have the pleasure of directing the messenger to ask if there are any letters for you?"

" I thank him, but I know there can be none."

" We are afraid," said Pet, sitting down beside her, shyly and half tenderly, " that you will feel quite deserted when we are all gone."

" Indeed ! "

" Not," said Pet, apologetically and embarrassed by her eyes, " not, of course, that we are any company to you, or that we have been able to be so, or that we thought you wished it."

" I have not intended to make it understood that I did wish it."

" No. Of course. But—in short," said Pet, timidly touching her hand as it lay impassive on the sofa between them, " will you not allow Father to render you any slight assistance or service ? He will be very glad."

" Very glad," said Mr. Meagles, coming forward with his wife and Clennam. " Anything short of speaking the language, I shall be delighted to undertake, I am sure."

" I am obliged to you," she returned, " but my arrangements are made, and I prefer to go my own way in my own manner."

" *Do* you ? " said Mr. Meagles, to himself, as he surveyed her with a puzzled look. " Well ! There's character in that, too."

" I am not much used to the society of young ladies, and I am afraid I may not show my appreciation of it as others might. A pleasant journey to you. Good-bye ! "

She would not have put out her hand, it seemed, but that Mr. Meagles put out his so straight before her, that she could not pass it. She put hers in it, and it lay there just as it had lain upon the couch.

" Good-bye ! " said Mr. Meagles. " This is the last good-bye upon the list, for Mother and I have just said it to Mr. Clennam here, and he only waits to say it to Pet. Good-bye ! We may never meet again."

" In our course through life we shall meet the people who

are coming to meet *us*, from many strange places and by
many strange roads," was the composed reply; "and what it
is set to us to do to them, and what it is set to them to do
to us, will all be done."

There was something in the manner of these words that
jarred upon Pet's ear. It implied that what was to be
done was necessarily evil, and it caused her to say in a
whisper, "O, Father!" and to shrink childishly in her
spoilt way, a little closer to him. This was not lost on the
speaker.

"Your pretty daughter," she said, "starts to think of such
things. Yet," looking full upon her, "you may be sure that
there are men and women already on their road, who have
their business to do with *you*, and who will do it. Of a
certainty they will do it. They may be coming hundreds,
thousands, of miles over the sea there; they may be close at
hand now; they may be coming, for anything you know, or
anything you can do to prevent it, from the vilest sweepings
of this very town."

With the coldest of farewells, and with a certain worn
expression on her beauty that gave it, though scarcely yet
in its prime, a wasted look, she left the room.

Now, there were many stairs and passages that she had to
traverse in passing from that part of the spacious house to
the chamber she had secured for her own occupation. When
she had almost completed the journey, and was passing along
the gallery in which her room was, she heard an angry sound
of muttering and sobbing. A door stood open, and within
she saw the attendant upon the girl she had just left; the
maid with the curious name.

She stood still, to look at this maid. A sullen, passionate
girl! Her rich black hair was all about her face, her face
was flushed and hot, and as she sobbed and raged, she
plucked at her lips with an unsparing hand.

"Selfish brutes!" said the girl, sobbing and heaving
between whiles. "Not caring what becomes of me! Leaving

me here hungry and thirsty and tired, to starve, for anything they care! Beasts! Devils! Wretches!"

"My poor girl, what is the matter?"

She looked up suddenly, with reddened eyes, and with her hands suspended, in the act of pinching her neck, freshly disfigured with great scarlet blots. "It's nothing to you what's the matter. It don't signify to any one."

"O yes it does; I am sorry to see you so."

"You are not sorry," said the girl. "You are glad. You know you are glad. I never was like this but twice, over in the quarantine yonder; and both times you found me. I am afraid of you."

"Afraid of me?"

"Yes. You seem to come like my own anger, my own malice, my own—whatever it is—I don't know what it is. But I am ill-used, I am ill-used, I am ill-used!" Here the sobs and the tears, and the tearing hand, which had all been suspended together, since the first surprise, went on together anew.

The visitor stood looking at her with a strange attentive smile. It was wonderful to see the fury of the contest in the girl, and the bodily struggle she made as if she were rent by the Demons of old.

"I am younger than she is by two or three years, and yet it's me that looks after her, as if I was old, and it's she that's always petted and called Baby! I detest the name. I hate her! They make a fool of her, they spoil her. She thinks of nothing but herself, she thinks no more of me than if I was a stock and a stone!" So the girl went on.

"You must have patience."

"I *won't* have patience!"

"If they take much care of themselves, and little or none of you, you must not mind it."

"I *will* mind it!"

"Hush! Be more prudent. You forget your dependent position."

Under the Microscope

A FIERCE STRUGGLE

"I don't care for that. I'll run away. I'll do some mischief. I won't bear it; I can't bear it; I shall die if I try to bear it!"

The observer stood with her hand upon her own bosom, looking at the girl, as one afflicted with a diseased part might curiously watch the dissection and exposition of an analogous case.

The girl raged and battled with all the force of her youth and fulness of life, until by little and little her passionate exclamations trailed off into broken murmurs as if she were in pain. By corresponding degrees she sank into a chair, then upon her knees, then upon the ground beside the bed, drawing the coverlet with her, half to hide her shamed head and wet hair in it, and half, as it seemed, to embrace it, rather than have nothing to take to her repentant breast.

"Go away from me, go away from me.! When my temper comes upon me, I am mad. I know I might keep it off if I only tried hard enough, and sometimes I do try hard enough, and at other times I don't and won't. What have I said! I knew when I said it, it was all lies. They think I am being taken care of somewhere, and have all I want. They are nothing but good to me. I love them dearly; no people could ever be kinder to a thankless creature than they always are to me. Do, do go away, for I am afraid of you. I am afraid of myself when I feel my temper coming, and I am as much afraid of you. Go away from me, and let me pray and cry myself better!"

The day passed on; and again the wide stare stared itself out; and the hot night was on Marseilles; and through it the caravan of the morning, all dispersed, went their appointed ways. And thus ever, by day and night, under the sun and under the stars, climbing the dusty hills and toiling along the weary plains, journeying by land and journeying by sea, coming and going so strangely, to meet and to act and react on one another, move all we restless travellers through the pilgrimage of life.

CHAPTER III

HOME

It was a Sunday evening in London, gloomy, close and stale. Maddening church bells of all degrees of dissonance, sharp and flat, cracked and clear, fast and slow, made the brick-and-mortar echoes hideous. Melancholy streets in a penitential garb of soot, steeped the souls of the people who were condemned to look at them out of windows, in dire despondency. In every thoroughfare, up almost every alley, and down almost every turning, some doleful bell was throbbing, jerking, tolling, as if the Plague were in the city and the dead-carts were going round. Everything was bolted and barred that could by possibility furnish relief to an over-worked people. No pictures, no unfamiliar animals, no rare plants or flowers, no natural or artificial wonders of the ancient world—all *taboo* with that enlightened strictness, that the ugly South Sea gods in the British Museum might have supposed themselves at home again. Nothing to see but streets, streets, streets. Nothing to breathe but streets, streets, streets. Nothing to change the brooding mind, or raise it up. Nothing for the spent toiler to do, but to compare the monotony of his seventh day with the monotony of his six days, think what a weary life he led, and make the best of it—or the worst, according to the probabilities.

At such a happy time, so propitious to the interests of religion and morality, Mr. Arthur Clennam, newly arrived from Marseilles by way of Dover, and by Dover coach the

SUNDAY EVENING IN LONDON

Blue-eyed Maid, sat in the window of a coffee-house on
Ludgate Hill. Ten thousand responsible houses surrounded
him, frowning as heavily on the streets they composed,
as if they were every one inhabited by the ten young men of
the Calender's story, who blackened their faces and bemoaned
their miseries every night. Fifty thousand lairs surrounded
him where people lived so unwholesomely, that fair water
put into their crowded rooms on Saturday night, would
be corrupt on Sunday morning; albeit my lord, their county
member, was amazed that they failed to sleep in company
with their butcher's meat. Miles of close wells and pits
of houses, where the inhabitants gasped for air, stretched
far away towards every point of the compass. Through
the heart of the town a deadly sewer ebbed and flowed,
in the place of a fine fresh river. What secular want could
the million or so of human beings whose daily labour, six
days in the week, lay among these Arcadian objects, from
the sweet sameness of which they had no escape between the
cradle and the grave—what secular want could they possibly
have upon their seventh day ? Clearly they could want
nothing but a stringent policeman.

Mr. Arthur Clennam sat in the window of the coffee-house
on Ludgate Hill, counting one of the neighbouring bells,
making sentences and burdens of songs out of it in spite of
himself, and wondering how many sick people it might be
the death of in the course of the year. As the hour approached,
its changes of measure made it more and more exasperating.
At the quarter, it went off into a condition of deadly-lively
importunity, urging the populace in a voluble manner to
Come to church, Come to church, Come to church ! At the
ten minutes, it became aware that the congregation would be
scanty, and slowly hammered out in low spirits, They *won't*
come, they *won't* come, they *won't* come ! At the five
minutes, it abandoned hope, and shook every house in the
neighbourhood for three hundred seconds, with one dismal
swing per second, as a groan of despair.

" Thank Heaven ! " said Clennam, when the hour struck, and the bell stopped.

But its sound had revived a long train of miserable Sundays, and the procession would not stop with the bell, but continued to march on. " Heaven forgive me," said he, " and those who trained me. How I have hated this day ! "

There was the dreary Sunday of his childhood, when he sat with his hands before him, scared out of his senses by a horrible tract which commenced business with the poor child by asking him in its title, why he was going to Perdition ?—a piece of curiosity that he, really in a frock and drawers, was not in a condition to satisfy—and which, for the further attraction of his infant mind, had a parenthesis in every other line with some such hiccupping reference as 2 Ep. Thess. c. iii. v. 6 & 7. There was the sleepy Sunday of his boyhood, when, like a military deserter, he was marched to chapel by a picquet of teachers three times a day, morally handcuffed to another boy ; and when he would willingly have bartered two meals of indigestible sermon for another ounce or two of inferior mutton at his scanty dinner in the flesh. There was the interminable Sunday of his nonage ; when his mother, stern of face and unrelenting of heart, would sit all day behind a Bible—bound, like her own construction of it, in the hardest, barest, and straitest boards, with one dinted ornament on the cover like the drag of a chain, and a wrathful sprinkling of red upon the edges of the leaves—as if it, of all books ! were a fortification against sweetness of temper, natural affection, and gentle intercourse. There was the resentful Sunday of a little later, when he sat glowering and glooming through the tardy length of the day, with a sullen sense of injury in his heart, and no more real knowledge of the beneficent history of the New Testament, than if he had been bred among idolaters. There was a legion of Sundays, all days of unserviceable bitterness and mortification, slowly passing before him.

" Beg pardon, sir," said a brisk waiter, rubbing the table. " Wish see bedroom ? "

"Yes. I have just made up my mind to do it."

"Chaymaid!" cried the waiter. "Gelen box num seven wish see room!"

"Stay!" said Clennam, rousing himself. "I was not thinking of what I said; I answered mechanically. I am not going to sleep here. I am going home."

"Deed, sir? Chaymaid! Gelen box num seven, not go sleep here, gome."

He sat in the same place as the day died, looking at the dull houses opposite, and thinking, if the disembodied spirits of former inhabitants were ever conscious of them, how they must pity themselves for their old places of imprisonment. Sometimes a face would appear behind the dingy glass of a window, and would fade away into the gloom as if it had seen enough of life and had vanished out of it. Presently the rain began to fall in slanting lines between him and those houses, and people began to collect under cover of the public passage opposite, and to look out hopelessly at the sky as the rain dropped thicker and faster. Then wet umbrellas began to appear, draggled skirts, and mud. What the mud had been doing with itself, or where it came from, who could say? But it seemed to collect in a moment, as a crowd will, and in five minutes to have splashed all the sons and daughters of Adam. The lamplighter was going his rounds now; and as the fiery jets sprang up under his touch, one might have fancied them astonished at being suffered to introduce any show of brightness into such a dismal scene.

Mr. Arthur Clennam took up his hat and buttoned his coat, and walked out. In the country, the rain would have developed a thousand fresh scents, and every drop would have had its bright association with some beautiful form of growth or life. In the city, it developed only foul stale smells, and was a sickly, lukewarm, dirt-stained, wretched addition to the gutters.

He crossed by St. Paul's and went down, at a long angle, almost to the water's edge, through some of the crooked and descending streets which lie (and lay more crookedly and closely then) between the river and Cheapside. Passing, now the mouldy hall of some obsolete Worshipful Company, now the illuminated windows of a Congregationless Church that seemed to be waiting for some adventurous Belzoni to dig it out and discover its history; passing silent warehouses and wharves, and here and there a narrow alley leading to the river, where a wretched little bill, FOUND DROWNED, was weeping on the wet wall; he came at last to the house he sought. An old brick house, so dingy as to be all but black, standing by itself within a gateway. Before it, a square court-yard where a shrub or two and a patch of grass were as rank (which is saying much) as the iron railings enclosing them were rusty; behind it, a jumble of roots. It was a double house, with long, narrow, heavily-framed windows. Many years ago, it had had it in its mind to slide down sideways; it had been propped up, however, and was leaning on some half-dozen gigantic crutches: which gymnasium for the neighbouring cats, weather-stained, smoke-blackened, and overgrown with weeds, appeared in these latter days to be no very sure reliance.

"Nothing changed," said the traveller, stopping to look round. "Dark and miserable as ever. A light in my mother's window, which seems never to have been extinguished since I came home twice a year from school, and dragged my box over this pavement. Well, well, well!"

He went up to the door, which had a projecting canopy in carved work, of festooned jack-towels and children's heads with water on the brain, designed after a once-popular monumental pattern; and knocked. A shuffling step was soon heard on the stone floor of the hall, and the door was opened by an old man; bent and dried, but with keen eyes.

He had a candle in his hand, and he held it up for a moment to assist his keen eyes. "Ah, Mr. Arthur?" he said, without any emotion, "you are come at last? Step in."

Mr. Arthur stepped in and shut the door.

"Your figure is filled out, and set," said the old man, turning to look at him with the light raised again, and shaking his head; "but you don't come up to your father in my opinion. Nor yet your mother."

"How is my mother?"

"She is as she always is now. Keeps her room when not actually bedridden, and hasn't been out of it fifteen times in as many years, Arthur." They had walked into a spare, meagre dining-room. The old man had put the candlestick upon the table, and, supporting his right elbow with his left hand, was smoothing his leathern jaws while he looked at the visitor. The visitor offered his hand. The old man took it coldly enough, and seemed to prefer his jaws; to which he returned, as soon as he could.

"I doubt if your mother will approve of your coming home on the Sabbath, Arthur," he said, shaking his head warily.

"You wouldn't have me go away again?"

"Oh! I? I? I am not the master. It's not what *I* would have. I have stood between your father and mother for a number of years. I don't pretend to stand between your mother and you."

"Will you tell her that I have come home?"

"Yes, Arthur, yes. Oh to be sure! I'll tell her that you have come home. Please to wait here. You won't find the room changed." He took another candle from a cupboard, lighted it, left the first on the table, and went upon his errand. He was a short, bald old man, in a high-shouldered black coat and waistcoat, drab breeches, and long drab gaiters. He might, from his dress, have been either clerk or servant, and in fact had long been both. There was nothing about him in the way of decoration but a watch, which was lowered into the depths of its proper pocket by an old black ribbon, and had a tarnished copper key moored above it, to show where it was sunk. His head was awry, and he had a one-sided, crab-like way with him, as if his foundations had

39

yielded at about the same time as those of the house, and he ought to have been propped up in a similar manner.

"How weak am I," said Arthur Clennam, when he was gone, "that I could shed tears at this reception! I, who have never experienced anything else; who have never expected anything else."

He not only could, but did. It was the momentary yielding of a nature that had been disappointed from the dawn of its perceptions, but had not quite given up all its hopeful yearnings yet. He subdued it, took up the candle and examined the room. The old articles of furniture were in their old places; the Plagues of Egypt, much the dimmer for the fly and smoke plagues of London, were framed and glazed upon the walls. There was the old cellaret with nothing in it, lined with lead, like a sort of coffin in compartments; there was the old dark closet, also with nothing in it, of which he had been many a time the sole contents, in days of punishment, when he had regarded it as the veritable entrance to that bourne to which the tract had found him galloping. There was the large, hard-featured clock on the sideboard, which he used to see bending its figured brows upon him with a savage joy when he was behind-hand with his lessons, and which, when it was wound up once a week with an iron handle, used to sound as if it were growling in ferocious anticipation of the miseries into which it would bring him. But here was the old man come back, saying, "Arthur, I'll go before and light you."

Arthur followed him up the staircase, which was panelled off into spaces like so many mourning tablets, into a dim bed-chamber, the floor of which had gradually so sunk and settled, that the fireplace was in a dell. On a black bier-like sofa in this hollow, propped up behind with one great angular black bolster, like the block at a state execution in the good old times, sat his mother in a widow's dress.

She and his father had been at variance from his earliest remembrance. To sit speechless himself in the midst of rigid silence, glancing in dread from the one averted face to the other, had been the peacefullest occupation of his childhood. She gave him one glassy kiss, and four stiff fingers muffled in worsted. This embrace concluded, he sat down on the opposite side of her little table. There was a fire in the grate, as there had been night and day for fifteen years. There was a kettle on the hob, as there had been night and day for fifteen years. There was a little mound of damped ashes on the top of the fire, and another little mound swept together under the grate, as there had been night and day for fifteen years. There was a smell of black dye in the airless room, which the fire had been drawing out of the crape and stuff of the widow's dress for fifteen months, and out of the bier-like sofa for fifteen years.

"Mother, this is a change from your old active habits."

"The world has narrowed to these dimensions, Arthur," she replied, glancing round the room. "It is well for me that I never set my heart upon its hollow vanities."

The old influence of her presence and her stern strong voice, so gathered about her son, that he felt conscious of a renewal of the timid chill and reserve of his childhood.

"Do you never leave your room, mother?"

"What with my rheumatic affection, and what with its attendant debility or nervous weakness—names are of no matter now—I have lost the use of my limbs. I never leave my room. I have not been outside this door for—tell him for how long," she said, speaking over her shoulder.

"A dozen year next Christmas," returned a cracked voice out of the dimness behind.

"Is that Affery?" said Arthur, looking towards it.

The cracked voice replied that it was Affery: and an old woman came forward into what doubtful light there was, and kissed her hand once; then subsided again into the dimness.

"I am able," said Mrs. Clennam, with a slight motion of her worsted-muffled right hand towards a chair on wheels,

41

standing before a tall writing cabinet close shut up, "I am able to attend to my business duties, and I am thankful for the privilege. It is a great privilege. But no more of business on this day. It is a bad night, is it not?"

"Yes, mother."

"Does it snow?"

"Snow, mother? And we only yet in September?"

"All seasons are alike to me," she returned, with a grim kind of luxuriousness. "I know nothing of summer and winter, shut up here. The Lord has been pleased to put me beyond all that." With her cold grey eyes and her cold grey hair, and her immovable face, as stiff as the folds of her stony head-dress,—her being beyond the reach of the seasons, seemed but a fit sequence to her being beyond the reach of all changing emotions.

On her little table lay two or three books, her handkerchief, a pair of steel spectacles newly taken off, and an old-fashioned gold watch in a heavy double case. Upon this last object her son's eyes and her own now rested together.

"I see that you received the packet I sent you on my father's death, safely, mother."

"You see."

"I never knew my father to show so much anxiety on any subject, as that his watch should be sent straight to you."

"I keep it here as a remembrance of your father."

"It was not until the last, that he expressed the wish. When he could only put his hand upon it, and very indistinctly say to me 'your mother.' A moment before, I thought him wandering in his mind, as he had been for many hours—I think he had no consciousness of pain in his short illness—when I saw him turn himself in his bed and try to open it."

"Was your father, then, not wandering in his mind when he tried to open it?"

"No. He was quite sensible at that time."

Mrs. Clennam shook her head; whether in dismissal of the

deceased or opposing herself to her son's opinion, was not clearly expressed.

"After my father's death I opened it myself, thinking there might be, for anything I knew, some memorandum there. However, as I need not tell you, mother, there was nothing but the old silk watch-paper worked in beads, which you found (no doubt) in its place between the cases, where I found and left it."

Mrs. Clennam signified assent; then added, "No more of business on this day," and then added, "Affery, it is nine o'clock."

Upon this, the old woman cleared the little table, went out of the room, and quickly returned with a tray, on which was a dish of little rusks and a small precise pat of butter, cool, symmetrical, white, and plump. The old man who had been standing by the door in one attitude during the whole interview, looking at the mother up-stairs as he had looked at the son down-stairs, went out at the same time, and, after a longer absence, returned with another tray on which was the greater part of a bottle of port wine (which, to judge by his panting, he had brought from the cellar), a lemon, a sugar-basin, and a spice box. With these materials and the aid of the kettle, he filled a tumbler with a hot and odorous mixture, measured out and compounded with as much nicety as a physician's prescription. Into this mixture, Mrs. Clennam dipped certain of the rusks and ate them; while the old woman buttered certain other of the rusks, which were to be eaten alone. When the invalid had eaten all the rusks and drunk all the mixture, the two trays were removed; and the books and the candle, watch, handkerchief, and spectacles were replaced upon the table. She then put on the spectacles and read certain passages aloud from a book—sternly, fiercely, wrathfully—praying that her enemies (she made them by her tone and manner expressly hers) might be put to the edge of the sword, consumed by fire, smitten by plagues and leprosy, that their bones might be ground to dust, and that they might be utterly exterminated. As she read on, years seemed to fall away from her son like the imaginings of a dream, and all the old dark horrors of his usual preparation for the sleep of an innocent child to overshadow him.

She shut the book and remained for a little time with her face shaded by her hand. So did the old man, otherwise still unchanged in attitude; so, probably, did the old woman in her dimmer part of the room. Then the sick woman was ready for bed.

"Good night, Arthur. Affery will see to your accommodation. Only touch me, for my hand is tender." He touched the worsted muffling of her hand—that was nothing; if his mother had been sheathed in brass there would have been no new barrier between them—and followed the old man and woman down-stairs.

The latter asked him, when they were alone together among the heavy shadows of the dining-room, would he have some supper?

"No, Affery, no supper."

"You shall if you like," said Affery. "There's her to-morrow's partridge in the larder—her first this year; say the word and I'll cook it."

No, he had not long dined, and could eat nothing.

"Have something to drink, then," said Affery; "you shall have some of her bottle of port, if you like. I'll tell Jeremiah that you ordered me to bring it you."

No; nor would he have that, either.

"It's no reason, Arthur," said the old woman, bending over him to whisper, "that because I am afeared of my life of 'em. you should be. You've got half the property, haven't you?"

"Yes, yes."

"Well then, don't *you* be cowed. You're clever, Arthur, an't you?"

He nodded, as she seemed to expect an answer in the affirmative.

44

A CLEVER ONE!

"Then stand up against them! She's awful clever, and none but a clever one durst say a word to her. *He's* a clever one—oh, he's a clever one!—and he gives it her when he has a mind to 't, he does!"

"Your husband does?"

"Does? It makes me shake from head to foot, to hear him give it her. My husband, Jeremiah Flintwinch, can conquer even your mother. What can he be but a clever one to do that!"

His shuffling footstep coming towards them caused her to retreat to the other end of the room. Though a tall hard-favoured sinewy old woman, who in her youth might have enlisted in the Food Guards without much fear of discovery, she collapsed before the little keen-eyed crab-like old man.

"Now Affery," said he, "now woman, what are you doing? Can't you find Master Arthur something or another to pick at?"

Master Arthur repeated his recent refusal to pick at anything.

"Very well, then," said the old man; "make his bed. Stir yourself." His neck was so twisted, that the knotted ends of his white cravat usually dangled under one ear; his natural acerbity and energy, always contending with a second nature of habitual repression, gave his features a swollen and suffused look; and altogether, he had a weird appearance of having hanged himself at one time or other, and of having gone about ever since, halter and all, exactly as some timely hand had cut him down.

"You'll have bitter words together to-morrow, Arthur; you and your mother," said Jeremiah. "Your having given up the business on your father's death—which she suspects, though we have left it to you to tell her—won't go off smoothly."

"I have given up everything in life for the business, and the time came for me to give up that."

"Good!" cried Jeremiah, evidently meaning Bad. "Very

good! only don't expect me to stand between your mother and you, Arthur. I stood between your mother and your father, fending off this, and fending off that, and getting crushed and pounded betwixt 'em; and I've done with such work."

"You will never be asked to begin it again for me, Jeremiah."

"Good. I'm glad to hear it; because I should have had to decline it, if I had been. That's enough—as your mother says—and more than enough of such matters on a Sabbath night. Affery, woman, have you found what you want yet?"

She had been collecting sheets and blankets from a press, and hastened to gather them up, and to reply, "Yes, Jeremiah." Arthur Clennam helped her by carrying the load himself, wished the old man good night, and went up-stairs with her to the top of the house.

They mounted up and up, through the musty smell of an old close house, little used, to a large garret bedroom. Meagre and spare, like all the other rooms, it was even uglier and grimmer than the rest, by being the place of banishment for the worn-out furniture. Its movables were ugly old chairs with worn-out seats, and ugly old chairs without any seats; a threadbare patternless carpet, a maimed table, a crippled wardrobe, a lean set of fire-irons like the skeleton of a set deceased, a washing-stand that looked as if it had stood for ages in a hail of dirty soapsuds, and a bedstead with four bare atomies of posts, each terminating in a spike, as if for the dismal accommodation of lodgers who might prefer to impale themselves. Arthur opened the long low window, and looked out upon the old blasted and blackened forest of chimneys, and the old red glare in the sky which had seemed to him once upon a time but a nightly reflection of the fiery environment that was presented to his childish fancy in all directions, let it look where it would.

He drew in his head again, sat down at the bedside, and looked on at Affery Flintwinch making the bed.

"Affery, you were not married when I went away."

She screwed her mouth into the form of saying, "No," shook her head, and proceeded to get a pillow into its case.

"How did it happen?"

"Why, Jeremiah, o' course," said Affery, with an end of the pillow-case between her teeth.

"Of course he proposed it, but how did it all come about? I should have thought that neither of you would have married; least of all should I have thought of your marrying each other."

"No more should I," said Mrs. Flintwinch, tying the pillow tightly in its case.

"That's what I mean. When did you begin to think otherwise?"

"Never begun to think otherwise at all," said Mrs. Flintwinch.

Seeing, as she patted the pillow into its place on the bolster, that he was still looking at her, as if waiting for the rest of her reply, she gave it a great poke in the middle, and asked, "How could I help myself?"

"How could you help yourself from being married!"

"O' course," said Mrs. Flintwinch. "It was no doing o' mine. I'd never thought of it. I'd got something to do, without thinking, indeed! She kept me to it (as well as he) when she could go about, and she could go about then."

"Well?"

"Well?" echoed Mrs. Flintwinch. "That's what I said myself. Well! What's the use of considering? If them two clever ones have made up their minds to it, what's left for *me* to do? Nothing."

"Was it my mother's project, then?"

"The Lord bless you, Arthur, and forgive me the wish!" cried Affery, speaking always in a low tone. "If they hadn't been both of a mind in it, how could it ever have been? Jeremiah never courted me; t'ant likely that he would, after living in the house with me and ordering me about for as many years as he'd done. He said to me one day, he said,

47

'Affery,' he said, 'now I am going to tell you something. What do you think of the name of Flintwinch?' 'What do I think of it?' I says. 'Yes,' he said, 'because you're going to take it,' he said. 'Take it?' I says. 'Jere-*mi*-ah?' Oh! he's a clever one!"

Mrs. Flintwinch went on to spread the upper sheet over the bed, and the blanket over that, and the counterpane over that, as if she had quite concluded her story.

"Well?" said Arthur again.

"Well?" echoed Mrs. Flintwinch again. "How could I help myself? He said to me, 'Affery, you and me must be married, and I'll tell you why. She's failing in health, and she'll want pretty constant attendance up in her room, and we shall have to be much with her, and there'll be nobody about now but ourselves when we're away from her, and altogether it will be more convenient. She's of my opinion,' he said, 'so if you'll put your bonnet on, next Monday morning at eight, we'll get it over.'" Mrs. Flintwinch tucked up the bed.

"Well?"

"Well?" repeated Mrs. Flintwinch, "I think so! I sits me down and says it. Well!—Jeremiah then says to me, 'As to banns, next Sunday being the third time of asking (for I've put 'em up a fortnight), is my reason for naming Monday. She'll speak to you about it herself, and now she'll find you prepared, Affery.' That same day she spoke to me, and she said, 'So, Affery, I understand that you and Jeremiah are going to be married. I am glad of it, and so are you, with reason. It is a very good thing for you, and very welcome under the circumstances to me. He is a sensible man, and a trustworthy man, and a persevering man, and a pious man.' What could I say when it had come to that? Why, if it had been—a Smothering instead of a Wedding," Mrs. Flintwinch cast about in her mind with great pains for this form of expression, "I couldn't have said a word upon it, against them two clever ones."

"In good faith, I believe so."

" And so you may, Arthur."

" Affery, what girl was that in my mother's room just now."

" Girl ? " said Mrs. Flintwinch in a rather sharp key.

" It was a girl, surely, whom I saw near you—almost hidden in the dark corner ? "

" Oh ! She ? Little Dorrit ? *She's* nothing ; she's a whim of—hers." It was a peculiarity of Affery Flintwinch that she never spoke of Mrs. Clennam by name. " But there's another sort of girls than that about. Have you forgot your old sweetheart ? Long and long ago, I'll be bound."

" I suffered enough from my mother's separating us, to remember her. I recollect her very well."

" Have you got another ? "

" No."

" Here's news for you, then. She's well to do now, and a widow. And if you like to have her, why you can."

" And how do you know that, Affery ? "

" Them two clever ones have been speaking about it.— There's Jeremiah on the stairs ! " She was gone in a moment.

Mrs. Flintwinch had introduced into the web that his mind was busily weaving, in that old workshop where the loom of his youth had stood, the last thread wanting to the pattern. The airy folly of a boy's love had found its way even into that house, and he had been as wretched under its hopeless-ness as if the house had been a castle of romance. Little more than a week ago at Marseilles, the face of the pretty girl from whom he had parted with regret, had had an unusual interest for him, and a tender hold upon him, because of some resemblance, real or imagined, to this first face that had soared out of his gloomy life into the bright glories of fancy. He leaned upon the sill of the long low window, and looking out upon the blackened forest of chimneys again, began to dream. For, it had been the uniform tendency of this man's life—so much was wanting in it to think about, so much that might have been better directed and happier to speculate upon—to make him a dreamer, after all.

CHAPTER IV

MRS. FLINTWINCH HAS A DREAM

When Mrs. Flintwinch dreamed, she usually dreamed, unlike the son of her old mistress, with her eyes shut. She had a curiously vivid dream that night, and before she had left the son of her old mistress many hours. In fact it was not at all like a dream, it was so very real in every respect. It happened in this wise.

The bed-chamber occupied by Mr. and Mrs. Flintwinch was within a few paces of that to which Mrs. Clennam had been so long confined. It was not on the same floor, for it was a room at the side of the house, which was approached by a steep descent of a few odd steps, diverging from the main staircase nearly opposite to Mrs. Clennam's door. It could scarcely be said to be within call, the walls, doors, and panelling of the old place were so cumbrous; but it was within easy reach, in any undress, at any hour of the night, in any temperature. At the head of the bed, and within a foot of Mrs. Flintwinch's ear, was a bell, the line of which hung ready to Mrs. Clennam's hand. Whenever this bell rang, up started Affery, and was in the sick room before she was awake.

Having got her mistress into bed, lighted her lamp, and given her good night, Mrs. Flintwinch went to roost as usual, saving that her lord had not yet appeared. It was her lord himself who became—unlike the last theme in the mind, according to the observation of most philosophers—the subject of Mrs. Flintwinch's dream.

MR. FLINTWINCH'S DOUBLE

It seemed to her that she awoke, after sleeping some hours, and found Jeremiah not yet abed. That she looked at the candle she had left burning, and, measuring the time like king Alfred the Great, was confirmed by its wasted state in her belief that she had been asleep for some considerable period. That she arose thereupon, muffled herself up in a wrapper, put on her shoes, and went out on the staircase much surprised, to look for Jeremiah.

The staircase was as wooden and solid as need be, and Affery went straight down it without any of those deviations peculiar to dreams. She did not skim over it, but walked down it, and guided herself by the banisters on account of her candle having died out. In one corner of the hall, behind the house-door, there was a little waiting-room, like a well-shaft, with a long narrow window in it as if it had been ripped up. In this room, which was never used, a light was burning.

Mrs. Flintwinch crossed the hall, feeling its pavement cold to her stockingless feet, and peeped in between the rusty hinges of the door, which stood a little open. She expected to see Jeremiah fast asleep or in a fit, but he was calmly seated in a chair, awake, and in his usual health. But what—hey ? —Lord forgive us !—Mrs. Flintwinch muttered some ejaculation to this effect, and turned giddy.

For, Mr. Flintwinch awake, was watching Mr. Flintwinch asleep. He sat on one side of a small table, looking keenly at himself on the other side with his chin sunk on his breast, snoring. The waking Flintwinch had his full front face presented to his wife ; the sleeping Flintwinch was in profile. The waking Flintwinch was the old original ; the sleeping Flintwinch was the double. Just as she might have distinguished between a tangible object and its reflection in a glass, Affery made out this difference with her head going round and round.

If she had had any doubt which was her own Jeremiah, it would have been resolved by his impatience. He looked about him for an offensive weapon, caught up the snuffers, and, before applying them to the cabbage-headed candle, lunged at the sleeper as though he would have run him through the body.

"Who's that? What's the matter?" cried the sleeper, starting.

Mr. Flintwinch made a movement with the snuffers, as if he would have enforced silence on his companion by putting them down his throat; the companion coming to himself, said, rubbing his eyes, "I forgot where I was."

"You have been asleep," snarled Jeremiah, referring to his watch, "two hours. You said you would be rested enough if you had a short nap."

"I have had a short nap," said Double.

"Half-past two o'clock in the morning," muttered Jeremiah. "Where's your hat? Where's your coat? Where's the box?"

"All here," said Double, tying up his throat with sleepy carefulness in a shawl. "Stop a minute. Now give me the sleeve—not that sleeve, the other one. Ha! I'm not as young as I was." Mr. Flintwinch had pulled him into his coat with vehement energy. "You promised me a second glass after I was rested."

"Drink it!" returned Jeremiah, "and—choke yourself, I was going to say—but go, I mean." At the same time he produced the identical port-wine bottle, and filled a wine-glass.

"Her port-wine, I believe?" said Double, tasting it as if he were in the Docks, with hours to spare. "Her health."

He took a sip.

"Your health!"

He took another sip.

"His health!"

He took another sip.

"And all friends round St. Paul's." He emptied and put down the wine-glass half-way through this ancient civic toast, and took up the box. It was an iron box some two

52

feet square, which he carried under his arms pretty easily. Jeremiah watched his manner of adjusting it, with jealous eyes; tried it with his hands, to be sure that he had a firm hold of it; bade him for his life be careful what he was about; and then stole out on tiptoe to open the door for him. Affery, anticipating the last movement, was on the staircase. The sequence of things was so ordinary and natural, that, standing there, she could hear the door open, feel the night air, and see the stars outside.

But now came the most remarkable part of the dream. She felt so afraid of her husband, that being on the staircase, she had not the power to retreat to her room (which she might easily have done before he had fastened the door), but stood there staring. Consequently when he came up the staircase to bed, candle in hand, he came full upon her. He looked astonished, but said not a word. He kept his eyes upon her, and kept advancing; and she, completely under his influence, kept retiring before him. Thus, she walking backward and he walking forward, they came into their own room. They were no sooner shut in there, than Mr. Flintwinch took her by the throat, and shook her until she was black in the face.

"Why, Affery, woman—Affery!" said Mr. Flintwinch. "What have you been dreaming of? Wake up, wake up! What's the matter?"

"The—the matter, Jeremiah?" gasped Mrs. Flintwinch, rolling her eyes.

"Why, Affery, woman—Affery! You have been getting out of bed in your sleep, my dear! I come up, after having fallen asleep myself, below, and find you in your wrapper here, with the nightmare. Affery, woman," said Mr. Flintwinch, with a friendly grin on his expressive countenance, "if you ever have a dream of this sort again, it'll be a sign of your being in want of physic. And I'll give you such a dose, old woman—such a dose!"

Mrs. Flintwinch thanked him and crept into bed.

CHAPTER V

FAMILY AFFAIRS

As the city clocks struck nine on Monday morning, Mrs. Clennam was wheeled by Jeremiah Flintwinch of the cut-down aspect, to her tall cabinet. When she had unlocked and opened it, and had settled herself at its desk, Jeremiah withdrew—as it might be, to hang himself more effectually—and her son appeared.

" Are you any better this morning, mother ? "

She shook her head, with the same austere air of luxuriousness that she had shown over-night when speaking of the weather. " I shall never be better any more. It is well for me, Arthur, that I know it and can bear it."

Sitting with her hands laid separately upon the desk, and the tall cabinet towering before her, she looked as if she were performing on a dumb church organ. Her son thought so (it was an old thought with him), while he took his seat beside it.

She opened a drawer or two, looked over some business papers, and put them back again. Her severe face had no thread of relaxation in it, by which any explorer could have been guided to the gloomy labyrinth of her thoughts.

" Shall I speak of our affairs, mother ? Are you inclined to enter upon business ? "

" Am I inclined, Arthur ? Rather, are you ? Your father has been dead a year and more. I have been at your disposal, and waiting your pleasure, ever since."

"There was much to arrange before I could leave; and when I did leave, I travelled a little for rest and relief."

She turned her face towards him, as not having heard or understood his last words.

"For rest and relief."

She glanced round the sombre room, and appeared from the motion of her lips to repeat the words to herself, as calling it to witness how little of either it afforded her.

"Besides, mother, you being sole executrix, and having the direction and management of the estate, there remained little business, or I might say none, that I could transact, until you had had time to arrange matters to your satisfaction."

"The accounts are made out," she returned. "I have them here. The vouchers have all been examined and passed. You can inspect them when you like, Arthur; now, if you please."

"It is quite enough, mother, to know that the business is completed. Shall I proceed then?"

"Why not?" she said, in her frozen way.

"Mother, our House has done less and less for some years past, and our dealings have been progressively on the decline. We have never shown much confidence, or invited much; we have attached no people to us; the track we have kept is not the track of the time; and we have been left far behind. I need not dwell on this to you, mother. You know it necessarily."

"I know what you mean," she answered, in a qualified tone.

"Even this old house in which we speak," pursued her son, "is an instance of what I say. In my father's earlier time, and in his uncle's time before him, it was a place of business —really a place of business, and business resort. Now, it is a mere anomaly and incongruity here, out of date and out of purpose. All our consignments have long been made to Rovinghams' the commission-merchants; and although, as a check upon them, and in the stewardship of my father's

resources, your judgment and watchfulness have been actively
exerted, still those qualities would have influenced my father's
fortunes equally, if you had lived in any private dwelling:
would they not?"

"Do you consider," she returned, without answering his
question, "that a house serves no purpose, Arthur, in sheltering your infirm and afflicted—justly infirm and righteously
afflicted—mother?"

"I was speaking only of business purposes."

"With what object?"

"I am coming to it."

"I foresee," she returned, fixing her eyes upon him, "what
it is. But the Lord forbid that I should repine under any
visitation. In my sinfulness I merit bitter disappointment,
and I accept it."

"Mother, I grieve to hear you speak like this, though I
have had my apprehensions that you would—"

"You knew I would. You knew *me*," she interrupted.

Her son paused for a moment. He had struck fire out of
her, and was surprised.

"Well!" she said, relapsing into stone. "Go on. Let
me hear."

"You have anticipated, mother, that I decide for my part,
to abandon the business. I have done with it. I will not
take upon myself to advise you: you will continue-it, I see. If
I had any influence with you, I would simply use it to soften
your judgment of me in causing you this disappointment: to
represent to you that I have lived the half of a long term of
life, and have never before set my own will against yours. I
cannot say that I have been able to conform myself, in heart
and spirit, to your rules; I cannot say that I believe my
forty years have been profitable or pleasant to myself, or any
one; but I have habitually submitted, and I only ask you to
remember it."

Woe to the suppliant, if such a one there were or ever had
been, who had any concession to look for in the inexorable

face at the cabinet. Woe to the defaulter whose appeal lay to the tribunal where those severe eyes presided. Great need had the rigid woman of her mystical religion, veiled in gloom and darkness, with lightnings of cursing, vengeance, and destruction, flashing through the sable clouds. Forgive us our debts as we forgive our debtors, was a prayer too poor in spirit for her. Smite Thou my debtors, Lord, wither them, crush them; do Thou as I would do, and Thou shalt have my worship: this was the impious tower of stone she built up to scale Heaven.

"Have you finished, Arthur, or have you anything more to say to me? I think there can be nothing else. You have been short, but full of matter!"

"Mother, I have yet something more to say. It has been upon my mind, night and day, this long time. It is far more difficult to say than what I have said. That concerned myself; this concerns us all."

"Us all! Who are us all?"

"Yourself, myself, my dead father."

She took her hands from the desk; folded them in her lap; and sat looking towards the fire, with the impenetrability of an old Egyptian sculpture.

"You knew my father infinitely better than I ever knew him; and his reserve with me yielded to you. You were much the stronger, mother, and directed him. As a child, I knew it as well as I know it now. I knew that your ascendency over him was the cause of his going to China to take care of the business there, while you took care of it here (though I do not even now know whether these were really terms of separation that you agreed upon); and that it was your will that I should remain with you until I was twenty, and then go to him as I did. You will not be offended by my recalling this, after twenty years?"

"I am waiting to hear why you recall it."

He lowered his voice, and said, with manifest reluctance, and against his will:

"I want to ask you, mother, whether it ever occurred to you to suspect— "

At the word Suspect, she turned her eyes momentarily upon her son, with a dark frown. She then suffered them to seek the fire, as before; but with the frown fixed above them, as if the sculptor of old Egypt had indented it in the hard granite face, to frown for ages.

"—that he had any secret remembrance which caused him trouble of mind—remorse? Whether you ever observed anything in his conduct suggesting that; or ever spoke to him upon it, or ever heard him hint at such a thing?"

"I do not understand what kind of secret remembrance you mean to infer that your father was a prey to," she returned, after a silence. "You speak so mysteriously."

"Is it possible, mother," her son leaned forward to be the nearer to her while he whispered it, and laid his hand nervously upon her desk, "is it possible, mother, that he had unhappily wronged any one, and made no reparation?"

Looking at him wrathfully, she bent herself back in her chair to keep him further off, but gave him no reply.

"I am deeply sensible, mother, that if this thought has never at any time flashed upon you, it must seem cruel and unnatural in me, even in this confidence, to breathe it. But I cannot shake it off. Time and change (I have tried both before breaking silence) do nothing to wear it out. Remember, I was with my father. Remember, I saw his face when he gave the watch into my keeping, and struggled to express that he sent it as a token you would understand, to you. Remember, I saw him at the last with the pencil in his failing hand, trying to write some word for you to read, but to which he could give no shape. The more remote and cruel this vague suspicion that I have, the stronger the circumstances that could give it any semblance of probability to me. For Heaven's sake, let us examine sacredly whether there is any wrong entrusted to us to set right. No one can help towards it, mother, but you."

Still so recoiling in her chair that her overpoised weight moved it, from time to time, a little on its wheels, and gave her the appearance of a phantom of fierce aspect gliding away from him, she interposed her left arm, bent at the elbow with the back of her hand towards her face, between herself and him, and looked at him in a fixed silence.

"In grasping at money and in driving hard bargains—I have begun, and I must speak of such things now, mother —some one may have been grievously deceived, injured, ruined. You were the moving power of all this machinery before my birth; your stronger spirit has been infused into all my father's dealings, for more than two score years. You can set these doubts at rest, I think, if you will really help me to discover the truth. Will you, mother?"

He stopped in the hope that she would speak. But her grey hair was not more immovable in its two folds, than were her firm lips.

"If reparation can be made to any one, if restitution can be made to any one, let us know it and make it. Nay, mother, if within my means, let *me* make it. I have seen so little happiness come of money; it has brought within my knowledge so little peace to this house, or to any one belonging to it; that it is worth less to me than to another. It can buy me nothing that will not be a reproach and misery to me, if I am haunted by a suspicion that it darkened my father's last hours with remorse, and that it is not honestly and justly mine."

There was a bell-rope hanging on the panelled wall, some two or three yards from the cabinet. By a swift and sudden action of her foot, she drove her wheeled chair rapidly back to it and pulled it violently—still holding her arm up in its shield-like posture, as if he were striking at her, and she warding off the blow.

A girl came hurrying in, frightened.

"Send Flintwinch here!"

In a moment the girl had withdrawn, and the old man

stood within the door. "What! You're hammer and tongs, already, you two?" he said, coolly stroking his face. "I thought you would be. I was pretty sure of it."

"Flintwinch!" said the mother, "look at my son. Look at him!"

"Well! I *am* looking at him," said Flintwinch.

She stretched out the arm with which she had shielded herself, and as she went on, pointed at the object of her anger.

"In the very hour of his return almost—before the shoe upon his foot is dry—he asperses his father's memory to his mother! Asks his mother to become, with him, a spy upon his father's transactions through a lifetime! Has misgivings that the goods of this world which we have painfully got together early and late, with wear and tear, and toil and self-denial, are so much plunder; and asks to whom they shall be given up, as reparation and restitution!"

Although she said this raging, she said it in a voice so far from being beyond her control, that it was even lower than her usual tone. She also spoke with great distinctness.

"Reparation!" said she. "Yes truly! It is easy for him to talk of reparation, fresh from journeying and junketing in foreign lands, and living a life of vanity and pleasure. But let him look at me, in prison, and in bonds here. I endure without murmuring, because it is appointed that I shall so make reparation for my sins. Reparation! Is there none in this room? Has there been none here this fifteen years?"

Thus was she always balancing her bargain with the Majesty of heaven, posting up the entries to her credit, strictly keeping her set-off, and claiming her due. She was only remarkable in this, for the force and emphasis with which she did it. Thousands upon thousands do it, according to their varying manner, every day.

"Flintwinch, give me that book!"

The old man handed it to her from the table. She put two fingers between the leaves, closed the book upon them, and held it up to her son in a threatening way.

A TERRIBLE THREAT

"In the days of old, Arthur, treated of in this commentary, there were pious men, beloved of the Lord, who would have cursed their sons for less than this: who would have sent them forth, and sent whole nations forth, if such had supported them, to be avoided of God and man, and perish, down to the baby at the breast. But I only tell you that if you ever renew that theme with me, I will renounce you; I will so dismiss you through that doorway, that you had better have been motherless from your cradle. I will never see or know you more. And if, after all, you were to come into this darkened room to look upon me lying dead, my body should bleed, if I could make it, when you came near me."

In part relieved by the intensity of this threat, and in part (monstrous as the fact is) by a general impression that it was in some sort a religious proceeding, she handed back the book to the old man, and was silent.

"Now," said Jeremiah; "premising that I'm not going to stand between you two, will you let me ask (as I *have* been called in, and made a third) what is all this about?"

"Take your version of it," returned Arthur, finding it left to him to speak, "from my mother. Let it rest there. What I have said, was said to my mother only."

"Oh!" returned the old man. "From your mother? Take it from your mother? Well! But your mother mentioned that you had been suspecting your father. That's not dutiful, Mr. Arthur. Who will you be suspecting next?"

"Enough," said Mrs. Clennam, turning her face so that it was addressed for the moment to the old man only. "Let no more be said about this."

"Yes, but stop a bit, stop a bit," the old man persisted. "Let us see how we stand. Have you told Mr. Arthur, that he mustn't lay offences at his father's door? That he has no right to do it? That he has no ground to go upon?"

"I tell him so now."

"Ah! Exactly," said the old man. "You tell him so

now. You hadn't told him so before, and you tell him so now. Ay, ay! That's right! You know I stood between you and his father so long, that it seems as if death had made no difference, and I was still standing between you. So I will, and so in fairness I require to have that plainly put forward. Arthur, you please to hear that you have no right to mistrust your father, and have no ground to go upon."

He put his hands to the back of the wheeled chair, and muttering to himself, slowly wheeled his mistress back to her cabinet. "Now," he resumed, standing behind her: "in case I should go away leaving things half done, and so should be wanted again when you come to the other half and get into one of your flights, has Arthur told you what he means to do about the business?"

"He has relinquished it."

"In favour of nobody, I suppose?"

Mrs. Clennam glanced at her son, leaning against one of the windows. He observed the look and said, "To my mother, of course. She does what she pleases."

"And if any pleasure," she said after a short pause, "could arise for me out of the disappointment of my expectations, that my son, in the prime of his life would infuse new youth and strength into it, and make it of great profit and power, it would be in advancing an old and faithful servant. Jeremiah, the captain deserts the ship, but you and I will sink or float with it."

Jeremiah, whose eyes glistened as if they saw money, darted a sudden look at the son, which seemed to say, " I owe *you* no thanks for this ; *you* have done nothing towards it !" and then told the mother that he thanked her, and that Affery thanked her, and that he would never desert her, and that Affery would never desert her. Finally, he hauled up his watch from its depths, said "Eleven. Time for your oysters !" and with that change of subject, which involved no change of expression or manner, rang the bell.

Mr. Flintwinch mediates as a Friend of the Family

MRS. CLENNAM'S OYSTERS

But Mrs. Clennam, resolved to treat herself with the greater rigour for having been supposed to be unacquainted with reparation, refused to eat her oysters when they were brought. They looked tempting; eight in number, circularly set out on a white plate on a tray covered with a white napkin, flanked by a slice of buttered French roll, and a little compact glass of cool wine and water; but she resisted all persuasions, and sent them down again—placing the act to her credit, no doubt, in her Eternal Day-Book.

This refection of oysters was not presided over by Affery, but by the girl who had appeared when the bell was rung; the same who had been in the dimly-lighted room last night. Now that he had an opportunity of observing her, Arthur found that her diminutive figure, small features, and slight spare dress, gave her the appearance of being much younger than she was. A woman, probably of not less than two-and-twenty, she might have been passed in the street for little more than half that age. Not that her face was very youthful, for in truth there was more consideration and care in it than naturally belonged to her utmost years; but she was so little and light, so noiseless and shy, and appeared so conscious of being out of place among the three hard elders, that she had all the manner and much of the appearance of a subdued child.

In a hard way, and in an uncertain way that fluctuated between patronage and putting down, the sprinkling from a watering-pot and hydraulic pressure, Mrs. Clennam showed an interest in this dependant. Even in the moment of her entrance upon the violent ringing of the bell, when the mother shielded herself with that singular action from the son, Mrs. Clennam's eyes had had some individual recognition in them, which seemed reserved for her. As there are degrees of hardness in the hardest metal, and shades of colour in black itself, so, even in the asperity of Mrs. Clennam's demeanour towards all the rest of humanity and towards Little Dorrit, there was a fine gradation.

Little Dorrit let herself out to do needlework. At so much a day—or at so little—from eight to eight, Little Dorrit was to be hired. Punctual to the moment, Little Dorrit appeared ; punctual to the moment, Little Dorrit vanished. What became of Little Dorrit between the two eights, was a mystery.

Another of the moral phenomena of Little Dorrit. Besides her consideration money, her daily contract included meals. She had an extraordinary repugnance to dining in company ; would never do so, if it were possible to escape. Would always plead that she had this bit of work to begin first, or that bit of work to finish first; and would, of a certainty, scheme and plan—not very cunningly, it would seem, for she deceived no one—to dine alone. Successful in this, happy in carrying off her plate anywhere, to make a table of her lap, or a box, or the ground, or even, as was supposed, to stand on tiptoe, dining moderately at a mantel-shelf ; the great anxiety of Little Dorrit's day was set at rest.

It was not easy to make out Little Dorrit's face ; she was so retiring, plied her needle in such removed corners, and started away so scared if encountered on the stairs. But it seemed to be a pale transparent face, quick in expression, though not beautiful in feature, its soft hazel eyes excepted. A delicately bent head, a tiny form, a quick little pair of busy hands, and a shabby dress—it must needs have been very shabby to look at all so, being so neat—were Little Dorrit as she sat at work.

For these particulars or generalities concerning Little Dorrit, Mr. Arthur was indebted in the course of the day to his own eyes and to Mrs. Affery's tongue. If Mrs. Affery had had any will or way of her own, it would probably have been unfavourable to Little Dorrit. But as " them two clever ones "—Mrs. Affery's perpetual reference, in whom her personality was swallowed up—were agreed to accept Little Dorrit as a matter of course, she had nothing for it but to follow suit. Similarly, if the two clever ones had agreed to murder Little Dorrit by candlelight, Mrs. Affery, being required to hold the candle, would no doubt have done it.

In the intervals of roasting the partridge for the invalid chamber, and preparing a baking-dish of beef and pudding for the dining-room, Mrs. Affery made the communications above set forth; invariably putting her head in at the door again after she had taken it out, to enforce resistance to the two clever ones. It appeared to have become a perfect passion with Mrs. Flintwinch, that the only son should be pitted against them.

In the course of the day too, Arthur looked through the whole house. Dull and dark he found it. The gaunt rooms, deserted for years upon years, seemed to have settled down into a gloomy lethargy from which nothing could rouse them again. The furniture, at once spare and lumbering, hid in the rooms rather than furnished them, and there was no colour in all the house; such colour as had ever been there, had long ago started away on lost sunbeams—got itself absorbed, perhaps, into flowers, butterflies, plumage of birds, precious stones, what not. There was not one straight floor, from the foundation to the roof; the ceilings were so fantastically clouded by smoke and dust, that old women might have told fortunes in them better than in grouts of tea; the dead-cold hearths showed no traces of having ever been warmed, but in heaps of soot that had tumbled down the chimneys, and eddied about in little dusky whirlwinds when the doors were opened. In what had once been a drawing-room, there were a pair of meagre mirrors, with dismal processions of black figures carrying black garlands, walking round the frames; but even these were short of heads and legs, and one undertaker-like Cupid had swung round on his own axis and got upside down, and another had fallen off altogether. The room Arthur Clennam's deceased father had occupied for business purposes, when he first remembered him, was so unaltered that he might have been imagined still to keep it invisibly, as his visible relict kept her room up-stairs; Jeremiah Flintwinch still going between them negotiating. His picture, dark and gloomy, earnestly speechless on the wall, with the eyes intently looking at his son as they had looked when life departed from them, seemed to urge him awfully to the task he had attempted; but as to any yielding on the part of his mother, he had now no hope, and as to any other means of setting his distrust at rest, he had abandoned hope a long time. Down in the cellars, as up in the bed-chambers, old objects that he well remembered were changed by age and decay, but were still in their old places; even to empty beer-casks hoary with cobwebs, and empty wine-bottles with fur and fungus choking up their throats. There, too, among unused bottle-racks and pale slants of light from the yard above, was the strong room stored with old ledgers, which had as musty and corrupt a smell as if they were regularly balanced, in the dead small hours, by a nightly resurrection of old book-keepers.

The baking-dish was served up in a penitential manner, on a shrunken cloth at an end of the dining-table, at two o'clock; when he dined with Mr. Flintwinch, the new partner. Mr. Flintwinch informed him that his mother had recovered her equanimity now, and that he need not fear her again alluding to what had passed in the morning. "And don't you lay offences at your father's door, Mr. Arthur," added Jeremiah, "once for all, don't do it! Now, we have done with the subject."

Mr. Flintwinch had been already re-arranging and dusting his own particular little office, as if to do honour to his accession to new dignity. He resumed this occupation when he was replete with beef, had sucked up all the gravy in the baking-dish with the flat of his knife, and had drawn liberally on a barrel of small beer in the scullery. Thus refreshed, he tucked up his shirt-sleeves and went to work again; and Mr. Arthur, watching him as he set about it, plainly saw that his father's picture, or his father's grave, would be as communicative with him as this old man.

"Now, Affery, woman," said Mr. Flintwinch, as she crossed the hall. "You hadn't made Mr. Arthur's bed when I was up there last. Stir yourself. Bustle."

But Mr. Arthur found the house so blank and dreary, and was so unwilling to assist at another implacable consignment of his mother's enemies (perhaps himself among them) to mortal disfigurement and immortal ruin, that he announced his intention of lodging at the coffee-house where he had left his luggage. Mr. Flintwinch taking kindly to the idea of getting rid of him, and his mother being indifferent, beyond considerations of saving, to most domestic arrangements that were not bounded by the walls of her own chamber, he easily carried this point without new offence. Daily business hours were agreed upon, which his mother, Mr. Flintwinch, and he, were to devote together to a necessary checking of books and papers; and he left the home he had so lately found, with a depressed heart.

But Little Dorrit?

The business hours, allowing for intervals of invalid regimen of oysters and partridges, during which Clennam refreshed himself with a walk, were from ten to six for about a fortnight. Sometimes Little Dorrit was employed at her needle, sometimes not, sometimes appeared as a humble visitor: which must have been her character on the occasion of his arrival. His original curiosity augmented every day, as he watched for her, saw or did not see her, and speculated about her. Influenced by his predominant idea, he even fell into a habit of discussing with himself the possibility of her being in some way associated with it. At last he resolved to watch Little Dorrit and know more of her story.

CHAPTER VI

THE FATHER OF THE MARSHALSEA

THIRTY years ago there stood, a few doors short of the church of Saint George, in the borough of Southwark, on the left-hand side of the way going southward, the Marshalsea Prison. It had stood there many years before, and it remained there some years afterwards; but it is gone now, and the world is none the worse without it.

It was an oblong pile of barrack building, partitioned into squalid houses standing back to back, so that there were no back rooms; environed by a narrow paved yard, hemmed in by high walls duly spiked at top. Itself a close and confined prison for debtors, it contained within it a much closer and more confined jail for smugglers. Offenders against the revenue laws, and defaulters to excise or customs, who had incurred fines which they were unable to pay, were supposed to be incarcerated behind an iron-plated door, closing up a second prison, consisting of a strong cell or two, and a blind alley some yard and a half wide, which formed the mysterious termination of the very limited skittle-ground in which the Marshalsea debtors bowled down their troubles.

Supposed to be incarcerated there, because the time had rather outgrown the strong cells and the blind alley. In practice they had come to be considered a little too bad, though in theory they were quite as good as ever; which may be observed to be the case at the present day with other cells that are not at all strong, and with other blind alleys that are stone-blind. Hence the smugglers habitually consorted with the debtors (who received them with open arms), except at certain constitutional moments when somebody came from some Office, to go through some form of overlooking something, which neither he nor anybody else knew anything about. On those truly British occasions, the smugglers, if any, made a feint of walking into the strong cells and the blind alley, while this somebody pretended to do his something; and made a reality of walking out again as soon as he hadn't done it—neatly epitomising the administration of most of the public affairs, in our right little, tight little, island.

There had been taken to the Marshalsea Prison, long before the day when the sun shone on Marseilles and on the opening of this narrative, a debtor with whom this narrative has some concern.

He was, at that time, a very amiable and very helpless middle-aged gentleman, who was going out again directly. Necessarily, he was going out again directly, because the Marshalsea lock never turned upon a debtor who was not. He brought in a portmanteau with him, which he doubted its being worth while to unpack; he was so perfectly clear —like all the rest of them, the turnkey on the lock said— that he was going out again directly.

He was a shy, retiring man; well-looking, though in an effeminate style; with a mild voice, curling hair, and irresolute hands—rings upon the fingers in those days—which nervously wandered to his trembling lip a hundred times, in the first half-hour of his acquaintance with the jail. His principal anxiety was about his wife.

"Do you think, sir," he asked the turnkey, "that she will be very much shocked, if she should come to the gate to-morrow morning?"

The turnkey gave it as the result of his experience that some of 'em was and some of 'em wasn't. In general, more no than yes. "What like is she, you see?" he philosophically asked: "that's what it hinges on."

"She is very delicate and inexperienced indeed."

"That," said the turnkey, "is agen her."

"She is so little used to go out alone," said the debtor, "that I am at a loss to think how she will ever make her way here, if she walks."

"P'raps," quoth the turnkey, "she'll take a ackney coach."

"Perhaps." The irresolute fingers went to the trembling lip. "I hope she will. She may not think of it."

"Or p'raps," said the turnkey, offering his suggestions from the top of his well-worn wooden stool, as he might have offered them to a child for whose weakness he felt a compassion, "p'raps she'll get her brother, or her sister, to come along with her."

"She has no brother or sister."

"Niece, nevy, cousin, serwant, young 'ooman, greengrocer. —Dash it! One or another on 'em," said the turnkey, repudiating beforehand the refusal of all his suggestions.

"I fear—I hope it is not against the rules—that she will bring the children."

"The children?" said the turnkey. "And the rules? Why, lord set you up like a corner pin, we've a reg'lar playground o' children here. Children? Why, we swarm with 'em. How many a you got?"

"Two," said the debtor, lifting his irresolute hand to his lip again, and turning into the prison.

The turnkey followed him with his eyes. "And you another," he observed to himself, "which makes three on you. And your wife another, I'll lay a crown. Which makes four on you. And another coming, I'll lay half-a-crown. Which'll make five on you. And I'll go another seven and sixpence to name which is the helplessest, the unborn baby or you!"

He was right in all his particulars. She came next day with a little boy of three years old, and a little girl of two, and he stood entirely corroborated.

"Got a room now; haven't you?" the turnkey asked the debtor after a week or two.

"Yes, I have got a very good room."

"Any little sticks a coming, to furnish it?" said the turnkey.

"I expect a few necessary articles of furniture to be delivered by the carrier, this afternoon."

"Missis and little 'uns a coming, to keep you company?" asked the turnkey.

"Why, yes, we think it better that we should not be scattered, even for a few weeks."

"Even for a few weeks, *of* course," replied the turnkey. And he followed him again with his eyes, and nodded his head seven times when he was gone.

The affairs of this debtor were perplexed by a partnership, of which he knew no more than that he had invested money in it; by legal matters of assignment and settlement, conveyance here and conveyance there, suspicion of unlawful preference of creditors in this direction, and of mysterious spiriting away of property in that; and as nobody on the face of the earth could be more incapable of explaining any single item in the heap of confusion than the debtor himself, nothing comprehensible could be made of his case. To question him in detail, and endeavour to reconcile his answers; to closet him with accountants and sharp practitioners, learned in the wiles of insolvency and bankruptcy; was only to put the case out at compound interest of incomprehensibility. The irresolute fingers fluttered more and more ineffectually about the trembling lip on every such occasion, and the sharpest practitioners gave him up as a hopeless job.

"Out?" said the turnkey, "*he*'ll never get out. Unless his creditors take him by the shoulders and shove him out."

He had been there five or six months, when he came running to this turnkey one forenoon to tell him, breathless and pale, that his wife was ill.

"As anybody might a known she would be," said the turnkey.

"We intended," he returned, "that she should go to a country lodging only to-morrow. What am I to do! Oh, good heaven, what am I to do!"

"Don't waste your time in clasping your hands and biting your fingers," responded the practical turnkey, taking him by the elbow, "but come along with me."

The turnkey conducted him—trembling from head to foot, and constantly crying under his breath, What was he to do! while his irresolute fingers bedabbled the tears upon his face —up one of the common staircases in the prison, to a door on the garret story. Upon which door the turnkey knocked with the handle of his key.

"Come in!" cried a voice inside.

The turnkey opening the door, disclosed in a wretched, ill-smelling little room, two hoarse, puffy, red-faced personages seated at a rickety table, playing at all-fours, smoking pipes, and drinking brandy.

"Doctor," said the turnkey, "here's a gentleman's wife in want of you without a minute's loss of time!"

The doctor's friend was in the positive degree of hoarseness, puffiness, red-facedness, all-fours, tobacco, dirt, and brandy; the doctor in the comparative—hoarser, puffier, more red-faced, more all-fourey, tobaccoer, dirtier, and brandier. The doctor was amazingly shabby, in a torn and darned rough-weather sea-jacket, out at elbows and eminently short of buttons (he had been in his time the experienced surgeon carried by a passenger ship), the dirtiest white trousers conceivable by mortal man, carpet slippers, and no visible linen. "Child-bed?" said the doctor. "I'm the boy!" With that the doctor took a comb from the chimney-piece and stuck his hair upright—whch appeared to be his way of washing himself— produced a professional chest or case, of most abject appear-ance, from the cupboard where his cup and saucer and coals were, settled his chin in the frowsy wrapper round his neck, and became a ghastly medical scarecrow.

The doctor and the debtor ran down-stairs, leaving the

turnkey to return to the lock, and made for the debtor's room. All the ladies in the prison had got hold of the news, and were in the yard. Some of them had already taken possession of the two children, and were hospitably carrying them off; others were offering loans of little comforts from their own scanty store; others were sympathising with the greatest volubility. The gentlemen prisoners, feeling themselves at a disadvantage, had for the most part retired, not to say sneaked, to their rooms; from the open windows of which, some of them now complimented the doctor with whistles as he passed below, while others, with several stories between them, interchanged sarcastic references to the prevalent excitement.

It was a hot summer day, and the prison rooms were baking between the high walls. In the debtor's confined chamber, Mrs. Bangham, charwoman and messenger, who was not a prisoner (though she had been once), but was the popular medium of communication with the outer world, had volunteered her services as fly-catcher and general attendant. The walls and ceiling were blackened with flies. Mrs. Bangham, expert in sudden device, with one hand fanned the patient with a cabbage leaf, and with the other set traps of vinegar and sugar in gallipots; at the same time enunciating sentiments of an encouraging and congratulatory nature, adapted to the occasion.

"The flies trouble you, don't they, my dear?" said Mrs. Bangham. "But p'raps they'll take your mind off it, and do you good. What between the buryin ground, the grocer's, the waggon-stables, and the paunch trade, the Marshalsea flies gets very large. P'raps they're sent as a consolation, if we only know'd it. How are you now, my dear? No better? No, my dear, it ain't to be expected; you'll be worse before you're better, and you know it, don't you? Yes. That's right! And to think of a sweet little cherub being born inside the lock! Now ain't it pretty, ain't *that* something to carry you through it pleasant? Why, we ain't had such a thing happen here, my dear, not for I couldn't name the time when. And you a crying too?" said Mrs. Bangham, to rally the patient more and more. "You! Making yourself so famous! With the flies a falling into the gallipots by fifties! And everything a going on so well! And here if there ain't," said Mrs. Bangham as the door opened, "if there ain't your dear gentleman along with Dr. Haggage! And now indeed we *are* complete, I *think!*"

The doctor was scarcely the kind of apparition to inspire a patient with a sense of absolute completeness, but as he presently delivered the opinion, "We are as right as we can be, Mrs. Bangham, and we shall come out of this like a house a fire;" and as he and Mrs. Bangham took possession of the poor helpless pair as everybody else and anybody else had always done; the means at hand were as good on the whole as better would have been. The special feature in Dr. Haggage's treatment of the case, was his determination to keep Mrs. Bangham up to the mark. As thus:

"Mrs. Bangham," said the doctor, before he had been there twenty minutes, "go outside and fetch a little brandy, or we shall have you giving in."

"Thank you, sir. But none on my accounts," said Mrs. Bangham.

"Mrs. Bangham," returned the doctor, "I am in professional attendance on this lady, and don't choose to allow any discussion on your part. Go outside and fetch a little brandy, or I foresee that you'll break down."

"You're to be obeyed, sir," said Mrs. Bangham, rising. "If you was to put your own lips to it, I think you wouldn't be the worse, for you look but poorly, sir."

"Mrs. Bangham," returned the doctor, "I am not your business, thank you, but you are mine. Never you mind *me*, if you please. What you have got to do, is, to do as you are told, and to go and get what I bid you."

Mrs. Bangham submitted; and the doctor, having administered her potion, took his own. He repeated the treatment

74

every hour, being very determined with Mrs. Bangham. Three or four hours passed; the flies fell into the traps by hundreds; and at length one little life, hardly stronger than theirs, appeared among the multitude of lesser deaths.

"A very nice little girl indeed," said the doctor; "little, but well-formed. Halloa, Mrs. Bangham! You're looking queer! You be off, ma'am, this minute, and fetch a little more brandy, or we shall have you in hysterics."

By this time, the rings had begun to fall from the debtor's irresolute hands, like leaves from a wintry tree. Not one was left upon them that night, when he put something that chinked into the doctor's greasy palm. In the meantime Mrs. Bangham had been out on an errand to a neighbouring establishment decorated with three golden balls, where she was very well known.

"Thank you," said the doctor, "thank you. Your good lady is quite composed. Doing charmingly."

"I am very happy and very thankful to know it," said the debtor, "though I little thought once, that—"

"That a child would be born to you in a place like this?" said the doctor. "Bah, bah, sir, what does it signify? A little more elbow-room is all we want here. We are quiet here; we don't get badgered here; there's no knocker here, sir, to be hammered at by creditors and bring a man's heart into his mouth. Nobody comes here to ask if a man's at home, and to say he'll stand on the door mat till he is. Nobody writes threatening letters about money to this place. It's freedom, sir, it's freedom! I have had to-day's practice at home and abroad, on a march, and aboard ship, and I'll tell you this: I don't know that I have ever pursued it under such quiet circumstances, as here this day. Elsewhere, people are restless, worried, hurried about, anxious respecting one thing, anxious respecting another. Nothing of the kind here, sir. We have done all that—we know the worst of it; we have got to the bottom, we can't fall, and what have we found? Peace. That's the word for it. Peace." With this profession of faith, the doctor, who was an old jail-bird, and was more sodden than usual, and had the additional and unusual stimulus of money in his pocket, returned to his associate and chum in hoarseness, puffiness, red-facedness, all-fours, tobacco, dirt, and brandy.

Now, the debtor was a very different man from the doctor, but he had already begun to travel, by his opposite segment of the circle, to the same point. Crushed at first by his imprisonment, he had soon found a dull relief in it. He was under lock and key; but the lock and key that kept him in, kept numbers of his troubles out. If he had been a man with strength of purpose to face those troubles and fight them, he might have broken the net that held him, or broken his heart; but being what he was, he languidly slipped into this smooth descent, and never more took one step upward.

When he was relieved of the perplexed affairs that nothing would make plain, through having them returned upon his hands by a dozen agents in succession who could make neither beginning, middle, nor end of them, or him, he found his miserable place of refuge a quieter refuge than it had been before. He had unpacked the portmanteau long ago; and his elder children now played regularly about the yard, and everybody knew the baby, and claimed a kind of proprietorship in her.

"Why, I'm getting proud of you," said his friend the turnkey, one day. "You'll be the oldest inhabitant soon. The Marshalsea wouldn't be like the Marshalsea now, without you and your family."

The turnkey really was proud of him. He would mention him in laudatory terms to new-comers, when his back was turned. "You took notice of him," he would say, "that went out of the Lodge just now?"

New-comer would probably answer Yes.

"Brought up as a gentleman, he was, if ever a man was. Ed'cated at no end of expense. Went into the Marshal's

house once, to try a new piano for him. Played it, I understand, like one o'clock—beautiful! As to languages—speaks
anything. We've had a Frenchman here in his time, and it's
my opinion he knowed more French than the Frenchman did.
We've had an Italian here in his time, and he shut *him* up
in about half a minute. You'll find some characters behind
other locks, I don't say you won't; but if you want the top
sawyer, in such respects as I've mentioned, you must come to
the Marshalsea."

When his youngest child was eight years old, his wife, who
had long been languishing away—of her own inherent weakness, not that she retained any greater sensitiveness as to her
place of abode than he did—went upon a visit to a poor
friend and old nurse in the country, and died there. He
remained shut up in his room for a fortnight afterwards; and
an attorney's clerk, who was going through the Insolvent
Court, engrossed an address of condolence to him, which
looked like a Lease, and which all the prisoners signed.
When he appeared again he was greyer (he had soon begun
to turn grey); and the turnkey noticed that his hands went
often to his trembling lips again, as they had used to do
when he first came in. But he got pretty well over it in a
month or two; and in the meantime the children played
about the yard as regularly as ever, but in black.

Then Mrs. Bangham, long popular medium of communication with the outer world, began to be infirm, and to be
found oftener than usual comatose on pavements, with her
basket of purchases spilt, and the change of her clients ninepence short. His son began to supersede Mrs. Bangham, and
to execute commissions in a knowing manner, and to be of
the prison prisonous and of the streets streety.

Time went on, and the turnkey began to fail. His
chest swelled, and his legs got weak, and he was short of
breath. The well-worn wooden stool was "beyond him," he
complained. He sat in an arm-chair with a cushion, and
sometimes wheezed so, for minutes together, that he couldn't

77

turn the key. When he was overpowered by these fits, the debtor often turned it for him.

"You and me," said the turnkey, one snowy winter's night, when the lodge, with a bright fire in it, was pretty full of company, "is the oldest inhabitants. I wasn't here myself, above seven year before you. I shan't last long. When I'm off the lock for good and all, you'll be the Father of the Marshalsea."

The turnkey went off the lock of this world, next day. His words were remembered and repeated; and tradition afterwards handed down from generation to generation—a Marshalsea generation might be calculated as about three months —that the shabby old debtor with the soft manner and the white hair, was the Father of the Marshalsea.

And he grew to be proud of the title. If any impostor had arisen to claim it, he would have shed tears in resentment of the attempt to deprive him of his rights. A disposition began to be perceived in him, to exaggerate the number of years he had been there; it was generally understood that you must deduct a few from his account; he was vain, the fleeting generations of debtors said.

All new-comers were presented to him. He was punctilious in the exaction of this ceremony. The wits would perform the office of introduction with overcharged pomp and politeness, but they could not easily overstep his sense of its gravity. He received them in his poor room (he disliked an introduction in the mere yard, as informal—a thing that might happen to anybody), with a kind of bowed-down beneficence. They were welcome to the Marshalsea, he would tell them. Yes, he was the Father of the place. So the world was kind enough to call him; and so he was, if more than twenty years of residence gave him a claim to the title. It looked small at first, but there was very good company there—among a mixture—necessarily a mixture—and very good air.

It became a not unusual circumstance for letters to be put under his door at night, enclosing half-a-crown, two half-crowns, now and then at long intervals even half-a-sovereign, for the Father of the Marshalsea. "With the compliments of a collegian taking leave." He received the gifts as tributes, from admirers, to a public character. Sometimes these correspondents assumed facetious names, as the Brick, Bellows, Old Gooseberry, Wideawake, Snooks, Mops, Cutaway, the Dogs-meat Man; but he considered this in bad taste, and was always a little hurt by it.

In the fulness of time, this correspondence showing signs of wearing out, and seeming to require an effort on the part of the correspondents to which in the hurried circumstances of departure many of them might not be equal, he established the custom of attending collegians of a certain standing, to the gate, and taking leave of them there. The collegian under treatment, after shaking hands, would occasionally stop to wrap up something in a bit of paper, and would come back again, calling "Hi!"

He would look round surprised. "Me?" he would say, with a smile.

By this time the collegian would be up with him, and he would paternally add, "What have you forgotten? What can I do for you?"

"I forgot to leave this," the collegian would usually return, "for the Father of the Marshalsea."

"My good sir," he would rejoin, "he is infinitely obliged to you." But, to the last, the irresolute hand of old would remain in the pocket into which he had slipped the money, during two or three turns about the yard, lest the transaction should be too conspicuous to the general body of collegians.

One afternoon he had been doing the honours of the place to a rather large party of collegians, who happened to be going out, when, as he was coming back, he encountered one from the poor side who had been taken in execution for a small sum a week before, had "settled" in the course of that afternoon, and was going out too. The man was a mere

Plasterer in his working dress; had his wife with him, and a bundle; and was in high spirits.

"God bless you, sir," he said in passing.

"And you," benignantly returned the Father of the Marshalsea.

They were pretty far divided, going their several ways, when the Plasterer called out, "I say!—sir!" and came back to him.

"It an't much," said the Plasterer, putting a little pile of halfpence in his hand, "but it's well meant."

The Father of the Marshalsea had never been offered tribute in copper yet. His children often had, and with his perfect acquiescence it had gone into the common purse, to buy meat that he had eaten, and drink that he had drunk; but fustian splashed with white lime, bestowing halfpence on him, front to front, was new.

"How dare you!" he said to the man, and feebly burst into tears.

The Plasterer turned him towards the wall, that his face might not be seen; and the action was so delicate, and the man was so penetrated with repentance, and asked pardon so honestly, that he could make him no less acknowledgment than, "I know you meant it kindly. Say no more."

"Bless your soul, sir," urged the Plasterer, "I did indeed. I'd do more by you than the rest of 'em do, I fancy."

"What would you do?" he asked.

"I'd come back to see you, after I was let out."

"Give me the money again," said the other, eagerly, "and I'll keep it, and never spend it. Thank you for it, thank you! I shall see you again?"

"If I live a week you shall."

They shook hands and parted. The collegians, assembled in Symposium in the Snuggery that night, marvelled what had happened to their Father; he walked so late in the shadows of the yard, and seemed so downcast.

CHAPTER VII

THE baby whose first draught of air had been tinctured with Doctor Haggage's brandy, was handed down among the generations of collegians, like the tradition of their common parent. In the earlier stages of her existence, she was handed down in a literal and prosaic sense; it being almost a part of the entrance footing of every new collegian to nurse the child who had been born in the college.

" By rights," remarked the turnkey, when she was first shown to him, " I ought to be her godfather."

The debtor irresolutely thought of it for a minute, and said, " Perhaps you wouldn't object to really being her godfather?"

" Oh! *I* don't object," replied the turnkey, " if you don't."

Thus it came to pass that she was christened one Sunday afternoon, when the turnkey, being relieved, was off the lock; and that the turnkey went up to the font of Saint George's Church, and promised and vowed and renounced on her behalf, as he himself related when he came back, " like a good 'un."

This invested the turnkey with a new proprietary share in the child, over and above his former official one. When she began to walk and talk, he became fond of her; bought a little arm-chair and stood it by the high fender of the lodge fireplace; liked to have her company when he was on the lock; and used to bribe her with cheap toys to come and talk to him. The child, for her part, soon grew so fond of the

81

turnkey, that she would come climbing up the lodge-steps of her own accord at all hours of the day. When she fell asleep in the little arm-chair by the high fender, the turnkey would cover her with his pocket-handkerchief; and when she sat in it dressing and undressing a doll—which soon came to be unlike dolls on the other side of the lock, and to bear a horrible family resemblance to Mrs. Bangham—he would contemplate her from the top of his stool with exceeding gentleness. Witnessing these things, the collegians would express an opinion that the turnkey, who was a bachelor, had been cut out by nature for a family man. But the turnkey thanked them, and said, " No, on the whole it was enough to see other people's children there."

At what period of her early life the little creature began to perceive that it was not the habit of all the world to live locked up in narrow yards surrounded by high walls with spikes at the top, would be a difficult question to settle. But she was a very, very little creature indeed, when she had somehow gained the knowledge, that her clasp of her father's hand was to be always loosened at the door which the great key opened; and that while her own light steps were free to pass beyond it, his feet must never cross that line. A pitiful and plaintive look, with which she had begun to regard him when she was still extremely young, was perhaps a part of this discovery.

With a pitiful and plaintive look for everything indeed, but with something in it for only him that was like protection, this Child of the Marshalsea and child of the Father of the Marshalsea, sat by her friend the turnkey in the lodge, kept the family room, or wandered about the prison-yard, for the first eight years of her life. With a pitiful and plaintive look for her wayward sister; for her idle brother; for the high blank walls; for the faded crowd they shut in; for the games of the prison children as they whooped and ran, and played at hide-and-seek, and made the iron bars of the inner gateway " Home."

Wistful and wondering, she would sit in summer weather by the high fender in the lodge, looking up at the sky through the barred window, until bars of light would arise, when she turned her eyes away, between her and her friend, and she would see him through a grating, too.

"Thinking of the fields," the turnkey said once, after watching her, "ain't you?"

"Where are they?" she inquired.

"Why, they're—over there, my dear," said the turnkey, with a vague flourish of his key. "Just about there."

"Does anybody open them, and shut them? Are they locked?"

The turnkey was discomfited. "Well," he said. "Not in general."

"Are they very pretty, Bob?" She called him Bob, by his own particular request and instruction.

"Lovely. Full of flowers. There's buttercups, and there's daisies, and there's"—the turnkey hesitated, being short of floral nomenclature—"there's dandelions, and all manner of games."

"Is it very pleasant to be there, Bob?"

"Prime," said the turnkey.

"Was father ever there?"

"Hem!" coughed the turnkey. "O yes, he was there, sometimes."

"Is he sorry not to be there now?"

"N—not particular," said the turnkey.

"Nor any of the people?" she asked, glancing at the listless crowd within. "O are you quite sure and certain, Bob?"

At this difficult point of the conversation Bob gave in, and changed the subject to hard-bake: always his last resource when he found his little friend getting him into a political, social, or theological corner. But this was the origin of a series of Sunday excursions that these two curious companions made together. They used to issue from the lodge on

alternate Sunday afternoons with great gravity, bound for some
meadows or green lanes that had been elaborately appointed
by the turnkey in the course of the week; and there she
picked grass and flowers to bring home, while he smoked his
pipe. Afterwards, there were tea-gardens, shrimps, ale, and
other delicacies; and then they would come back hand in hand,
unless she was more than usually tired, and had fallen asleep
on his shoulder.

In those early days, the turnkey first began profoundly to
consider a question which cost him so much mental labour,
that it remained undetermined on the day of his death. He
decided to will and bequeath his little property of savings
to his godchild, and the point arose how could it be so
"tied up" as that only she should have the benefit of it?
His experience on the lock gave him such an acute perception
of the enormous difficulty of "tying up" money with any
approach to tightness, and contrariwise of the remarkable
ease with which it got loose, that through a series of years
he regularly propounded this knotty point to every new insolvent agent and other professional gentleman who passed
in and out.

"Supposing," he would say, stating the case with his key,
on the professional gentleman's waistcoat; "supposing a man
wanted to leave his property to a young female, and wanted
to tie it up so that nobody else should ever be able to make
a grab at it; how would you tie up that property?"

"Settle it strictly on herself," the professional gentleman
would complacently answer.

"But look here," quoth the turnkey. "Supposing she had,
say a brother, say a father, say a husband, who would be
likely to make a grab at that property when she came into
it—how about that?"

"It would be settled on herself, and they would have no
more legal claim on it than you," would be the professional
answer.

"Stop a bit," said the turnkey. "Supposing she was

tender-hearted, and they came over her. Where's your law for tying it up then?"

The deepest character whom the turnkey sounded, was unable to produce his law for tying such a knot as that. So, the turnkey thought about it all his life, and died intestate after all.

But that was long afterwards, when his god-daughter was past sixteen. The first half of that space of her life was only just accomplished, when her pitiful and plaintive look saw her father a widower. From that time the protection that her wondering eyes had expressed towards him, became embodied in action, and the Child of the Marshalsea took upon herself a new relation towards the Father.

At first, such a baby could do little more than sit with him, deserting her livelier place by the high fender, and quietly watching him. But this made her so far necessary to him that he became accustomed to her, and began to be sensible of missing her when she was not there. Through this little gate, she passed out of childhood into the care-laden world.

What her pitiful look saw, at that early time, in her father, in her sister, in her brother, in the jail; how much, or how little of the wretched truth it pleased God to make visible to her; lies hidden with many mysteries. It is enough that she was inspired to be something which was not what the rest were, and to be that something, different and laborious, for the sake of the rest. Inspired? Yes. Shall we speak of the inspiration of a poet or a priest, and not of the heart impelled by love and self-devotion to the lowliest work in the lowliest way of life!

With no earthly friend to help her, or so much as to see her, but the one so strangely assorted; with no knowledge even of the common daily tone and habits of the common members of the free community who are not shut up in prisons; born and bred, in a social condition, false even with a reference to the falsest condition outside the walls; drinking from infancy of a well whose waters had their own peculiar stain, their own unwholesome and unnatural taste; the Child of the Marshalsea began her womanly life.

No matter through what mistakes and discouragements, what ridicule (not unkindly meant, but deeply felt) of her youth and little figure, what humble consciousness of her own babyhood and want of strength, even in the matter of lifting and carrying; through how much weariness and hope-lessness, and how many secret tears; she trudged on, until recognised as useful, even indispensable. That time came. She took the place of eldest of the three, in all things but precedence; was the head of the fallen family; and bore, in her own heart, its anxieties and shames.

At thirteen, she could read and keep accounts—that is, could put down in words and figures how much the bare necessaries that they wanted would cost, and how much less they had to buy them with. She had been, by snatches of a few weeks at a time, to an evening school outside, and got her sister and brother sent to day-schools by desultory starts, during three or four years. There was no instruction for any of them at home; but she knew well—no one better— that a man so broken as to be the Father of the Marshalsea, could be no father to his own children.

To these scanty means of improvement, she added another of her own contriving. Once, among the heterogeneous crowd of inmates there appeared a dancing-master. Her sister had a great desire to learn the dancing-master's art, and seemed to have a taste that way. At thirteen years old, the Child of the Marshalsea presented herself to the dancing-master, with a little bag in her hand, and preferred her humble petition.

"If you please, I was born here, sir."

"Oh! You are the young lady, are you?" said the dancing-master, surveying the small figure and uplifted face.

"Yes, sir."

"And what can I do for you?" said the dancing-man.

"Nothing for me, sir, thank you," anxiously undrawing the strings of the little bag; "but if, while you stay here, you could be so kind as to teach my sister cheap—"

"My child, I'll teach her for nothing," said the dancing-master, shutting up the bag. He was as good-natured a dancing-master as ever danced to the Insolvent Court, and he kept his word. The sister was so apt a pupil, and the dancing-master had such abundant leisure to bestow upon her (for it took him a matter of ten weeks to set to his creditors, lead off, turn the Commissioners, and right and left back to his professional pursuits), that wonderful progress was made. Indeed the dancing-master was so proud of it, and so wishful to display it before he left, to a few select friends among the collegians, that at six o'clock on a certain fine morning, a minuet de la cour came off in the yard—the college-rooms being of too confined proportions for the purpose—in which so much ground was covered, and the steps were so conscientiously executed, that the dancing-master, having to play the kit besides, was thoroughly blown.

The success of this beginning, which led to the dancing-master's continuing his instruction after his release, emboldened the poor child to try again. She watched and waited months, for a seamstress. In the fulness of time a milliner came in, and to her she repaired on her own behalf.

"I beg your pardon, ma'am," she said, looking timidly round the door of the milliner, whom she found in tears and in bed: "but I was born here."

Everybody seemed to hear of her as soon as they arrived; for the milliner sat up in bed, drying her eyes, and said, just as the dancing-master had said:

"Oh! *You* are the child, are you?"

"Yes, ma'am."

"I am sorry I haven't got anything for you," said the milliner, shaking her head.

"It's not that, ma'am. If you please I want to learn needlework."

87

"Why should you do that," returned the milliner, "with me before you? It has not done me much good."

"Nothing—whatever it is—seems to have done anybody much good who comes here," she returned in all simplicity; "but I want to learn just the same."

"I am afraid you are so weak, you see," the milliner objected.

"I don't think I am weak, ma'am."

"And you are so very, very, little, you see," the milliner objected.

"Yes, I am afraid I am very little indeed," returned the Child of the Marshalsea; and so began to sob over that unfortunate defect of hers, which came so often in her way. The milliner—who was not morose or hard-hearted, only newly insolvent—was touched, took her in hand in good-will, found her the most patient and earnest of pupils, and made her a cunning work-woman in course of time.

In course of time, and in the very self-same course of time, the Father of the Marshalsea gradually developed a new flower of character. The more Fatherly he grew as to the Marshalsea, and the more dependent he became on the contributions of his changing family, the greater stand he made by his forlorn gentility. With the same hand that he pocketed a collegian's half-crown half an hour ago, he would wipe away the tears that streamed over his cheeks if any reference were made to his daughters' earning their bread. So, over and above her other daily cares, the Child of the Marshalsea had always upon her, the care of preserving the genteel fiction that they were all idle beggars together.

The sister became a dancer. There was a ruined uncle in the family group—ruined by his brother, the Father of the Marshalsea, and knowing no more how than his ruiner did, but accepting the fact as an inevitable certainty—on whom her protection devolved. Naturally a retired and simple man, he had shown no particular sense of being ruined, at the time when that calamity fell upon him, further than that he left

HER UNCLE

off washing himself when the shock was announced, and never
took to that luxury any more. He had been a very indifferent
musical amateur in his better days; and when he fell with
his brother, resorted for support to playing a clarionet as
dirty as himself in a small Theatre Orchestra. It was the
theatre in which his niece became a dancer; he had been a
fixture there a long time when she took her poor station in
it; and he accepted the task of serving as her escort and
guardian, just as he would have accepted an illness, a legacy,
a feast, starvation—anything but soap.

To enable this girl to earn her few weekly shillings, it was
necessary for the Child of the Marshalsea to go through an
elaborate form with the Father.

"Fanny is not going to live with us just now, father. She
will be here a good deal in the day, but she is going to live
outside with uncle."

"You surprise me. Why?"

"I think uncle wants a companion, father. He should be
attended to, and looked after."

"A companion? He passes much of his time here. And
you attend to him and look after him, Amy, a great deal
more than ever your sister will. You all go out so much;
you all go out so much."

This was to keep up the ceremony and pretence of his
having no idea that Amy herself went out by the day to work.

"But we are always very glad to come home, father; now,
are we not? And as to Fanny, perhaps besides keeping uncle
company and taking care of him, it may be as well for her
not quite to live here, always. She was not born here as I
was, you know, father."

"Well, Amy, well. I don't quite follow you, but it's
natural I suppose that Fanny should prefer to be outside,
and even that you often should, too. So, you and Fanny
and your uncle, my dear, shall have your own way. Good,
good. I'll not meddle; don't mind me."

To get her brother out of the prison; out of the succession

89

to Mrs. Bangham in executing commissions, and out of the slang interchange with very doubtful companions, consequent upon both; was her hardest task. At eighteen he would have dragged on from hand to mouth, from hour to hour, from penny to penny, until eighty. Nobody got into the prison from whom he derived anything useful or good, and she could find no patron for him but her old friend and godfather.

"Dear Bob," said she, "what is to become of poor Tip?" His name was Edward, and Ted had been transformed into Tip, within the walls.

The turnkey had strong private opinions as to what would become of poor Tip, and had even gone so far with the view of averting their fulfilment, as to sound Tip in reference to the expediency of running away and going to serve his country. But Tip had thanked him, and said he didn't seem to care for his country.

"Well, my dear," said the turnkey, "something ought to be done with him. Suppose I try and get him into the law?"

"That would be so good of you, Bob!"

The turnkey had now two points to put to the professional gentlemen as they passed in and out. He put this second one so perseveringly, that a stool and twelve shillings a week were at last found for Tip in the office of an attorney in a great National Palladium called the Palace Court; at that time one of a considerable list of everlasting bulwarks to the dignity and safety of Albion, whose places know them no more.

Tip languished in Clifford's Inn for six months, and at the expiration of that term, sauntered back one evening with his hands in his pockets, and incidentally observed to his sister that he was not going back again.

"Not going back again?" said the poor little anxious Child of the Marshalsea, always calculating and planning for Tip, in the front rank of her charges.

"I am so tired of it," said Tip, "that I have cut it."

HER BROTHER

Tip tired of everything. With intervals of Marshalsea lounging, and Mrs. Bangham succession, his small second mother, aided by her trusty friend, got him into a warehouse, into a market garden, into the hop trade, into the law again, into an auctioneer's, into a brewery, into a stockbroker's, into the law again, into a coach office, into a waggon office, into the law again, into a general dealer's, into a distillery, into the law again, into a wool house, into a dry goods house, into the Billingsgate trade, into the foreign fruit trade, and into the docks. But whatever Tip went into, he came out of tired, announcing that he had cut it. Wherever he went, this foredoomed Tip appeared to take the prison walls with him, and to set them up in such trade or calling; and to prowl about within their narrow limits in the old slip-shod, purposeless, down-at-heel way; until the real immovable Marshalsea walls asserted their fascination over him, and brought him back.

Nevertheless, the brave little creature did so fix her heart on her brother's rescue, that while he was ringing out these doleful changes, she pinched and scraped enough together to ship him for Canada. When he was tired of nothing to do, and disposed in its turn to cut even that, he graciously consented to go to Canada. And there was grief in her bosom over parting with him, and joy in the hope of his being put in a straight course at last.

"God bless you, dear Tip. Don't be too proud to come and see us, when you have made your fortune."

"All right!" said Tip, and went.

But not all the way to Canada; in fact, not further than Liverpool. After making the voyage to that port from London, he found himself so strongly impelled to cut the vessel, that he resolved to walk back again. Carrying out which intention, he presented himself before her at the expiration of a month, in rags, without shoes, and much more tired than ever.

At length, after another interval of successorship to Mrs. Bangham, he found a pursuit for himself, and announced it.

" Amy, I have got a situation."

" Have you really and truly, Tip ? "

" All right. I shall do now. You needn't look anxious about me any more, old girl."

" What is it, Tip ? "

" Why, you know Slingo by sight ? "

" Not the man they call the dealer ? "

" That's the chap. He'll be out on Monday, and he's going to give me a berth."

" What is he a dealer in, Tip ? "

" Horses. All right ! I shall do now, Amy."

She lost sight of him for months afterwards, and only heard from him once. A whisper passed among the elder collegians that he had been seen at a mock auction in Moorfields, pretending to buy plated articles for massive silver, and paying for them with the greatest liberality in bank notes ; but it never reached her ears. One evening she was alone at work—standing up at the window, to save the twilight lingering above the wall—when he opened the door and walked in.

She kissed and welcomed him ; but was afraid to ask him any question. He saw how anxious and timid she was, and appeared sorry.

" I am afraid, Amy, you'll be vexed this time. Upon my life I am ! "

" I am very sorry to hear you say so, Tip. Have you come back ? "

" Why—yes."

" Not expecting this time that what you had found would answer very well, I am less surprised and sorry than I might have been, Tip."

" Ah ! But that's not the worst of it."

" Not the worst of it ? "

" Don't look so startled. No, Amy, not the worst of it. I have come back, you see ; but—*don't* look so startled—I have come back in what I may call a new way. I am off the volunteer list altogether. I am in now, as one of the regulars."

"Oh! Don't say you are a prisoner, Tip! Don't, don't!"

"Well, I don't want to say it," he returned in a reluctant tone; "but if you can't understand me without my saying it, what am I to do? I am in for forty pound odd."

For the first time in all those years, she sunk under her cares. She cried, with her clasped hands lifted above her head, that it would kill their father if he ever knew it; and fell down at Tip's graceless feet.

It was easier for Tip to bring her to her senses, than for her to bring *him* to understand that the Father of the Marshalsea would be beside himself if he knew the truth. The thing was incomprehensible to Tip, and altogether a fanciful notion. He yielded to it in that light only, when he submitted to her entreaties, backed by those of his uncle and sister. There was no want of precedent for his return; it was accounted for to the father in the usual way; and the collegians, with a better comprehension of the pious fraud than Tip, supported it loyally.

This was the life, and this the history, of the Child of the Marshalsea, at twenty-two. With a still surviving attachment to the one miserable yard and block of houses as her birthplace and home, she passed to and fro in it shrinkingly now, with a womanly consciousness that she was pointed out to every one. Since she had begun to work beyond the walls, she had found it necessary to conceal where she lived, and to come and go as secretly as she could, between the free city and the iron gates, outside of which she had never slept in her life. Her original timidity had grown with this concealment, and her light step and her little figure shunned the thronged streets while they passed along them.

Worldly wise in hard and poor necessities, she was innocent in all things else. Innocent, in the mist through which she saw her father, and the prison, and the turbid living river that flowed through it and flowed on.

This was the life, and this the history, of Little Dorrit; now going home upon a dull September evening, observed at a distance by Arthur Clennam. This was the life, and this the history, of Little Dorrit; turning at the end of London Bridge, recrossing it, going back again, passing on to Saint George's Church, turning back suddenly once more, and flitting in at the open outer gate and little court-yard of the Marshalsea.

CHAPTER VIII

THE LOCK

ARTHUR CLENNAM stood in the street, waiting to ask some passer-by what place that was. He suffered a few people to pass him in whose faces there was no encouragement to make the inquiry, and still stood pausing in the street, when an old man came up and turned into the court-yard.

He stooped a good deal, and plodded along in a slow pre-occupied manner, which made the bustling London thorough-fares no very safe resort for him. He was dirtily and meanly dressed, in a threadbare coat, once blue, reaching to his ankles and buttoned to his chin, where it vanished in the pale ghost of a velvet collar. A piece of red cloth with which that phantom had been stiffened in its lifetime was now laid bare, and poked itself up, at the back of the old man's neck, into a confusion of grey hair and rusty stock and buckle which altogether nearly poked his hat off. A greasy hat it was, and a napless ; impending over his eyes, cracked and crumpled at the brim, and with a wisp of pocket-handkerchief dangling out below it. His trousers were so long and loose, and his shoes so clumsy and large, that he shuffled like an elephant ; though how much of this was gait, and how much trailing cloth and leather, no one could have told. Under one arm he carried a limp and worn-out case, containing some wind instrument ; in the same hand he had a pennyworth of snuff in a little packet of whitey-brown paper, from which he slowly comforted his poor old blue nose with a lengthened-out pinch, as Arthur Clennam looked at him.

To this old man, crossing the court-yard, he preferred his inquiry, touching him on the shoulder. The old man stopped and looked round, with the expression in his weak grey eyes of one whose thoughts had been far off, and who was a little dull of hearing also.

"Pray, sir," said Arthur, repeating his question, "what is this place?"

"Ay! This place?" returned the old man, staying his pinch of snuff on its road, and pointing at the place without looking at it. "This is the Marshalsea, sir."

"The debtors' prison?"

"Sir," said the old man, with the air of deeming it not quite necessary to insist upon that designation, "the debtors' prison."

He turned himself about, and went on.

"I beg your pardon," said Arthur, stopping him once more, "but will you allow me to ask you another question? Can any one go in here?"

"Any one can *go in*," replied the old man; plainly adding by the significance of his emphasis, "but it is not every one who can go out."

"Pardon me once more. Are you familiar with the place?"

"Sir," returned the old man, squeezing his little packet of snuff in his hand, and turning upon his interrogator as if such questions hurt him. "I am."

"I beg you to excuse me. I am not impertinently curious, but have a good object. Do you know the name of Dorrit here?"

"My name, sir," replied the old man most unexpectedly, "is Dorrit."

Arthur pulled off his hat to him. "Grant me the favour of half-a-dozen words. I was wholly unprepared for your

96

announcement, and hope that assurance is my sufficient apology for having taken the liberty of addressing you. I have recently come home to England after a long absence. I have seen at my mother's—Mrs. Clennam in the city—a young woman working at her needle, whom I have only heard addressed or spoken of as Little Dorrit. I have felt sincerely interested in her, and have had a great desire to know something more about her. I saw her, not a minute before you came up, pass in at that door."

The old man looked at him attentively. "Are you a sailor, sir?" he asked. He seemed a little disappointed by the shake of the head that replied to him. "Not a sailor? I judged from your sunburnt face that you might be. Are you in earnest, sir?"

"I do assure you that I am, and do entreat you to believe that I am, in plain earnest."

"I know very little of the world, sir," returned the other, who had a weak and quavering voice. "I am merely passing on, like the shadow over the sun-dial. It would be worth no man's while to mislead me ; it would really be too easy—too poor a success, to yield any satisfaction. The young woman whom you saw go in here is my brother's child. My brother is William Dorrit ; I am Frederick. You say you have seen her at your mother's (I know your mother befriends her), you have felt an interest in her, and you wish to know what she does here. Come and see."

He went on again, and Arthur accompanied him.

"My brother," said the old man, pausing on the step, and slowly facing round again, "has been here many years ; and much that happens even among ourselves, out of doors, is kept from him for reasons that I needn't enter upon now. Be so good as to say nothing of my niece's working at her needle. Be so good as to say nothing that goes beyond what is said among us. If you keep within our bounds, you cannot well be wrong. Now! Come and see."

Arthur followed him down a narrow entry, at the end of

which a key was turned, and a strong door was opened from within. It admitted them into a lodge or lobby, across which they passed, and so through another door and a grating into the prison. The old man always plodding on before, turned round, in his slow, stiff, stooping manner, when they came to the turnkey on duty, as if to present his companion. The turnkey nodded ; and the companion passed in without being asked whom he wanted.

The night was dark ; and the prison lamps in the yard, and the candles in the prison windows faintly shining behind many sorts of wry old curtain and blind, had not the air of making it lighter. A few people loitered about, but the greater part of the population was within doors. The old man taking the right-hand side of the yard, turned in at the third or fourth doorway, and began to ascend the stairs. " They are rather dark, sir, but you will not find anything in the way."

He paused for a moment before opening a door on the second story. He had no sooner turned the handle, than the visitor saw Dorrit, and saw the reason of her setting so much store by dining alone.

She had brought the meat home that she should have eaten herself, and was already warming it on a gridiron over the fire, for her father, clad in an old grey gown and a black cap, awaiting his supper at the table. A clean cloth was spread before him, with knife, fork, and spoon, salt-cellar, pepper-box, glass, and pewter ale-pot. Such zests as his particular little phial of cayenne pepper, and his pennyworth of pickles in a saucer, were not wanting.

She started, coloured deeply, and turned white. The visitor, more with his eyes than by the slight impulsive motion of his hand, entreated her to be reassured and to trust him.

" I found this gentleman," said the uncle—" Mr. Clennam, William, son of Amy's friend—at the outer gate, wishful, as he was going by, of paying his respects, but hesitating whether to come in or not. This is my brother William, sir."

" I hope," said Arthur, very doubtful what to say, " that my respect for your daughter may explain and justify my desire to be presented to you, sir."

"Mr. Clennam," returned the other, rising, taking his cap off in the flat of his hand, and so holding it, ready to put on again, "you do me honour. You are welcome, sir." With a low bow. "Frederick, a chair. Pray sit down, Mr. Clennam."

He put his black cap on again as he had taken it off, and resumed his own seat. There was a wonderful air of benignity and patronage in his manner. These were the ceremonies with which he received the collegians.

" You are welcome to the Marshalsea, sir. I have welcomed many gentlemen to these walls. Perhaps you are aware—my daughter Amy may have mentioned that I am the Father of this place."

" I—so I have understood," said Arthur, dashing at the assertion.

" You know, I dare say, that my daughter Amy was born here. A good girl, sir, a dear girl, and long a comfort and support to me. Amy, my dear, put this dish on ; Mr. Clennam will excuse the primitive customs to which we are reduced here. Is it a compliment to ask you if you would do me the honour, sir, to— "

"Thank you," returned Arthur. "Not a morsel."

He felt himself quite lost in wonder at the manner of the man, and that the probability of his daughter's having had a reserve as to her family history, should be so far out of his mind.

She filled his glass, put all the little matters on the table ready to his hand, and then sat beside him while he ate his supper. Evidently in observance of their nightly custom, she put some bread before herself, and touched his glass with her lips ; but Arthur saw she was troubled and took nothing.

Her look at her father, half admiring him and proud of him, half ashamed for him, all devoted and loving, went to his inmost heart.

The Father of the Marshalsea condescended towards his brother as an amiable, well-meaning man; a private character, who had not arrived at distinction. "Frederick," said he, "you and Fanny sup at your lodgings to-night, I know. What have you done with Fanny, Frederick?"

"She is walking with Tip."

"Tip—as you may know—is my son, Mr. Clennam. He has been a little wild, and difficult to settle, but his introduction to the world was rather"—he shrugged his shoulders with a faint sigh, and looked round the room—"a little adverse. Your first visit here, sir?"

"My first."

"You could hardly have been here since your boyhood without my knowledge. It very seldom happens that anybody—of any pretensions—any pretensions—comes here without being presented to me."

"As many as forty or fifty in a day have been introduced to my brother," said Frederick, faintly lighting up with a ray of pride.

"Yes!" the Father of the Marshalsea assented. "We have even exceeded that number. On a fine Sunday in term time, it is quite a Levee—quite a Levee. Amy, my dear, I have been trying half the day to remember the name of the gentleman from Camberwell who was introduced to me last Christmas week, by that agreeable coal-merchant who was remanded for six months."

"I don't remember his name, father."

"Frederick, do *you* remember his name?"

Frederick doubted if he had ever heard it. No one could doubt that Frederick was the last person upon earth to put such a question to, with any hope of information.

"I mean," said his brother, "the gentleman who did that handsome action with so much delicacy. Ha! Tush! The

100

name has quite escaped me. Mr. Clennam, as I have happened to mention handsome and delicate action, you may like, perhaps, to know what it was."

" Very much," said Arthur, withdrawing his eyes from the delicate head beginning to droop, and the pale face with a new solicitude stealing over it.

" It is so generous, and shows so much fine feeling, that it is almost a duty to mention it. I said at the time that I always would mention it on every suitable occasion, without regard to personal sensitiveness. A—well—a—it's of no use to disguise the fact—you must know, Mr. Clennam, that it does sometimes occur that people who come here, desire to offer some little—Testimonial—to the Father of the place."

To see her hand upon his arm in mute entreaty half-repressed, and her timid little shrinking figure turning away, was to see a sad, sad sight.

"Sometimes," he went on in a low, soft voice, agitated, and clearing his throat every now and then; "sometimes—hem—it takes one shape and sometimes another; but it is generally—ha—Money. And it is, I cannot but confess it, it is too often—hem—acceptable. This gentleman that I refer to, was presented to me, Mr. Clennam, in a manner highly gratifying to my feelings, and conversed not only with great politeness, but with great—ahem—information." All this time, though he had finished his supper, he was nervously going about his plate with his knife and fork, as if some of it were still before him. " It appeared from his conversation that he had a garden, though he was delicate of mentioning it at first, as gardens are—hem—are not accessible to me. But it came out, through my admiring a very fine cluster of geranium—beautiful cluster of geranium to be sure—which he had brought from his conservatory. On my taking notice of its rich colour, he showed me a piece of paper round it, on which was written, 'For the Father of the Marshalsea,' and presented it to me. But this was—hem—not all. He made a particular request, on taking leave, that I would remove the paper in half an hour. I—ha—I did so; and I found that it contained—ahem—two guineas. I assure you, Mr. Clennam, I have received—hem—Testimonials in many ways, and of many degrees of value, and they have always been—ha—unfortunately acceptable; but I never was more pleased than with this—ahem—this particular Testimonial."

Arthur was in the act of saying the little he could say on such a theme, when a bell began to ring, and footsteps approached the door. A pretty girl of a far better figure and much more developed than Little Dorrit, though looking much younger in the face when the two were observed together, stopped in the doorway on seeing a stranger; and a young man who was with her, stopped too.

"Mr. Clennam, Fanny. My eldest daughter and my son, Mr. Clennam. The bell is a signal for visitors to retire, and so they have come to say good night; but there is plenty of time, plenty of time. Girls, Mr. Clennam will excuse any household business you may have together. He knows, I dare say, that I have but one room here."

"I only want my clean dress from Amy, father," said the second girl.

"And I my clothes," said Tip.

Amy opened a drawer in an old piece of furniture that was a chest of drawers above, and a bedstead below, and produced two little bundles, which she handed to her brother and sister. "Mended and made up?" Clennam heard the sister ask in a whisper. To which Amy answered "Yes." He had risen now, and took the opportunity of glancing round the room. The bare walls had been coloured green, evidently by an unskilled hand, and were poorly decorated with a few prints. The window was curtained, and the floor carpeted; and there were shelves and pegs, and other such conveniences, that had accumulated in the course of years. It was a close, confined room, poorly furnished; and the chimney smoked to boot, or the tin screen at the top of the fireplace was superfluous; but constant pains and care had made it neat, and even, after its kind, comfortable.

All the while the bell was ringing, and the uncle was anxious to go. "Come, Fanny, come, Fanny," he said with his ragged clarionet case under his arm; "the lock, child, the lock!"

Fanny bade her father good night, and whisked off airily. Tip had already clattered down-stairs. "Now, Mr. Clennam," said the uncle, looking back as he shuffled out after them, "the lock, sir, the lock."

Mr. Clennam had two things to do before he followed; one, to offer his testimonial to the Father of the Marshalsea, without giving pain to his child; the other to say something to that child, though it were but a word, in explanation of his having come there.

"Allow me," said the Father, "to see you down-stairs."

She had slipped out after the rest, and they were alone. "Not on any account," said the visitor, hurriedly. "Pray allow me to—" chink, chink, chink.

"Mr. Clennam," said the Father, "I am deeply, deeply—" But his visitor had shut up his hand to stop the chinking, and had gone down-stairs with great speed.

He saw no Little Dorrit on his way down, or in the yard. The last two or three stragglers were hurrying to the lodge, and he was following, when he caught sight of her in the doorway of the first house from the entrance. He turned back hastily.

"Pray forgive me," he said, "for speaking to you here; pray forgive me for coming here at all! I followed you to-night. I did so, that I might endeavour to render you and your family some service. You know the terms on which I and my mother are, and may not be surprised that I have preserved our distant relations at her house, lest I should unintentionally make her jealous, or resentful, or do you any injury in her estimation. What I have seen here, in this short time, has greatly increased my heartfelt wish to be a friend to you. It would recompense me for much disappointment if I could hope to gain your confidence."

She was scared at first, but seemed to take courage while he spoke to her.

"You are very good, sir. You speak very earnestly to me. But I—but I wish you had not watched me."

He understood the emotion with which she said it, to arise in her father's behalf; and he respected it, and was silent.

"Mrs. Clennam has been of great service to me; I don't know what we should have done without the employment she has given me; I am afraid it may not be a good return to become secret with her; I can say no more to-night, sir. I am sure you mean to be kind to us. Thank you, thank you."

"Let me ask you one question before I leave. Have you known my mother long?"

"I think two years, sir.—The bell has stopped."

"How did you know her first? Did she send here for you?"

"No. She does not even know that I live here. We have a friend, father and I—a poor labouring man, but the best of friends—and I wrote out that I wished to do needlework, and gave his address. And he got what I wrote out displayed at a few places where it cost nothing, and Mrs. Clennam found me that way, and sent for me. The gate will be locked, sir!"

She was so tremulous and agitated, and he was so moved by compassion for her, and by deep interest in her story as it dawned upon him, that he could scarcely tear himself away. But the stoppage of the bell, and the quiet in the prison, were a warning to depart; and with a few hurried words of kindness he left her gliding back to her father.

But he had remained too late. The inner gate was locked, and the lodge closed. After a little fruitless knocking with his hand, he was standing there with the disagreeable conviction upon him that he had to get through the night, when a voice accosted him from behind.

104

"Caught, eh?" said the voice. "You won't go home till morning.—Oh! It's you, is it, Mr. Clennam?"

The voice was Tip's; and they stood looking at one another in the prison-yard, as it began to rain.

"You've done it," observed Tip; "you must be sharper than that next time."

"But you are locked in too," said Arthur.

"I believe I am!" said Tip, sarcastically. "About! But not in your way. I belong to the shop, only my sister has a theory that our governor must never know it. I don't see why, myself."

"Can I get any shelter?" asked Arthur. "What had I better do?"

"We had better get hold of Amy first of all," said Tip, referring any difficulty to her as a matter of course.

"I would rather walk about all night—it's not much to do—than give that trouble."

"You needn't do that, if you don't mind paying for a bed. If you don't mind paying, they'll make you up one on the Snuggery table, under the circumstances. If you'll come along, I'll introduce you there."

As they passed down the yard, Arthur looked up at the window of the room he had lately left, where the light was still burning. "Yes, sir," said Tip, following his glance. "That's the governor's. She'll sit with him for another hour reading yesterday's paper to him, or something of that sort; and then she'll come out like a little ghost, and vanish away without a sound."

"I don't understand you."

"The governor sleeps up in the room, and she has a lodging at the turnkey's. First house there," said Tip, pointing out the doorway into which she had retired. "First house, sky parlour. She pays twice as much for it as she would for one twice as good outside. But she stands by the governor, poor dear girl, day and night."

This brought them to the tavern-establishment at the

upper end of the prison where the collegians had just vacated their social evening club. The apartment on the ground-floor in which it was held, was the Snuggery in question ; the presidential tribune of the chairman, the pewter-pots, glasses, pipes, tobacco-ashes, and general flavour of members, were still as that convivial institution had left them on its adjournment. The Snuggery had two of the qualities popularly held to be essential to grog for ladies, in respect that it was hot and strong; but in the third point of analogy, requiring plenty of it, the Snuggery was defective: being but a cooped-up apartment.

The unaccustomed visitor from outside, naturally assumed everybody here to be prisoners—landlord, waiter, barmaid, potboy, and all. Whether they were or not, did not appear; but they all had a weedy look. The keeper of a chandler's shop in a front parlour, who took in gentlemen boarders, lent his assistance in making the bed. He had been a tailor in his time, and had kept a phaëton, he said. He boasted that he stood up litigiously for the interests of the college ; and he had undefined and undefinable ideas that the marshal intercepted a " Fund," which ought to come to the collegians. He liked to believe this, and always impressed the shadowy grievance on new-comers and strangers; though he could not, for his life, have explained what Fund he meant, or how the notion had got rooted in his soul. He had fully convinced himself, notwithstanding, that his own proper share of the Fund was three and ninepence a week ; and that in this amount he, as an individual collegian, was swindled by the marshal, regularly every Monday. Apparently, he helped to make the bed, that he might not lose an opportunity of stating this case; after which unloading of his mind, and after announcing (as it seemed he always did, without any-thing coming of it) that he was going to write a letter to the papers and show the marshal up, he fell into miscellaneous conversation with the rest. It was evident from the general tone of the whole party, that they had come to regard insolvency as the normal state of mankind, and the payment of debts as a disease that occasionally broke out.

In this strange scene, and with these strange spectres flitting about him, Arthur Clennam looked on at the preparations, as if they were part of a dream. Pending which, the long-initiated Tip, with an awful enjoyment of the Snuggery's resources, pointed out the common kitchen fire maintained by subscription of collegians, the boiler for hot water supported in like manner, and other premises generally tending to the deduction that the way to be healthy, wealthy, and wise, was to come to the Marshalsea.

The two tables put together in a corner, were, at length, converted into a very fair bed; and the stranger was left to the Windsor chairs, the presidential tribune, the beery atmosphere, sawdust, pipe-lights, spittoons and repose. But the last item was long, long, long, in linking itself to the rest. The novelty of the place, the coming upon it without preparation, the sense of being locked up, the remembrance of that room up-stairs, of the two brothers, and above all of the retiring childish form, and the face in which he now saw years of insufficient food, if not of want, kept him waking and unhappy.

Speculations, too, bearing the strangest relations towards the prison, but always concerning the prison, ran like nightmares through his mind while he lay awake. Whether coffins were kept ready for people who might die there, where they were kept, how they were kept, where people who died in the prison were buried, how they were taken out, what forms were observed, whether an implacable creditor could arrest the dead? As to escaping, what chances there were of escape? Whether a prisoner could scale the walls with a cord and grapple, how he would descend upon the other side: whether he could alight on a housetop, steal down a staircase, let himself out at a door, and get lost in the crowd? As to Fire in the prison, if one were to break out while he lay there?

LITTLE DORRIT

And these involuntary starts of fancy were, after all, but the setting of a picture in which three people kept before him. His father, with the steadfast look with which he had died, prophetically darkened forth in the portrait; his mother, with her arm up, warding off his suspicion; Little Dorrit, with her hand on the degraded arm, and her drooping head turned away.

What if his mother had an old reason she well knew for softening to this poor girl! What if the prisoner now sleeping quietly—Heaven grant it!—by the light of the great Day of Judgment should trace back his fall to her! What if any act of hers, and of his father's, should have even remotely brought the grey heads of those two brothers so low!

A swift thought shot into his mind. In that long imprisonment here, and in her own long confinement to her room, did his mother find a balance to be struck? I admit that I was accessory to that man's captivity. I have suffered for it in kind. He has decayed in his prison; I in mine. I have paid the penalty.

When all the other thoughts had faded out, this one held possession of him. When he fell asleep, she came before him in her wheeled chair, warding him off with this justification. When he awoke, and sprang up causelessly frightened, the words were in his ears, as if her voice had slowly spoken them at his pillow, to break his rest: "He withers away in his prison; I wither away in mine; inexorable justice is done; what do I owe on this score!"

CHAPTER IX

LITTLE MOTHER

THE morning light was in no hurry to climb the prison wall and look in at the Snuggery windows; and when it did come, it would have been more welcome if it had come alone, instead of bringing a rush of rain with it. But the equinoctial gales were blowing out at sea, and the impartial south-west wind, in its flight, would not neglect even the narrow Marshalsea. While it roared through the steeple of St. George's Church, and twirled all the cowls in the neighbourhood, it made a swoop to beat the Southwark smoke into the jail; and, plunging down the chimneys of the few early collegians who were yet lighting their fires, half suffocated them.

Arthur Clennam would have been little disposed to linger in bed, though his bed had been in a more private situation, and less affected by the raking out of yesterday's fire, the kindling of to-day's under the collegiate boiler, the filling of that Spartan vessel at the pump, the sweeping and sawdusting of the common room, and other such preparations. Heartily glad to see the morning, though little rested by the night, he turned out as soon as he could distinguish objects about him, and paced the yard for two heavy hours before the gate was opened.

The walls were so near to one another, and the wild clouds hurried over them so fast, that it gave him a sensation like the beginning of sea-sickness to look up at the gusty sky.

The rain, carried aslant by flaws of wind, blackened that side
of the central building which he had visited last night, but
left a narrow dry trough under the lee of the wall, where he
walked up and down among waifs of straw and dust and
paper, the waste droppings of the pump, and the stray leaves
of yesterday's greens. It was as haggard a view of life as a
man need look upon.

Nor was it relieved by any glimpse of the little creature
who had brought him there. Perhaps she glided out of her
doorway and in at that where her father lived, while his face
was turned from both; but he saw nothing of her. It was
too early for her brother; to have seen him once, was to have
seen enough of him to know that he would be sluggish to
leave whatever frowsy bed he occupied at night; so, as Arthur
Clennam walked up and down, waiting for the gate to open,
he cast about in his mind for future rather than for present
means of pursuing his discoveries.

At last the lodge-gate turned, and the turnkey, standing
on the step, taking an early comb at his hair, was ready
to let him out. With a joyful sense of release he passed
through the lodge, and found himself again in the little outer
court-yard where he had spoken to the brother last night.

There was a string of people already straggling in, whom
it was not difficult to identify as the nondescript messengers,
go-betweens, and errand-bearers of the place. Some of them
had been lounging in the rain until the gate should open;
others, who had timed their arrival with greater nicety, were
coming up now, and passing in with damp whitey-brown
paper bags from the grocers, loaves of bread, lumps of butter,
eggs, milk, and the like. The shabbiness of these attendants
upon shabbiness, the poverty of these insolvent waiters upon
insolvency, was a sight to see. Such threadbare coats and
trousers, such fusty gowns and shawls, such squashed hats
and bonnets, such boots and shoes, such umbrellas and walk-
ing-sticks, never were seen in Rag Fair. All of them wore
the cast-off clothes of other men and women; were made

110

up of patches and pieces of other people's individuality, and had no sartorial existence of their own proper. Their walk was the walk of a race apart. They had a peculiar way of doggedly slinking round the corner, as if they were eternally going to the pawnbroker's. When they coughed, they coughed like people accustomed to be forgotten on door-steps and in draughty passages, waiting for answers to letters in faded ink, which gave the recipients of those manuscripts great mental disturbance and no satisfaction. As they eyed the stranger in passing, they eyed him with borrowing eyes —hungry, sharp, speculative as to his softness if they were accredited to him, and the likelihood of his standing something handsome. Mendicity on commission stooped in their high shoulders, shambled in their unsteady legs, buttoned and pinned and darned and dragged their clothes, frayed their button-holes, leaked out of their figures in dirty little ends of tape, and issued from their mouths in alcoholic breathings.

As these people passed him standing still in the court-yard, and one of them turned back to inquire if he could assist him with his services, it came into Arthur Clennam's mind that he would speak to Dorrit again before he went away. She would have recovered her first surprise, and might feel easier with him. He asked this member of the fraternity (who had two red herrings in his hand, and a loaf and a blacking brush under his arm), where was the nearest place to get a cup of coffee at. The nondescript replied in en- couraging terms, and brought him to a coffee-shop in the street within a stone's throw.

"Do you know Miss Dorrit?" asked the new client.

The nondescript knew two Miss Dorrits; one who was born inside—That was the one! That was the one? The non- descript had known her many years. In regard of the other Miss Dorrit, the nondescript lodged in the same house with herself and uncle.

This changed the client's half-formed design of remaining at the coffee-shop until the nondescript should bring him word that Dorrit had issued forth into the street. He entrusted the nondescript with a confidential message to her, importing that the visitor who had waited on her father last night, begged the favour of a few words with her at her uncle's lodging; he obtained from the same source full directions to the house, which was very near; dismissed the nondescript gratified with half-a-crown; and having hastily refreshed himself at the coffee-shop, repaired with all speed to the clarionet-player's dwelling.

There were so many lodgers in this house, that the door-post seemed to be as full of bell-handles as a cathedral organ is of stops. Doubtful which might be the clarionet-stop, he was considering the point, when a shuttlecock flew out of the parlour window, and alighted on his hat. He then observed that in the parlour-window was a blind with the inscription, Mr. Cripples's Academy; also in another line, Evening Tuition; and behind the blind was a little white-faced boy, with a slice of bread-and-butter, and a battledore. The window being accessible from the footway, he looked in over the blind, returned the shuttlecock, and put his question.

" Dorrit ? " said the little white-faced boy (Master Cripples in fact). " *Mr.* Dorrit ? Third bell and one knock."

The pupils of Mr. Cripples appeared to have been making a copy-book of the street-door, it was so extensively scribbled over in pencil. The frequency of the inscriptions, " Old Dorrit," and " Dirty Dick," in combination, suggested intentions of personality on the part of Mr. Cripples's pupils. There was ample time to make these observations before the door was opened by the poor old man himself.

" Ha ! " said he, very slowly remembering Arthur, " you were shut in last night ? "

" Yes, Mr. Dorrit. I hope to meet your niece here presently."

" Oh ! " said he, pondering. " Out of my brother's way ? True. Would you come up-stairs and wait for her."

" Thank you."

Turning himself, as slowly as he turned in his mind whatever he heard or said, he led the way up the narrow stairs. The house was very close, and had an unwholesome smell. The little staircase windows looked in at the back windows of other houses as unwholesome as itself, with poles and lines thrust out of them, on which unsightly linen hung: as if the inhabitants were angling for clothes, and had had some wretched bites not worth attending to. In the back garret—a sickly room, with a turn-up bedstead in it, so hastily and recently turned up that the blankets were boiling over, as it were, and keeping the lid open—a half-finished breakfast of coffee and toast, for two persons, was jumbled down anyhow on a rickety table.

There was no one there. The old man mumbling to himself, after some consideration, that Fanny had run away, went to the next room to fetch her back. The visitor, observing that she held the door on the inside, and that when the uncle tried to open it, there was a sharp adjuration of " Don't, stupid ! " and an appearance of loose stocking and flannel, concluded that the young lady was in an undress. The uncle, without appearing to come to any conclusion, shuffled in again, sat down in his chair, and began warming his hands at the fire. Not that it was cold, or that he had any waking idea whether it was or not.

" What did you think of my brother, sir ? " he asked, when he by-and-by discovered what he was doing, left off, reached over to the chimney-piece, and took his clarionet case down.

" I was glad," said Arthur, very much at a loss, for his thoughts were on the brother before him ; " to find him so well and cheerful."

" Ha ! " muttered the old man, " Yes, yes, yes, yes, yes ! "

Arthur wondered what he could possibly want with the clarionet case. He did not want it at all. He discovered, in due time, that it was not the little paper of snuff (which was also on the chimney-piece), put it back again, took down

113

the snuff instead, and solaced himself with a pinch. He was as feeble, spare, and slow in his pinches as in everything else, but a certain little trickling of enjoyment of them played in the poor worn nerves about the corners of his eyes and mouth.

"Amy, Mr. Clennam. What do you think of her?"

"I am much impressed, Mr. Dorrit, by all that I have seen of her and thought of her."

"My brother would have been quite lost without Amy," he returned. "We should all have been lost without Amy. She is a very good girl, Amy. She does her duty."

Arthur fancied that he heard in these praises, a certain tone of custom which he had heard from the father last night, with an inward protest and feeling of antagonism. It was not that they stinted her praises, or were insensible to what she did for them; but that they were lazily habituated to her, as they were to all the rest of their condition. He fancied that although they had before them, every day, the means of comparison between her and one another and themselves, they regarded her as being in her necessary place; as holding a position towards them all which belonged to her, like her name or her age. He fancied that they viewed her, not as having risen away from the prison atmosphere, but as appertaining to it; as being vaguely what they had a right to expect, and nothing more.

Her uncle resumed his breakfast, and was munching toast sopped in coffee, oblivious of his guest, when the third bell rang. That was Amy, he said, and went down to let her in; leaving the visitor with as vivid a picture on his mind of his begrimed hands, dirt-worn face, and decayed figure, as if he were still drooping in his chair.

She came up after him, in the usual plain dress, and with the usual timid manner. Her lips were a little parted, as if her heart beat faster than usual.

"Mr. Clennam, Amy," said her uncle, "has been expecting you some time."

" I took the liberty of sending you a message."

" I received the message, sir."

" Are you going to my mother's this morning ? I think not, for it is past your usual hour."

" Not to-day, sir. I am not wanted to-day."

" Will you allow me to walk a little way in whatever direction you may be going ? I can then speak to you as we walk, both without detaining you here, and without intruding longer here myself."

She looked embarrassed, but said, if he pleased. He made a pretence of having mislaid his walking-stick, to give her time to set the bedstead right, to answer her sister's impatient knock at the wall, and to say a word softly to her uncle. Then he found it, and they went down-stairs ; she first, he following, the uncle standing at the stair-head, and probably forgetting them before they had reached the ground floor.

Mr. Cripples's pupils, who were by this time coming to school, desisted from their morning recreation of cuffing one another with bags and books, to stare with all the eyes they had at a stranger who had been to see Dirty Dick. They bore the trying spectacle in silence, until the mysterious visitor was at a safe distance ; when they burst into pebbles and yells, and likewise into reviling dances, and in all respects buried the pipe of peace with so many savage ceremonies, that if Mr. Cripples had been the chief of the Cripplewayboo tribe with his war-paint on, they could scarcely have done greater justice to their education.

In the midst of this homage, Mr. Arthur Clennam offered his arm to Little Dorrit, and Little Dorrit took it. " Will you go by the Iron Bridge," said he, "where there is an escape from the noise of the street ? " Little Dorrit answered, if he pleased, and presently ventured to hope that he would "not mind " Mr. Cripples's boys, for she had herself received her education, such as it was, in Mr. Cripples's evening academy. He returned, with the best will in the world, that Mr. Cripples's boys were forgiven out of the bottom of his soul. Thus did Cripples unconsciously become a master of the ceremonies between them, and bring them more naturally together than Beau Nash might have done if they had lived in his golden days, and he had alighted from his coach and six for the purpose.

The morning remained squally, and the streets were miserably muddy, but no rain fell as they walked towards the Iron Bridge. The little creature seemed so young in his eyes, that there were moments when he found himself thinking of her, if not speaking to her, as if she were a child. Perhaps he seemed as old in her eyes as she seemed young in his.

"I am sorry to hear you were so inconvenienced last night, sir, as to be locked in. It was very unfortunate."

It was nothing, he returned. He had had a very good bed.

"Oh yes!" she said quickly; "she believed there were excellent beds at the coffee-house." He noticed that the coffee-house was quite a majestic hotel to her, and that she treasured its reputation.

"I believe it is very expensive," said Little Dorrit, "but my father has told me that quite beautiful dinners may be got there. And wine," she added timidly.

"Were you ever there?"

"Oh no! Only into the kitchen, to fetch hot water."

To think of growing up with a kind of awe upon one as to the luxuries of that superb establishment, the Marshalsea Hotel!

"I asked you last night," said Clennam, "how you had become acquainted with my mother. Did you ever hear her name before she sent for you?"

"No, sir."

"Do you think your father ever did?"

"No, sir."

He met her eyes raised to his with so much wonder in them (she was scared when that encounter took place, and shrunk away again), that he felt it necessary to say:

"I have a reason for asking, which I cannot very well

116

explain; but you must, on no account, suppose it to be of a nature to cause you the least alarm or anxiety. Quite the reverse. And you think that at no time of your father's life was my name of Clennam ever familiar to him?"

"No, sir."

He felt, from the tone in which she spoke, that she was glancing up at him with those parted lips; therefore he looked before him, rather than make her heart beat quicker still by embarrassing her afresh.

Thus they emerged upon the Iron Bridge, which was as quiet after the roaring streets, as though it had been open country. The wind blew roughly, the wet squalls came rattling past them, skimming the pools on the road and pavement, and raining them down into the river. The clouds raced on furiously in the lead-coloured sky, the smoke and mist raced after them, the dark tide ran fierce and strong in the same direction. Little Dorrit seemed the least, the quietest, and weakest of Heaven's creatures.

"Let me put you in a coach," said Clennam, very nearly adding, "my poor child."

She hurriedly declined, saying that wet or dry made little difference to her; she was used to go about in all weathers. He knew it to be so, and was touched with more pity; thinking of the slight figure at his side, making its nightly way through the damp dark boisterous streets, to such a place of rest.

"You spoke so feelingly to me last night, sir, and I found afterwards that you had been so generous to my father, that I could not resist your message, if it was only to thank you; especially as I wished very much to say to you—" she hesitated and trembled, and tears rose in her eyes, but did not fall.

"To say to me—?"

"That I hope you will not misunderstand my father. Don't judge him, sir, as you would judge others outside the gates. He has been there so long! I never saw him outside, but

I can understand that he must have grown different in some things since."

" My thoughts will never be unjust or harsh towards him, believe me."

" Not," she said with a prouder air, as the misgiving evidently crept upon her that she might seem to be abandoning him, " Not that he has anything to be ashamed of for himself, or that I have anything to be ashamed of for him. He only requires to be understood. I only ask for him that his life may be fairly remembered. All that he said was quite true. It all happened just as he related it. He is very much respected. Everybody who comes in, is glad to know him. He is more courted than any one else. He is far more thought of than the Marshal is."

If ever pride were innocent, it was innocent in Little Dorrit when she grew boastful of her father.

" It is often said that his manners are a true gentleman's, and quite a study. I see none like them in that place, but he is admitted to be superior to all the rest. This is quite as much why they make him presents, as because they know him to be needy. He is not to be blamed for being in need, poor love. Who could be in prison a quarter of a century, and be prosperous ! "

What affection in her words, what compassion in her repressed tears, what a great soul of fidelity within her, how true the light that shed false brightness round him !

" If I have found it best to conceal where my home is, it is not because I am ashamed of him. GOD forbid ! Nor am I so much ashamed of the place itself as might be supposed. People are not bad because they come there. I have known numbers of good, persevering, honest people, come there through misfortune. They are almost all kind-hearted to one another. And it would be ungrateful indeed in me, to forget that I have had many quiet, comfortable hours there ; that I had an excellent friend there when I was quite a baby, who was very fond of me ; that I have been taught there,

118

and have worked there, and have slept soundly there. I think it would be almost cowardly and cruel not to have some little attachment for it, after all this."

She had relieved the faithful fulness of her heart, and modestly said, raising her eyes appealingly to her new friend's, "I did not mean to say so much, nor have I ever but once spoken about this before. But it seems to set it more right than it was last night. I said I wished you had not followed me, sir. I don't wish it so much now, unless you should think—indeed I don't wish it at all, unless I should have spoken so confusedly, that—that you can scarcely understand me, which I am afraid may be the case."

He told her with perfect truth that it was not the case; and putting himself between her and the sharp wind and rain, sheltered her as well as he could.

"I feel permitted now," he said, "to ask you a little more concerning your father. Has he many creditors?"

"Oh! a great number."

"I mean detaining creditors, who keep him where he is?"

"Oh yes! a great number."

"Can you tell me—I can get the information, no doubt, elsewhere, if you cannot—who is the most influential of them?"

Dorrit said, after considering a little, that she used to hear long ago of Mr. Tite Barnacle as a man of great power. He was a commissioner, or a board, or a trustee, "or something." He lived in Grosvenor Square, she thought, or very near it. He was under Government—high in the Circumlocution Office. She appeared to have acquired, in her infancy, some awful impression of the might of this formidable Mr. Tite Barnacle of Grosvenor Square, or very near it, and the Circumlocution Office, which quite crushed her when she mentioned him.

"It can do no harm," thought Arthur, "if I see this Mr. Tite Barnacle."

The thought did not present itself so quietly but that her

119

quickness intercepted it. " Ah ! " said Little Dorrit, shaking
her head with the mild despair of a lifetime. " Many people
used to think once of getting my poor father out, but you
don't know how hopeless it is."

She forgot to be shy at the moment, in honestly warning
him away from the sunken wreck he had a dream of raising ;
and looked at him with eyes which assuredly, in association
with her patient face, her fragile figure, her spare dress, and
the wind and rain, did not turn him from his purpose of
helping her.

" Even if it could be done," said she—" and it never can be
done now—where could father live, or how could he live ? I
have often thought that if such a change could come, it might
be anything but a service to him now. People might not
think so well of him outside as they do there. He might
not be so gently dealt with outside as he is there. He
might not be so fit himself for the life outside, as he is
for that."

Here for the first time she could not restrain her tears from
falling ; and the little thin hands he had watched when they
were so busy, trembled as they clasped each other.

" It would be a new distress to him even to know that I
earn a little money, and that Fanny earns a little money.
He is so anxious about us, you see, feeling helplessly shut up
there. Such a good, good father ! "

He let the little burst of feeling go by before he spoke. It
was soon gone. She was not accustomed to think of herself,
or to trouble any one with her emotions. He had but glanced
away at the piles of city roofs and chimneys among which
the smoke was rolling heavily, and at the wilderness of masts
on the river, and the wilderness of steeples on the shore, indistinctly mixed together in the stormy haze, when she was
again as quiet as if she had been plying her needle in his
mother's room.

" You would be glad to have your brother set at liberty ? "
" Oh very, very glad, sir ! "

"Well, we will hope for him at least. You told me last night of a friend you had?"

His name was Plornish, Little Dorrit said.

And where did Plornish live? Plornish lived in Bleeding Heart Yard. He was "only a plasterer," Little Dorrit said, as a caution to him not to form high social expectations of Plornish. He lived at the last house in Bleeding Heart Yard, and his name was over a little gateway.

Arthur took down the address and gave her his. He had now done all he sought to do for the present, except that he wished to leave her with a reliance upon him, and to have something like a promise from her that she would cherish it.

"There is one friend!" he said, putting up his pocket-book. "As I take you back—you are going back?"

"Oh yes! going straight home."

"As I take you back," the word home jarred upon him, "let me ask you to persuade yourself that you have another friend. I make no professions, and say no more."

"You are truly kind to me, sir. I am sure I need no more."

They walked back through the miserable muddy streets, and among the poor, mean shops, and were jostled by the crowds of dirty hucksters usual to a poor neighbourhood. There was nothing, by the short way, that was pleasant to any of the five senses. Yet it was not a common passage through common rain, and mire, and noise, to Clennam, having this little, slender, careful creature on his arm. How young she seemed to him, or how old he to her; or what a secret either to the other, in that beginning of the destined interweaving of their stories, matters not here. He thought of her having been born and bred among these scenes, and shrinking through them now, familiar yet misplaced; he thought of her long acquaintance with the squalid needs of life, and of her innocence; of her old solicitude for others, and her few years, and her childish aspect.

They were come into the High Street, where the prison

121

stood, when a voice cried, "Little mother, little mother!" Dorrit stopping and looking back, an excited figure of a strange kind bounced against them (still crying "little mother"), fell down, and scattered the contents of a large basket, filled with potatoes, in the mud.

"Oh, Maggy," said Dorrit, "what a clumsy child you are!"

Maggy was not hurt, but picked herself up immediately, and then began to pick up the potatoes, in which both Dorrit and Arthur Clennam helped. Maggy picked up very few potatoes, and a great quantity of mud; but they were all recovered, and deposited in the basket. Maggy then smeared her muddy face with her shawl, and presenting it to Mr. Clennam as a type of purity, enabled him to see what she was like.

She was about eight-and-twenty, with large bones, large features, large feet and hands, large eyes and no hair. Her large eyes were limpid and almost colourless; they seemed to be very little affected by light, and to stand unnaturally still. There was also that attentive listening expression in her face, which is seen in the faces of the blind; but she was not blind, having one tolerably serviceable eye. Her face was not exceedingly ugly, though it was only redeemed from being so by a smile; a good-humoured smile, and pleasant in itself, but rendered pitiable by being constantly there. A great white cap, with a quantity of opaque frilling that was always flapping about, apologised for Maggy's baldness, and made it so very difficult for her old black bonnet to retain its place upon her head, that it held on round her neck like a gipsy's baby. A commission of haberdashers could alone have reported what the rest of her poor dress was made of; but it had a strong general resemblance to seaweed, with here and there a gigantic tea-leaf. Her shawl looked particularly like a tea-leaf, after long infusion.

Arthur Clennam looked at Dorrit, with the expression of one saying, "May I ask who this is?" Dorrit, whose hand this Maggy, still calling her little mother, had begun to

Little Mother

fondle, answered in words (they were under a gateway into which the majority of the potatoes had rolled).

"This is Maggy, sir."

"Maggy, sir," echoed the personage presented. "Little mother!"

"She is the grand-daughter—" said Dorrit.

"Grand-daughter," echoed Maggy.

"Of my old nurse, who has been dead a long time. Maggy, how old are you?"

"Ten, mother," said Maggy.

"You can't think how good she is, sir," said Dorrit, with infinite tenderness:

"Good *she* is," echoed Maggy, transferring the pronoun in a most expressive way from herself to her little mother.

"Oh how clever," said Dorrit. "She goes on errands as well as any one." Maggy laughed. "And is as trustworthy as the Bank of England." Maggy laughed. "She earns her own living entirely. Entirely, sir!" said Dorrit in a lower and triumphant tone. "Really does!"

"What is her history?" asked Clennam.

"Think of that, Maggy?" said Dorrit, taking her two large hands and clapping them together. "A gentleman from thousands of miles away, wanting to know your history!"

"*My* history?" cried Maggy. "Little mother."

"She means me," said Dorrit, rather confused; "she is very much attached to me. Her old grandmother was not so kind to her as she should have been; was she, Maggy?"

Maggy shook her head, made a drinking vessel of her clenched left hand, drank out of it, and said, "Gin." Then beat an imaginary child, and said, "Broom-handles and pokers."

"When Maggy was ten years old," said Dorrit, watching her face while she spoke, "she had a bad fever, sir, and she has never grown any older ever since."

"Ten years old," said Maggy, nodding her head. "But what a nice hospital! So comfortable, wasn't it? Oh so nice it was. Such a Ev'nly place!"

"She had never been at peace before, sir," said Dorrit, turning towards Arthur for an instant and speaking low, "and she always runs off upon that."

"Such beds there is there!" cried Maggy. "Such lemonades! Such oranges! Such d'licious broth and wine! Such Chicking! Oh, AIN'T it a delightful place to go and stop at!"

"So Maggy stopped there as long as she could," said Dorrit, in her former tone of telling a child's story; the tone designed for Maggy's ear, "and at last, when she could stop there no longer, she came out. Then, because she was never to be more than ten years old, however long she lived— "

"However long she lived," echoed Maggy.

"And because she was very weak; indeed was so weak that when she began to laugh she couldn't stop herself —which was a great pity— "

(Maggy mighty grave of a sudden.)

"Her grandmother did not know what to do with her, and for some years was very unkind to her indeed. At length, in course of time, Maggy began to take pains to improve herself, and to be very attentive and very industrious; and by degrees was allowed to come in and out as often as she liked, and got enough to do to support herself, and does support herself. And that," said Little Dorrit, clapping the two great hands together again, "is Maggy's history, as Maggy knows!"

Ah! But Arthur would have known what was wanting to its completeness, though he had never heard the words Little mother; though he had never seen the fondling of the small spare hand; though he had had no sight for the tears now standing in the colourless eyes; though he had had no hearing for the sob that checked the clumsy laugh. The dirty gateway with the wind and rain whistling through it, and the basket of muddy potatoes waiting to be spilt again or taken up, never seemed the common hole it really was, when he looked back to it by these lights. Never, never!

They were very near the end of their walk, and they now

came out of the gateway to finish it. Nothing would serve Maggy but that they must stop at a grocer's window, short of their destination, for her to show her learning. She could read after a sort; and picked out the fat figures in the tickets of prices, for the most part correctly. She also stumbled, with a large balance of success against her failures, through various philanthropic recommendations to Try our Mixture, Try our Family Black, Try our Orange-flavoured Pekoe, challenging competition at the head of Flowery Teas; and various cautions to the public against spurious establishments and adulterated articles. When he saw how pleasure brought a rosy tint into Dorrit's face when Maggy made a hit, he felt that he could have stood there making a library of the grocer's window until the rain and wind were tired.

The court-yard received them at last, and there he said good-bye to Little Dorrit. Little as she had always looked, she looked less than ever when he saw her going into the Marshalsea lodge passage, the little mother attended by her big child.

The cage door opened, and when the small bird, reared in captivity, had tamely fluttered in, he saw it shut again; and then he came away.

CHAPTER X

THE Circumlocution Office was (as everybody knows without being told) the most important Department under Government. No public business of any kind could possibly be done at any time, without the acquiescence of the Circumlocution Office. Its finger was in the largest public pie, and in the smallest public tart. It was equally impossible to do the plainest right and to undo the plainest wrong, without the express authority of the Circumlocution Office. If another Gunpowder Plot had been discovered half an hour before the lighting of the match, nobody would have been justified in saving the parliament until there had been half a score of boards, half a bushel of minutes, several sacks of official memoranda, and a family-vault full of ungrammatical correspondence, on the part of the Circumlocution Office.

This glorious establishment had been early in the field, when the one sublime principle involving the difficult art of governing a country, was first distinctly revealed to statesmen. It had been foremost to study that bright revelation, and to carry its shining influence through the whole of the official proceedings. Whatever was required to be done, the Circumlocution Office was beforehand with all the public departments in the art of perceiving—HOW NOT TO DO IT.

Through this delicate perception, through the tact with which it invariably seized it, and through the genius with

126

which it always acted on it, the Circumlocution Office had risen to over-top all the public departments; and the public condition had risen to be—what it was.

It is true that How not to do it was the great study and object of all public departments and professional politicians all round the Circumlocution Office. It is true that every new premier and every new government, coming in because they had upheld a certain thing as necessary to be done, were no sooner come in than they applied their utmost faculties to discovering How not to do it. It is true that from the moment when a general election was over, every returned man who had been raving on hustings because it hadn't been done, and who had been asking the friends of the honourable gentleman in the opposite interest on pain of impeachment to tell him why it hadn't been done, and who had been asserting that it must be done, and who had been pledging himself that it should be done, began to devise, How it was not to be done. It is true that the debates of both Houses of Parliament the whole session through, uniformly tended to the protracted deliberation, How not to do it. It is true that the royal speech at the opening of such session virtually said, My lords and gentle-men, you have a considerable stroke of work to do, and you will please to retire to your respective chambers, and discuss, How not to do it. It is true that the royal speech, at the close of such session, virtually said, My lords and gentlemen, you have through several laborious months been considering with great loyalty and patriotism, How not to do it, and you have found out; and with the blessing of Providence upon the harvest (natural, not political), I now dismiss you. All this is true, but the Circumlocution Office went beyond it.

Because the Circumlocution Office went on mechanically, every day, keeping this wonderful, all-sufficient wheel of statesman-ship, How not to do it, in motion. Because the Circumlocu-tion Office was down upon any ill-advised public servant who was going to do it, or who appeared to be by any surprising

accident in remote danger of doing it, with a minute, and a
memorandum, and a letter of instructions, that extinguished
him. It was this spirit of national efficiency in the Circumlocution Office that had gradually led to its having something to do with everything. Mechanicians, natural philosophers, soldiers, sailors, petitioners, memorialists, people with
grievances, people who wanted to prevent grievances, people
who wanted to redress grievances, jobbing people, jobbed
people, people who couldn't get rewarded for merit, and
people who couldn't get punished for demerit, were all in-
discriminately turned up under the foolscap paper of the
Circumlocution Office.

Numbers of people were lost in the Circumlocution Office.
Unfortunates with wrongs, or with projects for the general
welfare (and they had better have had wrongs at first, than
have taken that bitter English recipe for certainly getting
them), who in slow lapse of time and agony had passed safely
through other public departments; who, according to rule,
had been bullied in this, over-reached by that, and evaded
by the other; got referred at last to the Circumlocution Office,
and never reappeared in the light of day. Boards sat upon
them, secretaries minuted upon them, commissioners gabbled
about them, clerks registered, entered, checked, and ticked
them off, and they melted away. In short, all the business
of the country went through the Circumlocution Office,
except the business that never came out of it; and *its* name
was Legion.

Sometimes, angry spirits attacked the Circumlocution Office.
Sometimes, parliamentary questions were asked about it, and
even parliamentary motions made or threatened about it, by
demagogues so low and ignorant as to hold that the real
recipe of government was, How to do it. Then would the
noble lord, or right honourable gentleman, in whose department it was to defend the Circumlocution Office, put an
orange in his pocket, and make a regular field-day of the
occasion. Then would he come down to that house with a

slap upon the table, and meet the honourable gentleman foot to foot. Then would he be there to tell that honourable gentleman that the Circumlocution Office not only was blameless in this matter, but was commendable in this matter, was extollable to the skies in this matter. Then would he be there to tell that honourable gentleman, that, although the Circumlocution Office was invariably right and wholly right, it never was so right as in this matter. Then would he be there to tell that honourable gentleman that it would have been more to his honour, more to his credit, more to his good taste, more to his good sense, more to half the dictionary of commonplaces, if he had left the Circumlocution Office alone, and never approached this matter. Then would he keep one eye upon a coach or crammer from the Circumlocution Office sitting below the bar, and smash the honourable gentleman with the Circumlocution Office account of this matter. And although one of two things always happened; namely, either that the Circumlocution Office had nothing to say and said it, or that it had something to say of which the noble lord, or right honourable gentleman, blundered one half and forgot the other; the Circumlocution Office was always voted immaculate, by an accommodating majority.

Such a nursery of statesmen had the Department become in virtue of a long career of this nature, that several solemn lords had attained the reputation of being quite unearthly prodigies of business, solely from having practised, How not to do it, at the head of the Circumlocution Office. As to the minor priests and acolytes of that temple, the result of all this was that they stood divided into two classes, and, down to the junior messenger, either believed in the Circumlocution Office as a heaven-born institution, that had an absolute right to do whatever it liked; or took refuge in total infidelity, and considered it a flagrant nuisance.

The Barnacle family had for some time helped to administer the Circumlocution Office. The Tite Barnacle Branch, indeed,

129

considered themselves in a general way as having vested rights in that direction, and took it ill if any other family had much to say to it. The Barnacles were a very high family, and a very large family. They were dispersed all over the public offices, and held all sorts of public places. Either the nation was under a load of obligation to the Barnacles, or the Barnacles were under a load of obligation to the nation. It was not quite unanimously settled which; the Barnacles having their opinion, the nation theirs.

The Mr. Tite Barnacle who at the period now in question usually coached or crammed the statesman at the head of the Circumlocution Office, when that noble or right honourable individual sat a little uneasily in his saddle, by reason of some vagabond making a tilt at him in a newspaper, was more flush of blood than money. As a Barnacle he had his place, which was a snug thing enough; and as a Barnacle he had of course put in his son Barnacle Junior, in the office. But he had intermarried with a branch of the Stiltstalkings, who were also better endowed in a sanguineous point of view than with real or personal property, and of this marriage there had been issue, Barnacle Junior, and three young ladies. What with the patrician requirements of Barnacle Junior, the three young ladies, Mrs. Tite Barnacle née Stiltstalking, and himself, Mr. Tite Barnacle found the intervals between quarter day and quarter day rather longer than he could have desired; a circumstance which he always attributed to the country's parsimony.

For Mr. Tite Barnacle, Mr. Arthur Clennam made his fifth inquiry one day at the Circumlocution Office; having on previous occasions awaited that gentleman successively in a hall, a glass case, a waiting room, and a fire-proof passage where the department seemed to keep its wind. On this occasion Mr. Barnacle was not engaged, as he had been before, with the noble prodigy at the head of the Department; but was absent. Barnacle Junior, however, was announced as a lesser star, yet visible above the office horizon.

With Barnacle Junior, he signified his desire to confer; and found that young gentleman singeing the calves of his legs at the parental fire, and supporting his spine against the mantel-shelf. It was a comfortable room, handsomely furnished in the higher official manner; and presenting stately suggestions of the absent Barnacle, in the thick carpet, the leather-covered desk to sit at, the leather-covered desk to stand at, the formidable easy-chair and hearth-rug, the interposed screen, the torn-up papers, the dispatch-boxes with little labels sticking out of them, like medicine bottles or dead game, the pervading smell of leather and mahogany, and a general bamboozling air of How not to do it.

The present Barnacle, holding Mr. Clennam's card in his hand, had a youthful aspect, and the fluffiest little whisker, perhaps, that ever was seen. Such a downy tip was on his callow chin, that he seemed half fledged like a young bird; and a compassionate observer might have urged, that if he had not singed the calves of his legs, he would have died of cold. He had a superior eye-glass dangling round his neck, but unfortunately had such flat orbits to his eyes, and such limp little eyelids, that it wouldn't stick in when he put it up, but kept tumbling out against his waistcoat buttons with a click that discomposed him very much.

"Oh, I say. Look here! My father's not in the way, and won't be in the way to-day," said Barnacle Junior. "Is this anything that I can do?"

(Click! Eye-glass down. Barnacle Junior quite frightened and feeling all round himself, but not able to find it.)

"You are very good," said Arthur Clennam. "I wish however to see Mr. Barnacle."

"But I say. Look here! You haven't got any appointment, you know," said Barnacle Junior.

(By this time he had found the eye-glass, and put it up again.)

"No," said Arthur Clennam. "That is what I wish to have."

131

"But I say. Look here! Is this public business?" asked Barnacle Junior.

(Click! Eye-glass down again. Barnacle Junior in that state of search after it, that Mr. Clennam felt it useless to reply at present.)

"Is it," said Barnacle Junior, taking heed of his visitor's brown face, "anything about—Tonnage—or that sort of thing?"

(Pausing for a reply, he opened his right eye with his hand, and stuck his glass in it, in that inflammatory manner that his eye began watering dreadfully.)

"No," said Arthur, "it is nothing about tonnage."

"Then look here. Is it private business?"

"I really am not sure. It relates to a Mr. Dorrit."

"Look here, I tell you what! You had better call at our house, if you are going that way. Twenty-four, Mews Street, Grosvenor Square. My father's got a slight touch of the gout, and is kept at home by it."

(The misguided young Barnacle evidently going blind on his eye-glass side, but ashamed to make any further alteration in his painful arrangements.)

"Thank you. I will call there now. Good morning." Young Barnacle seemed discomfited at this, as not having at all expected him to go.

"You are quite sure," said Barnacle Junior, calling after him when he got to the door, unwilling wholly to relinquish the bright business idea he had conceived; "that it's nothing about Tonnage?"

"Quite sure."

With which assurance, and rather wondering what might have taken place if it *had* been anything about tonnage, Mr. Clennam withdrew to pursue his inquiries.

Mews Street, Grosvenor Square, was not absolutely Grosvenor Square itself, but it was very near it. It was a hideous little street of dead wall, stables, and dunghills, with lofts over coach-houses inhabited by coachmen's families, who had a passion for drying clothes, and decorating their window-sills with miniature turnpike-gates. The principal chimney-sweep of that fashionable quarter lived at the blind end of Mews Street; and the same corner contained an establishment much frequented about early morning and twilight, for the purchase of wine-bottles and kitchen-stuff. Punch's shows used to lean against the dead wall in Mews Street, while their proprietors were dining elsewhere; and the dogs of the neighbourhood made appointments to meet in the same locality. Yet there were two or three small airless houses at the entrance end of Mews Street, which went at enormous rents on account of their being abject hangers-on to a fashionable situation; and whenever one of these fearful little coops was to be let (which seldom happened, for they were in great request), the house agent advertised it as a gentlemanly residence in the most aristocratic part of town, inhabited solely by the élite of the beau monde.

If a gentlemanly residence coming strictly within this narrow margin, had not been essential to the blood of the Barnacles, this particular branch would have had a pretty wide selection among let us say ten thousand houses, offering fifty times the accommodation for a third of the money. As it was, Mr. Barnacle, finding his gentlemanly residence extremely inconvenient, and extremely dear, always laid it, as a public servant, at the door of the country, and adduced it as another instance of the country's parsimony.

Arthur Clennam came to a squeezed house, with a ramshackle bowed front, little dingy windows, and a little dark area like a damp waistcoat-pocket, which he found to be number twenty-four, Mews Street, Grosvenor Square. To the sense of smell, the house was like a sort of bottle filled with a strong distillation of mews; and when the footman opened the door, he seemed to take the stopper out.

The footman was to the Grosvenor Square footmen, what the house was to the Grosvenor Square houses. Admirable in his way, his way was a back and a bye way. His gorgeousness was not unmixed with dirt; and both in complexion and consistency, he had suffered from the closeness of his pantry. A sallow flabbiness was upon him, when he took the stopper out, and presented the bottle to Mr. Clennam's nose.

"Be so good as to give that card to Mr. Tite Barnacle, and to say that I have just now seen the younger Mr. Barnacle who recommended me to call here."

The footman (who had as many large buttons with the Barnacle crest upon them, on the flaps of his pockets, as if he were the family strong box, and carried the plate and jewels about with him buttoned up) pondered over the card a little; then said, "Walk in." It required some judgment to do it without butting the inner hall-door open, and in the consequent mental confusion and physical darkness slipping down the kitchen stairs. The visitor, however, brought himself up safely on the door-mat.

Still the footman said "Walk in," so the visitor followed him. At the inner hall-door, another bottle seemed to be presented and another stopper taken out. This second vial appeared to be filled with concentrated provisions, and extract of Sink from the pantry. After a skirmish in the narrow passage, occasioned by the footman's opening the door of the dismal dining-room with confidence, finding some one there with consternation, and backing on the visitor with disorder, the visitor was shut up, pending his announcement, in a close back parlour. There he had an opportunity of refreshing himself with both the bottles at once, looking out at a low blinding back wall three feet off, and speculating on the number of Barnacle families within the bills of mortality who lived in such hutches of their own free flunkey choice.

Mr. Barnacle would see him. Would he walk up-stairs? He would, and he did; and in the drawing-room, with his leg on a rest, he found Mr. Barnacle himself, the express image and presentment of How not to do it.

Mr. Barnacle dated from a better time, when the country was not so parsimonious, and the Circumlocution Office was not so badgered. He wound and wound folds of white cravat round his neck, as he wound and wound folds of tape and paper round the neck of the country. His wristbands and collar were oppressive, his voice and manner were oppressive. He had a large watch-chain and bunch of seals, a coat buttoned up to inconvenience, a waistcoat buttoned up to inconvenience, an unwrinkled pair of trousers, a stiff pair of boots. He was altogether splendid, massive, overpowering, and impracticable. He seemed to have been sitting for his portrait to Sir Thomas Lawrence all the days of his life.

"Mr. Clennam?" said Mr. Barnacle. "Be seated."

Mr. Clennam became seated.

"You have called on me, I believe," said Mr. Barnacle, "at the Circumlocution—" giving it the air of a word of about five-and-twenty syllables, " Office."

"I have taken that liberty."

Mr. Barnacle solemnly bent his head as who should say, "I do not deny that it is a liberty; proceed to take another liberty, and let me know your business."

"Allow me to observe that I have been for some years in China, am quite a stranger at home, and have no personal motive or interest in the inquiry I am about to make."

Mr. Barnacle tapped his fingers on the table, and, as if he were now sitting for his portrait to a new and strange artist, appeared to say to his visitor, "If you will be good enough to take me with my present lofty expression, I shall feel obliged."

"I have found a debtor in the Marshalsea prison of the name of Dorrit, who has been there many years. I wish to investigate his confused affairs, so far as to ascertain whether it may not be possible, after this lapse of time, to ameliorate his unhappy condition. The name of Mr. Tite Barnacle has been mentioned to me as representing some highly influential interest among his creditors. Am I correctly informed?"

It being one of the principles of the Circumlocution Office

never, on any account whatever, to give a straightforward answer, Mr. Barnacle said, "Possibly."

"On behalf of the Crown, may I ask, or as a private individual?"

"The Circumlocution Department, sir," Mr. Barnacle replied, "may have possibly recommended—possibly—I cannot say—that some public claim against the insolvent estate of a firm or copartnership to which this person may have belonged, should be enforced. The question may have been, in the course of official business, referred to the Circumlocution Department for its consideration. The Department may have either originated, or confirmed, a Minute making that recommendation."

"I assume this to be the case, then."

"The Circumlocution Department," said Mr. Barnacle, "is not responsible for any gentleman's assumptions."

"May I inquire how I can obtain official information as to the real state of the case?"

"It is competent," said Mr. Barnacle, "to any member of the—Public," mentioning that obscure body with reluctance, as his natural enemy, "to memorialise the Circumlocution Department. Such formalities as are required to be observed in so doing, may be known on application to the proper branch of that Department."

"Which is the proper branch?"

"I must refer you," returned Mr. Barnacle, ringing the bell, "to the Department itself for a formal answer to that inquiry."

"Excuse my mentioning—"

"The Department is accessible to the—Public," Mr. Barnacle was always checked a little by that word of impertinent signification, "if the—Public approaches it according to the official forms ; if the—Public does not approach it according to the official forms, the—Public has itself to blame."

Mr. Barnacle made him a severe bow, as a wounded man

of family, a wounded man of place, and a wounded man of a gentlemanly residence, all rolled into one; and he made Mr. Barnacle a bow, and was shut out into Mews Street by the flabby footman.

Having got to this pass, he resolved as an exercise in perseverance, to betake himself again to the Circumlocution Office, and try what satisfaction he could get there. So he went back to the Circumlocution Office, and once more sent up his card to Barnacle Junior by a messenger who took it very ill indeed that he should come back again, and who was eating mashed potatoes and gravy behind a partition by the hall fire.

He was re-admitted to the presence of Barnacle Junior, and found that young gentleman singeing his knees now, and gaping his weary way on to four o'clock.

"I say. Look here. You stick to us in a devil of a manner," said Barnacle Junior, looking over his shoulder.

"I want to know——"

"Look here. Upon my soul you mustn't come into the place saying you want to know, you know," remonstrated Barnacle Junior, turning about and putting up the eye-glass.

"I want to know," said Arthur Clennam, who had made up his mind to persistence in one short form of words, "the precise nature of the claim of the Crown against a prisoner for debt named Dorrit."

"I say. Look here. You really are going it at a great pace, you know. Egad you haven't got an appointment," said Barnacle Junior, as if the thing were growing serious.

"I want to know," said Arthur. And repeated his case.

Barnacle Junior stared at him until his eye-glass fell out, and then put it in again and stared at him until it fell out again. "You have no right to come this sort of move," he then observed with the greatest weakness. "Look here. What do you mean? You told me you didn't know whether it was public business or not."

"I have now ascertained that it is public business," returned the suitor, " and I want to know "—and again repeated his monotonous inquiry.

Its effect upon young Barnacle was to make him repeat in a defenceless way, " Look here ! Upon my soul you mustn't come into the place, saying you want to know, you know ! " The effect of that upon Arthur Clennam was to make him repeat his inquiry in exactly the same words and tone as before. The effect of that upon young Barnacle was to make him a wonderful spectacle of failure and helplessness.'

" Well, I tell you what. Look here. You had better try the Secretarial Department," he said at last, sidling to the bell and ringing it. " Jenkinson," to the mashed potatoes messenger, " Mr. Wobbler ! "

Arthur Clennam, who now felt that he had devoted himself to the storming of the Circumlocution Office, and must go through with it, accompanied the messenger to another floor of the building, where that functionary pointed out Mr. Wobbler's room. He entered that apartment, and found two gentlemen sitting face to face at a large and easy desk, one of whom was polishing a gun-barrel on his pocket-handkerchief, while the other was spreading marmalade on bread with a paper-knife.

" Mr. Wobbler ? " inquired the suitor.

Both gentlemen glanced at him, and seemed surprised at his assurance.

" So he went," said the gentleman with the gun-barrel, who was an extremely deliberate speaker, " down to his cousin's place, and took the Dog with him by rail. In-estimable Dog. Flew at the porter fellow when he was put into the dog-box, and flew at the guard when he was taken out. He got half-a-dozen fellows into a Barn, and a good supply of Rats, and timed the Dog. Finding the Dog able to do it immensely, made the match, and heavily backed the Dog. When the match came off, some devil of a fellow was bought over, Sir, Dog was made drunk, Dog's master was cleaned out."

" Mr. Wobbler ? " inquired the suitor.

The gentleman who was spreading the marmalade returned, without looking up from that occupation, " What did he call the Dog ? "

" Called him Lovely," said the other gentleman. " Said the Dog was the perfect picture of the old aunt from whom he had expectations. Found him particularly like her when hocussed."

" Mr. Wobbler ? " said the suitor.

Both gentlemen laughed for some time. The gentleman with the gun-barrel, considering it on inspection in a satisfactory state, referred it to the other ; receiving confirmation of his views, he fitted it into its place in the case before him, and took out the stock and polished that, softly whistling.

" Mr. Wobbler ? " said the suitor.

" What's the matter ? " then said Mr. Wobbler, with his mouth full.

" I want to know— " and Arthur Clennam again mechanically set forth what he wanted to know.

" Can't inform you," observed Mr. Wobbler, apparently to his lunch. " Never heard of it. Nothing at all to do with it. Better try Mr. Clive, second door on the left in the next passage."

" Perhaps he will give me the same answer."

" Very likely. Don't know anything about it," said Mr. Wobbler.

The suitor turned away and had left the room, when the gentleman with the gun called out " Mister ! Hallo ! "

He looked in again.

" Shut the door after you. You're letting in a devil of a draught here ! "

A few steps brought him to the second door on the left in the next passage. In that room he found three gentlemen ; number one doing nothing particular, number two doing nothing particular, number three doing nothing particular.

They seemed, however, to be more directly concerned than the others had been in the effective execution of the great principle of the office, as there was an awful inner apartment with a double door, in which the Circumlocution Sages appeared to be assembled in council, and out of which there was an imposing coming of papers, and into which there was an imposing going of papers, almost constantly; wherein another gentleman, number four, was the active instrument.

"I want to know," said Arthur Clennam,—and again stated his case in the same barrel-organ way. As number one referred him to number two, and as number two referred him to number three, he had occasion to state it three times before they all referred him to number four. To whom he stated it again.

Number four was a vivacious, well-looking, well-dressed, agreeable young fellow—he was a Barnacle, but on the more sprightly side of the family—and he said in an easy way, "Oh! you had better not bother yourself about it, I think."

"Not bother myself about it?"

"No! I recommend you not to bother yourself about it."

This was such a new point of view that Arthur Clennam found himself at a loss how to receive it.

"You can if you like. I can give you plenty of forms to fill up. Lots of 'em here. You can have a dozen if you like. But you'll never go on with it," said number four.

"Would it be such hopeless work? Excuse me; I am a stranger in England."

"*I* don't say it would be hopeless," returned number four, with a frank smile. "I don't express an opinion about that; I only express an opinion about you. *I* don't think you'd go on with it. However, of course, you can do as you like. I suppose there was a failure in the performance of a contract, or something of that kind, was there?"

"I really don't know."

"Well! That you can find out. Then you'll find out

what Department the contract was in, and then you'll find out all about it there."

"I beg your pardon. How shall I find out?"

"Why, you'll—you'll ask till they tell you. Then you'll memorialise that Department (according to regular forms which you'll find out) for leave to memorialise this Department. If you get it (which you may after a time), that memorial must be entered in that Department, sent to be registered in this Department, sent back to be signed by that Department, sent back to be countersigned by this Department, and then it will begin to be regularly before that Department. You'll find out when the business passes through each of these stages, by asking at both Departments till they tell you."

"But surely this is not the way to do the business," Arthur Clennam could not help saying.

This airy young Barnacle was quite entertained by his simplicity in supposing for a moment that it was. This light in hand young Barnacle knew perfectly that it was not. This touch and go young Barnacle had "got up" the Department in a private secretaryship, that he might be ready for any little bit of fat that came to hand; and he fully understood the Department to be a politico-diplomatic hocus pocus piece of machinery, for the assistance of the nobs in keeping off the snobs. This dashing young Barnacle, in a word, was likely to become a statesman, and to make a figure.

"When the business is regularly before that Department, whatever it is," pursued this bright young Barnacle, "then you can watch it from time to time through that Department. When it comes regularly before this Department, then you must watch it from time to time through this Department. We shall have to refer it right and left; and when we refer it anywhere, then you'll have to look it up. When it comes back to us at any time, then you had better look *us* up. When it sticks anywhere, you'll have to try to give it a jog. When you write to another Department about it, and then

LITTLE DORRIT

to this Department about it, and don't hear anything satisfactory about it, why then you had better—keep on writing."

Arthur Clennam looked very doubtful indeed. "But I am obliged to you at any rate," said he, "for your politeness."

"Not at all," replied this engaging young Barnacle. "Try the thing, and see how you like it. It will be in your power to give it up at any time, if you don't like it. You had better take a lot of forms away with you. Give him a lot of forms!" With which instruction to number two, this sparkling young Barnacle took a fresh handful of papers from numbers one and three, and carried them into the sanctuary, to offer to the presiding Idol of the Circumlocution Office.

Arthur Clennam put his forms in his pocket gloomily enough, and went his way down the long stone passage and the long stone staircase. He had come to the swing doors leading into the street, and was waiting, not over patiently, for two people who were between him and them to pass out and let him follow, when the voice of one of them struck familiarly on his ear. He looked at the speaker and recognised Mr. Meagles. Mr. Meagles was very red in the face—redder than travel could have made him—and collaring a short man who was with him, said, "Come out, you rascal, come out!"

It was such an unexpected hearing, and it was also such an unexpected sight to see Mr. Meagles burst the swing doors open, and emerge into the street with the short man, who was of an unoffending appearance, that Clennam stood still for the moment exchanging looks of surprise with the porter. He followed, however, quickly; and saw Mr. Meagles going down the street with his enemy at his side. He soon came up with his old travelling companion, and touched him on the back. The choleric face which Mr. Meagles turned upon him smoothed when he saw who it was, and he put out his friendly hand.

"How are you?" said Mr. Meagles. "How d'ye *do?* I have only just come over from abroad. I am glad to see you."

142

" And I am rejoiced to see you."

" Thank'ee. Thank'ee ! "

" Mrs. Meagles and your daughter— ? "

" Are as well as possible," said Mr. Meagles. " I only wish you had come upon me in a more prepossessing condition as to coolness."

Though it was anything but a hot day, Mr. Meagles was in a heated state that attracted the attention of the passers-by ; more particularly as he leaned his back against a railing, took off his hat and cravat, and heartily rubbed his steaming head and face, and his reddened ears and neck, without the least regard for public opinion.

" Whew ! " said Mr. Meagles, dressing again. " That's comfortable. Now I am cooler."

" You have been ruffled, Mr. Meagles. What is the matter ? "

" Wait a bit, and I'll tell you. Have you leisure for a turn in the Park ? "

" As much as you please."

" Come along then. Ah ! you may well look at him." He happened to have turned his eyes towards the offender whom Mr. Meagles had so angrily collared. " He's something to look at, that fellow is."

He was not much to look at, either in point of size or in point of dress ; being merely a short, square, practical-looking man, whose hair had turned grey, and in whose face and forehead there were deep lines of cogitation, which looked as though they were carved in hard wood. He was dressed in decent black, a little rusty, and had the appearance of a sagacious master in some handicraft. He had a spectacle-case in his hand, which he turned over and over while he was thus in question, with a certain free use of the thumb that is never seen but in a hand accustomed to tools.

" You keep with us," said Mr. Meagles, in a threatening kind of way, " and I'll introduce you presently. Now then ! "

Clennam wondered within himself, as they took the nearest

143

way to the Park, what this unknown (who complied in the gentlest manner) could have been doing. His appearance did not at all justify the suspicion that he had been detected in designs on Mr. Meagles's pocket-handkerchief; nor had he any appearance of being quarrelsome or violent. He was a quiet, plain, steady man; made no attempt to escape; and seemed a little depressed, but neither ashamed nor repentant. If he were a criminal offender, he must surely be an incorrigible hypocrite; and if he were no offender, why should Mr. Meagles have collared him in the Circumlocution Office? He perceived that the man was not a difficulty in his own mind alone, but in Mr. Meagles's too; for such conversation as they had together on the short way to the Park was by no means well sustained, and Mr. Meagles's eye always wandered back to the man, even when he spoke of something very different.

At length, they being among the trees, Mr. Meagles stopped short, and said:

"Mr. Clennam, will you do me the favour to look at this man? His name is Doyce, Daniel Doyce. You wouldn't suppose this man to be a notorious rascal; would you?"

"I certainly should not." It was really a disconcerting question, with the man there.

"No. You would not. I know you would not. You wouldn't suppose him to be a public offender; would you?"

"No."

"No. But he is. He is a public offender. What has he been guilty of? Murder, manslaughter, arson, forgery, swindling, housebreaking, highway robbery, larceny, conspiracy, fraud? Which should you say, now?"

"I should say," returned Arthur Clennam, observing a faint smile in Daniel Doyce's face, "not one of them."

"You are right," said Mr. Meagles. "But he has been ingenious, and he has been trying to turn his ingenuity to his country's service. That makes him a public offender directly, sir."

Arthur looked at the man himself, who only shook his head.

"This Doyce," said Mr. Meagles, "is a smith and engineer. He is not in a large way, but he is well known as a very ingenious man. A dozen years ago, he perfects an invention (involving a very curious secret process) of great importance to his country and his fellow-creatures. I won't say how much money it cost him, or how many years of his life he had been about it, but he brought it to perfection a dozen years ago. Wasn't it a dozen?" said Mr. Meagles, addressing Doyce. "He is the most exasperating man in the world; he never complains!"

"Yes. Rather better than twelve years ago."

"Rather better?" said Mr. Meagles, "you mean rather worse. Well, Mr. Clennam. He addresses himself to the Government. The moment he addresses himself to the Government, he becomes a public offender! Sir," said Mr. Meagles, in danger of making himself excessively hot again, "he ceases to be an innocent citizen, and becomes a culprit. He is treated from that instant as a man who has done some infernal action. He is a man to be shirked, put off, brow-beaten, sneered at, handed over by this highly-connected young or old gentleman, to that highly-connected young or old gentleman, and dodged back again; he is a man with no rights in his own time, or his own property; a mere outlaw, whom it is justifiable to get rid of anyhow; a man to be worn out by all possible means."

It was not so difficult to believe, after the morning's experience, as Mr. Meagles supposed.

"Don't stand there, Doyce, turning your spectacle-case over and over," cried Mr. Meagles, "but tell Mr. Clennam what you confessed to me."

"I undoubtedly was made to feel," said the inventor, "as if I had committed an offence. In dancing attendance at the various offices, I was always treated, more or less, as if it was a very bad offence. I have frequently found it necessary to reflect, for my own self-support, that I really had not done anything to bring myself into the Newgate Calendar, but only wanted to effect a great saving and a great improvement.

"There!" said Mr. Meagles. "Judge whether I exaggerate. Now you'll be able to believe me when I tell you the rest of the case."

With this prelude, Mr. Meagles went through the narrative; the established narrative, which has become tiresome; the matter-of-course narrative which we all know by heart. How, after interminable attendance and correspondence, after infinite impertinences, ignorances, and insults, my lords made a Minute, number three thousand four hundred and seventy-two, allowing the culprit to make certain trials of his invention at his own expense. How the trials were made in the presence of a board of six, of whom two ancient members were too blind to see it, two other ancient members were too deaf to hear it, one other ancient member was too lame to get near it, and the final ancient member was too pig-headed to look at it. How there were more years; more impertinences, ignorances, and insults. How my lords then made a Minute, number five thousand one hundred and three, whereby they resigned the business to the Circumlocution Office. How the Circumlocution Office, in course of time, took up the business as if it were a bran-new thing of yesterday, which had never been heard of before; muddled the business, addled the business, tossed the business in a wet blanket. How the impertinences, ignorances, and insults went through the multiplication table. How there was a reference of the invention to three Barnacles and a Stiltstalking, who knew nothing about it; into whose heads nothing could be hammered about it; who got bored about it, and reported physical impossibilities about it. How the Circumlocution Office, in a Minute, number eight thousand seven hundred and forty, "saw no reason to reverse the decision at which my lords had arrived." How the Circumlocution Office, being reminded that my lords had arrived at no decision, shelved the business. How there had been a final interview with the head of the Circumlocution Office that very morning, and how the Brazen Head had spoken, and had been, upon the whole, and under all the circumstances, and looking at it from the various points of view, of opinion that one of two courses was to be pursued in respect of the business : that was to say, either to leave it alone for evermore, or to begin it all over again.

"Upon which," said Mr. Meagles, "as a practical man, I then and there, in that presence, took Doyce by the collar, and told him it was plain to me that he was an infamous rascal, and treasonable disturber of the government peace, and took him away. I brought him out of the office door by the collar, that the very porter might know I was a practical man who appreciated the official estimate of such characters ; and here we are !"

If that airy young Barnacle had been there, he would have frankly told them perhaps that the Circumlocution Office had achieved its functions. That what the Barnacles had to do, was to stick on to the national ship as long as they could. That to trim the ship, lighten the ship, clean the ship, would be to knock them off ; that they could but be knocked off once ; and that if the ship went down with them yet sticking to it, that was the ship's look out, and not theirs.

"There !" said Mr. Meagles, "now you know all about Doyce. Except, which I own does not improve my state of mind, that even now you don't hear him complain."

"You must have great patience," said Arthur Clennam, looking at him with some wonder, "great forbearance."

"No," he returned, "I don't know that I have more than another man."

"By the Lord, you have more than I have though !" cried Mr. Meagles.

Doyce smiled, as he said to Clennam, "You see, my experience of these things does not begin with myself. It has been in my way to know a little about them, from time to time. Mine is not a particular case. I am not worse used than a hundred others, who have put themselves in the same position—than all the others, I was going to say."

" I don't know that I should find that a consolation, if it were my case; but I am very glad that you do."

"Understand me ! I don't say," he replied in his steady, planning way, and looking into the distance before him as if his grey eye were measuring it, "that it's recompense for a man's toil and hope; but it's a certain sort of relief to know that I might have counted on this."

He spoke in that quiet deliberate manner, and in that undertone, which is often observable in mechanics who consider and adjust with great nicety. It belonged to him like his suppleness of thumb, or his peculiar way of tilting up his hat at the back every now and then, as if he were contemplating some half-finished work of his hand, and thinking about it.

" Disappointed ? " he went on, as he walked between them under the trees. " Yes. No doubt I am disappointed. Hurt ? Yes. No doubt I am hurt. That's only natural. But what I mean, when I say that people who put themselves in the same position, are mostly used in the same way— "

" In England," said Mr. Meagles.

"Oh! of course I mean in England. When they take their inventions into foreign countries, that's quite different. And that's the reason why so many go there."

Mr. Meagles very hot indeed again.

" What I mean is, that however this comes to be the regular way of our government, it is its regular way. Have you ever heard of any projector or inventor who failed to find it all but inaccessible, and whom it did not discourage and ill-treat ? "

" I cannot say that I ever have."

" Have you ever known it to be beforehand in the adoption of any useful thing ? Ever known it to set an example of any useful kind ? "

148

"I am a good deal older than my friend here," said Mr. Meagles, "and I'll answer that. Never."

"But we all three have known, I expect," said the inventor, "a pretty many cases of its fixed determination to be miles upon miles, and years upon years, behind the rest of us ; and of its being found out persisting in the use of things long superseded, even after the better things were well known and generally taken up?"

They all agreed upon that.

"Well then," said Doyce with a sigh, "as I know what such a metal will do at such a temperature, and such a body under such a pressure, so I may know (if I will only consider), how these great lords and gentlemen will certainly deal with such a matter as mine. I have no right to be surprised, with a head upon my shoulders, and memory in it, that I fall into the ranks with all who came before me. I ought to have let it alone. I have had warning enough, I am sure."

With that he put up his spectacle-case, and said to Arthur, "If I don't complain, Mr. Clennam, I can feel gratitude ; and I assure you that I feel it towards our mutual friend. Many's the day, and many's the way in which he has backed me."

"Stuff and nonsense," said Mr. Meagles.

Arthur could not but glance at Daniel Doyce in the ensuing silence. Though it was evidently in the grain of his character, and of his respect for his own case, that he should abstain from idle murmuring, it was evident that he had grown the older, the sterner, and the poorer, for his long endeavour. He could not but think what a blessed thing it would have been for this man, if he had taken a lesson from the gentlemen who were so kind as to take the nation's affairs in charge, and had learnt How not to do it.

Mr. Meagles was hot and despondent for about five minutes, and then began to cool and clear up.

"Come, come!" said he. "We shall not make this the better by being grim. Where do you think of going, Dan?"

"I shall go back to the factory," said Dan.

"Why then, we'll all go back to the factory, or walk in that direction," returned Meagles cheerfully. "Mr. Clennam won't be deterred by its being in Bleeding Heart Yard."

"Bleeding Heart Yard?" said Clennam. "I want to go there."

"So much the better," cried Mr. Meagles. "Come along!"

As they went along, certainly one of the party, and probably more than one, thought that Bleeding Heart Yard was no inappropriate destination for a man who had been in official correspondence with my lords and the Barnacles—and perhaps had a misgiving also that Britannia herself might come to look for lodgings in Bleeding Heart Yard, some ugly day or other, if she over-did the Circumlocution Office.

CHAPTER XI

A LATE, dull autumn night was closing in upon the river
Saone. The stream, like a sullied looking-glass in a gloomy
place, reflected the clouds heavily; and the low banks leaned
over here and there, as if they were half curious, and half
afraid, to see their darkening pictures in the water. The
flat expanse of country about Chalons lay a long heavy
streak, occasionally made a little ragged by a row of poplar
trees, against the wrathful sunset. On the banks of the
river Saone it was wet, depressing, solitary; and the night
deepened fast.

One man, slowly moving on towards Chalons, was the only
visible figure in the landscape. Cain might have looked as
lonely and avoided. With an old sheepskin knapsack at his
back, and a rough, unbarked stick cut out of some wood in
his hand; miry, footsore, his shoes and gaiters trodden out,
his hair and beard untrimmed; the cloak he carried over his
shoulder, and the clothes he wore, soddened with wet;
limping along in pain and difficulty; he looked as if the
clouds were hurrying from him, as if the wail of the wind
and the shuddering of the grass were directed against him,
as if the low mysterious plashing of the water murmured at
him, as if the fitful autumn night were disturbed by him.

He glanced here, and he glanced there, sullenly but
shrinkingly; and sometimes stopped and turned about, and

151

looked all round him. Then he limped on again, toiling and muttering.

"To the devil with this plain that has no end! To the devil with these stones that cut like knives! To the devil with this dismal darkness, wrapping itself about one with a chill! I hate you!"

And he would have visited his hatred upon it all with the scowl he threw about him, if he could. He trudged a little further; and looking into the distance before him, stopped again.

"I, hungry, thirsty, weary. You, imbeciles, where the lights are yonder, eating and drinking, and warming yourselves at fires! I wish I had the sacking of your town; I would repay you, my children!"

But the teeth he set at the town, and the hand he shook at the town, brought the town no nearer; and the man was yet hungrier, and thirstier, and wearier, when his feet were on its jagged pavement, and he stood looking about him.

There was the hotel with its gateway, and its savoury smell of cooking; there was the café, with its bright windows, and its rattling of dominoes; there was the dyer's, with its strips of red cloth on the doorposts; there was the silversmith's, with its ear-rings, and its offerings for altars; there was the tobacco-dealer's, with its lively group of soldier customers coming out pipe in mouth; there were the bad odours of the town, and the rain and the refuse in the kennels, and the faint lamps slung across the road, and the huge Diligence, and its mountain of luggage, and its six grey horses with their tails tied up, getting under weigh at the coach office. But no small cabaret for a straitened traveller being within sight, he had to seek one round the dark corner, where the cabbage leaves lay thickest, trodden about the public cistern at which women had not yet left off drawing water. There, in the back street he found one, the Break of Day. The curtained windows clouded the Break of Day, but it seemed light and warmed, and it announced in legible inscriptions, with appropriate pictorial embellishment of billiard cue and ball, that at the Break of Day one could play billiards; that there one could find meat, drink, and lodging, whether one came on horseback, or came on foot; and that it kept good wines, liqueurs, and brandy. The man turned the handle of the Break of Day door, and limped in.

He touched his discoloured slouched hat, as he came in at the door, to a few men who occupied the room. Two were playing dominoes at one of the little tables; three or four were seated round the stove, conversing as they smoked; the billiard-table in the centre was left alone for the time; the landlady of the Daybreak sat behind her little counter among her cloudy bottles of syrups, baskets of cakes, and leaden drainage for glasses, working at her needle.

Making his way to an empty little table, in a corner of the room, behind the stove, he put down his knapsack and his cloak upon the ground. As he raised his head from stooping to do so, he found the landlady beside him.

"One can lodge here to-night, madame?"

"Perfectly!" said the landlady in a high, sing-song cheery voice.

"Good. One can dine—sup—what you please to call it?"

"Ah, perfectly!" cried the landlady as before.

"Dispatch then, madame, if you please. Something to eat, as quickly as you can; and some wine at once. I am exhausted."

"It is very bad weather, monsieur," said the landlady.

"Cursed weather."

"And a very long road."

"A cursed road."

His hoarse voice failed him, and he rested his head upon his hands until a bottle of wine was brought from the counter. Having filled and emptied his little tumbler twice, and having broken off an end from the great loaf that was set before him with his cloth and napkin, soup-plate, salt, pepper, and oil, he rested his back against the corner of the

153

wall, made a couch of the bench on which he sat, and began to chew crust, until such time as his repast should be ready.

There had been that momentary interruption of the talk about the stove, and that temporary inattention to and distraction from one another, which is usually inseparable in such a company from the arrival of a stranger. It had passed over by this time; and the men had done glancing at him, and were talking again.

"That's the true reason," said one of them, bringing a story he had been telling, to a close, "that's the true reason why they said that the devil was let loose." The speaker was the tall Swiss belonging to the church, and he brought something of the authority of the church into the discussion—especially as the devil was in question.

The landlady having given her directions for the new guest's entertainment to her husband, who acted as cook to the Break of Day, had resumed her needlework behind her counter. She was a smart, neat, bright little woman, with a good deal of cap and a good deal of stocking, and she struck into the conversation with several laughing nods of her head, but without looking up from her work.

"Ah Heaven, then," said she. "When the boat came up from Lyons, and brought the news that the devil was actually let loose at Marseilles, some fly-catchers swallowed it. But I? No, not I."

"Madame, you are always right," returned the tall Swiss. "Doubtless you were enraged against that man, madame?"

"Ay, yes, then!" cried the landlady, raising her eyes from her work, opening them very wide, and tossing her head on one side. "Naturally, yes."

"He was a bad subject."

"He was a wicked wretch," said the landlady, "and well merited what he had the good fortune to escape. So much the worse."

"Stay, madame! Let us see," returned the Swiss, argumentatively turning his cigar between his lips. "It may have been his unfortunate destiny. He may have been the child of circumstances. It is always possible that he had, and has, good in him if one did but know how to find it out. Philosophical philanthropy teaches—"

The rest of the little knot about the stove murmured an objection to the introduction of that threatening expression. Even the two players at dominoes glanced up from their game, as if to protest against philosophical philanthropy being brought by name into the Break of Day.

"Hold there, you and your philanthropy," cried the smiling landlady, nodding her head more than ever. "Listen then. I am a woman, I. I know nothing of philosophical philanthropy. But I know what I have seen, and what I have looked in the face, in this world here, where I find myself. And I tell you this, my friend, that there are people (men and women both, unfortunately) who have no good in them—none. That there are people whom it is necessary to detest without compromise. That there are people who must be dealt with as enemies of the human race. That there are people who have no human heart, and who must be crushed like savage beasts and cleared out of the way. They are but few, I hope; but I have seen (in this world here where I find myself, and even at the little Break of Day) that there are such people. And I do not doubt that this man—whatever they call him, I forget his name—is one of them."

The landlady's lively speech was received with greater favour at the Break of Day, than it would have elicited from certain amiable whitewashers of the class she so unreasonably objected to, nearer Great Britain.

"My faith! If your philosophical philanthropy," said the landlady, putting down her work, and rising to take the stranger's soup from her husband, who appeared with it at a side door, "puts anybody at the mercy of such people by holding terms with them at all, in words or deeds, or both, take it away from the Break of Day, for it isn't worth a sou."

As she placed the soup before the guest, who changed his

attitude to a sitting one, he looked her full in the face, and
his moustache went up under his nose, and his nose came
down over his moustache.

"Well!" said the previous speaker, "let us come back
to our subject. Leaving all that aside, gentlemen, it was
because the man was acquitted on his trial, that people said
at Marseilles that the devil was let loose. That was how the
phrase began to circulate, and what it meant; nothing more."

"How do they call him?" said the landlady. "Biraud, is
it not?"

"Rigaud, madame," returned the tall Swiss.

"Rigaud! To be sure."

The traveller's soup was succeeded by a dish of meat, and
that by a dish of vegetables. He ate all that was placed
before him, emptied his bottle of wine, called for a glass of
rum, and smoked his cigarette with his cup of coffee. As he
became refreshed, he became overbearing; and patronised the
company at the Daybreak in certain small talk, at which he
assisted, as if his condition were far above his appearance.

The company might have had other engagements, or they
might have felt their inferiority, but in any case they dispersed
by degrees, and not being replaced by other company, left
their new patron in possession of the Break of Day. The
landlord was clinking about in his kitchen; the landlady was
quiet at her work; and the refreshed traveller sat smoking by
the stove, warming his ragged feet.

"Pardon me, madame—that Biraud."

"Rigaud, monsieur."

"Rigaud. Pardon me again—has contracted your displeasure, how?"

The landlady, who had been at one moment thinking within
herself that this was a handsome man, at another moment
that this was an ill-looking man, observed the nose coming
down and the moustache going up, and strongly inclined to
the latter decision. Rigaud was a criminal, she said, who
had killed his wife.

"Ay, ay? Death of my life, that's a criminal indeed. But how do you know it?"

"All the world knows it."

"Hah! And yet he escaped justice?"

"Monsieur, the law could not prove it against him to its satisfaction. So the law says. Nevertheless, all the world knows he did it. The people knew it so well, that they tried to tear him to pieces."

"Being all in perfect accord with their own wives?" said the guest. "Haha!"

The landlady of the Break of Day looked at him again, and felt almost confirmed in her last decision. He had a fine hand though, and he turned it with a great show. She began once more to think that he was not ill-looking after all.

"Did you mention, madame—or was it mentioned among the gentlemen—what became of him?"

The landlady shook her head; it being the first conversational stage at which her vivacious earnestness had ceased to nod it, keeping time to what she said. It had been mentioned at the Daybreak, she remarked, on the authority of the journals, that he had been kept in prison for his own safety. However that might be, he had escaped his deserts, so much the worse.

The guest sat looking at her as he smoked out his final cigarette, and as she sat with her head bent over her work, with an expression that might have resolved her doubts, and brought her to a lasting conclusion on the subject of his good or bad looks if she had seen it. When she did look up, the expression was not there. The hand was smoothing his shaggy moustache.

"May one ask to be shown to bed, madame?"

Very willingly, monsieur. Hola, my husband! My husband would conduct him up-stairs. There was one traveller there, asleep, who had gone to bed very early indeed, being overpowered by fatigue; but it was a large chamber with two beds in it, and space enough for twenty. This the landlady of the Break of Day chirpingly explained, calling between whiles, Hola, my husband ! out at the side door.

My husband answered at length, " It is I, my wife ! " and presenting himself in his cook's cap, lighted the traveller up a steep and narrow staircase ; the traveller carrying his own cloak and knapsack, and bidding the landlady good night with a complimentary reference to the pleasure of seeing her again to-morrow. It was a large room, with a rough splintery floor, unplastered rafters overhead, and two bedsteads on opposite sides. Here my husband put down the candle he carried, and with a sidelong look at his guest stooping over his knapsack, gruffly gave him the instruction, " The bed to the right ! " and left him to his repose. The landlord, whether he was a good or a bad physiognomist, had fully made up his mind that the guest was an ill-looking fellow.

The guest looked contemptuously at the clean coarse bedding prepared for him, and, sitting down on the rush chair at the bedside, drew his money out of his pocket, and told it over in his hand. " One must eat," he muttered to himself, " but by Heaven I must eat at the cost of some other man to-morrow ! "

As he sat pondering, and mechanically weighing his money in his palm, the deep breathing of the traveller in the other bed fell so regularly upon his hearing that it attracted his eyes in that direction. The man was covered up warm, and had drawn the white curtain at his head, so that he could be only heard, not seen. But the deep regular breathing, still going on while the other was taking off his worn shoes and gaiters, and still continuing when he had laid aside his coat and cravat, became at length a strong provocative to curiosity, and incentive to get a glimpse of the sleeper's face.

The waking traveller, therefore, stole a little nearer, and yet a little nearer, and a little nearer, to the sleeping traveller's bed, until he stood close beside it. Even then he could not see his face, for he had drawn the sheet over it. The regular breathing still continuing, he put his smooth white hand (such a treacherous hand it looked, as it went creeping from him!) to the sheet, and gently lifted it away.

"Death of my soul!" he whispered, falling back, "here's Cavalletto!"

The little Italian, previously influenced in his sleep perhaps by the stealthy presence at his bedside, stopped in his regular breathing, and with a long deep respiration opened his eyes. At first they were not awake, though open. He lay for some seconds looking placidly at his old prison companion, and then, all at once, with a cry of surprise and alarm, sprang out of bed.

"Hush! What's the matter? Keep quiet! It's I. You know me?" cried the other, in a suppressed voice.

But John Baptist, widely staring, muttering a number of invocations and ejaculations, tremblingly backing into a corner, slipping on his trousers, and tying his coat by the two sleeves round his neck, manifested an unmistakable desire to escape by the door rather than renew the acquaintance. Seeing this, his old prison comrade fell back upon the door, and set his shoulders against it.

"Cavalletto! Wake, boy! Rub your eyes and look at me. Not the name you used to call me—don't use that— Lagnier, say Lagnier!"

John Baptist, staring at him with eyes opened to their utmost width, made a number of those national, backhanded shakes of the right forefinger in the air, as if he were resolved on negativing beforehand everything that the other could possibly advance, during the whole term of his life.

"Cavalletto! Give me your hand. You know Lagnier the gentleman. Touch the hand of a gentleman!"

Submitting himself to the old tone of condescending authority, John Baptist, not at all steady on his legs as yet, advanced and put his hand in his patron's. Monsieur Lagnier laughed; and having given it a squeeze, tossed it up and let it go.

"Then you were—" faltered John Baptist.

LITTLE DORRIT

"Not shaved? No. See here!" cried Lagnier, giving his head a twirl; "as tight on as your own."

John Baptist, with a slight shiver, looked all round the room as if to recall where he was. His patron took that opportunity of turning the key in the door, and then sat down upon his bed.

"Look!" he said, holding up his shoes and gaiters. "That's a poor trim for a gentleman, you'll say. No matter, you shall see how soon I'll mend it. Come and sit down. Take your old place!"

John Baptist, looking anything but reassured, sat down on the floor at the bedside, keeping his eyes upon his patron all the time.

"That's well!" cried Lagnier. "Now we might be in the old infernal hole again, hey? How long have you been out?"

"Two days after you, my master."

"How do you come here?"

"I was cautioned not to stay there, and so I left the town at once, and since then I have changed about. I have been doing odds and ends at Avignon, at Pont Esprit, at Lyons; upon the Rhone, upon the Saone." As he spoke, he rapidly mapped the places out with his sunburnt hand on the floor.

"And where are you going?"

"Going, my master?"

"Ay!"

John Baptist seemed to desire to evade the question without knowing how. "By Bacchus!" he said at last, as if he were forced to the admission, "I have sometimes had a thought of going to Paris, and perhaps to England."

"Cavalletto. This is in confidence. I also am going to Paris and perhaps to England. We'll go together."

The little man nodded his head, and showed his teeth; and yet seemed not quite convinced that it was a surpassingly desirable arrangement.

"We'll go together," repeated Lagnier. "You shall see

how soon I will force myself to be recognised as a gentleman, and you shall profit by it. Is it agreed? Are we one?"

"Oh, surely, surely!" said the little man.

"Then you shall hear before I sleep—and in six words, for I want sleep—how I appear before you, I Lagnier. Remember that. Not the other."

"Altro, altro! Not Ri——" Before John Baptist could finish the name, his comrade had got his hand under his chin and fiercely shut up his mouth.

"Death! what are you doing? Do you want me to be trampled upon and stoned? Do *you* want to be trampled upon and stoned? You would be. You don't imagine that they would set upon me, and let my prison chum go? Don't think it!"

There was an expression in his face as he released his grip of his friend's jaw, from which his friend inferred, that if the course of events really came to any stoning and trampling, Monsieur Lagnier would so distinguish him with his notice as to ensure his having his full share of it. He remembered what a cosmopolitan gentleman Monsieur Lagnier was, and how few weak distinctions he made.

"I am a man," said Monsieur Lagnier, "whom society has deeply wronged since you last saw me. You know that I am sensitive and brave, and that it is my character to govern. How has society respected those qualities in me? I have been shrieked at through the streets. I have been guarded through the streets against men, and especially women, running at me armed with any weapons they could lay their hands on. I have lain in prison for security, with the place of my confinement kept a secret, lest I should be torn out of it and felled by a hundred blows. I have been carted out of Marseilles in the dead of night, and carried leagues away from it packed in straw. It has not been safe for me to go near my house; and, with a beggar's pittance in my pocket, I have walked through vile mud and weather ever since, until my feet are crippled—look at them! Such are the humiliations that society has inflicted upon me, possessing the qualities I have mentioned, and which you know me to possess. But society shall pay for it."

All this he said in his companion's ear, and with his hand before his lips.

"Even here," he went on in the same way, "even in this mean drinking-shop, society pursues me. Madame defames me, and her guests defame me. I, too, a gentleman with manners and accomplishments to strike them dead! But the wrongs society has heaped upon me are treasured in this breast."

To all of which John Baptist, listening attentively to the suppressed hoarse voice, said from time to time, "Surely, surely!" tossing his head and shutting his eyes, as if there were the clearest case against society that perfect candour could make out.

"Put my shoes there," continued Lagnier. "Hang my cloak to dry there by the door. Take my hat." He obeyed each instruction, as it was given. "And this is the bed to which society consigns me, is it? Hah. *Very* well!"

As he stretched out his length upon it, with a ragged handkerchief bound round his wicked head, and only his wicked head showing above the bedclothes, John Baptist was rather strongly reminded of what had so very nearly happened to prevent the moustache from any more going up as it did, and the nose from any more coming down as it did.

"Shaken out of destiny's dice-box again into your company, eh? By Heaven! So much the better for you. You'll profit by it. I shall need a long rest. Let me sleep in the morning."

John Baptist replied that he should sleep as long as he would, and wishing him a happy night, put out the candle. One might have supposed that the next proceeding of the Italian would have been to undress; but he did exactly the reverse, and dressed himself from head to foot, saving his shoes. When he had so done, he lay down upon his bed

Making Off

with some of its coverings over him, and his coat still tied round his neck, to get through the night.

When he started up, the Godfather Break of Day was peeping at its namesake. He rose, took his shoes in his hand, turned the key in the door with great caution, and crept down-stairs. Nothing was astir there but the smell of coffee, wine, tobacco, and syrups; and madame's little counter looked ghastly enough. But he had paid madame his little note at it over-night, and wanted to see nobody—wanted nothing but to get on his shoes and his knapsack, open the door, and run away.

He prospered in his object. No movement or voice was heard when he opened the door; no wicked head tied up in a ragged handkerchief looked out of the upper window. When the sun had raised his full disc above the flat line of the horizon, and was striking fire out of the long muddy vista of paved road with its weary avenue of little trees, a black speck moved along the road and splashed among the flaming pools of rain-water, which black speck was John Baptist Cavalletto running away from his patron.

CHAPTER XII

In London itself, though in the old rustic road towards a suburb of note where in the days of William Shakespeare, author and stage-player, there were Royal hunting-seats, howbeit no sport is left there now but for hunters of men, Bleeding Heart Yard was to be found. A place much changed in feature and in fortune, yet with some relish of ancient greatness about it. Two or three mighty stacks of chimneys, and a few large dark rooms which had escaped being walled and subdivided out of the recognition of their old proportions, gave the Yard a character. It was inhabited by poor people, who set up their rest among its faded glories, as Arabs of the desert pitch their tents among the fallen stones of the Pyramids; but there was a family sentimental feeling prevalent in the Yard, that it had a character.

As if the aspiring city had become puffed up in the very ground on which it stood, the ground had so risen about Bleeding Heart Yard that you got into it down a flight of steps which formed no part of the original approach, and got out of it by a low gateway into a maze of shabby streets, which went about and about, tortuously ascending to the level again. At this end of the Yard and over the gateway, was the factory of Daniel Doyce, often heavily beating like a bleeding heart of iron, with the clink of metal upon metal.

The opinion of the Yard was divided respecting the derivation of its name. The more practical of its inmates abided

164

by the tradition of a murder ; the gentler and more imaginative inhabitants, including the whole of the tender sex, were loyal to the legend of a young lady of former times closely imprisoned in her chamber by a cruel father for remaining true to her own true love, and refusing to marry the suitor he chose for her. The legend related how that the young lady used to be seen up at her window behind the bars, murmuring a love-lorn song of which the burden was, " Bleeding Heart, Bleeding Heart, bleeding away," until she died. It was objected by the murderous party that this Refrain was notoriously the invention of a tambour-worker, a spinster and romantic, still lodging in the Yard. But, forasmuch as all favourite legends must be associated with the affections, and as many more people fall in love than commit murder— which it may be hoped, howsoever bad we are, will continue until the end of the world to be the dispensation under which we shall live—the Bleeding Heart, Bleeding Heart, bleeding away story, carried the day by a great majority. Neither party would listen to the antiquaries who delivered learned lectures in the neighbourhood, showing the Bleeding Heart to have been the heraldic cognizance of the old family to whom the property had once belonged. And, considering that the hour-glass they turned from year to year was filled with the earthiest and coarsest sand, the Bleeding Heart Yarders had reason enough for objecting to be despoiled of the one little golden grain of poetry that sparkled in it.

Down into the Yard, by way of the steps, came Daniel Doyce, Mr. Meagles, and Clennam. Passing along the Yard, and between the open doors on either hand, all abundantly garnished with light children nursing heavy ones, they arrived at its opposite boundary, the gateway. Here Arthur Clennam stopped to look about him for the domicile of Plornish, plasterer : whose name, according to the custom of Londoners, Daniel Doyce had never seen or heard of to that hour.

It was plain enough, nevertheless, as Little Dorrit had said ; over a lime-splashed gateway in the corner, within which

Plornish kept a ladder and a barrel or two. The last house in Bleeding Heart Yard which she had described as his place of habitation, was a large house, let off to various tenants; but Plornish ingeniously hinted that he lived in the parlour, by means of a painted hand under his name, the forefinger of which hand (on which the artist had depicted a ring and a most elaborate nail of the genteelest form) referred all inquirers to that apartment.

Parting from his companions, after arranging another meeting with Mr. Meagles, Clennam went alone into the entry, and knocked with his knuckles at the parlour-door. It was opened presently by a woman with a child in her arms, whose unoccupied hand was hastily re-arranging the upper part of her dress. This was Mrs. Plornish, and this maternal action was the action of Mrs. Plornish during a large part of her waking existence.

Was Mr. Plornish at home? "Well, sir," said Mrs. Plornish, a civil woman, "not to deceive you, he's gone to look for a job."

Not to deceive you, was a method of speech with Mrs. Plornish. She would deceive you, under any circumstances, as little as might be; but she had a trick of answering in this provisional form.

"Do you think he will be back soon, if I wait for him?"

"I have been expecting him," said Mrs. Plornish, "this half-an-hour, at any minute of time. Walk in, sir."

Arthur entered the rather dark and close parlour (though it was lofty too), and sat down in the chair she placed for him.

"Not to deceive you, sir, I notice it," said Mrs. Plornish, "and I take it kind of you."

He was at a loss to understand what she meant; and by expressing as much in his looks, elicited her explanation.

"It ain't many that comes into a poor place, that deems it worth their while to move their hats," said Mrs. Plornish. "But people think more of it than people think."

Clennam returned, with an uncomfortable feeling in so very

slight a courtesy being unusual, Was that all! And stooping down to pinch the cheek of another young child who was sitting on the floor, staring at him, asked Mrs. Plornish how old that fine boy was?

"Four year just turned, sir," said Mrs. Plornish. "He *is* a fine little fellow, ain't he, sir? But this one is rather sickly." She tenderly hushed the baby in her arms, as she said it. "You wouldn't mind my asking if it happened to be a job as you was come about, sir, would you?" added Mrs. Plornish, wistfully.

She asked it so anxiously, that if he had been in possession of any kind of tenement, he would have had it plastered a foot deep, rather than answer No. But he was obliged to answer No; and he saw a shade of disappointment on her face, as she checked a sigh, and looked at the low fire. Then he saw, also, that Mrs. Plornish was a young woman, made somewhat slatternly in herself and her belongings by poverty; and so dragged at by poverty and the children together, that their united forces had already dragged her face into wrinkles.

"All such things as jobs," said Mrs. Plornish, "seems to me to have gone underground, they do indeed." (Herein Mrs. Plornish limited her remark to the plastering trade, and spoke without reference to the Circumlocution Office and the Barnacle Family).

"Is it so difficult to get work?" asked Arthur Clennam.

"Plornish finds it so," she returned. "He is quite unfortunate. Really he is."

Really he was. He was one of those many wayfarers on the road of life, who seem to be afflicted with supernatural corns, rendering it impossible for them to keep up even with their lame competitors. A willing, working, soft-hearted, not hard-headed fellow, Plornish took his fortune as smoothly as could be expected; but it was a rough one. It so rarely happened that anybody seemed to want him, it was such an exceptional case when his powers were in any request, that his misty mind could not make out how it happened. He took it as it came, therefore; he tumbled into all kinds of difficulties, and tumbled out of them; and, by tumbling through life, got himself considerably bruised.

"It's not for want of looking after jobs, I am sure," said Mrs. Plornish, lifting up her eyebrows, and searching for a solution of the problem between the bars of the grate; "nor yet for want of working at them, when they are to be got. No one ever heard my husband complain of work."

Somehow or other, this was the general misfortune of Bleeding Heart Yard. From time to time there were public complaints, pathetically going about, of labour being scarce —which certain people seemed to take extraordinarily ill, as though they had an absolute right to it on their own terms —but Bleeding Heart Yard, though as willing a Yard as any in Britain, was never the better for the demand. That high old family, the Barnacles, had long been too busy with their great principle to look into the matter; and indeed the matter had nothing to do with their watchfulness in outgeneralling all other high old families except the Stiltstalkings.

While Mrs. Plornish spoke in these words of her absent lord, her lord returned. A smooth-cheeked, fresh-coloured, sandy-whiskered man of thirty. Long in the legs, yielding at the knees, foolish in the face, flannel-jacketed, lime-whitened.

"This is Plornish, sir."

"I came," said Clennam, rising, "to beg the favour of a little conversation with you, on the subject of the Dorrit family."

Plornish became suspicious. Seemed to scent a creditor. Said, "Ah, Yes. Well. He didn't know what satisfaction *he* could give any gentleman respecting that family. What might it be about, now?"

"I know you better," said Clennam, smiling, "than you suppose."

Plornish observed, not smiling in return, And yet he hadn't the pleasure of being acquainted with the gentleman, neither.

"No," said Arthur, "I know your kind offices at second hand, but on the best authority. Through Little Dorrit.— I mean," he explained, "Miss Dorrit."

"Mr. Clennam, is it? Oh! I've heard of you, sir."

"And I of you," said Arthur.

"Please to sit down again, sir, and consider yourself welcome.—Why, yes," said Plornish, taking a chair, and lifting the elder child upon his knee, that he might have the moral support of speaking to a stranger over his head, "I have been on the wrong side of the Lock myself, and in that way we come to know Miss Dorrit. Me and my wife, we are well acquainted with Miss Dorrit."

"Intimate!" cried Mrs. Plornish. Indeed, she was so proud of the acquaintance, that she had awakened some bitterness of spirit in the Yard, by magnifying to an enormous amount the sum for which Miss Dorrit's father had become insolvent. The Bleeding Hearts resented her claiming to know people of such distinction.

"It was her father that I got acquainted with first. And through getting acquainted with him, you see—why—I got acquainted with her," said Plornish tautologically.

"I see."

"Ah! And there's manners! There's polish! There's a gentleman to have run to seed in the Marshalsea Jail! Why, perhaps you are not aware," said Plornish, lowering his voice, and speaking with a perverse admiration of what he ought to have pitied or despised, "not aware that Miss Dorrit and her sister dursn't let him know that they work for a living. No!" said Plornish, looking with a ridiculous triumph first at his wife, and then all round the room. "Dursn't let him know it, they dursn't!"

"Without admiring him for that," Clennam quietly observed, "I am very sorry for him." The remark appeared to suggest to Plornish, for the first time, that it might not be a very fine trait of character after all. He pondered about it for a moment, and gave it up.

"As to me," he resumed, "certainly Mr. Dorrit is as affable with me, I am sure, as I can possibly expect. Considering the differences and distances betwixt us, more so. But it's Miss Dorrit that we were speaking of."

"True. Pray how did you introduce her at my mother's!"

Mr. Plornish picked a bit of lime out of his whisker, put it between his lips, turned it with his tongue like a sugar-plum, considered, found himself unequal to the task of lucid explanation, and appealing to his wife, said, "Sally, *you* may as well mention how it was, old woman."

"Miss Dorrit," said Sally, hushing the baby from side to side, and laying her chin upon the little hand as it tried to disarrange the gown again, "came here one afternoon with a bit of writing, telling that how she wished for needlework, and asked if it would be considered any ill-conwenience in case she was to give her address here." (Plornish repeated, her address here, in a low voice, as if he were making responses at church.) "Me and Plornish says, No, Miss Dorrit, no ill-conwenience," (Plornish repeated, no ill-conwenience,) "and she wrote it in, according. Which then me and Plornish says, Ho Miss Dorrit!" (Plornish repeated, Ho Miss Dorrit.) "Have you thought of copying it three or four times, as the way to make it known in more places than one? No, says Miss Dorrit, I have not, but I will. She copied it out according, on this table, in a sweet writing, and Plornish, he took it where he worked, having a job just then," (Plornish repeated, job just then,) "and likewise to the landlord of the Yard; through which it was that Mrs. Clennam first happened to employ Miss Dorrit." Plornish repeated, employ Miss Dorrit; and Mrs. Plornish having come to an end, feigned to bite the fingers of the little hand as she kissed it.

"The landlord of the Yard," said Arthur Clennam, "is——"

"He is Mr. Casby, by name, he is," said Plornish, "and Pancks, he collects the rents. That," added Mr. Plornish,

170

dwelling on the subject, with a slow thoughtfulness that appeared to have no connexion with any specific object, and to lead him nowhere, "that is about what *they* are, you may believe me or not, as you think proper."

"Ay?" returned Clennam, thoughtful in his turn. "Mr. Casby, too! An old acquaintance of mine, long ago!"

Mr. Plornish did not see his road to any comment on this fact, and made none. As there truly was no reason why he should have the least interest in it, Arthur Clennam went on to the present purport of his visit; namely, to make Plornish the instrument of effecting Tip's release, with as little detriment as possible to the self-reliance and self-helpfulness of the young man, supposing him to possess any remnant of those qualities : without doubt a very wide stretch of supposition. Plornish, having been made acquainted with the cause of action from the Defendant's own mouth, gave Arthur to understand that the Plaintiff was a "Chaunter" —meaning, not a singer of anthems, but a seller of horses— and that he (Plornish) considered that ten shillings in the pound "would settle handsome," and that more would be a waste of money. The Principal and instrument soon drove off together to a stable-yard in High Holborn, where a remarkably fine grey gelding, worth, at the lowest figure, seventy-five guineas (not taking into account the value of the shot he had been made to swallow, for the improvement of his form), was to be parted with for a twenty-pound note, in consequence of his having run away last week with Mrs. Captain Barbary of Cheltenham, who wasn't up to a horse of his courage, and who, in mere spite, insisted on selling him for that ridiculous sum : or, in other words, on giving him away. Plornish, going up this yard alone and leaving his Principal outside, found a gentleman with tight drab legs, a rather old hat, a little hooked stick, and a blue neckerchief (Captain Maroon of Gloucestershire, a private friend of Captain Barbary); who happened to be there, in a friendly way, to mention these little circumstances concerning the remarkably fine grey gelding, to any real judge of a horse and quick snapper-up of a good thing, who might look in at that address as per advertisement. This gentleman, happening also to be the Plaintiff in the Tip case, referred Mr. Plornish to his solicitor, and declined to treat with Mr. Plornish, or even to endure his presence in the yard, unless he appeared there with a twenty-pound note : in which case only, the gentleman would augur from appearances that he meant business, and might be induced to talk to him. On this hint, Mr. Plornish retired to communicate with his Principal, and presently came back with the required credentials. Then said Captain Maroon, " Now, how much time do you want to make up the other twenty in ? Now, I'll give you a month." Then said Captain Maroon, when that wouldn't suit, " Now, I'll tell what I'll do with you. You shall get me a good bill at four months, made payable at a banking-house, for the other twenty !" Then said Captain Maroon, when *that* wouldn't suit, "Now, come! Here's the last I've got to say to you. You shall give me another ten down, and I'll run my pen clean through it." Then said Captain Maroon, when *that* wouldn't suit, "Now, I'll tell you what it is, and this shuts it up ; he has used me bad, but I'll let him off for another five down and a bottle of wine ; and if you mean done, say done, and if you don't like it, leave it." Finally said Captain Maroon, when *that* wouldn't suit either, " Hand over, then !"—And in consideration of the first offer, gave a receipt in full and discharged the prisoner.

" Mr. Plornish," said Arthur, " I trust to you, if you please, to keep my secret. If you will undertake to let the young man know that he is free, and to tell him that you were employed to compound for the debt by some one whom you are not at liberty to name, you will not only do me a service, but may do him one, and his sister also."

" The last reason, sir," said Plornish, " would be quite sufficient. Your wishes shall be attended to."

"A Friend has obtained his discharge, you can say if you please. A Friend who hopes that for his sister's sake, if for no one else's, he will make good use of his liberty."

"Your wishes, sir, shall be attended to."

"And if you will be so good, in your better knowledge of the family, as to communicate freely with me, and to point out to me any means by which you think I may be delicately and really useful to Little Dorrit, I shall feel under an obligation to you."

"Don't name it, sir," returned Plornish, "it'll be ekally a pleasure and a—it'll be ekally a pleasure and a—" Finding himself unable to balance his sentence after two efforts, Mr. Plornish wisely dropped it. He took Clennam's card, and appropriate pecuniary compliment.

He was earnest to finish his commission at once, and his Principal was in the same mind. So, his Principal offered to set him down at the Marshalsea Gate, and they drove in that direction over Blackfriars Bridge. On the way, Arthur elicited from his new friend a confused summary of the interior life of Bleeding Heart Yard. They was all hard up there, Mr. Plornish said, uncommon hard up, to be sure. Well, he couldn't say how it was; he didn't know as anybody *could* say how it was; all he know'd was, that so it was. When a man felt, on his own back and in his own belly, that poor he was, that man (Mr. Plornish gave it as his decided belief) know'd well that he was poor somehow or another, and you couldn't talk it out of him, no more than you could talk Beef into him. Then you see, some people as was better off said, and a good many such people lived pretty close up to the mark themselves if not beyond it so he'd heerd, that they was "improvident" (that was the favourite word) down the Yard. For instance, if they see a man with his wife and children going to Hampton Court in a Wan, perhaps once in a year, they says, "Hallo! I thought you was poor, my improvident friend!" Why, Lord, how hard it was upon a man! What was a man to do? He couldn't

173

go mollancholly mad, and even if he did, you wouldn't be the better for it. In Mr. Plornish's judgment you would be the worse for it. Yet you seemed to want to make a man mollancholly mad. You was always at it—if not with your right hand, with your left. What was they a doing in the Yard? Why, take a look at 'em and see. There was the girls and their mothers a working at their sewing, or their shoe-binding, or their trimming, or their waistcoat-making, day and night and night and day, and not more than able to keep body and soul together after all—often not so much. There was people of pretty well all sorts of trades you could name, all wanting to work, and yet not able to get it. There was old people, after working all their lives, going and being shut up in the workhouse, much worse fed and lodged and treated altogether, than—Mr. Plornish said manufacturers, but appeared to mean malefactors. Why, a man didn't know where to turn himself, for a crumb of comfort. As to who was to blame for it, Mr. Plornish didn't know who was to blame for it. He could tell you who suffered, but he couldn't tell you whose fault it was. It wasn't *his* place to find out, and who'd mind what he said, if he did find out? He only know'd that it wasn't put right by them what undertook that line of business, and that it didn't come right of itself. And in brief his illogical opinion was, that if you couldn't do nothing for him, you had better take nothing from him for doing of it; so far as he could make out, that was about what it come to. Thus, in a prolix, gently-growling, foolish way, did Plornish turn the tangled skein of his estate about and about, like a blind man who was trying to find some beginning or end to it; until they reached the prison gate. There, he left his Principal alone; to wonder, as he rode away, how many thousand Plornishes there might be within a day or two's journey of the Circumlocution Office, playing sundry curious variations on the same tune, which were not known by ear in that glorious institution.

CHAPTER XIII

PATRIARCHAL

THE mention of Mr. Casby again revived, in Clennam's memory, the smouldering embers of curiosity and interest which Mrs. Flintwinch had fanned on the night of his arrival. Flora Casby had been the beloved of his boyhood; and Flora was the daughter and only child of wooden-headed old Christopher (so he was still occasionally spoken of by some irreverent spirits who had had dealings with him, and in whom familiarity had bred its proverbial result perhaps), who was reputed to be rich in weekly tenants, and to get a good quantity of blood out of the stones of several un-promising courts and alleys.

After some days of inquiry and research, Arthur Clennam became convinced that the case of the Father of the Marshal-sea was indeed a hopeless one, and sorrowfully resigned the idea of helping him to freedom again. He had no hopeful inquiry to make, at present, concerning Little Dorrit either; but he argued with himself that it might, for anything he knew it might be serviceable to the poor child, if he renewed this acquaintance. It is hardly necessary to add, that beyond all doubt he would have presented himself at Mr. Casby's door, if there had been no Little Dorrit in existence; for we all know how we all deceive ourselves—that is to say, how people in general, our profounder selves excepted, deceive themselves—as to motives of action.

175

With a comfortable impression upon him, and quite an honest one in its way, that he was still patronising Little Dorrit in doing what had no reference to her, he found himself one afternoon at the corner of Mr. Casby's street. Mr. Casby lived in a street in Gray's Inn Road, which had set off from that thoroughfare with the intention of running at one heat down into the valley, and up again to the top of Pentonville Hill; but which had run itself out of breath in twenty yards, and had stood still ever since. There is no such place in that part now; but it remained there for many years, looking with a baulked countenance at the wilderness patched with unfruitful gardens and pimpled with eruptive summer-houses, that it had meant to run over in no time.

" The house," thought Clennam, as he crossed to the door, " is as little changed as my mother's, and looks almost as gloomy. But the likeness ends outside. I know its staid repose within. The smell of its jars of old rose-leaves and lavender seems to come upon me even here."

When his knock, at the bright brass knocker of obsolete shape, brought a woman-servant to the door, those faded scents in truth saluted him like wintry breath that had a faint remembrance in it of the bygone spring. He stepped into the sober, silent, air-tight house—one might have fancied it to have been stifled by Mutes in the Eastern manner—and the door, closing again, seemed to shut out sound and motion. The furniture was formal, grave, and quaker-like, but well-kept; and had as prepossessing an aspect as anything, from a human creature to a wooden stool, that is meant for much use and is preserved for little, can ever wear. There was a grave clock, ticking somewhere up the staircase; and there was a songless bird in the same direction, pecking at his cage, as if he were ticking too. The parlour-fire ticked in the grate. There was only one person on the parlour-hearth, and the loud watch in his pocket ticked audibly.

The servant-maid had ticked the two words " Mr. Clennam" so softly that she had not been heard; and he consequently stood, within the door she had closed, unnoticed. The figure of a man advanced in life, whose smooth grey eyebrows seemed to move to the ticking as the fire-light flickered on them, sat in an arm-chair, with his list shoes on the rug, and his thumbs slowly revolving over one another. This was old Christopher Casby—recognisable at a glance—as unchanged in twenty years and upward, as his own solid furniture—as little touched by the influence of the varying seasons, as the old rose-leaves and old lavender in his porcelain jars.

Perhaps there never was a man, in this troublesome world, so troublesome for the imagination to picture as a boy. And yet he had changed very little in his progress through life. Confronting him, in the room in which he sat, was a boy's portrait, which anybody seeing him would have identified as Master Christopher Casby, aged ten : though disguised with a haymaking rake, for which he had had, at any time, as much taste or use as for a diving-bell; and sitting (on one of his own legs) upon a bank of violets, moved to precocious contemplation by the spire of a village church. There was the same smooth face and forehead, the same calm blue eye, the same placid air. The shining bald head, which looked so very large because it shone so much ; and the long grey hair at its sides and back, like floss silk or spun glass, which looked so very benevolent because it was never cut; were not, of course, to be seen in the boy as in the old man. Nevertheless, in the Seraphic creature with the haymaking rake were clearly to be discerned the rudiments of the Patriarch with the list shoes.

Patriarch was the name which many people delighted to give him. Various old ladies in the neighbourhood spoke of him as The Last of the Patriarchs. So grey, so slow, so quiet, so impassionate, so very bumpy in the head, Patriarch was the word for him. He had been accosted in the streets, and respectfully solicited to become a Patriarch for painters and for sculptors ; with so much importunity, in sooth, that it would appear to be beyond the Fine Arts to remember the points of a Patriarch, or to invent one. Philanthropists of both sexes had asked who he was, and on being informed, "Old Christopher Casby, formerly Town-agent to Lord Decimus Tite Barnacle," had cried in a rapture of disappointment, "Oh! why, with that head, is he not a benefactor to his species! Oh! why, with that head, is he not a father to the orphan and a friend to the friendless!" With that head, however, he remained old Christopher Casby, proclaimed by common report rich in house property; and with that head, he now sat in his silent parlour. Indeed it would be the height of unreason to expect him to be sitting there without that head.

Arthur Clennam moved to attract his attention, and the grey eyebrows turned towards him.

"I beg your pardon," said Clennam, "I fear you did not hear me announced?"

"No, sir, I did not. Did you wish to see me, sir?"

"I wished to pay my respects."

Mr. Casby seemed a feather's weight disappointed by the last words, having perhaps prepared himself for the visitor's wishing to pay something else. "Have I the pleasure, sir," he proceeded—"take a chair, if you please—have I the pleasure of knowing—? Ah! truly, yes, I think I have! I believe I am not mistaken in supposing that I am acquainted with those features? I think I address a gentleman of whose return to this country I was informed by Mr. Flintwinch?"

"That is your present visitor."

"Really! Mr. Clennam?"

"No other, Mr. Casby."

"Mr. Clennam, I am glad to see you. How have you been since we met?"

Without thinking it worth while to explain that in the course of some quarter of a century he had experienced occasional slight fluctuations in his health and spirits, Clennam answered generally that he had never been better, or something equally to the purpose; and shook hands with the possessor of "that head" as it shed its patriarchal light upon him.

"We are older, Mr. Clennam," said Christopher Casby.

"We are—not younger," said Clennam. After this wise remark he felt that he was scarcely shining with brilliancy, and became aware that he was nervous.

"And your respected father," said Mr. Casby, "is no more! I was grieved to hear it, Mr. Clennam, I was grieved."

Arthur replied in the usual way that he felt infinitely obliged to him.

"There was a time," said Mr. Casby, "when your parents and myself were not on friendly terms. There was a little family misunderstanding among us. Your respected mother was rather jealous of her son, maybe; when I say her son, I mean your worthy self, your worthy self."

His smooth face had a bloom upon it, like ripe wall-fruit. What with his blooming face, and that head, and his blue eyes, he seemed to be delivering sentiments of rare wisdom and virtue. In like manner, his physiognomical expression seemed to teem with benignity. Nobody could have said where the wisdom was, or where the virtue was, or where the benignity was; but they all seemed to be somewhere about him.

"Those times, however," pursued Mr. Casby, "are past and gone, past and gone. I do myself the pleasure of making a visit to your respected mother occasionally, and of admiring the fortitude and strength of mind with which she bears her trials, bears her trials."

When he made one of these little repetitions, sitting with his hands crossed before him, he did it with his head on one side, and a gentle smile, as if he had something in his thoughts too sweetly profound to be put into words. As if he denied himself the pleasure of uttering it, lest he should soar too high; and his meekness therefore preferred to be unmeaning.

"I have heard that you were kind enough on one of those

occasions," said Arthur, catching at the opportunity as it drifted past him, " to mention Little Dorrit to my mother."

" Little—? Dorrit? That's the seamstress who was mentioned to me by a small tenant of mine? Yes, yes. Dorrit? That's the name. Ah, yes,' yes! You call her Little Dorrit?"

No road in that direction. Nothing came of the cross-cut. It led no further.

" My daughter Flora," said Mr. Casby, " as you may have heard probably, Mr. Clennam, was married and established in life, several years ago. She had the misfortune to lose her husband when she had been married a few months. She resides with me again. She will be glad to see you, if you will permit me to let her know that you are here."

" By all means," returned Clennam. " I should have preferred the request, if your kindness had not anticipated me."

Upon this Mr. Casby rose up in his list shoes, and with a slow, heavy step (he was of an elephantine build), made for the door. He had a long wide-skirted bottle-green coat on, and a bottle-green pair of trousers, and a bottle-green waistcoat. The Patriarchs were not dressed in bottle-green broadcloth, and yet his clothes looked patriarchal.

He had scarcely left the room, and allowed the ticking to become audible again, when a quick hand turned a latchkey in the house-door, opened it, and shut it. Immediately afterwards, a quick and eager short dark man came into the room with so much way upon him, that he was within a foot of Clennam before he could stop.

" Halloa!" he said.

Clennam saw no reason why he should not say " Halloa!" too.

" What's the matter?" said the short dark man.

"I have not heard that anything is the matter," returned Clennam.

" Where's Mr. Casby?" asked the short dark man, looking about.

" He will be here directly, if you want him."

" *I* want him?" said the short dark man. "Don't you?"

This elicited a word or two of explanation from Clennam, during the delivery of which the short dark man held his breath and looked at him. He was dressed in black and rusty iron grey; had jet black beads of eyes; a scrubby little black chin; wiry black hair striking out from his head in prongs, like forks or hair-pins; and a complexion that was very dingy by nature, or very dirty by art, or a compound of nature and art. He had dirty hands and dirty broken nails, and looked as if he had been in the coals; he was in a perspiration, and snorted and sniffed and puffed and blew, like a little labour-ing steam-engine.

"Oh!" said he, when Arthur had told him how he came to be there. "Very well. That's right. If he should ask for Pancks, will you be so good as to say that Pancks is come in?" And so, with a snort and a puff, he worked out by another door.

Now, in the old days at home, certain audacious doubts respecting the last of the Patriarchs, which were afloat in the air, had, by some forgotten means, come in contact with Arthur's sensorium. He was aware of motes and specks of suspicion, in the atmosphere of that time; seen through which medium, Christopher Casby was a mere Inn signpost without any Inn—an invitation to rest and be thankful, when there was no place to put up at, and nothing whatever to be thankful for. He knew that some of these specks even represented Christopher as capable of harbouring designs in "that head," and as being a crafty impostor. Other motes there were which showed him as a heavy, selfish, drifting Booby, who, having stumbled, in the course of his unwieldy jostlings against other men, on the discovery that to get through life with ease and credit, he had but to hold his tongue, keep the bald part of his head well polished, and leave his hair alone, had had just cunning enough to seize the

181

idea and stick to it. It was said that his being town-agent to
Lord Decimus Tite Barnacle was referable, not to his having
the least business capacity, but to his looking so supremely
benignant that nobody could suppose the property screwed
or jobbed under such a man; also, that for similar reasons
he now got more money out of his own wretched lettings,
unquestioned, than anybody with a less knobby and less
shining crown could possibly have done. In a word, it was
represented (Clennam called to mind, alone in the ticking
parlour) that many people select their models, much as the
painters, just now mentioned, select theirs; and that,
whereas in the Royal Academy some evil old ruffian of a
Dog-stealer will annually be found embodying all the cardinal
virtues, on account of his eyelashes, or his chin, or his legs
(thereby planting thorns of confusion in the breasts of the
more observant students of nature), so, in the great social
Exhibition, accessories are often accepted in lieu of the internal character.

Calling these things to mind, and ranging Mr. Pancks in a
row with them, Arthur Clennam leaned this day to the opinion,
without quite deciding on it, that the last of the Patriarchs
was the drifting Booby aforesaid, with the one idea of keeping the bald part of his head highly polished : and that, much
as an unwieldy ship in the Thames river may sometimes be
seen heavily driving with the tide, broadside on, stern first,
in its own way and in the way of everything else, though
making a great show of navigation, when all of a sudden, a
little coaly steam-tug will bear down upon it, take it in tow,
and bustle off with it; similarly the cumbrous Patriarch had
been taken in tow by the snorting Pancks, and was now
following in the wake of that dingy little craft.

The return of Mr. Casby, with his daughter Flora, put an
end to these meditations. Clennam's eyes no sooner fell
upon the subject of his old passion, than it shivered and
broke to pieces.

Most men will be found sufficiently true to themselves to

be true to an old idea. It is no proof of an inconstant mind, but exactly the opposite, when the idea will not bear close comparison with the reality, and the contrast is a fatal shock to it. Such was Clennam's case. In his youth he had ardently loved this woman, and had heaped upon her all the locked-up wealth of his affection and imagination. That wealth had been, in his desert home, like Robinson Crusoe's money; exchangeable with no one, lying idle in the dark to rust, until he poured it out for her. Ever since that memorable time, though he had, until the night of his arrival, as completely dismissed her from any association with his Present or Future as if she had been dead (which she might easily have been for anything he knew), he had kept the old fancy of the Past unchanged, in its old sacred place. And now, after all, the last of the Patriarchs coolly walked into the parlour, saying in effect, "Be good enough to throw it down and dance upon it. This is Flora."

Flora, always tall, had grown to be very broad too, and short of breath; but that was not much. Flora, whom he had left a lily, had become a peony; but that was not much. Flora, who had seemed enchanting in all she said and thought, was diffuse and silly. That was much. Flora, who had been spoiled and artless long ago, was determined to be spoiled and artless now. That was a fatal blow.

This is Flora!

"I am sure," giggled Flora, tossing her head with a caricature of her girlish manner, such as a mummy might have presented at her own funeral, if she had lived and died in classical antiquity, "I am ashamed to see Mr. Clennam, I am a mere fright, I know he'll find me fearfully changed, I am actually an old woman, it's shocking to be so found out, it's really shocking!"

He assured her that she was just what he had expected, and that time had not stood still with himself.

"Oh! But with a gentleman it's so different and really you look so amazingly well that you have no right to say anything of the kind, while, as to me you know—oh!" cried Flora with a little scream, " I am dreadful!"

The Patriarch, apparently not yet understanding his own part in the drama under representation, glowed with vacant serenity.

"But if we talk of not having changed," said Flora, who, whatever she said, never once came to a full stop, "look at Papa, is not Papa precisely what he was when you went away, isn't it cruel and unnatural of Papa to be such a reproach to his own child, if we go on in this way much longer people who don't know us will begin to suppose that I am Papa's Mama!"

That must be a long time hence, Arthur considered.

"Oh Mr. Clennam you insincerest of creatures," said Flora, "I perceive already you have not lost your old way of paying compliments, your old way when you used to pretend to be so sentimentally struck you know—at least I don't mean that, I—oh I don't know what I mean!" Here Flora tittered confusedly, and gave him one of her old glances.

The Patriarch, as if he now began to perceive that his part in the piece was to get off the stage as soon as might be, rose, and went to the door by which Pancks had worked out, hailing that Tug by name. He received an answer from some little Dock beyond, and was towed out of sight directly.

"You mustn't think of going yet," said Flora—Arthur had looked at his hat, being in a ludicrous dismay, and not knowing what to do : "you could never be so unkind as to think of going, Arthur—I mean Mr. Arthur—or I suppose Mr. Clennam would be far more proper—but I am sure I don't know what I'm saying—without a word about the dear old days gone for ever, however when I come to think of it I dare say it would be much better not to speak of them and it's highly probable that you have some much more agreeable engagment and pray let Me be the last person in the world to interfere with it though there *was* a time, but I am running into nonsense again."

FLORA TACKS A LITTLE

Was it possible that Flora could have been such a chatterer, in the days she referred to? Could there have been anything like her present disjointed volubility, in the fascinations that had captivated him?

"Indeed I have little doubt," said Flora, running on with astonishing speed, and pointing her conversation with nothing but commas, and very few of them, "that you are married to some Chinese lady, being in China so long and being in business and naturally desirous to settle and extend your connection nothing was more likely than that you should propose to a Chinese lady and nothing was more natural I am sure than that the Chinese lady should accept you and think herself very well off too, I only hope she's not a Pagodian dissenter."

"I am not," returned Arthur, smiling in spite of himself, "married to any lady, Flora."

"Oh good gracious me I hope you never kept yourself a bachelor so long on my account!" tittered Flora; "but of course you never did why should you, pray don't answer, I don't know where I'm running to, oh do tell me something about the Chinese ladies whether their eyes are really so long and narrow always putting me in mind of mother-of-pearl fish at cards and do they really wear tails down their back and plaited too or is it only the men, and when they pull their hair so very tight off their foreheads don't they hurt themselves, and why do they stick little bells all over their bridges and temples and hats and things or don't they really do it!" Flora gave him another of her old glances. Instantly she went on again, as if he had spoken in reply for some time.

"Then it's all true and they really do! good gracious Arthur!—pray excuse me—old habit—Mr. Clennam far more proper—what a country to live in for so long a time, and with so many lanterns and umbrellas too how very dark and wet the climate ought to be and no doubt actually is, and the sums of money that must be made by those two trades where everybody carries them and hangs them everywhere, the little shoes too and the feet screwed back in infancy is quite surprising, what a traveller you are!"

In his ridiculous distress, Clennam received another of the old glances, without in the least knowing what to do with it.

"Dear dear," said Flora, "only to think of the changes at home Arthur—cannot overcome it, seems so natural, Mr. Clennam far more proper—since you became familiar with the Chinese customs and language which I am persuaded you speak like a Native if not better for you were always quick and clever though immensely difficult no doubt, I am sure the tea chests alone would kill *me* if I tried, such changes Arthur —I am doing it again, seems so natural, most improper—as no one could have believed, who could have ever imagined Mrs. Finching when I can't imagine it myself!"

"Is that your married name?" asked Arthur, struck, in the midst of all this, by a certain warmth of heart that expressed itself in her tone when she referred, however oddly, to the youthful relation in which they had stood to one another. "Finching?"

"Finching oh yes isn't it a dreadful name, but as Mr. F said when he proposed to me which he did seven times and handsomely consented I must say to be what he used to call on liking twelve months after all, he wasn't answerable for it and couldn't help it could he, Excellent man, not at all like you but excellent man!"

Flora had at last talked herself out of breath for one moment. One moment; for she recovered breath in the act of raising a minute corner of her pocket-handkerchief to her eye, as a tribute to the ghost of the departed Mr. F, and began again.

"No one could dispute, Arthur—Mr. Clennam—that it's quite right you should be formally friendly to me under the altered circumstances and indeed you couldn't be any-thing else, at least I suppose not you ought to know, but I can't help recalling that there *was* a time when things were very different."

"My dear Mrs. Finching," Arthur began, struck by the good tone again.

"Oh not that nasty ugly name, say Flora!"

"Flora. I assure you, Flora, I am happy in seeing you once more, and in finding that, like me, you have not forgotten the old foolish dreams, when we saw all before us in the light of our youth and hope."

"You don't seem so," pouted Flora, "you take it very coolly, but however I know you are disappointed in me, I suppose the Chinese ladies—Mandarinesses if you call them so—are the cause or perhaps I am the cause myself, it's just as likely."

"No, no," Clennam entreated, "don't say that."

"Oh I must you know," said Flora, in a positive tone, "what nonsense not to, I know I am not what you expected, I know that very well."

In the midst of her rapidity, she had found that out with the quick perception of a cleverer woman. The inconsistent and profoundly unreasonable way in which she instantly went on, nevertheless, to interweave their long-abandoned boy and girl relations with their present interview, made Clennam feel as if he were lightheaded.

"One remark," said Flora, giving their conversation, without the slightest notice and to the great terror of Clennam, the tone of a love-quarrel, "I wish to make, one explanation I wish to offer, when your Mama came and made a scene of it with my Papa and when I was called down into the little breakfast-room where they were looking at one another with your Mama's parasol between them seated on two chairs like mad bulls what was I to do?"

"My dear Mrs. Finching," urged Clennam—"all so long ago and so long concluded, is it worth while seriously to——"

"I can't Arthur," returned Flora, "be denounced as heartless by the whole society of China without setting myself right when I have the opportunity of doing so, and you must be very well aware that there was Paul and Virginia which had to be returned and which was returned without note or comment, not that I mean to say you could have written to me watched as I was but if it had only come back with a red wafer on the cover I should have known that it meant Come to Pekin Nankeen and What's the third place barefoot."

"My dear Mrs. Finching, you were not to blame, and I never blamed you. We were both too young, too dependent and helpless, to do anything but accept our separation.—Pray think how long ago," gently remonstrated Arthur.

"One more remark," proceeded Flora with unslackened volubility, "I wish to make, one more explanation I wish to offer, for five days I had a cold in the head from crying which I passed entirely in the back drawing-room—there is the back drawing-room still on the first floor and still at the back of the house to confirm my words—when that dreary period had passed a lull succeeded years rolled on and Mr. F became acquainted with us at a mutual friend's, he was all attention he called next day he soon began to call three evenings a week and to send in little things for supper, it was not love on Mr. F's part it was adoration, Mr. F proposed with the full approval of Papa and what could I do?"

"Nothing whatever," said Arthur, with the cheerfulest readiness, "but what you did. Let an old friend assure you of his full conviction that you did quite right."

"One last remark," proceeded Flora, rejecting commonplace life with a wave of her hand, "I wish to make, one last explanation I wish to offer, there *was* a time ere Mr. F first paid attentions incapable of being mistaken, but that is past and was not to be, dear Mr. Clennam you no longer wear a golden chain you are free I trust you may be happy, here is Papa who is always tiresome and putting in his nose everywhere where he is not wanted."

With these words, and with a hasty gesture fraught with timid caution—such a gesture had Clennam's eyes been familiar with in the old time—poor Flora left herself, at

eighteen years of age, a long long way behind again; and
came to a full stop at last.

Or rather, she left about half of herself at eighteen years
of age behind, and grafted the rest on to the relict of the
late Mr. F; thus making a moral mermaid of herself, which
her once boy-lover contemplated with feelings wherein his
sense of the sorrowful and his sense of the comical were
curiously blended.

For example. As if there were a secret understanding
between herself and Clennam of the most thrilling nature; as
if the first of a train of post-chaises and four, extending all
the way to Scotland, were at that moment round the corner;
and as if she couldn't (and wouldn't) have walked into the
Parish Church with him, under the shade of the family
umbrella, with the Patriarchal blessing on her head, and the
perfect concurrence of all mankind; Flora comforted her soul
with agonies of mysterious signalling, expressing dread of
discovery. With the sensation of becoming more and more
lightheaded every minute, Clennam saw the relict of the late
Mr. F enjoying herself in the most wonderful manner, by
putting herself and him in their old places, and going through
all the old performances—now, when the stage was dusty,
when the scenery was faded, when the youthful actors were
dead, when the orchestra was empty, when the lights were
out. And still, through all this grotesque revival of what he
remembered as having once been prettily natural to her, he
could not but feel that it revived at sight of him, and that
there was a tender memory in it.

The Patriarch insisted on his staying to dinner, and Flora
signalled "Yes!" Clennam so wished he could have done
more than stay to dinner—so heartily wished he could have
found the Flora that had been, or that never had been—
that he thought the least atonement he could make for the
disappointment he almost felt ashamed of, was to give himself
up to the family desire. Therefore, he stayed to dinner.

Pancks dined with them. Pancks steamed out of his little

dock at a quarter before six, and bore straight down for the Patriarch, who happened to be then driving, in an inane manner, through a stagnant account of Bleeding Heart Yard. Pancks instantly made fast to him and hauled him out.

"Bleeding Heart Yard?" said Pancks, with a puff and a snort. "It's a troublesome property. Don't pay you badly, but rents are very hard to get there. You have more trouble with that one place, than with all the places belonging to you."

Just as the big ship in tow gets the credit, with most spectators, of being the powerful object, so the Patriarch usually seemed to have said himself whatever Pancks said for him.

"Indeed?" returned Clennam, upon whom this impression was so efficiently made by a mere gleam of the polished head, that he spoke the ship instead of the Tug. "The people are so poor there?"

"*You* can't say, you know," snorted Pancks, taking one of his dirty hands out of his rusty iron-grey pockets to bite his nails, if he could find any, and turning his beads of eyes upon his employer, "whether they're poor or not. They say they are, but they all say that. When a man says he's rich, you're generally sure he isn't. Besides, if they *are* poor, you can't help it. You'd be poor yourself if you didn't get your rents."

"True enough," said Arthur.

"You're not going to keep open house for all the poor of London," pursued Pancks. "You're not going to lodge 'em for nothing. You're not going to open your gates wide and let 'em come free. Not if you know it, you ain't."

Mr. Casby shook his head, in placid and benignant generality.

"If a man takes a room of you at half-a-crown a week, and when the week comes round hasn't got the half-crown, you say to that man, Why have you got the room, then? If you haven't got the one thing, why have you got the other? What have you been and done with your money? What do you mean by it? What are you up to? That's what *you*

say to a man of that sort; and if you didn't say it, more
shame for you!" Mr. Pancks here made a singular and
startling noise, produced by a strong blowing effort in the
region of the nose, unattended by any result but that
acoustic one.

"You have some extent of such property about the east
and north-east here, I believe?" said Clennam, doubtful
which of the two to address.

"Oh, pretty well," said Pancks. "You're not particular to
east or north-east, any point of the compass will do for you.
What you want is a good investment and a quick return.
You take it where you can find it. You ain't nice as to
situation—not you."

There was a fourth and most original figure in the Patriarchal tent, who also appeared before dinner. This was an
amazing little old woman, with a face like a staring wooden
doll too cheap for expression, and a stiff yellow wig perched
unevenly on the top of her head, as if the child who owned
the doll had driven a tack through it anywhere, so that it
only got fastened on. Another remarkable thing in this little
old woman was, that the same child seemed to have damaged
her face in two or three places with some blunt instrument
in the nature of a spoon; her countenance, and particularly
the tip of her nose, presenting the phenomena of several dints,
generally answering to the bowl of that article. A further
remarkable thing in this little old woman was, that she had
no name but Mr. F's Aunt.

She broke upon the visitor's view under the following
circumstances: Flora said when the first dish was being put
on the table, perhaps Mr. Clennam might not have heard
that Mr. F had left her a legacy? Clennam in return
implied his hope that Mr. F had endowed the wife whom
he adored, with the greater part of his worldly substance,
if not with all. Flora said, oh yes, she didn't mean that,
Mr. F had made a beautiful will, but he had left her as a
separate legacy, his Aunt. She then went out of the room

to fetch the legacy, and, on her return, rather triumphantly presented " Mr. F's Aunt."

The major characteristics discoverable by the stranger in Mr. F's Aunt, were extreme severity and grim taciturnity; sometimes interrupted by a propensity to offer remarks in a deep warning voice, which, being totally uncalled for by anything said by anybody, and traceable to no association of ideas, confounded and terrified the mind. Mr. F's Aunt may have thrown in these observations on some system of her own, and it may have been ingenious, or even subtle; but the key to it was wanted.

The neatly-served and well-cooked dinner (for everything about the Patriarchal household promoted quiet digestion) began with some soup, some fried soles, a butter-boat of shrimp sauce, and a dish of potatoes. The conversation still turned on the receipt of rents. Mr. F's Aunt, after regarding the company for ten minutes with a malevolent gaze, delivered the following fearful remark.

" When we lived at Henley, Barnes's gander was stole by tinkers."

Mr. Pancks courageously nodded his head and said, " All right, ma'am." But the effect of this mysterious communication upon Clennam was absolutely to frighten him. And another circumstance invested this old lady with peculiar terrors. Though she was always staring, she never acknowledged that she saw any individual. The polite and attentive stranger would desire, say, to consult her inclinations on the subject of potatoes. His expressive action would be hopelessly lost upon her, and what could he do? No man could say, " Mr. F's Aunt, will you permit me?" Every man retired from the spoon, as Clennam did, cowed and baffled.

There was mutton, a steak, and an apple-pie—nothing in the remotest way connected with ganders—and the dinner went on like a disenchanted feast, as it truly was. Once upon a time Clennam had sat at that table taking no heed of anything but Flora; now the principal heed he took of Flora was, to observe, against his will, that she was very fond of porter, that she combined a great deal of sherry with sentiment, and that if she were a little overgrown, it was upon substantial grounds. The last of the Patriarchs had always been a mighty eater, and he disposed of an immense quantity of solid food with the benignity of a good soul who was feeding some one else. Mr. Pancks, who was always in a hurry, and who referred at intervals to a little dirty note-book which he kept beside him (perhaps containing the names of the defaulters he meant to look up by way of dessert), took in his victuals much as if he were coaling; with a good deal of noise, a good deal of dropping about, and a puff and a snort occasionally, as if he were nearly ready to steam away.

All through dinner, Flora combined her present appetite for eating and drinking, with her past appetite for romantic love, in a way that made Clennam afraid to lift his eyes from his plate; since he could not look towards her without receiving some glance of mysterious meaning or warning, as if they were engaged in a plot. Mr. F's Aunt sat silently defying him with an aspect of the greatest bitterness, until the removal of the cloth and the appearance of the decanters, when she originated another observation—struck into the conversation like a clock, without consulting anybody.

Flora had just said, "Mr. Clennam, will you give me a glass of port for Mr. F's Aunt ?"

"The Monument near London Bridge," that lady instantly proclaimed, "was put up arter the Great Fire of London; and the Great Fire of London was not the fire in which your uncle George's workshops was burned down."

Mr. Pancks, with his former courage, said "Indeed, ma'am ? All right !" But appearing to be incensed by imaginary contradiction, or other ill-usage, Mr. F's Aunt, instead of relapsing into silence, made the following additional proclamation :

"I hate a fool !"

She imparted to this sentiment, in itself almost Solomonic, so extremely injurious and personal a character, by levelling it straight at the visitor's head, that it became necessary to lead Mr. F's Aunt from the room. This was quietly done by Flora; Mr. F's Aunt offering no resistance, but inquiring on her way out "What he come there for, then?" with implacable animosity.

When Flora returned, she explained that her legacy was a clever old lady, but was sometimes a little singular, and "took dislikes"—peculiarities of which Flora seemed to be proud rather than otherwise. As Flora's good nature shone in the case, Clennam had no fault to find with the old lady for eliciting it, now that he was relieved from the terrors of her presence; and they took a glass or two of wine in peace. Foreseeing then that the Pancks would shortly get under weigh, and that the Patriarch would go to sleep, he pleaded the necessity of visiting his mother, and asked Mr. Pancks in which direction he was going?

"Citywards, sir," said Pancks.

"Shall we walk together?" said Arthur.

"Quite agreeable," said Pancks.

Meanwhile Flora was murmuring in rapid snatches for his ear, that there *was* a time and that the past was a yawning gulf however and that a golden chain no longer bound him and that she revered the memory of the late Mr. F and that she should be at home to-morrow at half-past one and that the decrees of Fate were beyond recall and that she considered nothing so improbable as that he ever walked on the north-west side of Gray's-Inn Gardens at exactly four o'clock in the afternoon. He tried at parting to give his hand in frankness to the existing Flora—not the vanished Flora, or the Mermaid—but Flora wouldn't have it, couldn't have it, was wholly destitute of the power of separating herself and him from their bygone characters. He left the house miserably enough; and so much more lightheaded than ever, that if it had not been his good fortune to be towed away,

Mr. F's Aunt is conducted into Retirement

he might, for the first quarter of an hour, have drifted anywhere.

When he began to come to himself, in the cooler air and
the absence of Flora, he found Pancks at full speed, cropping
such scanty pasturage of nails as he could find, and snorting
at intervals. These, in conjunction with one hand in his
pocket and his roughened hat hind side before, were evidently
the conditions under which he reflected.

" A fresh night ! " said Arthur.

" Yes, it's pretty fresh," assented Pancks. " As a stranger
you feel the climate more than I do, I dare say. Indeed I
haven't got time to feel it."

" You lead such a busy life ? "

" Yes, I have always some of 'em to look up, or something to look after. But I like business," said Pancks, getting
on a little faster. " What's a man made for ? "

" For nothing else ? " said Clennam.

Pancks put the counter question, " What else ? " It
packed up, in the smallest compass, a weight that had rested
on Clennam's life ; and he made no answer.

" That's what I ask our weekly tenants," said Pancks.
" Some of 'em will pull long faces to me, and say, Poor
as you see us, master, we're always grinding, drudging,
toiling, every minute we're awake. I say to them, What
else are you made for ? It shuts them up. They haven't
a word to answer. What else are you made for ? That
clinches it."

"Ah dear, dear, dear ! " sighed Clennam.

" Here am I," said Pancks, pursuing his argument with
the weekly tenant. " What else do you suppose I think I
am made for ? Nothing. Rattle me out of bed early, set
me going, give me as short a time as you like to bolt my
meals in, and keep me at it. Keep me always at it, and I'll
keep you always at it, you keep somebody else always at it.
There you are with the Whole Duty of Man in a commercial
country."

When they had walked a little further in silence, Clennam said : " Have you no taste for anything, Mr. Pancks ? "

" What's taste ? " drily retorted Pancks.

" Let us say inclination."

" I have an inclination to get money, sir," said Pancks, " if you will show me how." He blew off that sound again, and it occurred to his companion for the first time that it was his way of laughing. He was a singular man in all respects ; he might not have been quite in earnest, but that the short, hard, rapid manner in which he shot out these cinders of principles, as if it were done by mechanical revolvency, seemed irreconcilable with banter.

" You are no great reader, I suppose ? " said Clennam.

" Never read anything but letters and accounts. Never collect anything but advertisements relative to next of kin. If *that's* a taste, I have got that. You're not of the Clennams of Cornwall, Mr. Clennam ? "

" Not that I ever heard of."

" I know you're not. I asked your mother, sir. She has too much character to let a chance escape her."

" Supposing I had been of the Clennams of Cornwall ? "

" You'd have heard of something to your advantage."

" Indeed ! I have heard of little enough to my advantage for some time."

" There's a Cornish property going a begging, sir, and not a Cornish Clennam to have it for the asking," said Pancks, taking his note-book from his breast pocket and putting it in again. " I turn off here. I wish you good night."

" Good night ! " said Clennam. But the Tug suddenly lightened, and, untrammelled by having any weight in tow, was already puffing away into the distance.

They had crossed Smithfield together, and Clennam was left alone at the corner of Barbican. He had no intention of presenting himself in his mother's dismal room that night, and could not have felt more depressed and cast away if he had been in a wilderness. He turned slowly down Aldersgate

Street, and was pondering his way along towards Saint Paul's, purposing to come into one of the great thoroughfares for the sake of their light and life, when a crowd of people flocked towards him on the same pavement, and he stood aside against a shop to let them pass. As they came up, he made out that they were gathered around a something that was carried on men's shoulders. He soon saw that it was a litter, hastily made of a shutter or some such thing; and a recumbent figure upon it, and the scraps of conversation in the crowd, and a muddy bundle carried by one man, and a muddy hat carried by another, informed him that an accident had occurred. The litter stopped under a lamp before it had passed him half-a-dozen paces, for some re-adjustment of the burden; and, the crowd stopping too, he found himself in the midst of the array.

"An accident going to the Hospital?" he asked an old man beside him, who stood shaking his head, inviting conversation.

"Yes," said the man, "along of them Mails. They ought to be prosecuted and fined, them Mails. They come a racing out of Lad Lane and Wood Street at twelve or fourteen mile a hour, them Mails do. The only wonder is, that people ain't killed oftener by them Mails."

"This person is not killed, I hope?"

"I don't know!" said the man, "it an't for the want of a will in them Mails, if he an't." The speaker having folded his arms, and set in comfortably to address his depreciation of them Mails to any of the bystanders who would listen, several voices, out of pure sympathy with the sufferer, confirmed him; one voice saying to Clennam, "They're a public nuisance, them Mails, sir;" another, "*I* see one on 'em pull up within half a inch of a boy, last night;" another, "*I* see one on 'em go over a cat, sir—and it might have been your own mother;" and all representing, by implication, that if he happened to possess any public influence, he could not use it better than against them Mails.

197

"Why, a native Englishman is put to it every night of his life, to save his life from them Mails," argued the first old man; "and *he* knows when they're a coming round the corner, to tear him limb from limb. What can you expect from a poor foreigner who don't know nothing about 'em!"

"Is this a foreigner?" said Clennam, leaning forward to look.

In the midst of such replies as "Frenchman, sir," "Porteghee, sir," "Dutchman, sir," "Prooshan, sir," and other conflicting testimony, he now heard a feeble voice asking, both in Italian and in French, for water. A general remark going round, in reply, of "Ah, poor fellow, he says he'll never get over it; and no wonder!" Clennam begged to be allowed to pass, as he understood the poor creature. He was immediately handed to the front, to speak to him.

"First, he wants some water," he said, looking round. (A dozen good fellows dispersed to get it.) "Are you badly hurt, my friend?" he asked the man on the litter, in Italian.

"Yes, sir; yes, yes, yes. It's my leg, it's my leg. But it pleases me to hear the old music, though I am very bad."

"You are a traveller! Stay! See the water! Let me give you some."

They had rested the litter on a pile of paving stones. It was at a convenient height from the ground, and by stooping he could lightly raise the head with one hand, and hold the glass to the lips with the other. A little, muscular, brown man, with black hair and white teeth. A lively face, apparently. Ear-rings in his ears.

"That's well. You are a traveller?"

"Surely, sir."

"A stranger in this city?"

"Surely, surely, altogether. I am arrived this unhappy evening."

"From what country?"

"Marseilles."

"Why, see there! I also! Almost as much a stranger

here as you, though born here, I came from Marseilles a little while ago. Don't be cast down." The face looked up at him imploringly, as he rose from wiping it, and gently replaced the coat that covered the writhing figure. "I won't leave you, till you shall be well taken care of. Courage! You will be very much better, half-an-hour hence."

"Ah! Altro, Altro!" cried the poor little man, in a faintly incredulous tone; and as they took him up, hung out his right hand to give the forefinger a back-handed shake in the air.

Arthur Clennam turned; and walking beside the litter, and saying an encouraging word now and then, accompanied it to the neighbouring hospital of Saint Bartholomew. None of the crowd but the bearers and he being admitted, the disabled man was soon laid on a table in a cool, methodical way, and carefully examined by a surgeon: who was as near at hand, and as ready to appear, as Calamity herself. "He hardly knows an English word," said Clennam; "is he badly hurt?" "Let us know all about it first," said the surgeon, continuing his examination with a business-like delight in it, "before we pronounce."

After trying the leg with a finger and two fingers, and one hand and two hands, and over and under, and up and down, and in this direction and in that, and approvingly remarking on the points of interest to another gentleman who joined him, the surgeon at last clapped the patient on the shoulder, and said, "He won't hurt. He'll do very well. It's difficult enough, but we shall not want him to part with his leg this time." Which Clennam interpreted to the patient, who was full of gratitude, and, in his demonstrative way, kissed both the interpreter's hand and the surgeon's several times.

"It's a serious injury, I suppose?" said Clennam.

"Ye-es," replied the surgeon, with the thoughtful pleasure of an artist, contemplating the work upon his easel. "Yes, it's enough. There's a compound fracture above the knee, and a dislocation below. They are both of a beautiful kind."

He gave the patient a friendly clap on the shoulder again, as if he really felt that he was a very good fellow indeed, and worthy of all commendation for having broken his leg in a manner interesting to science.

"He speaks French?" said the surgeon.

"Oh yes, he speaks French."

"He'll be at no loss here, then.—You have only to bear a little pain like a brave fellow, my friend, and to be thankful that all goes as well as it does," he added, in that tongue, "and you'll walk again to a marvel. Now, let us see whether there's anything else the matter, and how our ribs are?"

There was nothing else the matter, and our ribs were sound. Clennam remained until everything possible to be done had been skilfully and promptly done—the poor belated wanderer in a strange land movingly besought that favour of him—and lingered by the bed to which he was in due time removed, until he had fallen into a doze. Even then he wrote a few words for him on his card, with a promise to return to-morrow, and left it to be given to him when he should awake.

All these proceedings occupied so long, that it struck eleven o'clock at night as he came out at the Hospital Gate. He had hired a lodging for the present in Covent Garden, and he took the nearest way to that quarter, by Snow Hill and Holborn.

Left to himself again, after the solicitude and compassion of his last adventure, he was naturally in a thoughtful mood. As naturally, he could not walk on thinking for ten minutes, without recalling Flora. She necessarily recalled to him his life, with all its misdirection and little happiness.

When he got to his lodging, he sat down before the dying fire, as he had stood at the window of his old room looking out upon the blackened forest of chimneys, and turned his gaze back upon the gloomy vista by which he had come to that stage in his existence. So long, so bare, so blank. No childhood; no youth, except for one remembrance; that one remembrance proved, only that day, to be a piece of folly.

It was a misfortune to him, trifle as it might have been to another. For, while all that was hard and stern in his recollection, remained Reality on being proved—was obdurate to the sight and touch, and relaxed nothing of its old indomitable grimness—the one tender recollection of his experience would not bear the same test, and melted away. He had foreseen this, on the former night, when he had dreamed with waking eyes; but he had not felt it then; and he had now.

He was a dreamer in such wise, because he was a man who had, deep-rooted in his nature, a belief in all the gentle and good things his life had been without. Bred in meanness and hard dealing, this had rescued him to be a man of honourable mind and open hand. Bred in coldness and severity, this had rescued him to have a warm and sympathetic heart. Bred in a creed too darkly audacious to pursue, through its process of reversing the making of man in the image of his Creator to the making of his Creator in the image of an erring man, this had rescued him to judge not, and in humility to be merciful, and have hope and charity.

And this saved him still from the whimpering weakness and cruel selfishness of holding that because such a happiness or such a virtue had not come into his little path, or worked well for him, therefore it was not in the great scheme, but was reducible, when found in appearance, to the basest elements. A disappointed mind he had, but a mind too firm and healthy for such unwholesome air. Leaving himself in the dark, it could rise into the light, seeing it shine on others and hailing it.

Therefore, he sat before his dying fire, sorrowful to think upon the way by which he had come to that night, yet not strewing poison on the way by which other men had come to it. That he should have missed so much, and at his time of life should look so far about him for any staff to bear him company upon his downward journey and cheer it, was a just regret. He looked at the fire from which the blaze departed, from which the after-glow subsided, in which the ashes turned grey, from which they dropped to dust, and thought, "How soon I too shall pass through such changes, and be gone!"

To review his life was like descending a green tree in fruit and flower, and seeing all the branches wither and drop off one by one, as he came down towards them.

"From the unhappy suppression of my youngest days, through the rigid and unloving home that followed them, through my departure, my long exile, my return, my mother's welcome, my intercourse with her since, down to the afternoon of this day with poor Flora," said Arthur Clennam, "what have I found!"

His door was softly opened, and these spoken words startled him, and came as if they were an answer:

"Little Dorrit."

CHAPTER XIV

ARTHUR CLENNAM rose hastily, and saw her standing at the door. This history must sometimes see with Little Dorrit's eyes, and shall begin that course by seeing him.

Little Dorrit looked into a dim room, which seemed a spacious one to her, and grandly furnished. Courtly ideas of Covent Garden, as a place with famous coffee-houses, where gentlemen wearing gold-laced coats and swords had quarrelled and fought duels; costly ideas of Covent Garden, as a place where there were flowers in winter at guineas a-piece, pine-apples at guineas a pound, and peas at guineas a pint; picturesque ideas of Covent Garden, as a place where there was a mighty theatre, showing wonderful and beautiful sights to richly-dressed ladies and gentlemen, and which was for ever far beyond the reach of poor Fanny or poor uncle; desolate ideas of Covent Garden, as having all those arches in it, where the miserable children in rags among whom she had just now passed, like young rats, slunk and hid, fed on offal, huddled together for warmth, and were hunted about (look to the rats young and old, all ye Barnacles, for before God they are eating away our foundations, and will bring the roofs on our heads!); teeming ideas of Covent Garden, as a place of past and present mystery, romance, abundance, want, beauty, ugliness, fair country gardens, and foul street-gutters; all confused together,—made the room dimmer than it was, in Little Dorrit's eyes, as they timidly saw it from the door.

At first in the chair before the gone-out fire, and then turned round wondering to see her, was the gentleman whom she sought. The brown, grave gentleman, who smiled so pleasantly, who was so frank and considerate in his manner, and yet in whose earnestness there was something that reminded her of his mother, with the great difference that she was earnest in asperity and he in gentleness. Now he regarded her with that attentive and inquiring look before which Little Dorrit's eyes had always fallen, and before which they fell still.

"My poor child ! Here at midnight ? "

" I said Little Dorrit, sir, on purpose to prepare you. I knew you must be very much surprised."

" Are you alone ? "

" No, sir, I have got Maggy with me."

Considering her entrance sufficiently prepared for by this mention of her name, Maggy appeared from the landing outside, on the broad grin. She instantly suppressed that manifestation, however, and became fixedly solemn.

"And I have no fire," said Clennam. " And you are— " He was going to say so lightly clad, but stopped himself in what would have been a reference to her poverty, saying instead, " And it is so cold."

Putting the chair from which he had risen nearer to the grate, he made her sit down in it ; and hurriedly bringing wood and coal, heaped them together and got a blaze.

" Your foot is like marble, my child ; " he had happened to touch it, while stooping on one knee at his work of kindling the fire ; " put it nearer the warmth." Little Dorrit thanked him hastily. It was quite warm, it was very warm ! It smote upon his heart to feel that she hid her thin, worn shoe.

Little Dorrit was not ashamed of her poor shoes. He knew her story, and it was not that. Little Dorrit had a misgiving that he might blame her father, if he saw them ; that he might think, " why did he dine to-day, and leave this little creature to the mercy of the cold stones!" She had no belief that it would have been a just reflection ; she simply knew, by experience, that such delusions did sometimes present themselves to people. It was a part of her father's misfortunes that they did.

"Before I say anything else," Little Dorrit began, sitting before the pale fire, and raising her eyes again to the face which in its harmonious look of interest, and pity, and protection, she felt to be a mystery far above her in degree, and almost removed beyond her guessing at; "may I tell you something, sir ? "

"Yes, my child."

A slight shade of distress fell upon her, at his so often calling her a child. She was surprised that he should see it, or think of such a slight thing ; but he said directly :

"I wanted a tender word, and could think of no other. As you just now gave yourself the name they give you at my mother's, and as that is the name by which I always think of you, let me call you Little Dorrit."

"Thank you, sir, I should like it better than any name."

"Little Dorrit."

"Little mother," Maggy (who had been falling asleep) put in, as a correction.

"It's all the same, Maggy," returned Dorrit, "all the same."

"Is it all the same, mother ? "

"Just the same."

Maggy laughed, and immediately snored. In Little Dorrit's eyes and ears, the uncouth figure and the uncouth sound were as pleasant as could be. There was a glow of pride in her big child, overspreading her face, when it again met the eyes of the grave, brown gentleman. She wondered what he was thinking of, as he looked at Maggy and her. She thought what a good father he would be. How, with some such look, he would counsel and cherish his daughter.

" What I was going to tell you, sir," said Little Dorrit, " is, that my brother is at large."

Arthur was rejoiced to hear it, and hoped he would do well.

" And what I was going to tell you, sir," said Little Dorrit, trembling in all her little figure and in her voice, " is, that I am not to know whose generosity released him —am never to ask, and am never to be told, and am never to thank that gentleman with all my grateful heart ! "

He would probably need no thanks, Clennam said. Very likely he would be thankful himself (and with reason), that he had had the means and chance of doing a little service to her, who well deserved a great one.

" And what I was going to say, sir, is," said Little Dorrit, trembling more and more, " that if I knew him, and I might, I would tell him that he can never, never know how I feel his goodness, and how my good father would feel it. And what I was going to say, sir, is, that if I knew him, and I might—but I don't know him and I must not—I know that !—I would tell him that I shall never any more lie down to sleep, without having prayed to Heaven to bless him and reward him. And if I knew him, and I might, I would go down on my knees to him, and take his hand and kiss it, and ask him not to draw it away, but to leave it— O to leave it for a moment—and let my thankful tears fall on it, for I have no other thanks to give him ! "

Little Dorrit had put his hand to her lips, and would have kneeled to him, but he gently prevented her, and re-placed her in her chair. Her eyes, and the tones of her voice, had thanked him far better than she thought. He was not able to say, quite as composedly as usual, " There, Little Dorrit, there, there, there ! We will suppose that you did know this person, and that you might do all this, and that it was all done. And now tell me, who am quite another person —who am nothing more than the friend who begged you to trust him—why you are out at midnight, and what it is that brings you so far through the streets at this late hour, my slight, delicate," child was on his lips again, " Little Dorrit ! "

" Maggy and I have been to-night," she answered, subduing herself with the quiet effort that had long been natural to her, " to the theatre where my sister is engaged."

" And oh ain't it a Ev'nly place," suddenly interrupted Maggy, who seemed to have the power of going to sleep and waking up whenever she chose. " Almost as good as a hospital. Only there ain't no Chicking in it."

Here she shook herself, and fell asleep again.

" We went there," said Little Dorrit, glancing at her charge, " because I like sometimes to know, of my own knowledge, that my sister is doing well ; and like to see her there, with my own eyes, when neither she nor Uncle is aware. It is very seldom indeed that I can do that, because when I am not out at work I am with my father, and even when I am out at work, I hurry home to him. But I pretend to-night that I am at a party."

As she made the confession, timidly hesitating, she raised her eyes to the face, and read its expression so plainly that she answered it.

" Oh no, certainly ! I never was at a party in my life."

She paused a little under his attentive look, and then said, " I hope there is no harm in it. I could never have been of any use, if I had not pretended a little."

She feared that he was blaming her in his mind, for so devising to contrive for them, think for them, and watch over them, without their knowledge or gratitude ; perhaps even with their reproaches for supposed neglect. But what was really in his mind, was the weak figure with its strong purpose, the thin worn shoes, the insufficient dress, and the pretence of recreation and enjoyment. He asked where the supposititious party was ? At a place where she worked, answered Little Dorrit, blushing. She had said very little

207

about it; only a few words to make her father easy. Her father did not believe it to be a grand party—indeed he might suppose that. And she glanced for an instant at the shawl she wore.

"It is the first night," said Little Dorrit, "that I have ever been away from home. And London looks so large, so barren, and so wild." In Little Dorrit's eyes, its vastness under the black sky was awful; a tremor passed over her as she said the words.

"But this is not," she added, with the quiet effort again, "what I have come to trouble you with, sir. My sister's having found a friend, a lady she has told me of and made me rather anxious about, was the first cause of my coming away from home. And being away, and coming (on purpose) round by where you lived, and seeing a light in the window——"

Not for the first time. No, not for the first time. In Little Dorrit's eyes, the outside of that window had been a distant star on other nights than this. She had toiled out of her way, tired and troubled, to look up at it, and wonder about the grave, brown gentleman from so far off, who had spoken to her as a friend and protector.

"There were three things," said Little Dorrit, "that I thought I would like to say, if you were alone and I might come up-stairs. First, what I have tried to say, but never can—never shall——"

"Hush, hush! That is done with, and disposed of. Let us pass to the second," said Clennam, smiling her agitation away, making the blaze shine upon her, and putting wine and cake and fruit towards her on the table.

"I think," said Little Dorrit—"this is the second thing, sir—I think Mrs. Clennam must have found out my secret, and must know where I come from and where I go to. Where I live, I mean."

"Indeed!" returned Clennam, quickly. He asked her, after a short consideration, why she supposed so.

"I think," replied Little Dorrit, "that Mr. Flintwinch must have watched me."

And why, Clennam asked, as he turned his eyes upon the fire, bent his brows, and considered again; why did she suppose that?

"I have met him twice. Both times near home. Both times at night, when I was going back. Both times I thought (though that may easily be my mistake), that he hardly looked as if he had met me by accident."

"Did he say anything?"

"No; he only nodded and put his head on one side."

"The devil take his head!" mused Clennam, still looking at the fire; "it's always on one side."

He roused himself to persuade her to put some wine to her lips, and to touch something to eat—it was very difficult, she was so timid and shy—and then said, musing again:

"Is my mother at all changed to you?"

"Oh, not at all. She is just the same. I wondered whether I had better tell her my history. I wondered whether I might—I mean, whether you would like me to tell her. I wondered," said Little Dorrit, looking at him in a suppliant way, and gradually withdrawing her eyes as he looked at her, "whether you would advise me what I ought to do."

"Little Dorrit," said Clennam; and the phrase had already begun, between those two, to stand for a hundred gentle phrases, according to the varying tone and connexion in which it was used; "do nothing. I will have some talk with my old friend, Mrs. Affery. Do nothing, Little Dorrit—except refresh yourself with such means as there are here. I entreat you to do that."

"Thank you, I am not hungry. Nor," said Little Dorrit, as he softly put her glass towards her, "nor thirsty.—I think Maggy might like something, perhaps."

"We will make her find pockets presently for all there is here," said Clennam: "but before we awake her, there was a third thing to say."

"Yes. You will not be offended, sir?"

"I promise that, unreservedly."

"It will sound strange. I hardly know how to say it. Don't think it unreasonable or ungrateful in me," said Little Dorrit, with returning and increasing agitation.

"No, no, no. I am sure it will be natural and right. I am not afraid that I shall put a wrong construction on it, whatever it is."

"Thank you. You are coming back to see my father again?"

"Yes."

"You have been so good and thoughtful as to write him a note, saying that you are coming to-morrow?"

"Oh, that was nothing! Yes."

"Can you guess," said Little Dorrit, folding her small hands tight in one another, and looking at him with all the earnestness of her soul looking steadily out of her eyes, "what I am going to ask you not to do?"

"I think I can. But I may be wrong."

"No, you are not wrong," said Little Dorrit, shaking her head. "If we should want it so very, very badly that we cannot do without it, let me ask you for it."

"I will,—I will."

"Don't encourage him to ask. Don't understand him if he does ask. Don't give it to him. Save him and spare him that, and you will be able to think better of him!"

Clennam said—not very plainly, seeing those tears glistening in her anxious eyes—that her wish should be sacred with him.

"You don't know what he is," she said; "you don't know what he really is. How can you, seeing him there all at once, dear love, and not gradually, as I have done! You have been so good to us, so delicately and truly good, that I want him to be better in your eyes than in anybody's. And I cannot bear to think," cried Little Dorrit, covering her tears with her hands, "I cannot bear to think that you of all the world should see him in his only moments of degradation."

"Pray," said Clennam, "do not be so distressed. Pray, pray, Little Dorrit! This is quite understood now."

"Thank you, sir. Thank you! I have tried very much to keep myself from saying this; I have thought about it, days and nights; but when I knew for certain you were coming again, I made up my mind to speak to you. Not because I am ashamed of him," she dried her tears quickly, "but because I know him better than any one does, and love him, and am proud of him."

Relieved of this weight, Little Dorrit was nervously anxious to be gone. Maggy being broad awake, and in the act of distantly gloating over the fruit and cakes with chuckles of anticipation, Clennam made the best diversion in his power by pouring her out a glass of wine, which she drank in a series of loud smacks; putting her hand upon her windpipe after every one, and saying, breathless, with her eyes in a prominent state, "Oh ain't it d'licious! Ain't it hospitally!" When she had finished the wine and these encomiums, he charged her to load her basket (she was never without her basket) with every eatable thing upon the table, and to take especial care to leave no scrap behind. Maggy's pleasure in doing this, and her little mother's pleasure in seeing Maggy pleased, was as good a turn as circumstances could have given to the late conversation.

"But the gates will have been locked long ago," said Clennam, suddenly remembering it. "Where are you going?"

"I am going to Maggy's lodging," answered Little Dorrit. "I shall be quite safe, quite well taken care of."

"I must accompany you there," said Clennam. "I cannot let you go alone."

"Yes, pray leave us to go there by ourselves. Pray do!" begged Little Dorrit.

She was so earnest in the petition, that Clennam felt a delicacy in obtruding himself upon her: the rather, because

he could well understand that Maggy's lodging was of the
obscurest sort. "Come, Maggy," said Little Dorrit, cheerily,
"we shall do very well; we know the way, by this time,
Maggy?"

"Yes, yes, little mother; we know the way," chuckled
Maggy. And away they went. Little Dorrit turned at the
door to say "God bless you!" She said it very softly, but
perhaps she may have been as audible above—who knows!—
as a whole cathedral choir.

Arthur Clennam suffered them to pass the corner of the
street, before he followed at a distance; not with any idea
of encroaching a second time on Little Dorrit's privacy, but
to satisfy his mind by seeing her secure, in the neighbourhood to which she was accustomed. So diminutive she looked,
so fragile and defenceless against the bleak damp weather,
flitting along in the shuffling shadow of her charge, that he
felt, in his compassion, and in his habit of considering her a
child apart from the rest of the rough world, as if he would
have been glad to take her up in his arms and carry her to
her journey's end.

In course of time she came into the leading thoroughfare where the Marshalsea was, and then he saw them slacken
their pace, and soon turn down a by-street. He stopped,
felt that he had no right to go further, and slowly left them.
He had no suspicion that they ran any risk of being houseless
until morning; had no idea of the truth, until long, long
afterwards.

But, said Little Dorrit, when they stopped at a poor
dwelling all in darkness, and heard no sound on listening at
the door, "Now, this is a good lodging for you, Maggy, and
we must not give offence. Consequently, we will only knock
twice, and not very loud; and if we cannot wake them so,
we must walk about till day."

Once, Little Dorrit knocked with a careful hand, and
listened. Twice, Little Dorrit knocked with a careful hand,
and listened. All was close and still. "Maggy, we must

do the best we can, my dear. We must be patient, and wait for day."

It was a chill dark night, with a damp wind blowing, when they came out into the leading street again, and heard the clocks strike half-past one. "In only five hours and a half," said Little Dorrit, "we shall be able to go home." To speak of home, and to go and look at it, it being so near, was a natural sequence. They went to the closed gate, and peeped through into the court-yard. "I hope he is sound asleep," said Little Dorrit, kissing one of the bars, "and does not miss me."

The gate was so familiar, and so like a companion, that they put down Maggy's basket in a corner to serve for a seat, and keeping close together, rested there for some time. While the street was empty and silent, Little Dorrit was not afraid; but when she heard a footstep at a distance, or saw a moving shadow among the street lamps, she was startled, and whispered, "Maggy, I see some one. Come away!" Maggy would then wake up more or less fretfully, and they would wander about a little, and come back again.

As long as eating was a novelty and an amusement, Maggy kept up pretty well. But, that period going by, she became querulous about the cold, and shivered and whimpered. "It will soon be over, dear," said Little Dorrit, patiently. "Oh it's all very fine for you, little mother," returned Maggy, "but I'm a poor thing, only ten years old." At last, in the dead of the night, when the street was very still indeed, Little Dorrit laid the heavy head upon her bosom, and soothed her to sleep. And thus she sat at the gate, as it were alone; looking up at the stars, and seeing the clouds pass over them in their wild flight—which was the dance at Little Dorrit's party.

"If it really was a party!" she thought once, as she sat there. "If it was light and warm and beautiful, and it was our house, and my poor dear was its master, and had never been inside these walls. And if Mr. Clennam was one of our visitors, and we were dancing to delightful music, and were all as gay and light-hearted as ever we could be! I wonder—" Such a vista of wonder opened out before her, that she sat looking up at the stars, quite lost; until Maggy was querulous again, and wanted to get up and walk.

Three o'clock, and half-past three, and they had passed over London Bridge. They had heard the rush of the tide against obstacles; and looked down, awed, through the dark vapour on the river; had seen little spots of lighted water where the bridge lamps were reflected, shining like demon eyes, with a terrible fascination in them for guilt and misery. They had shrunk past homeless people, lying coiled up in nooks. They had run from drunkards. They had started from slinking men, whistling and signing to one another at bye corners, or running away at full speed. Though everywhere the leader and the guide, Little Dorrit, happy for once in her youthful appearance, feigned to cling to and rely upon Maggy. And more than once some voice, from among a knot of brawling or prowling figures in their path, had called out to the rest, to "let the woman and the child go by!"

So, the woman and the child had gone by, and gone on, and five had sounded from the steeples. They were walking slowly towards the east, already looking for the first pale streak of day, when a woman came after them.

"What are you doing with the child?" she said to Maggy.

She was young—far too young to be there, Heaven knows! —and neither ugly nor wicked-looking. She spoke coarsely, but with no naturally coarse voice; there was even something musical in its sound.

"What are you doing with yourself?" retorted Maggy, for want of a better answer.

"Can't you see, without my telling you?"

"I don't know as I can," said Maggy.

"Killing myself. Now I have answered you, answer me. What are you doing with the child?"

The supposed child kept her head drooped down, and kept her form close at Maggy's side.

"Poor thing!" said the woman. "Have you no feeling, that you keep her out in the cruel streets at such a time as this? Have you no eyes, that you don't see how delicate and slender she is? Have you no sense (you don't look as if you had much), that you don't take more pity on this cold and trembling little hand?"

She had stepped across to that side, and held the hand between her own two, chafing it. "Kiss a poor lost creature, dear," she said, bending her face, "and tell me where she's taking you."

Little Dorrit turned towards her.

"Why, my God!" she said recoiling, "you're a woman!"

"Don't mind that!" said Little Dorrit, clasping one of her hands that had suddenly released hers. "I am not afraid of you."

"Then you had better be," she answered. "Have you no mother?"

"No."

"No father?"

"Yes, a very dear one."

"Go home to him, and be afraid of me. Let me go. Good night!"

"I must thank you first; let me speak to you as if I really were a child."

"You can't do it," said the woman. "You are kind and innocent; but you can't look at me out of a child's eyes. I never should have touched you, but I thought that you were a child." And with a strange, wild cry, she went away.

No day yet in the sky, but there was day in the resounding stones of the streets; in the waggons, carts, and coaches; in the workers going to various occupations; in the opening of early shops; in the traffic at markets; in the stir of the river-side. There was coming day in the flaring lights, with a feebler colour in them than they would have had at another

215

time; coming day in the increased sharpness of the air, and the ghastly dying of the night.

They went back again to the gate, intending to wait there now until it should be opened; but the air was so raw and cold, that Little Dorrit, leading Maggy about in her sleep, kept in motion. Going round by the church, she saw lights there, and the door open; and went up the steps, and looked in.

"Who's that?" cried a stout old man, who was putting on a nightcap as if he were going to bed in a vault.

"It's no one particular, sir," said Little Dorrit.

"Stop!" cried the man. "Let's have a look at you!"

This caused her to turn back again, in the act of going out, and to present herself and her charge before him.

"I thought so!" said he. "I know *you*."

"We have often seen each other," said Little Dorrit, recognising the sexton, or the beadle, or the verger, or whatever he was, "when I have been at church here."

"More than that, we've got your birth in our Register, you know; you're one of our curiosities."

"Indeed?" said Little Dorrit.

"To be sure. As the child of the—by-the-bye, how did you get out so early?"

"We were shut out last night, and are waiting to get in."

"You don't mean it? And there's another hour good yet! Come into the vestry. You'll find a fire in the vestry, on account of the painters. I'm waiting for the painters, or I shouldn't be here, you may depend upon it. One of our curiosities mustn't be cold, when we have it in our power to warm her up comfortable. Come along."

He was a very good old fellow, in his familiar way; and having stirred the vestry fire, he looked round the shelves of registers for a particular volume. "Here you are, you see," he said, taking it down and turning the leaves. "Here you'll find yourself, as large as life. Amy, daughter of William and Fanny Dorrit. Born, Marshalsea Prison, Parish of St. George.

Little Dorrit's Party

And we tell people that you have lived there, without so much as a day's or a night's absence, ever since. Is it true ? "

" Quite true, till last night."

" Lord ! " But his surveying her with an admiring gaze suggested something else to him, to wit: " I am sorry to see, though, that you are faint and tired. Stay a bit. I'll get some cushions out of the church, and you and your friend shall lie down before the fire. Don't be afraid of not going in to join your father when the gate opens. *I'll* call you."

He soon brought in the cushions, and strewed them on the ground.

" There you are, you see. Again as large as life. Oh, never mind thanking. I've daughters of my own. And though they weren't born in the Marshalsea Prison, they might have been, if I had been, in my ways of carrying on, of your father's breed. Stop a bit. I must put something under the cushion for your head. Here's a burial volume. Just the thing ! We have got Mrs. Bangham in this book. But what makes these books interesting to most people is—not who's in 'em, but who isn't—who's coming, you know, and when. That's the interesting question."

Commendingly looking back at the pillow he had improvised, he left them to their hour's repose. Maggy was snoring already, and Little Dorrit was soon fast asleep, with her head resting on that sealed book of Fate, untroubled by its mysterious blank leaves.

This was Little Dorrit's party. The shame, desertion, wretchedness, and exposure, of the great capital; the wet, the cold, the slow hours, and the swift clouds, of the dismal night. This was the party from which Little Dorrit went home, jaded, in the first grey mist of a rainy morning.

CHAPTER XV

THE debilitated old house in the city, wrapped in its mantle of soot, and leaning heavily on the crutches that had partaken of its decay and worn out with it, never knew a healthy or a cheerful interval, let what would betide. If the sun ever touched it, it was but with a ray, and that was gone in half an hour; if the moonlight ever fell upon it, it was only to put a few patches on its doleful cloak, and make it look more wretched. The stars, to be sure, coldly watched it when the nights and the smoke were clear enough; and all bad weather stood by it with a rare fidelity. You should alike find rain, hail, frost, and thaw lingering in that dismal enclosure, when they had vanished from other places; and as to snow, you should see it there for weeks, long after it had changed from yellow to black, slowly weeping away its grimy life. The place had no other adherents. As to street noises, the rumbling of wheels in the lane merely rushed in at the gateway in going past, and rushed out again: making the listening Mistress Affery feel as if she were deaf, and recovered the sense of hearing by instantaneous flashes. So with whistling, singing, talking, laughing, and all pleasant human sounds. They leaped the gap in a moment, and went upon their way.

The varying light of fire and candle in Mrs. Clennam's room made the greatest change that ever broke the dead monotony of the spot. In her two long narrow windows, the fire shone sullenly all day, and sullenly all night. On rare occasions, it flashed up passionately, as she did; but for the most part it was suppressed, like her, and preyed upon itself evenly and slowly. During many hours of the short winter days, however, when it was dusk there early in the afternoon, changing distortions of herself in her wheeled chair, of Mr. Flintwinch with his wry neck, of Mistress Affery coming and going, would be thrown upon the house wall that was over the gateway, and would hover there like shadows from a great magic lantern. As the room-ridden invalid settled for the night, these would gradually disappear: Mistress Affery's magnified shadow always flitting about, last, until it finally glided away into the air, as though she were off upon a witch excursion. Then the solitary light would burn unchangingly, until it burned pale before the dawn, and at last died under the breath of Mistress Affery, as her shadow descended on it from the witch-region of sleep.

Strange, if the little sick-room fire were in effect a beacon fire, summoning some one, and that the most unlikely some one in the world, to the spot that *must* be come to. Strange, if the little sick-room light were in effect a watch-light, burning in that place every night until an appointed event should be watched out! Which of the vast multitude of travellers, under the sun and the stars, climbing the dusty hills and toiling along the weary plains, journeying by land and journeying by sea, coming and going so strangely, to meet and to act and re-act on one another, which of the host may, with no suspicion of the journey's end, be travelling surely hither?

Time shall show us. The post of honour and the post of shame, the general's station and the drummer's, a peer's statue in Westminster Abbey and a seaman's hammock in the bosom of the deep, the mitre and the workhouse, the woolsack and the gallows, the throne and the guillotine — the travellers to all are on the great high road; but it has wonderful divergences, and only Time shall show us whither each traveller is bound.

On a wintry afternoon at twilight, Mrs. Flintwinch, having been heavy all day, dreamed this dream :

She thought she was in the kitchen getting the kettle ready for tea, and was warming herself with her feet upon the fender and the skirt of her gown tucked up, before the collapsed fire in the middle of the grate, bordered on either hand by a deep cold black ravine. She thought that as she sat thus, musing upon the question, whether life was not for some people a rather dull invention, she was frightened by a sudden noise behind her. She thought that she had been similarly frightened once last week, and that the noise was of a mysterious kind—a sound of rustling, and of three or four quick beats like a rapid step ; while a shock or tremble was communicated to her heart, as if the step had shaken the floor, or even as if she had been touched by some awful hand. She thought that this revived within her, certain old fears of hers that the house was haunted ; and that she flew up the kitchen stairs, without knowing how she got up, to be nearer company.

Mistress Affery thought that on reaching the hall, she saw the door of her liege lord's office standing open, and the room empty. That she went to the ripped-up window, in the little room by the street door, to connect her palpitating heart, through the glass, with living things beyond and outside the haunted house. That she then saw, on the wall over the gateway, the shadows of the two clever ones in conversation above. That she then went up stairs with her shoes in her hand, partly to be near the clever ones as a match for most ghosts, and partly to hear what they were talking about.

" None of your nonsense with me," said Mr. Flintwinch. " I won't take it from you."

Mrs. Flintwinch dreamed that she stood behind the door, which was just ajar, and most distinctly heard her husband say these bold words.

"Flintwinch," returned Mrs. Clennam, in her usual strong low voice, "there is a demon of anger in you. Guard against it."

"I don't care whether there's one or a dozen," said Mr. Flintwinch, forcibly suggesting in his tone that the higher number was nearer the mark. "If there was fifty, they should all say, None of your nonsense with me, I won't take it from you—I'd make 'em say it, whether they liked it or not."

"What have I done, you wrathful man?" her strong voice asked.

"Done?" said Mr. Flintwinch. "Dropped down upon me."

"If you mean, remonstrated with you——"

"Don't put words in my mouth that I don't mean," said Jeremiah, sticking to his figurative expression with tenacious and impenetrable obstinacy: "I mean dropped down upon me."

"I remonstrated with you," she began again, "because——"

"I won't have it!" cried Jeremiah. "You dropped down upon me."

"I dropped down upon you, then, you ill-conditioned man," (Jeremiah chuckled at having forced her to adopt his phrase,) "for having been needlessly significant to Arthur that morning. I have a right to complain of it as almost a breach of confidence. You did not mean it——"

"I won't have it!" interposed the contradictory Jeremiah, flinging back the concession. "I did mean it."

"I suppose I must leave you to speak in soliloquy if you choose," she replied, after a pause that seemed an angry one. "It is useless my addressing myself to a rash and head-strong old man who has a set purpose not to hear me."

"Now, I won't take that from you either," said Jeremiah. "I have no such purpose. I have told you I did mean it. Do you wish to know why I meant it, you rash and head-strong old woman?"

221

" After all, you only restore me my own words," she said, struggling with her indignation. " Yes."

" This is why, then. Because you hadn't cleared his father to him, and you ought to have done it. Because, before you went into any tantrum about yourself, who are—— "

" Hold there, Flintwinch!" she cried out in a changed voice: " you may go a word too far."

The old man seemed to think so. There was another pause, and he had altered his position in the room, when he spoke again more mildly:

" I was going to tell you why it was. Because, before you took your own part, I thought you ought to have taken the part of Arthur's father. Arthur's father! I had no particular love for Arthur's father. I served Arthur's father's uncle, in this house, when Arthur's father was not much above me—was poorer as far as his pocket went—and when his uncle might as soon have left me his heir as have left him. He starved in the parlour, and I starved in the kitchen; that was the principal difference in our positions; there was not much more than a flight of break-neck stairs between us. I never took to him in those times; I don't know that I ever took to him greatly at any time. He was an undecided, irresolute chap, who had had everything but his orphan life scared out of him when he was young. And when he brought you home here, the wife his uncle had named for him, I didn't need to look at you twice (you were a good-looking woman at that time) to know who'd be master. You have stood of your own strength ever since. Stand of your own strength now. Don't lean against the dead."

" I do *not*—as you call it—lean against the dead."

" But you had a mind to do it, if I had submitted," growled Jeremiah, " and that's why you drop down upon me. You can't forget that I didn't submit. I suppose you are astonished that I should consider it worth my while to have justice done to Arthur's father? Hey? It doesn't matter whether you answer or not, because I know you are, and you know you are. Come, then, I'll tell you how it is. I may be a bit of an oddity in point of temper, but this is my temper—I can't let anybody have entirely their own way. You are a determined woman, and a clever woman; and when you see your purpose before you, nothing will turn you from it. Who knows that better than I do?"

"Nothing will turn me from it, Flintwinch, when I have justified it to myself. Add that."

"Justified it to yourself? I said you were the most determined woman on the face of the earth (or I meant to say so), and if you are determined to justify any object you entertain, of course you'll do it."

"Man! I justify myself by the authority of these Books," she cried, with stern emphasis, and appearing from the sound that followed to strike the dead-weight of her arm upon the table.

"Never mind that," returned Jeremiah, calmly, "we won't enter into that question at present. However that may be, you carry out your purposes, and you make everything go down before them. Now, I won't go down before them. I have been faithful to you, and useful to you, and I am attached to you. But I can't consent, and I won't consent, and I never did consent, and I never will consent, to be lost in you. Swallow up everybody else, and welcome. The peculiarity of my temper is, ma'am, that I won't be swallowed up alive."

Perhaps this had originally been the mainspring of the understanding between them. Descrying thus much of force of character in Mr. Flintwinch, perhaps Mrs. Clennam had deemed alliance with him worth her while.

"Enough and more than enough of the subject," said she gloomily.

"Unless you drop down upon me again," returned the persistent Flintwinch, "and then you must expect to hear of it again."

Mistress Affery dreamed that the figure of her lord here

began walking up and down the room, as if to cool his spleen, and that she ran away; but that, as he did not issue forth when she had stood listening and trembling in the shadowy hall a little time, she crept up-stairs again, impelled as before by ghosts and curiosity, and once more cowered outside the door.

"Please to light the candle, Flintwinch," Mrs. Clennam was saying, apparently wishing to draw him back into their usual tone. "It is nearly time for tea. Little Dorrit is coming, and will find me in the dark."

Mr. Flintwinch lighted the candle briskly, and said, as he put it down upon the table:

"What are you going to do with Little Dorrit? Is she to come to work here for ever? To come to tea here, for ever? To come backwards and forwards here, in the same way, for ever?"

"How can you talk about 'for ever' to a maimed creature like me? Are we not all cut down like the grass of the field, and was not I shorn by the scythe many years ago: since when, I have been lying here, waiting to be gathered into the barn?"

"Ay, ay! But since you have been lying here—not near dead—nothing like it—numbers of children and young people, blooming women, strong men, and what not, have been cut down and carried; and still here are you, you see, not much changed after all. Your time and mine may be a long one yet. When I say for ever, I mean (though I am not poetical) through all our time." Mr. Flintwinch gave this explanation with great calmness, and calmly waited for an answer.

"So long as Little Dorrit is quiet, and industrious, and stands in need of the slight help I can give her, and deserves it; so long, I suppose, unless she withdraws of her own act, she will continue to come here, I being spared."

"Nothing more than that?" said Flintwinch, stroking his mouth and chin.

"What should there be more than that! What could

224

there be more than that!" she ejaculated, in her sternly wondering way.

Mrs. Flintwinch dreamed, that, for the space of a minute or two, they remained looking at each other with the candle between them, and that she somehow derived an impression that they looked at each other fixedly.

"Do you happen to know, Mrs. Clennam," Affery's liege lord then demanded in a much lower voice, and with an amount of expression that seemed quite out of proportion to the simple purpose of his words, "where she lives?"

"No."

"Would you—now, would you like to know?" said Jeremiah, with a pounce as if he had sprung upon her.

"If I cared to know, I should know already. Could I not have asked her, any day?"

"Then you don't care to know?"

"I do not."

Mr. Flintwinch, having expelled a long significant breath, said with his former emphasis, "For I have accidentally—mind!—found out."

"Wherever she lives," said Mrs. Clennam, speaking in one unmodulated hard voice, and separating her words as distinctly as if she were reading them off from separate bits of metal that she took up one by one, "she has made a secret of it, and she shall always keep her secret from me."

"After all, perhaps you would rather not have known the fact, anyhow?" said Jeremiah; and he said it with a twist, as if his words had come out of him in his own wry shape.

"Flintwinch," said his mistress and partner, flashing into a sudden energy that made Affery start, "why do you goad me? Look round this room. If it is any compensation for my long confinement within these narrow limits—not that I complain of being afflicted; you know I never complain of that—if it is any compensation to me for my long confinement to this room, that while I am shut up from all pleasant change, I am also shut up from the knowledge of some things that I may prefer to avoid knowing, why should you, of all men, grudge me that relief?"

"I don't grudge it to you," returned Jeremiah.

"Then say no more. Say no more. Let Little Dorrit keep her secret from me, and do you keep it from me also. Let her come and go, unobserved and unquestioned. Let me suffer, and let me have what alleviation belongs to my condition. Is it so much, that you torment me like an evil spirit?"

"I asked you a question. That's all."

"I have answered it. So, say no more. Say no more." Here the sound of the wheeled chair was heard upon the floor, and Affery's bell rang with a hasty jerk.

More afraid of her husband at the moment than of the mysterious sound in the kitchen, Affery crept away as lightly and as quickly as she could, descended the kitchen stairs almost as rapidly as she had ascended them, resumed her seat before the fire, tucked up her skirt again, and finally threw her apron over her head. Then the bell rang once more, and then once more, and then kept on ringing; in despite of which importunate summons, Affery still sat behind her apron, recovering her breath.

At last Mr. Flintwinch came shuffling down the staircase into the hall, muttering and calling "Affery woman!" all the way. Affery still remaining behind her apron, he came stumbling down the kitchen stairs, candle in hand, sidled up to her, twitched her apron off, and roused her.

"O Jeremiah!" cried Affery, waking. "What a start you gave me!"

"What have you been doing, woman?" inquired Jeremiah. "You've been rung for, fifty times."

"O Jeremiah," said Mistress Affery, "I have been a-dreaming!"

Reminded of her former achievement in that way, Mr. Flintwinch held the candle to her head, as if he had some idea of lighting her up for the illumination of the kitchen.

" Don't you know it's her tea-time ? " he demanded with a vicious grin, and giving one of the legs of Mistress Affery's chair a kick.

" Jeremiah ? Tea-time ? I don't know what's come to me. But I got such a dreadful turn, Jeremiah, before I went— off a-dreaming, that I think it must be that."

" Yoogh ! Sleepy-Head ! " said Mr. Flintwinch, " what are you talking about ? "

" Such a strange noise, Jeremiah, and such a curious move-ment. In the kitchen here—just here."

Jeremiah held up his light and looked at the blackened ceiling, held down his light and looked at the damp stone floor, turned round with his light and looked about at the spotted and blotched walls.

" Rats, cats, water, drains," said Jeremiah.

Mistress Affery negatived each with a shake of her head. " No, Jeremiah ; I have felt it before. I have felt it up-stairs, and once on the staircase as I was going from her room to ours in the night—a rustle and a sort of trembling touch behind me."

" Affery, my woman," said Mr. Flintwinch, grimly, after advancing his nose to that lady's lips as a test for the detec-tion of spirituous liquors, " if you don't get tea pretty quick, old woman, you'll become sensible of a rustle and a touch that'll send you flying to the other end of the kitchen."

This prediction stimulated Mrs. Flintwinch to bestir herself, and to hasten up-stairs to Mrs. Clennam's chamber. But, for all that, she now began to entertain a settled conviction that there was something wrong in the gloomy house. Henceforth, she was never at peace in it after daylight departed ; and never went up or down stairs in the dark without having her apron over her head, lest she should see something.

What with these ghostly apprehensions, and her singular dreams, Mrs. Flintwinch fell that evening into a haunted state of mind, from which it may be long before this present narra-tive descries any trace of her recovery. In the vagueness and indistinctness of all her new experiences and perceptions, as everything about her was mysterious to herself, she began to be mysterious to others; and became as difficult to be made out to anybody's satisfaction, as she found the house and everything in it difficult to make out to her own.

She had not yet finished preparing Mrs. Clennam's tea, when the soft knock came to the door which always announced Little Dorrit. Mistress Affery looked on at Little Dorrit taking off her homely bonnet in the hall, and at Mr. Flint-winch scraping his jaws and contemplating her in silence, as expecting some wonderful consequence to ensue which would frighten her out of her five wits or blow them all three to pieces.

After tea there came another knock at the door, announcing Arthur. Mistress Affery went down to let him in, and he said on entering, "Affery, I am glad it's you. I want to ask you a question." Affery immediately replied, "For goodness' sake don't ask me nothing, Arthur! I am frightened out of one half of my life, and dreamed out of the other. Don't ask me nothing! I don't know which is which, or what is what!"—and immediately started away from him, and came near him no more.

Mistress Affery having no taste for reading, and no sufficient light for needlework in the subdued room, supposing her to have the inclination, now sat every night in the dimness from which she had momentarily emerged on the evening of Arthur Clennam's return, occupied with crowds of wild speculations and suspicions respecting her mistress and her husband, and the noises in the house. When the ferocious devotional exercises were engaged in, these speculations would distract Mistress Affery's eyes towards the door, as if she expected some dark form to appear at those propitious moments, and make the party one too many.

Otherwise, Affery never said or did anything to attract the attention of the two clever ones towards her in any marked degree, except on certain occasions, generally at about the quiet hour towards bed-time, when she would suddenly dart out of her dim corner, and whisper with a face of terror, to Mr. Flintwinch reading the paper near Mrs. Clennam's little table:

"There, Jeremiah! Now! What's that noise?"

Then the noise, if there were any, would have ceased, and Mr. Flintwinch would snarl, turning upon her as if she had cut him down that moment against his will, "Affery, old woman, you shall have a dose, old woman, such a dose! You have been dreaming again!"

CHAPTER XVI

THE time being come for the renewal of his acquaintance with the Meagles family, Clennam, pursuant to contract made between himself and Mr. Meagles, within the precincts of Bleeding Heart Yard, turned his face on a certain Saturday towards Twickenham, where Mr. Meagles had a cottage-residence of his own. The weather being fine and dry, and any English road abounding in interest for him who had been so long away, he sent his valise on by the coach, and set out to walk. A walk was in itself a new enjoyment to him, and one that had rarely diversified his life afar off.

He went by Fulham and Putney, for the pleasure of strolling over the heath. It was bright and shining there ; and when he found himself so far on his road to Twickenham, he found himself a long way on his road to a number of airier and less substantial destinations. They had risen before him fast, in the healthful exercise and the pleasant road. It is not easy to walk alone in the country without musing upon something. And he had plenty of unsettled subjects to meditate upon, though he had been walking to the Land's End.

First, there was the subject seldom absent from his mind, the question, what he was to do henceforth in life ; to what occupation he should devote himself, and in what direction he had best seek it. He was far from rich, and every day of indecision and inaction made his inheritance a source of greater anxiety to him. As often as he began to consider how to increase this inheritance, or to lay it by, so often his misgiving that there was some one with an unsatisfied claim upon his justice, returned ; and that alone was a subject to outlast the longest walk. Again, there was the subject of his relations with his mother, which were now upon an equable and peaceful but never confidential footing, and whom he saw several times a-week. Little Dorrit was a leading and a constant subject : for the circumstances of his life, united to those of her own story, presented the little creature to him as the only person between whom and himself there were ties of innocent reliance on one hand, and affectionate protection on the other ; ties of compassion, respect, unselfish interest, gratitude, and pity. Thinking of her, and of the possibility of her father's release from prison by the unbarring hand of death—the only change of circumstance he could foresee that might enable him to be such a friend to her as he wished to be, by altering her whole manner of life, smoothing her rough road, and giving her a home—he regarded her, in that perspective, as his adopted daughter, his poor child of the Marshalsea hushed to rest. If there were a last subject in his thoughts, and it lay towards Twickenham, its form was so indefinite that it was little more than the pervading atmosphere in which these other subjects floated before him.

He had crossed the heath and was leaving it behind, when he gained upon a figure which had been in advance of him for some time, and which, as he gained upon it, he thought he knew. He derived this impression from something in the turn of the head, and in the figures action of consideration, as it went on at a sufficiently sturdy walk. But when the man—for it was a man's figure—pushed his hat up at the back of his head, and stopped to consider some object before him, he knew it to be Daniel Doyce.

"How do you do, Mr. Doyce?" said Clennam, overtaking him. "I am glad to see you again, and in a healthier place than the Circumlocution office."

"Ha! Mr. Meagles's friend!" exclaimed that public criminal, coming out of some mental combinations he had been making, and offering his hand. "I am glad to see you, sir. Will you excuse me if I forget your name?"

"Readily. It's not a celebrated name. It's not Barnacle."

"No, no," said Daniel, laughing. "And now I know what it is. It's Clennam. How do you do, Mr. Clennam?"

"I have some hope," said Arthur, as they walked on together, "that we may be going to the same place, Mr. Doyce."

"Meaning Twickenham?" returned Daniel. "I am glad to hear it."

They were soon quite intimate, and lightened the way with a variety of conversation. The ingenious culprit was a man of great modesty and good sense; and, though a plain man, had been too much accustomed to combine what was original and daring in conception with what was patient and minute in execution, to be by any means an ordinary man. It was at first difficult to lead him to speak about himself, and he put off Arthur's advances in that direction by admitting slightly, oh yes, he had done this, and he had done that, and such a thing was of his making, and such another thing was his discovery, but it was his trade, you see, his trade; until, as he gradually became assured that his companion had a real interest in his account of himself, he frankly yielded to it. Then it appeared that he was the son of a north-country blacksmith, and had originally been apprenticed by his widowed mother to a lock-maker; that he had "struck out a few little things" at the lock-maker's, which had led to his being released from his indentures with a present, which present had enabled him to gratify his ardent wish to bind himself to a working engineer, under whom he had laboured hard, learned hard, and lived hard, seven years. His time being out, he had "worked in the shop" at weekly wages seven or eight years more; and had then betaken himself to the banks of the Clyde, where he had studied, and filed, and

232

hammered, and improved his knowledge, theoretical and practical, for six or seven years more. There he had had an offer to go to Lyons, which he had accepted ; and from Lyons had been engaged to go to Germany, and in Germany had had an offer to go to St. Petersburg, and there had done very well indeed—never better. However, he had naturally felt a preference for his own country, and a wish to gain distinction there, and to do whatever service he could do, there rather than elsewhere. And so he had come home. And so at home he had established himself in business, and had invented and executed, and worked his way on, until, after a dozen years of constant suit and service, he had been enrolled in the Great British Legion of Honour, the Legion of the Rebuffed of the Circumlocution Office, and had been decorated with the Great British Order of Merit, the Order of the Disorder of the Barnacles and Stiltstalkings.

"It is much to be regretted," said Clennam, "that you ever turned your thoughts that way, Mr. Doyce."

"True, sir, true to a certain extent. But what is a man to do ? If he has the misfortune to strike out something service-able to the nation, he must follow where it leads him."

"Hadn't he better let it go ?" asked Clennam.

"He can't do it," said Doyce, shaking his head with a thoughtful smile. "It's not put into his head to be buried. It's put into his head to be made useful. You hold your life on the condition that to the last you shall struggle hard for it. Every man holds a discovery on the same terms."

"This is to say," said Arthur, with a growing admiration of his quiet companion, "you are not finally discouraged even now ?"

"I have no right to be, if I am," returned the other. "The thing is as true as it ever was."

When they had walked a little way in silence, Clennam, at once to change the direct point of their conversation and not to change it too abruptly, asked Mr. Doyce if he had any

233

partner in his business, to relieve him of a portion of its anxieties?

"No," he returned, "not at present. I had when I first entered on it, and a good man he was. But he has been dead some years; and as I could not easily take to the notion of another when I lost him, I bought his share for myself and have gone on by myself ever since. And here's another thing," he said, stopping for a moment with a good-humoured laugh in his eyes, and laying his closed right hand, with its peculiar suppleness of thumb, on Clennam's arm, "no inventor can be a man of business, you know."

"No?" said Clennam.

"Why, so the men of business say," he answered, resuming the walk and laughing outright. "I don't know why we unfortunate creatures should be supposed to want common sense, but it is generally taken for granted that we do. Even the best friend I have in the world, our excellent friend over yonder," said Doyce, nodding towards Twickenham, "extends a sort of protection to me, don't you know, as a man not quite able to take care of himself."

Arthur Clennam could not help joining in the good-humoured laugh, for he recognised the truth of the description.

"So I find that I must have a partner who is a man of business and not guilty of any inventions," said Daniel Doyce, taking off his hat to pass his hand over his forehead, "if it's only in deference to the current opinion, and to uphold the credit of the Works. I don't think he'll find that I have been very remiss or confused in my way of conducting them; but that's for him to say—whoever he is—not for me."

"You have not chosen him yet, then?"

"No, sir, no. I have only just come to a decision to take one. The fact is, there's more to do than there used to be, and the Works are enough for me as I grow older. What with the books and correspondence, and foreign journeys for which a Principal is necessary, I can't do all. I am going to talk over the best way of negotiating the matter, if I find a

spare half-hour between this and Monday morning, with my
—my Nurse and protector," said Doyce, with laughing eyes
again. " He is a sagacious man in business, and has had a
good apprenticeship to it."

After this, they conversed on different subjects until they
arrived at their journey's end. A composed and unobtrusive
self-sustainment was noticeable in Daniel Doyce—a calm
knowledge that what was true must remain true, in spite of
all the Barnacles in the family ocean, and would be just the
truth, and neither more nor less, when even that sea had run
dry—which had a kind of greatness in it, though not of the
official quality.

As he knew the house well, he conducted Arthur to it by
the way that showed it to the best advantage. It was a
charming place (none the worse for being a little eccentric),
on the road by the river, and just what the residence of the
Meagles family ought to be. It stood in a garden, no
doubt as fresh and beautiful in the May of the Year, as
Pet now was in the May of her life; and it was defended
by a goodly show of handsome trees and spreading evergreens,
as Pet was by Mr. and Mrs. Meagles. It was made out
of an old brick house, of which a part had been altogether
pulled down, and another part had been changed into the
present cottage; so there was a hale elderly portion, to
represent Mr. and Mrs. Meagles, and a young picturesque,
very pretty portion to represent Pet. There was even
the later addition of a conservatory sheltering itself against
it, uncertain of hue in its deep-stained glass, and in its more
transparent portions flashing to the sun's rays, now like
fire and now like harmless water drops ; which might have
stood for Tattycoram. Within view was the peaceful river
and the ferry-boat, to moralise to all the inmates, saying :
Young or old, passionate or tranquil, chafing or content,
you, thus runs the current always. Let the heart swell
into what discord it will, thus plays the rippling water on
the prow of the ferry-boat ever the same tune. Year after

year, so much allowance for the drifting of the boat, so many miles an hour the flowing of the stream, here the rushes, there the lilies, nothing uncertain or unquiet, upon this road that steadily runs away ; while you, upon your flowing road of time, are so capricious and distracted.

The bell at the gate had scarcely sounded when Mr. Meagles came out to receive them. Mr. Meagles had scarcely come out, when Mrs. Meagles came out. Mrs. Meagles had scarcely come out, when Pet came out. Pet had scarcely come out, when Tattycoram came out. Never had visitors a more hospitable reception.

"Here we are, you see," said Mr. Meagles, "boxed up, Mr. Clennam, within our own home-limits, as if we were never going to expand—that is, travel—again. Not like Marseilles, eh ? No allonging and marshonging here ! "

" A different kind of beauty, indeed ! " said Clennam, looking about him.

"But, Lord bless me ! " cried Mr. Meagles, rubbing his hands with a relish, " it was an uncommonly pleasant thing being in quarantine, wasn't it ? Do you know, I have often wished myself back again ? We were a capital party."

This was Mr. Meagles's invariable habit. Always to object to everything while he was travelling, and always to want to get back to it when he was not travelling.

" If it was summer-time," said Mr. Meagles, " which I wish it was on your account, and in order that you might see the place at its best, you would hardly be able to hear yourself speak for birds. Being practical people, we never allow anybody to scare the birds ; and the birds, being practical people too, come about us in myriads. We are delighted to see you, Clennam (if you'll allow me, I shall drop the Mister) ; I heartily assure you, we are delighted."

"I have not had so pleasant a greeting," said Clennam—then he recalled what Little Dorrit had said to him in his own room, and faithfully added " except once—since we last walked to and fro, looking down at the Mediterranean."

"Ah!" returned Mr. Meagles. "Something like a look out, *that* was, wasn't it? I don't want a military government, but I shouldn't mind a little allonging and marshonging— just a dash of it—in this neighbourhood sometimes. It's Devilish still."

Bestowing this eulogium on the retired character of his retreat with a dubious shake of the head, Mr. Meagles led the way into the house. It was just large enough, and no more; was as pretty within as it was without, and was perfectly well-arranged and comfortable. Some traces of the migratory habits of the family were to be observed in the covered frames and furniture, and wrapped-up hangings; but it was easy to see that it was one of Mr. Meagles's whims to have the cottage always kept, in their absence, as if they were always coming back the day after to-morrow. Of articles collected on his various expeditions, there was such a vast miscellany that it was like the dwelling of an amiable Corsair. There were antiquities from Central Italy, made by the best modern houses in that department of industry; bits of mummy from Egypt (and perhaps Birmingham); model gondolas from Venice; model villages from Switzerland; morsels of tesselated pavement from Herculaneum and Pompeii, like petrified minced veal; ashes out of tombs, and lava out of Vesuvius; Spanish fans, Spezzian straw hats, Moorish slippers, Tuscan hair-pins, Carrara sculpture, Trastaverini scarves, Genoese velvets and filigree, Neapolitan coral, Roman cameos, Geneva jewellery, Arab lanterns, rosaries blest all round by the Pope himself, and an infinite variety of lumber. There were views, like and unlike, of a multitude of places; and there was one little picture-room devoted to a few of the regular sticky old Saints, with sinews like whipcord, hair like Neptune's, wrinkles like tattooing, and such coats of varnish that every holy personage served for a fly-trap, and became what is now called in the vulgar tongue a Catch-em-alive O. Of these pictorial acquisitions Mr. Meagles spoke in the usual manner. He was no

237

judge, he said, except of what pleased himself; he had picked them up, dirt-cheap, and people *had* considered them rather fine. One man, who at any rate ought to know something of the subject, had declared that "Sage, Reading" (a specially oily old gentleman in a blanket, with a swan's-down tippet for a beard, and a web of cracks all over him like rich pie-crust), to be a fine Guercino. As for Sebastian del Piombo there, you would judge for yourself; if it were not his later manner, the question was, Who was it? Titian, that might or might not be—perhaps he had only touched it. Daniel Doyce said perhaps he hadn't touched it, but Mr. Meagles rather declined to overhear the remark.

When he had shown all his spoils, Mr. Meagles took them into his own snug room overlooking the lawn, which was fitted up in part like a dressing-room and in part like an office, and in which, upon a kind of counter-desk, were a pair of brass scales for weighing gold, and a scoop for shovelling out money.

"Here they are, you see," said Mr. Meagles. "I stood behind these two articles five-and-thirty years running, when I no more thought of gadding about than I now think of —staying at home. When I left the Bank for good, I asked for them, and brought them away with me. I mention it at once, or you might suppose that I sit in my counting-house (as Pet says I do), like the king in the poem of the four-and-twenty blackbirds, counting out my money."

Clennam's eyes had strayed to a natural picture on the wall, of two pretty little girls with their arms entwined. "Yes, Clennam," said Mr. Meagles in a lower voice. "There they both are. It was taken some seventeen years ago. As I often say to Mother, they were babies then."

"Their names?" said Arthur.

"Ah, to be sure! You have never heard any name but Pet. Pet's name is Minnie; her sister's Lillie."

"Should you have known, Mr. Clennam, that one was

meant for me?" asked Pet herself, now standing in the doorway.

"I might have thought that both of them were meant for you, both are still so like you. Indeed," said Clennam, glancing from the fair original to the picture and back, "I cannot even now say which is not your portrait."

"D'ye hear that, Mother?" cried Mr. Meagles to his wife, who had followed her daughter. "It's always the same, Clennam; nobody can decide. The child to your left is Pet."

The picture happened to be near a looking-glass. As Arthur looked at it again, he saw, by the reflection of the mirror, Tattycoram stop in passing outside the door, listen to what was going on, and pass away with an angry and contemptuous frown upon her face that changed its beauty into ugliness.

"But come!" said Mr. Meagles. "You have had a long walk, and will be glad to get your boots off. As to Daniel here, I suppose he'd never think of taking *his* boots off, unless we showed him a boot-jack."

"Why not?" asked Daniel, with a significant smile at Clennam.

"Oh! You have so many things to think about," returned Mr. Meagles, clapping him on the shoulder, as if his weakness must not be left to itself on any account. "Figures, and wheels, and cogs, and levers, and screws, and cylinders, and a thousand things."

"In my calling," said Daniel, amused, "the greater usually includes the less. But never mind, never mind! Whatever pleases you, pleases me."

Clennam could not help speculating, as he seated himself in his room by the fire, whether there might be in the breast of this honest, affectionate, and cordial Mr. Meagles, any microscopic portion of the mustard-seed that had sprung up into the great tree of the Circumlocution Office. His curious sense of a general superiority to Daniel Doyce, which seemed to be founded, not so much on anything in Doyce's personal character, as on the mere fact of his being an originator and a man out of the beaten track of other men, suggested the idea. It might have occupied him until he went down to dinner an hour afterwards, if he had not had another question to consider, which had been in his mind so long ago as before he was in quarantine at Marseilles, and which had now returned to it, and was very urgent with it. No less a question than this: Whether he should allow himself to fall in love with Pet?

He was twice her age. (He changed the leg he had crossed over the other, and tried the calculation again, but could not bring out the total at less.) He was twice her age. Well! He was young in appearance, young in health and strength, young in heart. A man was certainly not old at forty; and many men were not in circumstances to marry, or did not marry, until they had attained that time of life. On the other hand, the question was, not what he thought of the point, but what she thought of it.

He believed that Mr. Meagles was disposed to entertain a ripe regard for him, and he knew that he had a sincere regard for Mr. Meagles and his good wife. He could foresee that to relinquish this beautiful only child, of whom they were so fond, to any husband, would be a trial of their love which perhaps they never yet had had the fortitude to contemplate. But the more beautiful and winning and charming she, the nearer they must always be to the necessity of approaching it. And why not in his favour, as well as in another's?

When he had got so far, it came again into his head, that the question was, not what they thought of it, but what she thought of it.

Arthur Clennam was a retiring man, with a sense of many deficiencies; and he so exalted the merits of the beautiful Minnie in his mind, and depressed his own, that when he pinned himself to this point, his hopes began to fail him. He came to the final resolution, as he made himself ready for dinner, that he would *not* allow himself to fall in love with Pet.

They were only five, at a round table, and it was very pleasant indeed. They had so many places and people to recall, and they were all so easy and cheerful together (Daniel Doyce either sitting out like an amused spectator at cards, or coming in with some shrewd little experiences of his own, when it happened to be to the purpose), that they might have been together twenty times, and not have known so much of one another.

"And Miss Wade," said Mr. Meagles, after they had re-called a number of fellow-travellers. "Has anybody seen Miss Wade?"

"I have," said Tattycoram.

She had brought a little mantle which her young mistress had sent for, and was bending over her, putting it on, when she lifted up her dark eyes, and made this unexpected answer.

"Tatty!" her young mistress exclaimed. "You seen Miss Wade?—where?"

"Here, miss," said Tattycoram.

"How?"

An impatient glance from Tattycoram seemed, as Clennam saw it, to answer "With my eyes!" But her only answer in words was : "I met her near the church."

"What was she doing there I wonder!" said Mr. Meagles. "Not going to it, I should think."

"She had written to me first," said Tattycoram.

"Oh, Tatty!" murmured her mistress, "take your hands away. I feel as if some one else was touching me!"

She said it in a quick involuntary way, but half playfully, and not more petulantly or disagreeably than a favourite child might have done, who laughed next moment. Tatty-coram set her full red lips together, and crossed her arms upon her bosom.

"Did you wish to know, sir," she said, looking at Mr. Meagles, "what Miss Wade wrote to me about?"

241

" Well, Tattycoram," returned Mr. Meagles, " since you ask the question, and we are all friends here, perhaps you may as well mention it, if you are so inclined."

" She knew, when we were travelling, where you lived," said Tattycoram, " and she had seen me not quite—not quite——"

" Not quite in a good temper, Tattycoram ? " suggested Mr. Meagles, shaking his head at the dark eyes with a quiet caution. " Take a little time—count five-and twenty, Tatty-coram."

She pressed her lips together again, and took a long deep breath.

" So she wrote to me to say that if I ever felt myself hurt," she looked down at her young mistress, " or found myself worried," she looked down at her again, " I might go to her, and be considerately treated. I was to think of it, and could speak to her by the church. So I went there to thank her."

" Tatty," said her young mistress, putting her hand up over her shoulder that the other might take it, " Miss Wade almost frightened me when we parted, and I scarcely liked to think of her just now as having been so near me without my knowing it. Tatty dear ! "

Tatty stood for a moment, immovable.

" Hey ? " cried Mr. Meagles. " Count another five-and-twenty, Tattycoram."

She might have counted a dozen, when she bent and put her lips to the caressing hand. It patted her cheek, as it touched the owner's beautiful curls, and Tattycoram went away.

" Now, there," said Mr. Meagles, softly, as he gave a turn to the dumb-waiter on his right hand, to twirl the sugar towards himself. " There's a girl who might be lost and ruined, if she wasn't among practical people. Mother and I know, solely from being practical, that there are times when that girl's whole nature seems to roughen itself against seeing us so bound up in Pet. No father and mother were bound up in her, poor soul. I don't like to think of the way in which that unfortunate child, with all that passion and protest in her, feels when she hears the Fifth Commandment on a Sunday. I am always inclined to call out, Church, Count five-and-twenty, Tattycoram."

Besides his dumb-waiter, Mr. Meagles had two other not dumb waiters, in the persons of two parlour-maids, with rosy faces and bright eyes, who were a highly ornamental part of the table decoration. "And why not, you see?" said Mr. Meagles on this head. "As I always say to Mother, why not have something pretty to look at, if you have anything at all?"

A certain Mrs. Tickit, who was Cook and Housekeeper when the family were at home, and Housekeeper only when the family were away, completed the establishment. Mr. Meagles regretted that the nature of the duties in which she was engaged, rendered Mrs. Tickit unpresentable at present, but hoped to introduce her to the new visitor to-morrow. She was an important part of the cottage, he said, and all his friends knew her. That was her picture up in the corner. When they went away, she always put on the silk-gown and the jet-black row of curls represented in that portrait (her hair was reddish-grey in the kitchen), established herself in the breakfast-room, put her spectacles between two particular leaves of Doctor Buchan's Domestic Medicine, and sat looking over the blind all day until they came back again. It was supposed that no persuasion could be invented which would induce Mrs. Tickit to abandon her post at the blind, however long their absence, or to dispense with the attendance of Dr. Buchan: the lucubrations of which learned practitioner, Mr. Meagles implicitly believed she had never yet consulted to the extent of one word in her life.

In the evening, they played an old-fashioned rubber; and Pet sat looking over her father's hand, or singing to herself by fits and starts at the piano. She was a spoilt child; but how could she be otherwise? Who could be much with so pliable and beautiful a creature, and not yield to her endearing influence? Who could pass an evening in the house, and not love her for the grace and charm of her very presence in the room? This was Clennam's reflection, notwithstanding the final conclusion at which he had arrived up-stairs.

In making it, he revoked. "Why, what are you thinking of, my good sir?" asked the astonished Mr. Meagles, who was his partner. "I beg your pardon. Nothing," returned Clennam. "Think of something, next time; that's a dear fellow," said Mr. Meagles. Pet laughingly believed he had been thinking of Miss Wade. "Why of Miss Wade, Pet?" asked her father. "Why indeed!" said Arthur Clennam. Pet coloured a little, and went to the piano again.

As they broke up for the night, Arthur overheard Doyce ask his host if he could give him half-an-hour's conversation before breakfast in the morning? The host replying willingly, Arthur lingered behind a moment, having his own word to add on that topic.

"Mr. Meagles," he said, on their being left alone, "do you remember when you advised me to go straight to London?"

"Perfectly well."

"And when you gave me some other good advice, which I needed at that time?"

"I won't say what it was worth," answered Mr. Meagles; "but of course I remember our being very pleasant and confidential together."

"I have acted on your advice; and having disembarrassed myself of an occupation that was painful to me for many reasons, wish to devote myself and what means I have, to another pursuit."

"Right! You can't do it too soon," said Mr. Meagles.

"Now, as I came down to-day, I found that your friend, Mr. Doyce, is looking for a partner in his business—not a partner in his mechanical knowledge, but in the ways and means of turning the business arising from it to the best account."

"Just so," said Mr. Meagles, with his hands in his pockets, and with the old business expression of face that had belonged to the scales and scoop.

"Mr. Doyce mentioned incidentally, in the course of our conversation, that he was going to take your valuable advice on the subject of finding such a partner. If you should think our views and opportunities at all likely to coincide, perhaps you will let him know my available position. I speak, of course, in ignorance of the details, and they may be unsuitable on both sides."

"No doubt, no doubt," said Mr. Meagles, with the caution belonging to the scales and scoop.

"But they will be a question of figures and accounts——"

"Just so, just so," said Mr. Meagles, with the arithmetical solidity belonging to the scales and scoop.

"—And I shall be glad to enter into the subject, provided Mr. Doyce responds, and you think well of it. If you will at present, therefore, allow me to place it in your hands, you will much oblige me."

"Clennam, I accept the trust with readiness," said Mr. Meagles. "And without anticipating any of the points which you, as a man of business, have of course reserved, I am free to say to you that I think something may come of this. Of one thing you may be perfectly certain. Daniel is an honest man."

"I am so sure of it, that I have promptly made up my mind to speak to you."

"You must guide him, you know; you must steer him; you must direct him; he is one of a crotchety sort," said Mr. Meagles, evidently meaning nothing more than that he did new things and went new ways, "but he is as honest as the sun, and so good night!"

Clennam went back to his room, sat down again before his fire, and made up his mind that he was glad he had resolved not to fall in love with Pet. She was so beautiful, so amiable, so apt to receive any true impression given to her gentle nature and her innocent heart, and make the man who should be so happy as to communicate it, the most fortunate and enviable of all men, that he was very glad indeed he had come to that conclusion.

But, as this might have been a reason for coming to the opposite conclusion, he followed out the theme again a little way in his mind. To justify himself, perhaps.

" Suppose that a man," so his thoughts ran, " who had been of age some twenty years or so ; who was a diffident man, from the circumstances of his youth ; who was rather a grave man, from the tenor of his life ; who knew himself to be deficient in many little engaging qualities which he admired in others, from having been long in a distant region, with nothing softening near him ; who had no kind sisters to present to her ; who had no congenial home to make her known in ; who was a stranger in the land ; who had not a fortune to compensate, in any measure, for these defects ; who had nothing in his favour but his honest love and his general wish to do right—suppose such a man were to come to this house, and were to yield to the captivation of this charming girl, and were to persuade himself that he could hope to win her ; what a weakness it would be ! "

He softly opened his window, and looked out upon the serene river. Year after year so much allowance for the drifting of the ferry-boat, so many miles an hour the flowing of the stream, here the rushes, there the lilies, nothing uncertain or unquiet.

Why should he be vexed or sore at heart ? It was not his weakness that he had imagined. It was nobody's, nobody's within his knowledge, why should it trouble him ? And yet it did trouble him. And he thought—who has not thought for a moment, sometimes ?—that it might be better to flow away monotonously, like the river, and to compound for its insensibility to happiness with its insensibility to pain.

CHAPTER XVII

NOBODY'S RIVAL

BEFORE breakfast in the morning, Arthur walked out to look about him. As the morning was fine, and he had an hour on his hands, he crossed the river by the ferry, and strolled along a footpath through some meadows. When he came back to the towing-path, he found the ferry-boat on the opposite side, and a gentleman hailing it and waiting to be taken over.

This gentleman looked barely thirty. He was well dressed, of a sprightly and gay appearance, a well-knit figure, and a rich dark complexion. As Arthur came over the stile and down to the water's edge, the lounger glanced at him for a moment, and then resumed his occupation of idly tossing stones into the water with his foot. There was something in his way of spurning them out of their places with his heel, and getting them into the required position, that Clennam thought had an air of cruelty in it. Most of us have more or less frequently derived a similar impression, from a man's manner of doing some very little thing : plucking a flower, clearing away an obstacle, or even destroying an insentient object.

The gentleman's thoughts were pre-occupied, as his face showed, and he took no notice of a fine Newfoundland dog, who watched him attentively, and watched every stone too, in its turn, eager to spring into the river on receiving his master's sign. The ferry-boat came over, however, without his receiving any sign, and when it grounded his master took him by the collar and walked him into it.

"Not this morning," he said to the dog. "You won't do for ladies' company, dripping wet. Lie down."

Clennam followed the man and the dog into the boat, and took his seat. The dog did as he was ordered. The man remained standing, with his hands in his pockets, and towered between Clennam and the prospect. Man and dog both jumped lightly out as soon as they touched the other side, and went away. Clennam was glad to be rid of them.

The church clock struck the breakfast hour, as he walked up the little lane by which the garden-gate was approached. The moment he pulled the bell a deep loud barking assailed him from within the wall.

"I heard no dog last night," thought Clennam. The gate was opened by one of the rosy maids, and on the lawn were the Newfoundland dog and the man.

"Miss Minnie is not down yet, gentlemen," said the blushing portress, as they all came together in the garden. Then she said to the master of the dog, "Mr. Clennam, sir," and tripped away.

"Odd enough, Mr. Clennam, that we should have met just now," said the man. Upon which the dog became mute. "Allow me to introduce myself—Henry Gowan. A pretty place this, and looks wonderfully well this morning!"

The manner was easy, and the voice agreeable; but still Clennam thought, that if he had not made that decided resolution to avoid falling in love with Pet, he would have taken a dislike to this Henry Gowan.

"It's new to you, I believe?" said this Gowan, when Arthur had extolled the place.

"Quite new. I made acquaintance with it only yesterday afternoon."

"Ah! Of course this is not its best aspect. It used to look charming in the spring, before they went away last time. I should like you to have seen it then."

The Ferry

But for that resolution so often recalled, Clennam might have wished him in the crater of Mount Etna, in return for this civility.

"I have had the pleasure of seeing it under many circumstances during the last three years, and it's—a Paradise."

It was (at least it might have been, always excepting for that wise resolution) like his dexterous impudence to call it a Paradise. He only called it a Paradise because he first saw her coming, and so made her out within her hearing to be an angel, Confusion to him!

And ah, how beaming she looked, and how glad! How she caressed the dog, and how the dog knew her! How expressive that heightened colour in her face, that fluttered manner, her downcast eyes, her irresolute happiness! When had Clennam seen her look like this? Not that there was any reason why he might, could, would, or should have ever seen her look like this, or that he had ever hoped for himself to see her look like this; but still—when had he ever known her do it!

He stood at a little distance from them. This Gowan, when he had talked about a Paradise, had gone up to her and taken her hand. The dog had put his great paws on her arm and laid his head against her dear bosom. She had laughed and welcomed them, and made far too much of the dog, far, far, too much—that is to say, supposing there had been any third person looking on who loved her.

She disengaged herself now, and came to Clennam, and put her hand in his and wished him good morning, and gracefully made as if she would take his arm and be escorted into the house. This Gowan had no objection. No, he knew he was too safe.

There was a passing cloud on Mr. Meagles's good-humoured face, when they all three (four, counting the dog, and he was the most objectionable but one of the party) came in to breakfast. Neither it, nor the touch of uneasiness on Mrs. Meagles as she directed her eyes towards it, was unobserved by Clennam.

"Well, Gowan," said Mr. Meagles, even suppressing a sigh; "how goes the world with you this morning?"

"Much as usual, sir. Lion and I being determined not to waste anything of our weekly visit, turned out early, and came over from Kingston, my present head-quarters, where I am making a sketch or two." Then he told how he had met Mr. Clennam at the ferry, and they had come over together.

"Mrs. Gowan is well, Henry?" said Mrs. Meagles. (Clennam became attentive.)

"My mother is quite well, thank you." (Clennam became inattentive.) "I have taken the liberty of making an addition to your family dinner-party to-day, which I hope will not be inconvenient to you or to Mr. Meagles. I couldn't very well get out of it," he explained, turning to the latter. "The young fellow wrote to propose himself to me; and as he is well connected, I thought you would not object to my transferring him here."

"Who *is* the young fellow?" asked Mr. Meagles with peculiar complacency.

"He is one of the Barnacles. Tite Barnacle's son, Clarence Barnacle, who is in his father's Department. I can at least guarantee that the river shall not suffer from his visit. He won't set it on fire."

"Aye, aye?" said Meagles. "A Barnacle is he? *We* know something of that family, eh, Dan? By George, they are at the top of the tree, though! Let me see. What relation will this young fellow be to Lord Decimus now? His Lordship married, in seventeen ninety-seven, Lady Jemima Bilberry, who was the second daughter by the third marriage—no! There I am wrong! That was Lady Seraphina—Lady Jemima was the first daughter by the second marriage of the fifteenth Earl of Stiltstalking with the Honourable Clementina Toozellem. Very well. Now this young fellow's father married a Stiltstalking and *his* father married his cousin who was a Barnacle. The father of that father who married a Barnacle, married a Joddleby.—I am getting a little too far back, Gowan; I want to make out what relation this young fellow is to Lord Decimus."

"That's easily stated. His father is nephew to Lord Decimus."

"Nephew—to—Lord—Decimus," Mr. Meagles luxuriously repeated with his eyes shut, that he might have nothing to distract him from the full flavour of the genealogical tree. "By George, you are right, Gowan. So he is."

"Consequently, Lord Decimus is his great uncle."

"But stop a bit!" said Mr. Meagles, opening his eyes with a fresh discovery. "Then, on the mother's side, Lady Stiltstalking is his great aunt."

"Of course she is."

"Aye, aye, aye?" said Mr. Meagles, with much interest. "Indeed, indeed? We shall be glad to see him. We'll entertain him as well as we can, in our humble way; and we shall not starve him, I hope, at all events."

In the beginning of this dialogue, Clennam had expected some great harmless outburst from Mr. Meagles, like that which had made him burst out of the Circumlocution Office, holding Doyce by the collar. But his good friend had a weakness which none of us need go into the next street to find, and which no amount of Circumlocution experience could long subdue in him. Clennam looked at Doyce; but Doyce knew all about it beforehand, and looked at his plate, and made no sign, and said no word.

"I am much obliged to you," said Gowan, to conclude the subject. "Clarence is a great ass, but he is one of the dearest and best fellows that ever lived!"

It appeared, before the breakfast was over, that everybody whom this Gowan knew was either more or less of an ass, or more or less of a knave; but was, notwithstanding, the most lovable, the most engaging, the simplest, truest, kindest, dearest, best fellow that ever lived. The process by which this unvarying result was attained, whatever the premises, might have been stated by Mr. Henry Gowan thus: "I

251

claim to be always book-keeping, with a peculiar nicety, in every man's case, and posting up a careful little account of Good and Evil with him. I do this so conscientiously, that I am happy to tell you I find the most worthless of men to be the dearest old fellow too; and am in a condition to make the gratifying report, that there is much less difference than you are inclined to suppose between an honest man and a scoundrel." The effect of this cheering discovery happened to be, that while he seemed to be scrupulously finding good in most men, he did in reality lower it where it was, and set it up where it was not; but that was its only disagreeable or dangerous feature.

It scarcely seemed, however, to afford Mr. Meagles as much satisfaction as the Barnacle genealogy had done. The cloud that Clennam had never seen upon his face before that morning, frequently overcast it again; and there was the same shadow of uneasy observation of him on the comely face of his wife. More than once or twice when Pet caressed the dog, it appeared to Clennam that her father was unhappy in seeing her do it; and, in one particular instance when Gowan stood on the other side of the dog, and bent his head at the same time, Arthur fancied that he saw tears rise to Mr. Meagles's eyes as he hurried out of the room. It was either the fact too, or he fancied further, that Pet herself was not insensible to these little incidents; that she tried, with a more delicate affection than usual, to express to her good father how much she loved him; that it was on this account that she fell behind the rest, both as they went to church and as they returned from it, and took his arm. He could not have sworn but that as he walked alone in the garden afterwards, he had an instantaneous glimpse of her in her father's room, clinging to both her parents with the greatest tenderness, and weeping on her father's shoulder.

The latter part of the day turning out wet, they were fain to keep the house, look over Mr. Meagles's collection, and beguile the time with conversation. This Gowan had plenty to say for himself, and said it in an off-hand and amusing manner. He appeared to be an artist by profession, and to have been at Rome some time; yet he had a slight, careless, amateur way with him—a perceptible limp, both in his devotion to art and his attainments—which Clennam could scarcely understand.

He applied to Daniel Doyce for help, as they stood together, looking out of window.

" You know Mr. Gowan?" he said in a low voice.

" I have seen him here. Comes here every Sunday, when they are at home."

" An artist, I infer from what he says?"

" A sort of a one," said Daniel Doyce, in a surly tone.

" What sort of a one?" asked Clennam, with a smile.

" Why, he has sauntered into the Arts at a leisurely Pall-Mall pace," said Doyce, " and I doubt if they care to be taken quite so coolly."

Pursuing his inquiries, Clennam found that the Gowan family were a very distant ramification of the Barnacles; and that the paternal Gowan, originally attached to a legation abroad, had been pensioned off as a Commissioner of nothing particular somewhere or other, and had died at his post with his drawn salary in his hand, nobly defending it to the last extremity. In consideration of this eminent public service, the Barnacle then in power had recommended the Crown to bestow a pension of two or three hundred a-year on his widow; to which the next Barnacle in power had added certain shady and sedate apartments in the Palace at Hampton Court, where the old lady still lived, deploring the degeneracy of the times, in company with several other old ladies of both sexes. Her son, Mr. Henry Gowan, inheriting from his father, the Commissioner, that very questionable help in life, a very small independence, had been difficult to settle; the rather, as public appointments chanced to be scarce, and his genius, during his earlier manhood, was of that exclusively agricultural character which applies itself to the cultivation of wild oats. At last he had declared that he would become a Painter; partly because he had always had an idle knack that way, and partly to grieve the souls of the Barnacles-in-chief who had not provided for him. So it had come to pass successively, first, that several distinguished ladies had been frightfully shocked; then, that portfolios of his performances had been handed about o' nights, and declared with ecstasy to be perfect Claudes, perfect Cuyps, perfect phænomena; then, that Lord Decimus had bought his picture, and had asked the President and Council to dinner at a blow, and had said, with his own magnificent gravity, "Do you know, there appears to me to be really immense merit in that work?" and, in short, that people of condition had absolutely taken pains to bring him into fashion. But, somehow it had all failed. The prejudiced public had stood out against it obstinately. They had determined not to admire Lord Decimus's picture. They had determined to believe that in every service, except their own, a man must qualify himself, by striving, early and late, and by working heart and soul, might and main. So now Mr. Gowan, like that worn-out old coffin which never was Mahomet's nor anybody else's, hung midway between two points: jaundiced and jealous as to the one he had left: jaundiced and jealous as to the other that he couldn't reach.

Such was the substance of Clennam's discoveries concerning him, made that rainy Sunday afternoon and afterwards.

About an hour or so after dinner time, Young Barnacle appeared, attended by his eye-glass; in honour of whose family connections, Mr. Meagles had cashiered the pretty parlour-maids for the day, and had placed on duty in their stead two dingy men. Young Barnacle was in the last degree amazed and disconcerted at sight of Arthur, and had murmured involuntarily, "Look here!—upon my soul, you know!" before his presence of mind returned.

Even then, he was obliged to embrace the earliest opportunity of taking his friend into a window, and saying, in a nasal way that was a part of his general debility :

"I want to speak to you, Gowan. I say. Look here. Who is that fellow?"

"A friend of our host's. None of mine."

"He's a most ferocious Radical, you know," said Young Barnacle.

"Is he? How do you know?"

"Egod, sir, he was Pitching into our people the other day, in the most tremendous manner. Went up to our place and Pitched into my father to that extent that it was necessary to order him out. Came back to our department, and Pitched into me. Look here. You never saw such a fellow."

"What did he want?"

"Egod, sir," returned Young Barnacle, "He said he wanted to know, you know! Pervaded our department—without an appointment—and said he wanted to know!"

The stare of indignant wonder with which Young Barnacle accompanied this disclosure, would have strained his eyes injuriously but for the opportune relief of dinner. Mr. Meagles (who had been extremely solicitous to know how his uncle and aunt were) begged him to conduct Mrs. Meagles to the dining-room. And when he sat on Mrs. Meagles's right hand, Mr. Meagles looked as gratified as if his whole family were there.

All the natural charm of the previous day was gone. The eaters of the dinner, like the dinner itself, were lukewarm, insipid, over-done—and all owing to this poor little dull Young Barnacle. Conversationless at any time, he was now the victim of a weakness special to the occasion, and solely referable to Clennam. He was under a pressing and continual necessity of looking at that gentleman, which occasioned his eye-glass to get into his soup, into his wine-glass, into Mrs. Meagles's plate, to hang down his back like a bell-rope, and be several times disgracefully restored to his bosom by one of the dingy men. Weakened in mind by his frequent losses of this instrument, and its determination not to stick in his eye, and more and more enfeebled in intellect every time he looked at the mysterious Clennam, he applied spoons to his eye, forks, and other foreign matters connected with the furniture of the dinner-table. His discovery of these mistakes greatly increased his difficulties, but never released him from the necessity of looking at Clennam. And whenever Clennam spoke, this ill-starred young man was clearly seized with a dread that he was coming, by some artful device, round to that point of wanting to know, you know.

It may be questioned, therefore, whether any one but Mr. Meagles had much enjoyment of the time. Mr. Meagles, however, thoroughly enjoyed Young Barnacle. As a mere flask of the golden water in the tale became a full fountain when it was poured out, so Mr. Meagles seemed to feel that this small spice of Barnacle imparted to his table the flavour of the whole family-tree. In its presence, his frank, fine, genuine qualities paled; he was not so easy, he was not so natural, he was striving after something that did not belong to him, he was not himself. What a strange peculiarity on the part of Mr. Meagles, and where should we find such another case!

At last the wet Sunday wore itself out in a wet night; and Young Barnacle went home in a cab, feebly smoking; and the objectionable Gowan went away on foot, accompanied by the objectionable dog. Pet had taken the most amiable pains all day to be friendly with Clennam, but Clennam had been a little reserved since breakfast—that is to say, would have been, if he had loved her.

When he had gone to his own room, and had again thrown himself into the chair by the fire, Mr. Doyce knocked at the door, candle in hand, to ask him how and at what hour he purposed returning on the morrow? After settling this question, he said a word to Mr. Doyce about this Gowan—who would have run in his head a good deal, if he had been his rival.

"Those are not good prospects for a painter," said Clennam.

"No," returned Doyce.

Mr. Doyce stood, chamber-candlestick in hand, the other hand in his pocket, looking hard at the flame of his candle, with a certain quiet perception in his face that they were going to say something more.

"I thought our good friend a little changed, and out of spirits, after he came this morning?" said Clennam.

"Yes," returned Doyce.

"But not his daughter?" said Clennam.

"No," said Doyce.

There was a pause on both sides. Mr. Doyce, still looking at the flame of his candle, slowly resumed:

"The truth is, he has twice taken his daughter abroad, in the hope of separating her from Mr. Gowan. He rather thinks she is disposed to like him, and he has painful doubts (I quite agree with him, as I dare say you do,) of the hopefulness of such a marriage."

"There——" Clennam choked, and coughed, and stopped.

"Yes, you have taken cold," said Daniel Doyce. But without looking at him.

"——There is an engagement between them, of course?" said Clennam airily.

"No, as I am told, certainly not. It has been solicited on the gentleman's part, but none has been made. Since their recent return, our friend has yielded to a weekly visit, but that is the utmost. Minnie would not deceive her father and mother. You have travelled with them, and I believe you know what a bond there is among them, extending even beyond this present life. All that there is between Miss Minnie and Mr. Gowan, I have no doubt we see."

"Ah! We see enough!" cried Arthur.

Mr. Doyce wished him Good Night, in the tone of a man who had heard a mournful, not to say despairing, exclamation, and who sought to infuse some encouragement and hope into the mind of the person by whom it had been uttered. Such tone was probably a part of his oddity, as one of a crotchety band; for how could he have heard anything of that kind without Clennam's hearing it too?

The rain fell heavily on the roof, and pattered on the ground, and dripped among the evergreens, and the leafless branches of the trees. The rain fell heavily, drearily. It was a night of tears.

If Clennam had not decided against falling in love with Pet; if he had had the weakness to do it; if he had, little by little, persuaded himself to set all the earnestness of his nature, all the might of his hope, and all the wealth of his matured character, on that cast; if he had done this and found that all was lost; he would have been, that night, unutterably miserable. As it was——

As it was, the rain fell heavily, drearily.

CHAPTER XVIII

LITTLE DORRIT'S LOVER

LITTLE DORRIT had not attained her twenty-second birthday
without finding a lover. Even in the shallow Marshalsea,
the ever young Archer shot off a few featherless arrows now
and then from a mouldy bow, and winged a Collegian or two.

Little Dorrit's lover, however, was not a Collegian. He
was the sentimental son of a turnkey. His father hoped, in
the fulness of time, to leave him the inheritance of an
unstained key; and had from his early youth familiarised
him with the duties of his office, and with an ambition to
retain the prison-lock in the family. While the succession
was yet in abeyance, he assisted his mother in the conduct of
a snug tobacco business round the corner of Horsemonger
Lane (his father being a non-resident turnkey), which could
usually command a neat connection within the College walls.

Years agone, when the object of his affections was wont to
sit in her little arm-chair, by the high Lodge-fender, Young
John (family name, Chivery), a year older than herself, had
eyed her with admiring wonder. When he had played with
her in the yard, his favourite game had been to counterfeit
locking her up in corners, and to counterfeit letting her out
for real kisses. When he grew tall nough to peep through
the keyhole of the great lock of the main door, he had
divers times set down his father's dinner, or supper, to get
on as it might on the outer side thereof, while he stood

taking cold in one eye by dint of peeping at her through that airy perspective.

If Young John had ever slackened in his truth in the less penetrable days of his boyhood, when youth is prone to wear its boots unlaced and is happily unconscious of digestive organs, he had soon strung it up again and screwed it tight. At nineteen, his hand had inscribed in chalk on that part of the wall which fronted her lodging, on the occasion of her birthday, "Welcome sweet nursling of the Fairies!" At twenty-three, the same hand falteringly presented cigars on Sundays to the Father of the Marshalsea, and Father of the queen of his soul.

Young John was small of stature, with rather weak legs and very weak light hair. One of his eyes (perhaps the eye that used to peep through the keyhole) was also weak, and looked larger than the other, as if it couldn't collect itself. Young John was gentle likewise. But he was great of soul. Poetical, expansive, faithful.

Though too humble before the ruler of his heart to be sanguine, Young John had considered the object of his attachment in all its lights and shades. Following it out to blissful results, he had descried, without self-commendation, a fitness in it. Say things prospered, and they were united. She, the child of the Marshalsea; he, the lock-keeper. There was a fitness in that. Say he became a resident turnkey. She would officially succeed to the chamber she had rented so long. There was a beautiful propriety in that. It looked over the wall, if you stood on tip-toe; and, with a trellis-work of scarlet beans and a canary or so, would become a very Arbour. There was a charming idea in that. Then, being all in all to one another, there was even an appropriate grace in the lock. With the world shut out (except that part of it which would be shut in); with its troubles and disturbances only known to them by hearsay, as they would be described by the pilgrims tarrying with them on their way to the Insolvent Shrine; with the Arbour above, and the

Lodge below; they would glide down the stream of time, in pastoral domestic happiness. Young John drew tears from his eyes by finishing the picture with a tombstone in the adjoining churchyard, close against the prison wall, bearing the following touching inscription: "Sacred to the Memory of JOHN CHIVERY, Sixty years Turnkey, and fifty years Head Turnkey, Of the neighbouring Marshalsea, Who departed this life, universally respected, on the thirty-first of December, One thousand eight hundred and eighty-six, Aged eighty-three years. Also of his truly beloved and truly loving wife, AMY, whose maiden name was DORRIT, Who survived his loss not quite forty-eight hours, And who breathed her last in the Marshalsea aforesaid. There she was born, There she lived, There she died."

The Chivery parents were not ignorant of their son's attachment—indeed it had, on some exceptional occasions, thrown him into a state of mind that had impelled him to conduct himself with irascibility towards the customers, and damage the business—but they, in their turns, had worked it out to desirable conclusions. Mrs. Chivery, a prudent woman, had desired her husband to take notice that their John's prospects of the Lock would certainly be strengthened by an alliance with Miss Dorrit, who had herself a kind of claim upon the College, and was much respected there. Mrs. Chivery had desired her husband to take notice that if, on the one hand, their John had means and a post of trust, on the other hand, Miss Dorrit had family; and that her (Mrs. Chivery's) sentiment was, that two halves made a whole. Mrs. Chivery, speaking as a mother and not as a diplomatist, had then, from a different point of view, desired her husband to recollect that their John had never been strong, and that his love had fretted and worrited him enough as it was, without his being driven to do himself a mischief, as nobody couldn't say he wouldn't be if he was crossed. These arguments had so powerfully influenced the mind of Mr. Chivery, who was a man of few words, that he had on sundry Sunday mornings, given his boy what he termed "a lucky touch," signifying that he considered such commendation of him to Good Fortune, preparatory to his that day declaring his passion and becoming triumphant. But Young John had never taken courage to make the declaration; and it was principally on these occasions that he had returned excited to the tobacco shop, and flown at the customers.

In this affair, as in every other, Little Dorrit herself was the last person considered. Her brother and sister were aware of it, and attained a sort of station by making a peg of it on which to air the miserably ragged old fiction of the family gentility. Her sister asserted the family gentility, by flouting the poor swain as he loitered about the prison for glimpses of his dear. Tip asserted the family gentility, and his own, by coming out in the character of the aristocratic brother, and loftily swaggering in the little skittle-ground respecting seizures by the scruff of the neck, which there were looming probabilities of some gentleman unknown executing on some little puppy not mentioned. These were not the only members of the Dorrit family who turned it to account. No, no. The Father of the Marshalsea was supposed to know nothing about the matter, of course: his poor dignity could not see so low. But he took the cigars, on Sundays, and was glad to get them; and sometimes even condescended to walk up and down the yard with the donor (who was proud and hopeful then), and benignantly to smoke one in his society. With no less readiness and condescension did he receive attentions from Chivery Senior, who always relinquished his arm-chair and newspaper to him, when he came into the Lodge during one of his spells of duty; and who had even mentioned to him, that if he would like at any time after dusk, quietly to step out into the fore-court, and take a look at the street, there was not much to prevent him. If he did not avail himself of this latter civility, it was only because he had lost the relish for it; inasmuch as he took everything else he could get, and would say at times, "Extremely civil person, Chivery; very attentive man and very respectful. Young Chivery, too; really almost with a delicate perception of one's position here. A very well conducted family indeed, the Chiveries. Their behaviour gratifies me."

The devoted Young John all this time regarded the family with reverence. He never dreamed of disputing their pretensions, but did homage to the miserable Mumbo Jumbo they paraded. As to resenting any affront from *her* brother, he would have felt, even if he had not naturally been of a most pacific disposition, that to wag his tongue or lift his hand against that sacred gentleman would be an unhallowed act. He was sorry that his noble mind should take offence; still, he felt the fact to be not incompatible with its nobility, and sought to propitiate and conciliate that gallant soul. Her father, a gentleman in misfortune—a gentleman of a fine spirit and courtly manners, who always bore with him—he deeply honoured. Her sister, he considered somewhat vain and proud, but a young lady of infinite accomplishments, who could not forget the past. It was an instinctive testimony to Little Dorrit's worth, and difference from all the rest, that the poor young fellow honoured and loved her for being simply what she was.

The tobacco business round the corner of Horsemonger Lane was carried on in a rural establishment one story high, which had the benefit of the air from the yards of Horsemonger Lane Jail, and the advantage of a retired walk under the wall of that pleasant establishment. The business was of too modest a character to support a life-size Highlander, but it maintained a little one on a bracket on the door-post, who looked like a fallen Cherub that had found it necessary to take to a kilt.

From the portal thus decorated, one Sunday after an early dinner of baked viands, Young John issued forth on his usual Sunday errand; not empty-handed, but with his offering of cigars. He was neatly attired in a plum-coloured coat, with as large a collar of black velvet as his figure could carry; a silken waistcoat, bedecked with golden sprigs; a chaste neckerchief much in vogue at that day, representing a preserve of lilac pheasants on a buff ground; pantaloons so highly decorated with side-stripes, that each leg was a three-stringed lute, and a hat of state very high and hard. When the prudent Mrs. Chivery perceived that in addition to these adornments her John carried a pair of white kid gloves, and a cane like a little finger-post, surmounted by an ivory hand marshalling him the way that he should go; and when she saw him, in this heavy marching order, turn the corner to the right; she remarked to Mr. Chivery, who was at home at the time, that she thought she knew which way the wind blew.

The Collegians were entertaining a considerable number of visitors that Sunday afternoon, and their Father kept his room for the purpose of receiving presentations. After making the tour of the yard, Little Dorrit's lover with a hurried heart went up-stairs, and knocked with his knuckles at the Father's door.

"Come in, come in!" said a gracious voice. The Father's voice, her father's, the Marshalsea's father's. He was seated in his black velvet cap, with his newspaper, three-and-six-pence accidentally left on the table, and two chairs arranged. Everything prepared for holding his Court.

"Ah, Young John! How do you do, how do you do!"

"Pretty well, I thank you, sir. I hope you are the same."

"Yes, John Chivery; yes. Nothing to complain of."

"I have taken the liberty, sir, of—— "

"Eh?" The Father of the Marshalsea always lifted up his eyebrows at this point, and became amiably distraught and smilingly absent in mind.

" —A few cigars, sir."

"Oh!" (For the moment, excessively surprised.) "Thank you, Young John, thank you. But really, I am afraid I am too— No? Well then, I will say no more about it. Put

264

them on the mantel-shelf, if you please, Young John. And sit down, sit down. You are not a stranger, John."

"Thank you, sir, I am sure—Miss;" here Young John turned the great hat round and round upon his left hand, like a slowly twirling mouse-cage; "Miss Amy quite well, sir?"

"Yes, John, yes; very well. She is out."

"Indeed, sir?"

"Yes, John. Miss Amy is gone for an airing. My young people all go out a good deal. But at their time of life, it's natural, John."

"Very much so, I am sure, sir."

"An airing. An airing. Yes." He was blandly tapping his fingers on the table, and casting his eyes up at the window. "Amy has gone for an airing on the Iron Bridge. She has become quite partial to the Iron Bridge of late, and seems to like to walk there better than anywhere." He returned to conversation. "Your father is not on duty at present, I think, John?"

"No, sir, he comes on later in the afternoon." Another twirl of the great hat, and then Young John said, rising, "I am afraid I must wish you good day, sir."

"So soon? Good day, Young John. Nay, nay," with the utmost condescension, "never mind your glove, John. Shake hands with it on. You are no stranger here, you know."

Highly gratified by the kindness of his reception, Young John descended the staircase. On his way down he met some Collegians bringing up visitors to be presented, and at that moment Mr. Dorrit happened to call over the banisters with particular distinctness, "Much obliged to you for your little testimonial, John!"

Little Dorrit's lover very soon laid down his penny on the toll-plate of the Iron Bridge, and came upon it looking about him for the well-known and well-beloved figure. At first he feared she was not there; but as he walked on towards the Middlesex side, he saw her standing still, looking at the water. She was absorbed in thought, and he wondered what she might be thinking about. There were the piles of city roofs and chimneys, more free from smoke than on week-days; and there were the distant masts and steeples. Perhaps she was thinking about them.

Little Dorrit mused so long, and was so entirely pre-occupied, that although her lover stood quiet for what he thought was a long time, and twice or thrice retired and came back again to the former spot, still she did not move. So, in the end, he made up his mind to go on, and seem to come upon her casually in passing, and speak to her. The place was quiet, and now or never was the time to speak to her.

He walked on, and she did not appear to hear his steps until he was close upon her. When he said, " Miss Dorrit ! " she started, and fell back from him, with an expression in her face of fright and something like dislike that caused him unutterable dismay. She had often avoided him before— always, indeed, for a long, long while. She had turned away, and glided off, so often, when she had seen him coming towards her, that the unfortunate Young John could not think it accidental. But he had hoped that it might be shyness, her retiring character, her foreknowledge of the state of his heart, anything short of aversion. Now, that momen-tary look had said, " You, of all people ! I would rather have seen any one on earth, than you ! "

It was but a momentary look, inasmuch as she checked it, and said in her soft little voice, " Oh, Mr. John ! Is it you ? " But she felt what it had been, as he felt what it had been; and they stood looking at one another equally confused.

" Miss Amy, I am afraid I disturbed you by speaking to you."

" Yes, rather. I—I came here to be alone, and I thought I was."

" Miss Amy, I took the liberty of walking this way,

266

because Mr. Dorrit chanced to mention, when I called upon him just now, that you——"

She caused him more dismay than before by suddenly murmuring, "O, father, father!" in a heart-rending tone, and turning her face away.

"Miss Amy, I hope I don't give you any uneasiness by naming Mr. Dorrit. I assure you I found him very well, and in the best of spirits, and he showed me even more than his usual kindness; being so very kind as to say that I was not a stranger there, and in all ways gratifying me very much."

To the inexpressible consternation of her lover, Little Dorrit, with her hands to her averted face, and rocking herself where she stood, as if she were in pain, murmured, "O, father, how can you! O dear, dear father, how can you, can you, do it!"

The poor fellow stood gazing at her, overflowing with sympathy, but not knowing what to make of this, until, having taken out her handkerchief and put it to her still averted face, she hurried away. At first he remained stock still; then hurried after her.

"Miss Amy, pray! Will you have the goodness to stop a moment? Miss Amy, if it comes to that, let *me* go. I shall go out of my senses, if I have to think that I have driven you away like this."

His trembling voice and unfeigned earnestness brought Little Dorrit to a stop. "O, I don't know what to do," she cried, "I don't know what to do!"

To Young John, who had never seen her bereft of her quiet self-command, who had seen her from her infancy ever so reliable and self-suppressed, there was a shock in her distress, and in having to associate himself with it as its cause, that shook him from his great hat to the pavement. He felt it necessary to explain himself. He might be misunderstood —supposed to mean something, or to have done something, that had never entered into his imagination. He begged her

267

to hear him explain himself, as the greatest favour she could show him.

"Miss Amy, I know very well that your family is far above mine. It were vain to conceal it. There never was a Chivery a gentleman that ever I heard of, and I will not commit the meanness of making a false representation on a subject so momentous. Miss Amy, I know very well that your high-souled brother, and likewise your spirited sister, spurn me from a height. What I have to do is to respect them, to wish to be admitted to their friendship, to look up at the eminence on which they are placed, from my lowlier station—for, whether viewed as tobacco or viewed as the lock, I well know it is lowly—and ever wish them well and happy."

There really was a genuineness in the poor fellow, and a contrast between the hardness of his hat and the softness of his heart (albeit, perhaps, of his head, too), that was moving. Little Dorrit entreated him to disparage neither himself nor his station, and, above all things, to divest himself of any idea that she supposed hers to be superior. This gave him a little comfort.

"Miss Amy," he then stammered, "I have had for a long time—ages they seem to me—Revolving ages—a heart-cherished wish to say something to you. May I say it?"

Little Dorrit involuntarily started from his side again, with the faintest shadow of her former look; conquering that, she went on at great speed half across the Bridge without replying!

"May I—Miss Amy, I but ask the question humbly—may I say it? I have been so unlucky already in giving you pain, without having any such intentions, before the holy Heavens! that there is no fear of my saying it unless I have your leave. I can be miserable alone, I can be cut up by myself; why should I also make miserable, and cut up one, that I would fling myself off that parapet to give half a moment's joy to! Not that that's much to do, for I'd do it for twopence."

The mournfulness of his spirits, and the gorgeousness of his appearance, might have made him ridiculous, but that his delicacy made him respectable. Little Dorrit learnt from it what to do.

"If you please, John Chivery," she returned, trembling, but in a quiet way, "since you are so considerate as to ask me whether you shall say any more—if you please, no."

"Never, Miss Amy?"

"No, if you please. Never."

"Oh Lord!" gasped Young John.

"But perhaps, you will let me, instead, say something to you. I want to say it earnestly, and with as plain a meaning as it is possible to express. When you think of us, John—I mean my brother and sister, and me—don't think of us as being any different from the rest; for, whatever we once were (which I hardly know) we ceased to be long ago, and never can be any more. It will be much better for you, and much better for others, if you will do that, instead of what you are doing now."

Young John dolefully protested that he would try to bear it in mind, and would be heartily glad to do anything she wished.

"As to me," said Little Dorrit, "think as little of me as you can; the less, the better. When you think of me at all, John, let it only be as the child you have seen grow up in the prison, with one set of duties always occupying her; as a weak, retired, contented, unprotected girl. I particularly want you to remember, that when I come outside the gate, I am unprotected and solitary."

He would try to do anything she wished. But why did Miss Amy so much want him to remember that?

"Because," returned Little Dorrit, "I know I can then quite trust you not to forget to-day, and not to say any more to me. You are so generous that I know I can trust to you for that; and I do and I always will. I am going to show you, at once, that I fully trust you. I like this place where we are speaking, better than any place I know;" her slight colour had faded, but her lover thought he saw it coming back just then; "and I may be often here. I know it is only necessary for me to tell you so, to be quite sure that you will never come here again in search of me. And I am —quite sure!"

She might rely upon it, said Young John. He was a miserable wretch, but her word was more than a law for him.

"And good-bye, John," said Little Dorrit. "And I hope you will have a good wife one day, and be a happy man. I am sure you will deserve to be happy, and you will be, John."

As she held out her hand to him with these words, the heart that was under the waistcoat of sprigs—mere slop-work, if the truth must be known—swelled to the size of the heart of a gentleman; and the poor common little fellow, having no room to hold it, burst into tears.

"O don't cry!" said Little Dorrit piteously. "Don't, don't! Good-bye, John. God bless you!"

"Good-bye, Miss Amy. Good-bye!"

And so he left her: first observing that she sat down on the corner of a seat, and not only rested her little hand upon the rough wall, but laid her face against it too, as if her head were heavy, and her mind were sad.

It was an affecting illustration of the fallacy of human projects, to behold her lover with the great hat pulled over his eyes, the velvet collar turned up as if it rained, the plum-coloured coat buttoned to conceal the silken waistcoat of golden sprigs, and the little direction-post pointing inexorably home, creeping along by the worst back streets, and composing, as he went, the following new inscription for a tombstone in St. George's Churchyard:

"Here lie the mortal remains of JOHN CHIVERY, Never anything worth mentioning, Who died about the end of the year one thousand eight hundred and twenty-six, Of a broken heart, Requesting with his last breath that the word AMY might be inscribed over his ashes, Which was accordingly directed to be done, By his afflicted Parents."

CHAPTER XIX

THE brothers William and Frederick Dorrit, walking up and down the College-yard—of course on the aristocratic or Pump side, for the Father made it a point of his state to be chary of going among his children on the Poor side, except on Sunday mornings, Christmas Days, and other occasions of ceremony, in the observance whereof he was very punctual, and at which times he laid his hand upon the heads of their infants, and blessed those young Insolvents with a benignity that was highly edifying—the brothers, walking up and down the College-yard together, were a memorable sight. Frederick the free, was so humbled, bowed, withered, and faded; William the bond, was so courtly, condescending, and benevolently conscious of a position; that in this regard only, if in no other, the brothers were a spectacle to wonder at.

They walked up and down the yard, on the evening of Little Dorrit's Sunday interview with her lover on the Iron Bridge. The cares of state were over for that day, the Drawing Room had been well attended, several new presentations had taken place, the three-and-sixpence accidentally left on the table had accidentally increased to twelve shillings, and the Father of the Marshalsea refreshed himself with a whiff of cigar. As he walked up and down, affably accommodating his step to the shuffle of his brother, not proud in his superiority, but considerate of that poor creature, bearing

271

with him, and breathing toleration of his infirmities in every little puff of smoke that issued from his lips and aspired to get over the spiked wall, he was a sight to wonder at.

His brother Frederick of the dim eye, palsied hand, bent form, and groping mind, submissively shuffled at his side, accepting his patronage as he accepted every incident of the labyrinthian world in which he had got lost. He held the usual screwed bit of whity-brown paper in his hand, from which he ever and again unscrewed a spare pinch of snuff. That falteringly taken, he would glance at his brother not unadmiringly, put his hands behind him, and shuffle on so at his side until he took another pinch, or stood still to look about him—perchance suddenly missing his clarionet.

The College visitors were melting away as the shades of night drew on, but the yard was still pretty full, the Collegians being mostly out, seeing their friends to the Lodge. As the brothers paced the yard, William the bond looked about him to receive salutes, returned them by graciously lifting off his hat, and, with an engaging air, prevented Frederick the free from running against the company, or being jostled against the wall. The Collegians as a body were not easily impressible, but even they, according to their various ways of wondering, appeared to find in the two brothers a sight to wonder at.

"You are a little low this evening, Frederick," said the Father of the Marshalsea. "Anything the matter?"

"The matter?" He stared for a moment, and then dropped his head and eyes again. "No, William, no. Nothing is the matter."

"If you could be persuaded to smarten yourself up a little, Frederick——"

"Aye, aye!" said the old man hurriedly. "But I can't be. I can't be. Don't talk so. That's all over."

The Father of the Marshalsea glanced at a passing Collegian with whom he was on friendly terms, as who should say, "An enfeebled old man, this; but he is my brother, sir, my

The Brothers

brother, and the voice of Nature is potent!" and steered his brother clear of the handle of the pump by the threadbare sleeve. Nothing would have been wanting to the perfection of his character as a fraternal guide, philosopher, and friend, if he had only steered his brother clear of ruin, instead of bringing it upon him.

"I think, William," said the object of his affectionate consideration, "that I am tired, and will go home to bed."

"My dear Frederick," returned the other. "Don't let me detain you; don't sacrifice your inclinations to me."

"Late hours, and a heated atmosphere, and years, I suppose," said Frederick, "weaken me."

"My dear Frederick," returned the Father of the Marshalsea, "do you think you are sufficiently careful of yourself? Do you think your habits are as precise and methodical as— shall I say as mine are? Not to revert again to that little eccentricity which I mentioned just now, I doubt if you take air and exercise enough, Frederick. Here is the parade, always at your service. Why not use it more regularly than you do?"

"Hah!" sighed the other. "Yes, yes, yes, yes."

"But it is of no use saying yes, yes, my dear Frederick," the Father of the Marshalsea in his mild wisdom persisted, "unless you act on that assent. Consider my case, Frederick. I am a kind of example. Necessity and time have taught me what to do. At certain stated hours of the day, you will find me on the parade, in my room, in the Lodge, reading the paper, receiving company, eating and drinking. I have impressed upon Amy during many years, that I must have my meals (for instance) punctually. Amy has grown up in a sense of the importance of these arrangements, and you know what a good girl she is."

The brother only sighed again, as he plodded dreamily along, "Hah! Yes, yes, yes, yes."

"My dear fellow," said the Father of the Marshalsea, laying his hand upon his shoulder, and mildly rallying him—mildly, because of his weakness, poor dear soul; "you said that before, and it does not express much, Frederick, even if it means much. I wish I could rouse you, my good Frederick; you want to be roused."

"Yes, William, yes. No doubt," returned the other, lifting his dim eyes to his face. "But I am not like you."

The Father of the Marshalsea said, with a shrug of modest self-depreciation, "Oh! You might be like me, my dear Frederick; you might be, if you chose!" and forbore, in the magnanimity of his strength, to press his fallen brother further.

There was a deal of leave-taking going on in corners, as was usual on Sunday nights; and here and there in the dark, some poor woman, wife or mother, was weeping with a new Collegian. The time had been when the Father himself had wept, in the shades of that yard, as his own poor wife had wept. But it was many years ago; and now he was like a passenger aboard ship in a long voyage, who has recovered from sea-sickness, and is impatient of that weakness in the fresher passengers taken aboard at the last port. He was inclined to remonstrate, and to express his opinion that people who couldn't get on without crying, had no business there. In manner, if not in words, he always testified his displeasure at these interruptions of the general harmony; and it was so well understood, that delinquents usually withdrew if they were aware of him.

On this Sunday evening, he accompanied his brother to the gate with an air of endurance and clemency; being in a bland temper and graciously disposed to overlook the tears. In the flaring gaslight of the Lodge, several Collegians were basking; some taking leave of visitors, and some who had no visitors, watching the frequent turning of the key, and conversing with one another and with Mr. Chivery. The paternal entrance made a sensation of course; and Mr. Chivery, touching his hat (in a short manner though) with his key, hoped he found himself tolerable.

AMIABLE SOLICITUDE

"Thank you, Chivery, quite well. And you?"

Mr. Chivery said in a low growl, "Oh! *he* was all right." Which was his general way of acknowledging inquiries after his health, when a little sullen.

"I had a visit from Young John to-day, Chivery. And very smart he looked, I assure you."

So Mr. Chivery had heard. Mr. Chivery must confess, however, that his wish was that the boy didn't lay out so much money upon it. For what did it bring him in? It only brought him in Wexation. And he could get that anywhere, for nothing.

"How vexation, Chivery?" asked the benignant father.

"No odds," returned Mr. Chivery. "Never mind. Mr. Frederick going out?"

"Yes, Chivery, my brother is going home to bed. He is tired, and not quite well. Take care, Frederick, take care. Good night, my dear Frederick!"

Shaking hands with his brother, and touching his greasy hat to the company in the Lodge, Frederick slowly shuffled out of the door which Mr. Chivery unlocked for him. The Father of the Marshalsea showed the amiable solicitude of a superior being that he should come to no harm.

"Be so kind as to keep the door open a moment, Chivery, that I may see him go along the passage and down the steps. Take care, Frederick! (He is very infirm.) Mind the steps! (He is so very absent.) Be careful how you cross, Frederick. (I really don't like the notion of his going wandering at large, he is so extremely liable to be run over.)"

With these words, and with a face expressive of many uneasy doubts and much anxious guardianship, he turned his regards upon the assembled company in the Lodge: so plainly indicating that his brother was to be pitied for not being under lock and key, that an opinion to that effect went round among the Collegians assembled.

But he did not receive it with unqualified assent; on the contrary, he said, No, gentlemen, no; let them not misunderstand him. His brother Frederick was much broken, no doubt, and it might be more comfortable to himself (the Father of the Marshalsea) to know that he was safe within the walls. Still, it must be remembered that to support an existence there during many years, required a certain combination of qualities—he did not say high qualities, but qualities —moral qualities. Now, had his brother Frederick that peculiar union of qualities? Gentlemen, he was a most excellent man, a most gentle, tender, and estimable man, with the simplicity of a child; but would he, though unsuited for most other places, do for that place? No; he said confidently, no! And, he said, Heaven forbid that Frederick should be there in any other character than in his present voluntary character! Gentlemen, whoever came to that College, to remain there a length of time, must have strength of character to go through a good deal and to come out of a good deal. Was his beloved brother Frederick that man? No. They saw him, even as it was, crushed. Misfortune crushed him. He had not power of recoil enough, not elasticity enough, to be a long time in such a place, and yet preserve his self-respect and feel conscious that he was a gentleman. Frederick had not (if he might use the expression) Power enough to see in any delicate little attentions and—and—Testimonials that he might under such circumstances receive, the goodness of human nature, the fine spirit animating the Collegians as a community, and at the same time no degradation to himself, and no depreciation of his claims as a gentleman. Gentlemen, God bless you!

Such was the homily with which he improved and pointed the occasion to the company in the Lodge, before turning into the sallow yard again, and going with his own poor shabby dignity past the Collegian in the dressing-gown who had no coat, and past the Collegian in the sea-side slippers who had no shoes, and past the stout greengrocer Collegian in the corduroy knee-breeches who had no cares, and past the lean clerk Collegian in buttonless black who had no hopes, up his own poor shabby staircase, to his own poor shabby room.

There, the table was laid for his supper, and his old grey gown was ready for him on his chair-back at the fire. His daughter put her little prayer-book in her pocket—had she been praying for pity on all prisoners and captives!—and rose to welcome him.

Uncle had gone home, then? she asked him, as she changed his coat and gave him his black velvet cap. Yes, uncle had gone home. Had her father enjoyed his walk? Why, not much, Amy; not much. No! Did he not feel quite well?

As she stood behind him, leaning over his chair so lovingly, he looked with downcast eyes at the fire. An uneasiness stole over him that was like a touch of shame; and when he spoke, as he presently did, it was in an unconnected and embarrassed manner.

"Something, I—hem!—I don't know what, has gone wrong with Chivery. He is not—ha!—not nearly so obliging and attentive as usual to-night. It—hem!—it's a little thing, but it puts me out, my love. It's impossible to forget," turning his hands over and over, and looking closely at them, "that—hem!—that in such a life as mine, I am unfortunately dependent on these men for something, every hour in the day."

Her arm was on his shoulder, but she did not look in his face while he spoke. Bending her head she looked another way.

"I—hem!—I can't think, Amy, what has given Chivery offence. He is generally so—so very attentive and respectful. And to-night he was quite—quite short with me. Other people there too! Why, good Heaven! if I was to lose the support and recognition of Chivery and his brother officers, I might starve to death here." While he spoke, he was opening and shutting his hands like valves; so conscious all the time of that touch of shame, that he shrunk before his own knowledge of his meaning.

277

"I—ha!—I can't think what it's owing to. I am sure I cannot imagine what the cause of it is. There was a certain Jackson here once, a turnkey of the name of Jackson (I don't think you can remember him, my dear, you were very young), and—hem!—and he had a—brother, and this—young brother paid his addresses to—at least, did not go so far as to pay his addresses to—but admired—respectfully admired—the —not the daughter, the sister—of one of us; a rather distinguished Collegian; I may say, very much so. His name was Captain Martin; and he consulted me on the question whether it was necessary that his daughter—sister—should hazard offending the turnkey brother by being too—ha!— too plain with the other brother. Captain Martin was a gentleman and a man of honour, and I put it to him first to give me his—his own opinion. Captain Martin (highly respected in the army) then unhesitatingly said, that it appeared to him that his—hem!—sister was not called upon to understand the young man too distinctly, and that she might lead him on—I am doubtful whether lead him on was Captain Martin's exact expression: indeed I think he said tolerate him—on her father's—I should say, brother's— account. I hardly know how I have strayed into this story. I suppose it has been through being unable to account for Chivery; but as to the connection between the two, I don't see——"

His voice died away, as if she could not bear the pain of hearing him, and her hand had gradually crept to his lips. For a little while, there was a dead silence and stillness; and he remained shrunk in his chair, and she remained with her arm round his neck, and her head bowed down upon his shoulder.

His supper was cooking in a saucepan on the fire, and, when she moved, it was to make it ready for him on the table. He took his usual seat, she took hers, and he began his meal. They did not, as yet, look at one another. By little and little he began; laying down his knife and fork with a noise, taking things up sharply, biting at his bread as if he were offended with it, and in other similar ways showing that he was out of sorts. At length he pushed his plate from him, and spoke aloud. With the strangest inconsistency.

"What does it matter whether I eat or starve? What does it matter whether such a blighted life as mine comes to an end, now, next week, or next year? What am I worth to any one? A poor prisoner, fed on alms and broken victuals; a squalid, disgraced wretch!"

"Father, father!" As he rose, she went on her knees to him, and held up her hands to him.

"Amy," he went on in a suppressed voice, trembling violently, and looking at her as wildly as if he had gone mad. "I tell you, if you could see me as your mother saw me, you wouldn't believe it to be the creature you have only looked at through the bars of this cage. I was young, I was accomplished, I was good-looking, I was independent—by God I was, child!—and people sought me out, and envied me. Envied me!"

"Dear father!" She tried to take down the shaking arm that he flourished in the air, but he resisted, and put her hand away.

"If I had but a picture of myself in those days, though it was ever so ill done, you would be proud of it, you would be proud of it. But I have no such thing. Now, let me be a warning! Let no man," he cried, looking haggardly about, "fail to preserve at least that little of the times of his prosperity and respect. Let his children have that clue to what was. Unless my face, when I am dead, subsides into the long departed look—they say such things happen, I don't know—my children will have never seen me."

"Father, father!"

"O despise me, despise me! Look away from me, don't listen to me, stop me, blush for me, cry for me—Even you, Amy! Do it, do it! I do it to myself! I am hardened now, I have sunk too low to care long even for that."

"Dear father, loved father, darling of my heart!" She was clinging to him with her arms, and she got him to drop into his chair again, and caught at the raised arm, and tried to put it round her neck.

"Let it lie there, father. Look at me, father, kiss me, father! Only think of me, father, for one little moment!"

Still he went on in the same wild way, though it was gradually breaking down into a miserable whining.

"And yet I have some respect here. I have made some stand against it. I am not quite trodden down. Go out and ask who is the chief person in the place. They'll tell you it's your father. Go out and ask who is never trifled with, and who is always treated with some delicacy. They'll say, your father. Go out and ask what funeral here (it must be here, I know it can be nowhere else) will make more talk, and perhaps more grief, than any that has ever gone out at the gate. They'll say your father's. Well then. Amy! Amy! Is your father so universally despised? Is there nothing to redeem him? Will you have nothing to remember him by, but his ruin and decay? Will you be able to have no affection for him when he is gone, poor castaway, gone?"

He burst into tears of maudlin pity for himself, and at length suffering her to embrace him, and take charge of him, let his grey head rest against her cheek, and bewail his wretchedness. Presently he changed the subject of his lamentations, and clasping his hands about her as she embraced him, cried, O Amy, his motherless, forlorn child! O the days that he had seen her careful and laborious for him! Then he reverted to himself, and weakly told her how much better she would have loved him if she had known him in his vanished character, and how he would have married her to a gentleman who should have been proud of her as his daughter, and how (at which he cried again) she should first have ridden at his fatherly side on her own horse, and how the crowd (by which he meant in effect the people who had given him the twelve shillings he then had in his pocket) should have trudged the dusty roads respectfully.

Thus, now boasting, now despairing, in either fit a captive with the jail-rot upon him, and the impurity of his prison worn into the grain of his soul, he revealed his degenerate state to his affectionate child. No one else ever beheld him in the details of his humiliation. Little recked the Collegians who were laughing in their rooms over his late address in the Lodge, what a serious picture they had in their obscure gallery of the Marshalsea that Sunday night.

There was a classical daughter once—perhaps—who ministered to her father in his prison as her mother had ministered to her. Little Dorrit, though of the unheroic modern stock, and mere English, did much more, in comforting her father's wasted heart upon her innocent breast, and turning to it a fountain of love and fidelity that never ran dry or waned, through all his years of famine.

She soothed him ; asked him for his forgiveness if she had been, or seemed to have been, undutiful ; told him, Heaven knows truly, that she could not honour him more if he were the favourite of Fortune and the whole world acknowledged him. When his tears were dried, and he sobbed in his weakness no longer, and was free from that touch of shame, and had recovered his usual bearing, she prepared the remains of his supper afresh, and, sitting by his side, rejoiced to see him eat and drink. For, now he sat in his black velvet cap and old grey gown, magnanimous again ; and would have comported himself towards any Collegian who might have looked in to ask his advice, like a great moral Lord Chesterfield, or Master of the ethical ceremonies of the Marshalsea.

To keep his attention engaged, she talked with him about his wardrobe ; when he was pleased to say, that Yes, indeed, those shirts she proposed would be exceedingly acceptable, for those he had were worn out, and, being ready-made, had never fitted him. Being conversational, and in a reasonable flow of spirits, he then invited her attention to his coat as it hung behind the door: remarking that the Father of the place would set an indifferent example to his children, already disposed to be slovenly, if he went among them out at elbows. He was jocular, too, as to the heeling of his shoes; but became grave on the subject of his cravat, and promised her that when she could afford it, she should buy him a new one.

While he smoked out his cigar in peace, she made his bed, and put the small room in order for his repose. Being weary then, owing to the advanced hour and his emotions, he came out of his chair to bless her and wish her Good night. All this time he had never once thought of *her* dress, her shoes, her need of anything. No other person upon earth, save herself, could have been so unmindful of her wants.

He kissed her many times with "Bless you, my love. Good night, my dear!"

But her gentle breast had been so deeply wounded by what she had seen of him, that she was unwilling to leave him alone, lest he should lament and despair again. "Father, dear, I am not tired; let me come back presently, when you are in bed, and sit by you."

He asked her with an air of protection, if she felt solitary?

"Yes, father."

"Then come back by all means, my love."

"I shall be very quiet, father."

"Don't think of me, my dear," he said, giving her his kind permission fully. "Come back by all means."

He seemed to be dozing when she returned, and she put the low fire together very softly lest she should awake him. But he overheard her, and called out who was that?

"Only Amy, father."

"Amy, my child, come here. I want to say a word to you."

He raised himself a little in his low bed, as she kneeled beside it to bring her face near him; and put his hand between hers. O! Both the private father and the Father of the Marshalsea were strong within him then.

282

"My love, you have had a life of hardship here. No companions, no recreations, many cares I am afraid?"

"Don't think of that, dear. I never do."

"You know my position, Amy. I have not been able to do much for you; but all I have been able to do, I have done."

"Yes, my dear father," she rejoined, kissing him. "I know, I know."

"I am in the twenty-third year of my life here," he said, with a catch in his breath that was not so much a sob as an irrepressible sound of self-approval, the momentary outburst of a noble consciousness. "It is all I could do for my children—I have done it. Amy, my love, you are by far the best loved of the three; I have had you principally in my mind—whatever I have done for your sake, my dear child, I have done freely and without murmuring."

Only the wisdom that holds the clue to all hearts and all mysteries, can surely know to what extent a man, especially a man brought down as this man had been, can impose upon himself. Enough, for the present place, that he lay down with wet eyelashes, serene, in a manner majestic, after bestowing his life of degradation as a sort of portion on the devoted child upon whom its miseries had fallen so heavily, and whose love alone had saved him to be even what he was.

That child had no doubts, asked herself no questions, for she was but too content to see him with a lustre round his head. Poor dear, good dear, truest, kindest, dearest, were the only words she had for him, as she hushed him to rest.

She never left him all that night. As if she had done him a wrong which her tenderness could hardly repair, she sat by him in his sleep, at times softly kissing him with suspended breath, and calling him in a whisper by some endearing name. At times she stood aside, so as not to intercept the low firelight, and, watching him when it fell upon his sleeping face, wondered did he look now at all as he had looked when he was prosperous and happy; as he had so touched her by

283

imagining that he might look once more in that awful time. At the thought of that time, she kneeled beside his bed again, and prayed, "O spare his life! O save him to me! O look down upon my dear, long-suffering, unfortunate, much-changed, dear dear father!"

Not until the morning came to protect him and encourage him, did she give him a last kiss and leave the small room. When she had stolen down-stairs, and along the empty yard, and had crept up to her own high garret, the smokeless housetops and the distant country hills were discernible over the wall in the clear morning. As she gently opened the window, and looked eastward down the prison yard, the spikes upon the wall were tipped with red, then made a sullen purple pattern on the sun as it came flaming up into the heavens. The spikes had never looked so sharp and cruel, nor the bars so heavy, nor the prison space so gloomy and contracted. She thought of the sunrise on rolling rivers, of the sunrise on wide seas, of the sunrise on rich landscapes, of the sunrise on great forests where the birds were waking and the trees were rustling; and she looked down into the living grave on which the sun had risen, with her father in it, three-and-twenty years, and said, in a burst of sorrow and compassion, "No, no, I have never seen him in my life!"

CHAPTER XX

If Young John Chivery had had the inclination, and the power, to write a satire on family pride, he would have had no need to go for an avenging illustration out of the family of his beloved. He would have found it amply in that gallant brother and that dainty sister, so steeped in mean experiences, and so loftily conscious of the family name ; so ready to beg or borrow from the poorest, to eat of anybody's bread, spend anybody's money, drink from anybody's cup and break it afterwards. To have painted the sordid facts of their lives, and they throughout invoking the death's head apparition of the family gentility to come and scare their benefactors, would have made Young John a satirist of the first water.

Tip had turned his liberty to hopeful account by becoming a billiard-marker. He had troubled himself so little as to the means of his release, that Clennam scarcely needed to have been at the pains of impressing the mind of Mr. Plornish on that subject. Whoever had paid him the compliment, he very readily accepted the compliment with *his* compliments, and there was an end of it. Issuing forth from the gate on these easy terms, he became a billiard-marker ; and now occasionally looked in at the little skittle-ground in a green Newmarket coat (second-hand), with a shining collar and bright buttons (new), and drank the beer of the Collegians.

285

One solid stationary point in the looseness of this gentleman's character, was, that he respected and admired his sister Amy. The feeling had never induced him to spare her a moment's uneasiness, or to put himself to any restraint or inconvenience on her account; but with that Marshalsea taint upon his love, he loved her. The same rank Marshalsea flavour was to be recognised in his distinctly perceiving that she sacrificed her life to her father, and in his having no idea that she had done anything for himself.

When this spirited young man, and his sister, had begun systematically to produce the family skeleton for the over-awing of the College, this narrative cannot precisely state. Probably at about the period when they began to dine on the College charity. It is certain that the more reduced and necessitous they were, the more pompously the skeleton emerged from its tomb; and that when there was anything particularly shabby in the wind, the skeleton always came out with the ghastliest flourish.

Little Dorrit was late on the Monday morning, for her father slept late, and afterwards there was his breakfast to prepare and his room to arrange. She had no engagement to go out to work, however, and therefore stayed with him until, with Maggy's help, she had put everything right about him, and had seen him off upon his morning walk (of twenty yards or so) to the coffee-house to read the paper. She then got on her bonnet and went out, having been anxious to get out much sooner. There was, as usual, a cessation of the small-talk in the Lodge as she passed through it; and a Collegian who had come in on Saturday night, received the intimation from the elbow of a more seasoned Collegian, "Look out. Here she is!"

She wanted to see her sister, but when she got round to Mr. Cripples's, she found that both her sister and her uncle had gone to the theatre where they were engaged. Having taken thought of this probability by the way, and having settled that in such case she would follow them, she set off afresh for the theatre, which was on that side of the river, and not very far away.

Little Dorrit was almost as ignorant of the ways of theatres as of the ways of gold mines, and when she was directed to a furtive sort of door, with a curious up-all-night air about it, that appeared to be ashamed of itself and to be hiding in an alley, she hesitated to approach it; being further deterred by the sight of some half-dozen close-shaved gentlemen, with their hats very strangely on, who were lounging about the door, looking not at all unlike Collegians. On her applying to them, reassured by this resemblance, for a direction to Miss Dorrit, they made way for her to enter a dark hall—it was more like a great grim lamp gone out than anything else—where she could hear the distant playing of music and the sound of dancing feet. A man so much in want of airing that he had a blue mould upon him, sat watching this dark place from a hole in a corner, like a spider; and he told her that he would send a message up to Miss Dorrit by the first lady or gentleman who went through. The first lady who went through had a roll of music, half in her muff and half out of it, and was in such a tumbled condition altogether, that it seemed as if it would be an act of kindness to iron her. But as she was very good-natured, and said, "Come with me; I'll soon find Miss Dorrit for you," Miss Dorrit's sister went with her, drawing nearer and nearer at every step she took in the darkness, to the sound of music and the sound of dancing feet.

At last they came into a maze of dust, where a quantity of people were tumbling over one another, and where there was such a confusion of unaccountable shapes of beams, bulkheads, brick walls, ropes, and rollers, and such a mixing of gaslight and daylight, that they seemed to have got on the wrong side of the pattern of the universe. Little Dorrit, left to herself, and knocked against by somebody every moment, was quite bewildered when she heard her sister's voice.

"Why, good gracious, Amy, what ever brought you here?"

"I wanted to see you, Fanny dear; and as I am going out all day to-morrow, and knew you might be engaged all day to-day, I thought——"

"But the idea, Amy, of *you* coming behind! I never did!" As her sister said this in no very cordial tone of welcome, she conducted her to a more open part of the maze, where various golden chairs and tables were heaped together, and where a number of young ladies were sitting on anything they could find, chattering. All these young ladies wanted ironing, and all had a curious way of looking everywhere while they chattered.

Just as the sisters arrived here, a monotonous boy in a Scotch cap put his head round a beam on the left, and said, "Less noise there, ladies!" and disappeared. Immediately after which, a sprightly gentleman with a quantity of long black hair looked round a beam on the right, and said, "Less noise there, darlings!" and also disappeared.

"The notion of you among professionals, Amy, is really the last thing I could have conceived!" said her sister. "Why, how did you ever get here?"

"I don't know. The lady who told you I was here, was so good as to bring me in."

"Like you quiet little things! You can make your way anywhere, I believe. *I* couldn't have managed it, Amy, though I know so much more of the world."

It was the family custom to lay it down as family law, that she was a plain domestic little creature, without the great and sage experience of the rest. This family fiction was the family assertion of itself against her services. Not to make too much of them.

"Well! And what have you got on your mind, Amy? Of course you have got something on your mind, about me?" said Fanny. She spoke as if her sister, between two and three years her junior, were her prejudiced grandmother.

"It is not much; but since you told me of the lady who gave you the bracelet, Fanny——"

Miss Dorrit and Little Dorrit

The monotonous boy put his head round the beam on the left, and said, "Look out there, ladies!" and disappeared. The sprightly gentleman with the black hair as suddenly put his head round the beam on the right, and said, "Look out there, darlings!" and also disappeared. Thereupon all the young ladies rose, and began shaking their skirts out behind.

"Well, Amy?" said Fanny, doing as the rest did; "what were you going to say?"

"Since you told me a lady had given you the bracelet you showed me, Fanny, I have not been quite easy on your account, and indeed want to know a little more if you will confide more to me."

"Now, ladies!" said the boy in the Scotch cap. "Now, darlings!" said the gentleman with the black hair. They were every one gone in a moment, and the music and the dancing feet were heard again.

Little Dorrit sat down in a golden chair, made quite giddy by these rapid interruptions. Her sister and the rest were a long time gone; and during their absence a voice (it appeared to be that of the gentleman with the black hair) was continually calling out through the music, "One, two, three, four, five, six—go! One, two, three, four, five, six—go! Steady, darlings! One, two, three, four, five, six—go!" Ultimately the voice stopped, and they all came back again, more or less out of breath, folding themselves in their shawls, and making ready for the streets. "Stop a moment, Amy, and let them get away before us," whispered Fanny. They were soon left alone; nothing more important happening, in the meantime, than the boy looking round his old beam, and saying, "Everybody at eleven to-morrow, ladies!" and the gentleman with the black hair looking round his old beam, and saying, "Everybody at eleven to-morrow, darlings!" each in his own accustomed manner.

When they were alone, something was rolled up or by other means got out of the way, and there was a great empty

289

well before them, looking down into the depths of which
Fanny said, " Now, uncle ! "   Little Dorrit, as her eyes became
used to the darkness, faintly made him out, at the bottom of
the well, in an obscure corner by himself, with his instrument
in its ragged case under his arm.

The old man looked as if the remote high gallery windows,
with their little strip of sky, might have been the point of his
better fortunes, from which he had descended, until he had
gradually sunk down below there to the bottom. He had
been in that place six nights a week for many years, but had
never been observed to raise his eyes above his music-book,
and was confidently believed to have never seen a play.
There were legends in the place that he did not so much as
know the popular heroes and heroines by sight, and that the
low comedian had " mugged " at him in his richest manner
fifty nights for a wager, and he had shown no trace of consciousness. The carpenters had a joke to the effect that he
was dead without being aware of it ; and the frequenters of
the pit supposed him to pass his whole life, night and day, and
Sunday and all, in the orchestra. They had tried him a few
times with pinches of snuff offered over the rails, and he had
always responded to this attention with a momentary waking
up of manner that had the pale phantom of a gentleman in
it : beyond this he never, on any occasion, had any other
part in what was going on than the part written out for the
clarionet ; in private life, where there was no part for the
clarionet, he had no part at all. Some said he was poor,
some said he was a wealthy miser ; but he said nothing, never
lifted up his bowed head, never varied his shuffling gait by
getting his springless foot from the ground. Though expecting now to be summoned by his niece, he did not hear
her until she had spoken to him three or four times ; nor
was he at all surprised by the presence of two nieces instead
of one, but merely said in his tremulous voice, " I am coming,
I am coming ! " and crept forth by some underground way
which emitted a cellarous smell.

"And so, Amy," said her sister, when the three together passed out, at the door that had such a shame-faced consciousness of being different from other doors: the uncle instinctively taking Amy's arm as the arm to be relied on: "so, Amy, you are curious about me?"

She was pretty, and conscious, and rather flaunting; and the condescension with which she put aside the superiority of her charms, and of her worldly experience, and addressed her sister on almost equal terms, had a vast deal of the family in it.

"I am interested, Fanny, and concerned in anything that concerns you."

"So you are, so you are, and you are the best of Amys. If I am ever a little provoking, I am sure you'll consider what a thing it is to occupy my position and feel a consciousness of being superior to it. I shouldn't care," said the Daughter of the Father of the Marshalsea, "if the others were not so common. None of them have come down in the world as we have. They are all on their own level. Common."

Little Dorrit mildly looked at the speaker, but did not interrupt her. Fanny took out her handkerchief, and rather angrily wiped her eyes. "I was not born where you were, you know, Amy, and perhaps that makes a difference. My dear child, when we get rid of Uncle, you shall know all about it. We'll drop him at the cook's shop where he is going to dine."

They walked on with him until they came to a dirty shop-window in a dirty street, which was made almost opaque by the steam of hot meats, vegetables, and puddings. But glimpses were to be caught of a roast leg of pork bursting into tears of sage and onion in a metal reservoir full of gravy, of an unctuous piece of roast beef and blisterous Yorkshire pudding, bubbling hot in a similar receptacle, of a stuffed fillet of veal in rapid cut, of a ham in a perspiration with the pace it was going at, of a shallow tank of baked potatoes glued together by their own richness, of a truss or two of boiled greens, and other substantial delicacies. Within, were a few wooden partitions, behind which such customers as found it more convenient to take away their dinners in stomachs than in their hands, packed their purchases in solitude. Fanny opening her reticule, as they surveyed these things, produced from that repository a shilling and handed it to Uncle. Uncle, after not looking at it a little while, divined its object, and muttering "Dinner? Ha! Yes, yes, yes!" slowly vanished from them into the mist.

"Now, Amy," said her sister, "come with me, if you are not too tired to walk to Harley Street, Cavendish Square."

The air with which she threw off this distinguished address, and the toss she gave her new bonnet (which was more gaudy than serviceable), made her sister wonder; however, she expressed her readiness to go to Harley Street, and thither they directed their steps. Arrived at that grand destination, Fanny singled out the handsomest house, and knocking at the door, inquired for Mrs. Merdle. The footman who opened the door, although he had powder on his head and was backed up by two other footmen likewise powdered, not only admitted Mrs. Merdle to be at home, but asked Fanny to walk in. Fanny walked in, taking her sister with her; and they went up-stairs with powder going before and powder stopping behind, and were left in a spacious semicircular drawing-room, one of several drawing-rooms, where there was a parrot on the outside of a golden cage holding on by its beak with its scaly legs in the air, and putting itself into many strange upside-down postures. This peculiarity has been observed in birds of quite another feather, climbing upon golden wires.

The room was far more splendid than anything Little Dorrit had ever imagined, and would have been splendid and costly in any eyes. She looked in amazement at her sister and would have asked a question, but that Fanny with a warning frown pointed to a curtained doorway of communication with another room. The curtain shook next moment, and a lady, raising it with a heavily ringed hand, dropped it behind her again as she entered.

The lady was not young and fresh from the hand of Nature, but was young and fresh from the hand of her maid. She had large unfeeling handsome eyes, and dark unfeeling handsome hair, and a broad unfeeling handsome bosom, and was made the most of in every particular. Either because she had a cold, or because it suited her face, she wore a rich white fillet tied over her head and under her chin. And if ever there were an unfeeling handsome chin that looked as if, for certain, it had never been, in familiar parlance, "chucked" by the hand of man, it was the chin curbed up so tight and close by that laced bridle.

"Mrs. Merdle," said Fanny. "My sister, ma'am."

"I am glad to see your sister, Miss Dorrit. I did not remember that you had a sister."

"I did not mention that I had," said Fanny.

"Ah!" Mrs. Merdle curled the little finger of her left hand as who should say, "I have caught you. I know you didn't!" All her action was usually with her left hand because her hands were not a pair; the left being much the whiter and plumper of the two. Then she added, "Sit down," and composed herself voluptuously, in a nest of crimson and gold cushions, on an ottoman near the parrot.

"Also professional?" said Mrs. Merdle, looking at Little Dorrit through an eye-glass.

Fanny answered No. "No," said Mrs. Merdle, dropping her glass. "Has not a professional air. Very pleasant; but not professional."

"My sister, ma'am," said Fanny, in whom there was a singular mixture of deference and hardihood, "has been asking me to tell her, as between sisters, how I came to have the honour of knowing you. And as I had engaged to call upon you once more, I thought I might take the liberty of bringing her with me, when perhaps you would tell her. I wish her to know, and perhaps you will tell her?"

"Do you think, at your sister's age——" hinted Mrs. Merdle.

"She is much older than she looks," said Fanny; "almost as old as I am."

"Society," said Mrs. Merdle, with another curve of her little finger, "is so difficult to explain to young persons (indeed is so difficult to explain to most persons), that I am glad to hear that. I wish Society was not so arbitrary, I wish it was not so exacting—Bird, be quiet!"

The parrot had given a most piercing shriek, as if its name were Society and it asserted its right to its exactions.

"But," resumed Mrs. Merdle, "we must take it as we find it. We know it is hollow and conventional and worldly and very shocking, but unless we are Savages in the Tropical seas (I should have been charmed to be one myself—most delightful life and perfect climate I am told), we must consult it. It is the common lot. Mr. Merdle is a most extensive merchant, his transactions are on the vastest scale, his wealth and influence are very great, but even he—Bird, be quiet!"

The parrot had shrieked another shriek; and it filled up the sentence so expressively that Mrs. Merdle was under no necessity to end it.

"Since your sister begs that I would terminate our personal acquaintance," she began again, addressing Little Dorrit, "by relating the circumstances that are much to her credit, I cannot object to comply with her request, I am sure. I have a son (I was first married extremely young) of two or three-and-twenty."

Fanny set her lips, and her eyes looked half triumphantly at her sister.

"A son of two or three-and-twenty. He is a little gay, a thing Society is accustomed to in young men, and he is very impressible. Perhaps he inherits that misfortune. I am very impressible myself, by nature. The weakest of creatures. My feelings are touched in a moment."

She said all this, and everything else, as coldly as a woman of snow; quite forgetting the sisters except at odd times, and apparently addressing some abstraction of Society. For whose behoof, too, she occasionally arranged her dress, or the composition of her figure upon the ottoman.

"So he is very impressible. Not a misfortune in our natural state, I dare say, but we are not in a natural state. Much to be lamented, no doubt, particularly by myself, who am a child of nature if I could but show it; but so it is. Society suppresses us and dominates us—Bird, be quiet!"

The parrot had broken into a violent fit of laughter, after twisting divers bars of his cage with his crooked bill, and licking them with his black tongue.

"It is quite unnecessary to say to a person of your good sense, wide range of experience, and cultivated feelings," said Mrs. Merdle, from her nest of crimson and gold—and there put up her glass to refresh her memory as to whom she was addressing,—"that the stage sometimes has a fascination for young men of that class of character. In saying the stage, I mean the people on it of the female sex. Therefore, when I heard that my son was supposed to be fascinated by a dancer, I knew what that usually meant in Society, and confided in her being a dancer at the Opera, where young men moving in Society are usually fascinated."

She passed her white hands over one another, observant of the sisters now; and the rings upon her fingers grated against each other, with a hard sound.

"As your sister will tell you, when I found what the theatre was, I was much surprised and much distressed. But when I found that your sister, by rejecting my son's advances (I must add, in an unexpected manner), had brought him to the point of proposing marriage, my feelings were of the profoundest anguish—acute."

She traced the outline of her left eyebrow, and put it right.

"In a distracted condition which only a mother—moving in Society—can be susceptible of, I determined to go myself to the theatre, and represent my state of mind to the dancer. I made myself known to your sister. I found her, to my surprise, in many respects different from my expectations; and certainly in none more so, than in meeting me with—what shall I say?—a sort of family assertion on her own part?"

Mrs. Merdle smiled.

"I told you, ma'am," said Fanny, with a heightening colour, "that although you found me in that situation, I was so far above the rest, that I considered my family as good as your son's; and that I had a brother who, knowing the circumstances, would be of the same opinion, and would not consider such a connection any honour."

"Miss Dorrit," said Mrs. Merdle, after frostily looking at her through her glass, "precisely what I was on the point of telling your sister, in pursuance of your request. Much obliged to you for recalling it so accurately and anticipating me. I immediately," addressing Little Dorrit, "(for I am the creature of impulse), took a bracelet from my arm, and begged your sister to let me clasp it on hers, in token of the delight I had in our being able to approach the subject so far on a common footing." (This was perfectly true, the lady having bought a cheap and showy article on her way to the interview, with a general eye to bribery.)

"And I told you, Mrs. Merdle," said Fanny, "that we might be unfortunate, but were not common."

"I think, the very words, Miss Dorrit," assented Mrs. Merdle.

"And I told you, Mrs. Merdle," said Fanny, "that if you spoke to me of the superiority of your son's standing in Society, it was barely possible that you rather deceived yourself in your suppositions about my origin; and that my father's standing, even in the Society in which he now moved (what that was, was best known to myself), was eminently superior, and was acknowledged by every one."

"Quite accurate," rejoined Mrs. Merdle. "A most admirable memory."

"Thank you, ma'am. Perhaps you will be so kind as to tell my sister the rest."

"There is very little to tell," said Mrs. Merdle, reviewing the breadth of bosom which seemed essential to her having room enough to be unfeeling in, "but it is to your sister's credit. I pointed out to your sister the plain state of the case; the impossibility of the Society in which we moved recognising the Society in which she moved—though charming, I have no doubt; the immense disadvantage at which she would consequently place the family she had so high an opinion of, upon which we should find ourselves compelled to look down with contempt, and from which (socially speaking) we should feel obliged to recoil with abhorrence. In short, I made an appeal to that laudable pride in your sister."

"Let my sister know, if you please, Mrs. Merdle," Fanny pouted, with a toss of her gauzy bonnet, "that I had already had the honour of telling your son that I wished to have nothing whatever to say to him."

"Well, Miss Dorrit," assented Mrs. Merdle, "perhaps I might have mentioned that before. If I did not think of it, perhaps it was because my mind reverted to the apprehensions I had at the time, that he might persevere and you might have something to say to him. I also mentioned to your sister—I again address the non-professional Miss Dorrit—that my son would have nothing in the event of such a marriage, and would be an absolute beggar. (I mention that, merely as a fact which is part of the narrative, and not as supposing it to have influenced your sister, except in the prudent and legitimate way in which, constituted as our artificial system is, we must all be influenced by such considerations.) Finally, after some high words and high spirit on the part of your sister; we came to the complete understanding that there was no danger; and your sister was so obliging as to allow me to present her with a mark or two of my appreciation at my dressmaker's."

Little Dorrit looked sorry, and glanced at Fanny with a troubled face.

"Also," said Mrs. Merdle, "as to promise to give me the present pleasure of a closing interview, and of parting with her on the best of terms. On which occasion," added Mrs. Merdle, quitting her nest, and putting something in Fanny's hand, "Miss Dorrit will permit me to say Farewell with best wishes, in my own dull manner."

The sisters rose at the same time, and they all stood near the cage of the parrot, as he tore at a claw-full of biscuit and spat it out, seemed to mock them with a pompous dance of his body without moving his feet, and suddenly turned himself upside down and trailed himself all over the outside of his golden cage, with the aid of his cruel beak and his black tongue.

"Adieu, Miss Dorrit, with best wishes," said Mrs. Merdle. "If we could only come to a Millennium, or something of that sort, I for one might have the pleasure of knowing a number of charming and talented persons from whom I am at present excluded. A more primitive state of society would be delicious to me. There used to be a poem when I learnt lessons, something about Lo the poor Indian whose something mind! If a few thousand persons moving in Society, could only go and be Indians, I would put my name down directly; but as, moving in Society, we can't be Indians, unfortunately—Good morning!"

They came down-stairs with powder before them and powder behind, the elder sister haughty and the younger sister humbled, and were shut out into unpowdered Harley Street, Cavendish Square.

"Well?" said Fanny, when they had gone a little way without speaking. " Have you nothing to say, Amy?"

" Oh, I don't know what to say!" she answered, distressed.

" You didn't like this young man, Fanny?"

"Like him? He is almost an idiot."

"I am so sorry—don't be hurt—but, since you ask me

what I have to say, I am so very sorry, Fanny, that you suffered this lady to give you anything."

"You little Fool!" returned her sister, shaking her with the sharp pull she gave her arm. "Have you no spirit at all? But that's just the way! You have no self-respect, you have no becoming pride. Just as you allow yourself to be followed about by a contemptible little Chivery of a thing," with the scornfullest emphasis, "you would let your family be trodden on, and never turn."

"Don't say that, dear Fanny. I do what I can for them."

"You do what you can for them!" repeated Fanny, walking her on very fast. "Would you let a woman like this, whom you could see, if you had any experience of anything, to be as false and insolent as a woman can be—would you let her put her foot upon your family, and thank her for it?"

"No, Fanny, I am sure."

"Then make her pay for it, you mean little thing. What else can you make her do? Make her pay for it, you stupid child; and do your family some credit with the money!"

They spoke no more, all the way back to the lodging where Fanny and her uncle lived. When they arrived there, they found the old man practising his clarionet in the dolefullest manner, in a corner of the room. Fanny had a composite meal to make, of chops, and porter, and tea: and indignantly pretended to prepare it for herself, though her sister did all that in quiet reality. When, at last, Fanny sat down to eat and drink, she threw the table implements about and was angry with her bread, much as her father had been last night.

"If you despise me," she said, bursting into vehement tears, "because I am a dancer, why did you put me in the way of being one? It was your doing. You would have me stoop as low as the ground before this Mrs. Merdle, and let her say what she liked and do what she liked, and hold us all in contempt, and tell me so to my face. Because I am a dancer!"

"O Fanny!"

"And Tip too, poor fellow. She is to disparage him just as much as she likes, without any check—I suppose because he has been in the law, and the docks, and different things. Why, it was your doing, Amy. You might at least approve of his being defended."

All this time the uncle was dolefully blowing his clarionet in the corner, sometimes taking it an inch or so from his mouth for a moment while he stopped to gaze at them, with a vague impression that somebody had said something.

"And your father, your poor father, Amy. Because he is not free, to show himself and to speak for himself, you would let such people insult him with impunity. If you don't feel for yourself because you go out to work, you might at least feel for him, I should think, knowing what he has undergone so long."

Poor Little Dorrit felt the injustice of this taunt rather sharply. The remembrance of last night added a barbed point to it. She said nothing in reply, but turned her chair from the table towards the fire. Uncle, after making one more pause, blew a dismal wail and went on again.

Fanny was passionate with the tea-cups and the bread as long as her passion lasted, and then protested that she was the wretchedest girl in the world, and she wished she was dead. After that, her crying became remorseful, and she got up and put her arms round her sister. Little Dorrit tried to stop her from saying anything, but she answered that she would, she must! Thereupon she said again, and again, "I beg your pardon, Amy," and "Forgive me, Amy," almost as passionately as she had said what she regretted.

"But indeed, indeed, Amy," she resumed when they were seated in sisterly accord side by side, "I hope and I think you would have seen this differently, if you had known a little more of Society."

"Perhaps I might, Fanny," said the mild Little Dorrit.

"You see, while you have been domestic and resignedly shut

300

up there, Amy," pursued her sister, gradually beginning to patronise, "I have been out, moving more in Society, and may have been getting proud and spirited—more than I ought to be, perhaps?"

Little Dorrit answered "Yes. O yes!"

"And while you have been thinking of the dinner or the clothes, I may have been thinking, you know, of the family. Now, may it not be so, Amy?"

Little Dorrit again nodded "Yes," with a more cheerful face than heart.

"Especially as we know," said Fanny, "that there certainly is a tone in the place to which you have been so true, which does belong to it, and which does make it different from other aspects of Society. So kiss me once again, Amy dear, and we will agree that we may both be right, and that you are a tranquil, domestic, home-loving, good girl."

The clarionet had been lamenting most pathetically during this dialogue, but was cut short now by Fanny's announcement that it was time to go; which she conveyed to her uncle by shutting up his scrap of music, and taking the clarionet out of his mouth.

Little Dorrit parted from them at the door, and hastened back to the Marshalsea. It fell dark there sooner than elsewhere, and going into it that evening was like going into a deep trench. The shadow of the wall was on every object. Not least upon the figure in the old grey gown and the black velvet cap, as it turned towards her when she opened the door of the dim room.

"Why not upon me too!" thought Little Dorrit, with the door yet in her hand. "It was not unreasonable in Fanny."

CHAPTER XXI.

MR. MERDLE'S COMPLAINT.

UPON that establishment of state, the Merdle establishment in Harley Street, Cavendish Square, there was the shadow of no more common wall than the fronts of other establishments of state on the opposite side of the street. Like unexceptionable Society, the opposing rows of houses in Harley Street were very grim with one another. Indeed, the mansions and their inhabitants were so much alike in that respect, that the people were often to be found drawn up on opposite sides of dinner-tables, in the shade of their own loftiness, staring at the other side of the way with the dulness of the houses.

Everybody knows how like the street, the two dinner-rows of people who take their stand by the street will be. The expressionless uniform twenty houses, all to be knocked at and rung at in the same form, all approachable by the same dull steps, all fended off by the same pattern of railing, all with the same impracticable fire-escapes, the same inconvenient fixtures in their heads, and everything without exception to be taken at a high valuation—who has not dined with these? The house so drearily out of repair, the occasional bow-window, the stuccoed house, the newly-fronted house, the corner house with nothing but angular rooms, the house with the blinds always down, the house with the hatchment always up, the house where the collector has called for one quarter of an Idea, and found nobody at home—who has not dined with these? The house that nobody will take, and is to be had a bargain—who does not know her? The showy house that was taken for life by the disappointed gentleman, and which does not suit him at all—who is unacquainted with that haunted habitation?

Harley Street, Cavendish Square, was more than aware of Mr. and Mrs. Merdle. Intruders there were in Harley Street, of whom it was not aware; but Mr. and Mrs. Merdle it delighted to honour. Society was aware of Mr. and Mrs. Merdle. Society had said "Let us license them; let us know them."

Mr. Merdle was immensely rich; a man of prodigious enterprise; a Midas without the ears, who turned all he touched to gold. He was in everything good, from banking to building. He was in Parliament, of course. He was in the City, necessarily. He was Chairman of this, Trustee of that, President of the other. The weightiest of men had said to projectors, "Now, what name have you got? Have you got Merdle?" And, the reply being in the negative, had said "Then I won't look at you."

This great and fortunate man had provided that extensive bosom, which required so much room to be unfeeling enough in, with a nest of crimson and gold some fifteen years before. It was not a bosom to repose upon, but it was a capital bosom to hang jewels upon. Mr. Merdle wanted something to hang jewels upon, and he bought it for the purpose. Storr and Mortimer might have married on the same speculation.

Like all his other speculations, it was sound and successful. The jewels showed to the richest advantage. The bosom moving in Society with the jewels displayed upon it, attracted general admiration. Society approving, Mr. Merdle was satisfied. He was the most disinterested of men,—did everything for Society, and got as little for himself out of all his gain and care, as a man might.

That is to say, it may be supposed that he got all he wanted, otherwise with unlimited wealth he would have got it. But his desire was to the utmost to satisfy Society (whatever that was), and take up all its drafts upon him for tribute. He did not shine in company; he had not very much to say for himself; he was a reserved man, with a broad, overhanging, watchful head, that particular kind of dull red colour in his cheeks which is rather stale than fresh, and a somewhat uneasy expression about his coat-cuffs, as if they were in his confidence, and had reasons for being anxious to hide his hands. In the little he said, he was a pleasant man enough; plain, emphatic about public and private confidence, and tenacious of the utmost deference being shown by every one, in all things, to Society. In this same Society (if that were it which came to his dinners, and to Mrs. Merdle's receptions and concerts), he hardly seemed to enjoy himself much, and was mostly to be found against walls and behind doors. Also when he went out to it, instead of its coming home to him, he seemed a little fatigued, and upon the whole rather more disposed for bed; but he was always cultivating it nevertheless, and always moving in it, and always laying out money on it with the greatest liberality.

Mrs. Merdle's first husband had been a colonel, under whose auspices the bosom had entered into competition with the snows of North America, and had come off at little disadvantage in point of whiteness, and at none in point of coldness. The colonel's son was Mrs. Merdle's only child. He was of a chuckle-headed high-shouldered make, with a general appearance of being, not so much a young man as a swelled boy. He had given so few signs of reason, that a by-word went among his companions that his brain had been frozen up in a mighty frost which prevailed at St. John's, New Brunswick, at the period of his birth there, and had never thawed from that hour. Another by-word represented him as having in his infancy, through the negligence of a nurse, fallen out of a high window on his head, which had been heard by responsible witnesses to crack. It is probable that both these representations were of ex post facto origin; the young gentleman (whose expressive name was Sparkler) being monomaniacal in offering marriage to all manner of undesirable young ladies, and in remarking of every successive young lady to whom he tendered a matrimonial proposal that she was " a doosed fine gal—well educated too—with no biggodd nonsense about her."

A son-in-law, with these limited talents, might have been a clog upon another man; but Mr. Merdle did not want a son-in-law for himself; he wanted a son-in-law for Society. Mr. Sparkler having been in the Guards, and being in the habit of frequenting all the races, and all the lounges, and all the parties, and being well known, Society was satisfied with its son-in-law. This happy result Mr. Merdle would have considered well attained, though Mr. Sparkler had been a more expensive article. And he did not get Mr. Sparkler by any means cheap for Society, even as it was.

There was a dinner given in the Harley Street establishment, while Little Dorrit was stitching at her father's new shirts by his side that night; and there were magnates from the Court and magnates from the City, magnates from the Commons and magnates from the Lords, magnates from the bench and magnates from the bar, Bishop magnates, Treasury magnates, Horse Guards magnates, Admiralty magnates,— all the magnates that keep us going, and sometimes trip us up.

" I am told," said Bishop magnate to Horse Guards, " that Mr. Merdle has made another enormous hit. They say a hundred thousand pounds."

Horse Guards had heard two.

Treasury had heard three.

Bar, handling his persuasive double eye-glass, was by no means clear but that it might be four. It was one of those happy strokes of calculation and combination, the result of which it was difficult to estimate. It was one of those instances of a comprehensive grasp, associated with habitual luck and characteristic boldness, of which an age presented us but few. But here was Brother Bellows, who had been in the great Bank case, and who could probably tell us more. What did Brother Bellows put this new success at?

Brother Bellows was on his way to make his bow to the bosom, and could only tell them in passing that he had heard it stated, with great appearance of truth, as being worth, from first to last, half-a-million of money.

Admiralty said Mr. Merdle was a wonderful man. Treasury said he was a new power in the country, and would be able to buy up the whole House of Commons. Bishop said he was glad to think that this wealth flowed into the coffers of a gentleman who was always disposed to maintain the best interests of Society.

Mr. Merdle himself was usually late on these occasions, as a man still detained in the clutch of giant enterprises when other men had shaken off their dwarfs for the day. On this occasion, he was the last arrival. Treasury said Merdle's work punished him a little. Bishop said he was glad to think that this wealth flowed into the coffers of a gentleman who accepted it with meekness.

Powder! There was so much Powder in waiting, that it flavoured the dinner. Pulverous particles got into the dishes, and Society's meats had a seasoning of first-rate footmen. Mr. Merdle took down a countess who was secluded some-where in the core of an immense dress, to which she was in the proportion of the heart to the overgrown cabbage. If so low a simile may be admitted, the dress went down the stair-case like a richly brocaded Jack in the Green, and nobody knew what sort of small person carried it.

Society had everything it could want, and could not want, for dinner. It had everything to look at, and everything to eat, and everything to drink. It is to be hoped it enjoyed itself; for Mr. Merdle's own share of the repast might have been paid for with eighteenpence. Mrs. Merdle was magnificent. The chief butler was the next magnificent institution of the day. He was the stateliest man in company. He did nothing, but he looked on as few other men could have done. He was Mr. Merdle's last gift to Society. Mr. Merdle didn't want him, and was put out of countenance when the great creature looked at him; but inappeasable Society would have him—and had got him.

The invisible countess carried out the Green at the usual stage of the entertainment, and the file of beauty was closed up by the bosom. Treasury said, Juno. Bishop said, Judith.

Bar fell into discussion with Horse Guards concerning courts-martial. Brother Bellows and Bench struck in. Other magnates paired off. Mr. Merdle sat silent, and looked at the table-cloth. Sometimes a magnate addressed him, to turn the stream of his own particular discussion towards him; but Mr. Merdle seldom gave much attention to it, or did more than rouse himself from his calculations and pass the wine.

When they rose, so many of the magnates had something to say to Mr. Merdle individually, that he held little levees by the sideboard, and checked them off as they went out at the door.

Treasury hoped he might venture to congratulate one of England's world-famed capitalists and merchant-princes (he had turned that original sentiment in the house a few times, and it came easy to him) on a new achievement. To extend the triumphs of such men, was to extend the triumphs and resources of the nation; and Treasury felt—he gave Mr. Merdle to understand—patriotic on the subject.

"Thank you, my lord," said Mr. Merdle; "thank you. I accept your congratulations with pride, and I am glad you approve."

"Why, I don't unreservedly approve, my dear Mr. Merdle. Because," smiling Treasury turned him by the arm towards the sideboard and spoke banteringly, " it never can be worth your while to come among us and help us."

Mr. Merdle felt honoured by the——

" No, no," said Treasury, " that is not the light in which one so distinguished for practical knowledge, and great foresight, can be expected to regard it. If we should ever be happily enabled, by accidentally possessing the control over circumstances, to propose to one so eminent to—to come among us, and give us the weight of his influence, knowledge, and character, we could only propose it to him as a duty. In fact, as a duty that he owed to Society."

Mr. Merdle intimated that Society was the apple of his eye, and that its claims were paramount to every other consideration. Treasury moved on, and Bar came up.

Bar, with his little insinuating Jury droop, and fingering his persuasive double eye-glass, hoped he might be excused if he mentioned to one of the greatest converters of the root of all evil into the root of all good, who had for a long time reflected a shining lustre on the annals even of our commercial country—if he mentioned, disinterestedly, and as, what we lawyers called in our pedantic way, amicus curiæ, a fact that had come by accident within his knowledge. He had been required to look over the title of a very considerable estate in one of the eastern counties—lying, in fact, for Mr. Merdle knew we lawyers loved to be particular, on the borders of two of the eastern counties. Now, the title was perfectly sound, and the estate was to be purchased by one who had the command of—Money (Jury droop and persuasive eye-glass), on remarkably advantageous terms. This had come to Bar's knowledge only that day, and it had occurred to him. " I shall have the honour of dining with my esteemed friend Mr. Merdle this evening, and, strictly between ourselves, I will mention the opportunity." Such a purchase would involve not only great legitimate political influence, but some half-dozen church presentations of considerable annual value. Now, that Mr. Merdle was already at no loss to discover means of occupying even his capital, and of fully employing even his active and vigorous intellect, Bar well knew: but he would venture to suggest that the question arose in his mind, whether one who had deservedly gained so high a position and so European a reputation did not owe it—we would not say to himself, but we would say to Society, to possess himself of such influences as these; and to exercise them—we would not say for his own, or for his party's, but we would say for Society's—benefit.

Mr. Merdle again expressed himself as wholly devoted to that object of his constant consideration, and Bar took his persuasive eye-glass up the grand staircase. Bishop then came undesignedly sliding in the direction of the sideboard.

Surely the goods of this world, it occurred in an accidental way to Bishop to remark, could scarcely be directed into happier channels than when they accumulated under the magic touch of the wise and sagacious, who, while they knew the just value of riches (Bishop tried here to look as if he were rather poor himself), were aware of their importance, judiciously governed and rightly distributed, to the welfare of our brethren at large.

Mr. Merdle with humility expressed his conviction that Bishop couldn't mean him, and with inconsistency expressed his high gratification in Bishop's good opinion.

Bishop then—jauntily stepping out a little with his well-shaped right leg, as though he said to Mr. Merdle "don't mind the apron; a mere form!"—put this case to his good friend:

Whether it had occurred to his good friend, that Society might not unreasonably hope that one so blest in his undertakings, and whose example on his pedestal was so influential with it, would shed a little money in the direction of a mission or so to Africa?

Mr. Merdle signifying that the idea should have his best attention, Bishop put another case:

Whether his good friend had at all interested himself in the proceedings of our Combined Additional Endowed Dignitaries Committee, and whether it had occurred to him that to shed a little money in *that* direction might be a great conception finely executed?

Mr. Merdle made a similar reply, and Bishop explained his reason for inquiring.

Society looked to such men as his good friend to do such things. It was not that *he* looked to them, but that Society looked to them. Just as it was not Our Committee who wanted the Additional Endowed Dignitaries, but it was Society that was in a state of the most agonising uneasiness of mind until it got them. He begged to assure his good friend, that he was extremely sensible of his good friend's regard on all occasions for the best interests of Society; and he considered that he was at once consulting those interests, and expressing the feeling of Society, when he wished him continued prosperity, continued increase of riches, and continued things in general.

Bishop then betook himself up-stairs, and the other magnates gradually floated up after him until there was no one left below but Mr. Merdle. That gentleman, after looking at the table-cloth until the soul of the chief butler glowed with a noble resentment, went slowly up after the rest, and became of no account in the stream of people on the grand staircase. Mrs. Merdle was at home, the best of the jewels were hung out to be seen, Society got what it came for, Mr. Merdle drank twopennyworth of tea in a corner and got more than he wanted.

Among the evening magnates was a famous physician, who knew everybody, and whom everybody knew. On entering at the door, he came upon Mr. Merdle drinking his tea in a corner, and touched him on the arm.

Mr. Merdle started. "Oh! It's you!"

"Any better to-day?"

"No," said Mr. Merdle, "I am no better."

THE PHYSICIAN

"A pity I didn't see you this morning. Pray come to me to-morrow, or let me come to you."

"Well!" he replied. "I will come to-morrow as I drive by."

Bar and Bishop had both been bystanders during this short dialogue, and as Mr. Merdle was swept away by the crowd, they made their remarks upon it to the Physician. Bar said, there was a certain point of mental strain beyond which no man could go; that the point varied with various textures of brain and peculiarities of constitution, as he had had occasion to notice in several of his learned brothers; but, the point of endurance passed by a line's breadth, depression and dyspepsia ensued. Not to intrude on the sacred mysteries of medicine, he took it, now (with the Jury droop and persuasive eye-glass), that this was Merdle's case? Bishop said that when he was a young man, and had fallen for a brief space into the habit of writing sermons on Saturdays, a habit which all young sons of the church should sedulously avoid, he had frequently been sensible of a depression, arising as he supposed from an over-taxed intellect, upon which the yolk of a new-laid egg, beaten up by the good woman in whose house he at that time lodged, with a glass of sound sherry, nutmeg, and powdered sugar, acted like a charm. Without presuming to offer so simple a remedy to the consideration of so profound a professor of the great healing art, he would venture to inquire whether the strain, being by way of intricate calculations, the spirits might not (humanly speaking) be restored to their tone by a gentle and yet generous stimulant?

"Yes," said the physician, "yes, you are both right. But I may as well tell you that I can find nothing the matter with Mr. Merdle. He has the constitution of a rhinoceros, the digestion of an ostrich, and the concentration of an oyster. As to nerves, Mr. Merdle is of a cool temperament, and not a sensitive man: is about as invulnerable, I should say, as Achilles. How such a man should suppose himself unwell without reason, you may think strange. But I have found nothing the matter with him. He may have some deep-seated recondite complaint. I can't say. I only say, that at present I have not found it out."

There was no shadow of Mr. Merdle's complaint on the bosom now displaying precious stones in rivalry with many similar superb jewel-stands; there was no shadow of Mr. Merdle's complaint on young Sparkler hovering about the rooms, monomaniacally seeking any sufficiently ineligible young lady with no nonsense about her; there was no shadow of Mr. Merdle's complaint on the Barnacles and Stiltstalkings, of whom whole colonies were present; or on any of the company. Even on himself, its shadow was faint enough as he moved about among the throng, receiving homage.

Mr. Merdle's complaint. Society and he had so much to do with one another in all things else, that it is hard to imagine his complaint, if he had one, being solely his own affair. Had he that deep-seated recondite complaint, and did any doctor find it out? Patience. In the meantime, the shadow of the Marshalsea wall was a real darkening influence, and could be seen on the Dorrit Family at any stage of the sun's course.

CHAPTER XXII

MR. CLENNAM did not increase in favour with the Father of the Marshalsea in the ratio of his increasing visits. His obtuseness on the great Testimonial question was not calculated to awaken admiration in the paternal breast, but had rather a tendency to give offence in that sensitive quarter, and to be regarded as a positive shortcoming in point of gentlemanly feeling. An impression of disappointment, occasioned by the discovery that Mr. Clennam scarcely possessed that delicacy for which, in the confidence of his nature, he had been inclined to give him credit, began to darken the fatherly mind in connection with that gentleman. The father went so far as to say, in his private family circle, that he feared Mr. Clennam was not a man of high instincts. He was happy, he observed, in his public capacity as leader and representative of the College, to receive Mr. Clennam when he called to pay his respects; but he didn't find that he got on with him personally. There appeared to be something (he didn't know what it was) wanting in him. Howbeit, the father did not fail in any outward show of politeness, but, on the contrary, honoured him with much attention; perhaps cherishing the hope that, although not a man of a sufficiently brilliant and spontaneous turn of mind to repeat his former testimonial unsolicited, it might still be within the compass of his nature to bear the part of a responsive gentleman, in any correspondence that way tending.

In the threefold capacity, of the gentleman from outside who had been accidentally locked in on the night of his first appearance, of the gentleman from outside who had inquired into the affairs of the Father of the Marshalsea with the stupendous idea of getting him out, and of the gentleman from outside who took an interest in the child of the Marshalsea, Clennam soon became a visitor of mark. He was not surprised by the attentions he received from Mr. Chivery when that officer was on the lock, for he made little distinction between Mr. Chivery's politeness and that of the other turnkeys. It was on one particular afternoon that Mr. Chivery surprised him all at once, and stood forth from his companions in bold relief.

Mr. Chivery, by some artful exercise of his power of clearing the Lodge, had contrived to rid it of all sauntering Collegians; so that Clennam, coming out of the prison, should find him on duty alone.

"(Private) I ask your pardon, sir," said Mr. Chivery in a secret manner; "but which way might you be going?"

"I am going over the Bridge." He saw in Mr. Chivery, with some astonishment, quite an Allegory of Silence, as he stood with his key on his lips.

"(Private) I ask your pardon again," said Mr. Chivery, "but could you go round by Horsemonger Lane? Could you by any means find time to look in at that address?" handing him a little card, printed for circulation among the connection of Chivery and Co., Tobacconists, Importers of pure Havannah Cigars, Bengal Cheroots, and fine-flavoured Cubas, Dealers in Fancy Snuffs, &c. &c.

"(Private) It an't tobacco business," said Mr. Chivery. "The truth is, it's my wife. She's wishful to say a word to you, sir, upon a point respecting—yes," said Mr. Chivery, answering Clennam's look of apprehension with a nod, "respecting *her*."

"I will make a point of seeing your wife directly."

"Thank you, sir. Much obliged. It an't above ten

minutes out of your way. Please to ask for *Mrs.* Chivery!"
These instructions, Mr. Chivery, who had already let him out,
cautiously called through a little slide in the outer door,
which he could draw back from within for the inspection of
visitors when it pleased him.

Arthur Clennam, with the card in his hand, betook himself
to the address set forth upon it, and speedily arrived there.
It was a very small establishment, wherein a decent woman
sat behind the counter working at her needle. Little jars of
tobacco, little boxes of cigars, a little assortment of pipes, a
little jar or two of snuff, and a little instrument like a
shoeing horn for serving it out, composed the retail stock in
trade.

Arthur mentioned his name, and his having promised to
call, on the solicitation of Mr. Chivery. About something
relating to Miss Dorrit, he believed. Mrs. Chivery at once
laid aside her work, rose up from her seat behind the counter,
and deploringly shook her head.

" You may see him now," said she, " if you'll condescend to
take a peep."

With these mysterious words, she preceded the visitor into
a little parlour behind the shop, with a little window in it
commanding a very little dull back-yard. In this yard a wash
of sheets and table-cloths tried (in vain, for want of air) to
get itself dried on a line or two; and among those flapping
articles was sitting in a chair, like the last mariner left alive
on the deck of a damp ship without the power of furling
the sails, a little woe-begone young man.

" Our John," said Mrs. Chivery.

Not to be deficient in interest, Clennam asked what he
might be doing there?

" It's the only change he takes," said Mrs. Chivery, shaking
her head afresh. " He won't go out, even in the back-yard,
when there's no linen; but when there's linen to keep the
neighbours' eyes off, he'll sit there, hours. Hours he will.
Says he feels as if it was groves!" Mrs. Chivery shook her

head again, put her apron in a motherly way to her eyes, and reconducted her visitor into the regions of the business.

"Please to take a seat, sir," said Mrs. Chivery. "Miss Dorrit is the matter with Our John, sir; he's a breaking his heart for her, and I would wish to take the liberty to ask how it's to be made good to his parents when bust?"

Mrs. Chivery, who was a comfortable-looking woman, much respected about Horsemonger Lane for her feelings and her conversation, uttered this speech with fell composure, and immediately afterwards began again to shake her head and dry her eyes.

"Sir," said she in continuation, "you are acquainted with the family, and have interested yourself with the family, and are influential with the family. If you can promote views calculated to make two young people happy, let me, for Our John's sake, and for both their sakes, implore you so to do."

"I have been so habituated," returned Arthur, at a loss, "during the short time I have known her, to consider Little —I have been so habituated to consider Miss Dorrit in a light altogether removed from that in which you present her to me, that you quite take me by surprise. Does she know your son?"

"Brought up together, sir," said Mrs. Chivery. "Played together."

"Does she know your son as her admirer?"

"Oh! bless you, sir," said Mrs. Chivery, with a sort of triumphant shiver, "she never could have seen him on a Sunday without knowing he was that. His cane alone would have told it long ago, if nothing else had. Young men like John don't take to ivory hands a pinting, for nothing. How did I first know it myself? Similarly."

"Perhaps Miss Dorrit may not be so ready as you, you see."

"Then she knows it, sir," said Mrs. Chivery, "by word of mouth."

"Are you sure?"

A TRUE VERSION OF THE MATTER

"Sir," said Mrs. Chivery, "sure and certain as in this house I am. I see my son go out with my own eyes when in this house I was, and I see my son come in with my own eyes when in this house I was, and I know he done it!" Mrs. Chivery derived a surprising force of emphasis from the foregoing circumstantiality and repetition.

"May I ask you how he came to fall into the desponding state which causes you so much uneasiness?"

"That," said Mrs. Chivery, "took place on that same day when to this house I see that John with these eyes return. Never been himself in this house since. Never was like what he has been since, not from the hour when to this house seven year ago me and his father, as tenants by the quarter, came!" An effect in the nature of an affidavit was gained for this speech, by Mrs. Chivery's peculiar power of construction.

"May I venture to inquire what is your version of the matter?"

"You may," said Mrs. Chivery, "and I will give it to you in honour and in word as true as in this shop I stand. Our John has every one's good word and every one's good wish. He played with her as a child when in that yard a child she played. He has known her ever since. He went out upon the Sunday afternoon when in this very parlour he had dined, and met her, with appointment or without appointment which I do not pretend to say. He made his offer to her. Her brother and sister is high in their views, and against Our John. Her father is all for himself in his views and against sharing her with any one. Under which circumstances she has answered Our John, 'No, John, I cannot have you, I cannot have any husband, it is not my intentions ever to become a wife, it is my intentions to be always a sacrifice, farewell, find another worthy of you, and forget me!' This is the way in which she is doomed to be a constant slave, to them that are not worthy that a constant slave she unto them should be. This is the way in which Our John has come to find no pleasure but in taking cold among the linen, and in showing in that yard, as in that yard I have myself shown you, a broken-down ruin that goes home to his mother's heart!" Here the good woman pointed to the little window, whence her son might be seen sitting disconsolate in the tuneless groves; and again shook her head and wiped her eyes, and besought him, for the united sakes of both the young people, to exercise his influence towards the bright reversal of these dismal events.

She was so confident in her exposition of the case, and it was so undeniably founded on correct premises in so far as the relative positions of Little Dorrit and her family were concerned, that Clennam could not feel positive on the other side. He had come to attach to Little Dorrit an interest so peculiar—an interest that removed her from, while it grew out of, the common and coarse things surrounding her—that he found it disappointing, disagreeable, almost painful, to suppose her in love with young Mr. Chivery in the backyard, or any such person. On the other hand, he reasoned with himself that she was just as good and just as true, in love with him, as not in love with him; and that to make a kind of domesticated fairy of her, on the penalty of isolation at heart from the only people she knew, would be but a weakness of his own fancy, and not a kind one. Still, her youthful and ethereal appearance, her timid manner, the charm of her sensitive voice and eyes, the very many respects in which she had interested him out of her own individuality, and the strong difference between herself and those about her, were not in unison, and were determined not to be in unison, with this newly presented idea.

He told the worthy Mrs. Chivery, after turning these things over in his mind—he did that, indeed, while she was yet speaking—that he might be relied upon to do his utmost at all times to promote the happiness of Miss Dorrit, and to further the wishes of her heart if it were in his power to do so, and if he could discover what they were. At the same time he cautioned her against assumptions and appearances:

enjoined strict silence and secrecy, lest Miss Dorrit should be made unhappy ; and particularly advised her to endeavour to win her son's confidence and so to make quite sure of the state of the case. Mrs. Chivery considered the latter precaution superfluous, but said she would try. She shook her head as if she had not derived all the comfort she had fondly expected from this interview, but thanked him nevertheless for the trouble he had kindly taken. They then parted good friends, and Arthur walked away.

The crowd in the street jostling the crowd in his mind, and the two crowds making a confusion, he avoided London Bridge, and turned off in the quieter direction of the Iron Bridge. He had scarcely set foot upon it, when he saw Little Dorrit walking on before him. It was a pleasant day, with a light breeze blowing, and she seemed to have that minute come there for air. He had left her in her father's room within an hour.

It was a timely chance, favourable to his wish of observing her face and manner when no one else was by. He quickened his pace ; but before he reached her, she turned her head.

" Have I startled you ? " he asked.

" I thought I knew the step," she answered, hesitating.

" And did you know it, Little Dorrit ? You could hardly have expected mine."

" I did not expect any. But when I heard a step, I thought it—sounded like yours."

" Are you going further ? "

" No, sir, I am only walking here for a little change."

They walked together, and she recovered her confiding manner with him, and looked up in his face, as she said, after glancing around :

" It is so strange. Perhaps you can hardly understand it. I sometimes have a sensation as if it was almost unfeeling to walk here ? "

" Unfeeling ? "

" To see the river, and so much sky, and so many objects, and such change and motion. Then to go back, you know, and find him in the same cramped place."

" Ah yes! But going back, you must remember that you take with you the spirit and influence of such things to cheer him."

" Do I? I hope I may! I am afraid you fancy too much, sir, and make me out too powerful. If you were in prison, could I bring such comfort to you?"

" Yes, Little Dorrit, I am sure of it!"

He gathered from a tremor on her lip, and a passing shadow of great agitation on her face, that her mind was with her father. He remained silent for a few moments, that she might regain her composure. The Little Dorrit, trembling on his arm, was less in unison than ever with Mrs. Chivery's theory, and yet was not irreconcilable with a new fancy which sprung up within him, that there might be some one else in the hopeless—newer fancy still—in the hopeless unattainable distance.

They turned, and Clennam said, Here was Maggy coming! Little Dorrit looked up, surprised, and they confronted Maggy, who brought herself at sight of them to a dead stop. She had been trotting along, so preoccupied and busy, that she had not recognised them until they turned upon her. She was now in a moment so conscience-stricken that her very basket partook of the change.

" Maggy, you promised me to stop near father."

" So I would, Little Mother, only he wouldn't let me. If he takes and sends me out I must go. If he takes and says, ' Maggy, you hurry away and back with that letter, and you shall have a sixpence if the answer's a good 'un,' I must take it. Lor, Little Mother, what's a poor thing of ten year old to do? And if Mr. Tip—if he happens to be a coming in as I come out, and if he says, ' Where are you going, Maggy?' and if I says, ' I'm a going So and So,' and if he says, ' I'll have a Try too,' and if he goes into the George and writes a letter, and if he gives it me and says, 'Take that one to the same place, and if the answer's a good 'un I'll give you a shilling,' it ain't my fault, mother!"

Arthur read, in Little Dorrit's downcast eyes, to whom she foresaw that the letters were addressed.

"I'm a going So and So. There! That's where I am a going to," said Maggy. "I'm a going So and So. It an't you, Little Mother, that's got anything to do with it—it's you, you know," said Maggy, addressing Arthur. "You'd better come, So and So, and let me take and give 'em to you."

"We will not be so particular as that, Maggy. Give them me here," said Clennam, in a low voice.

"Well, then, come across the road," answered Maggy, in a very loud whisper. "Little Mother wasn't to know nothing of it, and she would never have known nothing of it if you had only gone, So and So, instead of bothering and loitering about. It ain't my fault. I must do what I am told. They ought to be ashamed of themselves for telling me."

Clennam crossed to the other side, and hurriedly opened the letters. That from the father mentioned that most unexpectedly finding himself in the novel position of having been disappointed of a remittance from the City on which he had confidently counted, he took up his pen, being restrained by the unhappy circumstance of his incarceration during three-and-twenty years (doubly underlined), from coming himself, as he would otherwise certainly have done—took up his pen to entreat Mr. Clennam to advance him the sum of Three Pounds Ten Shillings upon his I.O.U., which he begged to enclose. That from the son set forth that Mr. Clennam would, he knew, be gratified to hear that he had at length obtained permanent employment of a highly satisfactory nature, accompanied with every prospect of complete success in life; but that the temporary inability of his employer to pay him his arrears of salary to that date (in which condition said employer had appealed to that generous forbearance in which he trusted he should never be wanting towards a fellow-creature), combined with the fraudulent conduct of a false friend, and the present high price of provisions, had reduced him to the verge of ruin, unless he could by a quarter before six that evening raise the sum of eight pounds. This sum, Mr. Clennam would be happy to learn, he had, through the promptitude of several friends who had a lively confidence in his probity, already raised, with the exception of a trifling balance of one pound seventeen and fourpence; the loan of which balance, for the period of one month, would be fraught with the usual beneficent consequences.

These letters Clennam answered with the aid of his pencil and pocket-book, on the spot; sending the father what he asked for, and excusing himself from compliance with the demand of the son. He then commissioned Maggy to return with his replies, and gave her the shilling of which the failure of her supplemental enterprise would have disappointed her otherwise.

When he rejoined Little Dorrit, and they had begun walking as before, she said all at once:

"I think I had better go. I had better go home."

"Don't be distressed," said Clennam, "I have answered the letters. They were nothing. You know what they were. They were nothing."

"But I am afraid," she returned, "to leave him, I am afraid to leave any of them. When I am gone, they pervert —but they don't mean it—even Maggy."

"It was a very innocent commission that she undertook, poor thing. And in keeping it secret from you, she supposed, no doubt, that she was only saving you uneasiness."

"Yes, I hope so, I hope so. But I had better go home! It was but the other day that my sister told me I had become so used to the prison that I had its tone and character. It must be so. I am sure it must be when I see these things. My place is there. I am better there. It is unfeeling in me to be here, when I can do the least thing there. Good-bye. I had far better stay at home!"

The agonised way in which she poured this out, as if it burst of itself from her suppressed heart, made it difficult for Clennam to keep the tears from his eyes as he saw and heard her.

"Don't call it home, my child!" he entreated. "It is always painful to me to hear you call it home."

"But it is home! What else can I call home? Why should I ever forget it for a single moment?"

"You never do, dear Little Dorrit, in any good and true service."

"I hope not, O I hope not! But it is better for me to stay there; much better, much more dutiful, much happier. Please don't go with me, let me go by myself. Good-bye, God bless you. Thank you, thank you."

He felt that it was better to respect her entreaty, and did not move while her slight form went quickly away from him. When it had fluttered out of sight, he turned his face towards the water and stood thinking.

She would have been distressed at any time by this discovery of the letters; but so much so, and in that unrestrainable way?

No.

When she had seen her father begging with his threadbare disguise on, when she had entreated him not to give her father money, she had been distressed, but not like this. Something had made her keenly and additionally sensitive just now. Now, was there some one in the hopeless unattainable distance? Or had the suspicion been brought into his mind, by his own associations of the troubled river running beneath the bridge with the same river higher up, its changeless tune upon the prow of the ferry-boat, so many miles an hour the peaceful flowing of the stream, here the rushes, there the lilies, nothing uncertain or unquiet?

LITTLE DORRIT

He thought of his poor child, Little Dorrit, for a long time there; he thought of her going home; he thought of her in the night; he thought of her when the day came round again. And the poor child Little Dorrit thought of him— too faithfully, ah, too faithfully!—in the shadow of the Marshalsea wall.

CHAPTER XXIII

MACHINERY IN MOTION

Mr. Meagles bestirred himself with such prompt activity in the matter of the negotiation with Daniel Doyce which Clennam had entrusted to him, that he soon brought it into business train, and called on Clennam at nine o'clock one morning to make his report.

"Doyce is highly gratified by your good opinion," he opened the business by saying, " and desires nothing so much as that you should examine the affairs of the Works for yourself, and entirely understand them. He has handed me the keys of all his books and papers—here they are jingling in this pocket—and the only charge he has given me is, ' Let Mr. Clennam have the means of putting himself on a perfect equality with me as to knowing whatever I know. If it should come to nothing after all, he will respect my confidence. Unless I was sure of that to begin with, I should have nothing to do with him.' And there, you see," said Mr. Meagles, " you have Daniel Doyce all over."

" A very honourable character."

"Oh, yes, to be sure. Not a doubt of it. Odd, but very honourable. Very odd though. Now, would you believe, Clennam," said Mr. Meagles, with a hearty enjoyment of his friend's eccentricity, " that I had a whole morning in What's-his-name Yard—— "

" Bleeding Heart ? "

" A whole morning in Bleeding Heart Yard, before I could induce him to pursue the subject at all ? "

" How was that ? "

" How was that, my friend ?   I no sooner mentioned your name in connection with it, than he declared off."

" Declared off, on my account ? "

" I no sooner mentioned your name, Clennam, than he said, ' That will never do ! '   What did he mean by that ? I asked him.   No matter, Meagles ; that would never do. Why would it never do ?   You'll hardly believe it, Clennam," said Mr. Meagles, laughing within himself, " but it came out that it would never do, because you and he, walking down to Twickenham together, had glided into a friendly con-versation, in the course of which he had referred to his intention of taking a partner, supposing at the time that you were as firmly and finally settled as St. Paul's Cathedral. ' Whereas,' says he, ' Mr. Clennam might now believe, if I entertained his proposition, that I had a sinister and designing motive in what was open free speech.   Which I can't bear,' says he, ' which I really am too proud to bear.' "

" I should as soon suspect—— "

" Of course you would," interrupted Mr. Meagles, " and so I told him.   But it took a morning to scale that wall ; and I doubt if any other man than myself (he likes me of old) could have got his leg over it.   Well, Clennam.   This business-like obstacle surmounted, he then stipulated that before resuming with you I should look over the books and form my own opinion.   I looked over the books, and formed my own opinion.   ' Is it, on the whole, for, or against ? ' says he.   ' For,' says I.   ' Then,' says he, ' you may now, my good friend, give Mr. Clennam the means of forming his opinion.   To enable him to do which, without bias, and with perfect freedom, I shall go out of town for a week.' And he's gone," said Mr. Meagles ; " that's the rich conclusion of the thing."

"Leaving me," said Clennam, "with a high sense, I must say, of his candour and his——"

"Oddity," Mr. Meagles struck in. "I should think so!"

It was not exactly the word on Clennam's lips, but he forbore to interrupt his good-humoured friend.

"And now," added Mr. Meagles, "you can begin to look into matters as soon as you think proper. I have undertaken to explain where you may want explanation, but to be strictly impartial, and to do nothing more."

They began their perquisitions in Bleeding Heart Yard that same forenoon. Little peculiarities were easily to be detected by experienced eyes in Mr. Doyce's way of managing his affairs, but they almost always involved some ingenious simplification of a difficulty, and some plain road to the desired end. That his papers were in arrear, and that he stood in need of assistance to develop the capacity of his business, was clear enough; but all the results of his undertakings during many years were distinctly set forth, and were ascertainable with ease. Nothing had been done for the purposes of the pending investigation; everything was in its genuine working dress, and in a certain honest rugged order. The calculations and entries, in his own hand, of which there were many, were bluntly written, and with no very neat precision; but were always plain, and directed straight to the purpose. It occurred to Arthur that a far more elaborate and taking show of business—such as the records of the Circumlocution Office made perhaps—might be far less serviceable, as being meant to be far less intelligible.

Three or four days of steady application rendered him master of all the facts it was essential to become acquainted with. Mr. Meagles was at hand the whole time, always ready to illuminate any dim place with the bright little safety-lamp belonging to the scales and scoop. Between them they agreed upon the sum it would be fair to offer for the purchase of a half-share in the business, and then Mr. Meagles unsealed a paper in which Daniel Doyce had noted the amount at which he valued it; which was even something less. Thus, when Daniel came back, he found the affair as good as concluded.

"And I may now avow, Mr. Clennam," said he, with a cordial shake of the hand, "that if I had looked high and low for a partner, I believe I could not have found one more to my mind."

"I say the same," said Clennam.

"And I say of both of you," added Mr. Meagles, "that you are well matched. You keep him in check, Clennam, with your common sense, and you stick to the Works, Dan, with your—— "

"Uncommon sense?" suggested Daniel, with his quiet smile.

"You may call it so, if you like—and each of you will be a right hand to the other. Here's my own right hand upon it, as a practical man, to both of you."

The purchase was completed within a month. It left Arthur in possession of private personal means not exceeding a few hundred pounds; but it opened to him an active and promising career. The three friends dined together on the auspicious occasion; the factory and the factory wives and children made holiday and dined too; even Bleeding Heart Yard dined and was full of meat. Two months had barely gone by in all, when Bleeding Heart Yard had become so familiar with short-commons again that the treat was forgotten there; when nothing seemed new in the partnership but the paint of the inscription on the door-posts, DOYCE AND CLENNAM; when it appeared even to Clennam himself, that he had had the affairs of the firm in his mind for years.

The little counting-house reserved for his own occupation, was a room of wood and glass at the end of a long low workshop, filled with benches, and vices, and tools, and straps, and wheels; which, when they were in gear with the steam-engine, went tearing round as though they had a suicidal mission to grind the business to dust and tear the factory to pieces. A communication of great trap-doors in the floor and roof with the workshop above and the workshop below, made a shaft of light in this perspective, which brought to Clennam's mind the child's old picture-book, where similar rays were the witnesses of Abel's murder. The noises were sufficiently removed and shut out from the counting-house to blend into a busy hum, interspersed with periodical clinks and thumps. The patient figures at work were swarthy with the filings of iron and steel that danced on every bench and bubbled up through every chink in the planking. The workshop was arrived at by a step-ladder from the outer yard below, where it served as a shelter for the large grindstone where tools were sharpened. The whole had at once a fanciful and practical air in Clennam's eyes, which was a welcome change; and, as often as he raised them from his first work of getting the array of business documents into perfect order, he glanced at these things with a feeling of pleasure in his pursuit that was new to him.

Raising his eyes thus one day, he was surprised to see a bonnet labouring up the step-ladder. The unusual apparition was followed by another bonnet. He then perceived that the first bonnet was on the head of Mr. F's Aunt, and that the second bonnet was on the head of Flora, who seemed to have propelled her legacy up the steep ascent with considerable difficulty.

Though not altogether enraptured at the sight of these visitors, Clennam lost no time in opening the counting-house door, and extricating them from the workshop; a rescue which was rendered the more necessary by Mr. F's Aunt already stumbling over some impediment, and menacing steam power as an Institution with a stony reticule she carried.

"Good gracious, Arthur,—I should say Mr. Clennam, far more proper—the climb we have had to get up here and how ever to get down again without a fire-escape and Mr. F's Aunt slipping through the steps and bruised all over and you in the machinery and foundry way too only think, and never told us!"

Thus Flora, out of breath. Meanwhile, Mr. F's Aunt rubbed her esteemed insteps with her umbrella, and vindictively glared.

"Most unkind never to have come back to see us since that day, though naturally it was not to be expected that there should be any attraction at *our* house and you were much more pleasantly engaged, that's pretty certain, and is she fair or dark blue eyes or black I wonder, not that I expect that she should be anything but a perfect contrast to me in all particulars for I am a disappointment as I very well know and you are quite right to be devoted no doubt though what I am saying Arthur never mind I hardly know myself Good gracious!"

By this time he had placed chairs for them in the counting-house. As Flora dropped into hers, she bestowed the old look upon him.

"And to think of Doyce and Clennam, and who Doyce can be," said Flora; "delightful man no doubt and married perhaps or perhaps a daughter, now has he really? then one understands the partnership and sees it all, don't tell me anything about it for I know I have no claim to ask the question the golden chain that once was forged, being snapped and very proper."

Flora put her hand tenderly on his, and gave him another of the youthful glances.

"Dear Arthur—force of habit, Mr. Clennam every way more delicate and adapted to existing circumstances—I must beg to be excused for taking the liberty of this intrusion but I thought I might so far presume upon old times for ever faded never more to bloom as to call with Mr. F's Aunt to congratulate and offer best wishes, A great deal superior to China not to be denied and much nearer though higher up!"

"I am very happy to see you," said Clennam, "and I thank you, Flora, very much for your kind remembrance."

"More than I can say myself at any rate," returned Flora, "for I might have been dead and buried twenty distinct

330

Visitors at the Works

times over and no doubt whatever should have been before
you had genuinely remembered Me or anything like it in
spite of which one last remark I wish to make, one last
explanation I wish to offer——"

"My dear Mrs. Finching," Arthur remonstrated in alarm.

"Oh not that disagreeable name, say Flora!"

"Flora, is it worth troubling yourself afresh to enter into
explanations? I assure you none are needed. I am satisfied
—I am perfectly satisfied."

A diversion was occasioned here, by Mr. F's Aunt making
the following inexorable and awful statement:

"There's mile-stones on the Dover road!"

With such mortal hostility towards the human race did
she discharge this missile, that Clennam was quite at a loss
how to defend himself; the rather as he had been already
perplexed in his mind by the honour of a visit from this
venerable lady, when it was plain she held him in the utmost
abhorrence. He could not but look at her with disconcert-
ment, as she sat breathing bitterness and scorn, and staring
leagues away. Flora, however, received the remark as if it
had been of a most apposite and agreeable nature; approvingly observing aloud that Mr. F's Aunt had a great deal
of spirit. Stimulated either by this compliment, or by her
burning indignation, that illustrious woman then added,
"Let him meet it if he can!" And, with a rigid movement
of her stony reticule (an appendage of great size, and of a
fossil appearance), indicated that Clennam was the unfortunate
person at whom the challenge was hurled.

"One last remark," resumed Flora, "I was going to say I
wish to make one last explanation I wish to offer, Mr. F's
Aunt and myself would not have intruded on business hours
Mr. F having been in business and though the wine trade
still business is equally business call it what you will and
business habits are just the same as witness Mr. F himself
who had his slippers always on the mat at ten minutes before
six in the afternoon and his boots inside the fender at ten

331

minutes before eight in the morning to the moment in all weathers light or dark—would not therefore have intruded without a motive which being kindly meant it may be hoped will be kindly taken Arthur, Mr. Clennam far more proper, even Doyce and Clennam probably more business-like."

"Pray say nothing in the way of apology," Arthur entreated. "You are always welcome."

"Very polite of you to say so Arthur—cannot remember Mr. Clennam until the word is out, such is the habit of times for ever fled, and so true it is that oft in the stilly night ere slumber's chain has bound people, fond memory brings the light of other days around people—very polite but more polite than true I am afraid, for to go into the machinery business without so much as sending a line or a card to papa —I don't say me though there was a time but that is past and stern reality has now my gracious never mind—does not look like it you must confess."

Even Flora's commas seemed to have fled on this occasion ; she was so much more disjointed and voluble than in the preceding interview.

"Though indeed," she hurried on, "nothing else is to be expected and why should it be expected, and if it's not to be expected why should it be, and I am far from blaming you or any one, When your mama and my papa worried us to death and severed the golden bowl—I mean bond but I dare say you know what I mean and if you don't you don't lose much and care just as little I will venture to add—when they severed the golden bond that bound us and threw us into fits of crying on the sofa nearly choked at least myself everything was changed and in giving my hand to Mr. F I know I did so with my eyes open but he was so very unsettled and in such low spirits that he had distractedly alluded to the river if not oil of something from the chemist's and I did it for the best."

"My good Flora, we settled that before. It was all quite right."

"It's perfectly clear you think so," returned Flora, "for you take it very coolly, if I hadn't known it to be China I should have guessed myself the Polar regions, dear Mr. Clennam you are right however and I cannot blame you but as to Doyce and Clennam papa's property being about here we heard it from Pancks and but for him we never should have heard one word about it I am satisfied."

"No no, don't say that."

"What nonsense not to say it Arthur—Doyce and Clennam —easier and less trying to me than Mr. Clennam—when I know it and you know it too and can't deny it."

"But I do deny it, Flora. I should soon have made you a friendly visit."

"Ah!" said Flora, tossing her head. "I dare say!" and she gave him another of the old looks. "However when Pancks told us I made up my mind that Mr. F's Aunt and I would come and call because when papa—which was before that—happened to mention her name to me and to say that you were interested in her I said at the moment Good gracious why not have her here then when there's anything to do instead of putting it out."

"When you say Her," observed Clennam, by this time pretty well bewildered, "do you mean Mr. F's—— "

"My goodness, Arthur—Doyce and Clennam really easier to me with old remembrances—who ever heard of Mr. F's Aunt doing needlework and going out by the day!"

"Going out by the day! Do you speak of Little Dorrit?"

"Why yes of course," returned Flora; "and of all the strangest names I ever heard the strangest, like a place down in the country with a turnpike, or a favourite pony or a puppy or a bird or something from a seed-shop to be put in a garden or a flower-pot and come up speckled."

"Then, Flora," said Arthur, with a sudden interest in the conversation, "Mr. Casby was so kind as to mention Little Dorrit to you, was he? What did he say?"

"Oh you know what papa is," rejoined Flora, "and how

aggravatingly he sits looking beautiful and turning his thumbs over and over one another till he makes one giddy if one keeps one's eyes upon him, he said when we were talking of you—I don't know who began the subject Arthur (Doyce and Clennam) but I am sure it wasn't me, at least I hope not but you really must excuse my confessing more on that point."

"Certainly," said Arthur. "By all means."

"You are very ready," pouted Flora, coming to a sudden stop in a captivating bashfulness, "that I must admit, Papa said you had spoken of her in an earnest way and I said what I have told you and that's all."

"That's all?" said Arthur, a little disappointed.

"Except that when Pancks told us of your having embarked in this business and with difficulty persuaded us that it was really you I said to Mr. F's Aunt then we would come and ask you if it would be agreeable to all parties that she should be engaged at our house when required for I know she often goes to your mama's and I know that your mama has a very touchy temper Arthur—Doyce and Clennam—or I never might have married Mr. F and might have been at this hour but I am running into nonsense."

"It was very kind of you, Flora, to think of this."

Poor Flora rejoined with a plain sincerity which became her better than her youngest glances, that she was glad he thought so. She said it with so much heart, that Clennam would have given a great deal to buy his old character of her on the spot, and throw it and the mermaid away for ever.

"I think, Flora," he said, "that the employment you can give Little Dorrit, and the kindness you can show her——"

"Yes and I will," said Flora, quickly.

"I am sure of it—will be a great assistance and support to her. I do not feel that I have the right to tell you what I know of her, for I acquired the knowledge confidentially, and under circumstances that bind me to silence. But I have an interest in the little creature, and a respect for her that I cannot express to you. Her life has been one of such trial and devotion, and such quiet goodness, as you can scarcely imagine. I can hardly think of her, far less speak of her, without feeling moved. Let that feeling represent what I could tell you, and commit her to your friendliness with my thanks."

Once more he put out his hand frankly to poor Flora ; once more poor Flora couldn't accept it frankly, found it worth nothing openly, must make the old intrigue and mystery of it. As much to her own enjoyment as to his dismay, she covered it with a corner of her shawl as she took it. Then, looking towards the glass front of the counting-house, and seeing two figures approaching, she cried with infinite relish, " Papa ! Hush, Arthur, for Mercy's sake !" and tottered back to her chair with an amazing imitation of being in danger of swooning, in the dread surprise and maidenly flutter of her spirits.

The Patriarch, meanwhile, came inanely beaming towards the counting-house, in the wake of Pancks. Pancks opened the door for him, towed him in, and retired to his own moorings in a corner.

"I heard from Flora," said the Patriarch, with his benevolent smile, " that she was coming to call, coming to call. And being out, I thought I'd come also, thought I'd come also."

The benign wisdom he infused into this declaration (not of itself profound), by means of his blue eyes, his shining head, and his long white hair, was most impressive. It seemed worth putting down among the noblest sentiments enunciated by the best of men. Also, when he said to Clennam, seating himself in the proffered chair, " And you are in a new business, Mr. Clennam ? I wish you well, sir, I wish you well !" he seemed to have done benevolent wonders.

" Mrs. Finching has been telling me, sir," said Arthur, after making his acknowledgments; the relict of the late Mr. F meanwhile protesting, with a gesture, against his use of that

335

respectable name; "that she hopes occasionally to employ the young needlewoman you recommended to my mother. For which I have been thanking her."

The Patriarch turning his head in a lumbering way towards Pancks, that assistant put up the note-book in which he had been absorbed, and took him in tow.

"You didn't recommend her, you know," said Pancks; "how could you? You knew nothing about her, you didn't. The name was mentioned to you, and you passed it on. That's what *you* did."

"Well!" said Clennam. "As she justifies any recommendation, it is much the same thing."

"You are glad she turns out well," said Pancks, "but it wouldn't have been your fault if she had turned out ill. The credit's not yours as it is, and the blame wouldn't have been yours as it might have been. You gave no guarantee. You knew nothing about her."

"You are not acquainted, then," said Arthur, hazarding a random question, "with any of her family?"

"Acquainted with any of her family?" returned Pancks. "How should you be acquainted with any of her family? You never heard of 'em. You can't be acquainted with people you never heard of, can you? You should think not!"

All this time the Patriarch sat serenely smiling; nodding or shaking his head benevolently, as the case required.

"As to being a reference," said Pancks, "you know in a general way, what being a reference means. It's all your eye, that is! Look at your tenants down the Yard here. They'd all be references for one another, if you'd let 'em. What would be the good of letting 'em? It's no satisfaction to be done by two men instead of one. One's enough. A person who can't pay, gets another person who can't pay, to guarantee that he can pay. Like a person with two wooden legs, getting another person with two wooden legs, to guarantee that he has got two natural legs. It don't make either of them able to do a walking-match. And four wooden legs are more troublesome to you than two, when you don't want any." Mr. Pancks concluded by blowing off that steam of his.

A momentary silence that ensued was broken by Mr. F's Aunt, who had been sitting upright in a cataleptic state since her last public remark. She now underwent a violent twitch, calculated to produce a startling effect on the nerves of the uninitiated, and with the deadliest animosity observed :

"You can't make a head and brains out of a brass knob with nothing in it. You couldn't do it when your Uncle George was living; much less when he's dead."

Mr. Pancks was not slow to reply, with his usual calmness, "Indeed, ma'am! Bless my soul! I'm surprised to hear it." Despite his presence of mind, however, the speech of Mr. F's Aunt produced a depressing effect on the little assembly; firstly, because it was impossible to disguise that Clennam's unoffending head was the particular temple of reason depreciated ; and secondly, because nobody ever knew on these occasions whose Uncle George was referred to, or what spectral presence might be invoked under that appellation.

Therefore Flora said, though still not without a certain boastfulness and triumph in her legacy, that Mr. F's Aunt was "very lively to-day, and she thought they had better go." But, Mr. F's Aunt proved so lively as to take the suggestion in unexpected dudgeon and declare that she would not go ; adding, with several injurious expressions, that if "He "—too evidently meaning Clennam—wanted to get rid of her, "let him chuck her out of winder;" and urgently expressing her desire to see "Him" perform that ceremony.

In this dilemma, Mr. Pancks, whose resources appeared equal to any emergency in the Patriarchal waters, slipped on his hat, slipped out at the counting-house door, and slipped in again a moment afterwards with an artificial freshness upon him, as if he had been in the country for some weeks. "Why, bless my heart, ma'am!" said Mr. Pancks, rubbing up his hair in great astonishment, "is that you? How do you *do*, ma'am ? You are looking charming to-day! I am delighted to see you. Favour me with your arm, ma'am; we'll have a little walk together, you and me, if you'll honour me with your company." And so escorted Mr. F's aunt down the private staircase of the counting-house, with great gallantry and success. The patriarchal Mr. Casby then rose with the air of having done it himself, and blandly followed : leaving his daughter, as she followed in her turn, to remark to her former lover in a distracted whisper (which she very much enjoyed), that they had drained the cup of life to the dregs ; and further to hint mysteriously that the late Mr. F was at the bottom of it.

Alone again, Clennam became a prey to his old doubts in reference to his mother and Little Dorrit, and revolved the old thoughts and suspicions. They were all in his mind, blending themselves with the duties he was mechanically discharging, when a shadow on his papers caused him to look up for the cause. The cause was Mr. Pancks. With his hat thrown back upon his ears as if his wiry prongs of hair had darted up like springs and cast it off, with his jet-black beads of eyes inquisitively sharp, with the fingers of his right hand in his mouth that he might bite the nails, and with the fingers of his left hand in reserve in his pocket for another course, Mr. Pancks cast his shadow through the glass upon the books and papers.

Mr. Pancks asked, with a little inquiring twist of his head, if he might come in again ? Clennam replied with a nod of his head in the affirmative. Mr. Pancks worked his way in, came alongside the desk, made himself fast by leaning his arms upon it, and started conversation with a puff and a snort.

" Mr. F's Aunt is appeased, I hope," said Clennam.

" All right, sir," said Pancks.

" I am so unfortunate as to have awakened a strong animosity in the breast of that lady," said Clennam. " Do you know why ? "

"Does *she* know why?" said Pancks.

"I suppose not."

"*I* suppose not," said Pancks.

He took out his note-book, opened it, shut it, dropped it into his hat, which was beside him on the desk, and looked in at it as it lay at the bottom of the hat: all with a great appearance of consideration.

"Mr. Clennam," he then began, "I am in want of information, sir."

"Connected with this firm?" asked Clennam.

"No," said Pancks.

"With what then, Mr. Pancks? That is to say, assuming that you want it of me."

"Yes, sir; yes, I want it of you," said Pancks, "if I can persuade you to furnish it. A, B, C, D. DA, DE, DI, DO. Dictionary order. Dorrit. That's the name, sir?"

Mr. Pancks blew off his peculiar noise again, and fell to at his right-hand nails. Arthur looked searchingly at him; he returned the look.

"I don't understand you, Mr. Pancks."

"That's the name that I want to know about."

"And what do you want to know?"

"Whatever you can and will tell me." This comprehensive summary of his desires was not discharged without some heavy labouring on the part of Mr. Pancks's machinery.

"This is a singular visit, Mr. Pancks. It strikes me as rather extraordinary that you should come, with such an object, to me."

"It may be all extraordinary together," returned Pancks. "It may be out of the ordinary course, and yet be business. In short, it is business. I am a man of business. What business have I in this present world, except to stick to business? No business."

With his former doubt whether this dry hard personage were quite in earnest, Clennam again turned his eyes attentively upon his face. It was as scrubby and dingy as ever, and as eager and quick as ever, and he could see nothing lurking in it that was at all expressive of a latent mockery that had seemed to strike upon his ear in the voice.

"Now," said Pancks, "to put this business on its own footing, it's not my proprietor's."

"Do you refer to Mr. Casby as your proprietor."

Pancks nodded. "My proprietor. Put a case. Say, at my proprietor's I hear name—name of young person Mr. Clennam wants to serve. Say, name first mentioned to my proprietor by Plornish in the Yard. Say, I go to Plornish. Say, I ask Plornish as a matter of business, for information. Say, Plornish, though six weeks in arrear to my proprietor, declines. Say, Mrs. Plornish declines. Say, both refer to Mr. Clennam. Put the case."

"Well?"

"Well, sir," returned Pancks, "say, I come to him. Say, here I am."

With those prongs of hair sticking up all over his head, and his breath coming and going very hard and short, the busy Pancks fell back a step (in Tug metaphor, took half a turn astern) as if to show his dingy hull complete, then forged a-head again, and directed his quick glance by turns into his hat where his note-book was, and into Clennam's face.

"Mr. Pancks, not to trespass on your ground of mystery, I will be as plain with you as I can. Let me ask two questions. First——"

"All right!" said Pancks, holding up his dirty forefinger with his broken nail. "I see! 'What's your motive?'"

"Exactly."

"Motive," said Pancks, "good. Nothing to do with my proprietor; not stateable at present, ridiculous to state at present; but good. Desiring to serve young person, name of Dorrit," said Pancks, with his forefinger still up as a caution. "Better admit motive to be good."

"Secondly, and lastly, what do you want to know?"

Mr. Pancks finished up his note-book before the question was put, and buttoning it with care in an inner breast-pocket, and looking straight at Clennam all the time, replied with a pause and a puff, " I want supplementary information of any sort."

Clennam could not withhold a smile, as the panting little steam-tug, so useful to that unwieldy ship the Casby, waited on and watched him as if it were seeking an opportunity of running in and rifling him of all it wanted, before he could resist its manœuvres; though there was that in Mr. Pancks's eagerness, too, which awakened many wondering speculations in his mind. After a little consideration, he resolved to supply Mr. Pancks with such leading information as it was in his power to impart to him; well knowing that Mr. Pancks, if he failed in his present research, was pretty sure to find other means of getting it.

He, therefore, first requesting Mr. Pancks to remember his voluntary declaration that his proprietor had no part in the disclosure, and that his own intentions were good (two declarations which that coaly little gentleman with the greatest ardour repeated), openly told him that as to the Dorrit lineage or former place of habitation, he had no information to communicate, and that his knowledge of the family did not extend beyond the fact that it appeared to be now reduced to five members; namely, to two brothers, of whom one was single, and one a widower with three children. The ages of the whole family he made known to Mr. Pancks, as nearly as he could guess at them; and finally he described to him the position of the Father of the Marshalsea, and the course of time and events through which he had become invested with that character. To all this, Mr. Pancks, snorting and blowing in a more and more portentous manner as he became more interested, listened with great attention; appearing to derive the most agreeable sensations from the painfullest parts of the narrative, and particularly to be quite charmed by the account of William Dorrit's long imprisonment.

"In conclusion, Mr. Pancks," said Arthur, "I have but to say this. I have reasons beyond a personal regard, for speaking as little as I can of the Dorrit family, particularly at my mother's house" (Mr. Pancks nodded), "and for knowing as much as I can. So devoted a man of business as you are—eh?"

For, Mr. Pancks had suddenly made that blowing effort with unusual force.

"It's nothing," said Pancks.

"So devoted a man of business as yourself has a perfect understanding of a fair bargain. I wish to make a fair bargain with you, that you shall enlighten me concerning the Dorrit family, when you have it in your power, as I have enlightened you. It may not give you a very flattering idea of my business habits, that I failed to make my terms beforehand," continued Clennam; "but I prefer to make them a point of honour. I have seen so much business done on sharp principles that, to tell you the truth, Mr. Pancks, I am tired of them."

Mr. Pancks laughed. "It's a bargain, sir," said he. "You shall find me stick to it."

After that, he stood a little while looking at Clennam, and biting his ten nails all round; evidently while he fixed in his mind what he had been told, and went over it carefully before the means of supplying a gap in his memory should be no longer at hand. "It's all right," he said at last, "and now I'll wish you good day, as it's collecting day in the Yard. By-the-bye, though. A lame foreigner with a stick."

"Ay, ay. You do take a reference sometimes, I see?" said Clennam.

"When he can pay, sir," replied Pancks. "Take all you can get, and keep back all you can't be forced to give up. That's business. The lame foreigner with the stick wants a top room down the Yard. Is he good for it?"

"I am," said Clennam, "and I will answer for him."

342

"That's enough. What I must have of Bleeding Heart Yard," said Pancks, making a note of the case in his book, " is my bond. I want my bond, you see. Pay up, or produce your property ! That's the watchword down the Yard. The lame foreigner with the stick represented that you sent him ; but he could represent (as far as that goes) that the Great Mogul sent him. He has been in the hospital, I believe ? "

" Yes. Through having met with an accident. He is only just now discharged."

" It's pauperising a man, sir, I have been shown, to let him into a hospital ? " said Pancks. And again blew off that remarkable sound.

" I have been shown so too," said Clennam, coldly.

Mr. Pancks, being by that time quite ready for a start, got under steam in a moment, and, without any other signal or ceremony, was snorting down the step-ladder and working into Bleeding Heart Yard, before he seemed to be well out of the counting-house.

Throughout the remainder of the day, Bleeding Heart Yard was in consternation, as the grim Pancks cruised in it; haranguing the inhabitants on their backslidings in respect of payment, demanding his bond, breathing notices to quit and executions, running down defaulters, sending a swell of terror on before him, and leaving it in his wake. Knots of people, impelled by a fatal attraction, lurked outside any house in which he was known to be, listening for fragments of his discourses to the inmates ; and, when he was rumoured to be coming down the stairs, often could not disperse so quickly but that he would be prematurely in among them, demanding their own arrears, and rooting them to the spot. Throughout the remainder of the day, Mr. Pancks's What were they up to ? and What did they mean by it ? sounded all over the Yard. Mr. Pancks wouldn't hear of excuses, wouldn't hear of complaints, wouldn't hear of repairs, wouldn't hear of anything but unconditional money down. Perspiring and puffing and darting about in eccentric directions, and becoming hotter and dingier every moment, he lashed the tide of the Yard into a most agitated and turbid state. It had not settled down into calm water again, full two hours after he had been seen fuming away on the horizon at the top of the steps.

There were several small assemblages of the Bleeding Hearts at the popular points of meeting in the Yard that night, among whom it was universally agreed that Mr. Pancks was a hard man to have to do with; and that it was much to be regretted, so it was, that a gentleman like Mr. Casby should put his rents in his hands, and never know him in his true light. For (said the Bleeding Hearts), if a gentleman with that head of hair and them eyes took his rents into his own hands, ma'am, there would be none of this worriting and wearing, and things would be very different.

At which identical evening hour and minute, the Patriarch —who had floated serenely through the Yard in the forenoon before the harrying began, with the express design of getting up this trustfulness in his shining bumps and silken locks— at which identical hour and minute, that first-rate humbug of a thousand guns was heavily floundering in the little Dock of his exhausted Tug at home, and was saying, as he turned his thumbs:

" A very bad day's work, Pancks, very bad day's work. It seems to me, sir, and I must insist on making the observation forcibly, in justice to myself, that you ought to have got much more money, much more money."

CHAPTER XXIV

LITTLE DORRIT received a call that same evening from Mr. Plornish, who, having intimated that he wished to speak to her, privately, in a series of coughs so very noticeable as to favour the idea that her father, as regarded her seamstress occupation, was an illustration of the axiom that there are no such stone-blind men as those who will not see, obtained an audience with her on the common staircase outside the door.

"There's been a lady at our place to-day, Miss Dorrit," Plornish growled, "and another one along with her as is a old wixen if ever I met with such. The way she snapped a person's head off, dear me ! "

The mild Plornish was at first quite unable to get his mind away from Mr. F's Aunt. "For," said he, to excuse himself, " she is, I do assure you, the winegariest party."

At length, by a great effort, he detached himself from the subject sufficiently to observe :

"But she's neither here nor there just at present. The other lady, she's Mr. Casby's daughter; and if Mr. Casby an't well off, none better, it an't through any fault of Pancks. For, as to Pancks, he does, he really does, he does indeed ! "

Mr. Plornish, after his usual manner, was a little obscure, but conscientiously emphatic.

" And what she come to our place for," he pursued, " was to leave word that if Miss Dorrit would step up to that card

345

—which it's Mr. Casby's house that is, and Pancks he has a office at the back, where he really does, beyond belief—she would be glad for to engage her. She was a old and a dear friend, she said particular, of Mr. Clennam, and hoped for to prove herself a useful friend to *his* friend. Them was her words. Wishing to know whether Miss Dorrit could come to-morrow morning, I said I would see you, Miss, and inquire, and look round there to-night, to say yes, or, if you was engaged to-morrow, when."

"I can go to-morrow, thank you," said Little Dorrit. "This is very kind of you, but you are always kind."

Mr. Plornish, with a modest disavowal of his merits, opened the room door for her re-admission, and followed her in with such an exceedingly bald pretence of not having been out at all, that her father might have observed it without being very suspicious. In his affable unconsciousness, however, he took no heed. Plornish, after a little conversation, in which he blended his former duty as a Collegian with his present privilege as a humble outside friend, qualified again by his low estate as a plasterer, took his leave; making the tour of the prison before he left, and looking on at a game of skittles, with the mixed feelings of an old inhabitant who had his private reasons for believing that it might be his destiny to come back again.

Early in the morning, Little Dorrit, leaving Maggy in high domestic trust, set off for the Patriarchal tent. She went by the Iron Bridge, though it cost her a penny, and walked more slowly in that part of her journey than in any other. At five minutes before eight, her hand was on the Patriarchal knocker, which was quite as high as she could reach.

She gave Mrs. Finching's card to the young woman who opened the door, and the young woman told her that "Miss Flora"—Flora having, on her return to the parental roof, re-invested herself with the title under which she had lived there—was not yet out of her bedroom, but she was to please to walk up into Miss Flora's sitting-room. She walked up into Miss Flora's sitting-room, as in duty bound, and there found a breakfast-table comfortably laid for two, with a supplementary tray upon it laid for one. The young woman, disappearing for a few moments, returned to say that she was to please to take a chair by the fire, and to take off her bonnet and make herself at home. But Little Dorrit, being bashful, and not used to make herself at home on such occasions, felt at a loss how to do it; so she was still sitting near the door with her bonnet on, when Flora came in in a hurry half-an-hour afterwards.

Flora was so sorry to have kept her waiting, and good gracious why did she sit out there in the cold when she had expected to find her by the fire reading the paper, and hadn't that heedless girl given her the message then, and had she really been in her bonnet all this time, and pray for goodness sake let Flora take it off! Flora taking it off in the best-natured manner in the world, was so struck with the face disclosed, that she said, " Why, what a good little thing you are, my dear!" and pressed the face between her hands like the gentlest of women.

It was the word and the action of a moment. Little Dorrit had hardly time to think how kind it was, when Flora dashed at the breakfast-table, full of business, and plunged over head and ears into loquacity.

"Really so sorry that I should happen to be late on this morning of all mornings because my intention and my wish was to be ready to meet you when you came in and to say that any one that interested Arthur Clennam half so much must interest me and that I gave you the heartiest welcome and was so glad, instead of which they never called me and there I still am snoring I dare say if the truth was known and if you don't like either cold fowl or hot boiled ham which many people don't I dare say besides Jews and theirs are scruples of conscience which we must all respect though I must say I wish they had them equally strong when they sell us false articles for real that certainly ain't worth the money I shall be quite vexed," said Flora.

Little Dorrit thanked her, and said, shyly, bread-and-butter and tea was all she usually——

"Oh nonsense my dear child I can never hear of that," said Flora, turning on the urn in the most reckless manner, and making herself wink by splashing hot water into her eyes as she bent down to look into the tea-pot. "You are come here on the footing of a friend and companion you know if you will let me take that liberty and I should be ashamed of myself indeed if you could come here upon any other, besides which Arthur Clennam spoke in such terms—you are tired my dear."

"No, ma'am."

"You turn so pale you have walked too far before breakfast and I dare say live a great way off and ought to have had a ride," said Flora, "dear dear is there anything that would do you good?"

"Indeed I am quite well, ma'am. I thank you again and again, but I am quite well."

"Then take your tea at once I beg," said Flora, "and this wing of fowl and bit of ham, don't mind me or wait for me because I always carry in this tray myself to Mr. F's Aunt who breakfasts in bed and a charming old lady too and very clever, Portrait of Mr. F behind the door and very like though too much forehead and as to a pillar with a marble pavement and balustrades and a mountain I never saw him near it nor not likely in the wine trade, excellent man but not at all in that way."

Little Dorrit glanced at the portrait, very imperfectly following the references to that work of art.

"Mr. F was so devoted to me that he never could bear me out of his sight," said Flora, "though of course I am unable to say how long that might have lasted if he hadn't been cut short while I was a new broom, worthy man but not poetical manly prose but not romance."

348

ROMANCE AND STERN REALITY

Little Dorrit glanced at the portrait again. The artist had given it a head that would have been, in an intellectual point of view, top-heavy for Shakespeare.

"Romance, however," Flora went on, busily arranging Mr. F's Aunt's toast, "as I openly said to Mr. F when he proposed to me and you will be surprised to hear that he proposed seven times once in a hackney-coach once in a boat once in a pew once on a donkey at Tunbridge Wells and the rest on his knees, Romance was fled with the early days of Arthur Clennam, our parents tore us asunder we became marble and stern reality usurped the throne, Mr. F said very much to his credit that he was perfectly aware of it and even preferred that state of things accordingly the word was spoken the fiat went forth and such is life you see my dear and yet we do not break but bend, pray make a good breakfast while I go in with the tray."

She disappeared, leaving Little Dorrit to ponder over the meaning of her scattered words. She soon came back again; and at last began to take her own breakfast, talking all the while.

"You see my dear," said Flora, measuring out a spoonful or two of some brown liquid that smelt like brandy, and putting it into her tea, "I am obliged to be careful to follow the directions of my medical man though the flavour is anything but agreeable being a poor creature and it may be have never recovered the shock received in youth from too much giving way to crying in the next room when separated from Arthur, have you known him long?"

As soon as Little Dorrit comprehended that she had been asked this question—for which time was necessary, the galloping pace of her new patroness having left her far behind—she answered that she had known Mr. Clennam ever since his return.

"To be sure you couldn't have known him before unless you had been in China or had corresponded neither of which is likely," returned Flora, "for travelling-people usually get

more or less mahogany and you are not at all so and as to
corresponding what about? that's very true unless tea, so it
was at his mother's was it really that you knew him first,
highly sensible and firm but dreadfully severe—ought to be
the mother of the man in the iron mask."

"Mrs. Clennam has been kind to me," said Little Dorrit.

"Really? I am sure I am glad to hear it because as
Arthur's mother it's naturally pleasant to my feelings to have
a better opinion of her than I had before, though what she
thinks of me when I run on as I am certain to do and she
sits glowering at me like Fate in a go-cart—shocking comparison really—invalid and not her fault—I never know or
can imagine."

"Shall I find my work anywhere, ma'am?" asked Little
Dorrit, looking timidly about; "can I get it?"

"You industrious little fairy," returned Flora, taking, in
another cup of tea, another of the doses prescribed by her
medical man, "there's not the slightest hurry and it's better
that we should begin by being confidential about our mutual
friend—too cold a word for me at least I don't mean that,
very proper expression mutual friend—than become through
mere formalities not you but me like the Spartan boy with
the fox biting him, which I hope you'll excuse my bringing
up for of all the tiresome boys that will go tumbling into
every sort of company that boy's the tiresomest."

Little Dorrit, her face very pale, sat down again to listen.
"Hadn't I better work the while?" she asked. "I can work
and attend too. I would rather, if I may."

Her earnestness was so expressive of her being uneasy
without her work, that Flora answered, "Well my dear
whatever you like best," and produced a basket of white
handkerchiefs. Little Dorrit gladly put it by her side, took
out her little pocket-housewife, threaded her needle, and
began to hem.

"What nimble fingers you have," said Flora, "but are you
sure you are well?"

THE STATUE BRIDE

" Oh yes, indeed ! "

Flora put her feet upon the fender, and settled herself for a thorough good romantic disclosure. She started off at score, tossing her head, sighing in the most demonstrative manner, making a great deal of use of her eyebrows, and occasionally, but not often, glancing at the quiet face that bent over the work.

" You must know my dear," said Flora, " but that I have no doubt you know already not only because I have already thrown it out in a general way but because I feel I carry it stamped in burning what's his names upon my brow that before I was introduced to the late Mr. F I had been engaged to Arthur Clennam—Mr. Clennam in public where reserve is necessary Arthur here—we were all in all to one another it was the morning of life it was bliss it was frenzy it was everything else of that sort in the highest degree, when rent asunder we turned to stone in which capacity Arthur went to China and I became the statue bride of the late Mr. F."

Flora, uttering these words in a deep voice, enjoyed herself immensely.

" To paint," said she, " the emotions of that morning when all was marble within and Mr. F's Aunt followed in a glass-coach which it stands to reason must have been in shameful repair or it never could have broken down two streets from the house and Mr. F's Aunt brought home like the fifth of November in a rush-bottomed chair I will not attempt, suffice it to say that the hollow form of breakfast took place in the dining-room down-stairs that papa partaking too freely of pickled salmon was ill for weeks and that Mr. F and myself went upon a continental tour to Calais where the people fought for us on the pier until they separated us though not for ever that was not yet to be."

The statue bride, hardly pausing for breath, went on, with the greatest complacency, in a rambling manner, sometimes incidental to flesh and blood.

"I will draw a veil over that dreamy life, Mr. F was in good spirits his appetite was good he liked the cookery he considered the wine weak but palatable and all was well, we returned to the immediate neighbourhood of Number Thirty Little Gosling Street London Docks and settled down, ere we had yet fully detected the housemaid in selling the feathers out of the spare bed Gout flying upwards soared with Mr. F to another sphere."

His relict, with a glance at his portrait, shook her head and wiped her eyes.

"I revere the memory of Mr. F as an estimable man and most indulgent husband, only necessary to mention Asparagus and it appeared or to hint at any little delicate thing to drink and it came like magic in a pint bottle it was not ecstasy but it was comfort, I returned to papa's roof and lived secluded if not happy during some years until one day papa came smoothly blundering in and said that Arthur Clennam awaited me below, I went below and found him ask me not what I found him except that he was still unmarried still unchanged!"

The dark mystery with which Flora now enshrouded herself might have stopped other fingers than the nimble fingers that worked near her. They worked on, without pause, and the busy head bent over them watching the stitches.

"Ask me not," said Flora, "if I love him still or if he still loves me or what the end is to be or when, we are surrounded by watchful eyes and it may be that we are destined to pine asunder it may be never more to be reunited not a word not a breath not a look to betray us all must be secret as the tomb wonder not therefore that even if I should seem comparatively cold to Arthur or Arthur should seem comparatively cold to me we have fatal reasons it is enough if we understand them hush!"

All of which Flora said with so much headlong vehemence as if she really believed it. There is not much doubt, that when she worked herself into full mermaid condition, she did actually believe whatever she said in it.

"Hush!" repeated Flora, "I have now told you all, confidence is established between us hush, for Arthur's sake I will always be a friend to you my dear girl and in Arthur's name you may always rely upon me."

The nimble fingers laid aside the work, and the little figure rose and kissed her hand. "You are very cold," said Flora, changing to her own natural kind-hearted manner, and gaining greatly by the change. "Don't work to-day. I am sure you are not well I am sure you are not strong."

"It is only that I feel a little overcome by your kindness, and by Mr. Clennam's kindness in confiding me to one he has known and loved so long."

"Well really my dear," said Flora, who had a decided tendency to be always honest when she gave herself time to think about it, "It's as well to leave that alone now, for I couldn't undertake to say after all, but it doesn't signify lie down a little!"

"I have always been strong enough to do what I want to do, and I shall be quite well directly," returned Little Dorrit, with a faint smile. "You have overpowered me with gratitude, that's all. If I keep near the window for a moment I shall be quite myself."

Flora opened a window, sat her in a chair by it, and considerately retired to her former place. It was a windy day, and the air stirring on Little Dorrit's face soon brightened it. In a very few minutes she returned to her basket of work, and her nimble fingers were as nimble as ever.

Quietly pursuing her task, she asked Flora if Mr. Clennam had told her where she lived? When Flora replied in the negative, Little Dorrit said that she understood why he had been so delicate, but that she felt sure he would approve of her confiding her secret to Flora, and that she would therefore do so now with Flora's permission. Receiving an encouraging answer, she condensed the narrative of her life into a few

353

scanty words about herself, and a glowing eulogy upon her father; and Flora took it all in with a natural tenderness that quite understood it, and in which there was no incoherence.

When dinner-time came, Flora drew the arm of her new charge through hers, and led her down-stairs, and presented her to the Patriarch and Mr. Pancks, who were already in the dining-room waiting to begin. (Mr. F's Aunt was, for the time, laid up in ordinary in her chamber.) By those gentlemen she was received according to their characters; the Patriarch appearing to do her some inestimable service in saying that he was glad to see her, glad to see her; and Mr. Pancks blowing off his favourite sound as a salute.

In that new presence she would have been bashful enough under any circumstances, and particularly under Flora's insisting on her drinking a glass of wine and eating of the best that was there; but her constraint was greatly increased by Mr. Pancks. The demeanour of that gentleman at first suggested to her mind that he might be a taker of likenesses, so intently did he look at her, and so frequently did he glance at the little note-book by his side. Observing that he made no sketch, however, and that he talked about business only, she began to have suspicions that he represented some creditor of her father's, the balance due to whom was noted in that pocket volume. Regarded from this point of view Mr. Pancks's puffings expressed injury and impatience, and each of his louder snorts became a demand for payment.

But, here again she was undeceived by anomalous and incongruous conduct on the part of Mr. Pancks himself. She had left the table half-an-hour, and was at work alone. Flora had " gone to lie down " in the next room, concurrently with which retirement a smell of something to drink had broken out in the house. The Patriarch was fast asleep, with his philanthropic mouth open, under a yellow pocket-handkerchief in the dining-room. At this quiet time, Mr. Pancks softly appeared before her, urbanely nodding.

"Find it a little dull, Miss Dorrit?" inquired Pancks, in a low voice.

"No, thank you, sir," said Little Dorrit.

"Busy, I see," observed Mr. Pancks, stealing into the room by inches. "What are those now, Miss Dorrit?"

"Handkerchiefs."

"Are they, though!" said Pancks. "I shouldn't have thought it." Not in the least looking at them, but looking at Little Dorrit. "Perhaps you wonder who I am. Shall I tell you? I am a fortune-teller."

Little Dorrit now began to think he was mad.

"I belong body and soul to my proprietor," said Pancks; "you saw my proprietor having his dinner below. But I do a little in the other way, sometimes; privately, very privately, Miss Dorrit."

Little Dorrit looked at him doubtfully, and not without alarm. "I wish you'd show me the palm of your hand," said Pancks. "I should like to have a look at it. Don't let me be troublesome."

He was so far troublesome that he was not at all wanted there, but she laid her work in her lap for a moment, and held out her right hand with her thimble on it.

"Years of toil, eh?" said Pancks, softly, touching it with his blunt forefinger. "But what else are we made for? Nothing. Hallo!" looking into the lines. "What's this with bars? It's a College! And what's this with a grey gown and a black velvet cap? It's a father! And what's this with a clarionet? It's an uncle! And what's this in dancing-shoes? It's a sister! And what's this straggling about in an idle sort of a way? It's a brother! And what's this thinking for 'em all? Why, this is you, Miss Dorrit!"

Her eyes met his as she looked up wonderingly into his face, and she thought that although his were sharp eyes, he was a brighter and gentler-looking man than she had supposed at dinner. His eyes were on her hand again directly, and

LITTLE DORRIT

her opportunity of confirming or correcting the impression was gone.

"Now, the deuce is in it," muttered Pancks, tracing out a line in her hand with his clumsy finger, "if this isn't me in the corner here! What do I want here? What's behind me?"

He carried his finger slowly down to the wrist, and round the wrist, and affected to look at the back of the hand for what was behind him.

"Is it any harm?" asked Little Dorrit, smiling.

"Deuce a bit!" said Pancks. "What do you think it's worth?"

"I ought to ask you that. I am not the fortune-teller."

"True," said Pancks. "What's it worth? You shall live to see, Miss Dorrit."

Releasing the hand by slow degrees, he drew all his fingers through his prongs of hair, so that they stood up in their most portentous manner; and repeated slowly, "Remember what I say, Miss Dorrit. You shall live to see."

She could not help showing that she was much surprised, if it were only by his knowing so much about her.

"Ah! That's it!" said Pancks, pointing at her. "Miss Dorrit, not that, ever!"

More surprised than before, and a little more frightened, she looked to him for an explanation of his last words.

"Not that," said Pancks, making, with great seriousness, an imitation of a surprised look and manner, that appeared to be unintentionally grotesque. "Don't do that. Never on seeing me, no matter when, no matter where. I am nobody. Don't take on to mind me. Don't mention me. Take no notice. Will you agree, Miss Dorrit?"

"I hardly know what to say," returned Little Dorrit, quite astounded. "Why?"

"Because I am a fortune-teller. Pancks the gipsy. I haven't told you so much of your fortune, yet, Miss Dorrit, as to tell you what's behind me on that little hand. I

356

have told you you shall live to see. Is it agreed, Miss Dorrit?"

"Agreed that I—am—to—— "

"To take no notice of me away from here, unless I take on first. Not to mind me when I come and go. It's very easy. I am no loss, I am not handsome, I am not good company, I am only my proprietor's grubber. You need do no more than think, 'Ah! Pancks the gipsy at his fortune-telling—he'll tell the rest of my fortune one day—I shall live to know it.' Is it agreed, Miss Dorrit?"

"Ye-es," faltered Little Dorrit, whom he greatly confused, "I suppose so, while you do no harm."

"Good!" Mr. Pancks glanced at the wall of the adjoining room, and stooped forward. "Honest creature, woman of capital points, but heedless and a loose talker, Miss Dorrit." With that he rubbed his hands as if the interview had been very satisfactory to him, panted away to the door, and urbanely nodded himself out again.

If Little Dorrit were beyond measure perplexed by this curious conduct on the part of her new acquaintance, and by finding herself involved in this singular treaty, her perplexity was not diminished by ensuing circumstances. Besides that Mr. Pancks took every opportunity afforded him in Mr. Casby's house of significantly glancing at her and snorting at her—which was not much, after what he had done already —he began to pervade her daily life. She saw him in the street, constantly. When she went to Mr. Casby's, he was always there. When she went to Mrs. Clennam's, he came there on any pretence, as if to keep her in his sight. A week had not gone by, when she found him to her astonishment, in the Lodge one night, conversing with the turnkey on duty, and to all appearance one of his familiar companions. Her next surprise was to find him equally at his ease within the prison; to hear of his presenting himself among the visitors at her father's Sunday levee; to see him arm in arm with a Collegiate friend about the yard; to learn, from Fame,

357

that he had greatly distinguished himself one evening at the social club that held its meetings in the Snuggery, by addressing a speech to the members of that institution, singing a song, and treating the company to five gallons of ale—report madly added a bushel of shrimps. The effect on Mr. Plornish of such of these phenomena as he became an eye-witness of in his faithful visits, made an impression on Little Dorrit only second to that produced by the phenomena themselves. They seemed to gag and bind him. He could only stare, and sometimes weakly mutter that it wouldn't be believed down Bleeding Heart Yard that this was Pancks; but he never said a word more, or made a sign more, even to Little Dorrit. Mr. Pancks crowned his mysteries by making himself acquainted with Tip in some unknown manner, and taking a Sunday saunter into the College on that gentleman's arm. Throughout he never took any notice of Little Dorrit, save once or twice when he happened to come close to her, and there was no one very near; on which occasions, he said in passing, with a friendly look and a puff of encouragement, " Pancks the gipsy—fortune-telling."

Little Dorrit worked and strove as usual, wondering at all this, but keeping her wonder, as she had from her earliest years kept many heavier loads, in her own breast. A change had stolen, and was stealing yet, over the patient heart. Every day found her something more retiring than the day before. To pass in and out of the prison unnoticed, and elsewhere to be overlooked and forgotten, were, for herself, her chief desires.

To her own room too, strangely assorted room for her delicate youth and character, she was glad to retreat as often as she could without desertion of any duty. There were afternoon times when she was unemployed, when visitors dropped in to play a hand at cards with her father, when she could be spared and was better away. Then she would flit along the yard, climb the scores of stairs that led to her room, and take her seat at the window. Many combinations did those spikes upon the wall assume, many light shapes did the strong iron weave itself into, many golden touches fell upon the rust, while Little Dorrit sat there musing. New zig-zags sprung into the cruel pattern sometimes, when she saw it through a burst of tears; but beautiful or hardened still, always over it and under it and through it, she was fain to look in her solitude, seeing everything with that ineffaceable brand.

A garret, and a Marshalsea garret without compromise, was Little Dorrit's room. Beautifully kept, it was ugly in itself, and had little but cleanliness and air to set it off; for what embellishment she had ever been able to buy, had gone to her father's room. Howbeit, for this poor place she showed an increasing love; and to sit in it alone became her favourite rest.

Insomuch, that on a certain afternoon, during the Pancks mysteries, when she was seated at her window, and heard Maggy's well-known step coming up the stairs, she was very much disturbed by the apprehension of being summoned away. As Maggy's step came higher up and nearer, she trembled and faltered; and it was as much as she could do to speak, when Maggy at length appeared.

"Please, Little Mother," said Maggy, panting for breath, "you must come down and see him. He's here."

"Who, Maggy?"

"Who, o' course Mr. Clennam. He's in your father's room, and he says to me, Maggy, will you be so kind and go and say it's only me?"

"I am not very well, Maggy. I had better not go. I am going to lie down. See! I lie down now, to ease my head. Say, with my grateful regard, that you left me so, or I would have come."

"Well, it an't very polite though, Little Mother," said the staring Maggy, "to turn your face away, neither!"

Maggy was very susceptible to personal slights, and very ingenious in inventing them. "Putting both your hands afore your face too!" she went on. "If you can't bear the looks of a poor thing, it would be. better to tell her so at once, and not go and shut her out like that, hurting her feelings and breaking her heart at ten year old, poor thing!"

"It's to ease my head, Maggy."

"Well, and if you cry to ease your head, Little Mother, let me cry too. Don't go and have all the crying to yourself," expostulated Maggy, "that an't not being greedy." And immediately began to blubber.

It was with some difficulty that she could be induced to go back with the excuse; but the promise of being told a story —of old her great delight—on condition that she concentrated her faculties upon the errand and left her little mistress to herself for an hour longer, combined with a misgiving on Maggy's part that she had left her good temper at the bottom of the staircase, prevailed. So away she went, muttering her message all the way to keep it in her mind, and, at the appointed time, came back.

"He was very sorry, I can tell you," she announced, "and wanted to send a doctor. And he's coming again to-morrow he is, and I don't think he'll have a good sleep to-night along o' hearing about your head, Little Mother. Oh my! Ain't you been a-crying!"

"I think I have, a little, Maggy."

"A little! Oh!"

"But it's all over now—all over for good, Maggy. And my head is much better and cooler, and I am quite comfortable. I am very glad I did not go down."

Her great staring child tenderly embraced her; and having smoothed her hair, and bathed her forehead and eyes with cold water (offices in which her awkward hands became skilful), hugged her again, exulted in her brighter looks, and stationed her in her chair by the window. Over against this chair, Maggy, with apoplectic exertions that were not at all required, dragged the box which was her seat on story-telling occasions, sat down upon it, hugged her own knees, and said, with a voracious appetite for stories, and with widely-opened eyes :

"Now, Little Mother, let's have a good 'un ! "

"What shall it be about, Maggy ? "

"Oh, let's have a Princess," said Maggy, "and let her be a reg'lar one. Beyond all belief, you know ! "

Little Dorrit considered for a moment ; and with a rather sad smile upon her face, which was flushed by the sunset, began :

"Maggy, there was once upon a time a fine King, and he had everything he could wish for, and a great deal more. He had gold and silver, diamonds and rubies, riches of every kind. He had palaces, and he had—— "

"Hospitals," interposed Maggy, still nursing her knees. "Let him have hospitals, because they're so comfortable. Hospitals with lots of Chicking."

"Yes, he had plenty of them, and he had plenty of every-thing."

"Plenty of baked potatoes, for instance ? " said Maggy.

"Plenty of everything."

"Lor ! " chuckled Maggy, giving her knees a hug. "Wasn't it prime ! "

"This King had a daughter, who was the wisest and most beautiful Princess that ever was seen. When she was a child she understood all her lessons before her masters taught them to her ; and when she was grown up, she was the wonder of the world. Now, near the Palace where this Princess lived, there was a cottage in which there was a poor little tiny woman, who lived all alone by herself."

"A old woman," said Maggy, with an unctuous smack of her lips.

"No, not an old woman. Quite a young one."

"I wonder she warn't afraid," said Maggy. "Go on, please."

"The Princess passed the cottage nearly every day, and whenever she went by in her beautiful carriage, she saw the poor tiny woman spinning at her wheel, and she looked at the tiny woman, and the tiny woman looked at her. So, one

361

day she stopped the coachman a little way from the cottage, and got out and walked on and peeped in at the door, and there, as usual, was the tiny woman spinning at her wheel, and she looked at the Princess, and the Princess looked at her."

"Like trying to stare one another out," said Maggy. "Please go on, Little Mother."

"The Princess was such a wonderful Princess that she had the power of knowing secrets, and she said to the tiny woman, Why do you keep it there? This showed her directly that the Princess knew why she lived all alone by herself spinning at her wheel, and she kneeled down at the Princess's feet, and asked her never to betray her. So, the Princess said, I never will betray you. Let me see it. So, the tiny woman closed the shutter of the cottage window and fastened the door, and trembling from head to foot for fear that any one should suspect her, opened a very secret place, and showed the Princess a shadow."

"Lor!" said Maggy.

"It was the shadow of Some one who had gone by long before: of Some one who had gone on far away quite out of reach, never, never to come back. It was bright to look at; and when the tiny woman showed it to the Princess, she was proud of it with all her heart, as a great, great treasure. When the Princess had considered it a little while, she said to the tiny woman, And you keep watch over this, every day? And she cast down her eyes, and whispered, Yes. Then the Princess said, Remind me why. To which the other replied, that no one so good and kind had ever passed that way, and that was why in the beginning. She said, too, that nobody missed it, that nobody was the worse for it, that Some one had gone on to those who were expecting him——"

"Some one was a man then?" interposed Maggy.

Little Dorrit timidly said Yes, she believed so; and resumed:

"——Had gone on to those who were expecting him, and

362

The Story of the Princess

that this remembrance was stolen or kept back from nobody. The Princess made answer, Ah! But when the cottager died it would be discovered there. The tiny woman told her No; when that time came, it would sink quietly into her own grave, and would never be found."

"Well, to be sure!" said Maggy. "Go on, please."

"The Princess was very much astonished to hear this, as you may suppose, Maggy."

("And well she might be," said Maggy.)

"So she resolved to watch the tiny woman, and see what came of it. Every day, she drove in her beautiful carriage by the cottage-door, and there she saw the tiny woman always alone by herself spinning at her wheel, and she looked at the tiny woman, and the tiny woman looked at her. At last one day the wheel was still, and the tiny woman was not to be seen. When the Princess made inquiries why the wheel had stopped, and where the tiny woman was, she was informed that the wheel had stopped because there was nobody to turn it, the tiny woman being dead."

("They ought to have took her to the Hospital," said Maggy, "and then she'd have got over it.")

"The Princess, after crying a very little for the loss of the tiny woman, dried her eyes and got out of her carriage at the place where she had stopped it before, and went to the cottage and peeped in at the door. There was nobody to look at her now, and nobody for her to look at, so she went in at once to search for the treasured shadow. But there was no sign of it to be found anywhere; and then she knew that the tiny woman had told her the truth, and that it would never give anybody any trouble, and that it had sunk quietly into her own grave, and that she and it were at rest together.

"That's all, Maggy."

The sunset flush was so bright on Little Dorrit's face when she came thus to the end of her story, that she interposed her hand to shade it.

"Had she got to be old?" Maggy asked.

"The tiny woman?"

"Ah!"

"I don't know," said Little Dorrit. "But it would have been just the same, if she had been ever and ever so old."

"Would it raly!" said Maggy. "Well, I suppose it would though." And sat staring and ruminating.

She sat so long with her eyes wide open, that at length Little Dorrit, to entice her from her box, rose and looked out of window. As she glanced down into the yard, she saw Pancks come in, and leer up with the corner of his eye as he went by.

"Who's he, Little Mother?" said Maggy. She had joined her at the window and was leaning on her shoulder. "I see him come in and out often."

"I have heard him called a fortune-teller," said Little Dorrit. "But I doubt if he could tell many people, even their past or present fortunes."

"Couldn't have told the Princess hers?" said Maggy.

Little Dorrit, looking musingly down into the dark valley of the prison, shook her head.

"Nor the tiny woman hers?" said Maggy.

"No," said Little Dorrit, with the sunset very bright upon her. "But let us come away from the window."

CHAPTER XXV

CONSPIRATORS AND OTHERS

THE private residence of Mr. Pancks was in Pentonville, where he lodged on the second-floor of a professional gentleman in an extremely small way, who had an inner-door within the street door, poised on a spring and starting open with a click like a trap; and who wrote up in the fan-light, RUGG, GENERAL AGENT, ACCOUNTANT, DEBTS RECOVERED.

This scroll, majestic in its severe simplicity, illuminated a little slip of front garden abutting on the thirsty high-road, where a few of the dustiest of leaves hung their dismal heads and led a life of choking. A professor of writing occupied the first-floor, and enlivened the garden railings with glass-cases containing choice examples of what his pupils had been before six lessons and while the whole of his young family shook the table, and what they had become after six lessons when the young family was under restraint. The tenancy of Mr. Pancks was limited to one airy bedroom; he covenanting and agreeing with Mr. Rugg his landlord, that in consideration of a certain scale of payments accurately defined, and on certain verbal notice duly given, he should be at liberty to elect to share the Sunday breakfast, dinner, tea, or supper, or each or any or all of those repasts or meals, of Mr. and Miss Rugg (his daughter) in the back-parlour.

Miss Rugg was a lady of a little property, which she had acquired, together with much distinction in the neighbourhood, by having her heart severely lacerated and her feelings mangled by a middle-aged baker, resident in the vicinity, against whom she had, by the agency of Mr. Rugg, found it necessary to proceed at law to recover damages for a breach of promise of marriage. The baker having been, by the counsel for Miss Rugg, witheringly denounced on that occasion up to the full amount of twenty guineas, at the rate of about eighteen-pence an epithet, and having been cast in corresponding damages, still suffered occasional persecution from the youth of Pentonville. But Miss Rugg, environed by the majesty of the law, and having her damages invested in the public securities, was regarded with consideration.

In the society of Mr. Rugg, who had a round white visage, as if all his blushes had been drawn out of him long ago, and who had a ragged yellow head like a worn-out hearth-broom; and in the society of Miss Rugg, who had little nankeen spots, like shirt buttons, all over her face, and whose own yellow tresses were rather scrubby than luxuriant; Mr. Pancks had usually dined on Sundays for some few years, and had twice a week, or so, enjoyed an evening collation of bread, Dutch cheese, and porter. Mr. Pancks was one of the very few marriageable men for whom Miss Rugg had no terrors, the argument with which he reassured himself being twofold; that is to say, firstly, "that it wouldn't do twice," and secondly, "that he wasn't worth it." Fortified within this double armour, Mr. Pancks snorted at Miss Rugg on easy terms.

Up to this time, Mr. Pancks had transacted little or no business at his quarters in Pentonville, except in the sleeping line; but now that he had become a fortune-teller, he was often closeted after midnight with Mr. Rugg in his little front-parlour office, and even after those untimely hours, burnt tallow in his bedroom. Though his duties as his proprietor's grubber were in no wise lessened; and though that service bore no greater resemblance to a bed of roses than was to be discovered in its many thorns; some new branch of industry made a constant demand upon him. When he cast off the Patriarch at night, it was only to take an anonymous craft in tow, and labour away afresh in other waters.

The advance from a personal acquaintance with the elder Mr. Chivery, to an introduction to his amiable wife and disconsolate son, may have been easy; but easy or not, Mr. Pancks soon made it. He nestled in the bosom of the tobacco business within a week or two after his first appearance in the College, and particularly addressed himself to the cultivation of a good understanding with Young John. In this endeavour he so prospered as to lure that pining shepherd forth from the groves, and tempt him to undertake mysterious missions; on which he began to disappear at uncertain intervals for as long a space as two or three days together. The prudent Mrs. Chivery, who wondered greatly at this change, would have protested against it as detrimental to the Highland typification on the doorpost, but for two forcible reasons; one, that her John was roused to take strong interest in the business which these starts were supposed to advance—and this she held to be good for his drooping spirits; the other, that Mr. Pancks confidentially agreed to pay her, for the occupation of her son's time, at the handsome rate of seven and sixpence per day. The proposal originated with himself, and was couched in the pithy terms, "If your John is weak enough, ma'am, not to take it, that is no reason why you should be, don't you see? So, quite between ourselves, ma'am, business being business, here it is!"

What Mr. Chivery thought of these things, or how much or how little he knew about them, was never gathered from himself. It has been already remarked that he was a man of few words; and it may be here observed, that he had imbibed a professional habit of locking everything up. He locked himself up as carefully as he locked up the Marshalsea debtors. Even his custom of bolting his meals may have been a part of an uniform whole; but there is no question, that, as to all other purposes, he kept his mouth as he kept the Marshalsea door. He never opened it without occasion. When it was necessary to let anything out, he opened it a little way, held it open just as long as sufficed for the purpose, and locked it again. Even as he would be sparing of his trouble at the Marshalsea door, and would keep a visitor who wanted to go out, waiting for a few moments if he saw another visitor coming down the yard, so that one turn of the key should suffice for both, similarly he would often reserve a remark if he perceived another on its way to his lips, and would deliver himself of the two together. As to any key to his inner knowledge being to be found in his face, the Marshalsea key was as legible an index to the individual characters and histories upon which it was turned.

That Mr. Pancks should be moved to invite any one to dinner at Pentonville, was an unprecedented fact in his calendar. But he invited Young John to dinner, and even brought him within range of the dangerous (because expensive) fascinations of Miss Rugg. The banquet was appointed for a Sunday, and Miss Rugg with her own hands stuffed a leg of mutton with oysters on the occasion, and sent it to the baker's—not *the* baker's, but an opposition establishment. Provision of oranges, apples, and nuts was also made. And rum was brought home by Mr. Pancks on Saturday night, to gladden the visitor's heart.

The store of creature comforts was not the chief part of the visitor's reception. Its special feature was a foregone family confidence and sympathy. When Young John appeared at half-past one, without the ivory hand and waistcoat of golden sprigs, the sun shorn of his beams by disastrous clouds, Mr. Pancks presented him to the yellow-haired Ruggs as the young man he had so often mentioned who loved Miss Dorrit.

"I am glad," said Mr. Rugg, challenging him specially in that character, "to have the distinguished gratification of making your acquaintance, sir. Your feelings do you honour. You are young; may you never outlive your feelings! If I was to outlive my own feelings, sir," said Mr. Rugg, who was a man of many words, and was considered to possess a remarkably good address; "if I was to outlive my own feelings, I'd leave fifty pound in my will to the man who would put me out of existence."

Miss Rugg heaved a sigh.

"My daughter, sir," said Mr. Rugg. "Anastatia, you are no stranger to the state of this young man's affections. My daughter has had her trials, sir," Mr. Rugg might have used the word more pointedly in the singular number, "and she can feel for you."

Young John, almost overwhelmed by the touching nature of this greeting, professed himself to that effect.

"What I envy you, sir, is," said Mr. Rugg, "allow me to take your hat—we are rather short of pegs—I'll put it in the corner, nobody will tread in it there—What I envy you, sir, is the luxury of your own feelings. I belong to a profession in which that luxury is sometimes denied us."

Young John replied, with acknowledgments, that he only hoped he did what was right, and what showed how entirely he was devoted to Miss Dorrit. He wished to be unselfish; and he hoped he was. He wished to do anything as laid in his power to serve Miss Dorrit, altogether putting himself out of sight; and he hoped he did. It was but little that he could do, but he hoped he did it.

"Sir," said Mr. Rugg, taking him by the hand, "you are a young man that it does one good to come across. You are a young man that I should like to put in the witness-box, to humanise the minds of the legal profession. I hope you have brought your appetite with you, and intend to play a good knife and fork?"

"Thank you, sir," returned Young John, "I don't eat much at present."

Mr. Rugg drew him a little apart. "My daughter's case, sir," said he, "at the time when, in vindication of her outraged feelings and her sex, she became the plaintiff in Rugg and Hawkins. I suppose I could have put it in evidence, Mr. Chivery, if I had thought it worth my while, that the amount of solid sustenance my daughter consumed at that period did not exceed ten ounces per week."

" I think I go a little beyond that, sir," returned the other, hesitating, as if he confessed it with some shame.

" But in your case there's no fiend in human form," said Mr. Rugg, with argumentative smile and action of hand. " Observe, Mr. Chivery ! No fiend in human form ! "

"No, sir, certainly," Young John added with simplicity, "I should be very sorry if there was."

" The sentiment," said Mr. Rugg, " is what I should have expected from your known principles. It would affect my daughter greatly, sir, if she heard it. As I perceive the mutton, I am glad she didn't hear it. Mr. Pancks, on this occasion, pray face me. My dear, face Mr. Chivery. For what we are going to receive, may we (and Miss Dorrit) be truly thankful ! "

But for a grave waggishness in Mr. Rugg's manner of delivering this introduction to the feast, it might have appeared that Miss Dorrit was expected to be one of the company. Pancks recognised the sally in his usual way, and took in his provender in his usual way. Miss Rugg, perhaps making up some of her arrears, likewise took very kindly to the mutton, and it rapidly diminished to the bone. A bread-and-butter pudding entirely disappeared, and a considerable amount of cheese and radishes vanished by the same means. Then came the dessert.

Then also, and before the broaching of the rum and water, came Mr. Pancks's note-book. The ensuing business proceedings were brief but curious, and rather in the nature of a conspiracy. Mr. Pancks looked over his note-book, which was now getting full, studiously ; and picked out little extracts, which he wrote on separate slips of paper on the table ; Mr. Rugg, in the meanwhile, looking at him with close attention, and Young John losing his uncollected eye in mists of meditation. When Mr. Pancks, who supported the character of chief conspirator, had completed his extracts, he looked them over, corrected them, put up his note-book, and held them like a hand at cards.

"Now, there's a churchyard in Bedfordshire," said Pancks. "Who takes it?"

"I'll take it, sir," returned Mr. Rugg, "if no one bids."

Mr. Pancks dealt him his card, and looked at his hand again.

"Now, there's an Enquiry in York," said Pancks. "Who takes it?"

"I'm not good for York," said Mr. Rugg.

"Then perhaps," pursued Pancks, "you'll be so obliging, John Chivery?" Young John assenting, Pancks dealt him his card, and consulted his hand again.

"There's a Church in London; I may as well take that. And a Family Bible; I may as well take that, too. That's two to me. Two to me," repeated Pancks, breathing hard over his cards. "Here's a Clerk at Durham for you, John, and an old seafaring gentleman at Dunstable for you, Mr. Rugg. Two to me, was it? Yes, two to me. Here's a Stone; three to me. And a Still-born Baby; four to me. And all, for the present, told."

When he had thus disposed of his cards, all being done very quietly and in a suppressed tone, Mr. Pancks puffed his way into his own breast-pocket and tugged out a canvas bag; from which, with a sparing hand, he told forth money for travelling expenses in two little portions. "Cash goes out fast," he said anxiously, as he pushed a portion to each of his male companions, "very fast."

"I can only assure you, Mr. Pancks," said Young John, "that I deeply regret my circumstances being such that I can't afford to pay my own charges, or that it's not advisable to allow me the time necessary for my doing the distances on foot. Because nothing would give me greater satisfaction than to walk myself off my legs without fee or reward."

This young man's disinterestedness appeared so very ludicrous in the eyes of Miss Rugg, that she was obliged to effect a precipitate retirement from the company, and to sit upon the stairs until she had had her laugh out. Meanwhile Mr. Pancks, looking, not without some pity at Young John, slowly and thoughtfully twisted up his canvas bag as if he were wringing its neck. The lady returning as he restored it to his pocket, mixed rum and water for the party, not forgetting her fair self, and handed to every one his glass. When all were supplied, Mr. Rugg rose, and silently holding out his glass at arm's length above the centre of the table, by that gesture invited the other three to add theirs, and to unite in a general conspiratorial clink. The ceremony was effective up to a certain point, and would have been wholly so throughout, if Miss Rugg, as she raised her glass to her lips in completion of it, had not happened to look at Young John; when she was again so overcome by the contemptible comicality of his disinterestedness, as to splutter some ambrosial drops of rum and water around, and withdraw in confusion.

Such was the dinner without precedent, given by Pancks at Pentonville; and such was the busy and strange life Pancks led. The only waking moments at which he appeared to relax from his cares, and to recreate himself by going anywhere or saying anything without a pervading object, were when he showed a dawning interest in the lame foreigner with the stick, down Bleeding Heart Yard.

The foreigner, by name John Baptist Cavalletto—they called him Mr. Baptist in the Yard—was such a chirping, easy, hopeful little fellow, that his attraction for Pancks was probably in the force of contrast. Solitary, weak, and scantily acquainted with the most necessary words of the only language in which he could communicate with the people about him, he went with the stream of his fortunes, in a brisk way that was new in those parts. With little to eat, and less to drink, and nothing to wear but what he wore upon him, or had brought tied up in one of the smallest bundles that ever were seen, he put as bright a face upon it as if he were in the most flourishing circumstances, when he first hobbled up and down the Yard, humbly propitiating the general good-will with his white teeth.

It was up-hill work for a foreigner, lame or sound, to make his way with the Bleeding Hearts. In the first place, they were vaguely persuaded that every foreigner had a knife about him; in the second, they held it to be a sound constitutional national axiom that he ought to go home to his own country. They never thought of inquiring how many of their own countrymen would be returned upon their hands from divers parts of the world, if the principle were generally recognised; they considered it practically and peculiarly British. In the third place, they had a notion that it was a sort of Divine visitation upon a foreigner that he was not an Englishman, and that all kinds of calamities happened to his country because it did things that England did not, and did not do things that England did. In this belief, to be sure, they had long been carefully trained by the Barnacles and Stiltstalkings, who were always proclaiming to them, officially and unofficially, that no country which failed to submit itself to those two large families could possibly hope to be under the protection of Providence; and who, when they believed it, disparaged them in private as the most prejudiced people under the sun.

This, therefore, might be called a political position of the Bleeding Hearts; but they entertained other objections to having foreigners in the Yard. They believed that foreigners were always badly off; and though they were as ill off themselves as they could desire to be, that did not diminish the force of the objection. They believed that foreigners were dragooned and bayoneted; and though they certainly got their own skulls promptly fractured if they showed any ill-humour, still it was with a blunt instrument, and that didn't count. They believed that foreigners were always immoral;

and though they had an occasional assize at home, and now
and then a divorce case or so, that had nothing to do with it.
They believed that foreigners had no independent spirit, as
never being escorted to the poll in droves by Lord Decimus
Tite Barnacle, with colours flying and the tune of Rule
Britannia playing. Not to be tedious, they had many other
beliefs of a similar kind.

Against these obstacles, the lame foreigner with the stick
had to make head as well as he could; not absolutely single-
handed, because Mr. Arthur Clennam had recommended him
to the Plornishes (he lived at the top of the same house),
but still at heavy odds. However, the Bleeding Hearts were
kind hearts; and when they saw the little fellow cheerily
limping about with a good-humoured face, doing no harm,
drawing no knives, committing no outrageous immoralities,
living chiefly on farinaceous and milk diet, and playing with
Mrs. Plornish's children of an evening, they began to think
that although he could never hope to be an Englishman, still
it would be hard to visit that affliction on his head. They
began to accommodate themselves to his level, calling him
"Mr. Baptist," but treating him like a baby, and laughing
immoderately at his lively gestures and his childish English
—more, because he didn't mind it, and laughed too. They
spoke to him in very loud voices as if he were stone deaf.
They constructed sentences, by way of teaching him the language in its purity, such as were addressed by the savages
to Captain Cook, or by Friday to Robinson Crusoe. Mrs.
Plornish was particularly ingenious in this art; and attained
so much celebrity by saying "Me ope you leg well soon,"
that it was considered in the Yard but a very short remove
indeed from speaking Italian. Even Mrs. Plornish herself
began to think that she had a natural call towards that
language. As he became more popular, household objects
were brought into requisition for his instruction in a copious
vocabulary; and whenever he appeared in the Yard ladies
would fly out at their doors crying "Mr. Baptist—tea-pot!"

"Mr. Baptist—dust-pan!" "Mr. Baptist—flour-dredger!" "Mr. Baptist—coffee-biggin!" At the same time exhibiting those articles, and penetrating him with a sense of the appalling difficulties of the Anglo-Saxon tongue.

It was in this stage of his progress, and in about the third week of his occupation, that Mr. Pancks's fancy became attracted by the little man. Mounting to his attic, attended by Mrs. Plornish as interpreter, he found Mr. Baptist with no furniture but his bed on the ground, a table, and a chair, carving with the aid of a few simple tools, in the blithest way possible.

"Now, old chap," said Mr. Pancks, "pay up!"

He had his money ready, folded in a scrap of paper, and laughingly handed it in; then with a free action, threw out as many fingers of his right hand as there were shillings, and made a cut crosswise in the air for an odd sixpence.

"Oh!" said Mr. Pancks, watching him, wonderingly. "That's it, is it? You're a quick customer. It's all right. I didn't expect to receive it, though."

Mrs. Plornish here interposed with great condescension, and explained to Mr. Baptist. "E please. E glad get money."

The little man smiled and nodded. His bright face seemed uncommonly attractive to Mr. Pancks. "How's he getting on in his limb?" he asked Mrs. Plornish.

"Oh, he's a deal better, sir," said Mrs. Plornish. "We expect next week he'll be able to leave off his stick entirely." (The opportunity being too favourable to be lost, Mrs. Plornish displayed her great accomplishment, by explaining, with pardonable pride, to Mr. Baptist, "E ope you leg well soon.")

"He's a merry fellow, too," said Mr. Pancks, admiring him as if he were a mechanical toy. "How does he live?"

"Why, sir," rejoined Mrs. Plornish, "he turns out to have quite a power of carving them flowers that you see him at now." (Mr. Baptist, watching their faces as they spoke, held up his work. Mrs. Plornish interpreted in her Italian manner, on behalf of Mr. Pancks, " E please. Double good ! ")

" Can he live by that ? " asked Mr. Pancks.

" He can live on very little, sir, and it is expected as he will be able, in time, to make a very good living. Mr. Clennam got it him to do, and gives him odd jobs besides, in at the Works next door—makes 'em for him, in short, when he knows he wants 'em."

"And what does he do with himself, now, when he ain't hard at it ? " said Mr. Pancks.

" Why, not much as yet, sir, on accounts I suppose of not being able to walk much ; but he goes about the Yard, and he chats without particular understanding or being understood, and he plays with the children, and he sits in the sun—he'll sit down anywhere, as if it was a arm-chair—and he'll sing, and he'll laugh ! "

" Laugh ! " echoed Mr. Pancks. " He looks to me as if every tooth in his head was always laughing.

"But whenever he gets to the top of the steps at t'other end of the Yard," said Mrs. Plornish, " he'll peep out in the curiousest way ! So that some of us thinks he's peeping out towards where his own country is, and some of us thinks he's looking for somebody he don't want to see, and some of us don't know what to think."

Mr. Baptist seemed to have a general understanding of what she said ; or perhaps his quickness caught and applied her slight action of peeping. In any case he closed his eyes and tossed his head with the air of a man who had his sufficient reasons for what he did, and said in his own tongue, it didn't matter. Altro !

" What's Altro ? " said Pancks.

" Hem ! It's a sort of a general kind of expression, sir," said Mrs. Plornish.

" Is it ? " said Pancks. " Why, then Altro to you, old chap. Good afternoon. Altro ! "

Mr. Baptist in his vivacious way repeating the word several

376

times, Mr. Pancks in his duller way gave it him back once. From that time it became a frequent custom with Pancks the gipsy, as he went home jaded at night, to pass round by Bleeding Heart Yard, go quietly up the stairs, look in at Mr. Baptist's door, and, finding him in his room, to say "Hallo, old chap! Altro!" To which Mr. Baptist would reply, with innumerable bright nods and smiles, "Altro, signore, altro, altro, altro!" After this highly condensed conversation, Mr. Pancks would go his way; with an appearance of being lightened and refreshed.

CHAPTER XXVI

If Arthur Clennam had not arrived at that wise decision firmly to restrain himself from loving Pet, he would have lived on in a state of much perplexity, involving difficult struggles with his own heart. Not the least of these would have been a contention, always waging within it, between a tendency to dislike Mr. Henry Gowan, if not to regard him with positive repugnance, and a whisper that the inclination was unworthy. A generous nature is not prone to strong aversions, and is slow to admit them even dispassionately; but when it finds ill-will gaining upon it, and can discern between-whiles that its origin is not dispassionate, such a nature becomes distressed.

Therefore Mr. Henry Gowan would have clouded Clennam's mind, and would have been far oftener present to it than more agreeable persons and subjects, but for the great prudence of his decision aforesaid. As it was, Mr. Gowan seemed transferred to Daniel Doyce's mind; at all events, it so happened that it usually fell to Mr. Doyce's turn, rather than to Clennam's, to speak of him in the friendly conversations they held together. These were of frequent occurrence now; as the two partners shared a portion of a roomy house in one of the grave old-fashioned City streets, lying not far from the Bank of England, by London Wall.

Mr. Doyce had been to Twickenham to pass the day. Clennam had excused himself. Mr. Doyce was just come

378

home. He put in his head at the door of Clennam's sitting-room to say Good night.

"Come in, come in!" said Clennam.

"I saw you were reading," returned Doyce, as he entered, "and thought you might not care to be disturbed."

But for the notable resolution he had made, Clennam really might not have known what he had been reading; really might not have had his eyes upon the book for an hour past, though it lay open before him. He shut it up, rather quickly.

"Are they well?" he asked.

"Yes," said Doyce; "they are well. They are all well."

Daniel had an old workmanlike habit of carrying his pocket-handkerchief in his hat. He took it out and wiped his forehead with it, slowly repeating "they are all well. Miss Minnie looking particularly well, I thought."

"Any company at the cottage?"

"No, no company."

"And how did you get on, you four?" asked Clennam, gaily.

"There were five of us," returned his partner. "There was What's-his-name. He was there."

"Who is he?" said Clennam.

"Mr. Henry Gowan."

"Ah, to be sure!" cried Clennam, with unusual vivacity. "Yes!—I forgot him."

"As I mentioned, you may remember," said Daniel Doyce, "he is always there, on Sunday."

"Yes, yes," returned Clennam; "I remember now."

Daniel Doyce, still wiping his forehead, ploddingly repeated, "Yes. He was there, he was there. Oh yes, he was there. And his dog. *He* was there too."

"Miss Meagles is quite attached to—the—dog," observed Clennam.

"Quite so," assented his partner. "More attached to the dog than I am to the man."

379

" You mean Mr.——? "

"I mean Mr. Gowan, most decidedly," said Daniel Doyce.

There was a gap in the conversation, which Clennam devoted to winding up his watch.

" Perhaps you are a little hasty in your judgment," he said. " Our judgments—I am supposing a general case—— "

" Of course," said Doyce.

" Are so liable to be influenced by many considerations, which, almost without our knowing it, are unfair, that it is necessary to keep a guard upon them. For instance, Mr.—— "

" Gowan," quietly said Doyce, upon whom the utterance of the name almost always devolved.

" Is young and handsome, easy and quick, has talent, and has seen a good deal of various kinds of life. It might be difficult to give an unselfish reason for being prepossessed against him."

" Not difficult for me, I think, Clennam," returned his partner. " I see him bringing present anxiety, and, I fear, future sorrow, into my old friend's house. I see him wearing deeper lines into my old friend's face, the nearer he draws to, and the oftener he looks at, the face of his daughter. In short, I see him with a net about the pretty and affectionate creature whom he will never make happy."

" We don't know," said Clennam, almost in the tone of a man in pain, " that he will not make her happy."

" We don't know," returned his partner, " that the earth will last another hundred years, but we think it highly probable."

" Well, well ! " said Clennam, " we must be hopeful, and we must at least try to be, if not generous (which, in this case, we have no opportunity of being), just. We will not disparage this gentleman, because he is successful in his addresses to the beautiful object of his ambition ; and we will not question her natural right to bestow her love on one whom she finds worthy of it."

"May be, my friend," said Doyce. "May be also, that she is too young and petted, too confiding and inexperienced, to discriminate well."

"That," said Clennam, "would be far beyond our power of correction."

Daniel Doyce shook his head gravely, and rejoined, "I fear so."

"Therefore, in a word," said Clennam, "we should make up our minds that it is not worthy of us to say any ill of Mr. Gowan. It would be a poor thing to gratify a prejudice against him. And I resolve, for my part, not to depreciate him."

"I am not quite so sure of myself, and therefore I reserve my privilege of objecting to him," returned the other. "But, if I am not sure of myself, I am sure of you, Clennam, and I know what an upright man you are, and how much to be respected. Good night, my friend and partner!" He shook his hand in saying this, as if there had been something serious at the bottom of their conversation ; and they separated.

By this time, they had visited the family on several occasions, and had always observed that even a passing allusion to Mr. Henry Gowan when he was not among them, brought back the cloud which had obscured Mr. Meagles's sunshine on the morning of the chance encounter at the Ferry. If Clennam had ever admitted the forbidden passion into his breast, this period might have been a period of real trial ; under the actual circumstances, doubtless it was nothing— nothing.

Equally, if his heart had given entertainment to that prohibited guest, his silent fighting of his way through the mental condition of this period might have been a little meritorious. In the constant effort not to be betrayed into a new phase of the besetting sin of his experience, the pursuit of selfish objects by low and small means, and to hold instead to some high principle of honour and generosity, there might have been a little merit. In the resolution not even to avoid

Mr. Meagles's house, lest, in the selfish sparing of himself, he should bring any slight distress upon the daughter through making her the cause of an estrangement which he believed the father would regret, there might have been a little merit. In the modest truthfulness of always keeping in view the greater equality of Mr. Gowan's years, and the greater attractions of his person and manner, there might have been a little merit. In doing all this and much more, in a perfectly unaffected way and with a manful and composed constancy, while the pain within him (peculiar as his life and history) was very sharp, there might have been some quiet strength of character. But, after the resolution he had made, of course he could have no such merits as these; and such a state of mind was nobody's—nobody's.

Mr. Gowan made it no concern of his whether it was nobody's or somebody's. He preserved his perfect serenity of manner on all occasions, as if the possibility of Clennam's presuming to have debated the great question were too distant and ridiculous to be imagined. He had always an affability to bestow on Clennam and an ease to treat him with, which might of itself (in the supposititious case of his not having taken that sagacious course) have been a very uncomfortable element in his state of mind.

"I quite regret you were not with us yesterday," said Mr. Henry Gowan, calling on Clennam the next morning. "We had an agreeable day up the river there."

So he had heard, Arthur said.

"From your partner?" returned Henry Gowan. "What a dear old fellow he is!"

"I have a great regard for him."

"By Jove, he is the finest creature!" said Gowan. "So fresh, so green, trusts in such wonderful things!"

Here was one of the many little rough points that had a tendency to grate on Clennam's hearing. He put it aside by merely repeating that he had a high regard for Mr. Doyce.

"He is charming! To see him mooning along to that time

of life, laying down nothing by the way and picking up nothing by the way, is delightful. It warms a man. So unspoilt, so simple, such a good soul! Upon my life, Mr. Clennam, one feels desperately worldly and wicked, in comparison with such an innocent creature. I speak for myself, let me add, without including you. You are genuine also."

"Thank you for the compliment," said Clennam, ill at ease; "you are too, I hope?"

"So so," rejoined the other. "To be candid with you, tolerably. I am not a great impostor. Buy one of my pictures, and I assure you, in confidence, it will not be worth the money. Buy one of another man's—any great professor who beats me hollow—and the chances are that the more you give him, the more he'll impose upon you. They all do it."

"All painters?"

"Painters, writers, patriots, all the rest who have stands in the market. Give almost any man I know, ten pounds, and he will impose upon you to a corresponding extent; a thousand pounds—to a corresponding extent; ten thousand pounds—to a corresponding extent. So great the success, so great the imposition. But what a capital world it is!" cried Gowan with warm enthusiasm. "What a jolly, excellent, lovable world it is!"

"I had rather thought," said Clennam, "that the principle you mention was chiefly acted on by——"

"By the Barnacles?" interrupted Gowan, laughing.

"By the political gentlemen who condescend to keep the Circumlocution Office."

"Ah! Don't be hard upon the Barnacles," said Gowan, laughing afresh, "they are darling fellows! Even poor little Clarence, the born idiot of the family, is the most agreeable and most endearing blockhead! And by Jupiter, with a kind of cleverness in him too, that would astonish you!"

"It would. Very much," said Clennam, drily.

"And after all," cried Gowan, with that characteristic balancing of his which reduced everything in the wide world to the same light weight, "though I can't deny that the Circumlocution Office may ultimately shipwreck everybody and everything, still, that will probably not be in our time—and it's a school for gentlemen."

"It's a very dangerous, unsatisfactory, and expensive school to the people who pay to keep the pupils there, I am afraid," said Clennam, shaking his head.

"Ah! You are a terrible fellow," returned Gowan, airily. "I can understand how you have frightened that little donkey, Clarence, the most estimable of moon-calves (I really love him), nearly out of his wits. But enough of him, and of all the rest of them. I want to present you to my mother, Mr. Clennam. Pray do me the favour to give me the opportunity."

In nobody's state of mind, there was nothing Clennam would have desired less, or would have been more at a loss how to avoid.

"My mother lives in the most primitive manner down in that dreary red-brick dungeon at Hampton Court," said Gowan. "If you would make your own appointment, suggest your own day for permitting me to take you there to dinner, you would be bored and she would be charmed. Really that's the state of the case."

What could Clennam say after this? His retiring character included a great deal that was simple in the best sense, because unpractised and unused; and in his simplicity and modesty, he could only say that he was happy to place himself at Mr. Gowan's disposal. Accordingly he said it, and the day was fixed. And a dreaded day it was on his part, and a very unwelcome day when it came, and they went down to Hampton Court together.

The venerable inhabitants of that venerable pile seemed, in those times, to be encamped there like a sort of civilised gipsies. There was a temporary air about their establishments, as if they were going away the moment they could get anything better; there was also a dissatisfied air about themselves, as if they took it very ill that they had not already got something much better. Genteel blinds and makeshifts were more or less observable as soon as their doors were opened; screens not half high enough, which made dining-rooms out of arched passages, and warded off obscure corners where footboys slept at night with their heads among the knives and forks; curtains which called upon you to believe that they didn't hide anything; panes of glass which requested you not to see them; many objects of various forms, feigning to have no connection with their guilty secret, a bed; disguised traps in walls, which were clearly coal-cellars; affectations of no thoroughfares, which were evidently doors to little kitchens. Mental reservations and artful mysteries grew out of these things. Callers looking steadily into the eyes of their receivers, pretended not to smell cooking three feet off; people, confronting closets accidentally left open, pretended not to see bottles; visitors, with their heads against a partition of thin canvas and a page and a young female at high words on the other side, made believe to be sitting in a primeval silence. There was no end to the small social accommodation-bills of this nature which the gipsies of gentility were constantly drawing upon, and accepting for, one another.

Some of these Bohemians were of an irritable temperament, as constantly soured and vexed by two mental trials: the first, the consciousness that they had never got enough out of the public; the second, the consciousness that the public were admitted into the building. Under the latter great wrong, a few suffered dreadfully—particularly on Sundays, when they had for some time expected the earth to open and swallow the public up; but which desirable event had not yet occurred, in consequence of some reprehensible laxity in the arrangements of the Universe.

Mrs. Gowan's door was attended by a family servant of several years' standing, who had his own crow to pluck with the public, concerning a situation in the Post-Office which he had been for some time expecting, and to which he was not yet appointed. He perfectly knew that the public could never have got him in, but he grimly gratified himself with the idea that the public kept him out. Under the influence of this injury (and perhaps of some little straitness and irregularity in the matter of wages), he had grown neglectful of his person and morose in mind; and now beholding in Clennam one of the degraded body of his oppressors, received him with ignominy.

Mrs. Gowan, however, received him with condescension. He found her a courtly old lady, formerly a Beauty, and still sufficiently well-favoured to have dispensed with the powder on her nose, and a certain impossible bloom under each eye. She was a little lofty with him; so was another old lady, dark-browed and high-nosed, and who must have had something real about her, or she could not have existed, but it was certainly not her hair or her teeth or her figure or her complexion; so was a grey old gentleman of dignified and sullen appearance; both of whom had come to dinner. But, as they had all been in the British Embassy way in sundry parts of the earth, and as a British Embassy cannot better establish a character with the Circumlocution Office than by treating its compatriots with illimitable contempt (else it would become like the Embassies of other countries), Clennam felt that on the whole they let him off lightly.

The dignified old gentleman turned out to be Lord Lancaster Stiltstalking, who had been maintained by the Circumlocution Office for many years as a representative of the Britannic Majesty abroad. This noble Refrigerator had iced several European courts in his time, and had done it with such complete success that the very name of Englishman yet struck cold to the stomachs of foreigners who had the distinguished honour of remembering him, at a distance of a quarter of a century.

He was now in retirement, and hence (in a ponderous white cravat, like a stiff snow-drift) was so obliging as to shade the dinner. There was a whisper of the pervading Bohemian character in the nomadic nature of the service, and its curious races of plates and dishes; but the noble Refrigerator, infinitely better than plate or porcelain, made it superb. He shaded the dinner, cooled the wines, chilled the gravy, and blighted the vegetables.

There was only one other person in the room: a microscopically small foot-boy, who waited on the malevolent man who hadn't got into the Post-Office. Even this youth, if his jacket could have been unbuttoned and his heart laid bare, would have been seen, as a distant adherent of the Barnacle family, already to aspire to a situation under Government.

Mrs. Gowan with a gentle melancholy upon her, occasioned by her son's being reduced to court the swinish public as a follower of the low Arts, instead of asserting his birthright and putting a ring through its nose as an acknowledged Barnacle, headed the conversation at dinner on the evil days. It was then that Clennam learned for the first time what little pivots this great world goes round upon.

"If John Barnacle," said Mrs. Gowan, after the degeneracy of the times had been fully ascertained, "if John Barnacle had but abandoned his most unfortunate idea of conciliating the mob, all would have been well, and I think the country would have been preserved."

The old lady with the high nose assented; but added that if Augustus Stiltstalking had in a general way ordered the cavalry out with instructions to charge, she thought the country would have been preserved.

The noble Refrigerator assented; but added that if William Barnacle and Tudor Stiltstalking, when they came over to one another and formed their ever-memorable coalition, had boldly muzzled the newspapers, and rendered it penal for any Editor-person to presume to discuss the conduct of any appointed authority abroad or at home, he thought the country would have been preserved.

It was agreed that the country (another word for the Barnacles and Stiltstalkings) wanted preserving, but how it came to want preserving was not so clear. It was only clear that the question was all about John Barnacle, Augustus Stiltstalking, William Barnacle and Tudor Stiltstalking, Tom, Dick, or Harry Barnacle or Stiltstalking, because there was nobody else but mob. And this was the feature of the conversation which impressed Clennam, as a man not used to it, very disagreeably: making him doubt if it were quite right to sit there, silently hearing a great nation narrowed to such little bounds. Remembering, however, that in the Parliamentary debates, whether on the life of that nation's body or the life of its soul, the question was usually all about and between John Barnacle, Augustus Stiltstalking, William Barnacle and Tudor Stiltstalking, Tom, Dick, or Harry Barnacle or Stiltstalking, and nobody else; he said nothing on the part of mob, bethinking himself that mob was used to it.

Mr. Henry Gowan seemed to have a malicious pleasure in playing off the three talkers against each other, and in seeing Clennam startled by what they said. Having as supreme a contempt for the class that had thrown him off, as for the class that had not taken him on, he had no personal disquiet in anything that passed. His healthy state of mind appeared even to derive a gratification from Clennam's position of embarrassment and isolation among the good company; and if Clennam had been in that condition with which Nobody was incessantly contending, he would have suspected it, and would have struggled with the suspicion as a meanness, even while he sat at the table.

In the course of a couple of hours the noble Refrigerator, at no time less than a hundred years behind the period, got about five centuries in arrear, and delivered solemn political oracles appropriate to that epoch. He finished by freezing a cup of tea for his own drinking, and retiring at his lowest temperature.

Then Mrs. Gowan, who had been accustomed in her days of state to retain a vacant arm-chair beside her to which to summon her devoted slaves, one by one, for short audiences as marks of her especial favour, invited Clennam with a turn of her fan to approach the presence. He obeyed, and took the tripod recently vacated by Lord Lancaster Stilt-stalking.

"Mr. Clennam," said Mrs. Gowan, "apart from the happiness I have in becoming known to you, though in this odiously inconvenient place—a mere barrack—there is a subject on which I am dying to speak to you. It is the subject in connection with which my son first had, I believe, the pleasure of cultivating your acquaintance."

Clennam inclined his head, as a generally suitable reply to what he did not yet quite understand.

"First," said Mrs. Gowan, "now is she really pretty?"

In nobody's difficulties, he would have found it very difficult to answer; very difficult indeed to smile, and say "Who?"

"Oh! You know!" she returned. "This flame of Henry's. This unfortunate fancy. There! If it is a point of honour that I should originate the name—Miss Mickles—Miggles."

"Miss Meagles," said Clennam, "is very beautiful."

"Men are so often mistaken on those points," returned Mrs. Gowan, shaking her head, "that I candidly confess to you I feel anything but sure of it, even now; though it is something to have Henry corroborated with so much gravity and emphasis. He picked the people up at Rome, I think?"

The phrase would have given nobody mortal offence. Clennam replied, "Excuse me, I doubt if I understand your expression."

"Picked the people up," said Mrs. Gowan, tapping the sticks of her closed fan (a large green one, which she used as a hand-screen) upon her little table. "Came upon them. Found them out. Stumbled against them."

"The people?"

"Yes. The Miggles people."

"I really cannot say," said Clennam, "where my friend Mr. Meagles first presented Mr. Henry Gowan to his daughter."

"I am pretty sure he picked her up at Rome ; but never mind where—somewhere. Now (this is entirely between ourselves), *is* she very plebeian ? "

"Really, ma'am," returned Clennam, "I am so undoubtedly plebeian myself, that I do not feel qualified to judge."

"Very neat ! " said Mrs. Gowan, coolly unfurling her screen. "Very happy ! From which I infer that you secretly think her manner equal to her looks ? "

Clennam, after a moment's stiffness, bowed.

"That's comforting, and I hope you may be right. Did Henry tell me you had travelled with them ? "

"I travelled with my friend Mr. Meagles, and his wife and daughter, during some months." (Nobody's heart might have been wrung by the remembrance.)

"Really comforting, because you must have had a large experience of them. You see, Mr. Clennam, this thing has been going on for a long time, and I find no improvement in it. Therefore to have the opportunity of speaking to one so well informed about it as yourself, is an immense relief to me. Quite a boon. Quite a blessing, I am sure."

"Pardon me," returned Clennam, "but I am not in Mr. Henry Gowan's confidence. I am far from being so well informed as you suppose me to be. Your mistake makes my position a very delicate one. No word on this topic has ever passed between Mr. Henry Gowan and myself."

Mrs. Gowan glanced at the other end of the room, where her son was playing écarté on a sofa, with the old lady who was for a charge of cavalry.

"Not in his confidence ? No," said Mrs. Gowan. "No word has passed between you ? No. That I can imagine. But there are unexpressed confidences, Mr. Clennam ; and as you have been together intimately among these people, I cannot doubt that a confidence of that sort exists in the present case. Perhaps you have heard that I have suffered the keenest distress of mind from Henry's having taken to a pursuit which—well!" shrugging her shoulders, "a very respectable pursuit, I dare say, and some artists are, as artists, quite superior persons; still, we never yet in our family have gone beyond an Amateur, and it is a pardonable weakness to feel a little—— "

As Mrs. Gowan broke off to heave a sigh, Clennam, however resolute to be magnanimous, could not keep down the thought that there was mighty little danger of the family's ever going beyond an Amateur, even as it was.

"Henry," the mother resumed, "is self-willed and resolute; and as these people naturally strain every nerve to catch him, I can entertain very little hope, Mr. Clennam, that the thing will be broken off. I apprehend the girl's fortune will be very small; Henry might have done much better; there is scarcely anything to compensate for the connection : still, he acts for himself; and if I find no improvement within a short time, I see no other course than to resign myself, and make the best of these people. I am infinitely obliged to you for what you have told me."

As she shrugged her shoulders, Clennam stiffly bowed again. With an uneasy flush upon his face, and hesitation in his manner, he then said, in a still lower tone than he had adopted yet :

"Mrs. Gowan, I scarcely know how to acquit myself of what I feel to be a duty, and yet I must ask you for your kind consideration in attempting to discharge it. A misconception on your part, a very great misconception if I may venture to call it so, seems to require setting right. You have supposed Mr. Meagles and his family to strain every nerve, I think you said—— "

"Every nerve," repeated Mrs. Gowan, looking at him in calm obstinacy, with her green fan between her face and the fire.

"To secure Mr. Henry Gowan ?"

The lady placidly assented.

"Now that is so far," said Arthur, "from being the case, that I know Mr. Meagles to be unhappy in this matter; and to have interposed all reasonable obstacles, with the hope of putting an end to it."

Mrs. Gowan shut up her great green fan, tapped him on the arm with it, and tapped her smiling lips. "Why, of course," said she. "Just what I mean."

Arthur watched her face for some explanation of what she did mean.

"Are you really serious, Mr. Clennam? Don't you see?"

Arthur did not see; and said so.

"Why, don't I know my son, and don't I know that this is exactly the way to hold him?" said Mrs. Gowan, contemptuously; "and do not these Miggles people know it, at least as well as I? Oh, shrewd people, Mr. Clennam: evidently people of business! I believe Miggles belonged to a Bank. It ought to have been a very profitable Bank, if he had much to do with its management. This is very well done, indeed."

"I beg and entreat you, ma'am——" Arthur interposed.

"Oh, Mr. Clennam, can you really be so credulous!"

It made such a painful impression upon him to hear her talking in this haughty tone, and to see her patting her contemptuous lips with her fan, that he said very earnestly, "Believe me, ma'am, this is unjust, a perfectly groundless suspicion."

"Suspicion?" repeated Mrs. Gowan. "Not suspicion, Mr. Clennam, Certainty. It is very knowingly done indeed, and seems to have taken *you* in completely." She laughed; and again sat tapping her lips with her fan, and tossing her head, as if she added, "Don't tell me. I know such people will do anything for the honour of such an alliance."

At this opportune moment, the cards were thrown up, and Mr. Henry Gowan came across the room saying, "Mother, if you can spare Mr. Clennam for this time, we have a long way to go, and it's getting late." Mr. Clennam thereupon rose, as he had no choice but to do; and Mrs. Gowan showed him, to the last, the same look and the same tapped contemptuous lips.

"You have had a portentously long audience of my mother," said Gowan, as the door closed upon them. "I fervently hope she has not bored you?"

"Not at all," said Clennam.

They had a little open phaeton for the journey, and were soon in it on the road home. Gowan, driving, lighted a cigar; Clennam declined one. Do what he would, he fell into such a mood of abstraction that Gowan said again, "I am very much afraid my mother has bored you?" To which he roused himself to answer, "Not at all;" and soon relapsed again.

In that state of mind which rendered nobody uneasy, his thoughtfulness would have turned principally on the man at his side. He would have thought of the morning when he first saw him rooting out the stones with his heel, and would have asked himself, "Does he jerk me out of the path in the same careless, cruel way?" He would have thought, had this introduction to his mother been brought about by him because he knew what she would say, and that he could thus place his position before a rival and loftily warn him off, without himself reposing a word of confidence in him? He would have thought, even if there were no such design as that, had he brought him there to play with his repressed emotions, and torment him? The current of these meditations would have been stayed sometimes by a rush of shame, bearing a remonstrance to himself from his own open nature, representing that to shelter such suspicions, even for the passing moment, was not to hold the high, unenvious course he had resolved to keep. At those times, the striving within him would have been hardest; and looking up and catching Gowan's eyes, he would have started as if he had done him an injury.

Then, looking at the dark road and its uncertain objects,

he would have gradually trailed off again into thinking, "Where are we driving, he and I, I wonder, on the darker road of life? How will it be with us, and with her, in the obscure distance?" Thinking of her, he would have been troubled anew with a reproachful misgiving that it was not even loyal to her to dislike him, and that in being so easily prejudiced against him he was less deserving of her than at first.

"You are evidently out of spirits," said Gowan; "I am very much afraid my mother must have bored you dreadfully."

"Believe me, not at all," said Clennam. "It's nothing—nothing!"

CHAPTER XXVII

FIVE-AND-TWENTY

A FREQUENTLY recurring doubt, whether Mr. Pancks's desire to collect information relative to the Dorrit family could have any possible bearing on the misgivings he had imparted to his mother on his return from his long exile, caused Arthur Clennam much uneasiness at this period. What Mr. Pancks already knew about the Dorrit family, what more he really wanted to find out, and why he should trouble his busy head about them at all, were questions that often perplexed him. Mr. Pancks was not a man to waste his time and trouble in researches prompted by idle curiosity. That he had a specific object Clennam could not doubt. And whether the attainment of that object by Mr. Pancks's industry might bring to light, in some untimely way, secret reasons which had induced his mother to take Little Dorrit by the hand, was a serious speculation.

Not that he ever wavered, either in his desire or his determination to repair a wrong that had been done in his father's time, should a wrong come to light, and be reparable. The shadow of a supposed act of injustice, which had hung over him since his father's death, was so vague and formless that it might be the result of a reality widely remote from his idea of it. But, if his apprehensions should prove to be well founded, he was ready at any moment to lay down all he had, and begin the world anew. As the fierce dark

395

teaching of his childhood had never sunk into his heart, so the first article in his code of morals was, that he must begin in practical humility, with looking well to his feet on Earth, and that he could never mount on wings of words to Heaven. Duty on Earth, restitution on earth, action on earth; these first, as the first steep steps upward. Strait was the gate and narrow was the way; far straiter and narrower than the broad high road paved with vain professions and vain repetitions, motes from other men's eyes and liberal delivery of others to the judgment—all cheap materials costing absolutely nothing.

No. It was not a selfish fear or hesitation that rendered him uneasy, but a mistrust lest Pancks might not observe his part of the understanding between them, and, making any discovery, might take some course upon it without imparting it to him. On the other hand, when he recalled his conversation with Pancks, and the little reason he had to suppose that there was any likelihood of that strange personage being on that track at all, there were times when he wondered that he made so much of it. Labouring in this sea, as all barks labour in cross seas, he tossed about and came to no haven.

The removal of Little Dorrit herself from their customary association, did not mend the matter. She was so much out, and so much in her own room, that he began to miss her and to find a blank in her place. He had written to her to inquire if she were better, and she had written back, very gratefully and earnestly, telling him not to be uneasy on her behalf, for she was quite well; but he had not seen her, for what, in their intercourse, was a long time.

He returned home one evening from an interview with her father, who had mentioned that she was out visiting—which was what he always said, when she was hard at work to buy his supper—and found Mr. Meagles in an excited state walking up and down his room. On his opening the door, Mr. Meagles stopped, faced round, and said,

" Clennam !—Tattycoram ! "

" What's the matter ? "

" Lost ! "

" Why, bless my heart alive ! " cried Clennam in amazement. " What do you mean ? "

" Wouldn't count five-and-twenty, sir ; couldn't be got to do it ; stopped at eight, and took herself off."

" Left your house ? "

" Never to come back," said Mr. Meagles, shaking his head. " You don't know that girl's passionate and proud character. A team of horses couldn't draw her back now ; the bolts and bars of the old Bastille couldn't keep her."

" How did it happen ? Pray sit down and tell me."

" As to how it happened, it's not so easy to relate : because you must have the unfortunate temperament of the poor impetuous girl herself, before you can fully understand it. But it came about in this way. Pet and Mother and I have been having a good deal of talk together of late. I'll not disguise from you, Clennam, that those conversations have not been of as bright a kind as I could wish ; they have referred to our going away again. In proposing to do which, I have had, in fact, an object."

Nobody's heart beat quickly.

" An object," said Mr. Meagles, after a moment's pause, " that I will not disguise from you, either, Clennam. There's an inclination on the part of my dear child which I am sorry for. Perhaps you guess the person. Henry Gowan."

" I was not unprepared to hear it."

" Well ! " said Mr. Meagles, with a heavy sigh, " I wish to God you had never had to hear it. However, so it is. Mother and I have done all we could to get the better of it, Clennam. We have tried tender advice, we have tried time, we have tried absence. As yet, of no use. Our late conversations have been upon the subject of going away for another year at least, in order that there might be an entire separation and breaking off for that term. Upon that question, Pet has been unhappy, and therefore Mother and I have been unhappy."

Clennam said that he could easily believe it.

"Well!" continued Mr. Meagles, in an apologetic way, "I admit as a practical man, and I am sure Mother would admit as a practical woman, that we do, in families, magnify our troubles and make mountains of our molehills, in a way that is calculated to be rather trying to people who look on —to mere outsiders you know, Clennam. Still, Pet's happiness or unhappiness is quite a life or death question with us; and we may be excused, I hope, for making much of it. At all events, it might have been borne by Tattycoram. Now, don't you think so?"

"I do indeed think so," returned Clennam, in most emphatic recognition of this very moderate expectation.

"No, sir," said Mr. Meagles, shaking his head ruefully. "She couldn't stand it. The chafing and firing of that girl, the wearing and tearing of that girl within her own breast, has been such that I have softly said to her again and again in passing her, 'Five-and-twenty, Tattycoram, five-and-twenty!' I heartily wish she could have gone on counting five-and-twenty day and night, and then it wouldn't have happened."

Mr. Meagles, with a despondent countenance in which the goodness of his heart was even more expressed than in his times of cheerfulness and gaiety, stroked his face down from his forehead to his chin, and shook his head again.

"I said to Mother (not that it was necessary, for she would have thought it all for herself), we are practical people, my dear, and we know her story; we see in this unhappy girl, some reflection of what was raging in her mother's heart before ever such a creature as this poor thing was, in the world; we'll gloss her temper over, Mother, we won't notice it at present, my dear, we'll take advantage of some better disposition in her, another time. So we said nothing. But, do what we would, it seems as if it was to be; she broke out violently one night."

"How, and why?"

"If you ask me Why," said Mr. Meagles, a little disturbed by the question, for he was far more intent on softening her case than the family's, "I can only refer you to what I have just repeated as having been pretty near my words to Mother. As to How, we had said Good night to Pet in her presence (very affectionately, I must allow), and she had attended Pet up-stairs—you remember she was her maid. Perhaps Pet, having been out of sorts, may have been a little more inconsiderate than usual in requiring services of her: but I don't know that I have any right to say so; she was always thoughtful and gentle."

"The gentlest mistress in the world."

"Thank you, Clennam," said Mr. Meagles, shaking him by the hand; "you have often seen them together. Well! We presently heard this unfortunate Tattycoram loud and angry, and before we could ask what was the matter, Pet came back in a tremble, saying she was frightened of her. Close after her came Tattycoram, in a flaming rage. 'I hate you all three,' says she, stamping her foot at us. 'I am bursting with hate of the whole house.'"

"Upon which you——?"

"I?" said Mr. Meagles, with a plain good faith, that might have commanded the belief of Mrs. Gowan herself: "I said, count five-and-twenty, Tattycoram."

Mr. Meagles again stroked his face and shook his head, with an air of profound regret.

"She was so used to do it, Clennam, that even then, such a picture of passion as you never saw, she stopped short, looked me full in the face, and counted (as I made out) to eight. But she couldn't control herself to go any further. There she broke down, poor thing, and gave the other seventeen to the four winds. Then it all burst out. She detested us, she was miserable with us, she couldn't bear it, she wouldn't bear it, she was determined to go away. She was younger than her young mistress, and would she remain to see *her* always held up as the only creature who was young and interesting, and to be cherished and loved? No. She wouldn't, she wouldn't, she wouldn't! What did we think she, Tattycoram, might have been if she had been caressed and cared for in her childhood, like her young mistress? As good as her? Ah! Perhaps fifty times as good. When we pretended to be so fond of one another, we exulted over her; that was what we did; we exulted over her and shamed her. And all in the house did the same. They talked about their fathers and mothers, and brothers and sisters; they liked to drag them up before her face. There was Mrs. Tickit, only yesterday, when her little grandchild was with her, had been amused by the child's trying to call her (Tattycoram) by the wretched name we gave her; and had laughed at the name. Why, who didn't; and who were we that we should have a right to name her like a dog or a cat? But, she didn't care. She would take no more benefits from us; she would fling us her name back again, and she would go. She would leave us that minute, nobody should stop her, and we should never hear of her again."

Mr. Meagles had recited all this with such a vivid remembrance of his original, that he was almost as flushed and hot by this time as he described her to have been.

"Ah, well!" he said, wiping his face. "It was of no use trying reason then, with that vehement panting creature (Heaven knows what her mother's story must have been); so I quietly told her that she should not go at that late hour of night, and I gave her my hand and took her to her room, and locked the house doors. But she was gone this morning."

"And you know no more of her?"

"No more," returned Mr. Meagles. "I have been hunting about all day. She must have gone very early and very silently. I have found no trace of her, down about us."

"Stay! You want," said Clennam, after a moment's reflection, "to see her? I assume that?"

"Yes, assuredly; I want to give her another chance;

Mother and Pet want to give her another chance; come! You yourself," said Mr. Meagles, persuasively, as if the provocation to be angry were not his own at all, "want to give the poor passionate girl another chance, I know, Clennam."

"It would be strange and hard indeed if I did not," said Clennam, "when you are all so forgiving. What I was going to ask you was, have you thought of that Miss Wade?"

"I have. I did not think of her until I had pervaded the whole of our neighbourhood, and I don't know that I should have done so then, but for finding Mother and Pet, when I went home, full of the idea that Tattycoram must have gone to her. Then, of course, I recalled what she said that day at dinner when you were first with us."

"Have you any idea where Miss Wade is to be found?"

"To tell you the truth," returned Mr. Meagles, "it's because I have an addled jumble of a notion on that subject, that you found me waiting here. There is one of those odd impressions in my house, which do mysteriously get into houses sometimes, which nobody seems to have picked up in a distinct form from anybody, and yet which everybody seems to have got hold of loosely from somebody and let go again, that she lives, or was living, thereabouts." Mr. Meagles handed him a slip of paper, on which was written the name of one of the dull by-streets in the Grosvenor region, near Park Lane.

"Here is no number," said Arthur, looking over it.

"No number, my dear Clennam?" returned his friend. "No anything! The very name of the street may have been floating in the air, for, as I tell you, none of my people can say where they got it from. However, it's worth an inquiry; and as I would rather make it in company than alone, and as you too were a fellow-traveller of that immovable woman's, I thought perhaps——" Clennam finished the sentence for him by taking up his hat again, and saying he was ready.

It was now summer-time; a grey, hot, dusty evening. They rode to the top of Oxford Street, and there alighting, dived in among the great streets of melancholy stateliness, and the little streets that try to be as stately and succeed in being more melancholy, of which there is a labyrinth near Park Lane. Wildernesses of corner houses, with barbarous old porticoes and appurtenances; horrors that came into existence under some wrong-headed person in some wrong-headed time, still demanding the blind admiration of all ensuing generations and determined to do so until they tumbled down; frowned upon the twilight. Parasite little tenements, with the cramp in their whole frame, from the dwarf hall-door on the giant model of His Grace's in the Square to the squeezed window of the boudoir commanding the dunghills in the Mews, made the evening doleful. Rickety dwellings of undoubted fashion, but of a capacity to hold nothing comfortably except a dismal smell, looked like the last result of the great mansions' breeding in-and-in; and, where their little supplementary bows and balconies were supported on thin iron columns, seemed to be scrofulously resting upon crutches. Here and there a Hatchment, with the whole science of Heraldry in it, loomed down upon the street, like an Archbishop discoursing on Vanity. The shops, few in number, made no show; for popular opinion was as nothing to them. The pastrycook knew who was on his books, and in that knowledge could be calm, with a few glass cylinders of dowager peppermint-drops in his window, and half-a-dozen ancient specimens of currant-jelly. A few oranges formed the greengrocer's whole concession to the vulgar mind. A single basket made of moss, once containing plovers' eggs, held all that the poulterer had to say to the rabble. Everybody in those streets seemed (which is always the case at that hour and season) to be gone out to dinner, and nobody seemed to be giving the dinners they had gone to. On the doorsteps there were lounging footmen with bright parti-coloured plumage and white polls, like an extinct race of monstrous birds; and butlers, solitary men of recluse demeanour, each of whom appeared distrustful of all other butlers. The roll of carriages in the Park was done for the day; the street lamps were lighting; and wicked little grooms in the tightest-fitting garments, with twists in their legs answering to the twists in their minds, hung about in pairs, chewing straws and exchanging fraudulent secrets. The spotted dogs who went out with the carriages, and who were so associated with splendid equipages, that it looked like a condescension in those animals to come out without them, accompanied helpers to and fro on messages. Here and there was a retiring public-house which did not require to be supported on the shoulders of the people, and where gentlemen out of livery were not much wanted.

This last discovery was made by the two friends in pursuing their inquiries. Nothing was there, or anywhere, known of such a person as Miss Wade, in connection with the street they sought. It was one of the parasite streets; long, regular, narrow, dull, and gloomy; like a brick and mortar funeral. They inquired at several little area gates, where a dejected youth stood spiking his chin on the summit of a precipitous little shoot of wooden steps, but could gain no information. They walked up the street on one side of the way, and down it on the other, what time two vociferous news-sellers, announcing an extraordinary event that had never happened and never would happen, pitched their hoarse voices into the secret chambers; but nothing came of it. At length they stood at the corner from which they had begun, and it had fallen quite dark, and they were no wiser.

It happened that in the street they had several times passed a dingy house, apparently empty, with bills in the windows, announcing that it was to let. The bills, as a variety in the funeral procession, almost amounted to a decoration. Perhaps because they kept the house separate in his mind, or perhaps because Mr. Meagles and himself had twice agreed in passing, "It is clear she don't live there," Clennam now proposed that they should go back and try that house before finally going away. Mr. Meagles agreed, and back they went.

They knocked once, and they rang once, without any response. "Empty," said Mr. Meagles, listening. "Once more," said Clennam, and knocked again. After that knock they heard a movement below, and somebody shuffling up towards the door.

The confined entrance was so dark, that it was impossible to make out distinctly what kind of person opened the door; but it appeared to be an old woman. "Excuse our troubling you," said Clennam. "Pray can you tell us where Miss Wade lives?" The voice in the darkness unexpectedly replied, "Lives here."

"Is she at home?"

No answer coming, Mr. Meagles asked again. "Pray is she at home?"

After another delay, "I suppose she is," said the voice abruptly; "you had better come in, and I'll ask."

They were summarily shut into the close black house; and the figure rustling away, and speaking from a higher level, said, "Come up, if you please; you can't tumble over anything." They groped their way up-stairs towards a faint light, which proved to be the light of the street shining through a window; and the figure left them shut up in an airless room.

"This is odd, Clennam," said Mr. Meagles, softly.

"Odd enough," assented Clennam, in the same tone, "but we have succeeded; that's the main point. Here's a light coming!"

The light was a lamp, and the bearer was an old woman: very dirty, very wrinkled and dry. "She's at home," she said (and the voice was the same that had spoken before); "she'll come directly." Having set the lamp down on the table, the old woman dusted her hands on her apron, which she might have done for ever without cleaning them, looked at the visitors with a dim pair of eyes, and backed out.

MISS WADE APPEARS

The lady whom they had come to see, if she were the present occupant of the house, appeared to have taken up her quarters there, as she might have established herself in an Eastern caravanserai. A small square of carpet in the middle of the room, a few articles of furniture that evidently did not belong to the room, and a disorder of trunks and travelling articles, formed the whole of her surroundings. Under some former regular inhabitant, the stifling little apartment had broken out into a pier-glass and a gilt table; but the gilding was as faded as last year's flowers, and the glass was so clouded that it seemed to hold in magic preservation all the fogs and bad weather it had ever reflected. The visitors had had a minute or two to look about them, when the door opened and Miss Wade came in.

She was exactly the same as when they had parted. Just as handsome, just as scornful, just as repressed. She manifested no surprise in seeing them, nor any other emotion. She requested them to be seated; and declining to take a seat herself, at once anticipated any introduction of their business.

"I apprehend," she said, "that I know the cause of your favouring me with this visit. We may come to it at once."

"The cause then, ma'am," said Mr. Meagles, "is Tattycoram."

"So I supposed."

"Miss Wade," said Mr. Meagles, "will you be so kind as to say whether you know anything of her?"

"Surely. I know she is here with me."

"Then, ma'am," said Mr. Meagles, "allow me to make known to you that I shall be happy to have her back, and that my wife and daughter will be happy to have her back. She has been with us a long time: we don't forget her claims upon us, and I hope we know how to make allowances."

"You hope to know how to make allowances?" she returned, in a level, measured voice. "For what?"

"I think my friend would say, Miss Wade," Arthur Clennam interposed, seeing Mr. Meagles rather at a loss,

405

" for the passionate sense that sometimes comes upon the poor girl, of being at a disadvantage. Which occasionally gets the better of better remembrances."

The lady broke into a smile, as she turned her eyes upon him. " Indeed ? " was all she answered.

She stood by the table so perfectly composed and still after this acknowledgment of his remark, that Mr. Meagles stared at her under a sort of fascination, and could not even look to Clennam to make another move. After waiting, awkwardly enough, for some moments, Arthur said :

" Perhaps it would be well if Mr. Meagles could see her, Miss Wade ? "

" That is easily done," said she. " Come here, child." She had opened a door while saying this, and now led the girl in by the hand. It was very curious to see them standing together : the girl with her disengaged fingers plaiting the bosom of her dress, half irresolutely, half passionately ; Miss Wade with her composed face attentively regarding her, and suggesting to an observer with extraordinary force, in her composure itself (as a veil will suggest the form it covers), the unquenchable passion of her own nature.

" See here," she said, in the same level way as before. " Here is your patron, your master. He is willing to take you back, my dear, if you are sensible of the favour and choose to go. You can be, again, a foil to his pretty daughter, a slave to her pleasant wilfulness, and a toy in the house showing the goodness of the family. You can have your droll name again, playfully pointing you out and setting you apart, as it is right that you should be pointed out and set apart. (Your birth, you know ; you must not forget your birth.) You can again be shown to this gentleman's daughter, Harriet, and kept before her, as a living reminder of her own superiority and her gracious condescension. You can recover all these advantages, and many more of the same kind which I dare say start up in your memory while I speak, and which you lose in taking

406

refuge with me—you can recover them all, by telling these gentlemen how humbled and penitent you are, and by going back to them to be forgiven. What do you say, Harriet? Will you go?"

The girl who, under the influence of these words, had gradually risen in anger and heightened in colour, answered, raising her lustrous black eyes for the moment, and clenching her hand upon the folds it had been puckering up, "I'd die sooner!"

Miss Wade, still standing at her side holding her hand, looked quietly round and said with a smile, "Gentlemen! What do you do upon that?"

Poor Mr. Meagles's inexpressible consternation in hearing his motives and actions so perverted, had prevented him from interposing any word until now; but now he regained the power of speech.

"Tattycoram," said he, "for I'll call you by that name still, my good girl, conscious that I meant nothing but kindness when I gave it to you, and conscious that you know it——"

"I don't!" said she, looking up again, and almost rending herself with the same busy hand.

"No, not now, perhaps," said Mr. Meagles; "not with that lady's eyes so intent upon you, Tattycoram," she glanced at them for a moment, "and that power over you which we see she exercises; not now, perhaps, but at another time. Tattycoram, I'll not ask that lady whether she believes what she has said, even in the anger and ill blood in which I and my friend here equally know she has spoken, though she subdues herself with a determination that any one who has once seen her is not likely to forget. I'll not ask you, with your remembrance of my house and all belonging to it, whether you believe it. I'll only say that you have no profession to make to me or mine, and no forgiveness to entreat ; and that all in the world that I ask you to do, is, to count five-and-twenty, Tattycoram."

She looked at him for an instant, and then said frowningly, " I won't. Miss Wade, take me away, please."

The contention that raged within her had no softening in it now ; it was wholly between passionate defiance and stubborn defiance. Her rich colour, her quick blood, her rapid breath, were all setting themselves against the opportunity of retracing her steps. " I won't. I won't. I won't ! " she repeated in a low, thick voice. " I'd be torn to pieces first. I'd tear myself to pieces first ! "

Miss Wade, who had released her hold, laid her hand protectingly on the girl's neck for a moment, and then said, looking round with her former smile, and speaking exactly in her former tone, " Gentlemen ! What do you do upon that ? "

" Oh, Tattycoram, Tattycoram ! " cried Mr. Meagles, adjuring her besides with an earnest hand. " Hear that lady's voice, look at that lady's face, consider what is in that lady's heart, and think what a future lies before you. My child, whatever you may think, that lady's influence over you— astonishing to us, and I should hardly go too far in saying terrible to us, to see—is founded in passion fiercer than yours and temper more violent than yours. What can you two be together ? What can come of it ? "

" I am alone here, gentlemen," observed Miss Wade, with no change of voice or manner. " Say anything you will."

" Politeness must yield to this misguided girl, ma'am," said Mr. Meagles, " at her present pass ; though I hope not altogether to dismiss it, even with the injury you do her so strongly before me. Excuse me for reminding you in her hearing—I must say it—that you were a mystery to all of us, and had nothing in common with any of us, when she unfortunately fell in your way. I don't know what you are, but you don't hide, can't hide, what a dark spirit you have within you. If it should happen that you are a woman, who, from whatever cause, has a perverted delight in making a sister-woman as wretched as she is (I am old enough to have

Five-and-twenty

heard of such), I warn her against you, and I warn you against yourself."

"Gentlemen!" said Miss Wade, calmly. "When you have concluded—Mr. Clennam, perhaps you will induce your friend——"

"Not without another effort," said Mr. Meagles, stoutly. "Tattycoram, my poor dear girl, count five-and-twenty."

"Do not reject the hope, the certainty, this kind man offers you," said Clennam in a low emphatic voice. "Turn to the friends you have not forgotten. Think once more!"

"I won't! Miss Wade," said the girl, with her bosom swelling high, and speaking with her hand held to her throat, "take me away!"

"Tattycoram," said Mr. Meagles. "Once more yet! The only thing I ask of you in the world, my child! Count five-and-twenty!"

She put her hands tightly over her ears, confusedly tumbling down her bright black hair in the vehemence of the action, and turned her face resolutely to the wall. Miss Wade, who had watched her under this final appeal with that strange attentive smile, and that repressing hand upon her own bosom, with which she had watched her in her struggle at Marseilles, then put her arm about her waist as if she took possession of her for evermore.

And there was a visible triumph in her face when she turned it to dismiss the visitors.

"As it is the last time I shall have this honour," she said, "and as you have spoken of not knowing what I am, and also of the foundation of my influence here, you may now know that it is founded in a common cause. What your broken plaything is as to birth, I am. She has no name, I have no name. Her wrong is my wrong. I have nothing more to say to you."

This was addressed to Mr. Meagles, who sorrowfully went out. As Clennam followed, she said to him, with the same external composure and in the same level voice, but with a smile that is only seen on cruel faces : a very faint smile, lifting the nostril, scarcely touching the lips, and not breaking away gradually, but instantly dismissed when done with :

"I hope the wife of your dear friend, Mr. Gowan, may be happy in the contrast of her extraction to this girl's and mine, and in the high good fortune that awaits her."

CHAPTER XXVIII

NOBODY'S DISAPPEARANCE

Not resting satisfied with the endeavours he had made to recover his lost charge, Mr. Meagles addressed a letter of re- monstrance, breathing nothing but good-will, not only to her, but to Miss Wade too. No answer coming to these epistles, or to another written to the stubborn girl, by the hand of her late young mistress, which might have melted her if any- thing could (all three letters were returned weeks afterwards as having been refused at the house-door), he deputed Mrs. Meagles to make the experiment of a personal interview. That worthy lady being unable to obtain one, and being steadfastly denied admission, Mr. Meagles besought Arthur to essay once more what he could do. All that came of his compliance was, his discovery that the empty house was left in charge of the old woman, that Miss Wade was gone, that the waifs and strays of furniture were gone, and that the old woman would accept any number of half-crowns and thank the donor kindly, but had no information whatever to exchange for those coins, beyond constantly offering for perusal a memorandum relative to fixtures, which the house- agent's young man had left in the hall.

Unwilling, even under this discomfiture, to resign the ingrate and leave her hopeless, in case of her better disposi- tions obtaining the mastery over the darker side of her character, Mr. Meagles, for six successive days, published

411

a discreetly covert advertisement in the morning papers, to the effect that if a certain young person who had lately left home without reflection, would at any time apply at his address at Twickenham, everything would be as it had been before, and no reproaches need be apprehended. The unexpected consequences of this notification, suggested to the dismayed Mr. Meagles for the first time that some hundreds of young persons must be leaving their homes without reflection, every day; for, shoals of wrong young people came down to Twickenham, who, not finding themselves received with enthusiasm, generally demanded compensation by way of damages, in addition to coach-hire there and back. Nor were these the only uninvited clients whom the advertisement produced. The swarm of begging-letter writers, who would seem to be always watching eagerly for any hook, however small, to hang a letter upon, wrote to say that having seen the advertisement, they were induced to apply with confidence for various sums, ranging from ten shillings to fifty pounds: not because they knew anything about the young person, but because they felt that to part with those donations would greatly relieve the advertiser's mind. Several projectors, likewise, availed themselves of the same opportunity to correspond with Mr. Meagles; as, for example, to apprise him that their attention having been called to the advertisement by a friend, they begged to state that if they should ever hear anything of the young person, they would not fail to make it known to him immediately, and that in the meantime if he would oblige them with the funds necessary for bringing to perfection a certain entirely novel description of Pump, the happiest results would ensue to mankind.

Mr. Meagles and his family, under these combined discouragements, had begun reluctantly to give up Tattycoram as irrecoverable, when the new and active firm of Doyce and Clennam, in their private capacities, went down on a Saturday to stay at the cottage until Monday. The senior partner took the coach, and the junior partner took his walking-stick.

THE ROSES

A tranquil summer sunset shone upon him as he approached the end of his walk, and passed through the meadows by the river side. He had that sense of peace, and of being lightened of a weight of care, which country quiet awakens in the breasts of dwellers in towns. Everything within his view was lovely and placid. The rich foliage of the trees, the luxuriant grass diversified with wild flowers, the little green islands in the river, the beds of rushes, the water-lilies floating on the surface of the stream, the distant voices in boats borne musically towards him on the ripple of the water and the evening air, were all expressive of rest. In the occasional leap of a fish, or dip of an oar, or twittering of a bird not yet at roost, or distant barking of a dog, or lowing of a cow—in all such sounds, there was the prevailing breath of rest, which seemed to encompass him in every scent that sweetened the fragrant air. The long lines of red and gold in the sky, and the glorious track of the descending sun, were all divinely calm. Upon the purple tree-tops far away, and on the green height near at hand up which the shades were slowly creeping, there was an equal hush. Between the real landscape and its shadow in the water, there was no division; both were so untroubled and clear, and, while so fraught with solemn mystery of life and death, so hopefully reassuring to the gazer's soothed heart, because so tenderly and mercifully beautiful.

Clennam had stopped, not for the first time by many times, to look about him and suffer what he saw to sink into his soul, as the shadows, looked at, seemed to sink deeper and deeper into the water. He was slowly resuming his way, when he saw a figure in the path before him which he had, perhaps, already associated with the evening and its impressions.

Minnie was there, alone. She had some roses in her hand, and seemed to have stood still on seeing him, waiting for him. Her face was towards him, and she appeared to have been coming from the opposite direction. There was a flutter in her manner, which Clennam had never seen in it before, and as he came near her, it entered his mind all at once that she was there of a set purpose to speak to him.

She gave him her hand, and said, "You wonder to see me here by myself? But the evening is so lovely, I have strolled further than I meant at first. I thought it likely I might meet you, and that made me more confident. You always come this way, do you not?"

As Clennam said that it was his favourite way, he felt her hand falter on his arm, and saw the roses shake.

"Will you let me give you one, Mr. Clennam? I gathered them as I came out of the garden. Indeed, I almost gathered them for you, thinking it so likely I might meet you. Mr. Doyce arrived more than an hour ago, and told us you were walking down."

His own hand shook, as he accepted a rose or two from hers, and thanked her. They were now by an avenue of trees. Whether they turned into it on his movement or on hers matters little. He never knew how that was.

"It is very grave here," said Clennam, "but very pleasant at this hour. Passing along this deep shade, and out at that arch of light at the other end, we come upon the ferry and the cottage by the best approach, I think."

In her simple garden-hat and her light summer dress, with her rich brown hair naturally clustering about her, and her wonderful eyes raised to his for a moment, with a look in which regard for him and trustfulness in him were strikingly blended with a kind of timid sorrow for him, she was so beautiful, that it was well for his peace—or ill for his peace, he did not quite know which—that he had made that vigorous resolution he had so often thought about.

She broke a momentary silence by inquiring if he knew that papa had been thinking of another tour abroad? He said he had heard it mentioned. She broke another momentary silence by adding, with some hesitation, that papa had abandoned the idea.

At this, he thought directly, "they are to be married."

"Mr. Clennam," she said, hesitating more timidly yet, and speaking so low that he bent his head to hear her. "I should very much like to give you my confidence, if you would not mind having the goodness to receive it. I should have very much liked to have given it to you long ago, because—I felt that you were becoming so much our friend."

"How can I be otherwise than proud of it at any time! Pray give it to me. Pray trust me."

"I could never have been afraid of trusting you," she returned, raising her eyes frankly to his face. "I think I would have done so some time ago, if I had known how. But I scarcely know how, even now."

"Mr. Gowan," said Arthur Clennam, "has reason to be very happy. God bless his wife and him!"

She wept, as she tried to thank him. He reassured her, took her hand as it lay with the trembling roses in it on his arm, took the remaining roses from it, and put it to his lips. At that time, it seemed to him, he first finally resigned the dying hope that had flickered in nobody's heart so much to its pain and trouble; and from that time he became in his own eyes, as to any similar hope or prospect, a very much older man who had done with that part of life.

He put the roses in his breast and they walked on for a little while, slowly and silently, under the umbrageous trees. Then he asked her, in a voice of cheerful kindness, was there anything else that she would say to him as her friend and her father's friend, many years older than herself; was there any trust she would repose in him, any service she would ask of him, any little aid to her happiness that she could give him the lasting gratification of believing it was in his power to render?

She was going to answer, when she was so touched by some little hidden sorrow or sympathy—what could it have been?— that she said, bursting into tears again: "O, Mr. Clennam!

415

Good, generous, Mr. Clennam, pray tell me you do not blame me."

"I blame you?" said Clennam. "My dearest girl! I blame you? No!"

After clasping both her hands upon his arm, and looking confidentially up into his face, with some hurried words to the effect that she thanked him from her heart (as she did, if it be the source of earnestness), she gradually composed herself, with now and then a word of encouragement from him, as they walked on slowly and almost silently under the darkening trees.

"And, now, Minnie Gowan," at length said Clennam, smiling; "will you ask me nothing?"

"Oh! I have very much to ask of you."

"That's well! I hope so; I am not disappointed."

"You know how I am loved at home, and how I love home. You can hardly think it perhaps, dear Mr. Clennam," she spoke with great agitation, "seeing me going from it of my own free will and choice, but I do so dearly love it!"

"I am sure of that," said Clennam. "Can you suppose I doubt it?"

"No, no. But it is strange, even to me, that loving it so much and being so much beloved in it, I can bear to cast it away. It seems so neglectful of it, so unthankful."

"My dear girl," said Clennam, "it is in the natural progress and change of time. All homes are left so."

"Yes, I know; but all homes are not left with such a blank in them as there will be in mine when I am gone. Not that there is any scarcity of far better and more endearing and more accomplished girls than I am; not that I am much; but that they have made so much of me!"

Pet's affectionate heart was overcharged, and she sobbed while she pictured what would happen.

"I know what a change papa will feel at first, and I know that at first I cannot be to him anything like what I have been these many years. And it is then, Mr. Clennam, then more than at any time, that I beg and entreat you to remember him, and sometimes to keep him company when you can spare a little while ; and to tell him that you know I was fonder of him, when I left him, than I ever was in all my life. For there is nobody—he told me so himself when he talked to me this very day—there is nobody he likes so well as you, or trusts so much."

A clue to what had passed between the father and daughter dropped like a heavy stone into the well of Clennam's heart, and swelled the water to his eyes. He said, cheerily, but not quite so cheerily as he tried to say, that it should be done : that he gave her his faithful promise.

"If I do not speak of mama," said Pet, more moved by, and more pretty in, her innocent grief, than Clennam could trust himself even now to consider—for which reason he counted the trees between them and the fading light as they slowly diminished in number—" it is because mama will understand me better in this action, and will feel my loss in a different way, and will look forward in a different manner. But you know what a dear, devoted mother she is, and you will remember her, too ; will you not ? "

Let Minnie trust him, Clennam said, let Minnie trust him to do all she wished.

"And, dear Mr. Clennam," said Minnie, "because papa and one whom I need not name, do not fully appreciate and understand one another yet, as they will by-and-by ; and because it will be the duty, and the pride, and pleasure of my new life, to draw them to a better knowledge of one another, and to be a happiness to one another, and to be proud of one another, and to love one another, both loving me so dearly ; O, as you are a kind, true man ! when I am first separated from home (I am going a long distance away), try to reconcile papa to him a little more, and use your great influence to keep him before papa's mind, free from prejudice and in his real form. Will you do this for me, as you are a noble-hearted friend ? "

Poor Pet! Self-deceived, mistaken child! When were such changes ever made in men's natural relations to one another: when was such reconcilement of ingrain differences ever effected! It has been tried many times by other daughters, Minnie; it has never succeeded; nothing has ever come of it but failure.

So Clennam thought. So he did not say; it was too late. He bound himself to do all she asked, and she knew full well that he would do it.

They were now at the last tree in the avenue. She stopped, and withdrew her arm. Speaking to him with her eyes lifted up to his, and with the hand that had lately rested on his sleeve tremblingly touching one of the roses in his breast as an additional appeal to him, she said:

"Dear Mr. Clennam, in my happiness—for I am happy, though you have seen me crying—I cannot bear to leave any cloud between us. If you have anything to forgive me (not anything that I have wilfully done, but any trouble I may have caused you without meaning it, or having it in my power to help it), forgive me to-night out of your noble heart!"

He stooped to meet the guileless face that met his without shrinking. He kissed it, and answered, Heaven knew that he had nothing to forgive. As he stooped to meet the innocent face once again, she whispered "Good-bye!" and he repeated it. It was taking leave of all his old hopes—all nobody's old restless doubts. They came out of the avenue next moment, arm-in-arm as they had entered it; and the trees seemed to close up behind them in the darkness, like their own perspective of the past.

The voices of Mr. and Mrs. Meagles, and Doyce, were audible directly, speaking near the garden gate. Hearing Pet's name among them, Clennam called out, "She is here, with me." There was some little wondering and laughing until they came up; but as soon as they had all come together, it ceased, and Pet glided away.

Mr. Meagles, Doyce, and Clennam, without speaking, walked up and down on the brink of the river, in the light of the rising moon, for a few minutes; and then Doyce lingered behind, and went into the house. Mr. Meagles and Clennam walked up and down together for a few minutes more without speaking, until at length the former broke silence.

"Arthur," said he, using that familiar address for the first time in their communication, "do you remember my telling you, as we walked up and down one hot morning, looking over the harbour at Marseilles, that Pet's baby sister who was dead seemed to Mother and me to have grown as she had grown, and changed as she had changed?"

"Very well."

"You remembered my saying that our thoughts had never been able to separate those twin sisters, and that in our fancy whatever Pet was, the other was?"

"Yes, very well."

"Arthur," said Mr. Meagles, much subdued, "I carry that fancy further to-night. I feel to-night, my dear fellow, as if you had loved my dead child very tenderly, and had lost her when she was like what Pet is now."

"Thank you!" murmured Clennam, "thank you!" And pressed his hand.

"Will you come in?" said Mr. Meagles, presently.

"In a little while."

Mr. Meagles fell away, and he was left alone. When he had walked on the river's brink in the peaceful moonlight for some half-an-hour, he put his hand in his breast and tenderly took out the handful of roses. Perhaps he put them to his heart, perhaps he put them to his lips, but certainly he bent down on the shore, and gently launched them on the flowing river. Pale and unreal in the moonlight, the river floated them away.

The lights were bright within doors when he entered, and the faces on which they shone, his own face not excepted, were soon quietly cheerful. They talked of many subjects (his

419

partner never had had such a ready store to draw upon for the beguiling of the time), and so to bed, and to sleep. While the flowers, pale and unreal in the moonlight, floated away upon the river; and thus do greater things that once were in our breasts, and near our hearts, flow from us to the eternal seas.

CHAPTER XXIX

THE house in the city preserved its heavy dulness through all these transactions, and the invalid within it turned the same unvarying round of life. Morning, noon, and night, morning, noon, and night, each recurring with its accompanying monotony, always the same reluctant return of the same sequences of machinery, like a dragging piece of clockwork.

The wheeled chair had its associated remembrances and reveries, one may suppose, as every place that is made the station of a human being has. Pictures of demolished streets and altered houses, as they formerly were when the occupant of the chair was familiar with them; images of people as they too used to be, with little or no allowance made for the lapse of time since they were seen; of these, there must have been many in the long routine of gloomy days. To stop the clock of busy existence, at the hour when we were personally sequestered from it; to suppose mankind stricken motionless, when we were brought to a stand-still; to be unable to measure the changes beyond our view, by any larger standard than the shrunken one of our own uniform and contracted existence; is the infirmity of many invalids, and the mental unhealthiness of almost all recluses.

What scenes and actors the stern woman most reviewed, as she sat from season to season in her one dark room, none knew but herself. Mr. Flintwinch, with his wry presence brought to bear upon her daily like some eccentric mechanical force, would perhaps have screwed it out of her, if there had been less resistance in her; but she was too strong for him. So far as Mistress Affery was concerned, to regard her liege-lord and her disabled mistress with a face of blank wonder, to go about the house after dark with her apron over her head, always to listen for the strange noises and sometimes to hear them, and never to emerge from her ghostly, dreamy, sleep-waking state, was occupation enough for her.

There was a fair stroke of business doing, as Mistress Affery made out, for her husband had abundant occupation in his little office, and saw more people than had been used to come there for some years. This might easily be, the house having been long deserted; but he did receive letters, and comers, and keep books, and correspond. Moreover, he went about to other counting-houses, and to wharves, and docks, and to the Custom House, and to Garraway's Coffee House, and the Jerusalem Coffee House, and on 'Change; so that he was much in and out. He began, too, sometimes of an evening, when Mrs. Clennam expressed no particular wish for his society, to resort to a tavern in the neighbourhood to look at the shipping news and closing prices in the evening paper, and even to exchange small socialities with mercantile Sea Captains who frequented that establishment. At some period of every day, he and Mrs. Clennam held a council on matters of business; and it appeared to Affery, who was always groping about, listening and watching, that the two clever ones were making money.

The state of mind into which Mr. Flintwinch's dazed lady had fallen, had now begun to be so expressed in all her looks and actions, that she was held in very low account by the two clever ones, as a person, never of strong intellect, who was becoming foolish. Perhaps because her appearance was not of a commercial cast, or perhaps because it occurred to him that his having taken her to wife might expose his judgment to doubt in the minds of customers, Mr. Flintwinch

laid his commands upon her that she should hold her peace
on the subject of her conjugal relations, and should no longer
call him Jeremiah out of the domestic trio. Her frequent
forgetfulness of this admonition intensified her startled
manner, since Mr. Flintwinch's habit of avenging himself on
her remissness by making springs after her on the staircase,
and shaking her, occasioned her to be always nervously uncertain when she might be thus waylaid next.

Little Dorrit had finished a long day's work in Mrs.
Clennam's room, and was neatly gathering up her shreds and
odds and ends before going home. Mr. Pancks, whom Affery
had just shown in, was addressing an inquiry to Mrs. Clennam
on the subject of her health, coupled with the remark that,
"happening to find himself in that direction," he had looked
in to inquire, on behalf of his proprietor, how she found herself. Mrs. Clennam, with a deep contraction of her brows,
was looking at him.

"Mr. Casby knows," said she, "that I am not subject
to changes. The change that I await here is the great
change."

"Indeed, ma'am?" returned Mr. Pancks, with a wandering
eye towards the figure of the little seamstress on her knee
picking threads and fraying of her work from the carpet.
"You look nicely, ma'am."

"I bear what I have to bear," she answered. "Do you
what you have to do."

"Thank you, ma'am," said Mr. Pancks, "such is my
endeavour."

"You are often in this direction, are you not?" asked Mrs.
Clennam.

"Why, yes, ma'am," said Pancks, "rather so lately; I have
lately been round this way a good deal, owing to one thing
and another."

"Beg Mr. Casby and his daughter not to trouble themselves, by deputy, about me. When they wish to see me,
they know I am here to see them. They have no need to

trouble themselves to send. You have no need to trouble yourself to come."

"Not the least trouble, ma'am," said Mr. Pancks. "You really are looking uncommonly nicely, ma'am."

"Thank you. Good evening."

The dismissal, and its accompanying finger pointed straight at the door, was so curt and direct that Mr. Pancks did not see his way to prolonging his visit. He stirred up his hair with his sprightliest expression, glanced at the little figure again, said "Good evening, ma'am; don't come down, Mrs. Affery; I know the road to the door," and steamed out. Mrs. Clennam, her chin resting on her hand, followed him with attentive and darkly distrustful eyes; and Affery stood looking at her, as if she were spell-bound.

Slowly and thoughtfully, Mrs. Clennam's eyes turned from the door by which Pancks had gone out, to Little Dorrit, rising from the carpet. With her chin drooping more heavily on her hand, and her eyes vigilant and lowering, the sick woman sat looking at her until she attracted her attention. Little Dorrit coloured under such a gaze, and looked down. Mrs. Clennam still sat intent.

"Little Dorrit," she said, when she at last broke silence, " what do you know of that man?"

"I don't know anything of him, ma'am, except that I have seen him about, and that he has spoken to me."

"What has he said to you?"

"I don't understand what he has said, he is so strange. But nothing rough or disagreeable."

"Why does he come here to see you?"

"I don't know, ma'am," said Little Dorrit, with perfect frankness.

"You know that he does come here to see you?"

"I have fancied so," said Little Dorrit. "But why he should come here or anywhere, for that, ma'am, I can't think."

Mrs. Clennam cast her eyes towards the ground, and with

424

her strong, set face, as intent upon a subject in her mind as it had lately been upon the form that seemed to pass out of her view, sat absorbed. Some minutes elapsed before she came out of this thoughtfulness, and resumed her hard composure.

Little Dorrit in the meanwhile had been waiting to go, but afraid to disturb her by moving. She now ventured to leave the spot where she had been standing since she had risen, and to pass gently round by the wheeled chair. She stopped at its side to say " Good night, ma'am."

Mrs. Clennam put out her hand, and laid it on her arm. Little Dorrit, confused under the touch, stood faltering. Perhaps some momentary recollection of the story of the Princess may have been in her mind.

" Tell me, Little Dorrit," said Mrs. Clennam, " have you many friends now ? "

" Very few, ma'am. Besides you, only Miss Flora and—one more."

" Meaning," said Mrs. Clennam, with her unbent finger again pointing to the door, " that man ? "

" Oh no, ma'am ! "

" Some friend of his, perhaps ? "

" No, ma'am." Little Dorrit earnestly shook her head. " Oh no ! No one at all like him, or belonging to him."

" Well ! " said Mrs. Clennam, almost smiling. " It is no affair of mine. I ask, because I take an interest in you ; and because I believe I was your friend, when you had no other who could serve you. Is that so ? "

" Yes, ma'am ; indeed it is. I have been here many a time when, but for you and the work you gave me, we should have wanted everything."

" We," repeated Mrs. Clennam, looking towards the watch, once her dead husband's, which always lay upon her table. " Are there many of you ? "

" Only father and I, now. I mean, only father and I to keep regularly out of what we get."

" Have you undergone many privations ? You and your

father, and who else there may be of you?" asked Mrs. Clennam, speaking deliberately, and meditatively turning the watch over and over.

"Sometimes it has been rather hard to live," said Little Dorrit, in her soft voice, and timid uncomplaining way; "but I think not harder—as to that—than many people find it."

"That's well said!" Mrs. Clennam quickly returned. "That's the truth! You are a good, thoughtful girl. You are a grateful girl too, or I much mistake you."

"It is only natural to be that. There is no merit in being that," said Little Dorrit. "I am indeed."

Mrs. Clennam, with a gentleness of which the dreaming Affery had never dreamed her to be capable, drew down the face of her little seamstress, and kissed her on the forehead.

"Now go, Little Dorrit," said she, "or you will be late, poor child!"

In all the dreams Mistress Affery had been piling up since she first became devoted to the pursuit, she had dreamed nothing more astonishing than this. Her head ached with the idea that she would find the other clever one kissing Little Dorrit next, and then the two clever ones embracing each other and dissolving into tears of tenderness for all mankind. The idea quite stunned her, as she attended the light footsteps down the stairs, that the house door might be safely shut.

On opening it to let Little Dorrit out, she found Mr. Pancks, instead of having gone his way, as in any less wonderful place and among less wonderful phenomena he might have been reasonably expected to do, fluttering up and down the court outside the house. The moment he saw Little Dorrit, he passed her briskly, said with his finger to his nose (as Mistress Affery distinctly heard), "Pancks the gipsy, fortune-telling," and went away. "Lord save us, here's a gipsy and a fortune-teller in it now!" cried Mistress Affery. "What next!"

She stood at the open door, staggering herself with this

426

enigma, on a rainy, thundery evening. The clouds were flying fast, and the wind was coming up in gusts, banging some neighbouring shutters that had broken loose, twirling the rusty chimney-cowls and weather-cocks, and rushing round and round a confined adjacent churchyard as if it had a mind to blow the dead citizens out of their graves. The low thunder, muttering in all quarters of the sky at once, seemed to threaten vengeance for this attempted desecration, and to mutter, "Let them rest! Let them rest!"

Mistress Affery, whose fear of thunder and lightning was only to be equalled by her dread of the haunted house with a premature and preternatural darkness in it, stood undecided whether to go in or not, until the question was settled for her by the door blowing upon her in a violent gust of wind and shutting her out. "What's to be done now, what's to be done now!" cried Mistress Affery, wringing her hands in this last uneasy dream of all; "when she's all alone by herself inside, and can no more come down to open it than the churchyard dead themselves!"

In this dilemma, Mistress Affery, with her apron as a hood to keep the rain off, ran crying up and down the solitary paved enclosure several times. Why she should then stoop down and look in at the keyhole of the door, as if an eye would open it, it would be difficult to say; but it is none the less what most people would have done in the same situation, and it is what she did.

From this posture she started up suddenly, with a half scream, feeling something on her shoulder. It was the touch of a hand; of a man's hand.

The man was dressed like a traveller, in a foraging cap with fur about it, and a heap of cloak. He looked like a foreigner. He had a quantity of hair and moustache—jet black, except at the shaggy ends, where it had a tinge of red —and a high hook nose. He laughed at Mistress Affery's start and cry; and as he laughed, his moustache went up under his nose, and his nose came down over his moustache.

" What's the matter ? " he asked in plain English. " What are you frightened at ? ".

" At you," panted Affery.

" Me, madam ? "

" And the dismal evening, and—and everything," said Affery. " And here! The wind has been and blown the door to, and I can't get in."

" Hah ! " said the gentleman, who took that very coolly. " Indeed ! Do you know such a name as Clennam about here ? "

" Lord bless us, I should think I did, I should think I did ! " cried Affery, exasperated into a new wringing of hands by the inquiry.

" Where about here ? "

" Where ! " cried Affery, goaded into another inspection of the keyhole. " Where but here in this house ? And she's all alone in her room, and lost the use of her limbs and can't stir to help herself or me, and the t'other clever one's out, and Lord forgive me ! " cried Affery, driven into a frantic dance by these accumulated considerations, " if I ain't a-going headlong out of my mind ! "

Taking a warmer view of the matter now that it concerned himself, the gentleman stepped back to glance at the house, and his eye soon rested on the long narrow window of the little room near the hall-door.

" Where may the lady be who has lost the use of her limbs, madam ? " he inquired, with that peculiar smile which Mistress Affery could not choose but keep her eyes upon.

" Up there ! " said Affery. " Them two windows."

" Ha ! I am of a fair size, but could not have the honour of presenting myself in that room without a ladder. Now, madam, frankly—frankness is a part of my character—shall I open the door for you ? "

" Yes, bless you, sir, for a dear creetur, and do it at once," cried Affery, " for she may be a-calling to me at this very present minute, or may be setting herself afire and burning

428

herself to death, or there's no knowing what may be happening to her, and me a-going out of my mind at thinking of it!"

"Stay, my good madam!" He restrained her impatience with a smooth white hand. "Business-hours, I apprehend, are over for the day?"

"Yes, yes, yes," cried Affery. "Long ago."

"Let me make, then, a fair proposal. Fairness is a part of my character. I am just landed from the packet-boat, as you may see." He showed her that his cloak was very wet, and that his boots were saturated with water; she had previously observed that he was dishevelled and sallow, as if from a rough voyage, and so chilled that he could not keep his teeth from chattering. "I am just landed from the packet-boat, madam, and have been delayed by the weather: the infernal weather! In consequence of this, madam, some necessary business that I should otherwise have transacted here within the regular hours (necessary business because money-business), still remains to be done. Now, if you will fetch any authorised neighbouring somebody to do it, in return for my opening the door, I'll open the door. If this arrangement should be objectionable, I'll—— " and with the same smile he made a significant feint of backing away.

Mistress Affery, heartily glad to effect the proposed compromise, gave in her willing adhesion to it. The gentleman at once requested her to do him the favour of holding his cloak, took a short run at the narrow window, made a leap at the sill, clung his way up the bricks, and in a moment had his hand at the sash, raising it. His eyes looked so very sinister, as he put his leg into the room and glanced round at Mistress Affery, that she thought, with a sudden coldness, if he were to go straight up-stairs to murder the invalid, what could she do to prevent him?

Happily he had no such purpose; for he re-appeared, in a moment, at the house door. "Now, my dear madam," he said, as he took back his cloak and threw it on, "if you'll have the goodness to——what the Devil's that!"

The strangest of sounds. Evidently close at hand from the peculiar shock it communicated to the air, yet subdued as if it were far off. A tremble, a rumble, and a fall of some light dry matter.

"What the Devil is it?"

"I don't know what it is, but I've heard the like of it over and over again," said Affery, who had caught his arm.

He could hardly be a very brave man, even she thought in her dreamy start and fright, for his trembling lips had turned colourless. After listening a few moments, he made light of it.

"Bah! Nothing! Now, my dear madam, I think you spoke of some clever personage. Will you be so good as to confront me with that genius?" He held the door in his hand, as though he were quite ready to shut her out again if she failed.

"Don't you say anything about the door and me, then," whispered Affery.

"Not a word."

"And don't you stir from here, or speak if she calls, while I run round the corner."

"Madam, I am a statue."

Affery had so vivid a fear of his going stealthily up-stairs the moment her back was turned, that after hurrying out of sight, she returned to the gateway to peep at him. Seeing him still on the threshold, more out of the house than in it, as if he had no love for darkness and no desire to probe its mysteries, she flew into the next street, and sent a message into the tavern to Mr. Flintwinch, who came out directly. The two returning together—the lady in advance, and Mr. Flintwinch coming up briskly behind, animated with the hope of shaking her before she could get housed—saw the gentleman standing in the same place in the dark, and heard the strong voice of Mrs. Clennam calling from her room, "Who is it? What is it? Why does no one answer? Who *is* that, down there?"

CHAPTER XXX

When Mr. and Mrs. Flintwinch panted up to the door of the old house in the twilight, Jeremiah within a second of Affery, the stranger started back. "Death of my soul!" he exclaimed. "Why, how did you get here?"

Mr. Flintwinch, to whom these words were spoken, repaid the stranger's wonder in full. He gazed at him with blank astonishment; he looked over his own shoulder, as expecting to see some one he had not been aware of standing behind him; he gazed at the stranger again, speechlessly at a loss to know what he meant; he looked to his wife for explanation; receiving none, he pounced upon her, and shook her with such heartiness that he shook her cap off her head, saying between his teeth, with grim raillery, as he did it, "Affery, my woman, you must have a dose, my woman! This is some of your tricks! You have been dreaming again, mistress. What's it about? Who is it? What does it mean? Speak out or be choked! It's the only choice I'll give you."

Supposing Mistress Affery to have any power of election at the moment, her choice was decidedly to be choked; for she answered not a syllable to this adjuration, but, with her bare head wagging violently backwards and forwards, re-signed herself to her punishment. The stranger, however, picking up her cap with an air of gallantry, interposed.

431

"Permit me," said he, laying his hand on the shoulder of Jeremiah, who stopped, and released his victim. "Thank you. Excuse me. Husband and wife I know, from this playfulness. Haha! Always agreeable to see that relation playfully maintained. Listen! May I suggest that somebody upstairs, in the dark, is becoming energetically curious to know what is going on here?"

This reference to Mrs. Clennam's voice reminded Mr. Flintwinch to step into the hall and call up the staircase. "It's all right, I am here, Affery is coming with your light." Then he said to the latter flustered woman, who was putting her cap on, "Get out with you, and get up-stairs!" and then turned to the stranger, and said to him, "Now, sir, what might you please to want?"

"I am afraid," said the stranger, "I must be so troublesome as to propose a candle."

"True," assented Jeremiah. "I was going to do so. Please to stand where you are, while I get one."

The visitor was standing in the doorway, but turned a little into the gloom of the house as Mr. Flintwinch turned, and pursued him with his eyes into the little room, where he groped about for a phosphorus box. When he found it, it was damp, or otherwise out of order; and match after match that he struck into it lighted sufficiently to throw a dull glare about his groping face, and to sprinkle his hands with pale little spots of fire, but not sufficiently to light the candle. The stranger, taking advantage of this fitful illumination of his visage, looked intently and wonderingly at him. Jeremiah, when he at last lighted the candle, knew he had been doing this, by seeing the last shade of a lowering watchfulness clear away from his face, as it broke into the doubtful smile that was a large ingredient in its expression.

"Be so good," said Jeremiah, closing the house door, and taking a pretty sharp survey of the smiling visitor in his turn, "as to step into my counting-house.—It's all right, I tell you!" petulantly breaking off to answer the voice up-

Mr. Flintwinch has a mild Attack of Irritability

stairs, still unsatisfied, though Affery was there, speaking in persuasive tones. " Don't I tell you it's all right ? Preserve the woman, has she no reason at all in her ! "

" Timorous," remarked the stranger.

"Timorous ? " said Mr. Flintwinch, turning his head to retort, as he went before with the candle. " More courageous than ninety men in a hundred, sir, let me tell you."

" Though an invalid ? "

" Many years an invalid. Mrs. Clennam. The only one of that name left in the House now. My partner."

Saying something apologetically as he crossed the hall, to the effect that at that time of night they were not in the habit of receiving any one, and were always shut up, Mr. Flintwinch led the way into his own office, which presented a sufficiently business-like appearance. Here he put the light on his desk, and said to the stranger, with his wryest twist upon him, " Your commands."

" My name is Blandois."

" Blandois. I don't know it," said Jeremiah.

" I thought it possible," resumed the other, " that you might have been advised from Paris—— "

" We have had no advice from Paris, respecting anybody of the name of Blandois," said Jeremiah.

" No ? "

" No."

Jeremiah stood in his favourite attitude. The smiling Mr. Blandois, opening his cloak to get his hand to a breast-pocket, paused to say, with a laugh in his glittering eyes, which it occurred to Mr. Flintwinch were too near together :

" You are so like a friend of mine ! Not so identically the same as I supposed when I really did for the moment take you to be the same in the dusk—for which I ought to apologise ; permit me to do so ; a readiness to confess my errors is, I hope, a part of the frankness of my character— still, however, uncommonly like."

" Indeed ? " said Jeremiah, perversely. " But I have not

received any letter of advice from anywhere, respecting any-body of the name of Blandois."

"Just so," said the stranger.

"*Just* so," said Jeremiah.

Mr. Blandois, not at all put out by this omission on the part of the correspondents of the house of Clennam and Co., took his pocket-book from his breast-pocket, selected a letter from that receptacle, and handed it to Mr. Flintwinch. "No doubt you are well acquainted with the writing. Perhaps the letter speaks for itself, and requires no advice. You are a far more competent judge of such affairs than I am. It is my misfortune to be, not so much a man of business, as what the world calls (arbitrarily) a gentleman."

Mr. Flintwinch took the letter, and read, under date of Paris, "We have to present to you, on behalf of a highly esteemed correspondent of our Firm, M. Blandois, of this city," &c. &c. "Such facilities as he may require and such attentions as may lie in your power," &c. &c. Also have to add that if you will honour M. Blandois' drafts at sight to the extent of, say Fifty Pounds sterling (50*l.*)," &c. &c.

"Very good, sir," said Mr. Flintwinch. "Take a chair. To the extent of anything that our House can do—we are in a retired, old-fashioned, steady way of business, sir—we shall be happy to render you our best assistance. I observe, from the date of this, that we could not yet be advised of it. Probably you came over with the delayed mail that brings the advice."

"That I came over with the delayed mail, sir," returned Mr. Blandois, passing his white hand down his high-hooked nose, "I know to the cost of my head and stomach: the detestable and intolerable weather having racked them both. You see me in the plight in which I came out of the Packet within this half-hour. I ought to have been here hours ago, and then I should not have to apologise—permit me *to* apologise—for presenting myself so unseasonably, and frightening—no, by-the-bye, you said not frightening; permit me to apologise again—the esteemed lady, Mrs. Clennam, in her invalid chamber above stairs."

Swagger, and an air of authorised condescension, do so much, that Mr. Flintwinch had already begun to think this a highly gentlemanly personage. Not the less unyielding with him on that account, he scraped his chin and said, what could he have the honour of doing for Mr. Blandois to-night, out of business hours?

"Faith!" returned that gentleman, shrugging his cloaked shoulders, "I must change, and eat and drink, and be lodged somewhere. Have the kindness to advise me, a total stranger, where, and money is a matter of perfect indifference, until to-morrow. The nearer the place, the better. Next door, if that's all."

Mr. Flintwinch was slowly beginning, "For a gentleman of your habits, there is not in this immediate neighbourhood any hotel—" when Mr. Blandois took him up.

"So much for my habits! my dear sir," snapping his fingers. "A citizen of the world has no habits. That I am, in my poor way, a gentleman, by Heaven! I will not deny, but I have no unaccommodating prejudiced habits. A clean room, a hot dish for dinner, and a bottle of not absolutely poisonous wine, are all I want to-night. But I want that much, without the trouble of going one unnecessary inch to get it."

"There is," said Mr. Flintwinch, with more than his usual deliberation, as he met, for a moment, Mr. Blandois' shining eyes, which were restless; "there is a coffee-house and tavern close here, which, so far, I can recommend; but there's no style about it."

"I dispense with style!" said Mr. Blandois, waving his hand. "Do me the honour to show me the house, and introduce me there (if I am not too troublesome), and I shall be infinitely obliged."

Mr. Flintwinch, upon this, looked up his hat, and lighted Mr. Blandois across the hall again. As he put the candle on a bracket, where the dark old panelling almost served as an extinguisher for it, he bethought himself of going up to tell the invalid that he would not be absent five minutes.

"Oblige me," said the visitor, on his saying so, "by presenting my card of visit. Do me the favour to add, that I shall be happy to wait on Mrs. Clennam, to offer my personal compliments, and to apologise for having occasioned any agitation in this tranquil corner, if it should suit her convenience to endure the presence of a stranger for a few minutes, after he shall have changed his wet clothes and fortified himself with something to eat and drink."

Jeremiah made all despatch, and said, on his return, "She'll be glad to see you, sir; but, being conscious that her sick room has no attractions, wishes me to say that she won't hold you to your offer, in case you should think better of it."

"To think better of it," returned the gallant Blandois, "would be to slight a lady; to slight a lady would be to be deficient in chivalry towards the sex; and chivalry towards the sex is a part of my character!" Thus expressing himself, he threw the draggled skirt of his cloak over his shoulder, and accompanied Mr. Flintwinch to the tavern; taking up on the road a porter, who was waiting with his portmanteau on the outer side of the gateway.

The house was kept in a homely manner, and the condescension of Mr. Blandois was infinite. It seemed to fill to inconvenience the little bar in which the widow landlady and her two daughters received him; it was much too big for the narrow wainscoted room with a bagatelle-board in it, that was first proposed for his reception; it perfectly swamped the little private holiday sitting-room of the family, which was finally given up to him. Here, in dry clothes and scented linen, with sleeked hair, a great ring on each forefinger, and a massive show of watch-chain, Mr. Blandois waiting for his dinner, lolling on a window-seat with his knees drawn up, looked (for all the difference in the setting of the jewel) fearfully and wonderfully like a certain Monsieur

436

Rigaud who had once so waited for his breakfast, lying on the stone ledge of the iron grating of a cell in a villainous dungeon at Marseilles.

His greed at dinner, too, was closely in keeping with the greed of Monsieur Rigaud at breakfast. His avaricious manner of collecting all the eatables about him, and devouring some with his eyes, while devouring others with his jaws, was the same manner. His utter disregard of other people, as shown in his way of tossing the little womanly toys of furniture about, flinging favourite cushions under his boots for a softer rest, and crushing delicate coverings with his big body and his great black head, had the same brute selfishness at the bottom of it. The softly moving hands that were so busy among the dishes had the old wicked facility of the hands that had clung to the bars. And when he could eat no more, and sat sucking his delicate fingers one by one and wiping them on a cloth, there wanted nothing but the substitution of vine-leaves to finish the picture.

On this man, with his moustache going up and his nose coming down in that most evil of smiles, and with his surface eyes looking as if they belonged to his dyed hair, and had had their natural power of reflecting light stopped by some similar process, Nature, always true, and never working in vain, had set the mark, Beware! It was not her fault, if the warning were fruitless. She is never to blame in any such instance.

Mr. Blandois, having finished his repast and cleaned his fingers, took a cigar from his pocket, and, lying on the window-seat again, smoked it out at his leisure, occasionally apostrophising the smoke as it parted from his thin lips in a thin stream:

"Blandois, you shall turn the tables on society, my little child. Haha! Holy blue, you have begun well, Blandois! At a pinch, an excellent master in English or French; a man for the bosom of families! You have a quick perception, you have humour, you have ease, you have insinuating manners,

you have a good appearance; in effect, you are a gentleman!
A gentleman you shall live, my small boy, and a gentleman
you shall die. You shall win, however the game goes. They
shall all confess your merit, Blandois. You shall subdue
the society which has grievously wronged you, to your own
high spirit. Death of my soul! You are high-spirited by
right and by nature, my Blandois!"

To such soothing murmurs did this gentleman smoke out
his cigar and drink out his bottle of wine. Both being
finished, he shook himself into a sitting attitude; and with
the concluding serious apostrophe, "Hold then! Blandois,
you ingenious one, have all your wits about you!" arose and
went back to the house of Clennam and Co.

He was received at the door by Mistress Affery, who, under
instructions from her lord, had lighted up two candles in the
hall and a third on the staircase, and who conducted him to
Mrs. Clennam's room. Tea was prepared there, and such
little company arrangements had been made as usually
attended the reception of expected visitors. They were
slight on the greatest occasion, never extending beyond the
production of the China tea-service, and the covering of the
bed with a sober and sad drapery. For the rest, there was
the bier-like sofa with the block upon it, and the figure in
the widow's dress, as if attired for execution; the fire topped
by the mound of damped ashes; the grate with its second
little mound of ashes; the kettle and the smell of black dye;
all as they had been for fifteen years.

Mr. Flintwinch presented the gentleman commended to
the consideration of Clennam and Co. Mrs. Clennam, who
had the letter lying before her, bent her head and requested
him to sit. They looked very closely at one another. That
was but natural curiosity.

"I thank you, sir, for thinking of a disabled woman like
me. Few who come here on business have any remembrance
to bestow on one so removed from observation. It would be
idle to expect that they should have. Out of sight, out of

mind. When I am grateful for the exception, I don't complain of the rule."

Mr. Blandois, in his most gentlemanly manner, was afraid he had disturbed her by unhappily presenting himself at such an unconscionable time. For which he had already offered his best apologies to Mr. —— he begged pardon—but by name had not the distinguished honour—

"Mr. Flintwinch has been connected with the House many years."

Mr. Blandois was Mr. Flintwinch's most obedient humble servant. He entreated Mr. Flintwinch to receive the assurance of his profoundest consideration.

"My husband being dead," said Mrs. Clennam, "and my son preferring another pursuit, our old House has no other representative in these days than Mr. Flintwinch."

"What do you call yourself?" was the surly demand of that gentleman. "You have the head of two men."

"My sex disqualifies me," she proceeded with merely a slight turn of her eyes in Jeremiah's direction, "from taking a responsible part in the business, even if I had the ability; and therefore Mr. Flintwinch combines my interest with his own, and conducts it. It is not what it used to be; but some of our old friends (principally the writers of this letter) have the kindness not to forget us, and we retain the power of doing what they entrust to us as efficiently as we ever did. This however is not interesting to you. You are English, sir?"

"Faith, madam, no; I am neither born nor bred in England. In effect, I am of no country," said Mr. Blandois, stretching out his leg and smiting it: "I descend from half-a-dozen countries."

"You have been much about the world?"

"It is true. By Heaven, madam, I have been here and there and everywhere!"

"You have no ties, probably. Are not married?"

"Madam," said Mr. Blandois, with an ugly fall of his

eyebrows, " I adore your sex, but I am not married—never was."

Mistress Affery, who stood at the table near him, pouring out the tea, happened in her dreamy state to look at him as he said these words, and to fancy that she caught an expression in his eyes which attracted her own eyes so that she could not get them away. The effect of this fancy was, to keep her staring at him with the tea-pot in her hand, not only to her own great uneasiness, but manifestly to his, too ; and, through them both, to Mrs. Clennam's and Mr. Flintwinch's. Thus a few ghostly moments supervened, when they were all confusedly staring without knowing why.

" Affery," her mistress was the first to say, " what is the matter with you ? "

" I don't know," said Mistress Affery, with her disengaged left hand extended towards the visitor. " It ain't me. It's him ! "

" What does this good woman mean ? " cried Mr. Blandois, turning white, hot, and slowly rising with a look of such deadly wrath that it contrasted surprisingly with the slight force of his words. " How is it possible to understand this good creature ? "

" It's *not* possible," said Mr. Flintwinch, screwing himself rapidly in that direction. " She don't know what she means. She's an idiot, a wanderer in her mind. She shall have a dose, she shall have such a dose ! Get along with you, my woman," he added in her ear, " get along with you, while you know you're Affery, and before you're shaken to yeast."

Mistress Affery, sensible of the danger in which her identity stood, relinquished the tea-pot as her husband seized it, put her apron over her head, and in a twinkling vanished. The visitor gradually broke into a smile, and sat down again.

" You'll excuse her, Mr. Blandois," said Jeremiah, pouring out the tea himself ; " she's failing and breaking up ; that's what she's about. Do you take sugar, sir ? "

"Thank you; no tea for me.—Pardon my observing it, but that's a very remarkable watch!"

The tea-table was drawn up near the sofa, with a small interval between it and Mrs. Clennam's own particular table. Mr. Blandois in his gallantry had risen to hand that lady her tea (her dish of toast was already there), and it was in placing the cup conveniently within her reach that the watch, lying before her as it always did, attracted his attention. Mrs. Clennam looked suddenly up at him.

"May I be permitted? Thank you. A fine old-fashioned watch," he said, taking it in his hand. "Heavy for use, but massive and genuine. I have a partiality for everything genuine. Such as I am, I am genuine myself. Hah! A gentleman's watch with two cases in the old fashion. May I remove it from the outer case? Thank you. Aye? An old silk watch-lining, worked with beads! I have often seen these among old Dutch people and Belgians. Quaint things!"

"They are old-fashioned, too," said Mrs. Clennam.

"Very. But this is not so old as the watch, I think?"

"I think not."

"Extraordinary how they used to complicate these cyphers!" remarked Mr. Blandois, glancing up with his own smile again. "Now is this D. N. F.? It might be almost anything."

"Those are the letters."

Mr. Flintwinch, who had been observantly pausing all this time with a cup of tea in his hand, and his mouth open ready to swallow the contents, began to do so: always entirely filling his mouth before he emptied it at a gulp; and always deliberating again before he refilled it.

"D. N. F. was some tender lovely fascinating fair creature, I make no doubt," observed Mr. Blandois, as he snapped on the case again. "I adore her memory on the assumption. Unfortunately for my peace of mind, I adore but too readily. It may be a vice, it may be a virtue, but adoration of female beauty and merit constitutes three parts of my character, madam."

Mr. Flintwinch had by this time poured himself out another cup of tea, which he was swallowing in gulps as before, with his eyes directed to the invalid.

"You may be heart-free here, sir," she returned to Mr. Blandois. "Those letters are not intended, I believe, for the initials of any name."

"Of a motto, perhaps," said Mr. Blandois, casually.

"Of a sentence. They have always stood, I believe, for Do Not Forget!"

"And naturally," said Mr. Blandois, replacing the watch, and stepping backward to his former chair, "you do *not* forget."

Mr. Flintwinch, finishing his tea, not only took a longer gulp than he had taken yet, but made his succeeding pause under new circumstances: that is to say, with his head thrown back and his cup held still at his lips, while his eyes were still directed at the invalid. She had that force of face, and that concentrated air of collecting her firmness or obstinacy, which represented in her case what would have been gesture and action in another, as she replied with her deliberate strength of speech:

"No, sir, I do not forget. To lead a life as monotonous as mine has been during many years, is not the way to forget. To lead a life of self-correction is not the way to forget. To be sensible of having (as we all have, every one of us, all the children of Adam!) offences to expiate and peace to make, does not justify the desire to forget. Therefore I have long dismissed it, and I neither forget nor wish to forget."

Mr. Flintwinch, who had latterly been shaking the sediment at the bottom of his tea-cup, round and round, here gulped it down, and putting the cup in the tea-tray, as done with, turned his eyes upon Mr. Blandois, as if to ask him what he thought of that?

"All expressed, madam," said Mr. Blandois, with his smoothest bow and his white hand on his breast, "by the word 'naturally,' which I am proud to have had sufficient apprehension and appreciation (but without appreciation I could not be Blandois) to employ."

"Pardon me, sir," she returned, "if I doubt the likelihood of a gentleman of pleasure, and change, and politeness, accustomed to court and to be courted—"

"Oh madam! By Heaven!"

"—If I doubt the likelihood of such a character quite comprehending what belongs to mine in my circumstances. Not to obtrude doctrine upon you," she looked at the rigid pile of hard pale books before her, "(for you go your own way, and the consequences are on your own head), I will say this much: that I shape my course by pilots, strictly by proved and tried pilots, under whom I cannot be ship-wrecked—can not be—and that if I were unmindful of the admonition conveyed in those three letters, I should not be half as chastened as I am."

It was curious how she seized the occasion to argue with some invisible opponent. Perhaps with her own better sense, always turning upon herself and her own deception.

"If I forgot my ignorances in my life of health and freedom, I might complain of the life to which I am now condemned. I never do; I never have done. If I forgot that this scene, the Earth, is expressly meant to be a scene of gloom, and hardship, and dark trial, for the creatures who are made out of its dust, I might have some tenderness for its vanities. But I have no such tenderness. If I did not know that we are, every one, the subject (most justly the subject) of a wrath that must be satisfied, and against which mere actions are nothing, I might repine at the difference between me, imprisoned here, and the people who pass that gateway yonder. But I take it as a grace and favour to be elected to make the satisfaction I am making here, to know what I know for certain here, and to work out what I have

443

worked out here. My affliction might otherwise have had no meaning to me. Hence I would forget, and I do forget, nothing. Hence I am contented, and say it is better with me than with millions."

As she spoke these words, she put her hand upon the watch, and restored it to the precise spot on her little table which it always occupied. With her touch lingering upon it, she sat for some moments afterwards, looking at it steadily and half-defiantly.

Mr. Blandois, during this exposition, had been strictly attentive, keeping his eyes fastened on the lady, and thoughtfully stroking his moustache with his two hands. Mr. Flintwinch had been a little fidgety, and now struck in.

"There, there, there!" said he. "That is quite understood, Mrs. Clennam, and you have spoken piously and well. Mr. Blandois, I suspect, is not of a pious cast."

"On the contrary, sir!" that gentleman protested, snapping his fingers. "Your pardon! It's a part of my character. I am sensitive, ardent, conscientious, and imaginative. A sensitive, ardent, conscientious, and imaginative man, Mr. Flintwinch, must be that, or nothing!"

There was an inkling of suspicion in Mr. Flintwinch's face that he might be nothing, as he swaggered out of his chair (it was characteristic of this man, as it is of all men similarly marked, that whatever he did, he overdid, though it were sometimes by only a hair's-breadth), and approached to take his leave of Mrs. Clennam.

"With what will appear to you the egotism of a sick old woman, sir," she then said, "though really through your accidental allusion, I have been led away into the subject of myself and my infirmities. Being so considerate as to visit me, I hope you will be likewise so considerate as to overlook that. Don't compliment me, if you please." For he was evidently going to do it. "Mr. Flintwinch will be happy to render you any service, and I hope your stay in this city may prove agreeable."

Mr. Blandois thanked her, and kissed his hand several times. "This is an old room," he remarked, with a sudden sprightliness of manner, looking round when he got near the door. "I have been so interested that I have not observed it. But it's a genuine old room."

"It is a genuine old house," said Mrs. Clennam, with her frozen smile. "A place of no pretensions, but a piece of antiquity."

"Faith!" cried the visitor. "If Mr. Flintwinch would do me the favour to take me through the rooms on my way out, he could hardly oblige me more. An old house is a weakness with me. I have many weaknesses, but none greater. I love and study the picturesque in all its varieties. I have been called picturesque myself. It is no merit to be picturesque —I have greater merits, perhaps—but I may be, by an accident. Sympathy, sympathy!"

"I tell you beforehand, Mr. Blandois, that you'll find it very dingy, and very bare," said Jeremiah, taking up the candle. "It's not worth your looking at." But Mr. Blandois, smiting him in a friendly manner on the back, only laughed; so the said Blandois kissed his hand again to Mrs. Clennam, and they went out of the room together.

"You don't care to go up-stairs?" said Jeremiah, on the landing.

"On the contrary, Mr. Flintwinch; if not tiresome to you, I shall be ravished!"

Mr. Flintwinch, therefore, wormed himself up the staircase, and Mr. Blandois followed close. They ascended to the great garret bedroom, which Arthur had occupied on the night of his return. "There, Mr. Blandois!" said Jeremiah, showing it, "I hope you may think that worth coming so high, to see. I confess I don't."

Mr. Blandois being enraptured, they walked through other garrets and passages, and came down the staircase again. By this time, Mr. Flintwinch had remarked that he never found the visitor looking at any room, after throwing one quick glance around, but always found the visitor looking at him, Mr. Flintwinch. With this discovery in his thoughts, he turned about on the staircase for another experiment. He met his eyes directly; and on the instant of their fixing one another, the visitor, with that ugly play of nose and moustache, laughed (as he had done at every similar moment since they left Mrs. Clennam's chamber) a diabolically silent laugh.

As a much shorter man than the visitor, Mr. Flintwinch was at the physical disadvantage of being thus disagreeably leered at from a height; and as he went first down the staircase, and was usually a step or two lower than the other, this disadvantage was at the time increased. He postponed looking at Mr. Blandois again until this accidental inequality was removed by their having entered the late Mr. Clennam's room. But, then twisting himself suddenly round upon him, he found his look unchanged.

"A most admirable old house," smiled Mr. Blandois. "So mysterious. Do you never hear any haunted noises here?"

"Noises," returned Mr. Flintwinch. "No."

"Nor see any devils?"

"Not," said Mr. Flintwinch, grimly screwing himself at his questioner, "not any that introduce themselves under that name and in that capacity."

"Haha! A portrait here, I see."

(Still looking at Mr. Flintwinch, as if he were the portrait.)

"It's a portrait, sir, as you observe."

"May I ask the subject, Mr. Flintwinch?"

"Mr. Clennam, deceased. Her husband."

"Former owner of the remarkable watch, perhaps?" said the visitor.

Mr. Flintwinch, who had cast his eyes towards the portrait, twisted himself about again, and again found himself the subject of the same look and smile. "Yes, Mr. Blandois," he replied tartly. "It was his, and his uncle's before him, and Lord knows who before him; and that's all I can tell you of its pedigree."

"That's a strongly marked character, Mr. Flintwinch, our friend up-stairs."

"Yes, sir," said Jeremiah, twisting himself at the visitor again, as he did during the whole of this dialogue, like some screw-machine that fell short of its grip; for the other never changed, and he always felt obliged to retreat a little. "She is a remarkable woman. Great fortitude—great strength of mind."

"They must have been very happy," said Blandois.

"Who?" demanded Mr. Flintwinch, with another screw at him.

Mr. Blandois shook his right forefinger towards the sick room, and his left forefinger towards the portrait, and then putting his arms akimbo, and striding his legs wide apart, stood smiling down at Mr. Flintwinch with the advancing nose and the retreating moustache.

"As happy as most other married people, I suppose," returned Mr. Flintwinch. "I can't say. I don't know. There are secrets in all families."

"Secrets!" cried Mr. Blandois, quickly. "Say it again, my son."

"I say," replied Mr. Flintwinch, upon whom he had swelled himself so suddenly that Mr. Flintwinch found his face almost brushed by the dilated chest. "I say there are secrets in all families."

"So there are," cried the other, clapping him on both shoulders, and rolling him backwards and forwards. "Haha! you are right. So there are! Secrets! Holy Blue! There are the devil's own secrets in some families, Mr. Flintwinch!" With that, after clapping Mr. Flintwinch on both shoulders several times, as if, in a friendly and humorous way, he were rallying him on a joke he had made, he threw up his arms, threw back his head, hooked his hands together behind it, and burst into a roar of laughter. It was in vain for

447

Mr. Flintwinch to try another screw at him. He had his laugh out.

"But, favour me with the candle a moment," he said, when he had done. "Let us have a look at the husband of the remarkable lady. Hah!" holding up the light at arm's length. "A decided expression of face here too, though not of the same character. Looks as if he were saying—what is it—Do Not Forget—does he not, Mr. Flintwinch? By Heaven, sir, he does!"

As he returned him the candle, he looked at him once more; and then, leisurely strolling out with him into the hall, declared it to be a charming old house indeed, and one which had so greatly pleased him, that he would not have missed inspecting it for a hundred pounds.

Throughout these singular freedoms on the part of Mr. Blandois, which involved a general alteration in his demeanour, making it much coarser and rougher, much more violent and audacious, than before, Mr. Flintwinch, whose leathern face was not liable to many changes, preserved its immobility intact. Beyond now appearing, perhaps, to have been left hanging a trifle too long before that friendly operation of cutting down, he outwardly maintained an equable composure. They had brought their survey to a close in the little room at the side of the hall, and he stood there, eyeing Mr. Blandois.

"I am glad you are so well satisfied, sir," was his calm remark. "I didn't expect it. You seem to be quite in good spirits."

"In admirable spirits," returned Blandois. "Word of honour! never more refreshed in spirits. Do you ever have presentiments, Mr. Flintwinch?"

"I am not sure that I know what you mean by the term, sir," replied that gentleman.

"Say, in this case, Mr. Flintwinch, undefined anticipations of pleasure to come."

"I can't say I'm sensible of such a sensation at present,"

448

returned Mr. Flintwinch, with the utmost gravity. "If I should find it coming on, I'll mention it."

"Now I," said Blandois, "I, my son, have a presentiment to-night that we shall be well acquainted. Do you find it coming on?"

"N—no," returned Mr. Flintwinch, deliberately inquiring of himself. "I can't say I do."

"I have a strong presentiment that we shall become intimately acquainted.—You have no feeling of that sort yet?"

"Not yet," said Mr. Flintwinch.

Mr. Blandois, taking him by both shoulders again, rolled him about a little in his former merry way, then drew his arm through his own, and invited him to come off and drink a bottle of wine like a dear deep old dog as he was.

Without a moment's indecision, Mr. Flintwinch accepted the invitation, and they went out to the quarters where the traveller was lodged, through a heavy rain which had rattled on the windows, roofs, and pavements, ever since nightfall. The thunder and lightning had long ago passed over, but the rain was furious. On their arrival at Mr. Blandois' room, a bottle of port wine was ordered by that gallant gentleman; who (crushing every pretty thing he could collect, in the soft disposition of his dainty figure) coiled himself upon the window-seat, while Mr. Flintwinch took a chair opposite to him, with the table between them. Mr. Blandois proposed having the largest glasses in the house, to which Mr. Flintwinch assented. The bumpers filled, Mr. Blandois, with a roystering gaiety, clinked the top of his glass against the bottom of Mr. Flintwinch's, and the bottom of his glass against the top of Mr. Flintwinch's, and drank to the intimate acquaintance he foresaw. Mr. Flintwinch gravely pledged him, and drank all the wine he could get, and said nothing. As often as Mr. Blandois clinked glasses (which was at every replenishment), Mr. Flintwinch stolidly did his part of the clinking, and would have stolidly done his companion's part of the wine as well as his own: being, except in the article of palate, a mere cask.

In short, Mr. Blandois found that to pour port wine into the reticent Flintwinch was, not to open him but to shut him up. Moreover, he had the appearance of a perfect ability to go on all night; or, if occasion were, all next day, and all next night; whereas Mr. Blandois soon grew indistinctly conscious of swaggering too fiercely and boastfully. He therefore terminated the entertainment at the end of the third bottle.

"You will draw upon us to-morrow, sir," said Mr. Flintwinch, with a business-like face at parting.

"My Cabbage," returned the other, taking him by the collar with both hands. "I'll draw upon you; have no fear. Adieu, my Flintwinch. Receive at parting;" here he gave him a southern embrace, and kissed him soundly on both cheeks; "the word of a gentleman! By a thousand Thunders, you shall see me again!"

He did not present himself next day, though the letter of advice came duly to hand. Inquiring after him at night, Mr. Flintwinch found, with surprise, that he had paid his bill and gone back to the Continent by way of Calais. Nevertheless, Jeremiah scraped out of his cogitating face a lively conviction that Mr. Blandois would keep his word on this occasion, and would be seen again.

CHAPTER XXXI

SPIRIT

ANYBODY may pass, any day, in the thronged thoroughfares of the metropolis, some meagre, wrinkled, yellow old man who might be supposed to have dropped from the stars, if there were any star in the Heavens dull enough to be suspected of casting off so feeble a spark), creeping along with a scared air, as though bewildered and a little frightened by the noise and bustle. This old man is always a little old man. If he were ever a big old man, he has shrunk into a little old man; if he were always a little old man, he has dwindled into a less old man. His coat is of a colour, and cut, that never was the mode anywhere, at any period. Clearly, it was not made for him, or for any individual mortal. Some wholesale contractor measured Fate for five thousand coats of such quality, and Fate has lent this old coat to this old man, as one of a long unfinished line of many old men. It has always large dull metal buttons, similar to no other buttons. This old man wears a hat, a thumbed and napless and yet an obdurate hat, which has never adapted itself to the shape of his poor head. His coarse shirt and his coarse neckcloth have no more individuality than his coat and hat; they have the same character of not being his—of not being anybody's. Yet this old man wears these clothes with a certain unaccustomed air of being dressed and elaborated for the public ways; as though he passed the greater part of his time in a nightcap and gown. And so, like the country mouse in the second year of a famine, come to see the town mouse, and timidly threading his way to the town mouse's lodging through a city of cats, this old man passes in the streets.

Sometimes, on holidays towards the evening, he will be seen to walk with a slightly increased infirmity, and his old eyes will glimmer with a moist and marshy light. Then the little old man is drunk. A very small measure will overset him; he may be bowled off his unsteady legs with a half-pint pot. Some pitying acquaintance—chance acquaintance very often—has warmed up his weakness with a treat of beer, and the consequence will be the lapse of a longer time than usual before he shall pass again. For, the little old man is going home to the Workhouse; and on his good behaviour they do not let him out often (though methinks they might, considering the few years he has before him to go out in, under the sun); and on his bad behaviour they shut him up closer than ever, in a grove of two score and nineteen more old men, every one of whom smells of all the others.

Mrs. Plornish's father,—a poor little reedy piping old gentleman, like a worn-out bird; who had been in what he called the music-binding business, and met with great misfortunes, and who had seldom been able to make his way, or to see it or to pay it, or to do anything at all with it but find it no thoroughfare,—had retired of his own accord to the Workhouse which was appointed by law to be the Good Samaritan of his district (without the twopence, which was bad political economy), on the settlement of that execution which had carried Mr. Plornish to the Marshalsea College. Previous to his son-in-law's difficulties coming to that head, Old Nandy (he was always so called in his legal Retreat, but he was Old Mr. Nandy among the Bleeding Hearts) had sat in a corner of the Plornish fireside, and taken his bite and sup out of the Plornish cupboard. He still hoped to resume that domestic position, when Fortune should smile upon his son-in-law; in the meantime, while she preserved an immovable

452

countenance, he was and resolved to remain, one of these little old men in a grove of little old men with a community of flavour.

But, no poverty in him, and no coat on him that never was the mode, and no Old Men's Ward for his dwelling-place, could quench his daughter's admiration. Mrs. Plornish was as proud of her father's talents as she possibly could have been if they had made him Lord Chancellor. She had as firm a belief in the sweetness and propriety of his manners as she could possibly have had if he had been Lord Chamberlain. The poor little old man knew some pale and vapid little songs, long out of date, about Chloe, and Phyllis, and Strephon being wounded by the son of Venus; and for Mrs. Plornish there was no such music at the Opera, as the small internal flutterings and chirpings wherein he would discharge himself of these ditties, like a weak, little, broken barrel-organ, ground by a baby. On his "days out," those flecks of light in his flat vista of pollard old men, it was at once Mrs. Plornish's delight and sorrow, when he was strong with meat, and had taken his full halfpennyworth of porter, to say, "Sing us a song, Father." Then would he give them Chloe, and if he were in pretty good spirits, Phyllis also—Strephon he had hardly been up to, since he went into retirement—and then would Mrs. Plornish declare she did believe there never was such a singer as Father, and wipe her eyes.

If he had come from Court on these occasions, nay, if he had been the noble Refrigerator come home triumphantly from a foreign court to be presented and promoted on his last tremendous failure, Mrs. Plornish could not have handed him with greater elevation about Bleeding Heart Yard. "Here's Father," she would say, presenting him to a neighbour. "Father will soon be home with us for good, now. Ain't Father looking well? Father's a sweeter singer than ever; you'd never have forgotten it, if you'd aheard him just now." As to Mr. Plornish, he had married these articles of belief in marrying Mr. Nandy's daughter, and only wondered how it was that so gifted an old gentleman had not made a fortune. This he attributed, after much reflection, to his musical genius not having been scientifically developed in his youth. "For why," argued Mrs. Plornish, "why go a binding music when you've got it in yourself? That's where it is, I consider."

Old Nandy had a patron : one patron. He had a patron who in a certain sumptuous way—an apologetic way, as if he constantly took an admiring audience to witness that he really could not help being more free with this old fellow than they might have expected, on account of his simplicity and poverty—was mightily good to him. Old Nandy had been several times to the Marshalsea College, communicating with his son-in-law during his short durance there ; and had happily acquired to himself, and had by degrees and in course of time much improved the patronage of the Father of that national institution.

Mr. Dorrit was in the habit of receiving this old man, as if the old man held of him in vassalage under some feudal tenure. He made little treats and teas for him, as if he came in with his homage from some outlying district where the tenantry were in a primitive state. It seemed as if there were moments when he could by no means have sworn but that the old man was an ancient retainer of his, who had been meritoriously faithful. When he mentioned him, he spoke of him casually as his old pensioner. He had a wonderful satisfaction in seeing him, and in commenting on his decayed condition after he was gone. It appeared to him amazing that he could hold up his head at all, poor creature. "In the Workhouse, sir, the Union ; no privacy, no visitors, no station, no respect, no speciality. Most deplorable !"

It was Old Nandy's birthday, and they let him out. He said nothing about its being his birthday, or they might have kept him in ; for such old men should not be born. He passed along the streets as usual to Bleeding Heart Yard, and had his dinner with his daughter and son-in-law, and gave them Phyllis. He had hardly concluded, when Little Dorrit looked in to see how they all were.

"Miss Dorrit," said Mrs. Plornish. "Here's Father! Ain't he looking nice? And such voice he's in!"

Little Dorrit gave him her hand, and smilingly said she had not seen him this long time.

"No, they're rather hard on poor Father," said Mrs. Plornish with a lengthening face, "and don't let him have half as much change and fresh air as would benefit him. But he'll soon be home for good, now. Won't you, Father?"

"Yes, my dear, I hope so. In good time, please God."

Here Mr. Plornish delivered himself of an oration which he invariably made, word for word the same, on all such opportunities. It was couched in the following terms:

"John Edward Nandy. Sir. While there's a ounce of wittles or drink of any sort in this present roof, you're fully welcome to your share on it. While there's a handful of fire or a mouthful of bed in this present roof, you're fully welcome to your share on it. If so be as there should be nothing in this present roof, you should be as welcome to your share on it as if it was something much or little. And this is what I mean and so I don't deceive you, and consequently which is to stand out is to entreat of you, and therefore why not do it?"

To this lucid address, which Mr. Plornish always delivered as if he had composed it (as no doubt he had) with enormous labour, Mrs. Plornish's father pipingly replied:

"I thank you kindly, Thomas, and I know your intentions well, which is the same I thank you kindly for. But no, Thomas. Until such times as it's not to take it out of your children's mouths, which take it is, and call it by what name you will it do remain and equally deprive though may they come, and too soon they can not come, no Thomas, no!"

Mrs. Plornish, who had been turning her face a little away with a corner of her apron in her hand, brought herself back to the conversation again, by telling Miss Dorrit that Father was going over the water to pay his respects, unless she knew of any reason why it might not be agreeable.

Her answer was, "I am going straight home, and if he will come with me I shall be so glad to take care of him—so glad," said Little Dorrit, always thoughtful of the feelings of the weak, "of his company."

"There, Father!" cried Mrs. Plornish. "Ain't you a gay young man to be going for a walk along with Miss Dorrit! Let me tie your neck-handkerchief into a regular good bow, for you're a regular beau yourself, Father, if ever there was one."

With this filial joke his daughter smartened him up, and gave him a loving hug, and stood at the door with her weak child in her arms, and her strong child tumbling down the steps, looking after her little old father as he toddled away with his arm under Little Dorrit's.

They walked at a slow pace, and Little Dorrit took him by the Iron Bridge and sat him down there for a rest, and they looked over at the water and talked about the shipping, and the old man mentioned what he would do if he had a ship full of gold coming home to him (his plan was to take a noble lodging for the Plornishes and himself at a Tea Gardens, and live there all the rest of their lives, attended on by the waiter), and it was a special birthday for the old man. They were within five minutes of their destination, when, at the corner of her own street, they came upon Fanny in her new bonnet bound for the same port.

"Why, good gracious me, Amy!" cried that young lady starting. "You never mean it!"

"Mean what, Fanny dear?"

"Well! I could have believed a great deal of you," returned the young lady with burning indignation, "but I don't think even I could have believed this, of even you!"

"Fanny!" cried Little Dorrit, wounded and astonished.

"Oh! Don't Fanny me, you mean little thing, don't!

The idea of coming along the open streets, in the broad light of day, with a Pauper!" (firing off the last word as if it were a ball from an air-gun.)

"O Fanny!"

"I tell you not to Fanny me, for I'll not submit to it! I never knew such a thing. The way in which you are resolved and determined to disgrace us, on all occasions, is really infamous. You bad little thing!"

"Does it disgrace anybody," said Little Dorrit, very gently, "to take care of this poor old man?"

"Yes, Miss," returned her sister, "and you ought to know it does. And you do know it does, and you do it because you know it does. The principal pleasure of your life is to remind your family of their misfortunes. And the next great pleasure of your existence is to keep low company. But, however, if you have no sense of decency, I have. You'll please to allow me to go on the other side of the way, unmolested."

With this, she bounced across to the opposite pavement. The old disgrace, who had been deferentially bowing a pace or two off (for Little Dorrit had let his arm go in her wonder, when Fanny began), and who had been hustled and cursed by impatient passengers for stopping the way, rejoined his companion, rather giddy, and said, "I hope nothing's wrong with your honoured father, Miss? I hope there's nothing the matter in the honoured family?"

"No, no," returned Little Dorrit. "No, thank you. Give me your arm again, Mr. Nandy. We shall soon be there now."

So, she talked to him as she had talked before, and they came to the Lodge and found Mr. Chivery on the lock, and went in. Now, it happened that the Father of the Marshalsea was sauntering towards the Lodge at the moment when they were coming out of it, entering the Prison arm in arm. As the spectacle of their approach met his view, he displayed the utmost agitation and despondency of mind; and—altogether regardless of Old Nandy, who, making his reverence, stood with his hat in his hand, as he always did in that gracious presence—turned about, and hurried in at his own doorway and up the staircase.

Leaving the old unfortunate, whom in an evil hour she had taken under her protection, with a hurried promise to return to him directly, Little Dorrit hastened after her father, and, on the staircase, found Fanny following her, and flouncing up with offended dignity. The three came into the room almost together; and the Father sat down in his chair, buried his face in his hands, and uttered a groan.

"Of course," said Fanny. "Very proper. Poor, afflicted Pa! Now, I hope you believe me, Miss?"

"What is it, father?" cried Little Dorrit, bending over him. "Have I made you unhappy, father? Not I, I hope!"

"You hope, indeed! I dare say! Oh, you"—Fanny paused for a sufficiently strong expression —"you Common-minded little Amy! You complete prison-child!"

He stopped these angry reproaches with a wave of his hand, and sobbed out, raising his face, and shaking his melancholy head at his younger daughter, "Amy, I know that you are innocent in intention. But you have cut me to the soul."

"Innocent in intention!" the implacable Fanny struck in. "Stuff in intention! Low in intention! Lowering of the family in intention!"

"Father!" cried Little Dorrit, pale and trembling. "I am very sorry. Pray forgive me. Tell me how it is, that I may not do it again!"

"How it is, you prevaricating little piece of goods!" cried Fanny. "You know how it is. I have told you already, so don't fly in the face of Providence by attempting to deny it!"

"Hush! Amy," said the father, passing his pocket-handkerchief several times across his face, and then grasping it convulsively in the hand that dropped across his knee, "I have done what I could to keep you select here; I have done what I could to retain you a position here. I may have succeeded; I may not. You may know it; you may not. I give no opinion. I have endured everything here but humiliation. That I have happily been spared—until this day."

Here his convulsive grasp unclosed itself, and he put his pocket-handkerchief to his eyes again. Little Dorrit, on the ground beside him, with her imploring hand upon his arm, watched him remorsefully. Coming out of his fit of grief, he clenched his pocket-handkerchief once more.

"Humiliation I have happily been spared until this day. Through all my troubles there has been that—Spirit in myself, and that—that submission to it, if I may use the term, in those about me, which has spared me—ha—humiliation. But this day, this minute, I have keenly felt it."

"Of course! How could it be otherwise?" exclaimed the irrepressible Fanny. "Careering and prancing about with a Pauper!" (air-gun again.)

"But, dear father," cried Little Dorrit, "I don't justify myself for having wounded your dear heart—no! Heaven knows I don't!" She clasped her hands in quite an agony of distress. "I do nothing but beg and pray you to be comforted and overlook it. But if I had not known that you were kind to the old man yourself, and took much notice of him, and were always glad to see him, I would not have come here with him, father, I would not, indeed. What I have been so unhappy as to do, I have done in mistake. I would not wilfully bring a tear to your eyes, dear love!" said Little Dorrit, her heart well-nigh broken, "for anything the world could give me, or anything it could take away."

Fanny, with a partly angry and partly repentant sob, began to cry herself, and to say—as this young lady always said when she was half in a passion and half out of it, half spiteful with herself and half spiteful with everybody else—that she wished she was dead.

The Father of the Marshalsea in the meantime took his younger daughter to his breast, and patted her head.

"There, there! Say no more, Amy, say no more, my child, I will forget it as soon as I can. I," with hysterical cheerfulness, "I—shall soon be able to dismiss it. It is per-fectly true, my dear, that I *am* always glad to see my old pensioner—as such, as such—and that I do—ha—extend as much protection and kindness to the—hum—the bruised reed —I trust I may so call him without impropriety—as in my circumstances, I can. It is quite true that this is the case, my dear child. At the same time, I preserve in doing this, if I may—ha—if I may use the expression—Spirit. Becoming Spirit. And there are some things which are," he stopped to sob, "irreconcilable with that, and wound that—wound it deeply. It is not that I have seen my good Amy attentive, and—ha—condescending to my old pensioner—it is not *that* that hurts me. It is, if I am to close the painful subject by being explicit, that I have seen my child, my own child, my own daughter, coming into this College out of the public streets—smiling! smiling!—arm in arm with—O my God, a livery!"

This reference to the coat of no cut and no time, the un-fortunate gentleman gasped forth, in a scarcely audible voice, and with his clenched pocket-handkerchief raised in the air. His excited feelings might have found some further painful utterance, but for a knock at the door, which had been already twice repeated, and to which Fanny (still wishing herself dead, and indeed now going so far as to add, buried) cried "Come in!"

"Ah, Young John!" said the Father, in an altered and calmed voice. "What is it, Young John?"

"A letter for you, sir, being left in the Lodge just this minute, and a message with it, I thought, happening to be there myself, sir, I would bring it to your room." The speaker's attention was much distracted by the piteous spectacle of Little Dorrit at her father's feet, with her head turned away.

"Indeed, John? Thank you."

"The letter is from Mr. Clennam, sir—it's the answer—and the message was, sir, that Mr. Clennam also sent his compliments, and word that he would do himself the pleasure of calling this afternoon, hoping to see you, and likewise," attention more distracted than before, "Miss Amy."

"Oh!" As the Father glanced into the letter (there was a bank-note in it), he reddened a little, and patted Amy on the head afresh. "Thank you, Young John. Quite right. Much obliged to you for your attention. No one waiting?"

"No, sir, no one waiting."

"Thank you, John. How is your mother, Young John?"

"Thank you, sir, she's not quite as well as we could wish —in fact, we none of us are, except father—but she's pretty well, sir."

"Say we sent our remembrances, will you? Say, kind re-membrances, if you please, Young John."

"Thank you, sir, I will." And Mr. Chivery, junior, went his way, having spontaneously composed on the spot an entirely new epitaph for himself, to the effect that Here lay the body of John Chivery, Who, Having at such a date, Beheld the idol of his life, In grief and tears, And feeling unable to bear the harrowing spectacle, Immediately repaired to the abode of his inconsolable parents, And terminated his existence, by his own rash act.

"There, there, Amy!" said the Father, when Young John had closed the door, "let us say no more about it." The last few minutes had improved his spirits remarkably, and he was quite lightsome. "Where is my old pensioner all this while? We must not leave him by himself any longer, or he will begin to suppose he is not welcome, and that would pain me. Will you fetch him, my child, or shall I?"

"If you wouldn't mind, father," said Little Dorrit, trying to bring her sobbing to a close.

"Certainly I will go, my dear. I forgot; your eyes are rather. There! Cheer up, Amy. Don't be uneasy about me. I am quite myself again, my love, quite myself. Go to your room, Amy, and make yourself look comfortable and pleasant to receive Mr. Clennam."

"I would rather stay in my own room, father," returned Little Dorrit, finding it more difficult than before to regain her composure. "I would far rather not see Mr. Clennam."

"Oh, fie, fie, my dear, that's folly. Mr. Clennam is a very gentlemanly man—very gentlemanly. A little reserved at times; but I will say extremely gentlemanly. I couldn't think of your not being here to receive Mr. Clennam, my dear, especially this afternoon. So go and freshen yourself up, Amy; go and freshen yourself up, like a good girl."

Thus directed, Little Dorrit dutifully rose and obeyed: only pausing for a moment as she went out of the room, to give her sister a kiss of reconciliation. Upon which, that young lady, feeling much harassed in her mind, and having for the time worn out the wish with which she generally relieved it, conceived and executed the brilliant idea of wishing Old Nandy dead, rather than that he should come bothering there like a disgusting, tiresome, wicked wretch, and making mischief between two sisters.

The Father of the Marshalsea, even humming a tune, and wearing his black velvet cap a little on one side, so much improved were his spirits, went down into the yard, and found his old pensioner standing hat in hand just within the gate, as he had stood all this time. "Come, Nandy!" said he, with great suavity. "Come up-stairs, Nandy; you know the way; why don't you come up-stairs?" He went the length, on this occasion, of giving him his hand, and saying, "How are you, Nandy? Are you pretty well?" To which that vocalist returned, "I thank you, honoured sir, I am all the better for seeing your honour." As they went along the yard, the Father of the Marshalsea presented him to a Collegian of recent date. "An old acquaintance of mine, sir, an old pensioner." And then said, "Be covered, my good Nandy; put your hat on," with great consideration.

His patronage did not stop here; for he charged Maggy to get the tea ready, and instructed her to buy certain tea-cakes, fresh butter, eggs, cold ham, and shrimps: to purchase which collation, he gave her a bank-note for ten pounds, laying strict injunctions on her to be careful of the change. These preparations were in an advanced stage of progress, and his daughter Amy had come back with her work, when Clennam presented himself. Whom he most graciously received, and besought to join their meal.

"Amy, my love, you know Mr. Clennam even better than I have the happiness of doing. Fanny, my dear, you are acquainted with Mr. Clennam." Fanny acknowledged him haughtily; the position she tacitly took up in all such cases being that there was a vast conspiracy to insult the family by not understanding it, or sufficiently deferring to it, and here was one of the conspirators. "This, Mr. Clennam, you must know, is an old pensioner of mine, Old Nandy, a very faithful old man." (He always spoke of him as an object of great antiquity, but he was two or three years younger than himself.) "Let me see. You know Plornish, I think? I think my daughter Amy has mentioned to me that you know poor Plornish?"

"O yes!" said Arthur Clennam.

"Well, sir, this is Mrs. Plornish's father."

"Indeed? I am glad to see him."

"You would be more glad if you knew his many good qualities, Mr. Clennam."

"I hope I shall come to know them, through knowing him," said Arthur, secretly pitying the bowed and submissive figure.

"It is a holiday with him, and he comes to see his old friends who are always glad to see him," observed the Father of the Marshalsea. Then he added behind his hand, ("Union, poor old fellow. Out for the day.")

By this time Maggy, quietly assisted by her Little Mother, had spread the board, and the repast was ready. It being hot weather and the prison very close, the window was as wide open as it could be pushed. "If Maggy will spread that newspaper on the window-sill, my dear," remarked the Father complacently and in a half whisper to Little Dorrit, "my old pensioner can have his tea there, while we are having ours."

So, with a gulf between him and the good company of about a foot in width, standard measure, Mrs. Plornish's father was handsomely regaled. Clennam had never seen anything like his magnanimous protection by that other Father, he of the Marshalsea; and was lost in the contemplation of its many wonders.

The most striking of these was perhaps the relishing manner in which he remarked on the pensioner's infirmities and failings. As if he were a gracious Keeper, making a running commentary on the decline of the harmless animal he exhibited.

"Not ready for more ham, yet, Nandy? Why, how slow you are! (His last teeth," he explained to the company, "are going, poor old boy.")

At another time, he said, "No shrimps, Nandy?" and on his not instantly replying, observed, ("His hearing is becoming very defective. He'll be deaf directly.")

At another time, he asked him, "Do you walk much, Nandy, about the yard within the walls of that place of yours?"

"No, sir; no. I haven't any great liking for that."

"No, to be sure," he assented. "Very natural." Then he privately informed the circle ("Legs going.")

Once, he asked the pensioner, in that general clemency which asked him anything to keep him afloat, how old his younger grandchild was?

"John Edward," said the pensioner, slowly laying down his knife and fork to consider. "How old, sir? Let me think now."

The Father of the Marshalsea tapped his forehead. ("Memory weak.")

"John Edward, sir? Well, I really forget. I couldn't say at this minute, sir, whether it's two and two months, or whether it's two and five months. It's one or the other."

"Don't distress yourself by worrying your mind about it,"

The Pensioner Entertainment

he returned, with infinite forbearance. ("Faculties evidently decaying—old man rusts in the life he leads!")

The more of these discoveries that he persuaded himself he made in the pensioner, the better he appeared to like him; and when he got out of his chair after tea, to bid the pensioner good-bye, on his intimating that he feared, honoured sir, his time was running out, he made himself look as erect and strong as possible.

"We don't call this a shilling, Nandy, you know," he said, putting one in his hand. "We call it tobacco."

"Honoured sir, I thank you. It shall buy tobacco. My thanks and duty to Miss Amy and Miss Fanny. I wish you good night, Mr. Clennam."

"And mind you don't forget us, you know, Nandy," said the Father. "You must come again, mind, whenever you have an afternoon. "You must not come out without seeing us, or we shall be jealous. Good night, Nandy. Be very careful how you descend the stairs, Nandy; they are rather uneven and worn." With that he stood on the landing, watching the old man down : and when he came into the room again, said, with a solemn satisfaction on him, "A melancholy sight that, Mr. Clennam, though one has the consolation of knowing that he doesn't feel it himself. The poor old fellow is a dismal wreck. Spirit broken and gone—pulverised—crushed out of him, sir, completely!"

As Clennam had a purpose in remaining, he said what he could responsive to these sentiments, and stood at the window with their enunciator, while Maggy and her Little Mother washed the tea-service and cleared it away. He noticed that his companion stood at the window with the air of an affable and accessible Sovereign, and that, when any of his people in the yard below looked up, his recognition of their salutes just stopped short of a blessing.

When little Dorrit had her work on the table, and Maggy hers on the bedstead, Fanny fell to tying her bonnet as a preliminary to her departure. Arthur, still having his purpose, still remained. At this time the door opened, without any notice, and Mr. Tip came in. He kissed Amy as she started up to meet him, nodded to Fanny, nodded to his father, gloomed on the visitor without further recognition, and sat down.

"Tip, dear," said Little Dorrit, mildly, shocked by this, "don't you see— "

"Yes, I see, Amy. If you refer to the presence of any visitor you have here—I say, if you refer to that," answered Tip, jerking his head with emphasis towards his shoulder nearest Clennam, "I see!"

"Is that all you say?"

"That's all I say. And I suppose," added the lofty young man, after a moment's pause, "the visitor will understand me, when I say that's all I say. In short, I suppose the visitor will understand, that he hasn't used me like a gentleman."

"I do not understand that," observed the obnoxious personage referred to, with tranquillity.

"No? Why, then, to make it clearer to you, sir, I beg to let you know, that when I address what I call a properly-worded appeal, and an urgent appeal, and a delicate appeal, to an individual, for a small temporary accommodation, easily within his power—easily within his power mind!—and when that individual writes back word to me that he begs to be excused, I consider that he doesn't treat me like a gentleman."

The Father of the Marshalsea, who had surveyed his son in silence, no sooner heard this sentiment, than he began in an angry voice:—

"How dare you— " But his son stopped him.

"Now, don't ask me how I dare, father, because that's bosh. As to the fact of the line of conduct I choose to adopt towards the individual present, you ought to be proud of my showing a proper spirit."

"I should think so!" cried Fanny.

"A proper spirit?" said the Father. "Yes, a proper

spirit; a becoming spirit. Is it come to this that my son teaches me—*me*—spirit!"

"Now, don't let us bother about it, father, or have any row on the subject. I have fully made up my mind that the individual present has not treated me like a gentleman. And there's an end of it."

"But there is not an end of it, sir," returned the Father. "But there shall not be an end of it. You have made up your mind? You have made up your mind?"

"Yes, *I* have. What's the good of keeping on like that?"

"Because," returned the Father, in a great heat, "you had no right to make up your mind to what is monstrous, to what is—ha—immoral, to what is—hum—parricidal. No, Mr. Clennam, I beg, sir. Don't ask me to desist; there is a—hum—a general principle involved here, which rises even above considerations of—ha—hospitality. I object to' the assertion made by my son. I—ha—I personally repel it."

"Why, what is it to you, father?" returned the son, over his shoulder.

"What is it to me, sir? I have a—hum—a spirit, sir, that will not endure it. I," he took out his pocket-handkerchief again and dabbed his face. "I am outraged and insulted by it. Let me suppose the case that I myself may at a certain time—ha—or times, have made a—hum—an appeal, and a properly-worded appeal, and a delicate appeal, and an urgent appeal, to some individual for a small temporary accommodation. Let me suppose that that accommodation could have been easily extended, and was not extended, and that that individual informed me that he begged to be excused. Am I to be told by my own son, that I therefore received treatment not due to a gentleman, and that I—ha—I submitted to it?"

His daughter Amy gently tried to calm him, but he would not on any account be calmed. He said his spirit was up, and wouldn't endure this.

Was he to be told that, he wished to know again, by his

own son on his own hearth, to his own face? Was that humiliation to be put upon him by his own blood?

"You are putting it on yourself, father, and getting into all this injury of your own accord!" said the young gentleman morosely. "What I have made up my mind about has nothing to do with you. What I said had nothing to do with you. Why need you go trying on other people's hats?"

"I reply it has everything to do with me," returned the Father. "I point out to you, sir, with indignation, that— hum—the—ha—delicacy and peculiarity of your father's position should strike you dumb, sir, if nothing else should, in laying down such—ha—such unnatural principles. Besides; if you are not filial, sir, if you discard that duty, you are at least—hum—not a Christian? Are you—ha—an Atheist? And is it Christian, let me ask you, to stigmatise and denounce an individual for begging to be excused this time, when the same individual may—ha—respond with the required accommodation next time? Is it the part of a Christian not to— hum—not to try him again?" He had worked himself into quite a religious glow and fervour.

"I see precious well," said Mr. Tip, rising, "that I shall get no sensible or fair argument here to-night, and so the best thing I can do is to cut. Good night, Amy. Don't be vexed. I am very sorry it happens here, and you here, upon my soul I am; but I can't altogether part with my spirit, even for your sake, old girl."

With those words he put on his hat and went out, accompanied by Miss Fanny; who did not consider it spirited on her part to take leave of Clennam with any less opposing demonstration than a stare, importing that she had always known him for one of the large body of conspirators.

When they were gone, the Father of the Marshalsea was at first inclined to sink into despondency again, and would have done so, but that a gentleman opportunely came up within a minute or two to attend him to the Snuggery. It was the gentleman Clennam had seen on the night of his own

468

accidental detention there, who had that impalpable grievance about the misappropriated Fund on which the Marshal was supposed to batten. He presented himself as a deputation to escort the Father to the Chair; it being an occasion on which he had promised to preside over the assembled Collegians in the enjoyment of a little Harmony.

"Such, you see, Mr. Clennam," said the Father, "are the incongruities of my position here. But a public duty! No man, I am sure, would more readily recognise a public duty than yourself."

Clennam besought him not to delay a moment.

"Amy, my dear, if you can persuade Mr. Clennam to stay longer, I can leave the honours of our poor apology for an establishment with confidence in your hands, and perhaps you may do something towards erasing from Mr. Clennam's mind the—ha—untoward and unpleasant circumstance which has occurred since tea-time."

Clennam assured him that it had made no impression on his mind, and therefore required no erasure.

"My dear sir," said the Father, with a removal of his black cap and a grasp of Clennam's hand, combining to express the safe receipt of his note and enclosure that afternoon, "Heaven ever bless you!"

So, at last, Clennam's purpose in remaining was attained, and he could speak to Little Dorrit with nobody by. Maggy counted as nobody, and she was by.

CHAPTER XXXII

MAGGY sat at her work in her great white cap, with its quantity of opaque frilling hiding what profile she had (she had none to spare), and her serviceable eye brought to bear upon her occupation, on the window side of the room. What with her flapping cap, and what with her unserviceable eye, she was quite partitioned off from her Little Mother, whose seat was opposite the window. The tread and shuffle of feet on the pavement of the yard had much diminished since the taking of the Chair; the tide of Collegians having set strongly in the direction of Harmony. Some few who had no music in their souls, or no money in their pockets, dawdled about; and the old spectacle of the visitor-wife and the depressed unseasoned prisoner still lingered in corners, as broken cobwebs and such unsightly discomforts draggle in corners of other places. It was the quietest time the College knew, saving the night hours when the Collegians took the benefit of the act of sleep. The occasional rattle of applause upon the tables of the Snuggery, denoted the successful termination of a morsel of Harmony; or the responsive acceptance, by the united children, of some toast or sentiment offered to them by their Father. Occasionally, a vocal strain more sonorous than the generality informed the listener that some boastful bass was in blue water, or in the hunting field, or with the

470

reindeer, or on the mountain, or among the heather; but the Marshal of the Marshalsea knew better, and had got him hard and fast.

As Arthur Clennam moved to sit down by the side of Little Dorrit, she trembled so that she had much ado to hold her needle. Clennam gently put his hand upon her work, and said " Dear Little Dorrit, let me lay it down."

She yielded it to him, and he put it aside. Her hands were then nervously clasping together, but he took one of them.

" How seldom I have seen you lately, Little Dorrit!"

" I have been busy, sir."

" But I heard only to-day," said Clennam, " by mere accident, of your having been with those good people close by me. Why not come to me, then?"

" I—I don't know. Or rather, I thought you might be busy too. You generally are now, are you not?"

He saw her trembling little form and her downcast face, and the eyes that drooped the moment they were raised to his—he saw them almost with as much concern as tenderness.

" My child, your manner is so changed!"

The trembling was now quite beyond her control. Softly withdrawing her hand, and laying it in her other hand, she sat before him with her head bent and her whole form trembling.

" My own Little Dorrit," said Clennam, compassionately.

She burst into tears. Maggy looked round of a sudden, and stared for at least a minute; but did not interpose. Clennam waited some little while before he spoke again.

" I cannot bear," he said then, " to see you weep; but I hope this is a relief to an overcharged heart."

" Yes it is, sir. Nothing but that."

" Well, well! I feared you would think too much of what passed here just now. It is of no moment; not the least. I am only unfortunate to have come in the way. Let it

471

go by with these tears. It is not worth one of them. One of them? Such an idle thing should be repeated, with my glad consent, fifty times a day, to save you a moment's heart-ache, Little Dorrit."

She had taken courage now, and answered, far more in her usual manner, " You are so good! But even if there was nothing else in it to be sorry for and ashamed of, it is such a bad return to you—— "

" Hush ! " said Clennam, smiling and touching her lips with his hand. " Forgetfulness in you, who remember so many and so much, would be new indeed. Shall I remind you that I am not, and that I never was, anything but the friend whom you agreed to trust? No. You remember it, don't you? "

" I try to do so, or I should have broken the promise just now, when my mistaken brother was here. You will con-sider his bringing-up in this place, and will not judge him hardly, poor fellow, I know ! " In raising her eyes with these words, she observed his face more nearly than she had done yet, and said, with a quick change of tone, " You have not been ill, Mr. Clennam? "

" No ? "

" Nor tried? Nor hurt? " she asked him, anxiously.

It fell to Clennam, now, to be not quite certain how to answer. He said in reply:

" To speak the truth, I have been a little troubled, but it is over. Do I show it so plainly? I ought to have more fortitude and self-command than that. I thought I had. I must learn them of you. Who could teach me better ! "

He never thought that she saw in him what no one else could see. He never thought that in the whole world there were no other eyes that looked upon him with the same light and strength as hers.

" But it brings me to something that I wish to say," he continued, " and therefore I will not quarrel even with my own face for telling tales and being unfaithful to me.

Besides, it is a privilege and pleasure to confide in my Little Dorrit. Let me confess then, that, forgetting how grave I was, and how old I was, and how the time for such things had gone by me with the many years of sameness and little happiness that made up my long life far away, without marking it—that, forgetting all this, I fancied I loved some one."

"Do I know her, sir?" asked Little Dorrit.

"No, my child."

"Not the lady who has been kind to me for your sake?"

"Flora. No, no. Did you think——"

"I never quite thought so," said Little Dorrit, more to herself than him. "I did wonder at it a little."

"Well!" said Clennam, abiding by the feeling that had fallen on him in the avenue on the night of the roses, the feeling that he was an older man, who had done with that tender part of life, "I found out my mistake, and I thought about it a little—in short, a good deal—and got wiser. Being wiser, I counted up my years, and considered what I am, and looked back, and looked forward, and found that I should soon be grey. I found that I had climbed the hill, and passed the level ground upon the top, and was descending quickly."

If he had known the sharpness of the pain he caused the patient heart, in speaking thus! While doing it, too, with the purpose of easing and serving her.

"I found that the day when any such thing would have been graceful in me, or good in me, or hopeful or happy for me, or any one in connection with me, was gone, and would never shine again."

O! If he had known, if he had known! If he could have seen the dagger in his hand, and the cruel wounds it struck in the faithful bleeding breast of his Little Dorrit!

"All that is over, and I have turned my face from it. Why do I speak of this to Little Dorrit? Why do I show you, my child, the space of years that there is between us, and recall to you that I have passed, by the amount of your whole life, the time that is present to you?"

"Because you trust me, I hope. Because you know that nothing can touch you, without touching me; that nothing can make you happy or unhappy, but it must make me, who am so grateful to you, the same."

He heard the thrill in her voice, he saw her earnest face, he saw her clear true eyes, he saw the quickened bosom that would have joyfully thrown itself before him to receive a mortal wound directed at his breast, with the dying cry, "I love him!" and the remotest suspicion of the truth never dawned upon his mind. No. He saw the devoted little creature with her worn shoes, in her common dress, in her jail-home; a slender child in body, a strong heroine in soul; and the light of her domestic story made all else dark to him.

"For those reasons assuredly, Little Dorrit, but for another too. So far removed, so different, and so much older, I am the better fitted for your friend and adviser. I mean, I am the more easily to be trusted; and any little constraint that you might feel with another, may vanish before me. Why have you kept so retired from me? Tell me."

"I am better here. My place and use are here. I am much better here," said Little Dorrit, faintly.

"So you said that day, upon the bridge. I thought of it much afterwards. Have you no secret you could entrust to me, with hope and comfort, if you would!"

"Secret? No, I have no secret," said Little Dorrit in some trouble.

They had been speaking in low voices; more because it was natural to what they said, to adopt that tone, than with any care to reserve it from Maggy at her work. All of a sudden Maggy stared again, and this time spoke:

"I say! Little Mother!"

"Yes, Maggy."

"If you an't got no secret of your own to tell him, tell him that about the Princess. *She* had a secret, you know."

"The Princess had a secret?" said Clennam, in some surprise. "What Princess was that, Maggy?"

"Lor? How you do go and bother a gal of ten," said Maggy, "catching the poor thing up in that way. Whoever said the Princess had a secret? *I* never said so."

"I beg your pardon. I thought you did."

"No, I didn't. How could I, when it was her as wanted to find it out? It was the little woman as had the secret, and she was always a spinning at her wheel. And so she says to her, why do you keep it there? And so, the t'other one says to her, no I don't; and so the t'other one says to her, yes you do; and then they both goes to the cupboard, and there it is. And she wouldn't go into the Hospital, and so she died. *You* know, Little Mother; tell him that. For it was a reg'lar good secret, that was!" cried Maggy, hugging herself.

Arthur looked at Little Dorrit for help to comprehend this, and was struck by seeing her so timid and red. But, when she told him that it was only a Fairy Tale she had one day made up for Maggy, and that there was nothing in it which she wouldn't be ashamed to tell again to anybody else, even if she could remember it, he left the subject where it was.

However, he returned to his own subject, by first entreating her to see him oftener, and to remember that it was impossible to have a stronger interest in her welfare than he had, or to be more set upon promoting it than he was. When she answered fervently, she well knew that, she never forgot it, he touched upon his second and more delicate point—the suspicion he had formed.

"Little Dorrit," he said, taking her hand again, and speaking lower than he had spoken yet, so that even Maggy in the small room could not hear him, "another word. I have wanted very much to say this to you; I have tried for opportunities. Don't mind me, who, for the matter of years, might be your father or your uncle. Always think of me as quite an old man. I know that all your devotion centres in this room, and that nothing to the last will ever tempt you away from the duties you discharge here. If I were not sure of it, I should, before now, have implored you, and implored your father, to let me make some provision for you in a more suitable place. But, you may have an interest—I will not say, now, though even that might be—may have, at another time, an interest in some one else; an interest not incompatible with your affection here."

She was very, very pale, and silently shook her head.

"It may be, dear Little Dorrit."

"No. No. No." She shook her head, after each slow repetition of the word, with an air of quiet desolation that he remembered long afterwards. The time came when he remembered it well, long afterwards, within those prison walls; within that very room.

"But, if it ever should be, tell me so, my dear child. Entrust the truth to me, point out the object of such an interest to me, and I will try with all the zeal, and honour, and friendship and respect that I feel for you, good Little Dorrit of my heart, to do you a lasting service."

"O thank you, thank you! But, O no, O no, O no!" She said this, looking at him with her work-worn hands folded together, and in the same resigned accents as before.

"I press for no confidence now. I only ask you to repose unhesitating trust in me."

"Can I do less than that, when you are so good!"

"Then you will trust me fully? Will have no secret unhappiness, or anxiety, concealed from me?"

"Almost none."

"And you have none now?"

She shook her head. But she was very pale.

"When I lie down to-night, and my thoughts come back —as they will, for they do every night, even when I have not seen you—to this sad place, I may believe that there is no grief beyond this room, now, and its usual occupants, which preys on Little Dorrit's mind?"

She seemed to catch at these words—that he remembered, too, long afterwards—and said, more brightly, "Yes, Mr. Clennam; yes, you may!"

The crazy staircase, usually not slow to give notice when any one was coming up or down, here creaked under a quick tread, and a further sound was heard upon it, as if a little steam-engine with more steam than it knew what to do with, were working towards the room. As it approached, which it did very rapidly, it laboured with increased energy; and, after knocking at the door, it sounded as if it were stooping down and snorting in at the keyhole.

Before Maggy could open the door, Mr. Pancks, opening it from without, stood without a hat and with his bare head in the wildest condition, looking at Clennam and Little Dorrit, over her shoulder. He had a lighted cigar in his hand, and brought with him airs of ale and tobacco smoke.

"Pancks the gipsy," he observed out of breath, "fortune-telling."

He stood dingily smiling, and breathing hard at them, with a most curious air. As if, instead of being his proprietor's grubber, he were the triumphant proprietor of the Marshalsea, the Marshal, all the turnkeys, and all the Collegians. In his great self-satisfaction he put his cigar to his lips (being evidently no smoker), and took such a pull at it, with his right eye shut up tight for the purpose, that he underwent a convulsion of shuddering and choking. But even in the midst of that paroxysm, he still essayed to repeat his favourite introduction of himself, "Pa-ancks the gi-ipsy, fortune-telling."

"I am spending the evening with the rest of 'em," said Pancks. "I've been singing. I've been taking a part in White sand and grey sand. *I* don't know anything about it. Never mind. I'll take any part in anything. It's all the same, if you're loud enough."

At first Clennam supposed him to be intoxicated. But, he soon perceived that though he might be a little the worse

477

(or better) for ale, the staple of his excitement was not brewed from malt, or distilled from any grain or berry.

"How d'ye do, Miss Dorrit?" said Pancks. "I thought you wouldn't mind my running round, and looking in for a moment. Mr. Clennam I heard was here, from Mr. Dorrit. How are you, sir?"

Clennam thanked him, and said he was glad to see him so gay.

"Gay!" said Pancks. "I'm in wonderful feather, sir. I can't stop a minute, or I shall be missed, and I don't want 'em to miss me.—Eh, Miss Dorrit?"

He seemed to have an insatiate delight in appealing to her, and looking at her; excitedly sticking his hair up at the same moment, like a dark species of cockatoo.

"I haven't been here half-an-hour. I knew Mr. Dorrit was in the chair, and I said, 'I'll go and support him!' I ought to be down in Bleeding Heart Yard by rights; but I can worry them to-morrow.—Eh, Miss Dorrit?"

His little black eyes sparkled electrically. His very hair seemed to sparkle as he roughened it. He was in that highly-charged state that one might have expected to draw sparks and snaps from him by presenting a knuckle to any part of his figure.

"Capital company here," said Pancks.—"Eh, Miss Dorrit?"

She was half afraid of him, and irresolute what to say. He laughed, with a nod towards Clennam.

"Don't mind him, Miss Dorrit. He's one of us. We agreed that you shouldn't take on to mind me before people, but we didn't mean Mr. Clennam. He's one of us. He's in it. An't you, Mr. Clennam?—Eh, Miss Dorrit?"

The excitement of this strange creature was fast communicating itself to Clennam. Little Dorrit with amazement, saw this, and observed that they exchanged quick looks.

"I was making a remark," said Pancks, "but I declare I forget what it was. Oh, I know! Capital company here. I've been treating 'em all round.—Eh, Miss Dorrit?"

"Very generous of you," she returned, noticing another of the quick looks between the two.

"Not at all," said Pancks. "Don't mention it. I'm coming into my property, that's the fact. I can afford to be liberal. I think I'll give 'em a treat here. Tables laid in the yard. Bread in stacks. Pipes in faggots. Tobacco in hayloads. Roast beef and plum-pudding for every one. Quart of double stout a head. Pint of wine too, if they like it, and the authorities give permission.—Eh, Miss Dorrit?"

She was thrown into such a confusion by his manner, or rather by Clennam's growing understanding of his manner (for she looked to him after every fresh appeal and cockatoo demonstration on the part of Mr. Pancks), that she only moved her lips in answer, without forming any word.

"And oh, by-the-bye!" said Pancks, "you were to live to know what was behind us on that little hand of yours. And so you shall, you shall, my darling.—Eh, Miss Dorrit?"

He had suddenly checked himself. Where he got all the additional black prongs from, that now flew up all over his head, like the myriads of points that break out in the large change of a great firework, was a wonderful mystery.

"But I shall be missed;" he came back to that; "and I don't want 'em to miss me. Mr. Clennam, you and I made a bargain. I said you should find me stick to it. You shall find me stick to it now, sir, if you'll step out of the room a moment. Miss Dorrit, I wish you good night. Miss Dorrit, I wish you good fortune."

He rapidly shook her by both hands, and puffed down-stairs. Arthur followed him with such a hurried step, that he had very nearly tumbled over him on the last landing, and rolled him down into the yard.

"What is it, for Heaven's sake!" Arthur demanded, when they burst out there both together.

"Stop a moment, sir. Mr. Rugg. Let me introduce him."

With those words he presented another man without a hat, and also with a cigar, and also surrounded with a halo of ale and tobacco smoke, which man, though not so excited as himself, was in a state which would have been akin to lunacy but for its fading into sober method when compared with the rampancy of Mr. Pancks.

"Mr. Clennam, Mr. Rugg," said Pancks. "Stop a moment. Come to the pump."

They adjourned to the pump. Mr. Pancks, instantly putting his head under the spout, requested Mr. Rugg to take a good strong turn at the handle. Mr. Rugg complying to the letter, Mr. Pancks came forth snorting and blowing to some purpose, and dried himself on his handkerchief.

"I am the clearer for that," he gasped to Clennam standing astonished. "But upon my soul, to hear her father making speeches in that chair, knowing what we know, and to see her up in that room in that dress, knowing what we know, is enough to—give me a back, Mr. Rugg—a little higher, sir, —that'll do!"

Then and there, on that Marshalsea pavement, in the shades of evening, did Mr. Pancks, of all mankind, fly over the head and shoulders of Mr. Rugg, of Pentonville, General Agent, Accountant, and Recoverer of Debts. Alighting on his feet, he took Clennam by the button-hole, led him behind the pump, and pantingly produced from his pocket a bundle of papers.

Mr. Rugg, also, pantingly produced from his pocket a bundle of papers.

"Stay!" said Clennam in a whisper. "You have made a discovery."

Mr. Pancks answered, with an unction which there is no language to convey, "We rather think so."

"Does it implicate any one?"

"How implicate, sir?"

"In any suppression or wrong dealing of any kind?"

"Not a bit of it."

"Thank God!" said Clennam to himself. "Now show me."

"You are to understand"—snorted Pancks, feverishly

unfolding papers, and speaking in short high-pressure blasts of sentences. " Where's the Pedigree ? Where's Schedule number four, Mr. Rugg? Oh! all right! Here we are.— You are to understand that we are this very day virtually complete. We shan't be legally for a day or two. Call it at the outside a week. We've been at it, night and day, for I don't know how long. Mr. Rugg, you know how long? Never mind. Don't say. You'll only confuse me. You shall tell her, Mr. Clennam. Not till we give you leave. Where's that rough total, Mr. Rugg? Oh! Here we are! There, sir! That's what you'll have to break to her. That man's your Father of the Marshalsea ! "

CHAPTER XXXIII

RESIGNING herself to inevitable fate, by making the best of those people the Miggleses, and submitting her philosophy to the draught upon it, of which she had foreseen the likelihood in her interview with Arthur, Mrs. Gowan handsomely resolved not to oppose her son's marriage. In her progress to, and happy arrival at, this resolution, she was possibly influenced, not only by her maternal affections, but by three politic considerations.

Of these, the first may have been, that her son had never signified the smallest intention to ask her consent, or any mistrust of his ability to dispense with it; the second, that the pension bestowed upon her by a grateful country (and a Barnacle) would be freed from any little filial inroads, when her Henry should be married to the darling only child of a man in very easy circumstances; the third, that Henry's debts must clearly be paid down upon the altar-railing by his father-in-law. When, to these three-fold points of prudence, there is added the fact that Mrs. Gowan yielded her consent the moment she knew of Mr. Meagles having yielded his, and that Mr. Meagles's objection to the marriage had been the sole obstacle in its way all along, it becomes the height of probability that the relict of the deceased Commissioner of nothing particular, turned these ideas in her sagacious mind.

A VISIT OF SELF-CONDOLENCE

Among her connections and acquaintances, however, she maintained her individual dignity, and the dignity of the blood of the Barnacles, by diligently nursing the pretence that it was a most unfortunate business ; that she was sadly cut up by it ; that this was a perfect fascination under which Henry laboured ; that she had opposed it for a long time, but what could a mother do ; and the like. She had already called Arthur Clennam to bear witness to this fable, as a friend of the Meagles family ; and she followed up the move by now impounding the family itself for the same purpose. In the first interview she accorded to Mr. Meagles, she slided herself into the position of disconsolately but gracefully yielding to irresistible pressure. With the utmost politeness and good-breeding, she feigned that it was she—not he—who had made the difficulty, and who at length gave way ; and that the sacrifice was hers—not his. The same feint, with the same polite dexterity, she foisted on Mrs. Meagles, as a conjurer might have forced a card on that innocent lady ; and, when her future daughter-in-law was presented to her by her son, she said on embracing her, " My dear, what have you done to Henry that has bewitched him so ! " at the same time allowing a few tears to carry before them, in little pills, the cosmetic powder on her nose ; as a delicate but touching signal that she suffered much inwardly, for the show of composure with which she bore her misfortune.

Among the friends of Mrs. Gowan (who piqued herself at once on being Society, and on maintaining intimate and easy relations with that Power), Mrs. Merdle occupied a front row. True, the Hampton Court Bohemians, without exception, turned up their noses at Merdle as an upstart ; but they turned them down again, by falling flat on their faces to worship his wealth. In which compensating adjustment of their noses, they were pretty much like Treasury, Bar, and Bishop, and all the rest of them.

To Mrs. Merdle, Mrs. Gowan repaired on a visit of self-condolence, after having given the gracious consent aforesaid.

LITTLE DORRIT

She drove into town for the purpose, in a one-horse carriage, irreverently called at that period of English history, a pill-box. It belonged to a job-master in a small way, who drove it himself, and who jobbed it by the day, or hour, to most of the old ladies in Hampton Court Palace; but it was a point of ceremony, in that encampment, that the whole equipage should be tacitly regarded as the private property of the jobber for the time being, and that the job-master should betray personal knowledge of nobody but the jobber in possession. So, the Circumlocution Barnacles, who were the largest job-masters in the universe, always pretended to know of no other job but the job immediately in hand.

Mrs. Merdle was at home, and was in her nest of crimson and gold, with the parrot on a neighbouring stem watching her with his head on one side, as if he took her for another splendid parrot of a larger species. To whom entered Mrs. Gowan, with her favourite green fan, which softened the light on the spots of bloom.

"My dear soul," said Mrs. Gowan, tapping the back of her friend's hand with this fan, after a little indifferent conversation, "you are my only comfort. That affair of Henry's that I told you of, is to take place. Now, how does it strike you? I am dying to know, because you represent and express Society so well."

Mrs. Merdle reviewed the bosom which Society was accustomed to review; and having ascertained that show-window of Mr. Merdle's and the London jewellers' to be in good order, replied:

"As to marriage on the part of a man, my dear, Society requires that he should retrieve his fortunes by marriage. Society requires that he should gain by marriage. Society requires that he should found a handsome establishment by marriage. Society does not see, otherwise, what he has to do with marriage. Bird, be quiet!"

For, the parrot on his cage above them, presiding over

Society expresses its Views on a Question of Marriage

the conference as if he were a Judge (and indeed he looked rather like one), had wound up the exposition with a shriek.

"Cases there are," said Mrs. Merdle, delicately crooking the little finger of her favourite hand, and making her remarks neater by that neat action; "cases there are where a man is not young or elegant, and is rich, and has a handsome establishment already. Those are of a different kind. In such cases——"

Mrs. Merdle shrugged her snowy shoulders and put her hand upon the jewel-stand, checking a little cough, as though to add, "why a man looks out for this sort of thing, my dear." Then the parrot shrieked again, and she put up her glass to look at him, and said, "Bird! Do be quiet!"

"But, young men," resumed Mrs. Merdle, "and by young men you know what I mean, my love—I mean people's sons who have the world before them—they must place themselves in a better position towards Society by marriage, or Society really will not have any patience with their making fools of themselves. Dreadfully worldly all this sounds," said Mrs. Merdle, leaning back in her nest and putting up her glass again, "does it not?"

"But it is true," said Mrs. Gowan, with a highly moral air.

"My dear, it is not to be disputed for a moment," returned Mrs. Merdle; "because Society has made up its mind on the subject, and there is nothing more to be said. If we were in a more primitive state, if we lived under roofs of leaves, and kept cows and sheep and creatures, instead of banker's accounts (which would be delicious; my dear, I am pastoral to a degree, by nature), well and good. But we don't live under leaves, and keep cows and sheep and creatures. I perfectly exhaust myself sometimes, in pointing out the distinction to Edmund Sparkler."

Mrs. Gowan, looking over her green fan when this young gentleman's name was mentioned, replied as follows:

"My love, you know the wretched state of the country

—those unfortunate concessions of John Barnacle's!—and you therefore know the reasons for my being as poor as Thingummy."

"A church mouse?" Mrs. Merdle suggested with a smile.

"I was thinking of the other proverbial church person— Job," said Mrs. Gowan. "Either will do. It would be idle to disguise, consequently, that there is a wide difference between the position of your son and mine. I may add, too, that Henry has talent——"

"Which Edmund certainly has not," said Mrs. Merdle, with the greatest suavity.

"—And that his talent, combined with disappointment," Mrs. Gowan went on, "has led him into a pursuit which— ah dear me! *You* know, my dear. Such being Henry's different position, the question is what is the most inferior class of marriage to which I can reconcile myself."

Mrs. Merdle was so much engaged with the contemplation of her arms (beautifully formed arms, and the very thing for bracelets), that she omitted to reply for a while. Roused at length by the silence, she folded the arms, and with admirable presence of mind looked her friend full in the face, and said interrogatively, "Ye-es? And then?"

"And then, my dear," said Mrs. Gowan not quite so sweetly as before, "I should be glad to hear what you have to say to it."

Here the parrot, who had been standing on one leg since he screamed last, burst into a fit of laughter, bobbed himself derisively up and down on both legs, and finished by standing on one leg again, and pausing for a reply, with his head as much awry as he could possibly twist it.

"Sounds mercenary, to ask what the gentleman is to get with the lady," said Mrs. Merdle; "but Society *is* perhaps a little mercenary, you know, my dear."

"From what I can make out," said Mrs. Gowan, "I believe I may say that Henry will be relieved from debt——"

"Much in debt?" asked Mrs. Merdle through her eye-glass.

"Why tolerably, I should think," said Mrs. Gowan.

"Meaning the usual thing; I understand; just so," Mrs. Merdle observed in a comfortable sort of way.

"And that the father will make them an allowance of three hundred a-year, or perhaps altogether something more. Which, in Italy——"

"Oh! Going to Italy?" said Mrs. Merdle.

"For Henry to study. You need be at no loss to guess why, my dear. That dreadful Art——"

True. Mrs. Merdle hastened to spare the feelings of her afflicted friend. She understood. Say no more!

"And that," said Mrs. Gowan, shaking her despondent head, "that's all. That," repeated Mrs. Gowan, furling her green fan for the moment, and tapping her chin with it (it was on the way to being a double chin; might be called a chin and a half at present), "that's all! On the death of the old people, I suppose there will be more to come; but how it may be restricted or locked up, I don't know. And as to that, they may live for ever. My dear, they are just the kind of people to do it."

Now, Mrs. Merdle, who really knew her friend Society pretty well, and who knew what Society's mothers were, and what Society's daughters were, and what Society's matrimonial market was, and how prices ruled in it, and what scheming and counter-scheming took place for the high buyers, and what bargaining and huckstering went on, thought in the depths of her capacious bosom that this was a sufficiently good catch. Knowing, however, what was expected of her, and perceiving the exact nature of the fiction to be nursed, she took it delicately in her arms, and put her required contribution of gloss upon it.

"And that is all, my dear?" said she, heaving a friendly sigh. "Well, well! The fault is not yours. You have nothing to reproach yourself with. You must exercise the strength of mind for which you are renowned, and make the best of it."

" The girl's family have made," said Mrs. Gowan, " of course, the most strenuous endeavours to—as the lawyers say —to have and to hold Henry."

" Of course they have, my dear," said Mrs. Merdle.

" I have persisted in every possible objection, and have worried myself morning, noon, and night, for means to detach Henry from the connection."

" No doubt you have, my dear," said Mrs. Merdle.

" And all of no use. All has broken down beneath me. Now tell me, my love. Am I justified in at last yielding my most reluctant consent to Henry's marrying among people not in Society; or, have I acted with inexcusable weakness?"

In answer to this direct appeal, Mrs. Merdle assured Mrs. Gowan (speaking as a Priestess of Society) that she was highly to be commended, that she was much to be sympathised with, that she had taken the highest of parts, and had come out of the furnace refined. And Mrs. Gowan, who of course saw through her own threadbare blind perfectly, and who knew that Mrs. Merdle saw through it perfectly, and who knew that Society would see through it perfectly, came out of this form, notwithstanding, as she had gone into it, with immense complacency and gravity.

The conference was held at four or five o'clock in the afternoon, when all the region of Harley Street, Cavendish Square, was resonant of carriage-wheels and double-knocks. It had reached this point when Mr. Merdle came home, from his daily occupation of causing the British name to be more and more respected in all parts of the civilised globe, capable of the appreciation of world-wide commercial enterprise and gigantic combinations of skill and capital. For, though nobody knew with the least precision what Mr. Merdle's business was, except that it was to coin money, these were the terms in which everybody defined it on all ceremonious occasions, and which it was the last new polite reading of the parable of the camel and the needle's eye to accept without inquiry.

For a gentleman who had this splendid work cut out for him, Mr: Merdle looked a little common, and rather as if, in the course of his vast transactions, he had accidentally made an interchange of heads with some inferior spirit. He presented himself before the two ladies, in the course of a dismal stroll through his mansion, which had no apparent object but escape from the presence of the chief butler.

"I beg your pardon," he said, stopping short in confusion; "I didn't know there was anybody here but the parrot."

However, as Mrs. Merdle said, "You can come in!" and as Mrs. Gowan said she was just going, and had already risen to take her leave, he came in, and stood looking out at a distant window, with his hands crossed under his uneasy coat-cuffs, clasping his wrists as if he were taking himself into custody. In this attitude he fell directly into a reverie, from which he was only aroused by his wife's calling to him from her ottoman, when they had been for some quarter-of-an-hour alone.

"Eh? Yes?" said Mr. Merdle, turning towards her. "What is it?"

"What is it?" repeated Mrs. Merdle. "It is, I suppose, that you have not heard a word of my complaint."

"Your complaint, Mrs. Merdle?" said Mr. Merdle. "I didn't know that you were suffering from a complaint. What complaint?"

"A complaint of you," said Mrs. Merdle.

"Oh! A complaint of me," said Mr. Merdle. "What is the—what have I—what may you have to complain of in me, Mrs. Merdle?"

In his withdrawing, abstracted, pondering way, it took him some time to shape this question. As a kind of faint attempt to convince himself that he was the master of the house, he concluded by presenting his forefinger to the parrot, who expressed his opinion on that subject by instantly driving his bill into it.

" You were saying, Mrs. Merdle," said Mr. Merdle, with his wounded finger in his mouth, " that you had a complaint against me ? "

" A complaint which I could scarcely show the justice of more emphatically, than by having to repeat it," said Mrs. Merdle. " I might as well have stated it to the wall. I had far better have stated it to the bird. He would at least have screamed."

" You don't want me to scream, Mrs. Merdle, I suppose," said Mr. Merdle, taking a chair.

" Indeed I don't know," retorted Mrs. Merdle, " but that you had better do that, than be so moody and distraught. One would at least know that you were sensible of what was going on around you."

" A man might scream, and yet not be that, Mrs. Merdle," said Mr. Merdle, heavily.

" And might be dogged, as you are at present, without screaming," returned Mrs. Merdle. " That's very true. If you wish to know the complaint I make against you, it is, in so many plain words, that you really ought not to go into Society, unless you can accommodate yourself to Society."

Mr. Merdle, so twisting his hands into what hair he had upon his head that he seemed to lift himself up by it as he started out of his chair, cried :

" Why, in the name of all the infernal powers, Mrs. Merdle, who does more for Society than I do ? Do you see these premises, Mrs. Merdle ? Do you see this furniture, Mrs. Merdle ? Do you look in the glass and see yourself, Mrs. Merdle ? Do you know the cost of all this, and who it's all provided for ? And yet will you tell me that I oughtn't to go into Society ? I, who shower money upon it in this way ? I, who might be almost said—to—to—to harness myself to a watering-cart full of money, and go about, saturating Society, every day of my life ? "

" Pray, don't be violent, Mr. Merdle," said Mrs. Merdle.

" Violent ? " said Mr. Merdle. " You are enough to

make me desperate. You don't know half of what I do to accommodate Society. You don't know anything of the sacrifices I make for it."

"I know," returned Mrs. Merdle, "that you receive the best in the land. I know that you move in the whole Society of the country. And I believe I know (indeed, not to make any ridiculous pretence about it, I know I know) who sustains you in it, Mr. Merdle."

"Mrs. Merdle," retorted that gentleman, wiping his dull red and yellow face, "I know that, as well as you do. If you were not an ornament to Society, and if I was not a benefactor to Society, you and I would never have come together. When I say a benefactor to it, I mean a person who provides it with all sorts of expensive things to eat and drink and look at. But, to tell me that I am not fit for it after all I have done for it—after all I have done for it," repeated Mr. Merdle, with a wild emphasis that made his wife lift up her eyelids, "after all—all!—to tell me I have no right to mix with it after all, is a pretty reward."

"I say," answered Mrs. Merdle composedly, "that you ought to make yourself fit for it by being more *dégagé*, and less preoccupied. There is a positive vulgarity in carrying your business affairs about with you as you do."

"How do I carry them about, Mrs. Merdle?" asked Mr. Merdle.

"How do you carry them about?" said Mrs. Merdle. "Look at yourself in the glass."

Mr. Merdle involuntarily turned his eyes in the direction of the nearest mirror, and asked, with a slow determination of his turbid blood to his temples, whether a man was to be called to account for his digestion?

"You have a physician," said Mrs. Merdle.

"He does me no good," said Mr. Merdle.

Mrs. Merdle changed her ground.

"Besides," said she, "your digestion is nonsense. I don't speak of your digestion. I speak of your manner."

491

" Mrs. Merdle," returned her husband, " I look to you for that. You supply manner, and I supply money."

" I don't expect you," said Mrs. Merdle, reposing easily among her cushions, " to captivate people. I don't want you to take any trouble upon yourself, or to try to be fascinating. I simply request you to care about nothing—or seem to care about nothing—as everybody else does."

" Do I ever say I care about anything ? " asked Mr. Merdle.

" Say ? No ! Nobody would attend to you if you did. But you show it."

" Show what ? What do I show ? " demanded Mr. Merdle hurriedly.

" I have already told you. You show that you carry your business cares and projects about, instead of leaving them in the City, or wherever else they belong to," said Mrs. Merdle. " Or sceming to. Seeming would be quite enough : I ask no more. Whereas you couldn't be more occupied with your day's calculations and combinations than you habitually show yourself to be, if you were a carpenter."

" A carpenter ! " repeated Mr. Merdle, checking something like a groan. " I shouldn't so much mind being a carpenter, Mrs. Merdle."

" And my complaint is," pursued the lady, disregarding the low remark, " that it is not the tone of Society, and that you ought to correct it, Mr. Merdle. If you have any doubt of my judgment, ask even Edmund Sparkler." The door of the room had opened, and Mrs. Merdle now surveyed the head of her son through her glass. " Edmund ; we want you here."

Mr. Sparkler, who had merely put in his head and looked round the room without entering (as if he were searching the house for that young lady with no nonsense about her), upon this followed up his head with his body, and stood before them. To whom, in a few easy words adapted to his capacity, Mrs. Merdle stated the question at issue.

The young gentleman, after anxiously feeling his shirt-

492

collar as if it were his pulse and he were hypochondriacal, observed, "That he had heard it noticed by fellers."

"Edmund Sparkler has heard it noticed," said Mrs. Merdle, with languid triumph. "Why, no doubt everybody has heard it noticed!" Which in truth was no unreasonable inference; seeing that Mr. Sparkler would probably be the last person, in any assemblage of the human species, to receive an impression from anything that passed in his presence.

"And Edmund Sparkler will tell you, I dare say," said Mrs. Merdle, waving her favourite hand towards her husband, "how he has heard it noticed."

"I couldn't," said Mr. Sparkler, after feeling his pulse as before, "couldn't undertake to say what led to it—'cause memory desperate loose. But being in company with the brother of a doosed fine gal—well educated too—with no biggodd nonsense about her—at the period alluded to——"

"There! Never mind the sister," remarked Mrs. Merdle, a little impatiently. "What did the brother say?"

"Didn't say a word, ma'am," answered Mr. Sparkler. "As silent a feller as myself. Equally hard up for a remark."

"Somebody said something," returned Mrs. Merdle. "Never mind who it was."

("Assure you I don't in the least," said Mr. Sparkler.)

"But tell us what it was."

Mr. Sparkler referred to his pulse again, and put himself through some severe mental discipline before he replied:

"Fellers referring to my Governor—expression not my own—occasionally compliment my Governor in a very handsome way on being immensely rich and knowing—perfect phenomenon of Buyer and Banker and that—but say the Shop sits heavily on him. Say he carries the Shop about, on his back rather—like Jew clothesmen with too much business."

"Which," said Mrs. Merdle, rising, with her floating drapery about her, "is exactly my complaint. Edmund, give me your arm up-stairs."

Mr. Merdle, left alone to meditate on a better conformation

of himself to Society, looked out of nine windows in succession, and appeared to see nine wastes of space. When he had thus entertained himself he went down-stairs, and looked intently at all the carpets on the ground-floor; and then came up-stairs again, and looked intently at all the carpets on the first-floor; as if they were gloomy depths, in unison with his oppressed soul. Through all the rooms he wandered, as he always did, like the last person on earth who had any business to approach them. Let Mrs. Merdle announce, with all her might, that she was at Home ever so many nights in a season, she could not announce more widely and unmistakably than Mr. Merdle did that he was never at home.

At last he met the chief butler, the sight of which splendid retainer always finished him. Extinguished by this great creature, he sneaked to his dressing-room, and there remained shut up until he rode out to dinner, with Mrs. Merdle, in her own handsome chariot. At dinner, he was envied and flattered as a being of might, was Treasuried, Barred, and Bishoped, as much as he would; and an hour after midnight came home alone, and being instantly put out again in his own hall, like a rushlight, by the chief butler, went sighing to bed.

CHAPTER XXXIV

Mr. Henry Gowan and the dog were established frequenters of the cottage, and the day was fixed for the wedding. There was to be a convocation of Barnacles on the occasion ; in order that that very high and very large family might shed as much lustre on the marriage, as so dim an event was capable of receiving.

To have got the whole Barnacle family together, would have been impossible for two reasons. Firstly, because no building could have held all the members and connections of that illustrious house. Secondly, because wherever there was a square yard of ground in British occupation under the sun or moon, with a public post upon it, sticking to that post was a Barnacle. No intrepid navigator could plant a flagstaff upon any spot of earth, and take possession of it in the British name, but to that spot of earth, so soon as the discovery was known, the Circumlocution Office sent out a Barnacle and a despatch-box. Thus the Barnacles were all over the world, in every direction—despatch-boxing the compass.

But, while the so-potent art of Prospero himself would have failed in summoning the Barnacles from every speck of ocean and dry land on which there was nothing (except mischief) to be done, and anything to be pocketed, it was perfectly feasible to assemble a good many Barnacles. This

495

Mrs. Gowan applied herself to do; calling on Mr. Meagles frequently, with new additions to the list, and holding conferences with that gentleman when he was not engaged (as he generally was at this period) in examining and paying the debts of his future son-in-law, in the apartment of the scales and scoop.

One marriage guest there was, in reference to whose presence Mr. Meagles felt a nearer interest and concern than in the attendance of the most elevated Barnacle expected; though he was far from insensible of the honour of having such company. This guest was Clennam. But, Clennam had made a promise he held sacred, among the trees that summer night, and, in the chivalry of his heart, regarded it as binding him to many implied obligations. In forgetfulness of himself, and delicate service to her on all occasions, he was never to fail; to begin it, he answered Mr. Meagles cheerfully, "I shall come, of course."

His partner, Daniel Doyce, was something of a stumbling-block in Mr. Meagles's way, the worthy gentleman being not at all clear in his own anxious mind but that the mingling of Daniel with official Barnacleism might produce some explosive combination, even at a marriage breakfast. The national offender, however, lightened him of his uneasiness by coming down to Twickenham to represent that he begged, with the freedom of an old friend, and as a favour to one, that he might not be invited. "For," said he, "as my business with this set of gentlemen was to do a public duty and a public service, and as their business with me was to prevent it by wearing my soul out, I think we had better not eat and drink together with a show of being of one mind." Mr. Meagles was much amused by his friend's oddity; and patronised him with a more protecting air of allowance than usual, when he rejoined: "Well, well, Dan, you shall have your own crotchety way."

To Mr. Henry Gowan, as the time approached, Clennam tried to convey by all quiet and unpretending means, that he was frankly and disinterestedly desirous of tendering him any friendship he would accept. Mr. Gowan treated him in return with his usual ease, and with his usual show of confidence, which was no confidence at all.

"You see, Clennam," he happened to remark in the course of conversation one day, when they were walking near the Cottage within a week of the marriage, "I am a disappointed man. That, you know already."

"Upon my word," said Clennam, a little embarrassed, "I scarcely know how."

"Why," returned Gowan, "I belong to a clan, or a clique, or a family, or a connection, or whatever you like to call it, that might have provided for me in any one of fifty ways, and that took it into its head not to do it at all. So here I am, a poor devil of an artist."

Clennam was beginning, "But on the other hand——" when Gowan took him up.

"Yes, yes, I know. I have the good fortune of being beloved by a beautiful and charming girl whom I love with all my heart."

("Is there much of it?" Clennam thought. And as he thought it, felt ashamed of himself.)

"And of finding a father-in-law who is a capital fellow and a liberal good old boy. Still, I had other prospects washed and combed into my childish head when it was washed and combed for me, and I took them to a public school when I washed and combed it for myself, and I am here without them, and thus I am a disappointed man."

Clennam thought (and as he thought it, again felt ashamed of himself), was this notion of being disappointed in life, an assertion of station which the bridegroom brought into the family as his property, having already carried it detrimentally into his pursuit? And was it a hopeful or a promising thing anywhere?

"Not bitterly disappointed, I think," he said aloud.

"Hang it, no; not bitterly," laughed Gowan. "My

people are not worth that—though they are charming fellows, and I have the greatest affection for them. Besides, it's pleasant to show them that I can do without them, and that they may all go to the Devil. And besides again, most men are disappointed in life, somehow or other, and influenced by their disappointment. But it's a dear good world, and I love it!"

"It lies fair before you now," said Arthur.

"Fair as this summer river," cried the other, with enthusiasm, "and by Jove I glow with admiration of it, and with ardour to run a race in it. It's the best of old worlds! And my calling! The best of old callings, isn't it?"

"Full of interest and ambition, I conceive," said Clennam.

"And imposition," added Gowan, laughing; "we won't leave out the imposition. I hope I may not break down in that; but there, my being a disappointed man may show itself. I may not be able to face it out gravely enough. Between you and me, I think there is some danger of my being just enough soured not to be able to do that."

"To do what?" asked Clennam.

"To keep it up. To help myself in my turn, as the man before me helps himself in his, and pass the bottle of smoke. To keep up the pretence as to labour, and study, and patience, and being devoted to my art, and giving up many solitary days to it, and abandoning many pleasures for it, and living in it, and all the rest of it—in short, to pass the bottle of smoke, according to rule."

"But it is well for a man to respect his own vocation, whatever it is; and to think himself bound to uphold it, and to claim for it the respect it deserves; is it not?" Arthur reasoned. "And your vocation, Gowan, may really demand this suit and service. I confess I should have thought that all Art did."

"What a good fellow you are, Clennam!" exclaimed the other, stopping to look at him, as if with irrepressible

498

admiration. " What a capital fellow ! *You* have never been disappointed. That's easy to see."

It would have been so cruel if he had meant it, that Clennam firmly resolved to believe he did not mean it. Gowan, without pausing, laid his hand upon his shoulder, and laughingly and lightly went on :

"Clennam, I don't like to dispel your generous visions, and I would give any money (if I had any) to live in such a rose-coloured mist. But what I do in my trade, I do to sell. What all we fellows do, we do to sell. If we didn't want to sell it for the most we can get for it, we shouldn't do it. Being work, it has to be done ; but it's easily enough done. All the rest is hocus-pocus. Now here's one of the advantages, or disadvantages, of knowing a disappointed man. You hear the truth."

Whatever he had heard, and whether it deserved that name or another, it sank into Clennam's mind. It so took root there, that he began to fear Henry Gowan would always be a trouble to him, and that so far he had gained little or nothing from the dismissal of Nobody, with all his inconsistencies, anxieties, and contradictions. He found a contest still always going on in his breast, between his promise to keep Gowan in none but good aspects before the mind of Mr. Meagles, and his enforced observation of Gowan in aspects that had no good in them. Nor could he quite support his own conscientious nature against misgivings that he distorted and discoloured him, by reminding himself that he never sought those discoveries, and that he would have avoided them with willingness and great relief. For, he never could forget what had been ; and he knew that he had once disliked Gowan, for no better reason than that he had come in his way.

Harassed by these thoughts, he now began to wish the marriage over, Gowan and his young wife gone, and himself left to fulfil his promise, and discharge the generous function he had accepted. This last week was, in truth, an uneasy

interval for the whole house. Before Pet, or before Gowan,
Mr. Meagles was radiant; but, Clennam had more than once
found him alone, with his view of the scales and scoop much
blurred, and had often seen him look after the lovers, in
the garden or elsewhere when he was not seen by them, with
the old clouded face on which Gowan had fallen like a
shadow. In the arrangement of the house for the great
occasion, many little reminders of the old travels of the
father and mother and daughter had to be disturbed, and
passed from hand to hand; and sometimes, in the midst of
these mute witnesses to the life they had had together, even
Pet herself would yield to lamenting and weeping. Mrs.
Meagles, the blithest and busiest of mothers, went about
singing and cheering everybody; but she, honest soul, had
her flights into store-rooms, where she would cry until her
eyes were red, and would then come out, attributing that
appearance to pickled onions and pepper, and singing clearer
than ever. Mrs. Tickit, finding no balsam for a wounded
mind in Buchan's Domestic Medicine, suffered greatly from
low spirits, and from moving recollections of Minnie's infancy.
When the latter were powerful with her, she usually sent up
secret messages importing that she was not in parlour condition as to her attire, and that she solicited a sight of " her
child" in the kitchen; there, she would bless her child's face,
and bless her child's heart, and hug her child, in a medley
of tears and congratulations, chopping-boards, rolling-pins,
and pie-crust, with the tenderness of an attached old servant,
which is a very pretty tenderness indeed.

But, all days come that are to be; and the marriage-day
was to be, and it came; and with it came all the Barnacles
who were bidden to the feast.

There was Mr. Tite Barnacle, from the Circumlocution
Office, and Mews Street, Grosvenor Square, with the expensive
Mrs. Tite Barnacle *née* Stiltstalking, who made the Quarter
Days so long in coming, and the three expensive Miss Tite
Barnacles, double-loaded with accomplishments and ready to

go off, and yet not going off with the sharpness of flash and bang that might have been expected, but rather hanging fire. There was Barnacle Junior, also from the Circumlocution Office, leaving the Tonnage of the country, which he was somehow supposed to take under his protection, to look after itself, and, sooth to say, not at all impairing the efficiency of its protection by leaving it alone. There was the engaging Young Barnacle, deriving from the sprightly side of the family, also from the Circumlocution Office, gaily and agreeably helping the occasion along, and treating it, in his sparkling way, as one of the official forms and fees of the Church Department of How not to do it. There were three other Young Barnacles, from three other offices, insipid to all the senses, and terribly in want of seasoning, doing the marriage as they would have "done" the Nile, Old Rome, the new singer, or Jerusalem.

But, there was greater game than this. There was Lord Decimus Tite Barnacle himself, in the odour of Circumlocution—with the very smell of Despatch-Boxes upon him. Yes, there was Lord Decimus Tite Barnacle, who had risen to official heights on the wings of one indignant idea, and that was, My Lords, that I am yet to be told that it behoves a Minister of this free country to set bounds to the philanthropy, to cramp the charity, to fetter the public spirit, to contract the enterprise, to damp the independent self-reliance, of its people. That was, in other words, that this great statesman was always yet to be told that it behoved the Pilot of the ship to do anything but prosper in the private loaf and fish trade ashore, the crew being able, by dint of hard pumping, to keep the ship above water without him. On this sublime discovery, in the great art How not to do it, Lord Decimus had long sustained the highest glory of the Barnacle family; and let any ill-advised member of either House but try How to do it, by bringing in a Bill to do it, that Bill was as good as dead and buried when Lord Decimus Tite Barnacle rose up in his place, and solemnly said, soaring into indignant majesty as the Circumlocution cheering soared around him, that he was yet to be told, My Lords, that it behoved him as the Minister of this free country, to set bounds to the philanthropy, to cramp the charity, to fetter the public spirit, to contract the enterprise, to damp the independent self-reliance, of its people. The discovery of this Behoving Machine was the discovery of the political perpetual motion. It never wore out, though it was always going round and round in all the state Departments.

And there, with his noble friend and relative Lord Decimus, was William Barnacle, who had made the ever-famous coalition with Tudor Stiltstalking, and who always kept ready his own particular recipe for How not to do it; sometimes tapping the Speaker, and drawing it fresh out of him, with a "First, I will beg you, sir, to inform the House what Precedent we have for the course into which the honourable gentleman would precipitate us;" sometimes asking the honourable gentleman to favour him with his own version of the Precedent; sometimes telling the honourable gentleman that he (William Barnacle) would search for a Precedent; and oftentimes crushing the honourable gentleman flat on the spot, by telling him there was no Precedent. But, Precedent and Precipitate were, under all circumstances, the well-matched pair of battle-horses of this able Circumlocutionist. No matter that the unhappy honourable gentleman had been trying in vain, for twenty-five years, to precipitate William Barnacle into this—William Barnacle still put it to the House, and (at second-hand or so) to the country, whether he was to be precipitated into this. No matter that it was utterly irreconcilable with the nature of things and course of events, that the wretched honourable gentleman could possibly produce a Precedent for this—William Barnacle would nevertheless thank the honourable gentleman for that ironical cheer, and would close with him upon that issue, and would tell him to his teeth that there was no Precedent for this. It might perhaps have been objected that the William

PARLIAMENTARY BARNACLES

Barnacle wisdom was not high wisdom, or the earth it bamboozled would never have been made, or, if made in a rash mistake, would have remained blank mud. But, Precedent and Precipitate together frightened all objection out of most people.

And there, too, was another Barnacle, a lively one, who had leaped through twenty places in quick succession, and was always in two or three at once, and who was the much-respected inventor of an art which he practised with great success and admiration in all Barnacle Governments. This was, when he was asked a Parliamentary question on any one topic, to return an answer on any other. It had done immense service, and brought him into high esteem with the Circumlocution Office.

And there, too, was a sprinkling of less distinguished Parliamentary Barnacles, who had not as yet got anything snug, and were going through their probation to prove their worthiness. These Barnacles perched upon staircases and hid in passages, waiting their orders to make houses or not to make houses; and they did all their hearing, and ohing, and cheering, and barking, under directions from the heads of the family; and they put dummy motions on the paper in the way of other men's motions; and they stalled disagreeable subjects off until late in the night and late in the session, and then with virtuous patriotism cried out that it was too late; and they went down into the country, whenever they were sent, and swore that Lord Decimus had revived trade from a swoon, and commerce from a fit, and had doubled the harvest of corn, quadrupled the harvest of hay, and prevented no end of gold from flying out of the Bank. Also these Barnacles were dealt, by the heads of the family, like so many cards below the court-cards, to public meetings and dinners; where they bore testimony to all sorts of services on the part of their noble and honourable relatives, and buttered the Barnacles on all sorts of toasts. And they stood, under similar orders, at all sorts of elections; and they turned out of their own

503

seats, on the shortest notice and the most unreasonable terms, to let in other men; and they fetched and carried, and toadied and jobbed, and corrupted, and ate heaps of dirt, and were indefatigable in the public service. And there was not a list, in all the Circumlocution Office, of places that might fall vacant anywhere within half a century, from a lord of the Treasury to a Chinese consul, and up again to a governor-general of India, but, as applicants for such places, the names of some or of every one of these hungry and adhesive Barnacles were down.

It was necessarily but a sprinkling of any class of Barnacles that attended the marriage, for there were not two score in all, and what is that subtracted from Legion! But, the sprinkling was a swarm in the Twickenham cottage, and filled it. A Barnacle (assisted by a Barnacle) married the happy pair, and it behoved Lord Decimus Tite Barnacle himself to conduct Mrs. Meagles to breakfast.

The entertainment was not as agreeable and natural as it might have been. Mr. Meagles, hove down by his good company while he highly appreciated it, was not himself. Mrs. Gowan was herself, and that did not improve him. The fiction that it was not Mr. Meagles who had stood in the way, but that it was the Family greatness, and that the Family greatness had made a concession, and there was now a soothing unanimity, pervaded the affair, though it was never openly expressed. Then the Barnacles felt that they for their parts would have done with the Meagleses, when the present patronising occasion was over; and the Meagleses felt the same for their parts. Then Gowan asserting his rights as a disappointed man who had his grudge against the family, and who perhaps had allowed his mother to have them there, as much in the hope that it might give them some annoyance as with any other benevolent object, aired his pencil and his poverty ostentatiously before them, and told them he hoped in time to settle a crust of bread and cheese on his wife, and that he begged such of them as (more fortunate than himself) came in for any good thing, and could buy a picture, to please to remember the poor painter. Then Lord Decimus, who was a wonder on his own Parliamentary pedestal, turned out to be the windiest creature here: proposing happiness to the bride and bridegroom in a series of platitudes, that would have made the hair of any sincere disciple and believer stand on end; and trotting, with the complacency of an idiotic elephant, among howling labyrinths of sentences which he seemed to take for high roads, and never so much as wanted to get out of. Then Mr. Tite Barnacle could not but feel that there was a person in company, who would have disturbed his life-long sitting to Sir Thomas Lawrence in full official character, if such disturbance had been possible: while Barnacle Junior did, with indignation, communicate to two vapid young gentlemen his relatives, that there was a feller here, look here, who had come to our Department without an appointment and said he wanted to know, you know; and that, look here, if he was to break out now, as he might you know (for you never could tell what an ungentlemanly Radical of that sort would be up to next), and was to say, look here, that he wanted to know this moment, you know, that would be Jolly; wouldn't it?

The pleasantest part of the occasion, by far, to Clennam, was the painfullest. When Mr. and Mrs. Meagles at last hung about Pet, in the room with the two pictures (where the company were not), before going with her to the threshold which she could never re-cross to be the old Pet and the old delight, nothing could be more natural and simple than the three were. Gowan himself was touched, and answered Mr. Meagles's "O, Gowan, take care of her, take care of her!" with an earnest "Don't be so broken-hearted, sir. By Heaven I will!"

And so, with last sobs and last loving words, and a last look to Clennam of confidence in his promise, Pet fell back in the carriage, and her husband waved his hand, and they were away for Dover. Though not until the faithful Mrs. Tickit, in her silk gown and jet black curls, had rushed out from some hiding-place, and thrown both her shoes after the carriage ; an apparition which occasioned great surprise to the distinguished company at the windows.

The said company being now relieved from further attendance, and the chief Barnacles being rather hurried (for they had it in hand just then to send a mail or two, which was in danger of going straight to its destination, beating about the seas like the Flying Dutchman, and to arrange with complexity for the stoppage of a good deal of important business otherwise in peril of being done), went their several ways ; with all affability conveying to Mr. and Mrs. Meagles, that general assurance that what they had been doing there, they had been doing at a sacrifice for Mr. and Mrs. Meagles's good, which they always conveyed to Mr. John Bull in their official condescension to that most unfortunate creature.

A miserable blank remained in the house, and in the hearts of the father and mother and Clennam. Mr. Meagles called only one remembrance to his aid, that really did him good.

" It's very gratifying, Arthur," he said, " after all, to look back upon."

" The past ? " said Clennam.

" Yes—but I mean the company."

It had made him much more low and unhappy at the time, but now it really did him good. " It's very gratifying," he said, often repeating the remark in the course of the evening. " Such high company ! "

CHAPTER XXXV

It was at this time, that Mr. Pancks, in discharge of his compact with Clennam, revealed to him the whole of his gipsy story, and told him Little Dorrit's fortune. Her father was heir-at-law to a great estate that had long lain unknown of, unclaimed, and accumulating. His right was now clear, nothing interposed in his way, the Marshalsea gates stood open, the Marshalsea walls were down, a few flourishes of his pen, and he was extremely rich.

In his tracking out of the claim to its complete establishment, Mr. Pancks had shown a sagacity that nothing could baffle, and a patience and secrecy that nothing could tire. "I little thought, sir," said Pancks, "when you and I crossed Smithfield that night, and I told you what sort of a Collector I was, that this would come of it. I little thought, sir, when I told you you were not of the Clennams of Cornwall, that I was ever going to tell you who *were* of the Dorrits of Dorsetshire." He then went on to detail, How, having that name recorded in his note-book, he was first attracted by the name alone. How, having often found two exactly similar names, even belonging to the same place, to involve no traceable consanguinity, near or distant, he did not at first give much heed to this; except in the way of speculation as to what a surprising change would be made in the condition of a little seamstress,

507

if she could be shown to have any interest in so large a property. How he rather supposed himself to have pursued the idea into its next degree, because there was something uncommon in the quiet little seamstress, which pleased him and provoked his curiosity. How he had felt his way inch by inch, and "Moled it out, sir" (that was Mr. Pancks's expression), grain by grain. How, in the beginning of the labour described by this new verb, and to render which the more expressive Mr. Pancks shut his eyes in pronouncing it and shook his hair over them, he had alternated from sudden lights and hopes to sudden darkness and no hopes, and back again, and back again. How he had made acquaintances in the Prison, expressly that he might come and go there as all other comers and goers did; and how his first ray of light was unconsciously given him by Mr. Dorrit himself and by his son: to both of whom he easily became known; with both of whom he talked much, casually ("but always Moleing you'll observe," said Mr. Pancks): and from whom he derived, without being at all suspected, two or three little points of family history which, as he began to hold clues of his own, suggested others. How it had at length become plain to Mr. Pancks, that he had made a real discovery of the heir-at-law to a great fortune, and that his discovery had but to be ripened to legal fulness and perfection. How he had, thereupon, sworn his landlord, Mr. Rugg, to secrecy in a solemn manner, and taken him into Moleing partnership. How they had employed John Chivery as their sole clerk and agent, seeing to whom he was devoted. And how, until the present hour, when authorities mighty in the Bank and learned in the law declared their successful labours ended, they had confided in no other human being.

"So if the whole thing had broken down, sir," concluded Pancks, "at the very last, say the day before the other day when I showed you our papers in the Prison yard, or say that very day, nobody but ourselves would have been cruelly disappointed, or a penny the worse."

Clennam, who had been almost incessantly shaking hands with him throughout the narrative, was reminded by this to say, in an amazement which even the preparation he had had for the main disclosure scarcely smoothed down, "My dear Mr. Pancks, this must have cost you a great sum of money."

"Pretty well, sir," said the triumphant Pancks. "No trifle, though we did it as cheap as it could be done. And the outlay was a difficulty, let me tell you."

"A difficulty!" repeated Clennam. "But the difficulties you have so wonderfully conquered in the whole business!" shaking his hand again.

"I'll tell you how I did it," said the delighted Pancks, putting his hair into a condition as elevated as himself. "First, I spent all I had of my own. That wasn't much."

"I am sorry for it," said Clennam; "not that it matters now, though. Then, what did you do?"

"Then," answered Pancks, "I borrowed a sum of my proprietor."

"Of Mr. Casby?" said Clennam. "He's a fine old fellow."

"Noble old boy; an't he?" said Mr. Pancks, entering on a series of the dryest of snorts. "Generous old buck. Confiding old boy. Philanthropic old buck. Benevolent old boy! Twenty per cent. I engaged to pay him, sir. But we never do business for less, at our shop."

Arthur felt an awkward consciousness of having, in his exultant condition, been a little premature.

"I said to that boiling-over old Christian," Mr. Pancks pursued, appearing greatly to relish this descriptive epithet, "that I had got a little project on hand; a hopeful one; I told him a hopeful one; which wanted a certain small capital. I proposed to him to lend me the money on my note. Which he did, at twenty; sticking the twenty on in a business-like way, and putting it into the note, to look like a part of the principal. If I had broken down after that, I should have been his grubber for the next seven years at half wages and double grind. But he's a perfect Patriarch; and it would do a man good to serve him on such terms—on any terms."

Arthur for his life could not have said with confidence whether Pancks really thought so or not.

"When that was gone, sir," resumed Pancks, "and it did go, though I dribbled it out like so much blood, I had taken Mr. Rugg into the secret. I proposed to borrow of Mr. Rugg (or of Miss Rugg; it's the same thing; she made a little money by a speculation in the Common Pleas once). He lent it at ten, and thought that pretty high. But Mr. Rugg's a red-haired man, sir, and gets his hair cut. And as to the crown of his hat, it's high. And as to the brim of his hat, it's narrow. And there's no more benevolence bubbling out of *him*, than out of a ninepin."

"Your own recompense for all this, Mr. Pancks," said Clennam, "ought to be a large one."

"I don't mistrust getting it, sir," said Pancks. "I have made no bargain. I owed you one on that score; now, I have paid it. Money out of pocket made good, time fairly allowed for, and Mr. Rugg's bill settled, a thousand pounds would be a fortune to me. That matter I place in your hands. I authorise you, now, to break all this to the family in any way you think best. Miss Amy Dorrit will be with Mrs. Finching this morning. The sooner done the better. Can't be done too soon."

This conversation took place in Clennam's bedroom, while he was yet in bed. For, Mr. Pancks had knocked up the house and made his way in, very early in the morning; and, without once sitting down or standing still, had delivered himself of the whole of his details (illustrated with a variety of documents) at the bedside. He now said he would "go and look up Mr. Rugg," from whom his excited state of mind appeared to require another back; and bundling up his papers, and exchanging one more hearty shake of the hand with Clennam, he went at full speed down-stairs, and steamed off.

Clennam, of course, resolved to go direct to Mr. Casby's. He dressed and got out so quickly, that he found himself at the corner of the patriarchal street nearly an hour before her time; but he was not sorry to have the opportunity of calming himself with a leisurely walk.

When he returned to the street, and had knocked at the bright brass knocker, he was informed that she had come, and was shown up-stairs to Flora's breakfast-room. Little Dorrit was not there herself, but Flora was, and testified the greatest amazement at seeing him.

"Good gracious, Arthur—Doyce and Clennam!" cried that lady, "who would have ever thought of seeing such a sight as this and pray excuse a wrapper for upon my word I really never and a faded check too which is worse but our little friend is making me a, not that I need mind mentioning it to you for you must know that there are such things a skirt, and having arranged that a trying on should take place after breakfast is the reason though I wish not so badly starched."

"I ought to make an apology," said Arthur, "for so early and abrupt a visit; but you will excuse it when I tell you the cause."

"In times for ever fled Arthur," returned Mrs. Finching, "pray excuse me Doyce and Clennam infinitely more correct and though unquestionably distant still 'tis distance lends enchantment to the view, at least I don't mean that and if I did I suppose it would depend considerably on the nature of the view, but I'm running on again and you put it all out of my head."

She glanced at him tenderly, and resumed:

"In times for ever fled I was going to say it would have sounded strange indeed for Arthur Clennam—Doyce and Clennam naturally quite different—to make apologies for coming here at any time, but that is past and what is past can never be recalled except in his own case as poor Mr. F said when he was in spirits Cucumber and therefore never ate it."

She was making the tea when Arthur came in, and now hastily finished that operation.

"Papa," she said, all mystery and whisper, as she shut down the tea-pot lid, "is sitting prosingly breaking his new laid egg in the back parlour over the City article exactly like the Woodpecker Tapping and need never know that you are here, and our little friend you are well aware may be fully trusted when she comes down from cutting out on the large table overhead."

Arthur then told her, in the fewest words, that it was their little friend he came to see; and what he had to announce to their little friend. At which astounding intelligence, Flora clasped her hands, fell into a tremble, and shed tears of sympathy and pleasure, like the good-natured creature she really was.

"For gracious sake let me get out of the way first," said Flora, putting her hands to her ears, and moving towards the door, "or I know I shall go off dead and screaming and make everybody worse, and the dear little thing only this morning looking so nice and neat and good and yet so poor and now a fortune is she really and deserves it too! and might I mention it to Mr. F's Aunt Arthur not Doyce and Clennam for this once or if objectionable not on any account."

Arthur nodded his free permission, since Flora shut out all verbal communication. Flora nodded in return to thank him, and hurried out of the room.

Little Dorrit's step was already on the stairs, and in another moment she was at the door. Do what he would to compose his face, he could not convey so much of an ordinary expression into it, but that the moment she saw it she dropped her work, and cried, "Mr. Clennam! What's the matter?"

"Nothing, nothing. That is, no misfortune has happened. I have come to tell you something, but it is a piece of great good-fortune."

"Good-fortune?"

"Wonderful fortune!"

They stood in a window, and her eyes, full of light, were fixed upon his face. He put an arm about her, seeing her likely to sink down. She put a hand upon that arm, partly to rest upon it, and partly so to preserve their relative positions as that her intent look at him should be shaken by no change of attitude in either of them. Her lips seemed to repeat "Wonderful fortune?" He repeated it again, aloud.

"Dear Little Dorrit! Your father."

The ice of the pale face broke at the word, and little lights and shoots of expression passed all over it. They were all expressions of pain. Her breath was faint and hurried. Her heart beat fast. He would have clasped the little figure closer, but he saw that the eyes appealed to him not to be moved.

"Your father can be free within this week. He does not know it; we must go to him from here, to tell him of it. Your father will be free within a few days. Your father will be free within a few hours. Remember we must go to him from here, to tell him of it!"

That brought her back. Her eyes were closing, but they opened again.

"This is not all the good-fortune. This is not all the wonderful good-fortune, my dear Little Dorrit. Shall I tell you more?"

Her lips shaped "Yes."

"Your father will be no beggar when he is free. He will want for nothing. Shall I tell you more? Remember! He knows nothing of it; we must go to him, from here, to tell him of it!"

She seemed to entreat him for a little time. He held her in his arm, and, after a pause, bent down his ear to listen.

"Did you ask me to go on?"

"Yes."

"He will be a rich man. He is a rich man. A great sum of money is waiting to be paid over to him as his inheritance;

513

you are all henceforth very wealthy. Bravest and best of
children, I thank Heaven that you are rewarded!"

As he kissed her, she turned her head towards his shoulder,
and raised her arm towards his neck; cried out "Father!
Father! Father!" and swooned away.

Upon which Flora returned to take care of her, and
hovered about her on a sofa, intermingling kind offices
and incoherent scraps of conversation in a manner so con-
founding, that whether she pressed the Marshalsea to take a
spoonful of unclaimed dividends, for it would do her good; or
whether she congratulated Little Dorrit's father on coming
into possession of a hundred thousand smelling-bottles; or
whether she explained that she put seventy-five thousand
drops of spirits of lavender on fifty thousand pounds of lump
sugar, and that she entreated Little Dorrit to take that
gentle restorative; or whether she bathed the foreheads of
Doyce and Clennam in vinegar, and gave the late Mr. F
more air; no one with any sense of responsibility could have
undertaken to decide. A tributary stream of confusion,
moreover, poured in from an adjoining bedroom, where Mr.
F's Aunt appeared, from the sound of her voice, to be in a
horizontal posture, awaiting her breakfast; and from which
bower that inexorable lady snapped off short taunts, whenever
she could get a hearing, as, "Don't believe it's his doing!"
and "He needn't take no credit to himself for it!" and "It'll
be long enough, I expect, afore he'll give up any of his own
money!" all designed to disparage Clennam's share in the
discovery, and to relieve those inveterate feelings with which
Mr. F's Aunt regarded him.

But, Little Dorrit's solicitude to get to her father, and to
carry the joyful tidings to him, and not to leave him in his
jail a moment with this happiness in store for him and still
unknown to him, did more for her speedy restoration than all
the skill and attention on earth could have done. "Come
with me to my dear father. Pray come and tell my dear
father!" were the first words she said. Her father, her father.

She spoke of nothing but him, thought of nothing but him. Kneeling down and pouring out her thankfulness with uplifted hands, her thanks were for her father.

Flora's tenderness was quite overcome by this, and she launched out among the cups and saucers into a wonderful flow of tears and speech.

"I declare," she sobbed, "I never was so cut up since your mama and my papa not Doyce and Clennam for this once but give the precious little thing a cup of tea and make her put it to her lips at least pray Arthur do, not even Mr. F's last illness for that was of another kind and gout is not a child's affection though very painful for all parties and Mr. F a martyr with his leg upon a rest and the wine trade in itself inflammatory for they will do it more or less among themselves and who can wonder, it seems like a dream I am sure to think of nothing at all this morning and now Mines of money is it really, but you must you know my darling love because you never will be strong enough to tell him all about it upon teaspoons, mightn't it be even best to try the directions of my own medical man for though the flavour is anything but agreeable still I force myself to do it as a prescription and find the benefit, you'd rather not why no my dear I'd rather not but still I do it as a duty, everybody will congratulate you some in earnest and some not and many will congratulate you with all their hearts but none more so I do assure you than from the bottom of my own I do myself though sensible of blundering and being stupid, and will be judged by Arthur not Doyce and Clennam for this once so good-bye darling and God bless you and may you be very happy and excuse the liberty, vowing that the dress shall never be finished by anybody else but shall be laid by for a keepsake just as it is and called Little Dorrit though why that strangest of denominations at any time I never did myself and now I never shall!"

Thus Flora, in taking leave of her favourite. Little Dorrit thanked her, and embraced her, over and over again; and

515

finally came out of the house with Clennam, and took coach for the Marshalsea.

It was a strangely unreal ride through the old squalid streets, with a sensation of being raised out of them, into an airy world of wealth and grandeur. When Arthur told her that she would soon ride in her own carriage through very different scenes, when all the familiar experiences would have vanished away, she looked frightened. But, when he substituted her father for herself, and told her how he would ride in his carriage, and how great and grand he would be, her tears of joy and innocent pride fell fast. Seeing that the happiness her mind could realise was all shining upon him, Arthur kept that single figure before her; and so they rode brightly through the poor streets in the prison neighbourhood, to carry him the great news.

When Mr. Chivery, who was on duty, admitted them into the Lodge, he saw something in their faces which filled him with astonishment. He stood looking after them, when they hurried into the prison, as though he perceived that they had come back accompanied by a ghost a-piece. Two or three Collegians whom they passed, looked after them too, and presently joining Mr. Chivery, formed a little group on the Lodge steps, in the midst of which there spontaneously originated a whisper that the Father was going to get his discharge. Within a few minutes, it was heard in the remotest room in the College.

Little Dorrit opened the door from without, and they both entered. He was sitting in his old grey gown, and his old black cap, in the sunlight by the window, reading his newspaper. His glasses were in his hand, and he had just looked round; surprised at first, no doubt, by her step upon the stairs, not expecting her until night; surprised again, by seeing Arthur Clennam in her company. As they came in, the same unwonted look in both of them which had already caught attention in the yard below, struck him. He did not rise or speak, but laid down his glasses and his newspaper on the table beside him, and looked at them with his mouth a little open, and his lips trembling. When Arthur put out his hand, he touched it, but not with his usual state; and then he turned to his daughter, who had sat down close beside him with her hands upon his shoulder, and looked attentively in her face.

"Father! I have been made so happy this morning!"

"You have been made so happy, my dear?"

"By Mr. Clennam, father. He brought me such joyful and wonderful intelligence about you! If he had not, with his great kindness and gentleness, prepared me for it, father —prepared me for it, father—I think I could not have borne it."

Her agitation was exceedingly great, and the tears rolled down her face. He put his hand suddenly to his heart, and looked at Clennam.

"Compose yourself, sir," said Clennam, "and take a little time to think. To think of the brightest and most fortunate accidents of life. We have all heard of great surprises of joy. They are not at an end, sir. They are rare, but not at an end."

"Mr. Clennam? Not at an end? Not at an end for——" He touched himself upon the breast, instead of saying "me."

"No," returned Clennam.

"What surprise," he asked, keeping his left hand over his heart, and there stopping in his speech, while with his right hand he put his glasses exactly level on the table: "what such surprise can be in store for me?"

"Let me answer with another question. Tell me, Mr. Dorrit, what surprise would be the most unlooked for and the most acceptable to you. Do not be afraid to imagine it, or to say what it would be."

He looked steadfastly at Clennam, and, so looking at him, seemed to change into a very old haggard man. The sun was bright upon the wall beyond the window, and on the

517

spikes at top. He slowly stretched out the hand that had been upon his heart, and pointed at the wall.

"It is down," said Clennam. " Gone !"

He remained in the same attitude, looking steadfastly at him.

"And in its place," said Clennam, slowly and distinctly, " are the means to possess and enjoy the utmost that they have so long shut out. Mr. Dorrit, there is not the smallest doubt that within a few days you will be free, and highly prosperous. I congratulate you with all my soul on this change of fortune, and on the happy future into which you are soon to carry the treasure you have been blest with here —the best of all the riches you can have elsewhere—the treasure at your side."

With those words, he pressed his hand and released it; and his daughter, laying her face against his, encircled him in the hour of his prosperity with her arms, as she had in the long years of his adversity encircled him with her love and toil and truth; and poured out her full heart in gratitude, hope, joy, blissful ecstasy, and all for him.

"I shall see him, as I never saw him yet. I shall see my dear love, with the dark cloud cleared away. I shall see him, as my poor mother saw him long ago. O my dear, my dear ! O father, father ! O thank God, thank God !"

He yielded himself to her kisses and caresses, but did not return them, except that he put an arm about her. Neither did he say one word. His steadfast look was now divided between her and Clennam, and he began to shake as if he were very cold. Explaining to Little Dorrit that he would run to the coffee-house for a bottle of wine, Arthur fetched it with all the haste he could use. While it was being brought from the cellar to the bar, a number of excited people asked him what had happened : when he hurriedly informed them, that Mr. Dorrit had succeeded to a fortune.

On coming back with the wine in his hand, he found that she had placed her father in his easy-chair, and had loosened his shirt and neckcloth. They filled a tumbler with wine, and held it to his lips. When he had swallowed a little, he took the glass himself and emptied it. Soon after that, he leaned back in his chair and cried, with his handkerchief before his face.

After this had lasted a while, Clennam thought it a good season for diverting his attention from the main surprise, by relating its details. Slowly, therefore, and in a quiet tone of voice, he explained them as he best could, and enlarged on the nature of Pancks's service.

" He shall be—ha—he shall be handsomely recompensed, sir," said the Father, starting up and moving hurriedly about the room. " Assure yourself, Mr. Clennam, that everybody concerned shall be—ha—shall be nobly rewarded. No one, my dear sir, shall say that he has an unsatisfied claim against me. I shall repay the—hum—the advances I have had from you, sir, with peculiar pleasure. I beg to be informed at your early convenience, what advances you have made my son."

He had no purpose in going about the room, but he was not still a moment.

" Everybody," he said, " shall be remembered. I will not go away from here in anybody's debt. All the people who have been—ha—well behaved towards myself and my family, shall be rewarded. Chivery shall be rewarded. Young John shall be rewarded. I particularly wish, and intend, to act munificently, Mr. Clennam."

" Will you allow me," said Arthur, laying his purse on the table, " to supply any present contingencies, Mr. Dorrit? I thought it best to bring a sum of money for the purpose."

" Thank you, sir, thank you. I accept with readiness at the present moment, what I could not an hour ago have conscientiously taken. I am obliged to you for the temporary accommodation. Exceedingly temporary, but well timed— well timed." His hand had closed upon the money, and he carried it about with him. " Be so kind, sir, as to add the amount to those former advances to which I have already

519

referred; being careful, if you please, not to omit advances made to my son. A mere verbal statement of the gross amount is all I shall—ha—all I shall require."

His eye fell upon his daughter at this point, and he stopped for a moment to kiss her, and to pat her head.

" It will be necessary to find a milliner, my love, and to make a speedy and complete change in your very plain dress. Something must be done with Maggy too, who at present is —ha—barely respectable, barely respectable. And your sister, Amy, and your brother. And *my* brother, your uncle— poor soul, I trust this will arouse him—messengers must be despatched to fetch them. They must be informed of this. We must break it to them cautiously, but they must be informed directly. We owe it as a duty to them, and to ourselves, from this moment, not to let them—hum—not to let them do anything."

This was the first intimation he had ever given, that he was privy to the fact that they did something for a liveli- hood.

He was still jogging about the room, with the purse clutched in his hand, when a great cheering arose in the yard. " The news has spread already," said Clennam, looking down from the window. " Will you show yourself to them, Mr. Dorrit ? They are very earnest, and they evidently wish it."

" I—hum—ha—I confess I could have desired, Amy my dear," he said, jogging about in a more feverish flutter than before, " to have made some change in my dress first, and to have bought a—hum—a watch and chain. But if it must be done as it is, it—ha—it must be done. Fasten the collar of my shirt, my dear. Mr. Clennam, would you oblige me— hum—with a blue neckcloth you will find in that drawer at your elbow ? Button my coat across at the chest, my love. It looks—ha—it looks broader, buttoned."

With his trembling hand he pushed his grey hair up, and then, taking Clennam and his daughter for supporters, appeared at the window leaning on an arm of each. The Collegians cheered him very heartily, and he kissed his hand to them with great urbanity and protection. When he withdrew into the room again, he said "Poor creatures!" in a tone of much pity for their miserable condition.

Little Dorrit was deeply anxious that he should lie down to compose himself. On Arthur's speaking to her of his going to inform Pancks that he might now appear as soon as he would, and pursue the joyful business to its close, she entreated him in a whisper to stay with her, until her father should be quite calm and at rest. He needed no second entreaty; and she prepared her father's bed, and begged him to lie down. For another half-hour or more he would be persuaded to do nothing but go about the room, discussing with himself the probabilities for and against the Marshal's allowing the whole of the prisoners to go to the windows of the official residence which commanded the street, to see himself and family depart for ever in a carriage—which, he said, he thought would be a Sight for them. But, gradually he began to droop and tire, and at last stretched himself upon the bed.

She took her faithful place beside him, fanning him and cooling his forehead; and he seemed to be falling asleep (always with the money in his hand), when he unexpectedly sat up and said:

"Mr. Clennam, I beg your pardon. Am I to understand, my dear sir, that I could—ha—could pass through the Lodge at this moment, and—hum—take a walk?"

"I think not, Mr. Dorrit," was the unwilling reply. "There are certain forms to be completed; and although your detention here is now in itself a form, I fear it is one that for a little longer has to be observed too."

At this he shed tears again.

"It is but a few hours, sir," Clennam cheerfully urged upon him.

"A few hours, sir," he returned in a sudden passion. "You talk very easily of hours, sir! How long do you suppose, sir, that an hour is to a man who is choking for want of air?"

It was his last demonstration for that time; as, after shedding some more tears and querulously complaining that he couldn't breathe, he slowly fell into a slumber. Clennam had abundant occupation for his thoughts, as he sat in the quiet room watching the father on his bed, and the daughter fanning his face.

Little Dorrit had been thinking too. After softly putting his grey hair aside, and touching his forehead with her lips, she looked towards Arthur, who came nearer to her, and pursued in a low whisper the subject of her thoughts.

"Mr. Clennam, will he pay all his debts before he leaves here?"

"No doubt. All."

"All the debts for which he has been imprisoned here, all my life and longer?"

"No doubt."

There was something of uncertainty and remonstrance in her look; something that was not all satisfaction. He wondered to detect it, and said:

"You are glad that he should do so?"

"Are you?" asked Little Dorrit, wistfully.

"Am I? Most heartily glad!"

"Then I know I ought to be."

"And are you not?"

"It seems to me hard," said Little Dorrit, "that he should have lost so many years and suffered so much, and at last pay all the debts as well. It seems to me hard that he should pay in life and money both."

"My dear child—— " Clennam was beginning.

"Yes, I know I am wrong," she pleaded timidly, "don't think any worse of me; it has grown up with me here."

The prison, which could spoil so many things, had tainted Little Dorrit's mind no more than this. Engendered as the confusion was, in compassion for the poor prisoner, her father, it was the first speck Clennam had ever seen, it was the last speck Clennam ever saw, of the prison atmosphere upon her.

He thought this, and forbore to say another word. With the thought, her purity and goodness came before him in their brightest light. The little spot made them the more beautiful.

Worn out with her own emotions, and yielding to the silence of the room, her hand slowly slackened and failed in its fanning movement, and her head dropped down on the pillow at her father's side. Clennam rose softly, opened and closed the door without a sound, and passed from the prison, carrying the quiet with him into the turbulent streets.

CHAPTER XXXVI

THE MARSHALSEA BECOMES AN ORPHAN

AND now the day arrived, when Mr. Dorrit and his family were to leave the prison for ever, and the stones of its much-trodden pavement were to know them no more.

The interval had been short, but he had greatly complained of its length, and had been imperious with Mr. Rugg touching the delay. He had been high with Mr. Rugg, and had threatened to employ some one else. He had requested Mr. Rugg not to presume upon the place in which he found him, but to do his duty, sir, and to do it with promptitude. He had told Mr. Rugg that he knew what lawyers and agents were, and that he would not submit to imposition. On that gentleman's humbly representing that he exerted himself to the utmost, Miss Fanny was very short with him ; desiring to know what less he could do, when he had been told a dozen times that money was no object, and expressing her suspicion that he forgot whom he talked to.

Towards the Marshal, who was a Marshal of many years' standing, and with whom he had never had any previous difference, Mr. Dorrit comported himself with severity. That officer, on personally tendering his congratulations, offered the free use of two rooms in his house for Mr. Dorrit's occupation until his departure. Mr. Dorrit thanked him at the moment, and replied that he would think of it ; but the Marshal was no sooner gone than he sat down and wrote him a cutting note, in which he remarked that he had never on any former occasion had the honour of receiving his congratulations (which was true, though indeed there had not been anything particular to congratulate him upon), and that he begged, on behalf of himself and family, to repudiate the Marshal's offer, with all those thanks which its disinterested character and its perfect independence of all worldly considerations demanded.

Although his brother showed so dim a glimmering of interest in their altered fortunes, that it was very doubtful whether he understood them, Mr. Dorrit caused him to be measured for new raiment by the hosiers, tailors, hatters, and bootmakers whom he called in for himself; and ordered that his old clothes should be taken from him and burned. Miss Fanny and Mr. Tip required no direction in making an appearance of great fashion and elegance; and the three passed this interval together at the best hotel in the neighbourhood—though truly, as Miss Fanny said, the best was very indifferent. In connection with that establishment, Mr. Tip hired a cabriolet, horse, and groom, a very neat turnout, which was usually to be observed for two or three hours at a time, gracing the Borough High Street, outside the Marshalsea court-yard. A modest little hired chariot and pair was also frequently to be seen there; in alighting from and entering which vehicle, Miss Fanny fluttered the Marshal's daughters by the display of inaccessible bonnets.

A great deal of business was transacted in this short period. Among other items, Messrs. Peddle and Pool, solicitors, of Monument Yard, were instructed by their client Edward Dorrit, Esquire, to address a letter to Mr. Arthur Clennam, enclosing the sum of twenty-four pounds nine shillings and eightpence, being the amount of principal and interest computed at the rate of five per cent. per annum, in which their client believed himself to be indebted to Mr. Clennam. In making this communication and remittance, Messrs. Peddle and Pool were further instructed by their client to remind Mr. Clennam, that the favour of the advance now repaid (including gate-fees) had not been asked of him, and to inform him that it would not have been accepted if it had been openly proffered in his name. With which they requested a stamped receipt, and remained his obedient servants. A great deal of business had likewise to be done, within the so-soon-to-be-orphaned Marshalsea, by Mr. Dorrit so long its Father, chiefly arising out of applications made to him by Collegians for small sums of money. To these he responded with the greatest liberality, and with no lack of formality; always first writing to appoint a time at which the applicant might wait upon him in his room, and then receiving him in the midst of a vast accumulation of documents, and accompanying his donation (for he said in every such case, "it is a donation, not a loan") with a great deal of good counsel: to the effect that he, the expiring Father of the Marshalsea, hoped to be long remembered, as an example that a man might preserve his own and the general respect even there.

The Collegians were not envious. Besides that they had a personal and traditional regard for a Collegian of so many years' standing, the event was creditable to the College, and made it famous in the newspapers. Perhaps more of them thought, too, than were quite aware of it, that the thing might in the lottery of chances have happened to themselves, or that something of the sort might yet happen to themselves, some day or other. They took it very well. A few were low at the thought of being left behind, and being left poor; but even these did not grudge the family their brilliant reverse. There might have been much more envy in politer places. It seems probable that mediocrity of fortune would have been disposed to be less magnanimous than the Collegians, who lived from hand to mouth—from the pawnbroker's hand to the day's dinner.

They got up an address to him, which they presented in a neat frame and glass (though it was not afterwards displayed in the family mansion or preserved among the family papers); and to which he returned a gracious answer. In that document he assured them, in a Royal manner, that he received the profession of their attachment with a full conviction of its sincerity; and again generally exhorted them to follow his example—which, at least in so far as coming into a great property was concerned, there is no doubt they would have gladly imitated. He took the same occasion of inviting them to a comprehensive entertainment, to be given to the whole College in the yard, and at which he signified he would have the honour of taking a parting glass to the health and happiness of all those whom he was about to leave behind.

He did not in person dine at this public repast (it took place at two in the afternoon, and his dinners now came in from the hotel at six), but his son was so good as to take the head of the principal table, and to be very free and engaging. He himself went about among the company, and took notice of individuals, and saw that the viands were of the quality he had ordered, and that all were served. On the whole, he was like a baron of the olden time, in a rare good humour. At the conclusion of the repast, he pledged his guests in a bumper of old Madeira; and told them that he hoped they had enjoyed themselves, and what was more, that they would enjoy themselves for the rest of the evening; that he wished them well; and that he bade them welcome. His health being drunk with acclamations, he was not so baronial after all but that in trying to return thanks he broke down, in the manner of a mere serf with a heart in his breast, and wept before them all. After this great success, which he supposed to be a failure, he gave them "Mr. Chivery and his brother officers;" whom he had beforehand presented with ten pounds each, and who were all in attendance. Mr. Chivery spoke to the toast, saying, What you undertake to lock up, lock up; but remember that you are, in the words of the fettered African, a man and a brother ever. The list of toasts disposed of, Mr. Dorrit urbanely went through the motions of playing a game át skittles with the Collegian who was the next oldest inhabitant to himself; and left the tenantry to their diversions.

But all these occurrences preceded the final day. And now the day arrived when he and his family were to leave the prison for ever, and when the stones of its much-trodden pavement were to know them no more.

Noon was the hour appointed for the departure. As it approached, there was not a Collegian within doors, nor a turnkey absent. The latter class of gentlemen appeared in their Sunday clothes, and the greater part of the Collegians were brightened up as much as circumstances allowed. Two or three flags were even displayed, and the children put on odds and ends of ribbon. Mr. Dorrit himself, at this trying time, preserved a serious but graceful dignity. Much of his attention was given to his brother, as to whose bearing on the great occasion he felt anxious.

"My dear Frederick," said he, "if you will give me your arm, we will pass among our friends together. I think it is right that we should go out arm-in-arm, my dear Frederick."

"Hah!" said Frederick. "Yes, yes, yes, yes."

"And if, my dear Frederick—if you could, without putting any great constraint upon yourself, throw a little (pray excuse me, Frederick), a little polish into your usual demeanour—— "

"William, William," said the other, shaking his head, "it's for you to do all that. I don't know how. All forgotten, forgotten!"

"But, my dear fellow," returned William, "for that very reason, if for no other, you must positively try to rouse yourself. What you have forgotten you must now begin to recall, my dear Frederick. Your position—— "

"Eh?" said Frederick.

"Your position, my dear Frederick."

A VERY FINE POSITION

"Mine?" He looked first at his own figure, and then at his brother's, and then, drawing a long breath, cried, "Hah, to be sure! Yes, yes, yes."

"Your position, my dear Frederick, is now a fine one. Your position, as my brother, is a very fine one. And I know that it belongs to your conscientious nature, to try to become worthy of it, my dear Frederick, and to try to adorn it. To be no discredit to it, but to adorn it."

"William," said the other weakly, and with a sigh, "I will do anything you wish, my brother, provided it lies in my power. Pray be so kind as to recollect what a limited power mine is. What would you wish me to do to-day, brother? Say what it is, only say what it is."

"My dearest Frederick, nothing. It is not worth troubling so good a heart as yours with."

"Pray trouble it," returned the other. "It finds it no trouble, William, to do anything it can for you."

William passed his hands across his eyes, and murmured with august satisfaction, "Blessings on your attachment, my poor dear fellow!" Then he said aloud, "Well, my dear Frederick, if you will only try, as we walk out, to show that you are alive to the occasion—that you think about it——"

"What would you advise me to think about it?" returned his submissive brother.

"Oh! my dear Frederick, how can I answer you? I can only say what, in leaving these good people, I think myself."

"That's it!" cried his brother. "That will help me."

"I find that I think, my dear Frederick, and with mixed emotions in which a softened compassion predominates, What will they do without me!"

"True," returned his brother. "Yes, yes, yes, yes. I'll think that as we go, What will they do without my brother! Poor things! What will they do without him!"

Twelve o'clock having just struck, and the carriage being

529

reported ready in the outer court-yard, the brothers proceeded down-stairs arm-in-arm. Edward Dorrit, Esquire (once Tip), and his sister Fanny followed, also arm-in-arm; Mr. Plornish and Maggy, to whom had been entrusted the removal of such of the family effects as were considered worth removing, followed, bearing bundles and burdens to be packed in a cart.

In the yard, were the Collegians and turnkeys. In the yard, were Mr. Pancks and Mr. Rugg, come to see the last touch given to their work. In the yard, was Young John making a new epitaph for himself, on the occasion of his dying of a broken heart. In the yard, was the Patriarchal Casby, looking so tremendously benevolent that many enthusiastic Collegians grasped him fervently by the hand, and the wives and female relatives of many more Collegians kissed his hand, nothing doubting that he had done it all. In the yard, was the usual chorus of people proper to such a place. In the yard, was the man with the shadowy grievance respecting the Fund which the Marshal embezzled, who had got up at five in the morning to complete the copying of a perfectly unintelligible history of that transaction, which he had committed to Mr. Dorrit's care, as a document of the last importance, calculated to stun the Government and effect the Marshal's downfall. In the yard, was the insolvent whose utmost energies were always set on getting into debt, who broke into prison with as much pains as other men have broken out of it, and who was always being cleared and complimented; while the insolvent at his elbow—a mere little, snivelling, striving tradesman, half dead of anxious efforts to keep out of debt—found it a hard matter, indeed, to get a Commissioner to release him with much reproof and reproach. In the yard, was the man of many children and many burdens, whose failure astonished everybody; in the yard, was the man of no children and large resources, whose failure astonished nobody. There, were the people who were always going out to-morrow, and always putting it off; there, were the people who had come in yesterday, and who were much more jealous and resentful of this freak of fortune than the seasoned birds. There, were some who, in pure meanness of spirit, cringed and bowed before the enriched Collegian and his family; there, were others who did so really because their eyes, accustomed to the gloom of their imprisonment and poverty, could not support the light of such bright sunshine. There, were many whose shillings had gone into his pocket to buy him meat and drink ; but none who were now obtrusively Hail fellow well met! with him, on the strength of that assistance. It was rather to be remarked of the caged birds, that they were a little shy of the bird about to be so grandly free, and that they had a tendency to withdraw themselves towards the bars, and seem a little fluttered as he passed.

Through these spectators, the little procession, headed by the two brothers, moved slowly to the gate. Mr. Dorrit, yielding to the vast speculation how the poor creatures were to get on without him, was great, and sad, but not absorbed. He patted children on the head like Sir Roger de Coverley going to church, he spoke to people in the background by their Christian names, he condescended to all present, and seemed for their consolation to walk encircled by the legend in golden characters, " Be comforted, my people ! Bear it ! "

At last three honest cheers announced that he had passed the gate, and that the Marshalsea was an orphan. Before they had ceased to ring in the echoes of the prison walls, the family had got into their carriage, and the attendant had the steps in his hand.

Then, and not before, " Good Gracious ! " cried Miss Fanny all at once, " Where's Amy ! "

Her father had thought she was with her sister. Her sister had thought she was " somewhere or other." They had all trusted to finding her, as they had always done, quietly in the right place at the right moment. This going away was perhaps the very first action of their joint lives that they had got through without her.

A minute might have been consumed in the ascertaining of these points, when Miss Fanny, who, from her seat in the carriage, commanded the long narrow passage leading to the Lodge, flushed indignantly.

" Now I do say, Pa," cried she, " that this is dis-graceful ! "

" What is disgraceful, Fanny ? "

" I do say," she repeated, " this is perfectly infamous ! Really almost enough, even at such a time as this, to make one wish one was dead ! Here is that child Amy, in her ugly old shabby dress, which she was so obstinate about, Pa, which I over and over again begged and prayed her to change, and which she over and over again objected to, and promised to change to-day, saying she wished to wear it as long as ever she remained in there with you—which was absolutely romantic nonsense of the lowest kind—here is that child Amy disgracing us, to the last moment and at the last moment, by being carried out in that dress after all. And by that Mr. Clennam too ! "

The offence was proved, as she delivered the indictment. Clennam appeared at the carriage-door, bearing the little insensible figure in his arms.

" She has been forgotten," he said, in a tone of pity not free from reproach. " I ran up to her room (which Mr. Chivery showed me) and found the door open, and that she had fainted on the floor, dear child. She appeared to have gone to change her dress, and to have sunk down over-powered. It may have been the cheering, or it may have happened sooner. Take care of this poor cold hand, Miss Dorrit. Don't let it fall."

" Thank you, sir," returned Miss Dorrit, bursting into tears. " I believe I know what to do, if you will give me leave. Dear Amy, open your eyes, that's a love ! Oh, Amy, Amy, I really am so vexed and ashamed ! Do rouse yourself, darling ! Oh, why are they not driving on ! Pray, Pa, do drive on !"

The attendant, getting between Clennam and the carriage-door, with a sharp "By your leave, sir !" bundled up the steps, and they drove away.

NOTES ON LITTLE DORRIT

CHAPTER VI.

The Marshalsea.

Dickens's letter to Mr. Forster on the Marshalsea may here be cited "Shortly after the date of his letter he was in London on business connected with the purchase of Gadshill Place, and he went over to the Borough to see what traces were left of the prison of which his first impression was taken in his boyhood, which had played so important a part in this latest novel, and every brick and stone of which he had been able to rebuild in his book by the mere vividness of his marvellous memory. 'Went to the Borough yesterday morning before going to Gadshill, to see if I could find any ruins of the Marshalsea. Found a great part of the original building—now "Marshalsea Place." Found the rooms that have been in my mind's eye in the story. Found, nursing a very big boy, a very small boy, who, seeing me standing on the Marshalsea pavement, looking about, told me how it all used to be. God knows how he learned it (for he was a world too young to know anything about it), but he was right enough. . . . There is a room there—still standing, to my amazement—that I think of taking! It is the room through which the ever-memorable signers of Captain Porter's petition filed off in my boyhood. The spikes are gone, and the wall is lowered, and anybody can go out now who likes to go, and is not bedridden ; and I said to the boy, "Who lives there ?" and he said, "Jack Pithick." "Who is Jack Pithick ?" I asked him. And he said, "Joe Pithick's uncle." ' "

Dickens's pathetic account of his own experiences in the Marshalsea, when his father was confined there, are in the second chapter of his *Life* by Mr. Forster. His father was Chairman of the Club Committee.

CHAPTER XXXIII.

" Mr. Merdle, so twisting his hands into what hair he had upon his head that he seemed to lift himself up by it—— "

Have we not heard of the same feat in the case of Mr. Jellyby ?

This book, designed by
William B. Taylor
is a production of
Edito-Service S.A., Geneva

Printed in Switzerland
R 1